中鋼新進人員甄試

一、報名日期： 預計6月。（正確日期以正式公告為準）

二、考試日期： 預計7月。（正確日期以正式公告為準）

三、報名資格：

(一)師級：教育行政主管機關認可之大學（含）以上學校畢業，具有學士以上學位者。

(二)員級：教育行政主管機關認可之高職、高中（含）以上學校畢業，具相關證照者尤佳。

＊為適才適所，具碩士（含）以上學位者，請報考師級職位，如有隱匿學歷報考員級職位者，經查獲則不予錄用。

四、甄試方式：

各類組人員之甄試分二階段舉行：

(一)初試（筆試）：分「共同科目」及「專業科目」兩科，均為測驗題（題型為單選題或複選題），採2B鉛筆劃記答案卡方式作答。

1.共同科目：含國文（佔40%）、英文（佔60%），佔初試（筆試）之成績為30%。

2.專業科目：依各類組需要合併數個專業科目為一科，佔初試（筆試）之成績為70，有關各類組之專業科目，請參閱甄試職位類別之應考專業科目說明。

(二)複試（口試）：依應考人員初試（筆試）成績排序，按各類組（以代碼區分）預定錄取名額至少2倍人數，通知參加複試。

五、甄試類別、各類組錄取名額、測驗科目如下：

(一)師級職位：

類組	專業科目
機械	1.固力學及熱力學、2.流體力學、3.金屬材料與機械製造
電機	1.電路學及電子電路、2.電力系統及電機機械、3.控制系統

類組	專業科目
材料	1.物理冶金、2.熱力學
工業工程	1.工程經濟及效益評估、2.生產管理、3.統計及作業研究
資訊工程	1.程式設計、2.資料庫系統 3.資訊網路工程、4.計算機結構
財務會計	1.會計學、2.稅務法規、3.財務管理
人力資源	1.人力資源管理、2.勞動法規

(二)員級職位：

類組	專業科目
機械	1.機械概論、2. 機械製造與識圖
電機	1.電工及電子學、2.數位系統、3.電工機械
化工	1.化工基本概論、2.化學分析

六、進用待遇

(一)基本薪給：師級 NT$40,000 元/月；員級 NT$30,000 元/月。

(二)中鋼公司福利制度完善，每年並另視營運獲利情況及員工績效表現核發獎金等。

～以上資訊請以正式簡章公告為準～

千華數位文化股份有限公司
新北市中和區中山路三段136巷10弄17號
TEL: 02-22289070　FAX: 02-22289076

台灣電力(股)公司新進僱用人員甄試

壹、報名資訊

一、報名日期：2025年1月（正確日期以正式公告為準。）

二、報名學歷資格：公立或立案之私立高中（職）畢業

完整考試資訊

http://goo.gl/GFbwSu

貳、考試資訊

一、筆試日期：2025年5月（正確日期以正式公告為準。）

二、考試科目：

(一) 共同科目：國文為測驗式試題及寫作一篇，英文採測驗式試題。

(二) 專業科目：專業科目A採測驗式試題；專業科目B採非測驗式試題。

類別		專業科目
1.配電線路維護	國文(10%) 英文(10%)	A：物理(30%)、B：基本電學(50%)
2.輸電線路維護		A：輸配電學(30%) B：基本電學(50%)
3.輸電線路工程		
4.變電設備維護		
5.變電工程		
6.電機運轉維護		A：電工機械(40%) B：基本電學(40%)
7.電機修護		
8.儀電運轉維護		A：電子學(40%)、B：基本電學(40%)
9.機械運轉維護		A：物理(30%)、 B：機械原理(50%)
10.機械修護		
11.土木工程		A：工程力學概要(30%) B：測量、土木、建築工程概要(50%)
12.輸電土建工程		
13.輸電土建勘測		
14.起重技術		A：物理(30%)、B：機械及起重常識(50%)
15.電銲技術		A：物理(30%)、B：機械及電銲常識(50%)
16.化學		A：環境科學概論(30%) B：化學(50%)
17.保健物理		A：物理(30%)、B：化學(50%)
18.綜合行政類	國文(20%) 英文(20%)	A：行政學概要、法律常識(30%)、 B：企業管理概論(30%)
19.會計類	國文(10%) 英文(10%)	A：會計審計法規(含預算法、會計法、決算法與審計法)、採購法概要(30%)、 B：會計學概要(50%)

詳細資訊以正式簡章為準

歡迎至千華官網(http://www.chienhua.com.tw/)查詢最新考情資訊

經濟部所屬事業機構
新進職員甄試

一、報名方式：一律採「網路報名」。

二、學歷資格：教育部認可之國內外公私立專科以上學校畢業，並符合各甄試類別所訂之學歷科系者，學歷證書載有輔系者得依輔系報考。

三、應試資訊：

完整考試資訊

https://reurl.cc/bX0Qz6

(一)甄試類別：各類別考試科目及錄取名額：

類別	專業科目A(30%)	專業科目B(50%)
企管	企業概論 法學緒論	管理學 經濟學
人資	企業概論 法學緒論	人力資源管理 勞工法令
財會	政府採購法規 會計審計法規	中級會計學 財務管理
資訊	計算機原理 網路概論	資訊管理 程式設計
統計資訊	統計學 巨量資料概論	資料庫及資料探勘 程式設計
政風	政府採購法規 民法	刑法 刑事訴訟法
法務	商事法 行政法	民法 民事訴訟法
地政	政府採購法規 民法	土地法規與土地登記 土地利用
土地開發	政府採購法規 環境規劃與都市設計	土地使用計畫及管制 土地開發及利用

類別	專業科目A(30%)	專業科目B(50%)
土木	應用力學 材料力學	大地工程學 結構設計
建築	建築結構、構造與施工 建築環境控制	營建法規與實務 建築計畫與設計
機械	應用力學 材料力學	熱力學與熱機學 流體力學與流體機械
電機(一)	電路學 電子學	電力系統與電機機械 電磁學
電機(二)	電路學 電子學	電力系統 電機機械
儀電	電路學 電子學	計算機概論 自動控制
環工	環化及環微 廢棄物清理工程	環境管理與空污防制 水處理技術
職業安全衛生	職業安全衛生法規 職業安全衛生管理	風險評估與管理 人因工程
畜牧獸醫	家畜各論(豬學) 豬病學	家畜解剖生理學 免疫學
農業	民法概要 作物學	農場經營管理學 土壤學
化學	普通化學 無機化學	分析化學 儀器分析
化工製程	化工熱力學 化學反應工程學	單元操作 輸送現象
地質	普通地質學 地球物理概論	石油地質學 沉積學

(二)初(筆)試科目：

    1.共同科目：分國文、英文2科(合併1節考試)，國文為論文寫作，英文採測驗式試題，各占初(筆)試成績10%，合計20%。

    2.專業科目：占初(筆)試成績80%。除法務類之專業科目A及專業科目B均採非測驗式試題外，其餘各類別之專業科目A採測驗式試題，專業科目B採非測驗式試題。

    3.測驗式試題均為選擇題（單選題，答錯不倒扣）；非測驗式試題可為問答、計算、申論或其他非屬選擇題或是非題之試題。

(三)複試(含查驗證件、複評測試、現場測試、口試)。

四、待遇：人員到職後起薪及晉薪依各所用人之機構規定辦理，目前各機構起薪約為新臺幣4萬2仟元至4萬5仟元間。本甄試進用人員如有兼任車輛駕駛及初級保養者，屬業務上、職務上之所需，不另支給兼任司機加給。

※詳細資訊請以正式簡章為準！

 千華數位文化股份有限公司　■新北市中和區中山路三段136巷10弄17號
■TEL: 02-22289070　FAX: 02-22289076

桃園捷運公司新進職員招考

壹 應考資格

桃捷考情資訊

https://goo.gl/FD1mBt

(一) 國籍：具有中華民國國籍者，且不得兼具外國國籍。不限年齡。
(二) 招募人員體格須符合簡章要求。
(三) 國內外高中(職)以上學校畢業，並已取得畢業證書者即可報名。
(四) 原住民類職別，須具原住民身分者。
(五) 身心障礙類職別，須領有舊制身心障礙手冊或新制身心障礙證明者。

貳 應試資訊

(一) 筆試 (50%)：共同科目佔第一試(筆試)成績 40%、專業科目佔第一試(筆試)成績 60%。其中一科目零分或缺考者，不得參加第二試(口試)。
(二) 口試 (50%)：口試成績以 100 分計，並依與工作相關之構面及當日繳交各項資料進行綜合評分(職涯發展測驗成績不列入口試成績計算)。
(三) 共同科目：1.國文、2.英文、3.邏輯分析
(四) 專業科目：

類組	專業科目
技術員(維修機械類)	機械概論
技術員(維修電機類)	電機概論
技術員(維修電子類)	電子概論
技術員(維修軌道類)	機械工程
技術員(維修土木類)	土木概論
司機員(運務車務類)	大眾捷運概論

類組	專業科目
站務員(運務站務類)	大眾捷運概論
工程員(運務票務類)B103	1.程式語言 2.資料庫應用(50%)
工程員(運務票務類)B104	1.網路概論(50%) 2.Linux作業系統(50%)
助理工程員(運務票務類)	大眾捷運概論
助理工程員(企劃資訊)	1.計算機概論(50%) 2.程式設計(50%)
副管理師(會計類)	1.內部控制之理論與實務 2.會計審計法規與實務
副管理師(人力資源類)	1.人力資源管理實務 2.勞工法令與實務
技術員(運務票務類)	電子學概要

詳細資訊以正式簡章為準

歡迎至千華官網(http://www.chienhua.com.tw/)查詢最新考情資訊

 千華數位文化股份有限公司

新北市中和區中山路三段136巷10弄17號
TEL: 02-22289070　FAX: 02-22289076

目 次

Chapter 1 基礎實力演練

Chapter 2 進階金榜挑戰

Chapter 3 近年各類試題及解析

109 年

國民營考試試題分析

112年臺中捷運新進人員

臺中捷運股份有限公司112年度新進人員甄試英文試題共有25個選擇題，其中字彙7題、片語3題、文法7題、會話1題、閱讀測驗7題。現詳細分析如下：

（以下題號皆為原試題題號）

I. 字彙

1. 名詞
第28題：rank (n.)等級；crew (n.)全體船員；jail (n.)監獄；goal (n.)目標

第29題：kingdom (n.)王國；territory (n.)領土；audience(n.)聽眾；background(n.)背景

2. 形容詞
第27題：convincing (adj.)令人信服的；consuming (adj.)消耗的

第31題：suspicious (adj.)可疑的；anxious (adj.)焦慮的；potential (adj.)潛在的；normal (adj.)正常的

第32題：terrifying (adj.)可怕的；inferior (adj.)低等的；doubtful (adj.)懷疑的；universal (adj.)全世界的

第40題：latter (adj.)（兩者中）後者的；later (adj.)較晚的

3. 連接詞
第43題：although (conj.)雖然

II. 片語

4. 介系詞片語
第33題：in the end最後；for instance例如

5. **動詞片語**

第30題：figure out弄明白；dress up盛裝；look forward to期盼；result in導致

第37題：have access to可以使用

III. 文法

第26題：考動詞demand（要求）之後要用原形動詞。

第35題：考形容詞worth（值得做……）＋ N.的用法。

第36題：考關係代名詞which的用法。

第38題：考句型 "how + Adj. + S. + V." 的用法。

第39題：考過去分詞closed當形容詞的用法。

第41題：考 "should there be（如果有）" 的用法。本題選項中還有三個重要的句型：If it were not for（要不是有……，現在就會）；if it had not been for（要不是有……，過去就會……）；when it comes to（一說到）。

第42題：考 "hardly...when (before) = no sooner...than（一……就……）" 的用法。hardly或no sooner放在句首時，其後的主詞和動詞要倒裝。

IV. 會話

第34題：考表格忘記簽名時兩個人的對答。在這一題中出現幾個常見的片語：no problem（沒問題）；take your time（慢慢來）；a piece of cake（小事一樁）；it is very kind of you to say so（謝謝你的誇獎）等。

V. 閱讀測驗

第一篇閱讀測驗介紹園丁鳥的棲息地、外型顏色、生活型式、覓食方式、求偶行為等。全文有四段，文章中有不少艱澀的單字，例如：intricate（複雜精細的）；bower（涼亭）；saliva（唾液）；charcoal（木炭）；

entice（誘使）；satin（緞紋的）； polygynous（一夫多妻的）等等，算
是一篇很難讀懂的長文；但本篇考題只有三題，第一個考題是選出正確
的敘述，可以用刪除法，先刪去錯誤的選項，然後再針對剩下的選項，回
到原文中找到相關的字詞，即可找出正確答案。第二個考題考在地圖中找
出最不可能有園丁鳥的地方，要先看懂 "least likely（最不可能）" 這兩
個字的意思，才能找出正確答案。第三個考題要選出一張圖表可以最好地
組織最後一段，在這一題的四個選項中，只有圖形，沒有隻字片語，筆者
覺得這些選項不太合乎邏輯，如果要用一張圖表組織最後一段，一定要有
文字，否則只有圖形不能代表什麼，不用文字說明清楚的圖形是沒有意義
的。以下這份列表將本文最後一段整理出來，更易於閱讀和理解：

Feature	Description
Species	Bowerbirds
Courtship ritual	Males build and decorate bowers to attract females
Bower decoration	Brightly colored objects, such as flowers, berries, and feathers
Courtship display	Strutting around the bower, showing off his decorations and making calls
If impressed, the female	Enters the bower to mate and then goes off to perform nesting duties by herself

第二篇閱讀測驗談的是塑料汙染。全文用條列式簡短的敘述，來說明塑
料自然分解所需的時間和我們可以做些什麼來減少其對環境的影響。全
文中沒有艱深的單字，句型簡單，是一篇很容易看懂的文章。四個問答
題也很簡單，刪除原文中並未提到的選項，即可輕易找到正確答案。

111年中華郵政職階人員（專業(二)內勤）

今年試題跟去年一樣共有25題，分四大類：字彙（8題）、文法（7題）、克漏字測驗（5題）和閱讀測驗（5題）。現分析如下：

一、字彙

名 詞			
1	motion 運動；移動	2	hill 丘陵；小山
3	humidity 濕氣；濕度	4	crowd 人群；一伙；一幫
5	passion 熱情；激情；戀情	6	revision 修訂；校訂；修正
7	fingerprint 特色；特徵；指紋	8	polluting 汙染；玷汙；敗壞
9	promoting 促進；鼓勵；促銷；推銷	10	tracking 跟蹤；追蹤
11	staffing 人員編制；配備人員	--	--

動 詞（片 語）			
1	spare 赦免；饒恕；不傷害	2	spread 使伸展；使延伸；張開；塗
3	scatter 使分散；使消散	4	span 持續；延伸到；橫跨
5	double 變成兩倍；增加一倍	6	shoulder 肩起；挑起；擔負
7	relieve 解除；緩和；減輕	--	--

形容詞			
1	responsive 反應的；回答的	2	friendly 友好的；親切的
3	dazzling 耀眼的；眼花繚亂的	4	frosty 冷若冰霜的；霜凍的
5	courageous 勇敢的；英勇的	6	critical 批判的；緊要的
7	bold 大膽的；英勇的	8	noncredible 不可信的；不可靠的

副 詞			
1	cautiously 謹慎地；小心地	2	shapely 豐滿勻稱的；樣子好看的
3	technically 技術上；工藝上	4	massively 極度地；大規模地

二、文法（題號皆為原試卷題號，對應本書為第9-15題）

1. 第19題考現在式時態：is to雖然看起來是現在式，但它有未來的含意。

2. 第20題考現在分詞當形容詞：要先看清楚空格前後是否已經有動詞，要小心一個句子只能有一個動詞。

3. 第21題考動詞片語 find it hard to + V.的用法：此處的it是虛受詞，真正的受詞是後面的不定詞片語。

4. 第22題考分詞片語用法：including是由which includes簡化而來。

5. 第23題考形容詞extensive（廣大的）。

6. 第24題考對等連接詞片語not only...but (also)的用法：not only放在句首時，表示加強語氣，其後的主詞和動詞要交換位置成倒裝句，若動詞是一般動詞，則倒裝句的助動詞單複數要跟主詞的單複數一致，而時態要跟動詞的時態一致。

7. 第25題考關係代名詞which的用法：先行詞如果是物，則關係代名詞可以用which或that，但是因為空格前有介系詞of，所以that在本句中不能當關係代名詞。

三、克漏字測驗（題號皆為原試卷題號，對應本書為第16-20題）

本篇文章談一隻忠心的德國牧羊犬。此篇內容淺顯易懂，五個空格考題也很簡單：第26題考的是動詞seem，跟第19題一樣；第27題考介系詞at；第28題考關係代名詞that；第29題考不定詞片語當形容詞，修飾前面的名詞；第30題考被動語態的過去分詞。

四、閱讀測驗

　　本篇文章介紹新的網路應用程式Clubhouse。文章內容生活化且現代化，沒有生字，句型簡單，是一篇很有趣的文章，值得閱讀。五個問答題考的是主題為何、Clubhouse跟其它應用程式的不同之處為何、這個應用程式為台灣和中國大陸的人們做了甚麼、作者為何在文章中提到Facebook，以及找出錯誤的論述。只要在文章中找出考題句的關鍵字，即可找到正確答案。

基礎實力演練

一 字彙測驗

( ) **1** Evaluations provide an opportunity for all the teachers to review the _____ they have played throughout the course.
(A)games (B)audio-visual aids
(C)activities (D)roles

( ) **2** Air pollution is _____ the health of people in urban areas.
(A)threatening (B)enhancing
(C)improving (D)increasing

( ) **3** The market for low-cost notebooks has become very _____ because more and more companies start making low-cost notebooks.
(A)incredible (B)passive
(C)competitive (D)comprehensive

( ) **4** When searching for new _____, many companies would welcome reliable and hard-working people.
(A)retailers (B)consumers
(C)employers (D)employees

( ) **5** His proposal was _____ because the potential profit was too low.
(A)outlined (B)outdated
(C)outstanding (D)overturned

二　文法測驗

(　) **6** He got into the front seat _____ her, and they chatted as they drove down the highway.
　(A)along with
　(B)down to
　(C)next to
　(D)beside to

(　) **7** You can have your watch _____ at the Time Shop.
　(A)fixed
　(B)be fixed
　(C)fixing
　(D)being fixed

(　) **8** Many people will become vegetarians, because of the health risks _____ eating red meat.
　(A)which associated with
　(B)are associated with
　(C)being associated with
　(D)associated with

(　) **9** I used to _____ to the bank to wire money, but I do it online now.
　(A)goes
　(B)going
　(C)go
　(D)went

(　) **10** Mary wants to know if you _____ everyday.
　(A)work
　(B)works
　(C)worked
　(D)working

三　片語測驗

(　) **11** Lena tried to remain calm, but in the end she just _____.
　(A)got off her chest
　(B)lost her head
　(C)put her finger on
　(D)lent a hand

(　) **12** My husband and I like this couple very much, but their kids are _____.
　(A)the apple of our eye
　(B)a pearl of wisdom
　(C)a fish out of water
　(D)a pain in the neck

( ) **13** My husband's salary is good, but with inflation eating us up we could never educate the girls unless I _____.
(A)gave up (B)plough on
(C)pitched in (D)pitched up

( ) **14** Some people like to drive expensive cars to show _____.
(A)up (B)off
(C)out (D)down

( ) **15** A computer is _____ many different parts.
(A)make up of (B)made up of
(C)make up from (D)made up from

四 克漏字測驗

(一)

You are probably familiar with standardized tests like the Test of English as a Foreign Language (TOEFL), the test of English for International Communication (TOEIC), and college entrance examination in English. They are different from classroom tests, so preparing for them sometimes ___16.___ different kinds of strategies. The strategies for classroom tests will help you, but some additional strategies are ___17.___, too.

First of all, remember that standardized tests ___18.___ overall proficiency, so they are not based on a textbook or a course. On any one test, you can ___19.___ to see many different English grammar points, vocabulary, sounds, patterns, sentences, paragraphs, and conversations. So you cannot really study for these tests in the same ___20.___ you study for classroom tests. Your best preparation is to be ready for the types of items on the test, the skills (usually listening and reading) involved, and the time factor.

( ) **16** (A)requires (B)asks (C)knows (D)keeps
( ) **17** (A)disappointing (B)well-done (C)important (D)frustrating
( ) **18** (A)require (B)measure (C)help (D)demand
( ) **19** (A)look (B)regard (C)require (D)expect
( ) **20** (A)time (B)way (C)respect (D)perspective

(二)

　　Media plays an important role in the field of advertising. Media can easily ___21.___ the way people think and act. Advertising companies know this better than anyone else and they are willing to pay a lot of money every year to advertise their products through media. To attract people's attention, advertising companies sometimes ___22.___ claims about the value or effectiveness of their products. Many countries have laws ___23.___ companies that put misleading advertisements ___24.___. However, advertising companies also need ___25.___ themselves. It is their responsibility to make sure their ads are accurate.

(　) **21** (A)influence 　(B)affects 　(C)effecting 　(D)controlled
(　) **22** (A)understate 　(B)overcome 　(C)exaggerate 　(D)enlarge
(　) **23** (A)to 　(B)against 　(C)with 　(D)for
(　) **24** (A)on the air 　(B)in the air 　(C)for the air 　(D)of the air
(　) **25** (A)determine 　(B)to regulate 　(C)coordinating 　(D)in qualifying

解答與解析

一、字彙測驗

1 (D)。 評鑑為所有老師提供了機會，以回顧他們在課程中扮演的角色。
(A)遊戲　(B)視聽教材　(C)活動　(D)角色

2 (A)。 空氣污染正在威脅都市地區人們的健康。
(A)威脅　(B)增加（價值）　(C)促進　(D)增加（數量）

3 (C)。 低價位筆記型電腦的市場已經變得非常競爭，因為有愈來愈多公司開始生產低價位筆記型電腦。
(A)難以致信的　(B)被動的　(C)競爭的　(D)廣泛的

4 (D)。 許多公司在招募新員工時，較歡迎可信賴及認真工作的人。
(A)零售商　(B)消費者　(C)雇主　(D)雇員

5 (D)。 他的提案被推翻，是因為潛在利潤實在太低。
(A)略述　(B)過時　(C)傑出　(D)推翻

二、文法測驗

6 (C)。 在他們聊著天開下高速公路時，他坐到前座緊鄰著她。
(A)與……相處　(B)依賴　(C)緊鄰著　(D)在……旁邊

解 (D)beside（介）表「旁邊」之意，直接接受詞，不可和to連用。

7 (A)。 你可以把你的手錶拿到鐘錶店去修。

解 fix修理，句中have為使役動詞，受詞為人時，受詞補語表主動行為，以原形動詞為之；本題受詞為物（watch），受詞補語表被動行為，以過去分詞為之，故選(A)fixed。

8 (D)。 許多人將成為素食者，因為吃紅肉與健康風險有關。

解 becuase of ＋ N(片.)，原句為which are associated with, which are 可省略，故正確答案為(D)。

9 (C)。 我從前要到銀行去匯錢，但我現在只要在網路上做就好。

解 used to從前、曾經，後接原形動詞，故選(C)。

10 (A)。 Mary想知道你是否每天工作。

解 此題為間接疑問句，if引導名詞子句，子句中動詞隨主詞變化，如本題的everyday可知為現在簡單式，主詞又為you第二人稱，因此動詞為(A)work。

三、片語測驗

11 (B)。 Lena試圖要保持冷靜，但最後她還是失去理智。

(A)喘一口氣；解決事情 (B)失去理智 (C)指認、認出 (D)提供幫助

12 (D)。 我先生和我都很喜歡這對夫婦，但他們的孩子實在讓人頭痛。

(A)掌上明珠 (B)智慧之珠 (C)離水之魚 (D)眼中釘、使人難受

13 (C)。 我先生的薪水不錯，但因為通貨膨脹的消耗，除非我加入職場協力賺錢，要不然無法教育我們的女兒們。

(A)放棄 (B)耕犁 (C)協力 (D)選中

14 (B)。 有些人喜歡開名貴的車來炫耀。

解 show off 炫耀。

15 (B)。 一部電腦由許多不同的零件所組成。

解 電腦是「被」組成的，因此以(B)或(D)選項的「組成」進行考慮，(D)be made from是指物品製作的源起，從原料到完工進行的是化學變化，較難從外觀看得出來，而(B)的be made of是指物品組裝製成一個成品，是物理變化，較易從外觀看得出來。電腦主機中有許多電路板、線等，可看出其由不同零件組合而成。

四、克漏字測驗

(一)

你也許熟悉像托福、多益這樣的標準化測驗，或是大學入學英語考試。它們與課程測驗不同，因此在準備時，有時就需要不同型態的策略。在課程測驗準備的策略可以幫助你，但一些其他的策略也是相當的重要。

首先，記住所有標準化測驗都是要測出全面的英語精通能力，因此它們不會以一本教科書或一門課程為基礎。在任何的測驗，你可以期待你將看到許

多不同的英文文法重點、字彙、口音、題型、句子、段落及會話。所以你不可以用準備課程測驗的方式來準備這些測驗。朝測驗中的選項準備就是最好的準備，技巧（通常是聽力與閱讀）及時間因素也包括在準備的範圍內。

16 (A)。(A)需要　(B)問、要求　(C)知道　(D)保持

17 (C)。(A)使人失望的　(B)表現好　(C)重要的　(D)使人沮喪的

18 (B)。(A)需要　(B)測量　(C)幫助　(D)需求

19 (D)。(A)看　(B)不顧　(C)需要　(D)期待

20 (B)。(A)時間　(B)方式　(C)尊敬　(D)觀點

(二)

　　媒體在廣告界中扮演了很重要的角色。媒體可以輕易地影響人們思考或行為的模式。廣告公司比誰都清楚這一點，因此他們願意每年都付出很多金錢透過媒體廣告行銷他們的產品。為了吸引人們的注意，廣告公司有時會誇大它們產品的價值或效果。許多國家已制定法律來對抗在廣播中的不實誤導廣告。然而，廣告公司也需要自我管制，因為確保他們廣告正確性是他們的責任。

21 (A)。(A)影響　(B)影響　(C)造成　(D)控制

　　解 此題有助動詞can，後必須接原形動詞，故選(A)。

22 (C)。(A)少報、不充分陳述　(B)克服　(C)誇大　(D)使……變大

23 (B)。(A)給　(B)對抗　(C)與　(D)為

24 (A)。(A)在廣播　(B)在空中　(C)（無此用法）　(D)（無此用法）

25 (B)。(A)決定　(B)管制　(C)調合　(D)修正

一 字彙測驗

(   ) **1** How can I express my _____ for your help?
(A)appreciation   (B)application   (C)assumption   (D)attention

(   ) **2** You need to _____ the check to have it cashed.
(A)endorse   (B)invoice   (C)invalid   (D)revise

(   ) **3** No one is so _____ as the man who has no wish to learn.
(A)intelligent   (B)ignorant   (C)useless   (D)exclusive

(   ) **4** The policeman stopped him when he was driving home and_____ him of speeding.
(A)accounted   (B)arranged   (C)accused   (D)abused

(   ) **5** Since I know nothing about this, my answer to your question is "No _____."
(A)reliance   (B)discount   (C)elective   (D)comment

(   ) **6** A _____ for a product is the people or organizations who buy it or may buy it, or an area where it is sold.
(A)city   (B)downtown   (C)market   (D)village

(   ) **7** Excellent customer service helps maintain customer _____.
(A)fidelity   (B)loyalty   (C)piety   (D)reliability

(   ) **8** Although some people seem to have better verbal skills than others, almost everyone can _____ his or her first language easily and well.
(A)convince   (B)condense   (C)acquire   (D)attempt

二　文法測驗

(　) **9** It was careless _____ you to make the same mistake again and again.
(A)from 　(B)for 　(C)in 　(D)of

(　) **10** The manager hasn't been able to rest all day. In fact, he hasn't rested for _____ a minute.
(A)just 　(B)still 　(C)even 　(D)rather

(　) **11** After being away for thirty years, the artist finally came back to the town _____ he was born.
(A)where 　(B)which 　(C)from which 　(D)in that

(　) **12** Revenues or the quarter increased 12.2 _____ to $74.5bn.
(A)percents 　(B)percent 　(C)percentage 　(D)percentages

(　) **13** The United States _____ will remain a leading power if it continues to provide other countries with economic assistance.
(A)themselves 　(B)herselves 　(C)themselves 　(D)itself

(　) **14** To many Caucasians, the Koreans and the Japanese look so much _____ that they are often mistaken for each other.
(A)like 　(B)alike 　(C)liking 　(D)likable

(　) **15** I've lost my purse. I must _____ it somewhere.
(A)be dropping 　　　　　(B)be dropped
(C)have dropped 　　　　　(D)have being dropped

三　克漏字測驗

A terrible disease called polio struck the United States in the late 1940s and early 1950s. It crippled 300,000 people, mostly children, ___16.___ 57,000. There was no cure for the disease, ___17.___ scientists were working hard to find one. Finally, the National Foundation for Infantile Paralysis, ___18.___ the March of Dimes, with the contributions from millions of Americans, began a research program at the University of Pittsburgh Medical School. They asked Dr. Jonas Salk, ___19.___ his work on Flu viruses, to direct the program. Salk joined the fight ___20.___ polio.

(　) **16** (A)and kill　　(B)and killed　　(C)but killing　　(D)and kills

(　) **17** (A)because　　(B)and　　　　(C)as　　　　　(D)although

(　) **18** (A)good know as　　　　　(B)well knows as
　　　　　(C)better known as　　　　(D)well knew as

(　) **19** (A)which had been knew as
　　　　　(B)who was already known for
　　　　　(C)whom had already knowing to
　　　　　(D)whose had been know with

(　) **20** (A)to　　　　　(B)with　　　　(C)against　　　(D)on

四　閱讀測驗

　　When Maria was twelve, she made her first important decision about the course of her life. She decided that she wanted to continue her education. Most girls from middle-class families chose to stay home after primary school, though some attended private Catholic "finishing" schools. There they learned a little about music, art, needlework, and how to make polite conversation. This was not the sort of education that interested Maria - or her mother. By this time, she had begun to take her studies more seriously. She read constantly and brought her books everywhere. One time she even brought her math book to the theater and tried to study in the dark.

　　Maria knew that she wanted to go on learning in a serious way. That meant attending the public high school, something that very few girls did. In Italy at the time, there were two types of high schools: the "classical" schools and the "technical" schools. In the classical schools, the students followed a very traditional program of studies, with courses in Latin and Greek language and literature, and Italian literature and history. The few girls who continued studying after primary school usually chose these schools.

　　Maria, however, wanted to attend a technical school. The technical schools were more modern than the classical schools and they offered courses in modern language, mathematics, science, and accounting. Most people - including Maria's father - believed that girls would never be able to understand these subjects. Furthermore, they did not think it was proper for girls to study them.

(　　) **21** This passage is about ＿＿＿＿＿＿＿＿＿＿
　　　　(A)Maria's high school years.　　(B)technical schools in Italy.
　　　　(C)high school courses.　　　　(D)Maria's favorite courses.

(　　) **22** Maria wanted to attend ＿＿＿＿＿＿＿＿＿＿
　　　　(A)a private "finishing" school.　(B)a school with Latin and Greek.
　　　　(C)a technical high school.　　　(D)a school for art and music.

(　　) **23** In those days, most Italian girls ＿＿＿＿＿＿＿＿＿＿
　　　　(A)went to technical high school.　(B)went to "finishing" schools.
　　　　(C)did not go to high school.　　(D)went to classical schools.

(　　) **24** You can infer from this passage that ＿＿＿＿＿＿＿＿＿＿
　　　　(A)only girls attended classical schools.
　　　　(B)girls did not like going to school.
　　　　(C)girls usually attended private primary schools.
　　　　(D)only boys usually attended technical schools.

(　　) **25** Maria's father probably ＿＿＿＿＿＿＿＿＿＿
　　　　(A)had very modern views about women.
　　　　(B)had no opinion about women.
　　　　(C)thought women could not learn Latin.
　　　　(D)had very traditional views about women.

解答與解析

一、字彙測驗

1 (A)。我該怎麼表達你幫助我的謝意呢？
(A)感謝　(B)申請　(C)假定　(D)注意

2 (A)。你要在支票上背書才能將它兌現。
(A)背書　(B)發票　(C)無效的　(D)修改

3 (B)。沒有人比不想學習的人更無知。
(A)聰明的　(B)無知的　(C)無用的　(D)排他的

4 (C)。他開車回家的路上，警察把他攔下來，告他超速。
(A)說明　(B)安排　(C)控告　(D)虐待

5 (D)。我對這件事一無所知，所以我的回答是「不予置評」。
(A)依賴　(B)折扣　(C)選舉的　(D)評論

6 (C)。產品的市場，指的是會購買該產品的人或組織，或是該產品販售的地區。　(A)城市　(B)市中心　(C)市場　(D)村莊

7 (B)。絕佳的顧客服務有助於保住客戶的忠誠度。
(A)精確度　(B)忠誠　(C)虔誠　(D)可信賴度

8 (C)。雖然有些人的口語能力似乎比其他人還好，但幾乎所有人都能輕易地學好他們的第一語言。
(A)說服　(B)濃縮　(C)獲得　(D)試圖
解 人學語言的「學」，通常用「acquire（獲得）」而不用「learn（學習）」；不過，雖然不常見，但還是有些人以「learn」這個動詞來表示學習母語或外語。

二、文法測驗

9 (D)。一直重覆犯一樣的錯誤，你實在很不小心。
解 it be＋形容詞＋of＋某人＋to V，形容某人做某件事情是很……的，若此形容詞是形容「人的特質」，介係詞則需用of而非for。

10 (C)。經理整天都沒休息過。事實上，他甚至一分鐘都沒休息。
解 even在本句中用來強調「連一分鐘都沒有」。

11 (A)。離開家鄉三十年後，這位藝術家終於回到他出生的小鎮。
解 where當關係副詞用，也可以換成in which。

12 (B)。該季的稅收增加了12.2%，來到745億。
解 百分比單位為percent。

13 (D)。如果美國繼續對其他國家提供經濟援助，它將維持其自身的主導權。

解 the United States指一個國家，為單數，故反身代名詞用第三人稱單數。

14 (B)。對大多數白人來說，韓國人和日本人長得非常相似，所以常常被認錯。

解 look alike表示「看起來很像」。

15 (C)。我的包包不見了。我一定是把它掉在哪裡了。

解 現在完成式為have＋過去分詞。

三、克漏字測驗

　　1940年代晚期到1950年代早期，一種叫做polio（小兒麻痺症）的疾病席捲美國，重創了三十萬人口，其中大多是小孩，並有五萬七千人死於該疾病。雖然科學家非常努力想找出治療方法，但當時它仍是個不治之症。最後，以「the March of Dimes」之名廣為人所知的美國國家小兒麻痺基金會，帶著數百萬美國人的貢獻，在匹茲堡醫藥學院開始了一項研究計畫。他們請以研究流行感冒病毒著稱的喬那斯・沙克博士來主持該計畫。沙克博士於是加入對抗小兒麻痺症的行列。

16 (B)。解 and所連接的是「使殘廢（crippled）」和「殺害（killed）」兩個動詞，既然前文的crippled為過去式，killed也要用過去式。

17 (D)。(A)因為　(B)而且　(C)當時　(D)雖然

18 (C)。解 該組織以……的名稱「為人所知」，必須以過去分詞的形式表示被動，be known as＋名稱（身份）表示「以……的名稱（身份）為人所知」。

19 (B)。解 關係代名詞who代替Dr. Jonas Salk，who was already known for……表示「他已經以……的名聲被人所知」。

20 (C)。解 fight後接against（介）＋N. 表示對抗N.……。

四、閱讀測驗

　　瑪麗亞十二歲時，她為自己的人生做了第一個重要的決定。她決定繼續求學。大多數出身於中產階級家庭的女孩在完成小學學業後，都會選擇留在家裡，有一些是選擇就讀私立的天主教女子學堂，在女子學堂裡，她們學習一些音樂、美術、針線活、以及對話禮儀。這些都引不起瑪麗亞的興趣，她的母親對這些也一樣不感興趣。此時，瑪麗亞已經開始認真對待自己的學業。她定時讀書，且到哪都帶著書本。有一次她甚至帶著她的數學書籍到電影院裡，想在黑暗中讀書。

　　瑪麗亞知道自己想要繼續認真地學習，也就是上公立中學，這是很少女生會做的事。在當時的義大利，有兩種中學：「傳統」學校和「技術」學校。在傳統學校裡，學生的學習是遵循一套非常傳統的課程，課程含有拉丁文及

文學、希臘文及文學、義大利文學及歷史。那些在小學之後繼續求學的少數女生，通常都會選擇這種學校。

　　但是，瑪麗亞想要上技術學校。技術學校比傳統學校現代化的多，且技術學校提供當代語言、數學、科學、和會計等課程。大多數的人，包括瑪麗亞的父親，都認為女生不可能學會這些學問。而且，他們也認為女生不適合學習這些東西。

21 (A)。本文是關於_____。
(A)瑪麗亞的中學歲月
(B)義大利的技術學校
(C)中學課程
(D)瑪麗亞最喜歡的課程

22 (C)。瑪麗亞想要上_____。
(A)私立的女子學堂
(B)有拉丁文和希臘文的學校
(C)技術中學
(D)藝術和音樂學校

23 (C)。當時，大部分的義大利女孩_____。
(A)想要上技術學校
(B)上女子學堂
(C)不上中學
(D)上傳統學校

24 (D)。從本文可以推論_____。
(A)只有女生會上傳統學校
(B)女生不喜歡上學
(C)女生通常上私立小學
(D)通常只有男生才會上技術學校

25 (D)。瑪麗亞的父親可能_____。
(A)對女性抱持很進步的看法
(B)對女性沒有看法
(C)認為女性學不會拉丁文
(D)對女性抱持著很傳統的想法

解答與解析

一 字彙測驗

( ) **1** Consumers benefited from _____ competition between the two computer companies, which both cut their laptop prices in half.
(A)sparse (B)scarce (C)fierce (D)fraud

( ) **2** The _____ is poor because of the rain; therefore, you should drive slowly.
(A)region (B)scenery (C)eyesight (D)visibility

( ) **3** I'm sorry we cannot help you, sir, because that would be ____ the law.
(A)prohibiting (B)violating (C)completing (D)forbidding

( ) **4** Generally speaking, an attractive, well-written resume will ____ your chances of getting a good job.
(A)control (B)enhance (C)humiliate (D)comprehend

( ) **5** Although the police did not find out who stole the money from the bank, they have a strong _____ that it was a man who used to work there.
(A)hesitation (B)sensation (C)suspicion (D)extension

( ) **6** My father began to eat more fruit after the doctor determined that a vitamin _____ was causing his health problem.
(A)deficiency (B)deformity (C)disposition (D)discernment

( ) **7** A government officer should always try to make a clear _____ between right and wrong.
(A)imputation (B)extinction (C)distinction (D)assumption

( ) **8** Words of the offer gave some investors _____ although Buffett said a deal would only back municipal bonds, and not the risky and complicated financial instruments.
(A)relief (B)rebound (C)recluse (D)recreation

二 文法測驗

(　) **9** John has been invited to the party, but he doesn't know _____ or not.
(A)if to go (B)whether to go
(C)if he does go (D)whether does he go

(　) **10** Miss Chang is still looking for a job, but she hopes _____ something soon.
(A)to find (B)finding (C)to have found (D)having found

(　) **11** I've lost my purse. I must _____ it somewhere.
(A)be dropping (B)have dropped
(C)be dropped (D)have being dropped

(　) **12** Ang Lee _____ one of the best movie directors in the world.
(A)considers being (B)has considered to be
(C)may consider being (D)is considered to be

(　) **13** My number one advertising principle—_____—is to wake up the consumers.
(A)because I have one (B)but I have one
(C)if I have one (D)since I have one

(　) **14** In _____ of Taiwan lies the city of Kaohsiung, the major industrial and shipping center of the island.
(A)south-west (B)the south-west
(C)southern-west (D)south-western

(　) **15** Throughout the world, several _____ suffer from AIDS.
(A)millions of people (B)million of peoples
(C)million people (D)million of people

三　克漏字測驗

Many people often have the idea that a lawyer is a person who makes long speeches before a court. ___16.___, the average lawyer spends very little time in court. ___17.___ a trial lawyer does most of his work in his office. He often has to spend weeks or months studying related materials for a trial case, ___18.___ the trial may last only a day or two in the courtroom.

Most lawyers also spend a great deal of time in giving advice ___19.___ legal matters. They draw up contracts, wills, and other legal papers. They try to settle ___20.___ without lawsuits. In fact, many people agree that the best lawyer is the one who can protect the interests of his client without going to the court.

(　) **16** (A)To begin with　(B)Moreover　(C)In fact　　(D)In addition

(　) **17** (A)As　　　　　(B)Only　　　(C)Even　　　(D)Still

(　) **18** (A)once　　　　(B)while　　　(C)as for　　　(D)as though

(　) **19** (A)on　　　　　(B)from　　　(C)at　　　　(D)with

(　) **20** (A)exertions　　(B)benefits　　(C)documents　(D)compromises

四　閱讀測驗

Many economists warned that the U.S. economy is taking one of its cyclical snoozes. However, the predictions of a deep downturn are highly exaggerated, in part because Washington is rushing to revive the declining economy. GDP increased 0.6% in the fourth quarter of 2007, after a powerful 4.9% surge in the third quarter. Exports are booming, growing at an annual rate of 13%, thanks to the weak dollar. The employment picture is surprisingly resilient. Jobless claims, a reliable indicator of recession, have averaged about 325,000 for the past four weeks, far below the danger point. "We haven't seen the 25% increase in jobless claims we had before the last two recessions," says Michael Darda, chief economist with MKM Partners, an equity trading and research firm. "We're not getting a recession signal."

The forces weighing down the economy are soft consumer spending and plunging housing prices, along with far more expensive credit that's slowing everything from auto purchases to the creation of new businesses. Those factors are a serious drag on demand. But they pose their gravest threat in the first two quarters of 2008. In other words, if we're going to get a recession, it will most likely happen amid this turmoil, in the first half of this year.

(　　) **21** According to the passage, which of the following is true about the U.S. job market?
(A)There has been a 25% increase in jobless claims last year.
(B)The unemployment rate is now higher than the danger point.
(C)In the fourth quarter of 2007 the unemployment rate has increased about 13%.
(D)In the past four weeks the average of the jobless claims was about 325,000.

(　　) **22** According to the passage, which of the following is NOT a reason that may lead to a recession for the U.S. economy?
(A)Low GDP.　　　　　　　　(B)Falling housing prices.
(C)Weak consumer demand.　　(D)Expensive credit.

(　　) **23** The word "resilient" is closest in meaning to _____.
(A)high　　　　　　　　(B)weak
(C)durable　　　　　　　(D)changeable

(　　) **24** What may be inferred about the author's attitude about the U.S. economy?
(A)Pessimistic.　　　　　　(B)Optimistic.
(C)Neutral.　　　　　　　　(D)Indifferent.

(　　) **25** When was this passage was most likely written?
(A)September 2007.　　　　(B)December 2007.
(C)January 2008.　　　　　(D)June 2008.

解答與解析

一、字彙測驗

1 (C)。兩家電腦公司都將筆電價錢減半，激烈的競爭，使消費者因而受惠。
(A)稀少的　(B)缺乏的　(C)激烈的
(D)欺騙

2 (D)。因為下雨，能見度較低，你要開得慢一點。
(A)地區　(B)風景　(C)視力　(D)能見度

3 (B)。先生，很抱歉我們不能幫你，因為那會違反法律。
(A)妨礙　(B)違反　(C)完成　(D)禁止

4 (B)。一般而言，一篇吸引人的好履歷可以提高你得到好工作的機會。
(A)控制　(B)提高　(C)侮辱　(D)了解

5 (C)。雖然警察尚未確定誰偷了銀行的錢，但他們強烈懷疑是一個以前在這裡工作過的人偷的。
(A)猶豫　(B)感覺　(C)懷疑　(D)擴展

6 (A)。醫生說我父親的維他命不足，才引起健康問題，之後他就開始多吃水果。
(A)不足　(B)變形　(C)性情　(D)洞察力

7 (C)。政府官員應該試著明辨是非。
(A)歸罪　(B)滅絕　(C)分辨　(D)設想

8 (A)。雖然巴菲特所提供的擔保只針對市政債券，而不包括複雜的高風險金融工具，但這項提議仍然紓緩了投資者的擔憂。
(A)紓緩　(B)回彈　(C)隱遁者
(D)消遣

二、文法測驗

9 (B)。John受邀去那場宴會，但他不知道該不該去。
解 whether to go or not 與whether he should go or not 相同，表示他不知該去或不該去。

10 (A)。張小姐還在找工作，但她希望能盡快找到。
解 hope後接不定詞（to V）表示「希望做……」。

11 (B)。我的包包不見了。我一定是把它掉在哪了。
解 現在完成式為have/has＋過去分詞。

12 (D)。李安被視為現今世界上最好的導演之一。
解 A be considered to be B「A被視為B」是被動式，以be＋過去分詞來表達。

13 (C)。我對廣告的首要原則─如果我有的話─是要喚醒消費者。
解 破折號中的內容，用來補充說明前文提及的「我對廣告的首要原則」。

14 (B)。台灣西南部有高雄座落其中，高雄為本島主要的工業及船運中心。
　解 方向詞為名詞時，不可加-ern，-ern字尾為形容詞，且一般單數名詞要前接冠詞。

15 (A)。全世界有好幾百萬人罹患愛滋病。
　解 millions of ＋名詞，為「數以百萬的……」之意。

三、克漏字測驗

　　很多人都有一種觀念，就是律師是在法庭上長篇大論的人。事實上，一般律師只花很少的時間上法庭。即使是出庭律師，他大部分的工作也都在他的辦公室裡完成。他通常要花上好幾個星期或好幾個月來研究案件的相關資料，而案件通常只出庭一天或兩天。

　　大多數的律師也花很多時間對法律問題給出意見。他們草擬合約、遺囑、以及其他法律文件。他們試著不需上法庭就為客戶爭取到利益。事實上，很多人都認為最好的律師是能夠不用上法院就保護客戶權益的人。

16 (C)。　(A)首先　(B)再者；此外　(C)事實上　(D)此外

17 (C)。　(A)當……時　(B)只有　(C)即使　(D)仍然

18 (B)。　(A)一旦　(B)然而　(C)至於　(D)彷彿
　解 while在此連接前後兩句，表示意思轉折，或做對照用。

19 (A)。　針對……議題／主題來給與意見，用介系詞on。

20 (B)。　(A)盡力　(B)利益　(C)文件　(D)折衷

四、閱讀測驗

　　許多經濟學家警告，美國經濟正處於週期性休眠中。然而，這種認為經濟跌入谷底的預測實在言過其實，這麼說的部分原因是華府正在努力復甦蕭條中的經濟。2007年第三季，國內生產毛額漲了4.9%，第四季則上升6%。多虧了美元的下跌，對外貿易也蓬勃發展，全年上漲了13%。令人驚訝的是，就業市場更禁得起考驗。經濟蕭條最佳指標：失業聲明，前四週平均為32萬5千例，這個數字大幅低於危險低點。證券交易暨研究公司MKM Partners的首席經濟學家麥可‧達德說「上兩次經濟蕭條時，失業聲明增加了25%，但目前我們還沒見到這個數字。」他並表示「我們還沒看到經濟蕭條的信號。」

　　拖垮經濟的是消費者的消費走軟及房價猛跌，再加上昂貴的信貸，減緩了買車、創業等所有的消費。這些因素是當前的大問題。但它們最大的威脅是在2008年的上半年。也就是說，如果我們真的會有經濟蕭條，它最可能發生於現在的混亂狀況中，也就是今年的上半年。

21 (D)。　根據本文，關於美國就業市場的敘述，下列何者為真？
(A)去年失業聲明增加了25%
(B)目前失業率高於危險點

(C)2007年第四季的失業率增加約13%

(D)過去的四週中,失業聲明平均有
　　32萬5千例

22 (A)。 根據本文,下列何者不是美
國經濟蕭條的原因?

(A)國內生產毛額偏低

(B)房價下跌

(C)消費需求疲弱

(D)昂貴的信貸

23 (C)。「resilient」意思最接近
_____。

(A)高的　　　　(B)虛弱的

(C)耐用的　　　(D)可改變的

24 (C)。 由本文可以推論,作者對於
美國經濟的觀感為何?

(A)悲觀的　　　(B)樂觀的

(C)中性的　　　(D)冷漠的

25 (C)。 本文最可能寫於何時?

(A)2007年9月　(B)2007年12月

(C)2008年1月　(D)2008年6月

第四回

一 字彙測驗

(　　) **1** The three major banks in our country were arranged to _____ in order to become one of the world's largest financial institutions.
(A)blend　(B)merge　(C)immerse　(D)disperse

(　　) **2** Jacky's driver's license was _____ after he was caught speeding several times.
(A)resumed　(B)revoked　(C)reversed　(D)retrieved

(　　) **3** His religious belief is not _____ with reason.
(A)incompatible　(B)incomplete　(C)immortal　(D)interim

(　　) **4** Would you please _____ on your last statement? I'm not sure what you meant by that.
(A)insist　(B)promote　(C)retrieve　(D)elaborate

(　　) **5** Wall Street and European stocks finished mostly higher on Tuesday after Warren Buffett offered to help out troubled bond insurers, easing some of the market's concerns about further _____ in the credit markets.
(A)delirious　(B)deputy　(C)dimension　(D)deterioration

二 文法測驗

(　　) **6** Modern technology _____ the way we work and play, but it has also changed the way we receive information and communicate with others.
(A)will not only change　　(B)will only not change
(C)has only not changed　　(D)has not only changed

( ) **7** The car was three years old but _____ very much. So it still looked almost like new.

(A)hasn't used   (B)hadn't used

(C)hasn't been used   (D)hadn't been used

( ) **8** I really _____ to Taipei for the weekend.

(A)wish to going   (B)anticipate to going

(C)look forward to go   (D)feel like going

( ) **9** The _____ based on the principal unit "meter" to measure lengths, distances, weights, and other value is called the metric system.

(A)method being standard   (B)standard method is

(C)standard method   (D)standard method which

三 克漏字測驗

There was once a farmer who lived in a village miles away from a river. Every day the farmer had to go to river to carry water home for his family. He had two large buckets, each hung on the ends of a pole which he carried across his neck. One of the buckets had a crack in it, ___10.___ the other was perfect and always delivered a full portion of water.

At the end of each long walk from the river to the house, the cracked bucket arrived only half full. This went on for two years, ___11.___ the farmer delivering only one and a half buckets full of water to his house.

The perfect bucket was of course proud of its accomplishments. But the poor cracked bucket was ashamed of its own ___12.___. It felt sorry for being able to do only half of its job.

One day, the cracked bucket spoke to the farmer by the river. "I'm ashamed of myself. This crack in my side causes water to leak all the way back to your house. ___13.___ my flaws, you don't get full value from your efforts," the bucket apologized.

The farmer smiled. "Did you notice that there were flowers only on your side of the path? I've always ___14.___ your flaw, and I planted flower seeds on your side of the path. Every time when we walk back, you've watered them. For two years, I have been able to pick these beautiful flowers to decorate my dinner table, thanks to your crack."

(　　) **10** (A)as to 　　　(B)if only 　　(C)while 　　　(D)whether

(　　) **11** (A)to 　　　　(B)for 　　　(C)with 　　　(D)from

(　　) **12** (A)deception (B)negligence (C)ignorance (D)imperfection

(　　) **13** (A)In spite of (B)Because of (C)In relation to (D)In addition to

(　　) **14** (A)cared for 　(B)known to 　(C)known about (D)worried for

---

四 | 閱讀測驗

Of all the wars in Africa, the most deadly is between humans and mosquitoes. Thousands of Africans die every year of malaria, a disease spread by mosquito bites. One reason the mosquitoes are winning is that the world had discarded its most effective weapon, DDT.

DDT was the most important insecticide used to kill mosquitoes and get rid of malaria in the United States. It also played a key role in malaria control in southern Europe, Asia and Latin America. With DDT, malaria cases in Sri Lanka dropped from 2.8 million in 1946 to 17 in 1963.

But Rachel Carson's 1962 book Silent Spring documented how DDT, sprayed over crops and over cities, built up in the environment, killing birds and fish. William Ruckleshaus, the first head of the Environmental Protection Agency, thus banned DDT in 1972 for all but emergencies.

The ban on DDT, though a right decision for the United States, had deadly consequences overseas. Under American pressure, several Latin American countries that had controlled malaria stopped using DDT—and in most of them, malaria cases soared.

　　But the situation is now changing. As AIDS is spreading quickly in the third-world countries, diseases in this area, including malaria, have again attracted attention worldwide. Studies have also shown that in some areas the benefits from use of DDT far outweigh the risks. As a result, Washington recently resumed financing the use of DDT overseas. The World Health Organization also announced that it agrees on widespread indoor house spraying with DDT. This effective weapon, after being discarded for decades, is now back in the war to fight against mosquitoes.

(　　) **15** Which of the following is a reason why many Africans die of malaria every year?
　　(A)DDT has been banned for use all over the world.
　　(B)Africans have spent more money on weapons than on DDT.
　　(C)Their environment has been polluted from overuse of DDT.
　　(D)Spraying of DDT there has not been useful in killing mosquitoes.

(　　) **16** Who was William Ruchleshaus?
　　(A)The author of the book Silent Spring.
　　(B)The person who banned the use of DDT in 1972.
　　(C)The first head of the World Health Organization.
　　(D)The Minister of the Health Department in Sri Lanka.

(　　) **17** Why did some Latin American countries stop using DDT？
　　(A)Their use of DDT had not helped to reduce malaria cases.
　　(B)DDT was no longer needed after malaria had been controlled.
　　(C)The United States did not agree for them to continue using DDT.
　　(D)They were not able to balance risks and benefits from using DDT

(　　) **18** According to the passage, which of the following is NOT true？
　　(A)DDT kills not only mosquitoes, but also birds and fish.
　　(B)DDT use had been very helpful for malaria control in Asia.
　　(C)Malaria cases in Sri Lanka increased quickly between 1946 and 1963.
　　(D)After disuse of DDT, malaria cases increased quickly after disuse of DDT.

( ) **19** Why is the use of DDT allowed again？
　　(A)Malaria cases have suddenly increased in the United States.
　　(B)DDT use has been shown more beneficial than damaging in some areas.
　　(C)Some studies have proved that DDT is not harmful to our environment.
　　(D)The United States need to sell DDT to the third-world countries for financial reasons.

解答與解析

一、字彙測驗

1 (B)。 我國三家主要銀行正在計畫合併，以期成為世界最大的金融單位之一。
(A)混合　(B)合併　(C)浸沒　(D)解散
解 單位、組織、學校等的合併，多使用merge這個動詞。

2 (B)。 在Jacky被抓到超速駕駛好幾次之後，他的駕照被註銷了。
(A)重啟　(B)撤銷　(C)顛倒　(D)重獲

3 (A)。 他的宗教信仰與理性並不衝突。
(A)不相容的　(B)未完成的　(C)不死的　(D)過渡的

4 (D)。 能請你解釋最後一句話嗎？我不是很了解你的意思。
(A)堅持　(B)推廣　(C)收回　(D)解釋

5 (D)。 巴菲特表示願意幫助債券保險公司，這項消息減輕了投資者對於信貸市場進一步惡化的擔憂，星期二華爾街與歐洲股市都應聲上漲。
(A)精神錯亂的　(B)代理人　(C)範圍　(D)惡化

二、文法測驗

6 (D)。 現代化科技不只改變了我們工作和娛樂的方式，也改變了我們接受資訊和傳遞訊息的方法。
解 本句為「not only...but also...」的活用題，not only與but also所連接的兩個文法單位結構通常為平行結構，後句使用現在完成式為其時態時，前句亦為現在完成式。

7 (C)。 這輛車雖然已經三年了，但沒有很常被使用，因此看起來還幾乎是新的。
解 現在完成式加上被動態的組合，要用have/has＋been＋過去分詞。

8 (D)。 我真的很想去台北。
解 (A)wish後接不定詞，因此要改成wish to go。
(B)anticipate雖然可譯為「期

望」，但它不適合當「想要做某事」的意思，而是指「預期、預料會發生某事」。

(C)look forward to的to為介系詞，後接名詞或動名詞。

9 (C)。以「公制」為主要單位來測量長度、距離、重量以及其它數量等，這種標準方法稱為「公制/十進制」。

解 本句的結構為the standard method為主詞，後接形容詞片語（based on the principal unit... and other values）補充說明之，is called the metric system為主要動詞及補語。

三、克漏字測驗

以前有一位農夫住在離河幾哩遠的村莊中。每天他必須走到河邊提水回家給家人使用。他有兩個大水桶，他把水桶掛在一支竿子的兩端，將竿子扛在肩膀上。其中一個水桶有個裂縫，而另一個水桶完好無缺，且總是提滿水回家。

每次提水回到家時，有裂縫的水桶都只有半桶水。農夫每天提一桶半水回家的這種狀況持續了兩年。

完整的桶子當然對自己的成就感到很驕傲，但是另一個有裂縫的桶子就很可憐，它對自己的不完美感到很慚愧。它很抱歉自己只能夠完成一半的工作。

有一天，有裂縫的桶子在河邊跟農夫道歉說，「我很慚愧。在回你家的路上，我身上的這個裂縫讓水一直流掉。因為我的缺陷，你辛勤的工作無法得到你應得的全部利益。」

農夫微笑說，「你注意到沒？只有你那一側的路上才有花開著。我一直都知道你有缺口，所以就種了一些花的種子在你那一側的路上。每次我走回家時，你都為他們澆了水。兩年來，因為這樣我才得以摘一些花來裝飾我的餐桌，這都多謝了你的裂縫。」

10 (C)。解 while當連接詞，為「然而」之意，用來承接兩句，意思與but接近，表示上下文意的相反對比。with＋O.（受詞）＋O.C（受詞補語），此句受詞補語為Ving（delivering）

11 (C)。解 with在這裡用來表示持續了兩年的狀況是甚麼。with＋O.（受詞）＋O.C（受詞補語），此句受詞補語為V-ing（delivering）。

12 (D)。(A)欺騙　(B)疏忽　(C)無知　(D)不完美

13 (B)。(A)儘管　(B)因為　(C)與……有關　(D)除了……以外

14 (C)。(A)關心……　(B)被……所知　(C)知道關於……　(D)為……擔心

四、閱讀測驗

在非洲所有的戰爭中，最慘烈的是人和蚊子的戰爭。每年都有數以千計的非洲人死於由蚊蟲叮咬傳播的瘧疾。蚊子佔上風的原因之一是因為人們拋棄了最有效的武器：DDT殺蟲劑。

DDT殺蟲劑曾是美國最重要的殺蟲劑，用以撲滅蚊蟲，使美國擺脫瘧疾。在南歐、亞洲、及拉丁美洲控制瘧

疾的歷史上，ＤＤＴ也曾扮演重要的角色。在DDT的使用下，斯里蘭卡的瘧疾病例從1946年的兩百八十萬例降到1963年的十七例。

但是瑞秋・卡森1962年出版的《沉默的春天》，記錄了噴灑在農作物和城市中的DDT，如何堆積在環境中，並殺死鳥和魚。於是，環境保護局的第一位首長威廉・羅克勒蕭，在1972年下令，除非緊急狀況，禁止使用DDT。

ＤＤＴ的禁用對美國來說是正確的政策，但這項禁令對其他國家來說卻造成致命的危害。在美國的施壓下，許多已成功控制瘧疾的拉美國家也停止使用DDT，結果，這些國家瘧疾病例激增。

但是情況正在改變。由於愛滋病正在第三世界國家快速地蔓延開來，全世界於是再次注意到該地區的疾病，包括瘧疾。研究也指出，在某些地區，使用DDT的好處遠大過於其威脅。於是，華府最近重新援助其他國家使用DDT。世界衛生組織也宣布，他們同意DDT在室內噴灑。於是，在禁用了數十年後，這項有力的抗蚊武器再次回到人蚊大戰的戰場上。

15 (A)。 下列何者是每年許多非洲人死於瘧疾的原因？
(A)DDT在全世界被禁用。
(B)非洲花太多錢在ＤＤＴ以外的武器上。
(C)DDT的過度使用汙染了他們的環境。
(D)在那裡噴灑DDT無法有效消滅蚊子。

16 (B)。 威廉・羅克勒蕭是誰？
(A)《沉默的春天》的作者。
(B)1972年禁止使用DDT的人。
(C)世界衛生組織的第一位首長。
(D)斯里蘭卡的衛生部部長。

17 (C)。 拉美國家為何停用DDT？
(A)他們使用DDT並未有效控制瘧疾。
(B)瘧疾被控制後，他們不再需要DDT。
(C)美國不同意他們繼續用DDT。
(D)他們無法平衡ＤＤＴ帶來的威脅及其益處。

18 (C)。 根據本文，下列何者為誤？
(A)ＤＤＴ不只殺死蚊蟲，也殺死了鳥和魚。
(B)DDT的使用曾幫助亞洲控制瘧疾。
(C)1946到1963年間，斯里蘭卡瘧疾病例激增。
(D)DDT停用後，瘧疾病例激增。

19 (B)。 為何DDT再度被允許使用？
(A)美國的瘧疾病例突然增加。
(B)在某些地區，使用DDT的好處大過於壞處。
(C)一些研究證明DDT對環境無害。
(D)因財務關係，美國需要銷售DDT到第三世界國家。

解答與解析

一 字彙測驗

( ) **1** The ＿＿＿ employee was laid off, because he did not do his work efficiently. (A)lazy (B)angry (C)pretty (D)busy

( ) **2** He is a ＿＿＿ investor who buys only sound stocks.
(A)rich (B)rash (C)careful (D)stupid

( ) **3** Good economic news from the President usually ＿＿＿ the condition of the stock market.
(A)increases (B)improves (C)closes (D)opens

( ) **4** According to the expert's ＿＿＿, the economic growth rate of the whole nation will increase 2% by the end of this year.
(A)estimation (B)accumulation (C)institution (D)aspiration

( ) **5** When the boy said he could eat eighty dumplings, he was＿＿＿ exaggerating.
(A)generally (B)obviously (C)internally (D)curiously

( ) **6** Susan doesn't think this TV program is ＿＿＿ for children, so she won't let her son watch it.
(A)appropriate (B)fortunate (C)generous (D)mysterious

( ) **7** Only bring ＿＿＿ such as food and water when you hike because you don't want to carry so much extra weight.
(A)emergency (B)financial (C)essentials (D)proficiency

( ) **8** Many people like to make purchases in that company because it has a money-back ＿＿＿ for all of their new products.
(A)insurance (B)prejudice (C)guarantee (D)enhancement

( ) **9** A research team are planning an observation project on the____
of birds in Southern Taiwan.
(A)invention (B)migration (C)suggestion (D)regulation

( ) **10** As soon as a border conflict arose, the _____ ties between
these two nations were severed.
(A)diplomatic (B)characteristic (C)alphabetic (D)historic

( ) **11** Although the government has taken measures to ensure economic
recovery, some investors still feel _____ about the stock market.
(A)persuasive (B)sympathetic (C)aggressive (D) pessimistic

二 文法測驗

( ) **12** The news reports that America's financial problems were_____
expected.
(A)much worse than   (B)worse very much than
(C)bad more than   (D)very worse than

( ) **13** The staff are asked to enter the password before they _____ to
use the computer system.
(A)be allowed (B)allow (C)allowing (D)are allowed

( ) **14** There are a few shops at the end of the street but _____ of them
sell newspapers. (A)each (B)neither (C)every (D)none

( ) **15** They will put up a new building near the City Hall. All those old
buildings _____ down tomorrow.
(A)will knock   (B)will have knocked
(C)will be knocked   (D)will be knocking

( ) **16** A lot of people worked together _____ money for the people
killed in the earthquake.
(A)raise   (B)to raise
(C)raising   (D)raised

(　) **17** _____, we rushed to the scene of the accident.
　　(A)Hearing an explosion　　　(B)The man was shouting
　　(C)A big fire was seen by us　　(D)Heard loud noise

(　) **18** _____ the Internet, we would not have access to information so quickly.
　　(A)Were it not for　　　　　(B)Could it not be for
　　(C)Having no　　　　　　　(D)There was no

(　) **19** This is the _____ cell phone I want.
　　(A)same　(B)just　(C)very　(D)such

(　) **20** John is enthusiastic and patient. _____, he is always willing to help other people.
　　(A)However　(B)Nevertheless　(C)Moreover　(D)Although

三　克漏字測驗

　　In New York City, some high school students went to Cancun, Mexico for spring break and brought something back-swine flu, a new strain of the H1N1 influenza virus. Now, that small group ___21.___ hundreds of other teenagers, and fears are mounting that the new H1N1 influenza will be turning into a pandemic. The new H1N1 influenza virus has the potential to be very dangerous ___22.___ it can be spread between people. It most likely started when a pig was infected with a combination of avian and human flu.

　　The epicenter of the new H1N1 flu is Mexico, ___23.___ more than 150 people have died. The president of Mexico has ordered schools, churches and gyms closed. Restaurants are only serving carry-out meals, and the streets in many parts of Mexico City are deserted.

　　While the threat of a very serious global outbreak is looming, officials say that this has not happened and if it ___24.___ , they are ready. Health centers are asking for people who have been to Mexico recently, or have been in contact with those who have, to go to a hospital to be checked out.

Staying out of the crowded areas, frequently washing one's hands, or
____25.____ can prevent the new H1N1 flu strain. The government of Taiwan
says that they have two million vaccines on hand. If needed, the government
says that it can produce 200,000 vaccines per month as well as import them
from abroad in case the new H1N1 flu gets serious in Taiwan.

(   ) **21** (A)infecting   (B)is infected   (C)is infecting   (D)has infected

(   ) **22** (A)so that   (B)because   (C)for fear that (D)but also

(   ) **23** (A)where   (B)there   (C)which   (D)when

(   ) **24** (A)is   (B)were   (C)does   (D)will

(   ) **25** (A)getting vaccinated   (B)getting vaccinating
       (C)got vaccinating   (D)got vaccinated

四　閱讀測驗

Everyone loves money! But do you know where money originally came
from? Who were the first people to use money? Scientists say that over 10,000
years ago, people in Swaziland, Southern Africa, were using red dye as a type
of money. The aboriginal people of Australia were also using a similar dye as a
type of money around that period of time. Later, people in several places used
shells and other valuable things as a type of money to "buy" or "trade for" things
they wanted. This is known as a barter system, a form of trade where some
goods are exchanged for other goods.

Many things have been used as "money" from pigs to spices and salt.
For a long time, pepper could be used to "pay for" things in Europe. On the
Micronesian island of Yap, people used very big stone "coins," some of which
were up to eight feet wide and weighed more than a small car.

But the most convenient forms of money were pieces of valuable metals
like gold and silver. Historians think that the Lydians were the first people
to introduce the use of gold and silver coins around 650 BC. Gold and silver
are still quite valuable today.

　　The first banknotes appeared in China in the 7th century, and the first banknotes in Europe were issued in 1661.

　　Money has changed through the ages. However, it is more important today than ever before.

◎ Reference：G. J. Bahlmann & D.L. Boeuf & L. Jing (2009) Success With Reading : p.102～103

(　　) **26** What is the main idea of the article?
　　　　(A)Everyone loves money.
　　　　(B)Spending money is fun.
　　　　(C)People have used money for only a short time.
　　　　(D)People have used various forms of money for a long time.

(　　) **27** According to the article, what are some of the things that people have used for money?
　　　　(A)Pigs, spices, and dyes.　　(B)Dyes, coins, and bananas.
　　　　(C)Bananas, rocks, and pencils.　(D)Salt, dyes, and butterflies.

(　　) **28** How long ago did aboriginal people of Australia start using money?
　　　　(A)About 1,000 years ago.　　(B)About 2,650 years ago.
　　　　(C)About 10,000 years ago.　　(D)About 1,700 years ago.

(　　) **29** We can summarize the second paragraph of the article in the following sentence:
　　　　(A)The first money was used only in Swaziland.
　　　　(B)Shells were used as money long time ago.
　　　　(C)Small stones were once used as coins in Europe.
　　　　(D)A variety of things, large or small, have been used as money.

(　　) **30** Which of the following statements is true about banknotes?
　　　　(A)Banknotes were first used in China.
　　　　(B)Gold and silver were once used as banknotes in Lydia.
　　　　(C)The first banknotes appeared in 1661.
　　　　(D)Banknotes were very popular in Europe in the 7th century.

解答與解析

一、字彙測驗

1 (A)。懶惰的職員會遭解聘，因為他無法有效完成工作。
(A)懶惰 (B)憤怒 (C)美麗 (D)忙碌

2 (C)。他是名謹慎的投資者，只購買穩當的股票。
(A)富有 (B)匆忙 (C)小心謹慎 (D)愚笨的

3 (B)。來自總統關於經濟方面的好消息經常能夠改善股市的狀況。
(A)增加 (B)改善 (C)關閉 (D)開放

4 (A)。根據專家的估計，國家整體經濟成長率將於年底上升2%。
(A)估計 (B)累積 (C)直覺 (D)鼓舞

5 (B)。當那男孩說他可以吃八十顆水餃時，他顯然是誇大了。
(A)一般地 (B)明顯地 (C)內在地 (D)好奇地

6 (A)。Susan不認為這個節目適合兒童，所以她不讓她的兒子觀賞。
(A)合適 (B)幸運 (C)大方 (D)神秘

7 (C)。登山時只帶食物和水這些必需品，因為你不會想提太重的東西。
(A)緊急的 (B)財務的 (C)必要的 (D)精通

8 (C)。許多人喜歡在那家公司買東西，因為它針對所有新產品有退款保證。
(A)保險 (B)偏見 (C)保證 (D)提高

9 (B)。研究小組計劃針對臺灣南部的鳥類遷移進行觀察。
(A)創新 (B)遷移 (C)建議 (D)法規

10 (A)。一旦邊境的衝突提高，兩國間的外交關係就會展開。
(A)外交的 (B)特徵的 (C)字母順序 (D)歷史的

11 (D)。雖然政府已經採取措施以確保經濟復甦，某些投資者仍對股市感到悲觀。
(A)說服的 (B)同情的 (C)好鬥的 (D)悲觀的

二、文法測驗

12 (A)。根據新聞報導，美國的財務問題比預期地更糟糕。
解 worse是比較級形容詞，比worse更糟，用much worse。可修飾比較級之副詞有much／even／far／a lot

13 (D)。員工在使用電腦前必須先輸入密碼。
解 before後面接完整句（S＋V），句子中欠缺動詞，因為是被允許的，所以要用被動式。

14 (D)。這條街的盡頭有幾家店，但沒有一家店有賣報紙。
(A)每一 (B)兩者皆不 (C)每一 (D)一個都沒有

15 (C)。他們會在市政府附近蓋新大樓。所有的舊大樓將於明天拆除。
解 明天發生的事，用未來式；大樓是被拆除的，所以要用被動式。

16 (B)。為了在地震中身亡的人，許多人一起努力籌錢。
解 to raise ＝ in order to raise，表示目的。

17 (A)。聽到爆炸聲，我們趕忙跑往意外現場。
(A)聽到爆炸聲　(B)那名男子被射殺
(C)目睹一場大火　(D)聽到巨響
解 此為分詞構句，可還原為when we heard an explosion, we rushed to the scene of the accident. 去相同主詞（we），去連接詞（when），動詞改為分詞，此句為主動，用現在分詞（hearing）。

18 (A)。如果沒有網際網路，我們不可能那麼快得到這些資訊。
解 省略if的假設語氣，需要倒裝，原句為If it were not for...。

19 (C)。這正是我想要的那隻手機。
(A)相同的　(B)只是　(C)正是；恰為　(D)如此

20 (C)。John有熱忱又有耐心，而且，他總是願意幫助其他人。
(A)然而　(B)即使　(C)而且　(D)雖然

三、克漏字測驗

紐約市有許多高中生到墨西哥的坎昆過春假，並且帶了些東西回來——豬流感，一種新型的H1N1流行性感冒病毒。現在，那一小群人已經感染了許多其他年輕人，對於新H1N1流感會轉為大流行病的恐懼正在增加中。這種新型的H1N1流感病毒有變得非常危險的潛力，因為它會在人類間散布。當豬隻綜合感染了禽流感和人類感冒，它就非常可能開始。

新H1N1流感的中心在墨西哥，那裡已經有超過一百五十人身亡。墨西哥總統已經命令學校、教堂和健身房關閉。餐廳只提供外帶服務，墨西哥市許多街廓已無人煙。

一個非常嚴重的全球性爆發迫在眉睫，但官方說這不會發生，而且即使發生了，他們也準備好了。健康中心要求最近到過墨西哥的人，或曾與前往墨西哥的人接觸者，必須到醫院檢查。

遠離人潮擁擠的地方，常洗手，打預防針等可以預防H1N1病毒。臺灣政府表示，他們手中有兩百萬支疫苗。如果需要，政府每個月可以製造廿萬劑，同時也會從海外進口，以防新的H1N1情況在臺灣惡化。

21 (D)。**解** 已經感染了，要用完成式。

22 (B)。(A)以便　(B)因為　(C)害怕；唯恐　(D)但也……；而且……

23 (A)。**解** 先行詞Mexico是地名，關係代名詞用where ＝ in which。

24 (C)。 **解** 原句為this has not happened and if it happens.，用does來代替 happens。

25 (A)。 **解** 連接詞or前後的動詞形式要一致，staying, washing都是動名詞，所以要用getting，被接種get vaccinated。

四、閱讀測驗

每個人都愛錢，但你知道錢最早是由哪裡來的嗎？誰又是第一個使用錢的人？科學家認為，早在一萬年前，南非史瓦濟蘭人把紅色染料拿來當錢用。澳洲的原住民在同一時間也用同樣的染料為金錢。後來，許多地方的人用貝殼或其他有價值的東西當做錢來「買」或「交易」他們想要的東西。這就是所謂的「以物相易」，一種拿物品交換的貿易形式。

從豬到香料到鹽，許多東西都曾被當成「錢」來使用。有很長一段時間，胡椒可以在歐洲「購買」東西。在密克羅尼西亞的雅浦島，人類會用很大的石頭「硬幣」，某些石頭有八尺寬，重如一輛小車。

但金錢最方便的形式是像金或銀這種有價值的金屬薄片。歷史學家認為里底亞人最早使用金幣和銀幣，約當西元前六百五十年。金、銀至今仍然非常有價值。

中國第一張鈔票出現在西元七世紀，而歐洲的第一張鈔票在1661年發行。

金錢已經隨時間而有所改變，然而，比起過去，金錢在現今更為重要。

參考資料：G.J.Bahlmann & D.L.Boeuf & L.Jing (2009)《成功的閱讀》：第102至103頁。

26 (D)。 本文主旨為何？
(A)所有人都愛錢。
(B)花錢真有趣。
(C)人們用錢的時間很短。
(D)長久以來，人們有許多金錢的形式。

27 (A)。 根據本文，人們曾用哪些東西當做錢？
(A)豬、香料和染料
(B)染料、硬幣和香蕉
(C)香蕉、石頭和鉛筆
(D)鹽、染料和蝴蝶

28 (C)。 澳洲原住民在多久前開始使用金錢？
(A)大約一千年前
(B)大約2650年前
(C)大約一萬年前
(D)大約1700年前
解 文章中澳洲原住民用錢的時間和史瓦濟蘭around that period of time。

29 (D)。 用下列哪個句子可以總結本文的第二段？
(A)最早使用錢的只有史瓦濟蘭
(B)貝殼在很久以前就被用來做為金錢
(C)歐洲曾將小石頭當成硬幣
(D)或大或小，許多東西曾被視為金錢

30 (A)。 關於鈔票，下列敘述何者正確？
(A)最早在中國使用
(B)金銀曾在里底亞當成鈔票
(C)最早的鈔票出現在1661年
(D)七世紀的歐洲鈔票很流行

進階金榜挑戰

一 字彙測驗

( ) **1** One of Ms. Smith's _____ is to take care of the disadvantaged.
(A)readjustment (B)responsibility (C)irresponsibility (D) adjustment

( ) **2** After years of _____, flights commenced this summer between Java Airport and Stanley Island, about 270 kilometers from Casey Station.
(A)deception (B)recognition (C)perception (D)preparation

( ) **3** The board concluded that all policies and strategies must be discussed with all _____ personnel and staff.
(A)aboriginal (B)indulgent (C)industrious (D)managerial

( ) **4** Taiwan's enterprises should be _____ to establish themselves at home, network throughout the Asia-Pacific region, and position themselves globally.
(A)encouraged (B)discouraged (C)blamed (D)punished

( ) **5** The _____ is the highest administrative organ of the government or Republic of China.
(A)Examination Yuan　　　(B)Judicial Yuan
(C)Executive Yuan　　　(D)Control Yuan

( ) **6** To promote the upgrading of industry and to encourage exports, the government has _____ measures which include tax rebates for exports and reductions or exemptions of other taxes.
(A)admired (B)implemented (C)exposed (D)locked

( ) **7** Helen is managing director of Recruiting Services. She is
_____ developing a proven way to attract the best talent.
(A)committed to   (B)separated from
(C)removed from   (D)detached from

( ) **8** After the President's inauguration ceremony, new ministers
_____ office on May 20, 2008.
(A)presumed (B)resumed (C)assumed (D)consumed

( ) **9** Dr. Chen _____ a speech in which he commemorated the
Institute's achievements.
(A)threw (B)took (C)talked (D)delivered

( ) **10** Rampant _____ threatens many countrie's economic
performance. It is pervasive in some of their most vital sectors.
(A)benediction (B)corruption (C)fidelity (D)accuracy

( ) **11** The amendment was designed to _____ small business capital
formation by providing added investment flexibility to business
development companies.
(A)hinder (B)stem (C)facilitate (D)postpone

( ) **12** The young dancer made her very successful _____ last night.
(A)appearance (B)acquaintance (C)announcement (D)debut

( ) **13** The horrible earthquake has left our house in _____.
(A)place (B)shadows (C)shambles (D)smoke

( ) **14** Although the new investment plan looks lucrative, as an official
from the Bureau of Economic Affairs, one still has to examine all
possibilities of it being a _____ and jeopardizing national interests.
(A)sleuth (B)sham (C)shame (D)sphinx

( ) **15** It is easy to become _____ and feel good about oneself.
(A)complacent (B)contempt (C)contentious (D)contigent

( ) **16** I _____ any comments to the press.
(A)defused (B)dictated (C)deflected (D)declined

(　) **17** The billionaire is famed for his _____ to find gold and become rich overnight.
(A)settlement　(B)sacrifice　(C)serendipity　(D)originality

(　) **18** In a newspaper, the space _____ for news usually depends on the amount of advertising that is sold.
(A)anticipated　(B)allotted　(C)averted　(D)automated

(　) **19** Recently, I suffered serious insomnia so my family doctor prescribed some medicine to help _____ sleep.
(A)fall　(B)battle　(C)induce　(D)seduce

(　) **20** My boss is a typical Gemini and changes his mind about every 2 minutes—sometimes it is really _____ to be his subordinate.
(A)frustrating　(B)frustrated　(C)fortunate　(D)ingenious

二 文法測驗

(　) **21** _____ you have any further question, please feel free to ask.
(A)If　(B)Before　(C)After　(D)Don't

(　) **22** If Jane cannot finish the thesis on time, _____ present it on the symposium.
(A)she is able to　　　　　(B)unless she is able to
(C)she is going to　　　　(D)she won't be able to

(　) **23** A nationwide strike tomorrow against the government's plans to overhaul the pension system _____ some trains, flights and access to airports.
(A)disrupt to　(B)to be disrupted　(C)disrupted　(D)will disrupt

(　) **24** _____ their conclusions, the researchers matched the list of the most consumed foods with a list of black-hearted products and found an alarming degree of overlapping.
(A)To be reached　　　　(B)To be reaching
(C)To reach　　　　　　(D)The reach of

(　　) **25** Although the Williams are very strong, _____
(A) but they did not win every match.
(B)they did not win every match.
(C)though they did not win every match.
(D)so they win every match.

(　　) **26** Mr. Lee, Teng-hui, _____ from 1988 to 2000, was the President of the Republic of China.
(A)who served   (B)who serving
(C)be serving   (D)served

(　　) **27** Tom and Linda _____ to buy a new lamp.
(A)went to downtown yesterday
(B)went downtown during yesterday
(C)went downtown yesterday
(D)went to downtown during yesterday

(　　) **28** World leaders _____ concerted efforts to combat transnational threats, including terrorism.
(A)called out   (B)called in
(C)called at   (D)called for

(　　) **29** It has been raining for four hours. _____ forever.
(A)Either we go now or we remain here
(B)Neither we go now or we remain here
(C)Either we go now nor we remain here
(D)We are neither here nor there

(　　) **30** It is just _____ time. It will happen, but not today.
(A)a little of   (B)a lot of
(C)a matter of   (D)a few of

(　　) **31** _____ saving some money for your mortgage, I think you'd better not buy that fancy dress.
(A)By   (B)In addition to
(C)Away from   (D)In terms of

(　) **32** _____ Taiwan's 23 million people, the former President Chen sent a letter to the Secretary General of the United Nations to request the admission of Taiwan as a member to the United Nations.
(A)On behalf of　　　　　　(B)In the face of
(C)To be fond of　　　　　　(D)In favor of

(　) **33** You can't always say "Yes," to people. You have to _____ sometime and somewhere.
(A)drop a line　(B)draw a line　(C)drive a line　(D)dread a line

(　) **34** The new secretary is proficient _____ English and French.
(A)in　(B)on　(C)to　(D)with

(　) **35** We must be _____ guard against our competitor's new market release.
(A)in　(B)on　(C)at　(D)with

(　) **36** We are all _____ about your acquisition proposition.
(A)eyes　(B)breath　(C)hearts　(D)ears

(　) **37** The new administration's economic policies will _____ soon.
(A)come to an end　　　　　(B)come into force
(C)come into play　　　　　(D)come into words

(　) **38** We have scored _____ goals than our rivals.
(A)fewer　(B)less　(C)little　(D)much

(　) **39** What happened? You look _____ you have been in the rain.
(A)as　(B)as if　(C)such as　(D)like if

(　) **40** Almost every tourist will visit _____ Buckingham Palace when in London.
(A)(leave blank)　(B)the　(C)a　(D)an

三 閱讀測驗

(一)

The people of Taiwan have been proud of Taiwan's development experience, as the key to success has required the combined efforts of the entire nation. However, only rarely does one hear about the major role international assistance has played in Taiwan's economic construction and development. From the 1950s to 1980s, Taiwan received large amounts of money from donations and assistance from international organizations, as well as the United States and other wealthy nations. The total amount exceeded US$2.4 billin, not including US military assistance for safeguarding Taiwan. Most people remember the old days, when they consumed flour, drank milk and wore pants made from flour sacks, all of which came from the United States. However, they may not realize that many major infrastructures, including highways, electric railways, the Shih Men Dam and drinking water systems, were completed with preferential loans provided by international organizations and foreign countries. Even the eradication of malaria depended on assistance from the World Health Organization. Taiwan now has the ability to reciprocate as a result of the foreign aid it received in the past. In order to "give back to the inernational community and fulfill our responsibility as a member of the international community," Taiwan provides foreign aid to and shares our development experiences with friendly nations and diplomatic allies. This not only consolidates Taiwan's relations with them, but also lets us fulfill our obligations to the international community.

( ) **41** According to this paragraph, Taiwan _____.
  (A)did not receive any foreign aids in the past years.
  (B)is still receiving foreign aids.
  (C)only received foreign aids from the United States.
  (D)received foreign aids from the United States and other international organizations.

( ) **42** The total amount Taiwan received from intenational community are over _____.
(A)2400 million US dollars.　(B)24000 thousand US dollars.
(C)480000 million NT dollars.　(D)no reliable numbers.

( ) **43** Why preferential loan program is helpful to build up Taiwan's infrastructures?
(A)Because we don't need to pay back to the lenders.
(B)Because the interest rate is lower than the market rate.
(C)Because we can spend it as we wish.
(D)Because the Legislative Yuan cannot supervise its use.

( ) **44** Which international organization is specialized in the eradication of diseases?
(A)World Trade Organization　(B)International Labor Organization
(C)World Health Organization　(D)International Monetary Fund

( ) **45** Taiwan now provides foreign aid to its diplomatic allies, because _____.
(A)Taiwan is forced to do so by international laws.
(B)Taiwan has legal obligations to them.
(C)this policy serves Taiwan's overall national interests.
(D)this policy can control inflation.

(二)

A global "population explosion" brought to the postwar world a multitude of social problems. Symptoms of underlying social tensions were such disquieting contemporary phenomena as youth in revolt and upsurging crime.

The postwar years in America were marked by a curious mix of idealism and materialism. One striking example was the concurrent rise in both church membership and secularization.

Despite a record of unexampled physical growth, America found itself facing a host of danger signals, including depletion of natural resources, health hazards, a creaking governmental structure, and an overburdened educational system.

America's submerged minorities had achieved genuine progress, but the goal of a fully integrated society had not been attained. High on the agenda of unfinished business stood the incongruity of affluence for the majority of Americans while large minorities remained in poverty.

Once a revolutionary force in a world of conservatism, America had become a conservative force in a world of revolution. Yet America remained the world's last and perhaps still the best hope for freedom.

(　　) **46** According to the article, what main factor brought to the post World War II world a multitude of social problems?
(A)poverty　　　　　　　　　(B)population explosion
(C)loss of lives　　　　　　　(D)increased orphanage

(　　) **47** Which in the following is not a post-war danger signal in America?
(A)growing number of church goers
(B)health hazards
(C)depletion of natural resources
(D)an overburdened educational system

(　　) **48** Crime rate in post-war America has _____.
(A)become less organized　　　(B)declined
(C)climbed　　　　　　　　　(D)remained about the same

(　　) **49** Despite all the negative aspects he saw in post-war America, the author of the article still thinks America is _____.
(A)the best hope for rich and fame　(B)the best hope for freedom
(C)the worst hope for freedom　　(D)the last hope for survival

(　　) **50** According to the article, which problem is still remain to be solved for Americans?
(A)the generation gap between the elderly and the younger
(B)the wealth gap between the rich and the poor
(C)misbehavior of teenagers
(D)lack of job opportunities

解答與解析

一、字彙

1 (B)。 史密斯太太的責任之一就是照顧弱勢團體。
(A)重新調整　　(B)責任
(C)不負責　　　(D)調整

2 (D)。 在多年的準備後，班機今夏開始行駛於查亞機場和離凱西站約270公里遠的史丹利島之間。
(A)欺騙　　　　(B)辨認
(C)感知　　　　(D)準備

3 (D)。 有關當局決定所有的政策和策略必須與全部的管理者及職員討論過。
(A)原始的　　　(B)放縱的
(C)企業的　　　(D)管理的

4 (A)。 台灣的企業應該被鼓勵創立於台灣、連結亞太地區、並立足全球。
(A)被鼓勵　　　(B)受挫
(C)被責罵　　　(D)被處罰

5 (C)。 行政院是中華民國政府最高行政機關。
(A)考試院　　　(B)司法院
(C)行政院　　　(D)監察院

6 (B)。 為了推廣企業升級並鼓勵出口，政府執行了一些措施，像是出口減稅、其他稅項的減免等。
(A)崇拜　　　　(B)執行
(C)揭露　　　　(D)上鎖

7 (A)。 Helen是人事部經理。她致力於發展吸引人才的方法。
(A)致力於……　(B)與……分開
(C)被搬離……　(D)被脫離……

8 (C)。 總統就職後，新的部會首長也在2008年5月20日接掌辦公室。
(A)臆測　　　　(B)重返
(C)就任　　　　(D)消耗

9 (D)。 陳博士發表一場演說，演講中慶賀了該單位的成就。
(A)丟　(B)拿　(C)說　(D)遞送
🔑 deliver a speech 發表演說。

10 (B)。 猖獗的貪污腐敗威脅了許多國家的經濟表現。這常見於大多數的重要部門內。
(A)祝福　　　　(B)腐敗
(C)忠誠　　　　(D)精確

11 (C)。 這項修正案是要透過使商業發展公司有更多投資彈性，以幫助小型企業資本的形成。
(A)阻礙　　　　(B)紮根
(C)使容易　　　(D)延遲

12 (D)。 這位年輕的舞者昨晚表演了一場成功的處女秀。
(A)外觀　　　　(B)熟識
(C)宣布　　　　(D)初次登臺

13 (C)。 這場可怕的地震把我們的房子摧殘成廢墟。
(A)地方　　　　(B)影子
(C)廢墟　　　　(D)煙

14 (B)。 雖然新投資計畫看起來有利可圖，身為建設局的官員，還是應該要仔細檢驗各種可能性，不排除這是騙局或可能危及國家利益。
(A)大警犬　　　(B)騙局
(C)恥辱　　　　(D)獅身人面

15 (A)。 人很容易感到自滿以及自我感覺良好。
(A)自滿 　　　　(B)輕蔑
(C)爭議性的 　　(D)偶發的

16 (D)。 我謝絕對媒體發表任何評論。
(A)拆去雷管 　　(B)口述
(C)使偏斜 　　　(D)謝絕

17 (C)。 那位億萬富翁因意外發現金子、一夜致富而聞名。
(A)定居 　　　　(B)犧牲
(C)意外發現 　　(D)原創性

18 (B)。 在報上，新聞可佔的位置通常視廣告量而定。
(A)預計 　　　　(B)分配位置
(C)避開 　　　　(D)自動化

19 (C)。 近來我受嚴重失眠所苦，所以我的家庭醫生開了藥方幫助誘導睡眠。
(A)掉落 　　　　(B)戰爭
(C)誘導 　　　　(D)引誘

20 (A)。 我老闆是個典型的雙子座，他大概每兩分鐘就改變一次心意，有時候當他的下屬真的很令人挫折。
(A)令人挫折的 　(B)感到挫折的
(C)幸運的 　　　(D)巧妙的

二、文法

21 (A)。 如果你還有其他問題，請不要客氣，盡量發問。
(A)如果 　　　　(B)在……之前
(C)在……之後 　(D)不要

22 (D)。 如果Jane無法準時完成論文，她就不能在研討會上發表了。

解 if　S1＋V1（現在式），S2 will（not）V2。

23 (D)。 明天一場抗議政府改革退休金計畫的全國性罷工將會中斷火車、飛機、及通往機場的交通。

解 未來簡單式用will＋原形動詞。

24 (C)。 為了作出結論，研究員將賣得最好的食物清單與黑心食品清單比對，發現了相當程度的重疊。

解 to＋原形動詞表示「為了……」，也做「in order to＋原形動詞」。

25 (B)。 雖然威廉斯一家很屬害，他們還是沒有贏得比賽。

解 Although引導的副詞子句，後接主要子句，以逗點隔開，不需要其他任何連接詞。

26 (A)。 李登輝先生在1988至2000年間是中華民國的總統。

解 who引導形容詞子句補充説明主詞Mr. Lee, Teng-hui。

27 (C)。 Tom和Linda昨天去市區買了一個新的檯燈。

解 downtown和yesterday都是副詞，不需加任何介系詞就可以放在句中，downtown表示地點、yesterday表示時間。

28 (D)。 世界領袖呼籲協商努力抵抗跨國性威脅，包括恐怖主義。

解 call for……「呼籲大家做……，提倡……」。

29 (A)。 雨已經下四個小時了。我們現在不走，就要在這裡待一輩子了。

解 either A or B用來連接二擇一的情況，表示不是A就是B。

30 (C)。這只是時間的問題了。事情一定會發生的，只是不是今天而已。

　解 a matter of⋯⋯表示是「⋯⋯的問題」。

31 (D)。以你要省錢繳貸款的角度來說，我覺得你最好不要買那件亮麗的洋裝。

　(A)透過⋯⋯　　(B)除了⋯⋯以外

　(C)遠離⋯⋯　　(D)以⋯⋯的角度說來

32 (A)。代表著台灣兩千三百萬人民，前總統陳先生送信給聯合國秘書長，要求允許台灣加入聯合國。

　(A)代表　　　　(B)面對

　(C)喜歡　　　　(D)偏愛

33 (B)。你不能總是對人說「好」。你也要畫條底線。

　解 draw a line somewhere表示「要在某處畫條線」，這條線是底線的意思。

34 (A)。新祕書擅長英語和法語。

　解「在⋯⋯方面有專長、很專業、擅長」等，proficient / professional / good後接介系詞in再接專長。

35 (B)。我們必須提防競爭對手新的市場發佈。

　解 on guard against⋯⋯「對⋯⋯作提防」。against（介）反對；違抗＋N。

36 (D)。我們非常想聽聽你的收購提案。

解 be all ears：「很想聽／很想知道」。be all ears about⋯⋯「很想聽⋯⋯」。

37 (C)。新政府的經濟政策即將上場了。

　解 come into play意指「上場、開始運作」。

38 (A)。我們得分比對手少。

　解 本句為比較級，goals表示「得分」，為可數名詞，用fewer表示「較少」。little-less-least＋不可數N.

39 (B)。發生什麼事了？你看起來像是淋過雨。

　(A)身為⋯⋯　　　(B)就好像⋯⋯

　(C)比方說⋯⋯　　(D)像如果⋯⋯

40 (A)。幾乎每位遊客來到倫敦都會造訪白金漢宮。

　解 專有名詞前不需冠詞。

三、閱讀測驗

（一）

　　台灣人民以台灣的發展經驗為傲，因為成功的關鍵是需要整個國家一起努力。然而，人們很少聽到國際援助在台灣的經濟建設發展上所扮演的重要角色。從1950年代到1980年代之間，台灣收到國際組織、美國及其它富有國家的大筆捐款與援助。捐款總值超過24億美元，還不包括美國為了幫助保衛台灣所提供的軍事援助。大多數的人都記得以前，他們以麵粉為食、喝牛奶、穿麵粉袋做的褲子，這些都來自美國。然而，他們可能不知道許多基礎建設，像是高

速公路、鐵路電氣化、石門水庫、自來水系統等，都是靠著來自國際組織和其他國家的優惠借款建造的。甚至是瘧疾的撲滅也依賴了世界衛生組織的幫助。由於以前所受的國外援助，台灣現在有能力可以報答他們。為了「報答國際社會並實現我們身為國際成員的責任」，台灣也提供國際幫助、並分享我們的發展經驗給友好國家與邦交國。這不只鞏固台灣與他們的關係，也讓我們實現對國際社會的責任。

41 (D)。 根據本文，台灣_____。
(A)過去沒有收過任何國際援助
(B)還在接受國際援助
(C)只接受美國的援助
(D)曾受過美國及其他國際組織的幫助

42 (A)。 台灣接受國際社會幫助總額超過_____。
(A)24億美元　　(B)2400萬美元
(C)480億美元　　(D)沒有確切數字

43 (B)。 為什麼優惠貸款有助於台灣的基礎建設？
(A)因為我們不需要還錢給借款給我們的人
(B)因為利率低於市場利率
(C)因為我們可以照自己的意願花這些錢
(D)因為立法院不能監督它的用處

44 (C)。 哪一個國際組織專管疾病的撲滅？
(A)世界貿易組織
(B)國際勞工組織
(C)世界衛生組織
(D)國際貨幣基金會

45 (C)。 台灣現在提供國際幫助給邦交國是因為_____。
(A)台灣被國際法律強迫
(B)台灣對他們有法律責任
(C)這項政策是台灣主要的關注點
(D)這項政策可以控制通貨膨脹

(二)

　　全球性的「人口爆炸」為戰後的世界帶來了許多社會問題。社會緊張所帶來的症狀包括不安的當代社會現象，像是青少年叛逆和犯罪率高漲。

　　美國戰後年代的特徵是理想主義和現實主義的一種怪異混合。一個很顯著的例子是教會成員和世俗化數量同時增加。

　　儘管有著破記錄的空前成長，美國仍面臨許多危險警訊，包括自然資源耗竭，健康危機，運作不順的政府組織，及負荷過度的教育系統。

　　美國貧苦的少數族群的確得到了一些進步，但是社會完全融合的目標還沒有達成。未完成的事務清單上，富裕的多數族群與貧窮的少數族群間這種不協調現象，仍位居排行榜高處。

　　曾經身為保守世界中改革力量的美國，現在搖身一變成為改革世界中的保守勢力。然而美國仍然是世上最終的、可能也是最佳的自由希望所在。

46 (B)。 根據本文，何者是許多戰後社會問題的最主要因素？
(A)貧窮　　　　(B)人口爆炸
(C)死亡　　　　(D)孤兒增加

解答與解析

47 (A)。 下列何者不是美國的戰後警訊？
(A)上教堂的人數增加
(B)健康危機
(C)自然資源耗竭
(D)負荷過重的教育系統

48 (C)。 美國戰後犯罪率_____。
(A)變得較沒有組織　(B)降低
(C)攀升　　　　　　(D)與之前一樣

49 (B)。 儘管本文作者看到許多美國戰後負面情況，他仍然認為美國是_____。
(A)名利最佳希望所在
(B)自由的最佳希望所在
(C)最差的自由希望所在
(D)生存的最後希望

50 (B)。 根據本文內容，下列何者是美國尚未解決的問題？
(A)長者和年輕人間的代溝
(B)富者和窮人的貧富差距
(C)青少年的問題行為
(D)缺少就業機會

解 文中第四段中有提到，雖然底層的人民已有改善，但距離共融社會目標仍需努力，尤其首要問題為the incongruity of affluence，incongruity為不一致，affluence為富裕，因此可知道是貧富差距，因此此題答案選(B)。

第二回

一　字彙測驗

( )　**1** If you want to _____ money from one account to another, you need to fill out the form.
(A)transfer　(B)prefer　(C)inscribe　(D)describe

( )　**2** Sandra doesn't speak Spanish, so you'll have to _____ the speaker's words for her.
(A)penetrate　(B)translate　(C)indicate　(D)elevate

( )　**3** I feel sorry for those film stars. Reporters seem to follow them everywhere so they don't get much _____.
(A)evaluation　(B)momentum　(C)flashlight　(D)privacy

( )　**4** Some people never need to visit their bank. They use an _____ banking service to check their account and make payment using the internet.
(A)interest　(B)electronic　(C)overdraft　(D)accuracy

( )　**5** Mandarin Chinese is my mother tongue; it is the language I'm most _____ with.
(A)considerate　(B)comfortable　(C)convenient　(D)communicative

( )　**6** You'd better _____ smoking, or you'd endanger other people's health along with your own.
(A)break up　(B)end up　(C)back up　(D)give up

( )　**7** The car accident has caused _____ damage to her eyesight; she can hardly see anything now.
(A)permanent　(B)potential　(C)professional　(D)private

( )　**8** "The _____ from being childless to being a parent is extreme," said the new father. "Last week, only two quiet people lived at home. Suddenly, we have a third, noisy resident."
(A)explanation　(B)emergency　(C)proposal　(D)transition

(　　) **9** Shaking your head for "No" is not _____ ; in some cultures, shaking your head actually means "Yes."
(A)universal　(B)sensitive　(C)indifferent　(D)contemporary

(　　) **10** Among some business people, a _____ is concluded with a handshake. These business deals are never put in writing.
(A)document　(B)phenomenon　(C)transaction　(D)principle

二　文法測驗

(　　) **11** The bus company started offering reduced fares to older people last year, and so _____ .
(A)did one of the taxi companies
(B)one of the taxi companies has
(C)has one of the taxi companies
(D)one of the taxi companies did

(　　) **12** In the U.S. Senate, _____ , regardless of population, is equally represented.
(A)where each state　　　　(B)each state
(C)each state that is　　　　(D)for each state

(　　) **13** Spending the holidays in this small town _____ not what I'd like to do.
(A)is　(B)are　(C)being　(D)be

(　　) **14** Louise stayed there for a week, during _____ time he did nothing.
(A)this　(B)that　(C)where　(D)which

(　　) **15** If people were better educated in zoology, animals _____ treated differently.　(A)would be　(B)are　(C)were　(D)will be

(　　) **16** Not until I heard the scream _____ my car nearly ran over a little girl.　(A)I knew　(B)did I know　(C)do I know　(D)I did know

(　) **17** "The City of London" actually refers to only a small part of London, _____ there is a concentration of banks, insurance companies and financial markets.
(A)which　(B)where　(C)with which　(D)when

(　) **18** Why _____ at a given time is not known.
(A)does a drought occur　　(B)it is a drought occurred
(C)a drought should occur　(D)a drought that occurs

(　) **19** She'd rather _____ than _____ a public speech.
(A)die ... to give　　(B)dies ... gives
(C)to die ... to give　(D)die ... give

(　) **20** At thirteen _____ at a district school near her home, and when she was fifteen, she saw her first article in print.
(A)Mary Jane Hawes had her first teaching position
(B)the teaching position was Mary Jane Hawes' first
(C)the first teaching position that Mary Jane Hawes had
(D)when Mary Jane Hawes had her first teaching position

三　會話測驗

(　) **21** Terry: Have you ever been to Suntory?
Daniel: _____ What's it like?
Terry:It's interesting. It's a Japanese restaurant, and there's a beautiful garden in it.
(A)Yes, I do.　　(B)No, I haven't.
(C)A little.　　(D)What's wrong?

(　) **22** Ellen: Hello, Dad. I am at John's. We're just going to see a movie.
Dad: _____
(A)Really? Did you like it?　(B)How are you going to get in?
(C)Oh, we needed this!　　(D)OK. But come home early.

(   ) **23** Mother:Honey, why do you think our daughter Angel seems upset
all the time?

Father: Well, she's under a lot of pressure.

Mother: But she's one of the top students in her class.

Father:_____ When you're a gifted student, your daily
pressures are doubled-everyone has higher expectations of you.

(A)I don't see anything wrong.

(B)I'm watching.

(C)For God's sake, leave her alone.

(D)Maybe's that's where the problem is.

(   ) **24** Henry: I still can't believe we lost the big game.

Kyle: _____

We need to prepare for our next game.

(A)I like it.

(B)I can pretty much guarantee it.

(C)Get over it.

(D)I'm agreeing you more and more.

(   ) **25**   A:Excuse me. Would you please tell me where I can catch the
number 22 bus, please?

B: Yes, of course. _____

(A)Hurry up, or you'll miss it.

(B)The bus has been delayed by half an hour.

(C)The stop's around the corner in front of the bank.

(D)We apologize for the late arrival of the number 22 bus.

(   ) **26** Anna:Operator. This is Anna Hwang, Room 516. I'd like to place
a collect call to Taipei. The area code is 02. The number is
2234-5678.

Operator: _____

(A)Sorry, wrong number.

(B)May I take a message?

(C)Please hold. I will put you through.

(D)Please place a local call, all right?

(　　) **27** Tom: That cake looks delicious.

Willa:Well, it's not very fresh. I think it's at least a week old.

_____

(A)It's soft and tender. 　　　(B)I would even say it's a bit stale.

(C)It's absolutely tasty. 　　　(D)It's a bit overdone for my taste.

(　　) **28** A: You're from the States?

B: No, actually, from Canada.

A: _____

B: West, Vancouver.

(A)Canada? Is it very cold there?

(B)Oh, that's a nice place for visitors.

(C)Oh, really. What part?

(D)Terrific! I've been there several times.

(　　) **29** A:There are so many different computers-I don't know which one to buy.

B: Well, _____

A:Well, just my own writing mainly, you know. I'm working on a novel.

B: Are you going to write at home, or when you travel, or...when?

A: I do travel a lot. Maybe I'll think about a laptop.

(A)what are you going to use it for?

(B)what do you do for a living?

(C)it depends. How does a laptop sound to you?

(D)these laptops are on sale now. Would any of them be good enough?

(　　) **30** A: Cash or charge?

B: I'll put it on my Best Card.

A: OK. Thank you. _____

B: There you go.

A: Thank you. There you are. Have a nice day.

(A)You look nice in that color.

(B)That'll be $36.75. Here's your change, $3.25.

(C)Is it for here or to go?

(D)Could you sign here, please?

四 克漏字測驗

(一)

eBay was the first website where individual sellers could sell goods online. Now over 700,000 Americans earn a large part of their income selling things on eBay. This   31.   has spread very quickly around the globe.

Major companies now see the Asian market as   32.   the most potential. American companies Amazon.com and Yahoo! both recently cooperated with large Chinese   33. . In Shanghai, eBay offers a free hour of karaoke for registering as a new user. Selling on an Internet auction is quite simple. First, users pay a fee   34.   their goods.

Then buyers bid on the item. When the auction closes, the higher bidder wins. The seller is then   35.   for shipping it. After the sale, the buyer and seller can post comments about the sale on each other's profile.

( ) **31** (A)merchandise (B)reference (C)prospect (D)trend

( ) **32** (A)had (B)to have (C)having (D)will have

( ) **33** (A)scenes (B)scripts (C)sites (D)sheds

( ) **34** (A)who lists (B)to list (C)which listed (D)listed

( ) **35** (A)manageable (B)responsible (C)economical (D)fundamental

(二)

It is easy to recognize a college student because he or she is carrying books and usually wearing old jeans and a T-shirt. You will not see a college student driving a new car.   36. , you will see him or her at a bus stop or on a bicycle. And at mealtimes, a college student is more likely to be eating a slice of pizza than dining in a fine restaurant. Very few college students have extra money to spend   37.   cars, clothes, or good food. There are two main reasons why being poor is an unavoidable part of the college experience.

The first reason college students are poor is that they cannot work full-time. An eighteen-year-old is an adult with the needs and wants of an adult;　38.　, if that young person is taking courses at a university or a community college, he must spend as much time as possible studying. 　39.　, the student has to sacrifice the extra money that a job would provide in order to have the freedom to concentrate on classes.

A second reason college students have little money is that they have other expenses that working adults do not have. A college student must pay tuition fees every semester. A full-time student takes at least three classes each semester, and the fees for these classes can cost thousands of dollars per year. Also, students need to buy several expensive textbooks each semester. A single textbook can cost 　40.　 a hundred dollars. Other necessary expenses include computers, paper, pens, notebooks, and other items needed for school projects.

(　) **36** (A)In other words　(B)Instead　　(C)Meanwhile　(D)Likewise

(　) **37** (A)in　　　　　　　(B)for　　　　(C)on　　　　　(D)with

(　) **38** (A)moreover　　　(B)as a result　(C)otherwise　　(D)however

(　) **39** (A)Therefore　　　(B)Still　　　(C)In contrast　(D)In fact

(　) **40** (A)as many as　　(B)as little as　(C)as much as　(D)as few as

五　閱讀測驗

(一)
It's quiz time. Which of the following cannot be done with a cell phone? Would you guess you could not watch a television sports program, hold a video conference with somebody, turn your TV set on and off, or know the location of your best friend anywhere worldwide? Well, whatever your answer is, you are wrong. All of these functions are available now, enabled by the latest 3G wireless services.

What exactly is 3G wireless technology? 3G is an abbreviation for "third-generation", and the term refers particularly to mobile communication. The major advantage of 3G is that very large amounts of data can be sent at a much higher speed than ever before.

Phone users need this extra bandwidth, too. In the 1990s, cell phones were mainly used for simple voice calls.

Today's cell phones, on the other hand, are loaded with an incredible amount of functions. A phone can also be a powerful camera, a PDA, a video-game machine, a TV set, an e-mail reader, a GPS, or a digital music player.

The introduction of 3G seems like good news. After all, who wouldn't want to have a powerful multi-purpose phone with them at all times? In fact, not everybody would. In Japan and Europe there is a movement away from phones with all the bells and whistles. The price of cell phones is falling, so consumers can buy themselves two or three phones, depending on their needs. A person might have one phone for music, with a big hard drive. The second could be for doing business, with a big screen for e-mails or videoconferencing. The same person may own a third phone that is just cool, for taking out to parties. As desired, these phones could all share the same number, with only one being used at a time.

( ) **41** The first paragraph provides examples of _____.
　　　(A)problems most people have with new technology
　　　(B)things you can do with a new kind of technology
　　　(C)things that most people do with their earphones
　　　(D)things that cannot be done on new cell phones

( ) **42** According to the article, 3G cell phones _____.
　　　(A)used up very little bandwidth
　　　(B)were popular in the 1990s
　　　(C)are often advertised on TV
　　　(D)have lots of different uses

( ) **43** What does the article tell us about third-generation telephones?
(A)They have no special advantages over other cell phones.
(B)They can transmit a lot of information very quickly.
(C)They were an early kind of mobile communication.
(D)They are now used in most countries in the world.

( ) **44** In this article, what does the phrase "the bells and whistles" imply about the up-to-date cell phones?
(A)fancy but unnecessary functions
(B)musical instruments
(C)electrical equipment
(D)battery charger

( ) **45** What is happening with cell phones in Japan and Europe?
(A)3G cell phones are becoming much more expensive.
(B)Cell phones do not have as many functions as before.
(C)People are not always buying multi-function 3G phones.
(D)People are buying fewer cell phones than they used to .

(二)

Who becomes wealthy? Usually the wealthy individual is a businessman who has lived in the same town for all his adult life. This person owns a small factory, a chain of stores, or a service company. He has married once and remains married. He lives next door to people with much less money. He is a compulsive saver and investor.

And he has made his money on his own. Eighty percent of America's millionaires are first-generation rich.

Affluent people typically follow a lifestyle conducive to accumulating money. In the course of our investigations, we discovered seven features among those who successfully build wealth.

1. They live well below their means.
2. They allocate their time, energy, and money efficiently, in ways conducive to building wealth.

3. They believe that financial independence is more important than displaying high social status.

4. Their parents did not allow them to become financially dependent.

5. Their adult children are economically self-sufficient.

6. They are good at finding opportunities to make money.

7. They chose the right job or career.

(　　) **46** Which of the following is the best title for this passage?
(A)Shortcuts to Financial Independence
(B)The Millionaire Next Door
(C)Like Father, Like Son
(D)How to Get Rich Overnight

(　　) **47** According to this passage, wealthy people in America _____.
(A)lead an extravagant lifestyle
(B)were born with a silver spoon in their mouth
(C)spend much less than they earn
(D)always try to make both ends meet

(　　) **48** The word "conducive" in paragraph 2 is closest in meaning to _____.
(A)helpful　(B)contrary　(C)careful　(D)economical

(　　) **49** Which of the following statements is NOT supported by this passage?
(A)Most millionaires in America help themselves build wealth.
(B)Most millionaires in America cannot stop saving money and investing their savings.
(C)Most millionaires in America not only work hard but they also work smart.
(D)Most millionaires in America travel expensively for chances to make money.

( ) **50** Which of the following best describes the author's tone in this passage?

(A)informative   (B)sarcastic

(C)humorous   (D)subjective

解答與解析

一、字彙

1 (A)。 如果你想要從一個帳戶轉帳到另外一個帳戶，你必須填寫這些表格。

(A)轉帳 (B)偏好 (C)牢記 (D)描述

2 (B)。 Sandra不會說西班牙語，所以你必須替她翻譯演講者的講詞。

(A)識破 (B)翻譯 (C)指示 (D)振奮

3 (D)。 我替那些電影明星感到悲哀。記者似乎到處跟著他們，所以他們沒有太多的隱私。

(A)評估 (B)動力 (C)閃光燈 (D)隱私

4 (B)。 有些人從來不需要親臨銀行。他們在網路上使用電子銀行服務來檢查帳戶同時付款。

(A)興趣 (B)電子的 (C)透支 (D)正確

5 (B)。 國語是我的母語；這種語言是我使用起來最自在的。

(A)體貼的 (B)自在的 (C)方便的 (D)溝通的

6 (D)。 你最好戒菸，不然你將危及你自己以及其他人的健康。

(A)崩潰 (B)結束 (C)支持 (D)戒絕

7 (A)。 車禍造成她視力上永久的損害；她現在幾乎看不見東西了。

(A)永久的 (B)潛在的 (C)專業的 (D)私人的

8 (D)。 「從沒有子女到為人父母的轉變是很大的。」一個新手爸爸這樣說。「上個星期，只有兩個安靜的人住在這個屋子裡，忽然間，我們有了第三個吵鬧的住戶。」

(A)解釋 (B)緊急 (C)提案 (D)轉變

9 (A)。 搖頭表示「不是」並非眾所周知的；在某些文化中，搖頭竟然表示「是」的意思。

(A)眾所周知 (B)敏感的 (C)中立的 (D)當代的

10 (C)。 某些生意人握手就完成了交易，那些商業交易不需要寫下來。

(A)文件 (B)現象 (C)交易 (D)原則

11 **(A)**。去年，公車公司開始提供老人優惠票價，<u>有一家計程車公司也跟進了</u>。

解 so... 用於肯定句，表示「也……」的意思，要倒裝。

12 **(B)**。美國參議院中，無論人口多寡，每一州的代表性都一樣。

解 in the U.S. Senate是副詞，regardless of population是介係詞片語，真正的句子是Each state is equally represented. 這個句子已經有動詞is，還缺主詞，四個答案中只有each state是名詞，可以當主詞。

13 **(A)**。我並不會想要在這個小城渡假。

解 spending the holidays 是動名詞片語，視為單數，後接單數動詞。

14 **(D)**。Louise在那裡停留了一個星期，那段時間，他什麼事也沒做。

解 先行詞a week，關係代名詞可以用that，也可以用which，但前有介係詞during，先行詞不可用 that 取代。

15 **(A)**。如果人們接受更好的動物學教育，動物就會有不同的待遇了。

解 與現在事實相反的假設語氣，用過去式表示be動詞一律用were。「如果……那麼……」後面「那麼……」的句子要加入過去式，would 為 will 之過去式助動詞。

16 **(B)**。直到我聽到尖叫聲，我才知道我的車差點就碾過一個小女孩。

解 Not until後面要用倒裝句。（助V＋S＋V）

17 **(B)**。「倫敦市」事實上只是倫敦的一小部分，那裡是銀行、保險公司和金融市場的集中點。

解 先行詞London，因此關係代名詞要用where（＝in which）。

18 **(C)**。乾旱為何發生在特定季節原因不明。

解 why是關係副詞，後面要加主詞＋（助動詞）動詞＋（受詞）。

19 **(D)**。她寧死也不願公開演講。

解 rather...than寧可……也不願……，動詞前後要一致。因為前面已經有助動詞she'd（＝she would），所以要用原形動詞。

20 **(A)**。13歲時，Mary Jane Hawes得到她的第一個教職，15歲時，首次發表文章。

解 連接詞and要連接兩個完整的句子，主詞＋動詞＋受詞。

21 **(B)**。Terry：你去過Suntory嗎？
Daniel：<u>沒有</u>。那是怎樣的地方？
Terry：很有趣的地方，那是一家日本餐廳，裡面有一個漂亮的花園。

解 既然Daniel會問那是怎樣的地方，當然表示他沒有去過。用簡單句回答No, I haven't.即可。

22 **(D)**。Ellen：喂，爸爸，我在John家裡，我們正要去看電影。
Dad：<u>好，不過要早點回家。</u>
(A)真的嗎？你喜歡嗎？
(B)你要如何到達呢？

(C)喔，我們需要這個！
(D)好，不過要早點回家。

23 (D)。Mother：親愛的，為什麼你認為女兒Angel總是不開心？
Father：嗯，她有很多壓力。
Mother：但她是班上頂尖的學生啊！
Father：也許那正是問題所在。如果你是資優學生，你會有雙倍的壓力——大家都你有更高的期待。
(A)我看不出有什麼異狀。
(B)我正在觀察。
(D)老天爺啊！放過她吧。
(D)也許那正是問題所在。

24 (C)。Henry：我還是不相信我們輸了這場大比賽。
Kyle：別再想了，我們需要準備下一場比賽。
(A)我喜歡
(B)我相當程度能夠保證
(C)別再想了
(D)我越來越同意你了

25 (C)。A：對不起，可否告訴我去哪裡可以搭22號公車？
B：當然可以。公車站牌就在銀行前的轉角處。
(A)快一點，不然你會趕不上。
(B)公車已經遲到半小時了。
(C)公車站牌就在銀行前的轉角處。
(D)我們為22號公車晚到而道歉。

26 (C)。Anna：接線生，這是Anna Hwang，房號516，我想撥一通對方付費的電話到台北，區域號碼是02，電話號碼為2234-5678。

接線生：請稍候，我將為你轉接。
(A)抱歉，號碼錯誤。
(B)需要留言嗎？
(C)請稍候，我將為你轉接。
(D)請您撥市內電話，好嗎？

27 (B)。Tom：這蛋糕看起來真好吃。
Willa：它非常不新鮮，我想它至少放了一個禮拜了。我甚至認為它已經過期了。
(A)它又柔又軟。
(B)我甚至認為它已經過期了。
(C)它絕對好吃。
(D)對我的口味而言，它有點烤過頭了。

28 (C)。A：你從美國來的嗎？
B：不，事實上，從加拿大來。
A：喔，真的嗎？哪個區域？
B：西邊，溫哥華。
(A)加拿大？那裡很冷吧？
(B)喔，對訪客而言那是個好地方。
(C)喔，真的嗎？哪個區域？
(D)太棒了，我去過那裡好幾次。

29 (A)。A：這裡有好多電腦，我不知道該買哪一台。
B：你主要的用途是什麼？
A：你知道，我主要是在家裡寫作。我正在寫一本小說。
B：你要在家裡寫作嗎？或是旅行，或是當……
A：我的確常常旅行，也許我該考慮買筆記型電腦。
(A)你主要的用途是什麼？
(B)你謀生的方法是什麼？
(C)不一定，你覺得筆記型電腦如何？

(D)這些筆記型電腦正在打折,你有中意的嗎?

30 (D)。A:付現還是記帳?
B:我想記帳在Best Card上。
A:好的,謝謝你。可以麻煩您在這裡簽名嗎?
B:好了。
A:謝謝你,給你。祝你今天愉快。
(A)這個顏色你穿了很好看。
(B)總共是36.75元,這是你的零錢3.25元。
(C)這裡用或外帶?
(D)可以麻煩您在這裡簽名嗎?

二、克漏字測驗

(一)

eBay是第一個個人賣家可以上網出售商品的網站。現在有70萬名美國人靠著在eBay上面賣東西而賺取大部分的生活費。這個趨勢快速地在全球曼延。主要的公司現在認為,亞洲市場有最大的潛力。美國公司亞馬遜.com和Yahoo!最近都與大規模的中國網路合作。eBay在上海提供一個小時免費的卡拉OK給新註冊的使用者。在網路上拍賣商品非常容易。首先,使用者付費列出貨物清單,然後買家可以開始出價。拍賣結束時,出價最高的人獲勝。這時賣家負責送貨。買賣結束後,買賣雙方都可以在個人的檔案中發表對該次交易的意見。

31 (D)。(A)購買　(B)參考　(C)前景(D)趨勢

32 (C)。as介系詞後面要加Ving。

33 (C)。(A)場景　(B)劇本　(C)網路(D)庫房

34 (B)。pay 是動詞,後面加to V。

35 (B)。(A)管理的　(B)有責任的(C)經濟的　(D)基礎的

(二)

要認出大學生不難,因為他或她抱著書,而且經常穿舊牛仔褲和T恤。你很難看到大學生開新車。然而,你會在公車站牌看到他或她,或是看到他們騎腳踏車。同時,大學生比較可能吃一片比薩,而不是在高級餐廳用餐。非常少數的大學生有多餘的錢花費在車子、衣服或美食上。貧窮是大學經驗中不可避免的一部分,這有兩個主要的原因。

大學生之所以貧窮的第一個原因是,他們無法全職工作。十八歲已經成人了,有成人的需要和慾望。然而如果年輕人在大學或大專修課,他必須盡可能花時間唸書。因此,學生必須犧牲掉工作可以帶來的額外收入,才有辦法專心唸書。

大學生口袋總是少有現金的第二個原因是,他們有就業的成人不必花費的額外開銷。大學生每學期都要付學費。全職的學生每學期至少要修三門課,這些課程的費用一年可能要數千元。而且,每個學期還要買昂貴的教科書。一本教科書可能就要價數百元之譜。其他必要的花費還包括電腦、紙、筆、筆記本以及其他學校的研究計劃所需要的東西。

36 (B)。(A)換句話說　(B)然而　(C)同時　(D)同樣地

37 (C)。spend on＋N.：在……方面花錢；spend...＋V-ing

38 (D)。(A)而且　(B)結果　(C)否則　(D)然而

39 (A)。(A)因此　(B)仍然　(C)相反　(D)事實上

40 (C)。像……一樣多，用as many as 或as much as，這裡因為錢是不可數的，所以要用as much as。

三、閱讀測驗

(一)

　　小考時間！以下哪件事是手機辦不到的？你會猜看電視上的體育節目、和別人開視訊會議、開關電視或知道你最好的朋友現在在地球的何處？好了，不管你的答案是什麼，你都答錯了。這些功能現在都因為3G的無線服務而得以辦到。

　　到底什麼是3G科技？3G是「第三世代」的縮寫，這個名詞特別指行動溝通。3G主要的優點是可以用比從前更快的速度，傳輸大量的訊息。

　　手機的使用者也需要更多頻寬。1990年代，手機最主要的功能是簡單的語音通話。另一方面，今日的手機有非常許多功能。手機也可以是效能很強的相機、PDA、電玩、電視機、email讀取機、GPS和數位音樂播放器。

　　3G的問世似乎是個好消息。畢竟，誰不想要隨時攜帶一個高效能的多功用手機？事實上，並不是每個人都想要。在日本和歐洲，現在有一種不要手機有這些「鈴聲和哨音」（意指不必要

的附屬配件）的傾向。手機的價格下跌，所以消費者可以因需求而買兩、三支手機。人們可以有一支硬碟很大的手機來聽音樂，第二支手機要有大螢幕可以讀email和進行視訊會議，方便做生意，同一個人還可以有第三支手機，只是因為很酷，帶去宴會用的。只要你想要，這些手機都可以共用同一個號碼，只要一次使用一支手機即可。

41 (B)。第一段舉例說明＿＿＿＿＿＿
(A)多數人在面對新科技時會遇到的問題
(B)因為一種新科技你可做的事
(C)多數人用耳機來做的事
(D)新手機無法做到的事。

42 (D)。根據本文，3G手機是＿＿＿＿＿
(A)用很少的頻寬
(B)1990年代流行過
(C)常在電視上廣告
(D)有許多不同的功能

43 (B)。從本文中我們學習到第三世代手機的＿＿＿＿＿＿
(A)與其他手機相較沒什麼優勢
(B)它們可以快速地傳輸大量訊息
(C)它們是早期的行動溝通方式
(D)現在全球多數國家都在使用

44 (A)。在本文中，片語「鈴聲和哨音」暗示最新的手機有＿＿＿＿＿
(A)花俏但不必要的功能
(B)樂器
(C)電子設備
(D)充電器

45 (C)。　日本和歐洲的手機有什麼狀況？
(A)3G 手機變得非常昂貴
(B)手機的功能不如過去多
(C)人們常不買多功能的3G電話
(D)人們的手機支數不同從前

(二)

　　誰能變得富有？有錢人經常是成人後就住在同一個村鎮的商人。這種人有一個小工廠、連鎖商店或服務公司。他結過一次婚，而且婚姻還維持著。他的隔壁鄰居只有很少的錢。他是強制節儉的人和投資者。而且他的錢都是靠自己賺來的。80%美國的百萬富翁是第一代富有。

　　有錢人典型的生活方式有助於他們累積錢財。在我們的調查中，我們發現那些成功建立財富的人有七個特質：
1. 他們的生活低於他們的收入水平。
2. 他們用一種有助於建立財富的方法，有效率地分配時間、精力和錢財。
3. 他們相信，財務獨立遠比高社會地位更重要。
4. 他們的父母不容許他們經濟依賴。
5. 他們的成人子女在經濟上可以自足。
6. 他們精於找機會賺錢。
7. 他們選擇對的工作或職業。

46 (B)。　這篇文章最適合的標題是什麼？
(A)財務獨立的捷徑
(B)隔壁的百萬富翁
(C)有其父必有其子
(D)如何一夜致富

47 (C)。　根據本文，美國的富人＿＿＿
(A)引導奢華的生活型態
(B)含著銀湯匙出生
(C)花得比賺得少
(D)收支短絀，勉強維生

48 (A)。　第二段的conducive（有助益的）意義上與何字最接近？
(A)有幫助的　　　(B)相反的
(C)小心的　　　　(D)節儉的

49 (D)。　以下哪個論點不被本文支持？
(A)美國多數的百萬富翁靠自己建立財富
(B)美國多數的百萬富翁無法停下來不存錢或不投資
(C)美國多數的百萬富翁不止努力工作，也聰明地工作
(D)美國多數的百萬富翁奢侈地旅遊來賺錢

50 (A)。　本文作者的語氣是哪一種？
(A)見聞廣博的　　(B)諷刺的
(C)幽默的　　　　(D)主觀的

一 字彙測驗

( ) **1** A few political extremists _____ the crowd to attack the police.
(A)incited (B)stirred (C)agitated (D)animated

( ) **2** A thorough analysis of market _____ can increase the success rate of a new product.
(A)anticipation (B)recession (C)installment (D)discrimination

( ) **3** The suppliers will claim compensation if we partially _____ our contract with them.
(A)contaminate (B)propagate (C)delegate (D)terminate

( ) **4** In the face of energy crisis, scientists worldwide are now exploring _____ energy to replace fossil fuels.
(A)alleviating (B)alternative (C)allergic (D)altitudinal

( ) **5** The shopping _____ policy aimed to stimulate consumption in order to boost up droopy economy.
(A)voucher (B)diploma (C)redeem (D)rebate

( ) **6** I enjoyed the concert last night. But someone's cell phone rang during the concert and it was _____.
(A)constructive (B)disruptive (C)corruptive (D)destructive

( ) **7** Experiments in genetic engineering have created important _____ to find cures for many cancers.
(A)drawbacks   (B)breakthroughs
(C)accusations   (D)obstacles

( ) **8** The faucet in the kitchen had been _____ for days. We should call the plumber to fix the problem.
(A)leaking (B)sipping (C)rusting (D)blurring

(   ) **9** One of the most important decisions a company must make is how to _____ the company in its advertisements through photographs, graphic design, or other means.
(A)ascribe   (B)assess   (C)depict   (D)defame

(   ) **10** It was felt that the new bonus for increased production would provide an _____ to work overtime.
(A)incentive   (B)initiative   (C)attraction   (D)incitement

(   ) **11** A country's financial _____ is an essential factor in investment evaluation.
(A)depression   (B)boundary   (C)abstract   (D)infrastructure

(   ) **12** The special committee investigating the inside trading had accidentally _____ evidence of asset stripping.
(A)unearthed   (B)plagiarized   (C)embargoed   (D)retaliated

(   ) **13** Given the increasingly high rate of divorce, many couples, prior to marriage, are advised to consider getting a _____ agreement.
(A)bilingual   (B)biennial   (C)provisional   (D)prenuptial

(   ) **14** Most companies, faced with the economic downturn, need to have strong _____, with assets valuable enough to meet obligations and operations in the long term.
(A)restraint   (B)vigilance   (C)solvency   (D)commodity

(   ) **15** The Office of Media Relations issued a press _____ to clarify some recent doubts regarding the company's quarterly earnings report.
(A)religion   (B)release   (C)revolution   (D)reservation

二 文法測驗

( ) **16** The Review Board could be considering _____ the grants given to several non-governmental organizations.
(A)to discontinue
(B)discontinuing
(C)to be discontinued
(D)discontinue

( ) **17** A lot of debris _____ at the site of explosion for quite a while.
(A)was left
(B)were left
(C)have been left
(D)has been left

( ) **18** The key players in the energy market, _____ heavy capital investment, have little interest in innovation.
(A)which to require
(B)requiring
(C)which it requires
(D)required

( ) **19** Employees are required to follow the standard operating procedures and to act _____.
(A)according to
(B)in accordance with
(C)according
(D)accordingly

( ) **20** The social welfare system _____ provide the underprivileged people with sufficient support.
(A)had better to
(B)would rather to
(C)ought to
(D)due to

( ) **21** The day _____ I shall never forget is the one _____ I joined the army.
(A)that / where
(B)which / when
(C)when / in which
(D)on which / why

( ) **22** Little is known about the criteria, _____ the committee selects the final winners.
(A)in which
(B)by which
(C)according to what
(D)owing to what

(   ) **23** We can judge the success of your scheme only by taking _____ account the financial benefits over the next few years.
(A)out   (B)over
(C)from   (D)into

(   ) **24** If James had taken my advice, he _____ such a stupid mistake.
(A)had not made   (B)would not have made
(C)did not make   (D)won't make

(   ) **25** I don't regret _____ even if it might have upset her.
(A)telling what I thought   (B)to tell her what I thought
(C)telling her what I thought   (D)to have told her that I thought

(   ) **26** Seldom _____ any mistake during my past five years of service in the company.
(A)did I make   (B)I did make
(C)should I make   (D)would I make

(   ) **27** No matter how _____, many people have escaped from big cities to rural areas.
(A)inconvenient country life may be
(B)country life may be inconvenient
(C)may country life be inconvenient
(D)country life inconvenient may be

(   ) **28** _____ by transferring the blame to others is often called scapegoating.
(A)Eliminate problems   (B)Eliminating problems
(C)The eliminated problems   (D)Problems are eliminated

(   ) **29** Diamonds are precious stones buried deep under the ground, _____, are perfectly white.
(A)when, pure which   (B)when, which pure
(C)which, when pure   (D)which, pure when

(　　) **30** In the far distance _____.
　　　　(A)was a lake surrounded by trees seen
　　　　(B)was seen a lake surrounded by trees
　　　　(C)a lake surrounded was seen by trees
　　　　(D)seen a lake surrounded by trees was

三 克漏字測驗

(一)

　　Americans like to think of themselves as martyrs to work. They delight in telling stories about their pushing hours, and they even marvel at the laziness of their European cousins, particularly the French. But when it comes to the young the situation is ___31.___ . American children have it easier than most other children in the world, including the ___32.___ lazy Europeans. They have one of the shortest school years anywhere, a mere 180 days ___33.___ with an average of 195 of OECD (The Organization for Economic Cooperation and Development) and more than 200 for East Asian countries. German children spend 20 more days in school than American ones, and South Koreans over a month more. Over 12 years, a 15-day ___34.___ means American children lose out on 180 days of school, ___35.___ an entire year.

(　　) **31** (A)preserved　　(B)coerced　　　(C)reversed　　(D)devised

(　　) **32** (A)selflessly　　(B)supposedly　(C)pitilessly　　(D)confusedly

(　　) **33** (A)compared　　(B)comparing　(C)opposed　　(D)opposing

(　　) **34** (A)preference　(B)deficit　　　(C)advantage　(D)appointment

(　　) **35** (A)similar to　　(B)deprived of　(C)typical of　　(D)equivalent to

(二)

The World Health Organization (WHO) kept its pandemic swine flu alert at the second highest level on June 5, but said that future changes would reflect how severe an outbreak was. The U.N. agency has been evaluating how to adjust its pandemic alert scale to reflect both the severity of the flu as well as its ___36.___ spread around the world. This follows criticism that it may have caused unnecessary panic about the disease whose effects have been mainly mild ___37.___ in Mexico, where it is known to have killed 103 people. The experts, meeting as WHO's emergency committee, made recommendations on a number of factors to be taken into account to assess the severity of an epidemic. To date, the novel H1N1 strain, ___38.___ swine flu, has infected 21,940 people in 69 countries, killing 125 of them, according to the WHO.

Mexico, the United States and Canada have suffered the impact of the illness and a case was confirmed in Saudi Arabia for the first time. More than 13,000 cases have been detected in the U.S., with 27 deaths ___39.___, according to the federal Centers for Disease Control and Prevention. The WHO representative said this week that one idea was to add three severity notches to the highest marker of 6, so the overall level can reach the peak even if the flu's effects remain moderate, and then be adjusted again later if the virus causes more serious health problems. WHO's pandemic scale now remains at the second-highest level, phase 5 on a scale of 1 to 6, meaning a widespread infection is ___40.___. Production of seasonal influenza vaccines should also continue for now, as work proceeds on developing a vaccine against the new flu.

(   ) **36** (A)personal   (B)exciting   (C)outstanding (D)geographic

(   ) **37** (A)despite from (B)apart from   (C)away from   (D)depart from

(   ) **38** (A)mainly as   (B)so far as   (C)as well as   (D)also known as

(   ) **39** (A)segregated   (B)advised   (C)confirmed   (D)excluded

(   ) **40** (A)imminent   (B)exceptional (C)unlikely   (D)decided

四 閱讀測驗

(一)

Advertisement can be thought of "as the means of making known in order to buy or sell goods or services". Advertisement aims to increase people's awareness and arouse interest. It tries to inform and to persuade. The media are all used to spread the message. The press offers a fairly cheap method, and magazines are used to reach special sections of the market. The cinema and commercial radio are useful for local market. Television, although more expensive, can be very effective. Public notices are fairly cheap and more permanent in their power of attraction. Other ways of increasing consumer interest are through exhibitions and trade fairs as well as direct mail advertisement.

There can be no doubt that the growth in advertisement is one of the most striking features of the western world in this century. Many businesses such as those handling frozen foods, liquor, tobacco and medicines have been built up largely by advertisement.

We might ask whether the cost of advertisement is paid for by the producer or by the customer. Since advertisement forms part of the cost of production, which has to be covered by the selling price, it is clear that it is the customer who pays for advertisement. However, if large scale advertisement leads to increased demand, production costs are reduced, and the customer pays less.

It is difficult to measure exactly the influence of advertisement on sales. When the market is growing, advertisement helps to increase demand. When the market is shrinking, advertisement may prevent a bigger fall in sales than would occur without its support. What is clear is that businesses would not pay large sums for advertisement if they were not convinced of its value to them.

(　　) **41** Advertisement is mainly paid for by _____.
    (A)the producer　　　　　(B)the customer
    (C)increased sales　　　　(D)reduced prices

( ) **42** The word "media" in the first paragraph includes _____.
(A)radio only   (B)the press only
(C)television only   (D)all of the above

( ) **43** Advertisement is often used to _____.
(A)push the sale   (B)arouse suspicion
(C)deceive customers   (D)increase production

( ) **44** Advertisement can increase demand _____.
(A)all the time   (B)in any circumstances
(C)in a growing market   (D)in a shrinking market

( ) **45** From the last sentence of this passage we conclude that _____.
(A)businesses usually do not pay much for advertisement
(B)businessmen know well that advertisement could bring them more profits
(C)advertisement usually cost businesses large amounts of money
(D)advertisement could hardly convince people of the value of the goods

(二)

On October 17, 1904, Italian American A. P. Giannini established Bank of Italy in San Francisco. During its development, Giannini's bank survived several crises throughout the 20th century including a natural disaster and a major economic upheaval.

One major rest for Giannini's bank occurred in 1906, when a massive earthquake struck San Francisco, followed by a raging fire that destroyed much of the city. Giannini obtained two wagons and teams of horses, filled the wagons with the bank's reserves, mostly in the form of gold, and escaped from the chaos of the city with his clients' funds protected. After the disaster, Giannini opened up a temporary shop on the Washington Street Wharf and was the first to resume operations.

In the period following the 1906 fire, Bank of Italy continued to prosper and expand. By 1918 there were twenty-four branches of the bank, and ten years later Giannini had acquired numerous other banks, including Bank of

America located in New York City In 1930 he consolidated all the branches of Bank of Italy, Bank of America in New York City, and another Bank of America that he had formed in California into the Bank of America National Trust and Savings Association.

A second major crisis for the bank occurred during the Great Depression of the 1930s. Although Giannini had already retired prior to the darkest days of the Depression, he became incensed when his successor began selling off banks during the bad economic times. Giannini resumed leadership of the bank at the age of sixty-two. Under his leadership, the bank weathered the storm of the Depression and subsequently moved into a phase of overseas development.

(　　) **46** According to the passage, Giannini _____
　　　　(A)opened Bank of America in 1904.
　　　　(B)worked in a bank in Italy.
　　　　(C)later changed the name of Bank of Italy.
　　　　(D)merged Bank of America in California.

(　　) **47** Which of the following is not true about the San Francisco earthquake?
　　　　(A)It was a tremendous disaster.
　　　　(B)It occurred in the aftermath of a fire.
　　　　(C)It happened in 1906.
　　　　(D)It caused problems for Giannini's bank.

(　　) **48** When did Giannini acquire Bank of America in New York City?
　　　　(A)1908　　　　　　　　　(B)1918
　　　　(C)1928　　　　　　　　　(D)1930

(　　) **49** The passage states that after his retirement, Giannini _____
　　　　(A)returned to lead the bank running.
　　　　(B)was responsible for the economic misfortune to occur.
　　　　(C)began selling off banks.
　　　　(D)supported his successor to survive the Great Depression.

(　) **50** The paragraph following the passage would mostly likely talk about ＿＿＿＿＿

(A)the development of Bank of Italy during World War II.

(B)a third major crisis of Giannini's bank association.

(C)bank failures during the Great Depression.

(D)the international business of the Bank of America group.

解答與解析

一、字彙測驗

1 (A)。 少數的政治狂熱者煽動群眾攻擊警方。

(A)煽動　(B)攪拌　(C)攪動（液體）等；搖動　(D)鼓舞

2 (A)。 對市場預測的徹底分析可以增加新產品成功的機率。

(A)預測　(B)後退　(C)就任　(D)區辨

3 (D)。 供應商會訴請賠償，如果我們片面中斷與他們的合約。

(A)污染　(B)繁殖　(C)委派　(D)中斷

4 (B)。 面臨能源危機，全球的科學家現都致力於開發替代性能源，以取代化石燃料。

(A)減輕　(B)替代　(C)敏感　(D)高度

5 (A)。 消費券政策的目標是刺激消費以增強頹廢的經濟。

(A)憑單　(B)證書　(C)贖回　(D)折扣

6 (B)。 我喜歡昨晚的音樂會。但有人的手機在音樂會上一直響，十分破壞氣氛。

(A)結構性的　(B)破壞性的　(C)敗壞的　(D)毀滅的

7 (B)。 基因工程的實驗已經達到數種癌症治療方法的重要突破。

(A)短處　(B)突破　(C)指控　(D)干擾

8 (A)。 廚房的水龍頭已經漏了好幾天。我們應該找水電工來修理。

(A)漏　(B)啜飲　(C)生鏽　(D)模糊

9 (C)。 一個公司最重要的決策之一，是如何利用照片、圖片設計或其他方法在廣告中描繪這家公司。

(A)歸屬　(B)評價　(C)描述　(D)誹謗

10 (A)。 看來新的增產紅利會成為加班的誘因。

(A)誘因　(B)直覺　(C)吸引力　(D)激勵

11 (D)。 一個國家的財務基礎建設是投資評估時重要的因素。
(A)沮喪　(B)界域　(C)抽象　(D)基礎建設

12 (A)。 特別小組對內部交易的調查意外地洩露了資產拆賣的證據。
(A)洩露　(B)抄襲　(C)禁運　(D)報復

13 (D)。 因為離婚的代價變高了，許多伴侶在婚前會考慮簽訂婚前協議。
(A)雙語的　(B)兩年一次的　(C)暫時的　(D)婚前的

14 (C)。 大多數公司在面臨經濟低迷時，需要很強的償付能力，有足夠的資金足以長期應付支出和營運。
(A)限制　(B)警覺　(C)償付能力　(D)商品

15 (B)。 公關室發表一篇新聞稿，澄清近期關於公司季營收的種種疑慮。
(A)宗教　(B)發表　(C)革命　(D)保留

二、文法測驗

16 (B)。 覆核委員會可能考慮要中止對數個非政府組織的補助經費。
解 consider是以動名詞為受詞的及物動詞。consider＋V-ing。

17 (D)。 爆炸現場的許多破瓦礫已經滯留甚久。
解 for a while指出已經有一陣子了，是從過去到現在仍然持續存在的，所以動詞的時態要選用現在完成式。（have＋p.p.）

18 (B)。 能源市場中的主要玩家需要大量的資金投資，少有興趣從事創新的工作。
解 require和have的主詞都是players，當主詞相同時，分詞構句可省略主詞，因為是主動的，所以用現在分詞而非過去分詞。原句可還原為The key players in the energy market, require ...，and have...。

19 (D)。 雇員需要遵從標準運作程序，並據之行動。
解 根據……而行動，accordingly是形容act（V.），修飾動詞要用副詞。

20 (C)。 社會福利系統應該提供貧困者足夠的支持。
(A)最好是 had better＋原V.
(B)寧願去…… would rather＋原V.
(C)應該＋原V
(D)由於＋N／V-ing

21 (B)。 入伍的那天是我絕對不會忘記的日子。
解 本題考代名詞的觀念。第一個which代替日子，第二個when（＝on which＝on the day）是表示時間的副詞，引導「當……時候」的子句，先行詞是the one。

22 (B)。 很少人知道評審用來挑選冠軍的標準。
解 主要句子中的criteria是先行詞，因為是事物，所以關係代名詞為which，介系詞要放在關係代名詞前，所以答案是by which，by ～ 根據～。

23 (D)。唯有將接下來幾年的財務利益納入考慮，我們才能判斷你這計劃是成功的。

解 take ～ into account 考慮～

24 (B)。如果James採用我的建議，他就不會犯下這愚蠢的錯誤。

解 在假設語氣中使用過去完成式（had＋p.p.），表示與過去事實相反的狀態。動詞的時態和所要表現的時間有落差，要用助動詞的過去式（如would,could...）＋have＋過去分詞。

25 (C)。即便惹惱了他，我仍不後悔告訴他我的想法。

解 regret＋Ving，tell是及物動詞，補語前要有受詞。

26 (A)。過去五年，我在公司中很少犯錯。

解 表示否定的副詞置於句首時，要用倒裝句（助V＋S＋V.）。

27 (A)。不論鄉間生活多麼不便，許多人仍舊從大都市逃到鄉村地區。

解 how＋adj＋S＋V. 什麼東西多麼地……

28 (B)。怪罪他人以消滅問題，這通常稱為代罪羔羊。

解 本句缺少主詞，動名詞或不定詞才能夠當主詞，視為單數，後用單數動詞（is）。

29 (C)。鑽石是珍貴的石頭，被深埋在地底，純粹的鑽石是完全白晰的。

解 原句為which are perfectly white when they are pure. they are可省

略，因which＝they＝diamonds，同時將when pure用逗號斷開，成為插入的子句，答案為which, when pure, are perfectly white.

30 (B)。在遠方可以看見一個被樹圍繞的湖。

解 湖被樹圍繞，surrounded by trees，是省略了which was的形容詞子句，用來形容lake。地方副詞放句首＋倒裝句（V＋S）（In the far distance），原序為 A lake（which was）surrounded by trees was in the far distance.

三、克漏字測驗

(一)

美國人喜歡認為自己是工作的烈士。他們喜歡談論自己辛勤的工作，也對他們歐洲的表兄弟，特別是法國，對他們的懶惰感到驚訝。但到了年輕人身上，情況就相反了。美國的兒童比全世界所有的兒童，包括被認為懶惰的歐洲人，都過得更舒適。他們的上學時間最短，只有一百八十天，相較之下，OECD（經濟合作發展組織）的平均是一百九十五天，而東亞國家則超過兩百天。德國的小孩比美國學童多了廿個上學日，而韓國比美國多一個月。過去十二年，少上十五天課就表示美國學生少了一百八十天的上課日，那相當於是一個學年。

31 (C)。(A)保留的 (B)脅迫 (C)相反的 (D)設計

32 (B)。(A)無私地　(B)被認定　(C)無情地　(D)困惑地

33 (A)。**解** be compared with與～比較，be opposed to～反對～，本句已有動詞（have），故用分詞（compared）。

34 (B)。(A)喜好　(B)短缺　(C)利益　(D)約會

35 (D)。(A)相似　(B)剝奪　(C)典型　(D)相當於

（二）

六月五日，世界衛生組織仍將流行性豬流感的警報設定在第二高的等級，但表示未來的變化將反映爆發的情況有多嚴重。聯合國的官員也在評估如何調整警報規模來反映流感的嚴重性以及它在全世界散佈的情況。批評者認為，這可能導致除墨西哥外的國家那些疾病影響中等不必要的恐慌，這個疾病已經在墨西哥導致103人死亡。專家組成的世界衛生組織緊急委員會推薦幾項可能可以列入評估流行嚴重性的因素。根據世衛，至今，新型的H1N1品種，又稱為豬流感，已經造成六十九個國家兩萬一千九百四十人感染，一百廿五人致命。墨西哥、美國和加拿大受該疾病的衝擊。同時，沙烏地阿拉伯也出現了首樁病例。美國有超過一萬三千個感染案例，廿七名確認死亡，這份資料來自聯邦疾病管制及預防中心。世界衛生組織的代表表示，本週會有一個作法：將嚴重程度從三級增加到六級，如果流感的影響維持適中，整體的水準會達到高峰。如果病毒引發了更嚴重的問題，他們將再調整。世界衛生組織的普及規模現在維持在第二高等級，在一到六的等級中，目前是五級，這表示大規模的感染即將發生。季節性的感冒疫苗仍會繼續生產，但發展新疫苗以對抗新流感的工作也在持續。

36 (D)。(A)個人的　(B)興奮的　(C)傑出的　(D)地理上的

37 (B)。(A)despite（介）＋N. 儘管　(B)除……以外　(C)遠離　(D)分離

38 (D)。(A)主要是因為……　(B)迄今　(C)也……　(D)也稱為

39 (C)。(A)被隔離　(B)被建議採取的　(C)被確認　(D)被除外

40 (A)。(A)逼近的　(B)例外的　(C)不可能　(D)明確的

四、閱讀測驗

（一）

廣告可以被視為「讓人知道而去買或賣商品或服務的方法」。廣告的目標是增加人們的知覺並引發興趣。它試圖知會而且說服。媒體是用來傳播訊息的，新聞提供相當便宜的方法，而雜誌是用來觸及市場中的特定區塊。電影和商業電台對地方性的市場十分有用。電視雖然十分昂貴，但非常有效。公告非常便宜，而且它的吸引力更持久。其他增加消費者興趣的方法是經由展示、商業博覽會以及直接郵寄廣告。

本世紀，大量使用廣告是西方國家最突顯的特色之一，這是無庸置疑的。像是冷凍食品、煙酒和藥物的生意，都是靠大量的廣告而建立。

我們想知道，廣告的成本是製造商或消費者支付的。既然廣告是產品成本的一部分，就必須在售價中反映，因此很明顯地，消費者付了廣告的費用。然而如果大量的廣告導致需求增加，生產的成本降低，消費者就可以少付一些。

精準地測量廣告的影響是困難的。當市場成長時，廣告有助於增加需求。當市場萎縮，廣告可能會干預更大幅的銷售降低，而非任其發生而不援助。我們清楚的是，如果廣告無法有其價值，沒有人會大量付費在廣告上。

41 (B)。廣告的費用主要來自於
　　　　　　。
(A)廠商　(B)顧客　(C)增加的銷量
(D)降低的價格

42 (D)。第一段的「媒體 media」一字包括：　　　　　。
(A)只有廣播　(B)只有新聞　(C)只有電視　(D)以上皆是

43 (A)。廣告經常用來：　　　　　。
(A)推動銷售量　(B)引發猜疑　(C)欺騙消費者　(D)增加生產

44 (C)。廣告可以在　　　　　　增加需求。
(A)任何時刻　(B)任何狀況　(C)成長中的市場　(D)萎縮的市場

45 (B)。從本文的最後一句我們可以結論出：　　　　　。
(A)商業經常不必付出太多廣告費用
(B)商人知道廣告會為他們帶來更多利益
(C)廣告經常讓商業付出大量金錢
(D)廣告很難說服人們商品的價值

(二)

一九〇四年的十月十七日，義裔美籍人士A. P. Giannini在舊金山創立義大利銀行。在發展過程中，Giannini的銀行經歷廿世紀幾次天災和經濟遽變的危機。

Giannini的銀行在一九〇六年曾經休業，當時巨大的地震重創舊金山，引發好幾起大火，幾乎毀了這個城市。Giannini找了兩輛馬車和一隊馬匹，他將銀行的儲備金，主要是黃金，裝滿馬車，然後逃離那個混亂的城市，保全了客戶的基金。在災難結束後，Giannini在華盛頓街碼頭設立一個臨時的店面，這是第一個準備開始營運的銀行。

在一九〇六年的大火後，義大利銀行繼續繁榮且擴張。一九一八年，它已經有廿四家分行。十年後，Giannini獲得了數家銀行，包括座落在紐約市的美國銀行。一九三〇年，他合併義大利銀行的所有分行、紐約市的美國銀行以及他在加州成立的數家美國銀行，成為美國商業銀行國家信託儲蓄股份有限公司。

銀行的第二次大危機發生在一九三〇年代的大蕭條。雖然Giannini在經濟大蕭條最黑暗前已經退休，但他的後繼

者在經濟狀況不好時出售銀行，仍然惹惱了Giannini。他在六十二歲重新執掌銀行，在他的領導下，銀行平安度過經濟大蕭條的風暴而且進入海外擴張的另一個階段。

46 (C)。根據本文，Giannini _____
(A)在一九〇四年設立美國銀行
(B)在義大利的銀行上班
(C)後來變更義大利銀行的名字
(D)合併加州的美國銀行

47 (B)。關於舊金山地震，以下何者為非？
(A)是一場大災難
(B)在大火後發生
(C)在一九〇六年發生
(D)對Giannini銀行有影響

48 (C)。Giannini何時獲得紐約市的美國銀行？
(A)1908　(B)1918　(C)1928　(D)1930
解 本文提及一九一八年，它已經有廿四家分行。十年後，Giannini獲得了數家銀行，包括座落在紐約市的美國銀行。所以是一九二八年。

49 (A)。文章指出，Giannini退休後
(A)回來領導銀行　(B)對後來的經濟厄運有責任　(C)開始出售銀行　(D)支持他的後繼者渡過大蕭條

50 (D)。本文後的段落最可能會談及　(A)義大利銀行在二戰時的發展
(B)Giannini的第三次危機　(C)大蕭條時的失敗　(D)美國銀行集團的國際事業

解答與解析

一　字彙測驗

(　) **1** The congressmen have reached a _____ that smoking should be banned within thirty feet from the entrance of a building.
(A)consensus　(B)flexibility　(C)dispute　(D)subscription

(　) **2** When we receive text messages of promotions from a company, we must be _____ of possible false advertisement out of which the company wants to make profit.
(A)worried　(B)suspicious　(C)reluctant　(D)effective

(　) **3** I just learned that Tivoli Gardens in Copenhagen, Denmark was the _____ for the original Disneyland in L. A., California.
(A)organization　　　　　(B)substitution
(C)inspiration　　　　　(D)complication

(　) **4** Tom's desk was so _____ with papers that it was hard to find anything.
(A)cluttered　(B)muddled　(C)overrun　(D)burdened

(　) **5** All branch stores are required to fill out the _____ report to check if there is enough merchandise on shelf and in stock.
(A)finance　(B)inquiry　(C)customs　(D)inventory

(　) **6** Many journalists do not _____ whether or not it is appropriate to interview a child during a tragic event for he/she is usually too young to understand the trauma he/she is involved in.
(A)ascertain　(B)detect　(C)decide　(D)assume

(　) **7** The annual charity fundraising event is _____ by several financial institutions in Taiwan.
(A)isolated　(B)prohibited　(C)sponsored　(D)consumed

(　) **8** Public education _____ would need to be increased for small-size classes, teacher training programs and new E-learning facilities.
(A)excavation　(B)expulsion　(C)expenditures　(D)expectancies

(　) **9** Steve Jobs' _____ mastery of technological innovations and aesthetics successfully transformed the landscape of consumer electronics industry.
(A)aggravated　(B)unrivaled　(C)disclosed　(D)segmented

(　) **10** _____ production lines is the prioritized agenda in manufacturing industries.
(A)Eradicating　(B)Penetrating　(C)Optimizing　(D)Curbing

二　文法測驗

(　) **11** I want to see _____.
(A)what it tracks and manages data reporting
(B)what does it track and manage data reporting
(C)how it tracks and manages data reporting
(D)how does it track and manage data reporting

(　) **12** Not until Toyota debuted the model Prius in the late 1990s _____ the technology of hybrid engine.
(A)the auto industry introduced
(B)did the auto industry introduce
(C)the auto industry introducing
(D)does the auto industry introduce

(　) **13** _____ for the sales in the first quarter may not necessarily be the final sales volume at the end of the quarter.
(A)Although it projects　　　(B)What is projected
(C)Projected　　　　　　　(D)Despite its projection

(　) **14** _____ in 1952, the MIT Sloan School of Management is one of the world's most prestigious business school.
(A)Founding　　　　　　　(B)Founded
(C)To found　　　　　　　(D)To find

(　　) **15** To prevent sewage from entering the waterways and protect public health, the city councilman strongly demanded that the sewage system _____ in three months.

(A)improved   (B)to improve

(C)was improved   (D)be improved

(　　) **16** _____ you encounter any problems regarding the new system, please notify the tech support ASAP.

(A)Might   (B)Would

(C)Should   (D)Could

(　　) **17** The former CEO of Highhills Inc. was believed _____ a suicide.

(A)to commit   (B)to have committed

(C)committing   (D)having committed

(　　) **18** The original model has been _____ and replaced by the new one.

(A)rendered obsolete (B)rendering superior

(C)rendered catastrophic (D)rendering absolute

(　　) **19** _____ the lobbying groups been backing up the new protocol, but several industry labor unions are now voicing their stern support for it.

(A)Not until there have (B)There have never

(C)Not only have   (D)If they could have

(　　) **20** The representatives, with cigarettes in their hands, _____ over a few details when suddenly smoke detector set off the fire alarm.

(A)negotiated   (B)are negotiating

(C)are going to negotiate (D)were negotiating

(　　) **21** The Review Board could be considering _____ the grants given to several non-governmental organizations.

(A)to discontinue   (B)discontinuing

(C)to be discontinued (D)discontinue

(　　) **22** A lot of debris _____ at the site of explosion for quite a while.

(A)was left   (B)were left

(C)have been left   (D)has been left

(   ) **23** The key players in the energy market, _____ heavy capital investment, have little interest in innovation.
(A)which to require   (B)requiring
(C)which it requires   (D)required

(   ) **24** Employees are required to follow the standard operating procedures and to act _____.
(A)according to   (B)in accordance with
(C)according   (D)accordingly

(   ) **25** The social welfare system _____ provide the underprivileged people with sufficient support.
(A)had better to   (B)would rather to
(C)ought to   (D)due to

三　克漏字測驗

(一)

　　The digital age is dawning, and that's good news for Asian companies. Already, a high __26.__ of the world's new digital products, such as DVD players and digital cameras, are being produced there, not only because manufacturing costs are lower there than in North America and Europe, but also because Asia has become a center for __27.__. Japanese companies, of course, have long been admired for their ability to design and manufacture consumer products that incorporate the latest technology while __28.__ the most-desired functions. Now other Asian countries like Korea and Taiwan are __29.__. With the worldwide demand for digital products growing __30.__ a furious pace, the future looks bright for the Asian companies that make them.

(   ) **26** (A)level   (B)quality   (C)affluence   (D)percentage

(   ) **27** (A)animation   (B)innovation   (C)recreation   (D)organization

(   ) **28** (A)offering   (B)offered   (C)did offer   (D)would offer

(　　) **29** (A)taking its leave　　　　(B)making its exit
　　　　(C)following its lead　　　　(D)catching its breath

(　　) **30** (A)at　　　　(B)in　　　　(C)on　　　　(D)with

四　閱讀測驗

(一)

　　How men first learnt to invent words is unknown; in other words, the origin of language is a mystery. All we really know is that men, unlike animals, somehow invented certain sounds to express thoughts and feelings, actions and things, so that they could communicate with each other; and that later they agreed upon certain signs, called letters, which could be combined to represent those sounds, and which could be written down. Those sounds, whether spoken or written in letters, we call words.

　　The power of words, then, lies in their associations–the things they bring up before our minds, Words become filled with meaning for us by experience; and the longer we live, the more certain words recall to us the glad and sad events of our past; and the more we read and learn, the more the number of words that mean something to us increases.

　　Great writers are those who not only have great thoughts but also express these thoughts in words which appeal powerfully to our minds and emotions. This charming and telling use of words is what we call literary style. Above all, the real poet is a master of words. He can convey his meaning in words which like music and by their association can move men to tears. We should therefore learn to choose our words carefully and use them accurately, or they will make our speech silly and vulgar.

(　　) **31** The author of the passage advises us _____.
　　　　(A)to use emotional words
　　　　(B)to use words in a literary style
　　　　(C)not to use silly and rude words
　　　　(D)to use words carefully and accurately

( ) **32** What is true about the words?
(A)They are visual letters.
(B)They are signs called letters.
(C)They are represented by sounds.
(D)They are represented by thoughts.

( ) **33** One of the reasons why men invented certain sounds to express thoughts and feelings was that _____.
(A)they could agree upon letters
(B)they could write and combine them
(C)they could express actions and things
(D)they could communicate with each other

( ) **34** The secret of a writer's success is the use of words that _____.
(A)recall to us the glad and sad events of our past
(B)are as beautiful as music
(C)are arranged in a creative way
(D)agree with certain literary style

( ) **35** Which of the following statements is NOT TRUE?
(A)The more we read and learn, the more learned we are.
(B)The more we read and learn, the more the number of words that mean something to us decreases.
(C)The more we read and learn, the more illiterate we become.
(D)The more we read and learn, the more knowledge we will acquire.

解答與解析

一、字彙測驗

1 **(A)**。對於大樓門口三十呎內不應抽煙已經達成共識。
(A)共識 (B)彈性 (C)爭執 (D)訂閱

2 **(B)**。當我們收到公司促銷的短訊時,我們必須懷疑那可能是公司想要賺錢的假廣告。

(A)擔心 (B)懷疑 (C)勉強 (D)有效

3 **(C)**。我剛才習得丹麥哥本哈根的蒂沃利花園最初是得自加州迪士尼樂園的靈感。
(A)組織 (B)代替 (C)靈感 (D)完成

4 (A)。 Tom的桌子被紙張弄得如此混亂，很難找東西。
(A)混亂　(B)攪拌　(C)漫延　(D)負荷

5 (D)。 所有的分店都必須填寫庫存單以檢視架上和倉庫是否有足夠的商品。
(A)財務　(B)需求　(C)關稅　(D)庫存

6 (A)。 許多記者不確定是否合適採訪一些太年幼以致於不瞭解自己已經身陷悲痛的孩童。
(A)確定　(B)檢查　(C)決定　(D)假設

7 (C)。 每年的慈善募款是由臺灣數個財務機構贊助的。
(A)孤立　(B)禁止　(C)贊助　(D)消費

8 (C)。 因應小班制、教師訓練計劃和新的Ｅ化學習設施，公共教育經費必需增加。
(A)開鑿　(B)驅逐　(C)經費　(D)期望

9 (B)。 Steve Jobs無可匹敵地掌握技術創新和美學，已經成功地改變消費電器產業的版圖。
(A)嚴重的　(B)無對手的　(C)揭露的　(D)分割的

10 (C)。 優化生產線是製造業的優先議程。
(A)惡化　(B)有穿透力的　(C)優化　(D)控制

二、文法測驗

11 (C)。 我想瞭解它如何追蹤並管理資料報告。
解 本句缺少動詞後的受詞，可以當受詞的只有名詞，因此要從答案中尋找名詞子句。子句的順序還是主詞＋動詞＋受詞或補語，因此有助動詞的(B)和(D)就不是答案。以文意來說，(C)是較合適的答案。

12 (B)。 直到TOYOTA在一九九〇年代晚期推出Prius車款，汽車工業才開始引進混合動力車的技術。
解 以否定副詞開頭的句子，要用倒裝（助V＋S＋V）。

13 (B)。 第一季所預測的銷售量不必然是季末的銷售數字。
解 關係代名詞what（＝the thing which）引導的子句為名詞子句，前面沒有先行詞，表示「所……的事」，what is projected for the sales in the first quarter這整個名詞子句是整個句子的主詞。

14 (B)。 成立於一九五二年，MIT的Sloan管理學院是全球最知名的商學院之一。
解 學校是被成立的，所以要用被動式。

15 (D)。 為了預防污水進入水道，並為了保護大眾的健康，市議員強力要求污水系統要在三個月內改善。
解 系統被改善，所以要用被動式。原句應該為that the sewage system

should be improved in three months. 但是在美語中，that子句若表示必要做的事，should可省略。

16 (C)。 如果你使用新系統遇到任何問題，請立刻通知技術支援部門。

解 看到倒裝（should＋主詞＋動詞），就知道是省略if的假設語氣。只有were, had和should倒裝放在句首，才可以省略if。原句If you should encounter ...，shuold 萬一。

17 (B)。 Highhills的前執行長被證實自殺了。

解 be believed to＋V：被認為或被證實……。句子是過去式，自殺的行為已經完成了，所以用to have committed。

18 (A)。 最初的模型已經過時，已經被新的取代。
(A)過時　(B)卓越　(C)災難　(D)絕對

19 (C)。 不只遊說團體支持新的提案，許多產業的勞工工會也表達支持。

解 not only.... but (also)不只……而且……

20 (D)。 當煙霧偵測器引發警報時，代表們正手持香菸,協商某些細節。

解 當……時，表示過去正在進行的事，用過去進行式。

21 (B)。 覆核委員會可能考慮要中止對數個非政府組織的補助經費。

解 consider是以動名詞為受詞的及物動詞，consider＋V-ing。

22 (D)。 爆炸現場的許多破瓦礫已經滯留甚久。

解 for a while指出已經有一陣子了，是從過去到現在仍然持續存在的，所以動詞的時態要選用現在完成式（have＋p.p.）。

23 (B)。 能源市場中的主要玩家需要大量的資金投資，少有興趣從事創新的工作。

解 require和have的主詞都是players，當主詞相同時，分詞構句可省略主詞，因為是主動的，所以用現在分詞而非過去分詞。

24 (D)。 雇員需要遵從標準運作程序，並據之行動。

解 根據……而行動，accordingly是形容act（V.），修飾動詞要用副詞。

25 (C)。 社會福利系統應該提供貧困者足夠的支持。
(A)最好是 had better＋原V
(B)寧願去……would rather＋原V
(C)應該＋原V
(D)由於＋N／V-ing

三、克漏字測驗

(一)

數位時代已見曙光，這對亞洲公司是個好消息。全球新的數位產品，像是DVD播放器和數位相機，有很高的比例是在亞洲生產。這不只是因為生產成本比北美和歐洲為低，也是因為亞洲已經成為創新中心。當然，日本公司已經在

他們設計和生產消費商品的能力上備受推崇，他們的商品包含了最新的技術，並提供最受用的功能。現在，亞洲其他國家，像是韓國和臺灣也效法日本。當全世界對電子產品的需求以狂熱的步調成長時，製造電子商品的亞洲公司，其未來一片光明。

26 (D)。(A)層次　(B)品質　(C)豐富　(D)比例

27 (B)。(A)活潑　(B)創新　(C)娛樂　(D)組織

28 (A)。原句為while it is offering，it is 需一起省略。

29 (C)。(A)告辭　(B)退出　(C)效尤、模仿　(D)屏息

30 (A)。at...pace：以……的步調

四、閱讀測驗

(一)

　　一開始，人們如何發明語詞，已經不可考。換句話說，語言的起源是個謎團。我們真正知道的是不像動物，人發明了特定的聲音來表達思想和感覺、行動和事件，所以他們能夠彼此溝通。後來，他們對特定的符號，所謂的字母，達成一致的意見，它們可以結合起來代表聲音，也可以被寫下來。那些聲音，不論以字母言說或書寫，我們稱為語詞。

　　語詞的力量與它們的聯想有關，我們提及在心中想到的事件。藉由經驗，語詞變得充滿意義。我們活得越久，會有越特定的語詞讓我們回想起過去快樂和傷心的事件。而且我們閱讀和學習地越多，會有越多的語詞對我們產生意義。

　　偉大的作家不只是那些有思想，同時也能夠用語詞表達這些思想，那些語詞能夠強烈地感染我們的心智和情緒。如此有魅力且生動地使用語詞，即稱為文學風格。尤其，詩人是語詞大師。他可以用像音樂的方式，用語詞傳達他的意思，並用語詞聯想賺人熱淚。我們因而應學習小心地選擇我們的語言，並且正確地使用，否則，它們將使我們說的話變得愚蠢且粗俗。

31 (D)。本文作者建議我們_____。
(A)使用情緒的語詞
(B)以文學風格運用語詞
(C)不要用愚蠢且粗俗的話
(D)小心且正確地使用語詞

32 (C)。關於語詞何者正確？
(A)它們是視覺的字母
(B)它們是稱為字母的符號
(C)它們可以用聲音表現
(D)它們可以用思想表現

33 (D)。人們發明特定的聲音來表達思想和感覺的原因之一為_____。
(A)他們對字母意見一致
(B)他們可以寫也可以組合
(C)他們可以表達行動和事件
(D)他們可以彼此溝通

34 (A)。作家成功的秘密是因為他們使用語詞_____。
(A)喚起我們對過去高興和傷心事件的回憶
(B)如音樂般美麗
(C)用特定的方式安排
(D)與特定的文學風格一致

35 (B)。以下何者為非？
(A)我們閱讀和學習地越多，就越有知識。
(B)我們閱讀和學習地越多，對我們有意義的字就會減少。
(C)我們閱讀和學習地越多，我們會更無知。
(D)我們閱讀和學習地越多，我們會得到越多知識。

解答與解析

第五回

一 字彙測驗

( ) **1** If you _____ an organization, you become a member of it or start work as an employee of it.
(A)pay (B)leave (C)join (D)employ

( ) **2** _____ to lead is known to damage the brains of young children.
(A)Exposure (B)Expansion (C)Experience (D)Exchange

( ) **3** The Los Angeles riots _____ the bitterness between the black and Korean communities in the city.
(A)referred (B)reflected (C)replayed (D)received

( ) **4** A (n) _____ view or vision of a situation is one in which all the different aspects of it are considered.
(A)ominous (B)narrow (C)local (D)global

( ) **5** A _____ is a building or a room where scientific experiments, analyses and research are carried out.
(A)laboratory (B)library (C)limousine (D)lavatory

( ) **6** I am graduating this coming June and am seeking a career in _____ .
(A)employee (B)employer (C)business (D)compromise

( ) **7** If you say that someone is _____ , you mean that they are not perfect and are likely to make mistakes or to fail in what they are doing.
(A)perfect (B)fallible (C)plausible (D)placid

( ) **8** After a string of oil _____ , people find it hard to trust any oil product on the market.
(A)services (B)scandals (C)solutions (D)schedules

( ) **9** The government must take action to root out dishonest food-makers and ensure food _____ .
(A)safety (B)reality (C)charity (D)property

( ) **10** Drunk driving has caused a lot of tragic crashes. Such reckless behavior should be severely _____ .
(A)operated (B)recorded (C)punished (D)displayed

( ) **11** The restaurant's menu is _____ and surely can satisfy everyone's different tastes.
(A)diverse (B)stuffed (C)ancient (D)logical

( ) **12** _____ may be deceiving. All that glitters is not gold.
(A)Appearances (B)Relationships
(C)Entertainments (D)Transportations

( ) **13** I've _____ to run the marathon held in Hualien.If you want to join too, put your name down here.
(A)got on (B)signed up (C)looked up (D)held on

( ) **14** About two hours ago there was a very nasty accident on the highway; _____ , nobody was injured.
(A)instantly (B)regularly (C)personally (D)fortunately

( ) **15** In the film, Beyond Beauty-TAIWAN FROM ABOVE, the photographer successfully _____ Taiwan's natural beauty.
(A)captured (B)replaced (C)motivated (D)survived

二 文法測驗

( ) **16** With a little _____ from his parents, he should do well.
(A)encourage (B)encouragement
(C)to encourage (D)encouraging

( ) **17** Vitamins cannot be _____ by our bodies.
(A)manufacture (B)manufactured
(C)manufacturing (D)to manufacture

(　　) **18** We are here to provide the public _____ a service.

(A)with　(B)on　(C)for　(D)at

(　　) **19** You could see from his face that he was.

(A)lie　(B)lied　(C)lay　(D)lying

(　　) **20** If I were you, I _____ to talk to him.

(A)go　(B)will go　(C)would have gone　(D)may

(　　) **21** I _____ for more than 10 years, and now I am still taking English classes at school.

(A)study English　　　　　(B)studied English

(C)am studying English　　　(D)have been studying English

(　　) **22** _____ no specific treatment of Ebola virus infection, and the fatality rate can be up to 90%.

(A)It is　(B)It has　(C)That is　(D)There is

(　　) **23** It takes someone _____ is as smart as Sherlock Holmes to crack the case and solve the crime.

(A)who　(B)what　(C)when　(D)which

(　　) **24** The kind woman took the lost brother and sister in and made sure they had something _____ .

(A)eaten　(B)to eat　(C)eating　(D)can eat

(　　) **25** You cannot mask your messy room _____ throwing all your stuff under your bed or into your closet.

(A)as　(B)by　(C)on　(D)from

(　　) **26** Vivian could feel her heart _____ fast when Jason knelt down and popped the question.

(A)beaten　(B)to beat　(C)beating　(D)had beaten

(　　) **27** A: _____ is it to the shopping mall?

B: It's about 10 minutes on foot.

(A)How far　(B)How long　(C)How often　(D)How much

(　　) **28** Walter wasn't careful with his money, and ＿＿＿ .That was why they both got into heavy debt.

(A)so was his wife　　　　(B)his wife was too

(C)his wife was either　　　(D)neither was his wife

(　　) **29** It was an easy test and Tom should have passed, but he ＿＿＿ .

(A)didn't　(B)hadn't　(C)wasn't　(D)shouldn't

(　　) **30** ＿＿＿ wild animals tend to stay away from people, you still need to be careful while walking through the forest.

(A)Since　(B)For　(C)Though　(D)Because

三　克漏字測驗

(一)

It's not often that qualifications and experience totally match up to an advertised post, so it's preferable to emphasize other qualitied, like your willingness to learn and the fact that you work hard. __31.__ , you should be careful not to give the impression you are over-qualified for the job. I think that employers are often more interested in things like loyalty and ability to fit in. A high-flier who knows too much can create a bad working atmosphere and __32.__ a team. Personally, I want the employer to think that I am going to be easy to work with and won't create too many waves.

No one likes a "big head" but, on the other hand, don't be falsely modest either. Basically, your qualifications and experience tell their own story, so you're not going to __33.__ anyone by adding a lot of adjectives like "excellent" and "outstanding" to your CV. Usually this will make an experienced recruitment officer __34.__ . It doesn't hurt to acknowledge one or two weaknesses either-areas that you would like to __35.__ and you want a chance to develop. Above all, be honest, because if you exaggerate or like, in the end someone is going to catch you out and you'll end up looking stupid.

(   ) **31** (A)Likewise   (B)In fact   (C)Relatively   (D)On the other hand

(   ) **32** (A)form   (B)break   (C)lead   (D)help

(   ) **33** (A)imagine   (B)support   (C)include   (D)impress

(   ) **34** (A)important (B)considerate (C)suspicious (D)confident

(   ) **35** (A)improve   (B)replace   (C)abbuse   (D)release

(二)

How is it possible that two passengers sitting shoulder to shoulder in the same plane can pay such different prices for their ticket? Buying an air ticket has become a test of skill and timing,   36.   the customer is responsible for getting the best deal possible. With the online reservation systems of cut-price airlines it is your fault if you get a bad deal, because there is no travel agent to   37. .

Nowadays, all airlines have a "pricing" department which is responsible for "yield management". In other words, their job is to adjust the price of ticket in order to get the maximum possible profit for each seat on the flight. Ticket prices vary   38.   supply and demand and depend on how full the flight is, and when you make your reservation. The result is a   39.   difference in prices. In one investigation, Le Monde newspaper made enquiries at different times about Air France tickets on the same flight from Paris to New York in economy class. They were quoted 17 different prices, ranging from € 467 to € 3,228. Airlines justify these variable pricing policies on the extremely narrow profit margins of the business. To illustrate this, easyjet use a graphic which shows the seating plan of a plane with 155 seats. They need to sell 39 of these seats to   40.   airport costs. 37 seats go in fuel costs and 15 to pay the pilots and crew. That leaves just 9 seats for profit.

(   ) **36** (A)where   (B)which   (C)what   (D)how

(   ) **37** (A)fly   (B)blame   (C)plan   (D)buy

(   ) **38** (A)instead of (B)as for   (C)according to (D)aside from

(   ) **39** (A)brisk   (B)minimal   (C)vague   (D)tremendous

(   ) **40** (A)cover   (B)take   (C)remove   (D)accept

(三)

A good communication involves a lot more than simply having a large vocabulary and good pronunciation. It also includes having the ability to interpret peoples __41.__ and facial expressions. Something else that facilitates good communication is the awareness of personal space, which is that invisible boundary people create around themselves __42.__ feel comfortable and secure. Though personal space boundaries vary from culture to culture and person to person, everyone has one or a few. Psychologists generally __43.__ four different boundaries or zones. The largest is the public zone. It's the distance between the speaker and the audience. The next is the smaller social zone. It's a polite and safe distance, too far for any body contact. The even smaller is the friend zone, __44.__ , however, does allow for touch, for things like high five and hugs. __45.__ , the intimate zone is the closest space reserved for those you love and trust the most.

Being aware of personal space helps us avoid making people feel uncomfortable, which will help improve our communication.

(　　) **41** (A)mother tongue　　　　　(B)sign language
　　　　　(C)body language　　　　　(D)foreign language

(　　) **42** (A)so that　(B)such as　(C)in order to　(D)so as not to

(　　) **43** (A)care for　(B)point to　(C)try out　(D)look up

(　　) **44** (A)who　(B)what　(C)where　(D)which

(　　) **45** (A)Finally　(B)Likewise　(C)Besides　(D)Therefore

四　閱讀測驗

Hello, and welcome to Business Talk. This month we're looking at the role of ethics in business. According to Richard Reed, co-founder of Innocent Drinks, the company behind award-winning fruit-based smoothies, ethics are fundamental to the company's success. Innocent says that, as well as making money, the objective is always to leave things a little bit better than it finds them, an inspiring way to approach business.

So, how did the success of Innocent all begin? Innocent was founded back in 1998 by Richard and two friends from Cambridge University. They decided to set up a business together and spent £500 on fruit to make smoothies to sell at a music festival.

A sign above their stall said "Should we give up our jobs to make these smoothies? " They asked people to put their empty bottles in one of two bins marked "Yes" and "No". At the end of the festival the "Yes" bin was full, so they went into work the next day and resigned. Innocent continues to innovate and the product range now consists of vegetable pots and other healthy, natural products as well as smoothies, and the company is constantly working on new lines. Innocent sells to over 10,000 retailers in 13 European countries, and its market is constantly growing.

So what is it that makes Innocent an ethical company? Apart from only using packaging that can be recycled,it uses only 100% natural products and each year gives 10% of its profits to charities in the countries where its fruit comes from.

Innocent wasn't the first company to tap into the fruit market, but it was one of the first. It's always important to be different from the competition and, with Innocent, the combination of ethics and clever marketing is a recipe for success.

(　　) **46** What are the two important factors that make Innocent successful?
　　　　(A)Certificates from Cambridge University and the fruit market.
　　　　(B)Smoothies and European market.
　　　　(C)Ethics and clever marketing.
　　　　(D)Vegetable pots and healthy products.

(　　) **47** Who actually decided that Richard and his two friends should sell smoothies?
　　　　(A)They themselves.
　　　　(B)People who attended the festival.
　　　　(C)Their former employers.
　　　　(D)Retailers in 13 European countries.

( ) **48** Which of the following can be considered contributing to Innocent's being an ethical company?
(A)It competes with other companies.
(B)It was founded by well-educated people.
(C)Each year it gives 10% of its profits to charities.
(D)It produces healthy, natural products.

( ) **49** What area might be Innocent's main market?
(A)Europe.　　　　　　(B)Asia.
(C)North America.　　　(D)Africa.

( ) **50** What might be the main point that the author of the essay wants to make?
(A)Attending a festival may be important for a company to be successful.
(B)Making money is the primary goal of a successful company.
(C)A food company needs to use 100% natural products in order to succeed.
(D)Ethics may be an important factor for a company's success.

解答與解析

一、字彙測驗

1 (C)。加入機構，你便成為其中一份子或職員之一。
(A)付款　(B)離開　(C)加入　(D)雇用。
解 可從become a member／start work as an employee推斷出答案為加入組織開始工作，故選(C)。

2 (A)。暴露於鉛下會傷害兒童的大腦。
(A)暴露　(B)擴展　(C)經驗　(D)交換。

解 從語句可知某因素導致兒童腦受到損害，又lead為鉛之意，故選(A)。

3 (B)。洛杉磯暴動反映出該城市黑人及韓國社區的苦境。
(A)提到　(B)反映　(C)重播　(D)接受。
解 可從riots（暴動）及bitterness兩單字推估出答案為reflect（反映），故選(B)。

4 (D)。所謂局勢的全盤觀點或視野指的是針對該局勢的每個部

分都有考慮到 (A)不吉祥的 (B)狹窄的 (C)局部的 (D)總體的。

解 可從本句後面的different aspects of it are considered推出view／vision of a situation是相當全面的 故選(D)。

5 **(A)**。 實驗室為進行科學實驗、分析及研究的大樓或房間。
(A)實驗室 (B)圖書館 (C)豪華轎車 (D)廁所。

解 可從scientific experiments推估出答案為實驗室，故選(A)。

6 **(C)**。 我今年六月就會畢業，目前正在找商業相關的職業。
(A)職員 (B)雇主 (C)商業 (D)妥協。

解 可從seeking a career推估出答案為商業相關工作，故選(C)。

7 **(B)**。 如果你形容一個人易犯錯，代表你覺得他們不夠完美且極容易犯錯，或是搞砸他們正在做的事。
(A)完美的 (B)容易犯錯的 (C)貌似有理的 (D)平和的。

解 可從後句中的are not perfect……推估出someone易犯錯，故選(B)。

8 **(B)**。 黑心油醜聞後，人們很難再相信市場上的油相關商品了。
(A)服務 (B)醜聞 (C)解決辦法 (D)計畫表。

解 從後句的人們很難再相信油相關商品，可推估出前句為爆發黑心油醜聞，故選(B)。

9 **(A)**。 政府必須採取行動剷除黑心食品製造商，保障食物安全。
(A)安全 (B)真實 (C)慈善 (D)財產。

解 剷除黑心商保障食物安全，故選(A)。

10 **(C)**。 酒駕已經造成許多無法挽回的車禍悲劇，如此魯莽的行為應該被嚴格取締。(A)操作 (B)收錄 (C)處罰 (D)展出。

解 由車禍悲劇無法挽回可知酒駕應被懲罰，故選(C)。

11 **(A)**。 餐廳菜單多樣化，絕對可以滿足每個人不同的品味。
(A)多樣化的 (B)塞滿的 (C)古老的 (D)合邏輯的。

解 可從satisfy everyone's different tastes推估出餐廳菜單多樣化，故選(A)。

12 **(A)**。 外表會騙人，金玉其外敗絮其中。
(A)外觀 (B)關係 (C)娛樂 (D)交通。

解 "All that glitters is not gold"為英文諺語，意為「金玉其外，敗絮其中」，由此可推估外表不可信，故選(A)。

13 **(B)**。 我已經申請參加花蓮馬拉松，如果你也想參加的話，就把名字寫在這邊 (A)應付 (B)申請 (C)查詢 (D)停下來。

解 參加馬拉松需事先申請，(A)(C)(D)語意皆不合，故選(B)。

14 (D)。 大約兩小時前高速公路發生了一起相當嚴重的車禍，所幸沒有人受傷　(A)立刻地　(B)經常地　(C)私人的　(D)幸運地。

解 可從nasty accident／nobody was injured推估出車禍雖嚴重卻沒造成傷亡，為相當幸運之事，故選(D)。

15 (A)。 在電影「看見台灣」中，攝影師成功捕捉了台灣自然之美。(A)捕捉　(B)取代　(C)激發　(D)存活下來。

解 攝影師捕捉台灣之美呈現於電影中，故選(A)。

二、文法

16 (B)。 有他父母的加油打氣，他應該會表現良好。

解 with在此為「擁有」之意，加上後面的a，可知空格內應填入名詞，故選(B)。

17 (B)。 維他命無法由人體生成。

解 本句組成「受詞+be V.+過去分詞+by+主詞」為被動語態，可知動詞應選擇過去分詞manufactured表示被動語態，故選(B)。

18 (A)。 我們來此提供公眾服務。

解 此題出現的介系詞中文無法翻譯，故需思考每個介系詞本身隱含的詞意；(A)with有使用、藉由的含意　(B)on有在……之上的含意　(C)for有為誰、給誰的含意　(D)at有在某個點的含意；(A)意思最為接近，故選(A)。

19 (D)。 從他的臉就可以知道他在說謊。

解 此題由介系詞that連接You could see from his face及he was ＿＿＿ 兩個獨立句子，可直接由後句的He was（S+be V）推估出句子組成為過去進行式，需加Ving，故選(D)。

20 (C)。 如果我是你的話，我就會過去跟他說話。

解 英文在對「不可能發生」的情況或「過去沒有發生的事情」進行假設時，會使用「If+過去式……would／could／might」的句型，此句"I were you"由於是不可能發生的狀況，因此後面需用would，在加上講述過去未發生的狀況，故使用would have done to..，選擇(C)。

【觀念延伸】表達「如果我是你」時，需使用I were you而非I was you，需注意。

21 (D)。 我已經學英文學了十年，卻還是在學校上英文課。

解 英文要描述一段時間內持續進行某事時，需用現在完成式「S+has／have+過去分詞+(for時間)」的句型，如：I have studied English for 10 years.（我已經學英文學了十年）；此題因為要強調過去這段時間一直在學習，因此使用現在完成進行式have been studying English for more than 10 years，故選(D)。

解答與解析

22 (D)。 依波拉病毒並無特定治療方法，致死率高達90%。

解 英文可用There is來表示某事物存在的現象，如：There is a dog in the garden.（花園裡有一隻狗），此題主詞為Ebola，為描述Ebola存在的情況，故用There is no specific treatment of Ebola之句型，選擇(D)。

23 (A)。 要順利破案並解決犯罪問題需要一個像福爾摩斯般聰明的人。

解 關係代名詞who／which可用來修飾名詞，此題先點出主詞someone，並於後面補充說明someone is as smart as Sherlock Holmes，中間需要一個可以修飾人的關係代名詞who進行連接，故選(A)。

【補充字彙】crack the case：解開謎題、破案。

24 (B)。 那個好心的女人將迷路的兄妹帶進房裡且確保他們有東西可以吃。

解 they had something……此句型欲連接兩個動詞had及eat，用介系詞to連接，故選(B)。

25 (B)。 你將所有的東西藏進床下或塞進衣櫥，是沒辦法將髒亂的房間打理乾淨的。

解 介系詞by有藉由、透過……方法之意，放在此語意符合，故選之。

26 (C)。 當傑森跪下求婚時，薇薇安可以感受到她的心臟快要跳出來了。

解 表達五官感受的動詞後面再接動詞時，需使用原型V／Ving形式，如：

I	see hear feel	her	cry crying	in the garden.

故此題答案為(C)。

27 (A)。 A:購物中心離這裡多遠？B:走路大約十分鐘。

解 此題詢問距離長短，(C)How often詢問頻率以及(D)How much詢問價錢皆不合，故可先刪除；(B)How long後面需接does it take，代表詢問時間長短(若接is it會變成詢問長度)，語意不合可刪除；(A)How far is it有詢問距離多遠之意，故選之。

【補充字彙】debt (n.)負債

28 (D)。 華特沒有小心管理好錢，他太太也是，難怪他們都陷入巨額負債。

解 英文表達「A如何..B也是」時，肯定句使用too、否定句使用either，如：

【肯定】John is a teacher. Tom is a teacher, too.

可濃縮為John is a teacher, so is Tom.

【肯定】John is not a teacher. Tom is not a teacher, either.

可濃縮為John is not a teacher, neither is Tom.

以此模式推論，可知本題答案為(D)。

29 (A)。 這是個簡單的考試，湯姆應該要通過的，但他沒有。

　解 英文在描述過去「沒有發生的事情」時，會採用「S＋過去式……would／should／might+have+過去分詞」句型，由於前面已出現should have passed，可推估後面需使用過去式didn't，故選(A)。

30 (C)。 雖然野生動物會避開人類，但經過森林時還是要小心　(A)既然　(B)因為　(C)雖然　(D)因為。

　解 此題可從後面的still need to be careful判斷出句子採用轉折語氣，(A)(B)(D)語意皆不合，故選(C)。

　【觀念延伸】For在此可當「因為」解釋，比Because更為正式。

三、克漏字測驗

(一)

　由於資格與經驗通常無法兩立，因此在推銷自己時，最好再加入其他特質，如：願意學習及工作認真等事實。（31）事實上，你應該避免給人一種過於優秀的印象，比起資格，雇主更在乎應試者忠誠度及適應能力。一個太有潛力的新秀反而可能搞壞工作氣氛，（32）破壞團隊團結。個人而言，我更希望雇主認為我是一名好相處、不會興風作浪的新職員。

　「強出頭」雖然沒人愛，卻也不宜刻意低調，基本上你的資歷會說話，無需在簡歷表上加一堆如「優秀」、「傑出」等形容詞企圖讓人（33）印象深刻，經驗豐富的人事專員反而會覺得這樣的敘述（34）很可疑。可以的話，甚至可以加註一兩項你想要（34）改進或是找機會發展的弱點。總而言之，誠實為上策，因為如果你誇大不實，總有一天一定會露出馬腳，只會讓你看起來更笨。

31 (B)。 (A)同樣地　(B)事實上　(C)相對地　(D)另一方面。

　解 (A)(C)(D)語意皆不合，故選(B)。

32 (B)。 (A)形成　(B)破壞　(C)領導　(D)幫助。

　解 high-flier（潛力新秀）會破壞團隊，故選(B)。

33 (D)。 (A)想像　(B)支持　(C)含有　(D)使人產生印象。

　解 在CV中加入形容詞讓人印象深刻，故選(D)；CV為Curriculum Vitae的縮寫，意思為個人簡歷。

34 (C)。 (A)重要的　(B)貼心的　(C)存疑的　(D)有自信的。

　解 太多形容詞反而會弄巧成拙，讓經驗豐富的人事專員存疑，故選(C)；suspicious of可表示對……存疑，如：I am suspicious of her getting married so young.（她這麼早結婚令人感到很可疑。）

35 (A)。 (A)改善　(B)替代　(C)虐待　(D)釋放。

　解 缺點需要改善並找機會發展，故選(A)。

　【補充字彙】weakness (n.)弱項、缺點

解答與解析

(二)

　　兩個肩並肩、比鄰而坐的旅客買的機票價格怎麼可以差那麼多？買機票已成為技術與時機的考驗，（36）消費者必須憑本事買到最佳價格。假如乘客是透過飛機網站預訂折扣機票的話，那麼買貴了就得自己認栽，因為沒有旅行社可以（37）責怪。

　　現在各家航空公司都有個「議價部門」進行「讓價管理」，換句話說，他們的工作便是調整機票價格以確保飛機上的所有座位能為航空公司贏取最大利益。機票價格（38）隨著供需變化，飛機滿座狀況以及預定時間而有不同，價格變化（39）相當大。法國<世界報>曾做過一項調查，在不同時間點詢問法航同一班班機，從巴黎飛往紐約的機票價格，結果問出17種價格介於467歐元至3,228歐元之間的票價。航空公司為其辯護，解釋這是為因應極低利潤設下的多樣化票價方針。英國易捷航空則是乾脆以一架能容納155個座位的飛機售票情形進行解釋，表示航空公司必須售出39個機位才能（40）抵銷機場成本，賣出37個機位支付燃油成本，最後再用15個機位支付機長及空服人員的薪水，至於航空公司自己則是只預留9個機位的收入做為利潤。

36 (A)。🈁 此句可拆成兩個句子來看：
(1) Buying an air ticket has become a test of skill and timing.
(2) The customer is responsible for getting the best deal possible.

拆開之後會發現(2)可置於(1)之前，整個句子便可如此理解：The customer is responsible for getting the best deal possible in buying an air ticket.（顧客在買機票時能否買到好價格須自行負責。）
以此句為前提再回到原本的句子時，會發現後面句子要修飾的名詞並非skill and timing而是buying an air ticket這個動作，因此關係代名詞不可用which、而是要用in which，加上in which＝where，故此題答案為(A)。

37 (B)。(A)飛行　(B)責怪　(C)計劃　(D)購買。
🈁 從前句"it is your fault if you get a bad deal"可推估買不到票須自己負責任，因為沒有旅行社可以責怪，故選(B)。

38 (C)。(A)反而　(B)至於　(C)根據　(D)除此之外。
🈁 前面已提到航空公司有個部門負責調整票價變化，由此可推知機票價格是隨著supply and demand（供應及需求）變化的，故選(C)。

39 (D)。(A)繁榮的　(B)最小的　(C)模糊的　(D)巨大的。
🈁 同上題，從前面敘述可知機票價格會隨著供需變化、飛機滿座狀況及預定時間而有不同，可推知機票價格變化極大，故選(D)。

40 (A)。(A)覆蓋　(B)拿取　(C)移除　(D)接受。

解 airport cost為機場成本，(B)(D)語意皆不合可先刪除；另，成本已經存在只能抵銷無法移除，故(C)亦不合刪除之；(A)雖為覆蓋之意，用在此處cover the cost有抵銷成本之意，故選(A)。

（三）

　　良好的溝通不只包括龐大字彙量以及正確發音而已，還包括了理解對方（41）肢體語言及臉部表情的能力，其他讓溝通變得更好的元素則是對私人空間的認知，了解人們無形中會在自己與他人之間畫出界線，（42）以便讓自己感到舒適安全。雖然私人空間的界線隨著文化及個人而有不同，不過每個人至少都會有一至兩條。心理學家常（43）點明四個不同的界線或區域，最大的便是公眾區，這是講者和聽者之間的距離，另外則是小一點的社交區，同樣是禮貌但保持距離，不會有任何肢體接觸，再小一點則是朋友區，（44）允許擊掌或擁抱等肢體接觸。（45）最後的親密區只留給你最愛及信任的人，因為那是與你最緊密的空間。

　　了解私人空間可避免讓人感到不愉快，有助於日常生活溝通。

41 (C)。(A)母語　(B)手語　(C)肢體語言　(D)外語。

解 此題答案可從facial expressions（表情）推斷出與人溝通還得注意對方肢體語言釋放的訊息，故選(C)。

42 (C)。(A)以便於　(B)例如　(C)為了　(D)為了不要。

解 (A)so that後面接續句子須有主詞，例如：invisible boundary people create themselves so that they feel comfortable and safe.(B) such as用以舉例，此處語意不合，故刪除；(C)in order to畫出無形界線是為了讓自己感到舒適及安全，語意符合可選之；(D) so as not to語意剛好與正確答案相反，故刪除。

43 (B)。(A)計較　(B)表明　(C)試用(D)查詢。

解 前面敘述已說明每個人或多或少都會有私人空間界線，可推估出心理學家會對這些界線進行劃分，表明四種不同類型：公眾、社交、朋友、親密，故選(B)。

44 (D)。

解 The even smaller is the friend zone,_____, however, does allow for touch.由兩個句子組成：The even smaller is the friend zone. The friend zone, however, does allow for touch. 兩句主詞相同可用關係代名詞which連接做修飾，故選(D)。

45 (A)。(A)最後　(B)同樣地　(C)此外　(D)因此。

解 由於前面已提到public zone, social zone, friend zone等區，加上文章之前曾提到Psychologists

解答與解析

generally point to four different zones，可知最後會介紹intimate zone，故選(A)。

四、閱讀測驗

　　大家好！歡迎參加商業會談，這個月我們要探討良心在商業中的角色。根據一家得獎水果奶昔製造商「純真飲料公司」共同創辦人李察利德，良心是帶領一家公司邁向成功的基礎，純真飲料表示，訂定目標要像賺錢，永遠比實際情況再高一點，這會讓經營事業更有動力。那麼，純真飲料究竟如何成功？這家公司設立於1998年，由畢業於劍橋大學的李察及兩名友人創立，當時他們決心設立一家公司並花費500英鎊製作奶昔在音樂祭上販賣。

　　他們在攤位寫下：「我們應該放棄工作製作奶昔嗎？」然後要求大家將空瓶投入標示「贊成」或「反對」的塑膠桶裡，音樂祭結束後贊成的桶子全被塞滿，所以他們隔天便辭職了。

　　純真飲料不斷創新，現在產品已經包括了蔬菜鍋、健康自然食品以及奶昔等，即便如此，公司還是繼續開發新產品。純真飲料旗下商品銷售至歐洲13國超過一萬個零售商，市場不斷茁壯。

　　那麼，又是什麼讓純真飲料成為一家良心公司呢？除了只採用回收材質做包裝，它還只用百分之百天然食品，並於每年撥出10%的企業利潤做慈善，捐給水果原料來源國當作回饋。

　　純真飲料不是第一家涉足水果市場的公司，卻是最棒的公司之一。從競爭中與眾不同相當重要，純真飲料的經驗告訴我們，良心與聰明行銷是邁向成功的不二法門。

46 (C)。 純真飲料公司成功最重要的兩個因素為何？ (A)劍橋大學及水果市場核發的證照 (B)奶昔及歐洲市場 (C)良心及聰明行銷 (D)蔬菜鍋及健康食品。

解 本文最末段提到「良心與聰明行銷是邁向成功的不二法門」，故答案選擇(C)。

47 (B)。 誰決定李察跟他兩個朋友應該改賣奶昔？ (A)他們自己 (B)參加音樂祭的人 (C)他們的前雇主 (D)歐洲13國零售商。

解 本文第二段提到「他們在攤位寫下：『我們應該放棄工作製作奶昔嗎？』然後要求大家將空瓶投入標示『贊成』或『反對』的塑膠桶裡」，參加音樂祭的人決定了他們的未來，故選(B)。

48 (C)。 下列選項何者是純真飲料成為一家良心公司的因素？
(A)純真飲料與其他公司競爭
(B)純真飲料由高學歷人員設立
(C)每年純真飲料都捐10%利潤做慈善
(D)純真飲料生產健康、自然的產品。

解 本文第三段提到「是什麼讓純真飲料成為一家良心公司呢？除了只採用回收材質做包裝，它還只用百分之百天然食品，並於每年

撥出10%的企業利潤做慈善」，
故選(C)。

49 (A)。 下列何者可能是純真飲料的
主要市場？ (A)歐洲 (B)亞洲
(C)北美洲 (D)非洲。

解 本文第三段提到 「純真飲料旗
下商品銷售至歐洲13國超過一萬
個零售商」 可知主要市場在歐
洲，故選(A)。

50 (D)。 下列何者為本文主旨？
(A)公司要成功就應該多多參加節慶
活動
(B)賺錢是一家成功公司的主要目標
(C)食品公司要成功就得使用百分之
百的天然產品
(D)良心可以是一家公司成功的關鍵。

解 本文主要在介紹純真飲料公司如
何靠著良心做事業，故選(D)。

解答與解析

109年 台北捷運新進人員（技術員(電子類)、站務員）

( ) **1** Our newest station _____ in two months, so we need to start hiring new employees.
(A)will open (B)had opened
(C)would open (D)has opened

( ) **2** Julia is a famous and highly _____ doctor.
(A)respect (B)respected
(C)respecting (D)to respect

( ) **3** Fortunately, his response _____ both sides, and the conflict was resolved successfully.
(A)satisfaction (B)satisfied
(C)satisfactory (D)satisfactorily

( ) **4** By this time next year, the appearance of our station _____ greatly improved.
(A)has been (B)is
(C)is being (D)will be

( ) **5** We made an order for new components last week, and they told us that the package _____ yesterday.
(A)ship (B)shipped
(C)was shipped (D)are shipping

( ) **6** The contract with the new company expires _____ March.
(A)at (B)on
(C)for (D)in

(   ) **7** You need to _____ your request form for vacation days at least one week in advance.

(A)turn in   (B)turn on

(C)turn up   (D)turn out

(   ) **8** Since the main purpose of the trip was business, I don't have to pay _____ my plane tickets.

(A)with   (B)for

(C)to   (D)about

(   ) **9** There are several _____ from work this week because many people have the flu.

(A)absentees   (B)attendants

(C)workers   (D)owners

(   ) **10** Please enclose your resume with your _____ to this position.

(A)formation   (B)application

(C)stimulation   (D)creation

(   ) **11** His opinions are very personal. I don't think his views are _____ of all the workers here.

(A)preventive   (B)conservative

(C)negative   (D)representative

(   ) **12** We are _____ with new challenges in this new era.

(A)planned   (B)stayed

(C)faced   (D)talked

(   ) **13** All the basic _____ new employees need to know about our company is in this handbook.

(A)emotion   (B)information

(C)sensation   (D)deformation

(   ) **14** A: How about having the meeting on Sunday?

B: _____

(A)The weather is perfect.

(B)Let's have a picnic.

(C)Sorry. I already have plans.

(D)Yes. The food is delicious.

( ) **15** A: How did you get to work today?

B: _____

(A)I took another route by bike.

(B)I was late for work today.

(C)I am always early.

(D)Almost two hours.

( ) **16** A: Did you manage to get an appointment this week?

B: _____

(A)My manager wants to see me.

(B)Do you want an appointment?

(C)I just fixed my car last week.

(D)They are fully booked.

閱讀測驗（第17～19題）

Basic protective measures against the new coronavirus

Airborne viruses have been spreading around the world in the speed of light – and the most recent one has spread as far as North America and Europe with every single region of China having confirmed cases!

The WHO (Word Health Organization) has declared a global health emergency. During such a critical period, it's necessary to be careful about your health – any extra effort of protection is beneficial in order to decrease your chances of getting infected! Here are ways to protect yourself:

1. Regularly and thoroughly clean your hands with an alcohol-based hand rub or wash them with soap and water.

2. Maintain at least 1 meter (3 feet) distance between yourself and anyone who is coughing or sneezing.

3. Avoid touching eyes, nose and mouth.

Do all you can to protect yourself and others from getting sick.

(　) **17** What is the main idea of the passage?
(A)The government has controlled the spread of the infection.
(B)People should take showers every day.
(C)Tips for preventing the contraction of virus.
(D)It is very easy to travel around the world.

(　) **18** Which of the following is NOT a way of protecting yourself from getting sick?
(A)Wash your hands with soap and water regularly.
(B)Go to the emergency.
(C)Keep a distance from other sick people.
(D)Do not touch your face.

(　) **19** What does the word "airborne" mean?
(A)Transported by air.
(B)A world-wide virus.
(C)The virus is born in the air.
(D)Virus on the face.

(　) **20** Most of the audience had difficulty hearing the speaker _____ the first part of the speech.
(A)along　　　　　　　　(B)during
(C)while　　　　　　　　(D)on

(　) **21** You should keep quite in the library. No conversation or other types of noise _____ in this area.
(A)permit　　　　　　　　(B)are permitted
(C)are permitting　　　　　(D)been permitted

(　) **22** It is necessary to _____ potential dangers before selling your product.
(A)look to　　　　　　　　(B)look from
(C)look into　　　　　　　(D)look away

( ) **23** We have bought materials from them for many years. If they refuse to agree to our proposal, we should not _____ them in the future.
(A)stand up   (B)deal with
(C)keep to   (D)run into

( ) **24** Employees are encouraged to invite their family andfriends to the company picnic, and there will be _____ of food for everyone.
(A)service   (B)volume
(C)quantity   (D)plenty

( ) **25** A: Can you recall when the meeting is scheduled to begin?
B: _____
(A)It is a long schedule.
(B)I believe it starts at 10 AM.
(C)I will bring a bag with me.
(D)I need to make a phone call first.

解答與解析　答案標示為#者，表官方曾公告更正該題答案。

1 (A)。 我們最新的車站將在兩個禮拜後開放，所以我們必須開始徵才。

(A)will open　　　(B)had opened

(C)would open　　(D)has opened

解 「in＋時間」為「在（某個時間）後」，因此知道為最新的車站會在兩個禮拜後開放，因為是「未來」將要發生的事，因此要用未來式，此題選(A)。

2 (B)。 Julia是為家喻戶曉且備受景仰的醫生。

(A)respect　　　(B)respected

(C)respecting　　(D)to respect

解 highly respected為常見用法，用來指「地位崇高」、「受人景仰」，如果不知道這個用法也可從句意推敲出來，and前後連接的一定為相同詞性，and前的famous為形容詞，因此可知道空格中一定是和highly搭配的形容詞，highly為「高度的」，加上respect可推測要表示「受高度推崇的」，因此要用「被動式」，此題選(B)。

3 (B)。 很幸運地，他的答覆令雙方都很滿意且也成功化解了衝突。

(A)名詞　　　　(B)動詞

(C)形容詞　　　(D)副詞

解 此題可從詞性判斷答案，his response為主詞，both sides為受詞，因此缺少了動詞，選項中只有(B)為動詞，此題選(B)。

4 (D)。 明年的這個時候，我們車站的外觀將會大大地改變。

(A)has been　　(B)is

(C)is being　　(D)will be

解 "by this time next year"為明年的這個時候，因此時態為未來式，此題選(D)。

5 (C)。 我們在上個禮拜訂了新的零件,他們告訴我們包裹在昨天寄出了。

(A)ship　　　(B)shipped

(C)was shipped　(D)are shipping

解 yesterday為關鍵字，從yesterday可以判斷時態為過去式，因此(A)(D)刪去，package是物品所以一定是「被」人寄出，因此要用被動式，此題選(C)。

6 (D)。 和那間新公司的合約在三月到期。

(A)at　　　　(B)on

(C)for　　　　(D)in

解 沒有(C)的用法，因此優先刪去，expire at後面大多接地點，expire in後面接月份、年份或一段時間，此題空格後為月份，因此答案選(D)。

7 (A)。 你至少得在假期的一個禮拜前繳出申請表。

(A)交出　　　(B)打開

(C)露面　　　(D)結果為

解 受詞為"request form"，而turn in有「交出」、「繳交」的意思，

通常「交報告」、「交表格」這類紙本文件都是用turn in 作為動詞，此題選(A)。

8 (B)。 由於此旅遊是以出差為主要目的，所以我不用付機票錢。
(A)with　　　　　(B)for
(C)to　　　　　　(D)about
解 關鍵字為"business"，從此可看出要強調此次旅行目的為出差，所以可推論後面要表達不用自己付機票錢，而「人＋pay for something」為常見用法，介系詞為for時解釋為「為（某樣物品的）付錢」，此題選(B)。

9 (A)。 這週有好幾個人請假沒來上班，因為很多人都得了流感。
(A)缺席者　　　　(B)服務生
(C)員工　　　　　(D)雇主
解 此題要從後半句來看，後半句提到因為很多人都得了流感，所以可以回推前半句為請病假而缺席，若是不認得這個單字也有方法能判斷字意，absent為「缺席的」，因此從字根就可看出此單字的意思，此題選(A)。

10 (B)。 請附上履歷表及此職缺的申請表。
(A)形成方式　　　(B)申請書
(C)刺激　　　　　(D)創造
解 前面提到履歷表，且後面的受詞為職缺，因此可以判斷最合理選項為申請表，此題選(B)。

11 (D)。 他的想法很主觀，我覺得他的觀點並不代表這裡所有員工。
(A)防止的　　　　(B)保守的
(C)負面的　　　　(D)代表的
解 "personal"為「個人的」，所以可以知道第一句要表示這個人的意見僅代表「個人意見」，且空格後介系詞為of，因此可以推論為"be representative of"，此題選(D)。

12 (C)。 我們在這個新世代面臨著許多新挑戰。
(A)計畫　　　　　(B)停留
(C)面臨　　　　　(D)談論
解 後面為"new challenges"，且介系詞為with，因此可以判斷為"be faced with"，此題選(C)。

13 (B)。 所有我們公司的新員工需要知道的資訊都在這本手冊裡。
(A)情緒　　　　　(B)資訊
(C)感覺　　　　　(D)變形
解 此題關鍵為"new employees need to know about our company"且在手冊裡，因此可以判斷為information，此題選(B)。

14 (C)。 A：禮拜天開會如何？
B：抱歉，我已經有其他安排了。
(A)天氣很好
(B)我們來野餐吧
(C)抱歉，我已經有其他安排了
(D)是的，食物很美味
解 "have the meeting"為「開會」，"how about"為「如何」，因此可以知道為詢問開會時間，此題選(C)。

解答與解析

15 (A)。　A：你今天怎麼去上班的？
　　B：我騎腳踏車走另一條路。
　　(A)我騎腳踏車走另一條路
　　(B)我今天上班遲到了
　　(C)我總是早到
　　(D)大約兩小時
　　解 "get to work"為「去上班」，結合how為「如何」，因此答案選(A)。

16 (D)。
　　A：你有試看看預約這個禮拜嗎？
　　B：他們全部都訂滿了。
　　(A)我的主管想見我
　　(B)你要預約嗎？
　　(C)我上禮拜才剛把我的車修好
　　(D)他們全都訂滿了
　　解 "get an appointment"和"make an appointment"都是「預約」、「預訂」的意思，此題答案選(D)。

閱讀測驗（第17～19題）

對抗新型冠狀病毒的基本預防措施

　　經空氣傳播的病毒已用光速傳播至世界各地－－最近一次病例已擴散至北美和歐洲，而中國的各區域都已出現確診病例。

　　世界衛生組織（WHO）已宣布全球健康緊急事件，在這個關鍵的時期必須注意你的自身健康－－為了降低受感染的機會，任何額外的保護措施都是有益的，這裡有一些保護自己的措施：

1. 經常徹底地清洗雙手－基本的用酒精搓手或用肥皂和清水洗手。
2. 與其他咳嗽或打噴嚏的人保持至少一公尺（三步）的距離。
3. 避免觸碰眼、口、鼻。
努力防止自己和他人生病。

17 (C)。　本文主旨為何？
　　(A)政府已控制住感染的擴散
　　(B)人們要每天洗澡
　　(C)預防感染病毒的訣竅
　　(D)環遊世界很容易

18 (B)。　下列何者並非避免自己生病的方法？
　　(A)經常用手和肥皂洗手
　　(B)去急診室
　　(C)與其他生病的人保持距離
　　(D)不要觸碰你的臉
　　解 此題答案在文中最後一段，此題選(B)。

19 (A)。　"airborne"是什麼意思？
　　(A)經由空氣傳播
　　(B)世界性的病毒
　　(C)空氣中產生的病毒
　　(D)臉上的病毒
　　解 "airborne"為「空氣傳播的」，此題選(A)。

20 (B)。　大部分的觀眾在演講的第一段時聽不太到音響的聲音。
　　(A)沿著　　　　　(B)在……期間
　　(C)當時　　　　　(D)在
　　解 (A)(D)明顯不正確，而while和during雖意思相近但用法不同，while後面動詞或省略主詞接動

名詞，during後只能接名詞，此題空格後為名詞因此用during，此題選(B)。

21 (B)。 在圖書館你應該保持安靜，這裡禁止對話或任何其他的噪音。

(A)permit

(B)are permitted

(C)are permitting

(D)been permitted

解 注意空格前為conversation和noise，對話及噪音都並非「人」，因此不可能主動允許某事，一定是用被動式「be動詞＋p.p」表示「被」允許，兩句的時態皆為現在簡單式，為陳述某個事實，因此be動詞用are即可，此題選(B)。

22 (C)。 在賣產品之前先調查潛在的風險是必要的。

(A)照看　　　　(B)從某處看

(C)調查　　　　(D)看向別處

解 受詞為danger，因此以「調查」作為動詞最為合適，此題選(C)。

23 (B)。 我們已經從他們那邊購買材料好幾年了，如果他拒絕同意我們的提議，那我們將來不應再和他們有生意往來了。

(A)站立　　　　(B)做生意

(C)遵守（承諾）(D)偶然遇到

解 前面一句是重要的提示，前面表示已和他們買東西買很多年了，因此可以推論和「合作」、「生

意」相關，deal with除了是「處理」的意思外，還有「做生意」的意思，此題解釋為後者，此題選(B)。

24 (D)。 公司野餐歡迎員工邀請自己的家人和朋友，到時會提供多樣的食物給大家。

(A)服務　　　　(B)體積

(C)數量　　　　(D)豐富的

解 前面提到公司野餐，因此可推論後面要表達「很多食物」，且從介系詞為of也可推出為plenty of，plenty of為固定用法表示「豐富的」、「眾多的」，此題選(D)。

25 (B)。

A：你還記得會議訂在什麼時候開嗎？

B：我記得是早上10點開始。

(A)這個時間表很長

(B)我記得是早上10點開始

(C)我會帶一個包包

(D)我要先打個電話

解 recall為「回想」、「記得」，且when問的是「時間」，所以可以知道A在問B是否記得開會的時間，此題選(B)。

解答與解析

109年　台北捷運新進人員
（技術員(電機類、機械類、土木類)、司機員）

一、選擇題

( ) **1** Alice, like her sister Lisa, _____ studying to be a lawyer.
(A)also (B)are
(C)is (D)have been

( ) **2** No company is allowed to make its employees _____ overtime without extra pay on a national holiday.
(A)work (B)works
(C)be working (D)worked

( ) **3** The copy machine is not working well. The paper keeps getting stuck in the machine and the copies _____ very light.
(A)comes out (B)come out
(C)coming out (D)will coming

( ) **4** You should order the tickets _____ if you want to get a good seat.
(A)right away (B)as soon as
(C)once (D)at ease

( ) **5** If you leave a message on my voice mail, I will _____ as soon as possible.
(A)cut off (B)call back
(C)hold on (D)hang up

( ) **6** You can use the desk by the window _____ the table by the door.
(A)but (B)nor
(C)for (D)or

( ) **7** Mr. Lee moved to the country side because he was tired _____ city life.
(A)on (B)at
(C)of (D)to

( ) **8** Every once _____ a while, David treats his customers to lunch.
(A)at (B)in
(C)on (D)to

( ) **9** Having a good working relationship _____ management and the workforce is a challenge.
(A)between (B)among
(C)beside (D)inside

( ) **10** Even though it will mean higher rent, we have decided that the only good _____ for our station is right in the center of the city.
(A)location (B)situation
(C)position (D)placement

( ) **11** I would like to take a computer programming course, but it is hard to find one that _____ my schedule.
(A)avoids (B)meets
(C)expects (D)introduces

( ) **12** A book is being _____ by J. K. Rowling and will be published next year.
(A)write (B)writing
(C)wrote (D)written

( ) **13** The action movie is _____ to be released in the theaters next month.
(A)schedule (B)scheduling
(C)scheduled (D)to scheduling

(　　) **14** I like to have my desk _____ the window so I can take advantage of the natural light.

(A)near (B)about

(C)above (D)from

(　　) **15** In regard _____ your question, we have no answers at this time.

(A)about (B)to

(C)from (D)with

(　　) **16** A: When do you want to visit the bookstore?

B: _____

(A)Whenever you are available.

(B)Not quite right.

(C)Are you sure?

(D)Let's do lunch.

(　　) **17** A: It is really cold and windy today!

B: _____

(A)No. This is not my day.

(B)Best time of the year.

(C)Yes. Remember to keep warm.

(D)It is a sunny day.

(　　) **18** A: I need to know the details about the project.

B: _____

(A)Wait, I just signed up for a new course.

(B)No problem. I will come over as soon as I can.

(C)I forgot your number.

(D)The menu looks really attractive.

(　　) **19** A: Why was Mandy late to work today?

B: _____

(A)Her car broke down. (B)She woke up really early today.

(C)Me too. (D)So will Cindy.

(　) **20** A: Did anyone call while I was out?

B: _____

(A)I didn't call you.　　　　(B)Can I take a message?

(C)I will call back later.　　　(D)Not even one person.

(　) **21** A: Would you like to put the book in a paper or plastic bag?

B: _____

(A)Bags are recyclable.　　　(B)Either is fine.

(C)Only for this book.　　　　(D)Take your time.

(　) **22** A: The annual celebration is in two days.

B: _____

(A)I joined the party last week. (B)It happens twice a year.

(C)It is a long flight.　　　　(D)We are almost ready.

二、閱讀測驗

Stocking up to prepare for a crisis

When there is a crisis, people tend to clear supermarket shelves for the things they feel they might need. This behavior is called "panic buying". Stocking up on food and other supplies helps people feel they have some level of control over events. Unlike most animals, humans can perceive some future threats and prepare for them. The greater the perceived threat, the stronger the reaction will be. Buying up large stores of supplies – which can lead to empty supermarket shelves – may seem like an irrational emotion response. But emotions are not irrational, they help us decide how to focus our attention. Then, panic buying is not so bad after all.

(　) **23** What is the main idea of the passage?

(A)Panic buying might be a positive thing.

(B)Everyone should stock up on food and other supplies.

(C)When there is crisis, there is threat.

(D)Emotions lead to irrational behavior.

(　) **24** What does the author of the passage think about 'panic buying'?
(A)It is irrational.
(B)It is good for the supermarkets.
(C)It is a way to relieve emotional stress.
(D)It is animal-like.

(　) **25** Which word can replace "perceive"?
(A)prepare　　　　　　　(B)foresee
(C)receive　　　　　　　(D)accept

解答與解析　答案標示為# 者，表官方曾公告更正該題答案。

一、選擇題

1 (C)。 Alice跟她的姐姐Lisa一樣都正在學習成為律師。
(A)也　　　　　　(B)are
(C)is　　　　　　(D)have been
解 此句逗點和逗點中間只是補充資訊，真正的主詞仍然是Alice，因此be動詞要用單數，此題選(C)。

2 (A)。 沒有任何公司可以在國定假日請員工加班但不支付加班費。
(A)work　　　　　(B)works
(C)be working　　(D)worked
解 make為使役動詞，使役動詞後要接原形動詞，此題選(A)。

3 (B)。 那部印表機運作不太正常，一直卡紙而且印出來的影本墨水很淺。
(A)comes out　　　(B)come out
(C)coming out　　(D)will coming
解 空格前為copies，因為是複數所以後面動詞不加s，且此題時態用現在簡單式即可，此題答案選(B)。

4 (A)。 如果想要坐在好位置，你應該馬上去訂票。
(A)立即　　　　　(B)一……就……
(C)一旦　　　　　(D)自在
解 此題重點在「如果你想坐在好位置」，從後面可推論是應該「馬上」訂票才能搶到好位置，此題選(A)。

5 (B)。 如果你在我的語音信箱留言，我會盡速回撥。
(A)切斷　　　　　(B)回撥
(C)稍等　　　　　(D)掛斷（電話）
解 as soon as possible為「盡快」，因此可以判斷是聽到留言後會盡速回撥，此題選(B)。

6 (D)。 你可以用窗邊的桌子或門邊的桌子。
(A)但是　　　　　(B)也不是
(C)給　　　　　　(D)或
解 前半句後半句都在講桌子，因此or是最合適的，此題選(D)。

7 (C)。李先生因為厭倦城市生活所以搬去鄉下。

(A)on　(B)at　(C)of　(D)to

解 「tired of＋名詞/動名詞」為「厭倦某事」，為常見用法，因此看見tired就知道介系詞要接of，此題選(C)。

8 (B)。Davd每隔一段時間就會請他的客戶吃飯。

(A)at　(B)in　(C)on　(D)to

解 "once in a while"為固定用法，為「每隔一段時間」的意思，此題選(B)。

9 (A)。資方和勞方之間擁有良好的工作關係是個挑戰。

(A)之間　　　(B)之中

(C)旁　　　　(D)裡面

解 (C)(D)明顯不正確所以可先刪去，among和between雖然都是解釋成「之間」不過用法有所不同，among強調的是「整體性」，而非明確指出個別為何，而between則是強調「個別性」，會明確指出個別為何，舉例來說：There is a secret among three of them.（他們三個之間有個秘密），此句並沒有明確且個別點出是哪三個人因此要用among，若是要用between則應該是：There is a secret between Nick, Alex and Tom.（Nick、Alex、Tom之間有個秘密），因為有明確指出是哪三個人因此要用between，本題題目有明確指

出「勞方」和「資方」，因此要用between，此題選(A)。

10 (A)。即使租金更高，我們已決定市中心是我們車站座落的最佳地點。

(A)地點　　　(B)情況

(C)位置　　　(D)放置

解 (B)(D)明顯不符合因此先刪去，比較有疑慮的只有(C)的position，position雖然也有「位置」的意思但指的是某物體與其他物體相對的位置，而location才是指某物設置的地點，因此答案選(A)。

11 (B)。我想上程式設計的課程，但是很難找到能配合我行程的。

(A)避免　　　(B)符合

(C)期望　　　(D)介紹

解 but表示語氣轉折，因此可推論後半句內容會與前半段有所衝突，"it is hard to dosomething"為「很難做某事」，所以可以推論為很難配合行程表，meet除了是「會見」的意思也是「符合」的意思，如"meet one's expectation"也與本題的meet同樣解釋為「符合」，此題選(B)。

12 (D)。這本書為J.K.羅琳所著，且將在明年出版。

(A)write　　　(B)writing

(C)wrote　　　(D)written

解 書是「被」寫出來的，因此要用被動式，也就是「be動詞＋過去分詞」，答案選(D)。

解答與解析

13 (C)。那部動作片預定在下個月於電影院上映。

(A)schedule　　　　(B)scheduling

(C)scheduled　　　(D)to scheduling

解 動作片是「被」播映而不是主動播映，因此要用被動式，答案選(C)。

14 (A)。我想讓我的桌子靠近窗戶，這樣就能利用太陽光。

(A)近的　　　　(B)關於

(C)在……之上　(D)從

解 "take advantage of something"為「利用」的意思，因此從後半句表示能利用太陽光可以判斷是將桌子靠近窗邊，此題選(A)。

15 (B)。關於你的疑問，我們現在無法回應。

(A)about　　　　(B)to

(C)from　　　　(D)with

解 "in regard to"為固定用法，因此看到in regard就要反應後面介系詞為to，此題選(B)。

16 (A)。

A：你想要什麼時候去逛書店？

B：只要你有空的時候都可以。

(A)只要你有空的時候都可以

(B)不完全正確

(C)你確定嗎？

(D)我們吃午餐吧

解 此題問的是"when"因此可以知道A問的是「時間」，(A)是最合適的答案，"available"在此解釋為「空閒的」，此題選(A)。

17 (C)。

A：今天真的很冷風又很大！

B：是啊，注意保暖。

(A)不，我今天真不順

(B)一年中最棒的時刻

(C)是啊，注意保暖

(D)今天是晴天

解 A提到很冷且風很大，因此要從這兩個線索推測B的回覆，只有(C)有對應到A的內容，此題選(C)。

18 (B)。

A：我要知道關於這個計畫的細節。

B：沒問題，我會盡速過去。

(A)等一下，我剛報名一堂新課程

(B)沒問題，我會盡速過去

(C)我忘記你的電話號碼了

(D)菜單看來很吸引人

解 其他三個選項都答非所問，此題選(B)。

19 (A)。

A：Mandy今天上班怎麼會遲到？

B：她的車子壞掉了。

(A)她的車子壞掉了

(B)她今天很早起床

(C)我也是

(D)Cindy也會這樣做

解 題目問的是"why"，因此知道問的是遲到的「原因」，此題選(A)。

20 (D)。

A：我外出時有人打來嗎？

B：一個都沒有。

(A)我沒有打給你
(B)我可以留言嗎
(C)我等等會再回撥
(D)一個都沒有

解 A問的是打來，因此可判斷B的回覆應該跟「數量」、「人名」有關，此題選(D)。

21 (B)。
A：你的書要用紙袋裝還是塑膠袋裝？
B：任一種都可以。
(A)袋子是可回收的
(B)任一種都可以
(C)只有這本書
(D)慢慢來

解 A問的是要放在紙袋或塑膠袋，因此可推測B的回覆會是兩者之一，either有兩者之一的意思，此題選(B)。

22 (D)。
A：一年一度的慶典將在兩天後舉行。
B：我們差不多準備好了。
(A)我上禮拜參加了派對
(B)它兩年才會發生一次
(C)這是個長途的飛行
(D)我們差不多準備好了

解 其他三個選項與A的內容完全無關，此題選(D)。

二、閱讀測驗

為了緊急時刻而囤貨

當出現緊急狀況時，人們常將超市架上他們認為需要的物品全部清空，這個行為稱為「恐慌性購買」，囤積食物或其他物資使人們感到自己對於重大情況有某種程度上的掌控度，與其他大多數的動物不同，人類能察覺一些潛在的威脅並提前做準備，他們察覺的威脅越大，反應也會更激烈，將大型商店的物資一掃而空－－這造成超市的架上空蕩蕩的－－可能看似是不理智的情感表現，不過情感並非是不理智的，它幫助我們決定如何集中我們的注意力，這樣一來，恐慌性購買也不是那麼糟了。

23 (A)。本篇主旨為何？
(A)恐慌性購買可能是正向的
(B)大家都該囤積食物和其他物資
(C)有危機時就有威脅
(D)情感導致不理智的行為

解 本文的最後一句為本文重點，此題選(A)。

24 (C)。本文作者對於「恐慌性購買」的看法是？
(A)是很不理智的
(B)對於超市而言是好事
(C)是釋放情感壓力的一種方式
(D)與動物很相似

解 本文後半段有解釋雖然「恐慌性消費」看似不理性，但其實這行為本身能幫助我們決定如何集中注意力，因此答案選(C)。

25 (B)。哪個字能取代"perceive"？
(A)準備　　　　(B)預料
(C)接收　　　　(D)接受

解 "perceive"為「感知」、「察覺」之意，而"foresee"為「預料」、「預知」之意，兩者意思相近，此題選(B)。

109年　台北捷運新進人員
（工程員(二)、工程員(三)、專員(三)）

(　) **1** Please _____ the following changes regarding the English language courses offered at our Language Center this year.
(A)be aware of
(B)be conceived of
(C)be looking for
(D)be watching out

(　) **2** He _____ murder since he was barely 18 as he accidentally killed someone during a fight.
(A)has been in prison
(B)has been in jail
(C)has been locked for
(D)has been imprisoned for

(　) **3** The flowers and plants were the most _____ arranged creations I have ever seen in this garden.
(A)beautification
(B)beautiful
(C)beautifully
(D)beauty

(　) **4** Presbyterians, Methodists, _____ Baptists are the prevalent Protestant congregations in many places around the world.
(A)and
(B)but
(C)or
(D)nor

(　) **5** In April, _____ the snow has already melted in New York.
(A)countless of
(B)many of
(C)much of
(D)various of

(　) **6** There are over 1,500 _____ in our campus and they could provide an opportunity for every student to become involved.
(A)club and organization
(B)clubs and organizations
(C)coach and staff
(D)coaches and staffs

( ) **7** This is what we have discussed today for this topic, and call
_____ if you have questions so we could further discuss it later on.
(A)I (B)me
(C)us (D)we

( ) **8** To celebrate with it, we are going to have a party _____ the
Dragon Boat Festival Day.
(A)at (B)for
(C)in (D)on

( ) **9** Look at those cars in the parking lot over there. _____ is
really ugly, but ours is beautiful.
(A)Their (B)Theirs
(C)Them (D)They

( ) **10** After buying a new car for the eldest daughter, _____ adds a
double garage to their house.
(A)the Johnson (B)the Johnsons
(C)The Johnson (D)The Johnsons

( ) **11** When you order a copy of this newly published book, _____ include
cash payment with your order form.
(A)do (B)forget
(C)please (D)remember

( ) **12** It is _____ common belief that a newspaper should have
_____ obligation to seek out and tell the truth.
(A)a, a (B)an, an
(C)a, an (D)an, a

( ) **13** My grandfather refuses to go to bed early, _____ I am afraid
he is going to catch a bad cold.
(A)and (B)but
(C)or (D)however

(　) **14** It is difficult to become ＿＿＿＿＿ because sometimes you have to avoid telling the truth due to some reasons.
(A)an honest person　　　　　(B)a person who is honest
(C)an honorable person　　　　(D)a person who is honorable

(　) **15** What is ＿＿＿＿＿ color? ＿＿＿＿＿ green.
(A)its, Its　　　　　　　　　(B)it's, It's
(C)its, It's　　　　　　　　　(D)it's, Its

(　) **16** ＿＿＿＿＿ the football season has not yet begun, ＿＿＿＿＿ is overly anxious for information about the team.
(A)Although, the public　　　(B)Although, but the public
(C)Today, thepublic　　　　　(D)Spring, the public

(　) **17** When John bumps up against a complex problem, he thinks back to a lesson he ＿＿＿＿＿ in high school.
(A)is learning　　　　　　　(B)learn
(C)learned　　　　　　　　　(D)was learning

(　) **18** Today, some people argue that the easiest and simplest way to improve our democracy is to ＿＿＿＿＿ political parties as many of them only look for their own benefits, but not the benefits for the general public.
(A)abolish　　　　　　　　　(B)blow
(C)create　　　　　　　　　　(D)support

(　) **19** In English, ＿＿＿＿＿ letters are the "large" versions of the 26 alphabets, frequently used for the first letter of proper names.
(A)capital　　　　　　　　　(B)large
(C)mini　　　　　　　　　　(D)small

(　) **20** My dog would excitedly ＿＿＿＿＿ to me when I return home from school.
(A)bite into　　　　　　　　(B)cross over
(C)dash up　　　　　　　　　(D)jump down

(　) **21** The severe forest fire in New South Wales recently caused a terrible damage to the _____ of Australia and its south-eastern coast.
(A)ecology
(B)landform
(C)mountains
(D)valleys

(　) **22** When teachers ask you to _____, they want to see you move from the particular to the general or from the concrete to the abstract.
(A)entertain
(B)generalize
(C)speak
(D)talk

(　) **23** The roof of our greenhouse _____ leak when it rains heavily in the summer time.
(A)is apt to
(B)is excelled to
(C)is part to
(D)is up to

(　) **24** Although the surface of the egg shell looks smooth, when _____ it is actually full of bumps and holes.
(A)boiled
(B)dyed
(C)heated
(D)magnified

(　) **25** There are several ways to _____ the Sun, and for yourself, the easiest and safest is to project it by building your own pinhole camera.
(A)break
(B)catch
(C)observe
(D)spy

(　) **26** At age 16, John dropped out of school _____ the fact that it was necessary for him to help support his parents as they got sick and became weak.
(A)on account of
(B)on behalf of
(C)on the chain of
(D)on the cultivation of

(　　) **27** We encourage all our students to _____ in this important and transformative program as they will benefit a lot from it.
(A)conquer　　　　　　　　(B)participate
(C)prevent　　　　　　　　(D)stop

(　　) **28** Today, many students are _____ more challenging academic work at a younger age in spite of hardship in life they might deal with.
(A)not for　　　　　　　　(B)ready for
(C)waiting for　　　　　　(D)yet for

(　　) **29** To investigate the crime thoroughly, the policeman interviewed the two suspects _____ over several days.
(A)excellently　　　　　　(B)freely
(C)separately　　　　　　(D)singly

(　　) **30** Obtaining _____ is often considered as licensing, and when you have it, you have a license to use the work.
(A)permission　　　　　　(B)slip
(C)ticket　　　　　　　　(D)voucher

(　　) **31** I need to look for a new job as my working contract will _____ three months later.
(A)initiate　　　　　　　(B)terminate
(C)uphold　　　　　　　　(D)waive

(　　) **32** This is the final list with the names of winners _____ in red.
(A)underlined　　　　　　(B)underscored
(C)underutilized　　　　(D)underweight

(　　) **33** In old days, my grandmother loved to hand-knit sweaters in wool _____ for all her six grandchildren.
(A)floss　　　　　　　　(B)tinsels
(C)twigs　　　　　　　　(D)yarns

(　　) **34** Mom: Glad to see you home, and he's adorable!

Daughter: I think he's the one!

Mom: Oh, me, too. I watched you two coming up the path and I saw how you looked at him. Do I hear wedding bells?

What does the mother expect to see? She expects that _____

(A)her daughter should consider well before getting married.

(B)her daughter should ask the man to go away.

(C)the man shouldn't contact her daughter again.

(D)the young couple would get married soon.

(　　) **35** Woman: It's nice to be back but I do miss the excitement of the World Cup in Paris. I'm bored!

Man: Oh, thanks very much!

Woman: I didn't mean you! I just mean it's a bit hard to come back to reality; that's all.

Why does the woman respond in this way? She feels that _____

(A)she should continue her vacation.

(B)she should stay in Paris.

(C)the man might misunderstand her.

(D)the man should stop working.

(　　) **36** Man: What a great barbeque yesterday!

Woman: Oh no, I feel dreadful. I was throwing up all night long!

Man: Though the salmon looked gorgeous, I didn't have any of it.Did you?

Woman: Yes... oh, no!

What happened to the woman? She _____

(A)enjoyed the party last night.

(B)stayed up late last night.

(C)cooked for everyone.

(D)has been sick since last night.

(　　) **37** Woman: No wonders you love it here, your garden is beautiful.

　　　　Man:Thank you. Just my luck though, neither my wife nor my daughter has green fingers.

　　　　Woman: I love gardening, too!

　　　　Where is the man? He is _____

　　　　(A)in his garden.　　　　　　(B)in his living room.

　　　　(C)in his office.　　　　　　(D)in a wild field.

(　　) **38** Peter: Grace, we have to talk about something. My dad has had a heart attack.

　　　　Grace: Oh, that's awful, so you are flying over to visit him. How long are you going for?

　　　　Peter: Grace, it's a one-way ticket I've booked; I'm going back to USA for good.

　　　　What does Peter really mean? He would _____

　　　　(A)come back soon to continue his study.

　　　　(B)return home forever in order to take care of his father.

　　　　(C)run away from everything.

　　　　(D)travel with Grace to his home.

(　　) **39** Albert: How does this sound? Wanted: male student or young professional for bright, sunny room in mixed flat-share. Must be clean, tidy and easy-going. Close to shops, pubs and buses. Reasonable rent,...

　　　　Gina: Shouldn't we say something about the cat? He might be allergic.

　　　　Albert: Ooh, yeah, good point.

　　　　What are they doing? They are writing _____

　　　　(A)an advert to share their flat.

　　　　(B)a note left on their fridge.

　　　　(C)a reminder to their landlord.

　　　　(D)a sales poster to promote some items.

(　) **40** Woman: It's almost bedtime. Time for you to go to bed.

　　　　Kid: I don't want to go to bed. I want to stay here and watch TV.

　　　　Woman: I don't think that's a good idea. You have to get up early for school in the morning.

　　　　What is the woman doing this evening? She is _____

　　　　(A)babysitting the kid.　　　　(B)reading a book to the kid.

　　　　(C)watching TV alone.　　　　(D)writing a paper by herself.

(　) **41** Man: How can I help you, madam?

　　　　Woman: It's about this watch.

　　　　Man: What seems to be the problem?

　　　　Woman: The alarm doesn't work, and when I take it off, the strap leaves a brown mark on my wrist.

　　　　What could the woman be? She could be a _____

　　　　(A)customer complaining a watch bought earlier.

　　　　(B)designer testing the watch designed by herself.

　　　　(C)lady showing off her favorite fashion accessory.

　　　　(D)saleswoman promoting a commercial item.

(　) **42** Man: Can I talk to you?

　　　　Woman: OK, but nothing heavy. I'm not in the mood.

　　　　Man: It's just that I don't think I can make the rent this month.

　　　　Woman: Oh! What am I supposed to do?

　　　　What could the woman be? She could be a _____

　　　　(A)coach　(B)landlady　(C)manager　(D)shop owner

(　) **43** Woman: Don't cry, ... you might feel better if you talk about it.

　　　　Girl: I am so... I had a date with Ted last night. When I arrived, I heard he was talking to somebody on the phone. I heard he said "I can't wait to see you, darling. I love you." He is seeing someone else!

　　　　Woman: Oh, there could be a perfectly reasonable explanation.

　　　　What does the woman want to do? She wants _____

　　　　(A)her to look for a new boyfriend.

　　　　(B)her to stop crying.

　　　　(C)her to cool down before looking for an answer.

　　　　(D)to be a good consultant.

A young boy in Hubei Province witnessed his grandfather die and remained at home alone afterward because of COVID-19 restrictions, local media reported.

The news of the child's **ordeal** prompted an outpouring of anger online in China.

In Shiyan's Zhangwan District, which has implemented "wartime control" to prevent the spread of the coronavirus, local community workers on Monday afternoon found an elderly man surnamed Tan who had died at home.

His five or six-year-old grandson was also at home, Zhangwan District Department of Public Affairs vice deputy director Guo Ruibing told local media.

The official did not confirm details posted online that the man had died several days earlier and that the grandson had survived on cookies.

Asked by community workers why he did not seek help, the child reportedly said: "Grandpa said not to leave. There is a virus outside."

It is not possible that Tan died days earlier, Guo told Hongxing News, a government-affiliated media platform.

Under lockdown measures in which residents cannot leave their homes, community workers had been making daily visits to check on residents, asking for their temperatures and if they needed any food supplies.

The time and cause of Tan's death was still being investigated, Guo said, adding that the grandson was being taken into care "according to procedure" by the district.

The child's father is in Guangxi Province and cannot return because of the lockdown measures on the area.

Asked whether Tan's temperature was normal before his death, Guo said: "Certainly, it was normal."

The news caused **a flood of** criticism online, underlining public frustration and mistrust.

"Why do they always do such a crappy job of 'dispelling rumors'?" one user on Weibo wrote, adding that the official could have used community records to **back up** his statement. "The government always says: 'impossible' or 'absolutely,' but who can believe you?"

Earlier this month, Zhangwan District was the first to implement official "wartime" **quarantine** measures in response to COVID-19, which emerged in nearby Wuhan.

Commercial and residential buildings in Zhangwan were sealed and **no unapproved outside vehicles** could enter.

Only healthcare workers and those providing essential supplies were able to be out on the streets, policed by public security. Local committee districts were to arrange food and medicine for residents.

Those who broke the rules would be detained, an official notice said.

(　) **44** Which of the following is the best title for this passage?
(A)Grandpa died without any supportive care
(B)The kid is going to die soon
(C)Virus Outbreak: Child home alone with dead grandpa
(D)Virus Outbreak: One more to the dead toll

(　) **45** Ordeal is a very _____ that one might suffer from a man-made or natural disaster, such as plane crash, coronavirus spreading, earthquake, major flood, etc.
(A)arrogant, bossy, and cocky feeling
(B)ironic, mocking, and satirical sense
(C)joyful, sweet, and happy perception
(D)unpleasant, painful, and difficult experience

(　) **46** "It is not possible that Tan died days earlier" implies that Tan died _____ though it might not be true.
(A)four days ago　　　　　(B)three days ago
(C)two days ago　　　　　(D)yesterday

(　) **47** This group received a flood of input containing the target forms of various discourse markers taught in the class.
(A)a great deal of　　　　(B)rare
(C)incomplete　　　　　　(D)insufficient

(　　) **48** You don't need to plug your device into a computer or even be at home to <u>back up</u> with iCloud.
(A)edit a document　　　　　(B)make a redundant file
(C)make a spare copy　　　　(D)write a document

(　　) **49** Usually, the first response to the threat of an epidemic is to keep people out of the country or <u>quarantine</u> them.
(A)to bake something with high temperature
(B)to keep away from others for a period of time
(C)to make a pie to share with others
(D)to stand far away from everything

(　　) **50** The buildings were sealed and <u>no unapproved vehicles</u> could enter.
(A)a few authorized cars permitted
(B)some unauthorized cars released
(C)no any authorized cars allowed
(D)only authorized cars allowed

解答與解析　　答案標示為# 者，表官方曾公告更正該題答案。

1 (A)。 請知悉以下有關我們語言中心今年對於英語課程的更動。
(A)be aware of 知道；了解
(B)be conceived of 被設想；被想像
(C)be looking for 尋找
(D)be watching out 注意；小心
解 依照句型，空格處需填入動詞，依據題意應填入(A)be aware of（知道；了解）；(B)(C)(D)皆不符合題意。

2 (D)。 他在年僅18歲時不小心在一場糾紛中殺了人，自那時起他便因謀殺罪而被監禁至今。

(A)has been in prison 一直在監獄裡
(B)has been in jail 一直在監獄裡
(C)has been locked for 因……被鎖住
(D)has been imprisoned for 因……被監禁
解 依照句型，空格處後方接有名詞，因此(A)(B)並不符合文法。而依據題意應填入(D)has been imprisoned for（因……被監禁）。介系詞for通常會表示「因為……；為了……」之意，後方接續原因。

3 (C)。 這些花與植物是我在這座花園中所看過布置得最美麗的創作。
(A)beautification 美化；裝飾（名詞）

(B)beautiful 美麗的（形容詞）

(C)beautifully 美麗地（副詞）

(D)beauty 美麗（名詞）

解 依照句型，空格處前方為動詞（were）、後方為形容詞（arranged）與名詞（creations），此句句型完整，因此應放置副詞(C)beautifully，來修飾後方的形容詞arranged，代表「布置得美麗的」。(A)(B)(D)之詞性放入句中皆不符合文法。

4 (A)。長老會、衛理公會與浸禮會是世界上許多地方普遍流行的新教徒集會。

(A)and 和、與　　(B)but 但是

(C)or 或是　　(D)nor 兩者皆非

解 依照句型，空格處應連接三個名詞，依據題意應填入(A)and（與）最恰當。

5 (C)。四月時，紐約許多的雪都已經融了。

(A)countless of ＜無此用法＞

(B)many of 許多的（接複數可數名詞）

(C)much of 許多的（接不可數名詞）

(D)various of ＜無此用法＞

解 依照句型，後方是名詞snow，為不可數名詞，因此應填入(C)much of（許多的）。(B)應接複數可數名詞；並無(A)(D)等用法。

6 (B)。我們校園有超過1,500個社團與組織，他們提供每位學生參與的機會。

(A)club and organization 社團與組織（單數）

(B)clubs and organizations 社團與組織（複數）

(C)coach and staff 教練與員工（單數）

(D)coaches and staffs 教練與員工（複數）

解 選項分別有「社團與組織」和「教練與員工」兩類，根據後方題意，應選「社團與組織」，且應選複數型的(B)clubs and organizations。且staff為集合名詞，本身即代表複數概念，並無使用複數型「staffs」的習慣。

7 (B)。這就是我們今天針對此議題所討論的內容，如果你有任何問題，請打電話給我，以便我們之後更深入討論。

(A)I 我（主格）

(B)me 我（受格）

(C)us 我們（受格）

(D)we 我們（主格）

解 依照句型，空格前方為動詞call，因此此處應放入受格；而根據題意，應填入me（我），因此應選(B)。

8 (D)。為了慶祝，我們要在端午節那天舉辦派對。

(A)at 在……　　(B)for 為了……

(C)in 在……裡面　(D)on 在……

解 依照句型，後方是節慶the Dragon Boat Festival（端午節），表達在某個日子的介系詞為on，因此應選(D)。

9 (B)。看看停在停車場那邊的車輛。他們的真的好醜，但我們的很好看。

(A)Their 他們的（所有格）

(B)Theirs 他們的事物（所有格代名詞）

(C)Them 他們（受格）

(D)They 他們（主格）

解 依照句型，後方為be動詞is，空格處應填入一主格名詞，因此應填入(B)Theirs，此處Theirs＝Their car，指涉前方提過的名詞cars；(A)(C)(D)填入皆不符合文法。

10 (B)。 在買了新車給他們最年長的女兒後，強森一家為他們家添加了一個雙車位車庫。

(A)the Johnson　　(B)the Johnsons

(C)The Johnson　　(D)The Johnsons

解 此題考的是文法，若要指涉某家人，應使用「the+姓氏s」，如Smith一家人，即為「the Smiths」；因此此題應選(B)，指涉強森一家人。逗點後方開頭應小寫，因此(C)(D)皆不正確。

11 (C)。 當您訂購這本新出版的書時，請與訂購單一同附上您的現金款項。

(A)do 做　　　　(B)forget 忘記

(C)please 請　　(D)remember 記得

解 此題考的是文法，根據句型，應填入(C)please（請）。正式文法不能將兩個動詞擺在一起，因此(A)不正確；(B)的用法為forget to V（忘記做某事）或forget V-ing（忘記做過某事），此處文法不正確、題意也不符合；(D)的用法同(C)，為remember

to V（記得做某事）與remember V-ing（記得做過某事），若要填入此選項，應為remember to include...，因此並不正確。

12 (C)。 新聞報紙的義務是探求並告知大眾真相，此為公眾認同的信念。

(A)a, a　　　　　(B)an, an

(C)a, an　　　　　(D)an, a

解 此題考的是文法，不定冠詞a若碰到後方詞彙開頭為母音時，則應改為an；因此應選(C)a, an。

13 (A)。 我爺爺拒絕早點上床睡覺，而我怕他會因此得到重感冒。

(A)and 而（連接詞）

(B)but 但（連接詞）

(C)or 否則（連接詞）

(D)however 然而（副詞）

解 此題考的是文法，連接兩個句子應使用連接詞，(D)however為一副詞，因此並不正確；而根據題意，後方句子為補充接續前方句子，因此應選(A)and（而且；還有）。(B)but是使用在轉折語氣時；(C)or當句子連接詞時，意思為「否則……」。

14 (A)。 要當一個誠實的人是很困難的，因為有時候，由於一些原因你必須避免說實話。

(A)an honest person 一個誠實的人

(B)a person who is honest 一個誠實的人

(C)an honorable person 一個榮譽的人

(D)a person who is honorable 一個榮譽的人

解 此題考的是文法，根據題意，應填入(A)an honest person（一個誠實的人）；(B)為使用關係代名詞之限定用法，為在一範圍中需要限定時才會使用。

15 (C)。 它的顏色是什麼？它是綠色。
(A)its, Its　　　　(B)it's, It's
(C)its, It's　　　　(D)it's, Its

解 此題考的是文法，第一句空格處後方為名詞color，且此句已有動詞，應填入所有格its（它的）；第二句缺動詞，因此應填入It's（=It is），表示「它是……」。

16 (A)。 雖然足球賽季還沒開始，群眾已對於隊伍的消息過度焦慮。
(A)Although, the public
(B)Although, but the public
(C)Today, the public
(D)Spring, the public

解 此題考的是文法與題意，兩個句子應用一個連接詞串起，因此第一格應填入連接詞Although（雖然；儘管）；第二格根據題意應填入the public（公眾；群眾），但是要注意的是不能放入but（但是），因為but也是一個連接詞，兩個句子僅需一個連接詞即可，因此不能選(B)。在中文上，常常會說「雖然……但是……」，但在英文中需要避免落入這樣的中式英文陷阱。

17 (C)。 每當約翰碰到複雜的問題時，他會回想在高中所學的一課。
(A)is learning 正在學（現在進行式）
(B)learn 學習（現在式）
(C)learned 學習（過去式）
(D)was learning 正在學（過去進行式）

解 此題考的是文法時態，後面出現時間點「在高中的時候」，且前方動詞thinks為現在式，退回一步為過去式，因此選(C)。補充一點，若前方動詞為過去式，退回一步則應為過去完成式。

18 (A)。 現今有某些人抗辯，要改善我們民主制度最簡單的方式就是廢除政黨，因為許多政黨只會尋求己利，而非公眾的利益。
(A)abolish 廢除　　(B)blow 吹動
(C)create 創造　　(D)support 支持

解 此題考的是詞彙意義，根據題意，應選(A)abolish（廢除）。補充一點，此題句中的as為連接詞，表示「因為……」之意。

19 (A)。 在英語之中，大寫字母就是26個字母的「大」版本，常會用在專有名詞開頭的第一個字母。
(A)capital 大寫的　(B)large 大的
(C)mini 迷你的　　(D)small 小的

解 此題考的是詞彙意義，根據題意，應填入(A)capital（大寫的），capital letter即為「大寫字母」之意。

20 (C)。 在我從學校回家時，我的狗會很興奮地衝向我。
(A)bite into 咬；咬住
(B)cross over 穿越；橫越

解答與解析

(C)dash up 衝向；奔向

(D)jump down 跳下

解 此題考的是詞彙意義，根據題意，應填入(C)dash up（衝向；奔向）。

21 (A)。 新南威爾斯州的森林大火近期對澳洲與其東南海岸的生態造成嚴重破壞。

(A)ecology 生態　　(B)landform 地形

(C)mountains 山　　(D)valleys 山谷

解 此題考的是詞彙意義，根據題意，應填入(A)ecology（生態）。

22 (B)。 當老師要你歸納某件事時，就是要你將特定的事物轉換成攏統的、將具體的事物轉換成抽象的。

(A)entertain 使娛樂

(B)generalize 歸納；概括

(C)speak 開口説

(D)talk 談論

解 此題考的是詞彙意義，根據後方句子解釋空格處，應填入(B)generalize（歸納；概括）。

23 (A)。 每當夏天下大雨時，我們溫室的屋頂都很容易漏水。

(A)is apt to 易於……；有……的傾向

(B)is excelled to ＜無此用法＞

(C)is part to ＜無此用法＞

(D)is up to 正要做……

解 此題考的是詞彙意義，根據題意，應填入(A)is apt to，be apt to意為「易於……；有……的傾向」。

24 (D)。 雖然蛋殼的表面看起來很滑順，在放大看之後，它其實充滿凸粒與凹洞。

(A)boiled 被煮沸

(B)dyed 被染色

(C)heated 被加熱

(D)magnified 被放大

解 此題考的是詞彙意義，根據題意，應填入(D)magnified（被放大）。此題空格處為分詞構句，原句為「...when (it is)magnified it is...」，因主詞與前句相同，因此連接詞後省略主詞與動詞。

25 (C)。 觀察太陽的方法有許多種，對你來説，最簡單、安全的方式就是建造自己的針孔相機來投射太陽。

(A)break 打破　　(B)catch 抓住

(C)observe 觀察　(D)spy 暗中監視

解 此題考的是詞彙意義，根據題意，應填入(C)observe（觀察）。

26 (A)。 在16歲的時候，約翰因為要照顧生病且逐漸虛弱的雙親而退學了。

(A)on account of 因為；由於

(B)on behalf of 代表

(C)on the chain of ＜無此用法＞

(D)on the cultivation of ＜無此用法＞

解 此題考的是詞彙意義，根據題意，應填入(A)on account of（因為；由於）。

27 (B)。 我們鼓勵所有的學生參與這項重要且具顛覆性的計畫，因為他們將會從中受益良多。

(A)conquer 征服

(B)participate 參與

(C)prevent 預防

(D)stop 停止

解 此題考的是詞彙意義，根據題意，應填入(B)participate（參與）。

28 (B)。 在現今，許多學生在年紀很輕的時候就準備好面對較艱難的學業，儘管他們可能會遇到生活上的困難。
(A)not for 不是為了……
(B)ready for 準備好
(C)waiting for 等待
(D)yet for 還沒
解 此題考的是詞彙意義，根據題意，應填入(B)ready for（準備好）。

29 (C)。 為了要全面調查這起犯罪案件，員警在幾天的時間分別訪談了兩位嫌疑犯。
(A)excellently 極好地
(B)freely 自由地
(C)separately 分別地；各自地
(D)singly 單個地
解 此題考的是詞彙意義，根據題意，應填入(C)separately（分別地；各自地）。

30 (A)。 獲得許可通常被視為准許證明，當你擁有時，就代表有許可能使用該作品。
(A)permission 許可；准許
(B)slip 紙條
(C)ticket 票券
(D)voucher 代金券
解 此題考的是詞彙意義，根據題意，應填入(A)permission（許可；准許）。

31 (B)。 我需要找一份新工作，因為我的勞動契約三個月後即將終止。
(A)initiate 開始；創始
(B)terminate 終止；結束
(C)uphold 支持；支撐
(D)waive 放棄；撤回
解 此題考的是詞彙意義，根據題意，應填入(B)terminate（終止；結束）。

32 (A)。 這是最終確認名單，贏家的名字用紅筆畫了底線。
(A)underlined 在……底下畫線
(B)underscored 強調；在……底下畫線
(C)underutilized 未充分利用
(D)underweight 重量不足
解 此題考的是詞彙意義，根據題意，應填入(A)underlined（在……底下畫線）。(B)也有相同之意，唯此字極少使用在「畫底線」之意，其多指平時使用e-mail信箱時所提到的「_」底線，如「will_smith@mail.com」其中的底線，而非我們平常所指的畫重點之底線。

33 (D)。 在以前，我奶奶喜歡用羊毛線為六個子孫手工織毛衣。
(A)floss 牙線
(B)tinsels 金屬絲
(C)twigs 細枝；嫩枝
(D)yarns 紗線；毛線
解 此題考的是詞彙意義，根據題意，應填入(D)yarns（紗線；毛線）。

34 (D)。

媽媽：很高興妳回家，他真可愛！

女兒：我覺得就是他了！

媽媽：喔，我也這樣覺得。我看你們兩個從小徑走來，而我看到妳看他的眼神，我彷彿聽到婚禮鐘聲。

該位母親期待看到什麼？她期待＿＿＿＿＿＿＿。

(A) her daughter should consider well before getting married
她女兒在結婚前應該好好思考

(B) her daughter should ask the man to go away
她女兒應該要叫那個男子走開

(C) the man shouldn't contact her daughter again
那個男子不該再聯絡她女兒

(D) the young couple would get married soon
這對年輕情侶盡快結婚

解 此題考的是對話情境，根據對話，母親與女兒提及一名男子，而在對話最後母親提到「wedding bells」（婚禮鐘聲），表示她期待兩人盡快結婚，因此應填入(D)the young couple would get married soon（這對年輕情侶盡快結婚）。

35 (C)。

女子：回來真好，但我真想念巴黎世界盃的刺激，我好無聊！

男子：喔，還真是謝謝啊！

女子：我不是在說你啦！我只是覺得要回到現實有點難，僅此而已。

為什麼這位女子會這樣反應？她感覺＿＿＿＿＿＿＿。

(A) she should continue her vacation
她應該繼續她的假期

(B) she should stay in Paris
她應該待在巴黎

(C) the man might misunderstand her
這位男子可能誤解她了

(D) the man should stop working
這位男子應該要停止工作

解 此題考的是對話情境，根據對話，男子與女子在談論女子剛結束的假期，而題目問及為何女子會有這樣的反應（指I didn't mean you! I just...）。女子會有這樣的反應，是因為男子誤解女子在說跟他相處很無聊，因此應選(C)。

36 (D)。

男子：昨天的烤肉真棒啊！

女子：喔不，我覺得糟透了。我昨天吐一整晚！

男子：雖然那個鮭魚看起來很棒，但我一點都沒吃。妳呢？

女子：是的……喔不！

這位女子發生了什麼事？她＿＿＿＿＿＿＿。

(A) enjoyed the party last night 很享受昨晚的派對

(B) stayed up late last night 昨天熬夜到很晚

(C) cooked for everyone 為所有人做菜

(D) has been sick since last night 從昨晚開始就病了

解 此題考的是對話情境，根據對話，男子與女子在談論昨天的烤肉，而女子提及她昨天吐了一整晚，因此應選(D)。

37 (A)。
女子：難怪你會喜歡這裡，你的花園好漂亮。
男子：謝謝妳。只是我幸運，我老婆和我女兒都不擅長園藝。
女子：我也喜歡園藝！
這位男子在哪裡？他在_____。
(A)in his garden 他的花園
(B)in his living room 他的客廳
(C)in his office 他的辦公室
(D)in a wild field 野外
解 此題考的是對話情境，根據對話，男子與女子在談論男子的花園，因此應選(A)。

38 (B)。
彼特：葛瑞絲，我們需要談談，我爸心臟病發了。
葛瑞絲：喔，那真糟糕，所以你要飛去看他。你要去多久？
彼特：葛瑞絲，我訂的是單程票，我要永久回美國了。
彼特真正的意思是什麼？他要_____。
(A) come back soon to continue his study
很快就回來繼續他的學業
(B) return home forever in order to take care of his father
為了照顧他的父親回家定居
(C) run away from everything 逃避所有事情

(D) travel with Grace to his home 與葛瑞絲一同回家
解 此題考的是對話情境，根據對話，男子說他父親心臟病發，要永久回美國了，可推斷是要回去照顧生病的父親，因此應選(B)。補充一點，此對話最後的for good為一常見片語，意為「永久；永遠」。

39 (A)。
艾伯特：這聽起來怎麼樣？「徵求：男性學生或年輕教授尋找合租公寓中的明亮房間。務必愛乾淨、整齊且隨和。鄰近商店、俱樂部與公車站。合理的租金，……」
吉娜：我們應該要說說貓的事吧？他可能會過敏。
艾伯特：喔對，好提議。
他們在做什麼？他們正在寫_____。
(A)an advert to share their flat 一則分租他們公寓的廣告
(B)a note left on their fridge 一則留在他們冰箱的便籤
(C)a reminder to their landlord 一則給他們房東的提醒事項
(D)a sales poster to promote some items 一則宣傳某些產品的銷售海報
解 此題考的是對話情境，艾伯特所說的內容皆是針對徵求分租公寓的敘述，因此應選(A)。

解答與解析

40 (A)。

女子：到了睡覺時間了，你應該要上床睡覺了。

小孩：我不想上床睡覺，我想留在這裡看電視。

女子：我覺得這不是個好點子，你明天很早就要起床上學。

這名女子今晚在幹嘛？她在_____。

(A)babysitting the kid 照顧小孩

(B)reading a book to the kid 為小孩朗讀書籍

(C)watching TV alone 一個人看電視

(D)writing a paper by herself 獨自寫論文

解 此題考的是對話情境，根據對話，女子在催促小孩上床睡覺，因此應選(A)。

41 (A)。 男子：我能協助您嗎，女士？

女子：是有關這個手錶。

男子：有什麼問題嗎？

女子：鬧鐘不會響，而且當我取下時，錶帶會在我手腕上留下咖啡色的痕跡。

這名女子可能是誰？她可能是_____。

(A) customer complaining a watch bought earlier

抱怨稍早購買的錶的顧客

(B) designer testing the watch designed by herself

測試自己所設計的錶的設計師

(C) lady showing off her favorite fashion accessory

炫耀自己最喜歡的時尚配件的女士

(D) saleswoman promoting a commercial item

推銷商品的女性業務

解 此題考的是對話情境，根據對話，女子帶著錶回來向店員抱怨瑕疵，因此應選(A)。

42 (B)。 男子：可以跟妳談談嗎？

女子：好，但不要太沉重的事，我現在沒心情。

男子：我只是覺得，我這個月可能付不出房租。

女子：喔！我該怎麼辦呢？

這名女子可能是誰？她可能是_____。

(A)coach 教練

(B)landlady 房東

(C)manager 經理

(D)shop owner 店主

解 此題考的是對話情境，根據對話，男子與女子訴說自己這個月可能繳不出房租，推測女子應為房東，因此應選(B)。

43 (C)。

女子：別哭，……說出來妳可能會覺得好一點。

女孩：我覺得好……。我昨晚跟泰德約會，當我到達的時候，我聽到他正在跟某個人講電話。我聽到他說：「我等不及見妳了，親愛的，我愛妳。」他有其他對象！

女子：喔，可能有其他完全合理的解釋啊。

這位女子想做什麼？她想要_____。

(A) her to look for a new boyfriend
她找一個新男友

(B) her to stop crying 她不要再哭了

(C) her to cool down before looking for an answer
她在尋求真相前先冷靜

(D) to be a good consultant 當一個好顧問

解 此題考的是對話情境，根據對話，女孩哭訴男友可能有其他對象，而女子說「there could be a perfectly reasonable explanation.」（可能有完全合理的解釋），代表她想安慰她、可能不是她所想的那樣，因此應選(C)。

當地媒體報導，湖北省一名男孩目睹他爺爺因為新型冠狀病毒的限制而死在家中，並在之後獨自留在家中。

這名孩童所遭受的**磨難**被報導出，便激怒了中國網壇。

在十堰市張灣區，此區為了避免新型冠狀病毒擴散而進入「戰時管制」，一名當地社區工作人員在一個星期一下午，發現一名譚姓老人死在家中。

他年約五、六歲的孫子當時也在家，張灣區宣傳部副主任郭瑞兵會見媒體時如此表示。

對於網路上傳聞該名男子已死亡多日、孫子必須靠餅乾充饑度日的細節消息，官方並未予以確認。

當被社區工作人員問起為何不向外求助時，該名孩童表示：「爺爺叫我不要離開，他說外面有病毒。」

譚姓男子不可能在幾天前就去世，郭向紅星新聞表示，其為一家隸屬於政府的媒體平台。

在封閉管理下，居民不能離開住家，在這段期間社區工作人員會每日造訪居民、詢問體溫以及是否需要任何食物或供給品。

譚姓男子死亡的時間與原因尚在調查中，郭表示，並補充說道，該名孩童「按照程序」而被該區政府照護中。

孩童的父親人在廣西，因為封閉管制的關係而無法回到家中。

被詢問到譚姓男子在死前的體溫是否正常，郭表示：「當然，是正常的。」

這則新聞在網路造成**大量**批評聲浪，突顯出公眾的不滿與不信任。

「為什麼他們總是要做這種『闢謠』的爛工作？」一名微博用戶寫道，並說官方明明可以用社區紀錄來**支撐**他的陳述。「政府老是說『不可能』或『絕對』，但誰會相信？」

這個月稍早，張灣區是第一個實施官方「戰時」**隔離**措施的區域，因應鄰近武漢的新型冠狀病毒。

張灣區的商業與住宅大樓皆被封閉，**任何未經核准的外部車輛都不**能進入。

只有醫護人員與提供必要供給品的人員可以出外上街，公安局如此規範。

當地委員會地區將為居民安排食物與藥品供給。

違反規則的人將會被拘留，一則官方聲明表示。

44 (C)。下列何者最適合當本篇文章的標題？

(A) Grandpa died without any supportive care
爺爺在沒有任何照護下離世

(B) The kid is going to die soon 該名孩童即將死亡

(C) Virus Outbreak: Child home alone with dead grandpa
病毒爆發：孩童獨自與過世爺爺在家中

(D) Virus Outbreak: One more to the dead toll
病毒爆發：死亡名單再添一名

解 此題考最適合本文的標題，也就是本文概括的大意。根據本文，大致是在描述一名孩童的爺爺死在家中，而孩童獨自在家伴屍多日的新聞，因此應選(C)Virus Outbreak: Child home alone with dead grandpa（病毒爆發：孩童獨自與過世爺爺在家中）。

45 (D)。磨難是一種非常_____。

(A) arrogant, bossy, and cocky feeling
自傲、跋扈且過度自信的感覺

(B) ironic, mocking, and satirical sense 挖苦、嘲諷且諷刺的感覺

(C) joyful, sweet, and happy perception
喜悅、甜蜜且快樂的感覺

(D) unpleasant, painful, and difficult experience
不愉快、痛苦且艱困的經驗

解 此題考的是位於第二段「ordeal」的意思，ordeal意為「苦難；折磨；嚴峻考驗」，因此應選(D)。

46 (D)。「譚姓男子不可能在幾天前就去世」暗指譚姓男子在_____死亡，儘管這可能不是真的。

(A)four days ago 四天前

(B)three days ago 三天前

(C)two days ago 兩天前

(D)yesterday 昨天

解 此題考的是位於第七段，郭向媒體表示的話暗指譚姓男子在幾天前去世，而根據文中官方表示，每天皆會有社區工作人員巡視，因此推測應為(D) yesterday（昨天）。

47 (A)。這個團體獲得大量的輸入，包含了這堂課所教授的不同話語標記的目標格式。

(A)a great deal of 大量的

(B)rare 稀少的

(C)incomplete 不完整的

(D)insufficient 不充足的

解 此題考的是位於倒數第六段的「a flood of」，意為「大量的；如湧水般的」，因此應選(A)a great deal of（大量的）。

48 (C)。你不需要將你的裝置插入電腦，甚至不需要在家也可以用iCloud來備份。

(A)edit a document 編輯文件

(B)make a redundant file 製作多餘的檔案

(C)make a spare copy 製作備用的檔案

(D)write a document 撰寫文件

解 此題考的是位於倒數第五段的「back up」，意為「支撐；證實；備份」等意，在這題的語意中back up為「備份」之意，因此應選(C)make a spare copy（製作備用的檔案）。

49 **(B)**。 通常來說，流行性傳染病的首要因應措施是要禁止人們入境或是隔離。

(A)to bake something with high temperature 用高溫烘烤

(B)to keep away from others for a period of time 與他人隔離一段時間

(C)to make a pie to share with others 做一個派與他人分享

(D)to stand far away from everything 遠離所有事物

解 此題考的是位於倒數第四段的「quarantine」，意為「隔離」，因此應選(B)to keep away from others for a period of time（與他人隔離一段時間）。

50 **(D)**。 建築物皆被封閉，任何未經核准的車輛都不能進入。

(A)a few authorized cars permitted 只有一些授權的車輛獲准

(B)some authorized cars released 釋放一些核准的車輛

(C)no any authorized cars allowed 任何經授權的車輛都不允許

(D)only authorized cars allowed 僅允許經授權的車輛

解 此題考的是位於倒數第三段的「no unapproved vehicles」，意為「任何未經核准的車輛皆不……」，因此應選(D)only authorized cars allowed（僅允許經授權的車輛）。

109年 台北捷運新進人員（控制員、專員(二)）

( ) **1** He can't hear from her clearly as her voice was barely _____ above the noise of the machinery where he is working.
(A)audible (B)audio
(C)auditorium (D)auditory

( ) **2** An entirely new policy for dealing with an increasing academic suspension and withdrawal made by our students _____ by the executive committee in our college.
(A)has approved (B)have approved
(C)has been approved (D)have been approved

( ) **3** It is great to see Lincoln's famous advice to the young people: "You can fool some of the people all of the time, and all of the people _____, but you cannot fool all of the people all of the time."
(A)always (B)frequently
(C)now and then (D)some of the time

( ) **4** The ancient Egyptians preserved dead people's bodies by making mummies of them. The process, the so-called "_____," consisted of removing the internal organs, applying natural preservatives inside and out, and then wrapping the body in layers of bandages.
(A)mummificated (B)mummification
(C)mummified (D)mummify

( ) **5** After the party, I found that somebody _____ her purse on the chair.
(A)is left (B)was left
(C)has left (D)have left

( ) **6** The really important issue of the conference on the novel Coronavirus Disease 2019 this month, stripped of all other considerations, _____ the morality of doing a research project.
(A)are (B)is
(C)was (D)were

( ) **7** In sunny autumn days, all leaves are falling, coming down in _____ streams of gold and brown.
(A)dance (B)danced
(C)dancing (D)dancingly

( ) **8** Captain Lewis is famous for his expedition into the new territory and beyond, _____ few people know of his contributions to natural science.
(A)and (B)but
(C)nor (D)or

( ) **9** The sun is high, _____ put on some sunscreen because we will be out all day.
(A)and (B)but
(C)for (D)so

( ) **10** The congress criticize that the education _____ gets slowed down in spite of the total tax revenue has increased recently.
(A)give (B)giving
(C)spend (D)spending

( ) **11** Our class all really got into it and gave it our best effort, but _____ we still struggled a bit trying to solve this problem.
(A)despite (B)inspite
(C)despite that (D)inspite that

( ) **12** After serving twenty years in prison for murder of a shopkeeper, John will be free _____ next week.
(A)after a while (B)as far as
(C)as long as (D)at last

( ) **13** Asian countries, and _____ Taiwan, are good places to visit as they are populated with people who are very friendly with visitors.
(A)particular (B)specially
(C)in particular (D)in specie

( ) **14** Due to insufficient numbers of doctors and nurses recently, there are major barriers to getting surgery within the time frame wanted, including getting an appointment _____.
(A)firstly (B)secondly
(C)in the first place (D)in the second place

( ) **15** The protesters gathered and shouted in the street, and they had even turned nasty for several hours before the policemen _____.
(A)return (B)returns
(C)returning (D)returned

( ) **16** In our college, most students _____ ninety credits by the time they graduate.
(A)take (B)will take
(C)have taken (D)will have taken

( ) **17** Pablo Picasso did not speak often about _____, but when he did, it was a form either for decoration or for contradictory.
(A)abstraction (B)clarity
(C)explicitness (D)ignorance

( ) **18** The teacher _____ students in the back row as some of them dozed off in the class.
(A)call at (B)call for
(C)called on (D)call out

( ) **19** _____ is often defined as an economic system where private sectors are allowed to own and control the use of property in accord with their own interests.

(A)Capitalism   (B)Communism

(C)Corporatism   (D)Socialism

(   ) **20** Language learners are encouraged to use a _____ input strategy to accomplish his or her language acquisition, which has been popular since the 80's.

(A)comprehend   (B)comprehended

(C)comprehending   (D)comprehensible

(   ) **21** Our office allows a _____ to work abroad, which is that a person, or a group, authorizes someone to serve as his or her representative for a particular task of responsibility.

(A)consignment   (B)delegation

(C)promotion   (D)submission

(   ) **22** Our shop opens every day, _____ Chinese Lunar New Year, from 10:00 am to 5:30 pm.

(A)but   (B)close to

(C)except   (D)next to

(   ) **23** After my sister returned home from her 10 years studying in other city, I was shocked by her _____ on luxury items.

(A)cash   (B)extravagance

(C)money   (D)thriftiness

(   ) **24** The global sea level record from _____ is an important indicator of the evolution and impact of global climate change.

(A)bar ruler   (B)tape ruler

(C)tide gauges   (D)tide clock

(   ) **25** When sentences written full with errors often sound awkward, ridiculous, or confusing, they can be downright _____.

(A)analytical   (B)illogical

(C)irrational   (D)logical

(　) **26** In an era of social media and fake news, _____ who have survived the print plunge have new foes to face.
(A)journalists (B)novelists
(C)painters (D)writers

(　) **27** _____ involved certain behavioral patterns, such as a respect required between siblings of the opposite sex, children and parents, and between children-in-law and their parents-in-law.
(A)Brotherhood (B)Kinship
(C)Manhood (D)Relationship

(　) **28** As a courtesy to the long patronage of villagers, the filling station was _____ free gas for three days.
(A)given away (B)given up
(C)giving away (D)giving up

(　) **29** The committee who has been assigned to review this project _____ the papers carefully before giving its final comments.
(A)looks at (B)looks for
(C)looks in (D)looks over

(　) **30** The demarcation of the _____ coordinate is drawn hypothetically with circles on the globe parallel to the equator.
(A)horizontal (B)latitude
(C)longitude (D)vertical

(　) **31** Our company provides _____ protection for its officers and employees when acting within the scope of their employment.
(A)agility (B)docility
(C)fertility (D)liability

(　) **32** Doing a research, one should carefully _____ electronic resources to review past information and scholarly articles before selecting a topic.
(A)make out (B)make up
(C)pick out (D)pick up

( ) **33** _____ production has seen abundant growth over the past 10 years as the land in our area is prime for grazing and making feeds for all cows and sheep.
(A)Crops (B)Harvest
(C)Livestock (D)Poultry

( ) **34** In Taiwan, scientific _____ has become one of the country's strongest assets as the government has aimed to support the semiconductor industry in the last three decades.
(A)human (B)manpower
(C)staff (D)workers

( ) **35** Albert: This will be your room, and we share the housework together.
John: It's a very nice room, and you guys are great and everything, but I have to say, I think it's a little bit pricey. I wonder if it would be possible to reduce the rent a little bit?
Gina: I'm afraid it isn't up to us. We have to ask our landlord about that.
What is the context? The two residents are _____ to John for a leasing.
(A)citing a verse (B)introducing the room
(C)selling some books (D)telling a story

( ) **36** Man: Oh, that's the pager. What is it now? Oh, no, serious traffic incident. They want me right away.
Woman: Oh, I'll come, too. I'm sure they'll need some extra nurses.
Where are they working? They are probably working in a(n) _____.
(A)hospital (B)laundromat
(C)office (D)school

( ) **37** Man: Come in. Have a seat.
Girl: I am sorry that I didn't make an appointment earlier, but I really have to talk to you.
Man: It is OK. What's on your mind?
Girl: I've been neglecting my studies and I want to get back on the right track.

Man: That IS good news. What's brought on this change of heart?
What are they? They are a _____ and his _____ .
(A)consultant, consultee   (B)doctor, patient
(C)professor, student   (D)psychiatrist, patient

(   ) **38** Man: You're not scared, are you?
Woman: It's too high to climb up even for a brave one.
Man: Come on, take my hand. We'll go up slowly, I promise.
What is the man trying to do? He tries to _____ .
(A)demonstrate how easy it is
(B)encourage her to climb up
(C)show her how difficult it could be
(D)tell her nothing is easy

(   ) **39** Woman: The kitty is sick. Is she an indoor or an outdoor cat?
Man: Both really. She stays in at night, but she's out most of the day, playing with other cats.
Where could this conversation taken place?
It could be in a _____ .
(A)classroom   (B)market
(C)theater   (D)vet

(   ) **40** Woman: A friend of mine is retiring, and he's looking for someone to take care of his small business. I thought you might be the man for it.
Man: How would I do it? A business all of my own?
What does the woman mean? She proposes that _____ .
(A)he could accept the offer
(B)he could celebrate for the new job
(C)he should consider the cash flow first
(D)he should train himself to be a good manager

( ) **41** Woman: I'm finding it hard to get back into the books.

Man: I was exactly the same, but it does get easier, eventually.

Woman: Can I ask you a favor? How would you feel about having a study-buddy?

What is the woman? She is a _____.

(A)college student   (B)primary school teacher

(C)professor in a university   (D)watch-guard in the building

( ) **42** Man: How are you?

Woman: Exhausted. Just finished another long shift.

Man: Yes, it's been busy here lately as too many cases of surgery have been carried out.

Where are they working? The place would be a(n) _____.

(A)drawing room   (B)operating room in a hospital

(C)painting room   (D)woodworking room of a sawmill

( ) **43** Woman: Why should the bank lend you this money?

Man: I've been saving here for almost five years.

Woman: Haven't you been unemployed recently?

Man: Yes, but I've been living on my savings, not using an overdraft. I'm a reliable customer and I think my new business is an excellent investment. Some of your lending would be good for me and good for the bank, too.

What does the man do now? He is _____.

(A)applying a bank loan   (B)depositing some cash

(C)running up an overdraft   (D)saving a time-deposit

Dozens of viruses exist in the coronavirus family, but only seven **afflict** humans. Four are known to cause mild colds in people, while others are more novel, deadly, and thought to be transmitted from animals like bats and camels. Health officials have labeled this new virus SARS-CoV-2 and its disease COVID-19.

Ian Lipkin, director of the Columbia University's Center for Infection and Immunity, has been studying the novel coronavirus. He says sunlight, which is less abundant in winter, can also help break down viruses that have been transmitted to surfaces.

"**UV light** breaks down nucleic acid. It almost sterilizes surfaces. If you're outside, it's generally cleaner than inside simply because of that UV light," he says.

UV light is so effective at killing bacteria and viruses; it's often used in hospitals to **sterilize** equipment.

Another scholar, David Heymann from the London School of Hygiene and Tropical Medicine, says **not enough is known** about this new virus to predict how it will change with different weather conditions.

According to the Centers for Disease Control (CDC), people are most **contagious** when they're showing **symptoms**. However, some experts suspect official counts may underestimate the number of infected people, saying not everyone infected will develop a severe illness.

"We're only seeing the most severe cases," says Weston. "There may be some infection going on that isn't being detected."

Many experts are saying SARS-CoV-2 will likely become **endemic**, joining the other existing four coronaviruses that cause mild colds, or becoming a seasonal health hazard like the flu.

To prevent contracting an illness from any virus, the World Health Organization recommends frequently washing your hands, avoiding close contact with those showing symptoms like coughing or sneezing, and seeking treatment if sick.

(　　) **44** To _____ empty jars, we should put them right side up on the rack in a boiling-water canner.
(A)coat　　　　　　　　　(B)contaminate
(C)disinfect　　　　　　　(D)muddy

(　　) **45** Taiwan government has already _____ all the foreign tourist to visit Taiwan because of the COVID-19 outbreak.
(A)welcomed　　　　　　(B)asked
(C)banned　　　　　　　(D)greeted

( ) **46** The World Health Organization has cautioned against using ibuprofen to manage _____ of COVID-19.
(A)features
(B)information
(C)symptoms
(D)structure

( ) **47** A(n) _____ is an occurrence of a disease that affects many people over a very wide area.
(A)endemic
(B)ebola
(C)pandemic
(D)poliomyelitis

( ) **48** The scientists all over the world work together to find new ways to combat novel coronavirus that has already _____ more than 200,000 people globally.
(A)assisted
(B)relieved
(C)affected
(D)infected

( ) **49** UV light can _____ the bacteria and viruses.
(A)fertilize
(B)sanitize
(C)clean
(D)wash

( ) **50** All the citizens are now being told to _____ at least 14 days upon returning form travel.
(A)quarantine
(B)work
(C)rest
(D)excercise

解答與解析　答案標示為# 者，表官方曾公告更正該題答案。

1 (A)。他無法清楚聽見她，因為她的聲音在他工作時的機器噪音下幾乎讓人聽不到。
(A)audible 聽得到的；可聽見的
(B)audio 聲音；音頻
(C)auditorium 禮堂；觀眾席
(D)auditory 聽覺的

解 此題為詞彙意義題，依據題意應填入(A)audible（聽得到的；可聽見的）；(B)(C)(D)皆不符合題意。

2 (C)。我們學院的行政委員會已通過一項全新的規定，其為因應本校學生日漸升高的短期停學與退學率。

(A)has approved 已核准（單數動詞）

(B)have approved 已核准（複數動詞）

(C)has been approved 已被核准（單數動詞；被動式）

(D)have been approved 已被核准（複數動詞；被動式）

解 此題為文法題，此題句型為「名詞（An entirely ...by our students）＋動詞被動式（has been approved）＋by＋動作執行者（the executive ...in our college）」；因動詞應為被動式，因此應選(C)或(D)，而前述名詞為單數，因此應選單數動詞的(C)。

3 (D)。 聽到林肯給予年輕人的著名建言是很棒的：「你可以在長時間矇騙一些人，也可以在一時矇騙所有人，但不可能在長時間矇騙所有的人。」

(A)always 總是

(B)frequently 頻繁地

(C)now and then 有時；偶爾

(D)some of the time 有些時候

解 此題考的是林肯著名的建言，根據題意，應填入(D)some of the time（有些時候）。

4 (B)。 古埃及人靠製作木乃伊的方式來保存故人的屍體。這個叫作「木乃伊化」的過程包含了去除內臟、在裡外塗抹天然防腐劑以及用層層繃帶綑綁屍體。

(A)mummificated ＜無此字＞

(B)mummification 木乃伊化（名詞）

(C)mummified 被做成木乃伊（過去分詞）

(D)mummify 將……做成木乃伊（動詞）

解 依照句型，空格處應填入名詞，因此應填入(B)mummification（木乃伊化）。

5 (C)。 在派對結束後，我發現有人遺落她的錢包在椅子上。

(A)is left 被遺落（現在式；被動式）

(B)was left 被遺落（過去式；被動式）

(C)has left 已遺落（現在完成式；單數動詞）

(D)have left 已遺落（現在完成式；複數動詞）

解 依照句型，空格處應放入主動式動詞，且somebody為單數名詞，因此應選(C)has left（已遺落）。

6 (B)。 這個月關於2019年新型冠狀病毒會議真正重要的議題，撇除其他考慮因素，是有關做一個研究計畫的道德品行。

(A)are 是（現在式；複數）

(B)is 是（現在式；單數）

(C)was 是（過去式；單數）

(D)were 是（過去式；複數）

解 此題句型為「名詞（The really ... this month）＋分詞構句（stripped of ... considerations）＋動詞（is）＋補語（the morality ... project）；空格處應填入動詞，且根據時態與單複數，應填入(B)is。

7 (C)。 在秋天晴朗的時日，所有葉子都在掉落，金黃色與棕色的落葉以舞蹈般的線條落下。

(A)dance 跳舞（動詞；現在式）

(B)danced 跳舞（動詞；過去式）

(C)dancing 跳舞的（現在分詞）

(D)dancingly ＜無此字＞

解 依照句型，空格僅能填入(C) dancing（跳舞的），此處為現在分詞做形容詞使用，修飾後方的streams；填入其他選項皆不符合文法。

8 (B)。 路易斯船長以他深入新大陸的遠征為名，但很少人知道他對於自然科學的貢獻。

(A)and 而且　　　(B)but 但是

(C)nor 兩者皆非　(D)or 否則

解 依照句型，空格處應填入一連接詞以連接兩個句子；而根據題意，應填入but（但是）作轉折語氣，因此應選(B)。

9 (D)。 太陽很大，所以擦一些防曬乳吧，因為我們整天都要待在外面。

(A)and 而且　　　(B)but 但是

(C)for 因為　　　(D)so 所以

解 依照句型，總共有三個動詞（is、put、will be），因此應該要有兩個連接詞，題目僅有一個連接詞（because），所以空格處應填入一連接詞。依據題意，應填入(D)so（所以）。此處補充一點，for除了當作介系詞外，也可作為連接詞，意為「因為」。

10 (D)。 國會批判教育的花費降低了，儘管最近的總稅收額提升了。

(A)give 給（動詞）

(B)giving 給（動名詞）

(C)spend 花費（動詞）

(D)spending 花費（動名詞）

解 依照句型，空格處應填入名詞；而根據題意，應填入(D) spending（花費）。

11 (C)。 我們班真的全心投入並全力以赴了，但儘管如此，我們仍然很難解決這個問題。

(A)despite 儘管

(B)inspite ＜無此字＞

(C)despite that 儘管

(D)inspite that ＜無此用法＞

解 此題考的是文法，依據結構，應填入(C)despite that（儘管）。despite後加名詞，而despite that後應接一子句，因此此處放入despite that才正確。

12 (D)。 因謀殺一位商店老闆而入獄服役20年後，約翰終於將在下週重獲自由。

(A)after a while 在一陣子之後

(B)as far as 到達……的程度

(C)as long as 只要……

(D)at last 終於

解 此題考的是語意，根據題意，應填入(D)at last（終於）。

13 (C)。 亞洲國家，尤其是台灣，都非常適合造訪，因為這些地方的居民都對遊客相當友善。

(A)particular 特地的

(B)specially 特別地

(C)in particular 特別是……；尤其是……

(D)in specie 以實物

解 此題考的是一慣用語，in particular意為「特別是……；尤其是……」，多用在強調特定物件的時候使用，因此應選(C)。

14 (C)。 由於近期醫生與護理師的人數不足，在想要的時限內開刀變得非常困難，這包含想要事先預約的狀況。
(A)firstly 首要地
(B)secondly 次要地
(C)in the first place 首先
(D)in the second place 其次
解 此題考的是文法，根據題意，應填入(C)in the first place（首先）。

15 (D)。 抗議群眾在街上聚集咆哮，他們甚至在警方回來前變得很不耐煩、持續了幾個小時。
(A)return 回來　　(B)returns 回來
(C)returning 回來　(D)returned 回來
解 此題考的是文法時態，空格前方為過去完成式（had turned），在過去完成式之時間點之後所發生的事用過去式，因此應選(D)。

16 (D)。 在我們學院，大部分的學生在畢業前將會修滿90學分。
(A)take 修（現在式）
(B)will take 將修（未來式）
(C)have taken 已修了（現在完成式）
(D)will have taken 將修（未來完成式）
解 此題考的是文法時態，在未來某時間點之前將完成某件事時，應使用未來完成式「will have＋P.P.」，因此應選(D)。

17 (A)。 巴勃羅‧畢卡索並不常談論起抽象派，但當他談論時，其指涉裝飾的形式或矛盾的形式。
(A)abstraction 抽象
(B)clarity 清楚；明確
(C)explicitness 明確性
(D)ignorance 忽略
解 此題考的是語意，根據題意，應選(A)abstraction（抽象）。

18 (C)。 老師點名了坐在後排的學生，因為他們有些人在課堂中打瞌睡。
(A)call at 造訪某地
(B)call for 來取某物
(C)called on 點名
(D)call out 大聲呼喊
解 此題考的是詞彙意義，根據題意，應選(C)called on（點名）；且根據文法，主詞為teacher，因此(A)(B)(D)的動詞形式皆不正確。

19 (A)。 資本主義通常被定義為一種經濟體系，其體系下的私部門能夠依照個人利益擁有財產與財產控制權。
(A)Capitalism 資本主義
(B)Communism 共產主義
(C)Corporatism 集團主義
(D)Socialism 社會主義
解 此題考的是詞彙意義，根據題意，應填入(A)Capitalism（資本主義）。

20 (D)。 語言學習者被鼓勵使用可理解性輸入策略來習得語言，這個策略自80年代便盛行至今。
(A)comprehend 理解（動詞；現在式）
(B)comprehended 理解（動詞；過去式）

(C)comprehending 理解（動詞；現在分詞）

(D)comprehensible 可理解的（形容詞）

解 此題考的是詞彙意義，根據題意，應填入(D)comprehensible（可理解的），來修飾後方的input（輸入）。

21 (B)。 我們公司允許委任出差制度，也就是一個人或團體，授權某人代表負責特定的任務。

(A)consignment 寄售

(B)delegation 委任

(C)promotion 促銷

(D)submission 順從

解 此題考的是詞彙意義，根據題意，應填入(B)delegation（委任）。

22 (C)。 我們商店的營業時間為每天的早上10點至晚上5點半，除了農曆新年之外。

(A)but 但是

(B)close to 接近於

(C)except 除了……

(D)next to 在……隔壁

解 此題考的是詞彙意義，根據題意，應填入(C)except（除了……）。補充一點，but當作介系詞也有「除了……之外」的意思，但前方需放有anything、nobody、who、all等詞。

23 (B)。 我妹妹在其他城市讀書了十年回家後，我對於她在奢侈品上的浪費相當震驚。

(A)cash 現金

(B)extravagance 奢侈；浪費

(C)money 金錢

(D)thriftiness 節儉

解 此題考的是詞彙意義，根據題意，應填入(B)extravagance（奢侈；浪費）。

24 (C)。 測潮儀所記錄的全球海平面高度是對於氣候變遷的演變與影響相當重要的指標。

(A)bar ruler ＜無此用法＞

(B)tape ruler 捲尺

(C)tide gauges 測潮儀

(D)tide clock 潮位鐘

解 此題考的是詞彙意義，根據題意，應填入(C)tide gauges（測潮儀）；tide為「潮汐」之意，而gauge為「測量儀器」。

25 (B)。 充滿錯誤的句子通常會聽起來很怪、很荒謬或讓人困惑，它們有可能完全不合邏輯。

(A)analytical 分析的

(B)illogical 不合邏輯的

(C)irrational 不理智的

(D)logical 合邏輯的

解 此題考的是詞彙意義，根據題意，應填入(B)illogical（不合邏輯的）。

26 (A)。 在這個充滿社群媒體與假新聞的時代，從印刷品衰退潮倖存下來的記者有新的敵人要面對。

(A)journalists 記者

(B)novelists 小說家

(C)painters 畫家

(D)writers 作家

解 此題考的是詞彙意義，根據題意，
　　應填入(A)journalist（記者）。

27 (B)。 親屬關係涉及某種行為模
式，例如在異性的兄弟姐妹、小
孩、父母親之間的尊重，以及在兒
媳與親家之間的敬重。
(A)Brotherhood 兄弟之情
(B)Kinship 親屬關係
(C)Manhood 男子氣概
(D)Relationship 關係
解 此題考的是詞彙意義，根據題意，
　　應填入(B)Kinship（親屬關係）。

28 (C)。 為了感謝村民的長期光顧，
加油站免費發送三天的汽油。
(A)given away 免費發送（完成式）
(B)given up 放棄（完成式）
(C)giving away 免費發送（進行式）
(D)giving up 放棄（進行式）
解 此題考的是詞彙意義與文法，根
據句型結構，空格處應填入過去
進行式的動詞；而根據題意，應填
入(C)giving away（免費發送）。

29 (D)。 被指派審閱這份報告的委員
會在送出最終的評論前仔細地檢閱
文件。
(A)looks at 看；盯
(B)looks for 尋找
(C)looks in 往裡面看
(D)looks over 仔細檢查
解 此題考的是詞彙意義，根據題意，
　　應填入(D)looks over（仔細檢查）。

30 (B)。 緯度座標的劃分，是畫在地
球上與赤道平行的假定圓圈。

(A)horizontal 水平的
(B)latitude 緯度
(C)longitude 經度
(D)vertical 垂直的
解 此題考的是詞彙意義，根據題意，
　　應填入(B)latitude（緯度）。

31 (D)。 本公司為高級職員與僱員提供
在其工作範圍內行事的責任保護。
(A)agility 敏捷；靈活
(B)docility 順從；馴服
(C)fertility 肥沃；繁殖力
(D)liability 責任；義務
解 此題考的是詞彙意義，根據題
意，應填入(D)liability（責任；
義務）。

32 (C)。 做研究時，研究者在挑選主
題之前，應該謹慎地挑選網路資料
來檢視過往的資訊與學術文章。
(A)make out 了解；領會
(B)make up 編造
(C)pick out 挑選；辨認出
(D)pick up 撿起
解 此題考的是詞彙意義，根據題
意，應填入(C)pick out（挑選；
辨認出）。

33 (C)。 在過去的十年中，畜牧生產
業迅速地增長，因為我們這區的土
地是放牧以及為乳牛和綿羊生產飼
料的黃金地段。
(A)Crops 作物　　(B)Harvest 收成
(C)Livestock 牲畜 (D)Poultry 家禽
解 此題考的是詞彙意義，根據題意，
　　應填入(C)Livestock（牲畜）。

34 (B)。 在台灣，科技人力已變成國家最強而有力的資產，因為政府在過去30年間全力支持半導體產業的發展。

(A)human 人類

(B)manpower 人力

(C)staff 員工

(D)workers 工作人員

解 此題考的是詞彙意義，根據題意，應填入(B)manpower（人力）。

35 (B)。

艾伯特：這就是你的房間，我們一起分擔家務。

約翰：這是間很棒的房間，而且你們人都很好，但我想說，我覺得有一點貴。我在想有沒有可能降低一點租金呢？

吉娜：恐怕這不是我們能決定的。我們必須問一下房東。

情境脈絡為何？這兩位住戶正在向約翰為一間租屋_____。

(A)citing a verse 引用一首詩

(B)introducing the room 介紹房間

(C)selling some books 販賣一些書籍

(D)telling a story 說一個故事

解 此題考的是對話情境，根據對話，男子一開始在介紹房屋，而另一個男子問及房租的問題，女子則回答要問一下房東，可推測兩位住戶在向約翰介紹房間，因此應選(B)。

36 (A)。

男子：喔，呼叫器響了。情況怎麼了？喔不，是嚴重的交通事故，他們現在就需要我。

女子：喔，那我也去。我確信他們會需要更多的護理師。

他們在哪裡工作？他們也許在一間_____工作。

(A)hospital 醫院

(B)laundromat 自助洗衣店

(C)office 辦公室

(D)school 學校

解 此題考的是對話情境，根據對話，男子提及交通事故，而女子提及護理師，因此可推斷他們是在醫院工作，應選(A)。

37 (C)。 男子：請進，坐吧。

女孩：很抱歉我沒有更早預約，但我真的需要跟您談談。

男子：沒關係，妳怎麼了嗎？

女孩：我最近有些荒廢學業，而我想要振作起來。

男子：那真的是好消息啊，是什麼讓妳轉變心意的呢？

他們是誰？他們是_____和他的_____。

(A)consultant, consultee 顧問；尋求諮詢者

(B)doctor, patient 醫生；病人

(C)professor, student 教授；學生

(D)psychiatrist, patient 心理醫生；病人

解答與解析

解 此題考的是對話情境,根據對話,女子提及近期她荒廢學業而想要振作,因此可推斷她是一名學生,在和她的教授諮詢,因此應選(C)。

38 (B)。 男子:妳不會怕吧,對嗎?
女子:這個高度就算是勇敢的人來爬也有點太高了。
男子:來吧,拉我的手。我們慢慢上去,我保證。
這位男子試著想要做什麼?他試著_____。
(A)demonstrate how easy it is 示範這有多簡單
(B)encourage her to climb up 鼓勵她往上爬
(C)show her how difficult it could be 向她展示這有多難
(D)tell her nothing is easy 告訴她沒有任何事是簡單的
解 此題考的是對話情境,根據對話,女子說這高度對勇敢的人來說也太高了,而男子保證他們會慢慢爬上去,並且提議拉他的手,可推論男子想鼓勵女子往上爬,應選(B)。

39 (D)。
女子:這隻小貓病了。她是隻養在室內還是室外的貓?
男子:兩者都有。她晚上待在室內,但白天大多時間都在外面,和其他隻貓玩耍。
這則對話可能在哪裡發生?可能是在_____。

(A)classroom 教室 (B)market 市場
(C)theater 電影院 (D)vet 獸醫院
解 此題考的是對話情境,根據對話,女子說小貓病了,並詢問其是室內還室外的貓,男子則解釋小貓的生活情況,因此可推斷是在獸醫院,應選(D)。

40 (A)。
女子:我的一個朋友要退休了,他正在找人照看他的小型公司。我認為你可能是合適的人選。
男子:我要怎麼做?我自己獨立經營一家企業?
這位女子是什麼意思?她提議_____。
(A)he could accept the offer 他可以接受這個職務
(B)he could celebrate for the new job 他可以為新工作慶祝
(C)he should consider the cash flow first 他應該優先考量現金流
(D)he should train himself to be a good manager 他應該培訓自己成為一位好的主管
解 此題考的是對話情境,根據對話,女子提到自己一位朋友近期退休,在為自己的小公司找尋人選接管,女子認為這位男子可能是合適的人選,因此應選(A)。

41 (A)。
女子:我覺得要專注於書中有點困難。

男子：我完全也是，但這最後總會
　　　變得輕鬆的。

女子：我可以請你幫一個忙嗎？你
　　　覺得有一個學伴怎麼樣？

這位女子是誰？她是＿＿＿＿。

(A)college student 大學生

(B)primary school teacher 小學老師

(C)professor in a university 大學教授

(D)watch-guard in the building 大樓
　　保全

解 此題考的是對話情境，根據對
話，女子提及要專注於書本中有
點困難，並詢問男子是否想要有
一位學伴，因此應選(A)。

42 (B)。 男子：妳好嗎？

女子：累死了，又完成另一個長時
　　　輪班。

男子：是啊，最近這裡都很忙，因
　　　為有太多手術了。

他們在哪裡工作？這個地點可能
是＿＿＿＿。

(A)drawing room 客廳

(B)operating room in a hospital 醫院
　　手術室

(C)painting room 畫室

(D)woodworking room of a sawmill
　　鋸木廠的木工房

解 此題考的是對話情境，根據對
話，女子說她剛輪完班，而男子
說最近的手術很多，因此可推論
他們在手術室工作，應選(B)。

43 (A)。

女子：為什麼銀行應該借您這筆錢呢？

男子：我在這邊儲蓄將近五年了。

女子：但您最近不是沒有工作嗎？

男子：是的，但我都是靠我的儲蓄
　　　在生活，而非透支額度。我
　　　是一位可靠的顧客，而我相
　　　信我新的事業將會是一個很
　　　棒的投資。您們的借貸將會
　　　對我與貴銀行都有益。

現在這名男子在做什麼？他正
在＿＿＿＿。

(A)applying a bank loan 申請銀行借貸

(B)depositing some cash 存一些現金

(C)running up an overdraft 借貸透支

(D)saving a time-deposit 存一筆定期
　　存款

解 此題考的是對話情境，根據對
話，女子詢問為什麼銀行應該借
錢給這位男子，而男子針對自己
的財務狀況做說明，因此可推論
男子正在向銀行申請一筆貸款，
應選(A)。

　　在冠狀病毒的種類之中有許多不
同的病毒，但只有七種會**影響**人類。其
中有四種會讓人得比較不嚴重的感冒，
而其他的則較為新穎、容易致死，且被
認為是經由像是蝙蝠或駱駝等動物傳播
的。醫療官員已將此種新型病毒標示為
SARS-CoV-2，而其疾病為COVID-19。

　　哥倫比亞大學感染與免疫中心主
任伊恩·利普金一直在研究這種新冠病
毒。他說冬季的陽光較少，陽光也可以
幫助分解已傳播至地表的病毒。

「**紫外線**會分解核酸，這幾乎消毒了整個地表。如果你待在室外會比待在室內還要乾淨，僅僅是因為紫外線的緣故。」他說。

紫外線對於殺死細菌與病毒相當有效；這通常會使用在醫院來使設備**無菌化**。

另外一位學者，倫敦大學衛生與熱帶醫學院的戴維‧哈曼說道，我們對於這種新病毒的**所知還太少**，無法預防在不同天氣狀況下的變異。

根據衛生福利部疾病管制署（CDC），人在出現**症狀**時最**具有傳染性**。然而，一些專家懷疑官方的數據可能低估了感染的人數，說道不是每個感染的人都會演變成嚴重的疾病。

「我們只看到一些最嚴重的情況。」魏斯頓說，「可能有一些正在發生的感染是沒有被檢測到的。」

許多專家說SARS-CoV-2可能會變成**地方疾病**，加入其他四種造成溫和感冒的病毒，或是變成像是流行性感冒的季節性健康危害。

為了要避免感染任何病毒的疾病，世界衛生組織建議常洗手、避免與有咳嗽、打噴嚏症狀的人有近距離接觸，並且在生病時尋求治療。

44 (C)。為了要_____空罐，我們應該將它們放置於沸水罐中的架子上、正面朝上。
(A)coat 塗在……上
(B)contaminate 污染；弄髒

(C)disinfect 消毒
(D)muddy 沾滿爛泥
解 此題考的是詞彙語意，根據題意，應填入(C)disinfect（消毒）。

45 (C)。臺灣政府已因為新冠病毒爆發而_____所有外國旅客造訪台灣。
(A)welcomed 歡迎
(B)asked 詢問
(C)banned 禁止
(D)greeted 招待
解 此題考的是詞彙語意，根據題意，應填入(C)banned（禁止）。

46 (C)。世界衛生組織已針對使用布洛芬提出警告，來管理新冠病毒的____。
(A)features 特徵
(B)information 資訊
(C)symptoms 症狀
(D)structure 結構
解 此題考的是詞彙語意，根據題意，應填入(C)symptoms（症狀）。補充一點，此處的ibuprofen為一種治療關節炎的止痛退燒藥。

47 (C)。_____是一種在非常大地區影響許多人的疾病。
(A)endemic 地方疾病
(B)ebola 伊波拉病毒
(C)pandemic 流行疾病
(D)poliomyelitis 小兒麻痺症
解 此題考的是詞彙語意，根據題意，應填入(C)pandemic（流行疾病）。

48 (D)。 全球各地的科學家齊力在尋找對抗新冠病毒的新方法，全球已有超過200,000人_____此病毒。
(A)assisted 幫助
(B)relieved 緩和
(C)affected 影響
(D)infected 感染

解 此題考的是詞彙語意，根據題意，應填入(D)infected（感染）。

49 (B)。 紫外線能夠_____細菌與病毒。
(A)fertilize 使肥沃
(B)sanitize 給……消毒
(C)clean 清潔
(D)wash 清洗

解 此題考的是詞彙語意，根據題意與文章第四段提及的內容，應填入(B)sanitize（給……消毒）。

50 (A)。 現在所有的市民都被告知在旅遊回國後需要_____至少14天。
(A)quarantine 隔離
(B)work 工作
(C)rest 休息
(D)exercise 運動

解 此題考的是詞彙語意，根據題意，應填入(A)quarantine（隔離）。

109年 台灣電力新進僱用人員

( ) **1** The government is trying to _____ the economy by increasing public spending.
 (A)encourage   (B)stimulate
 (C)reduce   (D)remove

( ) **2** Because of _____, weather around the world has been unstable these years.
 (A)climate change   (B)temperature loss
 (C)warm increase   (D)global warm

( ) **3** At the request of the US government, TSMC has decided to set up a plant in Arizona to protect high-level technologies _____ getting stolen.
 (A)to   (B)of
 (C)for   (D)from

( ) **4** Mary doesn't work here anymore; she _____ two months ago.
 (A)has left   (B)was transferred
 (C)quieted   (D)gone out

( ) **5** In spite of Eddie's _____, Sara refused to forgive his rude behavior.
 (A)politics   (B)modesty
 (C)capability   (D)apologies

( ) **6** The manager left town for an emergency last night, so today's meeting has to be _____.
 (A)stopped   (B)continued
 (C)postponed   (D)late

(　) **7** Stores are forbidden to sell cigarettes or alcohol to minors. "Minors" are people _____ .
(A)working in mines 　 (B)not suitable to use such products
(C)under 18 years of age 　 (D)having some diseases

(　) **8** Oil prices are going up after Saudi Arabia decided to _____ production.
(A)reduce 　 (B)stop
(C)increase 　 (D)keep

(　) **9** After retirement, Mr. Wang chose to live in an old folks' home in order not to be a _____ children.
(A)response 　 (B)weight
(C)burden 　 (D)support

(　) **10** Some light bulbs in the office were broken, so I called the _____ crew.
(A)electric 　 (B)maintenance
(C)construction 　 (D)fix

(　) **11** Nancy likes pink color, but it _____ .
(A)doesn't look nice in her 　 (B)isn't fit her
(C)doesn't look nice on her 　 (D)doesn't suitable for her

(　) **12** It took us a few hours to get everything ready for the picnic, but, ____, it started to rain as soon as we walked out the door.
(A)luckily 　 (B)unfortunately
(C)quietly 　 (D)positively

(　) **13** Many ships travel _____ the Taiwan Strait to go from Southeast Asia to Japan.
(A)through 　 (B)across
(C)over 　 (D)in

(　) **14** What does the "e" in "e-commerce" mean?
(A)electric 　 (B)elective
(C)electronic 　 (D)elevated

(   ) **15** The MRT has _____ a lot of business from taxis.

(A)stolen   (B)brought out

(C)taken away   (D)gotten

(   ) **16** Harry was let go after his mistakes caused two important customers to switch to the company's competitors. Which is the closest to "let go" in meaning?

(A)quit   (B)fired

(C)given a warning   (D)transferred

(   ) **17** Most consumers have the _____ to prefer certain brands and this is called brand loyalty.

(A)hobby   (B)mood

(C)tendency   (D)choice

(   ) **18** Where _____ all day? Lots of people were looking for you!

(A)have you been   (B)are you

(C)did you   (D)you were

(   ) **19** The cell phone market is very _____ and every company tries to put out new models with improved functions each year.

(A)busy   (B)popular

(C)powerful   (D)competitive

(   ) **20** Taiwan's National Health Insurance is considered a _____ health insurance system that countries around the world would like to have.

(A)ideal   (B)model

(C)success   (D)interesting

(   ) **21** Apple is unable to _____ the latest i-Phone model because the manufacturers in China cannot resume production.

(A)show   (B)push

(C)forward   (D)release

(　) **22** More and more people use _____; they don't use cash or
credit cards.
(A)action pay　　　　　　(B)activity payment
(C)portable pay　　　　　(D)mobile payment

(　) **23** The city government urges every citizen not to waste any water
because it _____ for four months.
(A)hasn't rained　　　　(B)isn't raining
(C)hadn't rained　　　　(D)wasn't rainy

(　) **24** Lynn learns Japanese on Monday and Wednesday and English on
Tuesday and Thursday. Sometimes she gets _____ between
the two languages.
(A)loss　　　　　　　　(B)mistaken
(C)restless　　　　　　　(D)confused

(　) **25** Linda has always been good with numbers; it's not surprising that
she's a _____ teacher today.
(A)history　　　　　　　(B)math
(C)English　　　　　　　(D)geography

(　) **26** After spending one year at an aviation school in the US, Leon is
now a China Airlines pilot. What does "aviation" means?
(A)driving　　　　　　　(B)riding
(C)maintenance　　　　　(D)flying

(　) **27** Mark is extremely _____. He goes everywhere in the city by
bicycle in order not to create any carbon emissions.
(A)user-friendly　　　　(B)healthy
(C)eco-friendly　　　　　(D)unhealthy

(　) **28** Jack enjoys _____ people; he's a clown in a circus.
(A)to cheer　　　　　　(B)entertaining
(C)to amuse　　　　　　(D)welcoming

(   ) **29** Japan announced the 2020 Summer Olympics would be _____ for one year.
    (A)put off   (B)moved up
    (C)taken in   (D)slowed down

(   ) **30** The general manager offered me a promotion, but the job was really _____ my ability and I could only say no.
    (A)after   (B)above
    (C)into   (D)without

(   ) **31** The manager thinks some of the _____ in this report are wrong and wants you to check all the numbers once more.
    (A)sentences   (B)explanations
    (C)examples   (D)statistics

(   ) **32** The pizza place in the alley is not around anymore. They closed down last month. Which is the closest to "around" in meaning?
    (A)nearby   (B)close
    (C)existing   (D)buyable

(   ) **33** Night markets in Taiwan are _____ attractions that draw lots of foreigners.
    (A)tourist   (B)traveling
    (C)sightseeing   (D)scenic

(   ) **34** The game will continue until there is a winner _____ it rains.
    (A)even   (B)even if
    (C)although   (D)in case

(   ) **35** The government offers loans at reasonably low _____ rates to qualified young people who want to start their own businesses.
    (A)interest   (B)financial
    (C)funds   (D)money

(   ) **36** Jane has a terrible _____ and she often gets lost.
    (A)sense of direction   (B)feeling of map
    (C)old vehicle   (D)distance perception

(　) **37** Using credit cards online to buy things is convenient, but there is the _____ that your personal information might get stolen.
(A)risk　　　　　　(B)perhaps
(C)good chance　　　(D)unlucky

(　) **38** Simon has been training to swim _____ the Sun Moon Lake. He admits it's tough.
(A)over　　　(B)on
(C)in　　　　(D)across

(　) **39** Japan is one of the most popular travel _____ for Taiwanese.
(A)nations　　　(B)attractions
(C)locations　　(D)destinations

(　) **40** As the ice in the North Pole continues to melt, polar bears are losing their habitat. "Habitat" means _____.
(A)everyday habits　　　　　(B)place to live
(C)space polar bears are used to (D)houses

解答與解析　答案標示為# 者，表官方曾公告更正該題答案。

1 (B)。政府正嘗試透過提升公共支出的方式來刺激經濟。
(A)encourage(v.)鼓勵；助長
(B)stimulate(v.)刺激；激勵
(C)reduce(v.)減少；降低
(D)remove(v.)移動；消除
解 依照句型，空格處需填入動詞，依據題意應填入(B)stimulate（刺激；激勵）。(A)encourage雖為「鼓勵」之意，但受詞多接人物，句型為「encourage sb. to V」，意為「鼓勵某人做某事」；(C)與(D)皆不符合題意。

2 (A)。由於氣候變遷的關係，這幾年世界各地的天氣皆不穩定。
(A)climate change 氣候變遷
(B)temperature loss 溫度流失
(C)warm increase （無此用法）
(D)global warm （無此用法）
解 空格前方為Because of，因此空格處應填入名詞。依據題意應填入(A)climate change（氣候變遷）。(B)並不符合題意；並無(C)與(D)之用法。若是要填入「全球暖化」之意，應為「global warming」。

3 (D)。因應美國政府要求，台積電決定在亞利桑那州建立一座工廠，來保護高階科技不被竊取。

(A)to　　　　　(B)of
(C)for　　　　　(D)from

解 此題考的是文法句型〈protect ... from ...〉，意為「保護……不受……侵害」，from之後銜接可能帶來傷害或損害的事物。例：It's important to protect your skin from the harmful effects of the sun.（保護好你的肌膚不受陽光侵害是很重要的。）

4 (B)。瑪麗已不在這裡工作；她兩個月前被調職了。

(A)has left 已經離開（現在完成式）
(B)was transferred 被調職（過去式；被動式）
(C)quieted 使安靜（過去式）
(D)gone out 出去

解 依照句型，空格處應填入動詞，該句最後有過去時間點two months ago，有提及過去時間點應使用過去式，因此應選(B)was transferred（被調職）。(A)為現在完成式，應使用在有〈for ＋一段時間〉（做某事已持續多久時間）或〈since ＋過去時間點〉（從過去某時間點開始從事某事）之句型；(C)為動詞quiet（使安靜）的過去式，並不符合題意，且此選項為陷阱選項，故意選用與quit（辭職）相像之詞彙來混淆；(D)並不符合文法。

5 (D)。儘管艾迪道歉，莎拉依然拒絕原諒他的無禮行為。

(A)politics 政治　　(B)modesty 謙遜
(C)capability 能力　(D)apologies 道歉

解 依照句型，In spite of後方應接名詞，意為「儘管……；雖然……」。依據題意應填入(D)apologies（道歉）。(A)(B)(C)皆不符合題意。

6 (C)。經理昨晚因緊急事件出城了，所以今天的會議必須延期。

(A)stopped(v.)停止
(B)continued(v.)繼續
(C)postponed(v.)延期
(D)late (a.) 遲到的

解 依照句型，空格處可填入動詞被動式或形容詞。依據題意應填入(C)postponed（延期）。(A)(B)(D)皆不符合題意。

7 (C)。商店禁止販售菸酒給未成年人。「未成年人」是未滿18歲的人。

(A)working in mines 在礦井工作
(B)not suitable to use such products 不適合使用這種商品
(C)under 18 years of age 未滿18歲
(D)having some diseases 有某些疾病

解 依據題意，要描述「minors」為何種人，答案應為(C)under 18 years of age。(A)使用與minors相似的mines，mine在此處為名詞，意為「礦井；礦區」；(B)(D)皆不符合minors之意。

8 (A)。在沙烏地阿拉伯決定降低產量後，石油價格便上漲了。

(A)reduce(v.)降低
(B)stop(v.)停止
(C)increase(v.)增加
(D)keep(v.)保持
解 依照句型，空格處應填入動詞。production為「產量」之意，依據題意應填入(A)reduce（降低）。(B)(C)(D)皆不符合題意。

9 (C)。 在退休之後，為了不要成為孩子的負擔，王先生決定住進老人院。
(A)response(n.)回答
(B)weight(n.)重量
(C)burden(n.)負擔
(D)support(n.)支持
解 依照句型，空格處應填入名詞。依據題意填入(C)burden（負擔）。(A)(B)(D)皆不符合題意。

10 (B)。 辦公室裡有些電燈泡壞了，所以我打了電話給維修人員。
(A)electric (a.) 電的
(B)maintenance(n.)維修
(C)construction(n.)建設
(D)fix(v.)修理
解 依照句型，空格處應填入形容詞修飾後面的名詞crew、或是填入名詞與後面的名詞crew形成複合名詞。依據題意填入(B)maintenance（維修）。(A)(C)並不符合題意；(D)並不符合文法。

11 (C)。 南希喜歡粉紅色，但她穿粉紅色並不好看。
(A)doesn't look nice in her
(B)isn't fit her

(C)doesn't look nice on her
(D)doesn't suitable for her
解 此題考的是文法，(A)使用了錯誤的介系詞，穿在某人身上介系詞應用on；(B)並不符合文法，且fit作為動詞意為「合……身；適合於……」，多用於談論衣物是否合身、某人（物）的條件（品質）是否符合某事；(D)並不符合文法，且suitable作為形容詞意為「適宜的；合適的」，用於某事（物）對於某種場合是否合宜、妥當。只有(C)doesn't look nice on her正確，因此選(C)。

12 (B)。 我們花了幾個小時才準備好一切要去野餐，但是，不幸地，我們一出門那刻便開始下雨了。
(A)luckily (ad.)幸運地
(B)unfortunately (ad.)不幸地
(C)quietly (ad.)安靜地
(D)positively (ad.)肯定地；正面地
解 依照句型，空格處應填入副詞。依據題意應填入(B)unfortunately（不幸地）。(A)(C)(D)皆不符合題意。

13 (A)。 許多船隻會航行穿越台灣海峽，從東南亞前往日本
(A)through 穿過；通過
(B)across 橫越；穿過
(C)over 在……之上
(D)in 在……之內
解 依照句型，空格處應填入介系詞。(A)與(B)皆能表示「穿越；

橫過」之意，唯(B)across是用於穿越平面場域到達對面，如穿越馬路，而(A)through則是用於穿越一個立體空間、在內部空間裡穿越而到達對面，如穿越森林、公園等。台灣海峽為一立體場域，因此應選(A)。(C)(D)並不符合題意。

14 (C)。「e-commerce」中的e代表了什麼意思？

(A)electric (a.)電的

(B)elective (a.)選舉的；選擇的

(C)electronic (a.)電子的

(D)elevated (a.)升高的

解 此題考「e-commerce」中的e字代表了什麼意思，此處的e即為electronic（電子的）開頭的e，組合起來即為「電子商務」之意。

15 (C)。台北捷運搶走了計程車許多生意。

(A)stolen 偷竊

(B)brought about 帶來

(C)taken away 拿走；搶走

(D)gotten 得到；獲得

解 依照句型，空格處應填入現在完成式的過去分詞。依據題意應填入(C)taken away（拿走；搶走）。(A)(B)(D)皆不符合題意。

16 (B)。哈瑞的錯誤造成兩位重要的客戶移轉至公司的競爭對手，在這之後他便被解僱了。下列何者意思最接近於「let go」？

(A)quit 辭職

(B)fired 被開除

(C)given a warning 被警告

(D)transferred 被調職

解 此題詢問let go的意思最接近何者，let go的意思有「放開；鬆手；讓……走；解僱」等，在此處為「解僱」之意，fire為「開除」之意，因此選(B)。(A)(C)(D)皆不符合題意。

17 (C)。大部分的顧客都會有偏好特定品牌的傾向，這個即叫作品牌忠誠度。

(A)hobby 嗜好；興趣

(B)mood 心情；情緒

(C)tendency 傾向

(D)choice 選擇

解 依照句型，空格處應填入名詞。依據題意應填入(C)tendency（傾向）。(A)(B)(D)皆不符合題意。

18 (A)。你整天都跑哪去了？很多人都在找你！

(A)have you been　(B)are you

(C)did you　　　　(D)you were

解 此題考的是文法。根據後句的「... were looking for ...」可推斷事情發生在過去，因此不可選(B)。all day為一段時間，需配合完成式使用，因此選擇時態為現在完成式的(A)，「Where have you been?」為一常用問法，建議背起此問候語。(C)(D)皆不符合文法。

19 (D)。手機市場非常競爭,各間公司每年都試著推出改善功能的新機種。
(A)busy (a.)忙碌的
(B)popular (a.)受歡迎的;流行的
(C)powerful (a.)強而有力的;強大的
(D)competitive (a.)競爭的
解 依照句型,空格處應填入形容詞。依據題意應填入(D)competitive(競爭的)。(A)(B)(C)皆不符合題意。

20 (B)。台灣的國家健康保險被認為是模範健保制度,世界各國都想擁有。
(A)ideal (a.)理想的;完美的
(B)model (a.)模範的;榜樣的
(C)success (n.)成功;成就
(D)interesting (a.)有趣的
解 依照句型,空格處應填入形容詞。依據題意可填入(A)或(B),但ideal為母音開頭,前面的冠詞應為an;model作為名詞意為「模範;榜樣」,而作為形容詞則為「模範的;榜樣的」之意,因此應選(B)。(C)並不符合文法,若要放「成功的」應改為successful;(D)並不符合題意與文法。

21 (D)。蘋果無法發表最新的i-Phone機型,因為中國的製造商還不能恢復生產。
(A)show(v.)展現;秀出
(B)push(v.)推動;推進
(C)forward(v.)發送;轉交
(D)release(v.)發行;發表
解 依照句型,be unable to後應接續原形動詞,意為「無法……」。

依據題意應選(D)release(發行;發表)。(A)(C)(D)皆不符合題意。

22 (D)。越來越多人使用行動支付;他們不使用現金或信用卡。
(A)action pay
(B)activity payment
(C)portable pay
(D)mobile payment
解 後面的句子解釋了空格處之意,指出越來越多人不使用現金或信用卡,即為使用「行動支付」的人越來越多,行動支付為mobile payment,因此選(D)。

23 (A)。市政府激勵每位市民不要浪費水,因為已經四個月沒有下雨了。
(A)hasn't rained
(B)isn't raining
(C)hadn't rained
(D)wasn't rainy
解 此題考的是文法。根據後方的for four months得知應使用完成式,而依據前方的urges則可推斷應使用現在完成式,因此應選(A)。(B)為現在進行式,應使用在現在正在進行的動作;(C)為過去完成式,應有一個過去時間點,而使用在此過去時間點之前的動作;(D)並不符合文法。

24 (D)。林恩在星期一和星期三學日文、在星期二和星期四學英文。有時候她會在兩個語言之間搞混。
(A)loss(n.)損失;喪失
(B)mistaken (a.)弄錯的;誤解的
(C)restless (a.)煩躁的;焦躁不安的
(D)confused (a.)混亂的;困惑的
解 依照句型,空格處應填入形容詞。依據題意,後面寫道

「between the two languages」，因此應為「在兩者語言間混淆」，應填入(D)confused（混淆的；困惑的）。(A)(B)(C)皆不符合題意。

25 (B)。 琳達總是很擅長數字方面的事；她今天是位數學老師並不讓人驚訝。
(A)history 歷史　　(B)math 數學
(C)English 英文　　(D)geography 地理
解 此題考的是科目。be good at意思為「擅長……」，前面提及琳達擅長數字，因此依題意應填入(B)math（數學）。

26 (D)。 在美國的航空學校待了一年之後，里昂現在是一位中華航空的機師。「aviation」是什麼意思？
(A)driving 駕駛；操縱
(B)riding 搭乘；乘坐
(C)maintenance 維修；保養
(D)flying 飛行；航空
解 此題詢問aviation的意思為何，aviation為「航空；飛行」之意，且根據後句之意可推斷出aviation與機師有關，因此應選(D)flying（飛行的）。(A)(B)(C)皆不符合題意。

27 (C)。 馬克非常地環保。他為了不要製造任何碳排放量，在市內各處皆是騎乘腳踏車。
(A)user-friendly (a.) 便於使用的
(B)healthy (a.) 健康的
(C)eco-friendly(n.)環保的；不損害環境的
(D)unhealthy (a.) 不健康的

解 後面的句子解釋了空格處之意，指出馬克為了不製造碳排放量，在市內不管去哪都騎腳踏車，因此依據題意應選(C)eco-friendly（環保的；不損害環境的）。

28 (B)。 傑克喜歡娛樂人群；他是一位馬戲團的小丑。
(A)to cheer 喝采；鼓勵
(B)entertaining 使娛樂；使歡樂
(C)to amuse 使歡樂；逗……高興
(D)welcoming 歡迎；款待
解 依照句型，enjoy的用法為「enjoy V-ing」，因此(A)(C)並不正確；而根據題意應選(B)entertaining（使娛樂；使歡樂）。

29 (A)。 日本宣布2020夏季奧林匹克運動會將會延後一年舉辦。
(A)put off 延後；拖延
(B)moved up 提升
(C)taken in 理解；欺騙
(D)slowed down 減速
解 此題考了四個片語，根據題意應選(A)put off（延後；拖延）。

30 (B)。 總經理給了我升職的機會，但這份職務實在是超過我的能力，我只能拒絕。
(A)after 在……之後
(B)above 在……之上；超過
(C)into 進入到……
(D)without 沒有……
解 此題考了四個介系詞，根據題意應選(B)above（在……之上；超過），above one's ability意為「超過……的能力」。

31 (D)。經理認為這份報告有些統計資料有誤，希望你能再確認一次所有的數字。
(A)sentences(n.)句子
(B)explanations(n.)解釋
(C)examples(n.)例子
(D)statistics(n.)統計資料
解 後方句子提到numbers（數字），因此根據題意應選(D)statistics（統計資料）。

32 (C)。巷子裡的披薩店已經不在了，他們上個月歇業了。下列何者最接近「around」的意思？
(A)nearby (a.)附近的
(B)close(v.)關閉
(C)existing (a.)存在的
(D)buyable (a.)可買的
解 此題詢問around的意思最接近何者，後方提及該店上個月歇業了，可推斷出not around為「不在了」之意，因此應選(C)existing（存在的）。

33 (A)。台灣的夜市是吸引許多外國人的旅遊景點。
(A)tourist(n.)旅客
(B)traveling (a.)旅行的
(C)sightseeing (a.)觀光的
(D)scenic (a.)風景的
解 此題考的是一固定用法，tourist attraction為「旅遊景點；觀光勝地」之意。

34 (B)。即使下雨，這場比賽會持續進行到有贏家為止。

(A)even (ad.)甚至；連
(B)even if (conj.)即使
(C)although (conj.)雖然；儘管
(D)in case (conj.)萬一
解 依照句型，句中有三個動詞（will continue、there is、rains），但僅有一個連接詞（until），因此空格處需放入一連接詞。根據題意，可放入(B)或(C)，唯although是用在既定情況（已發生的事實），例如：He decides to go out although it is raining right now.（雖然現在在下雨，他還是決定要出門。）；even if用在描述假定的情況（未發生的情形），例如：He decides to go out even if the weather forecast said it might rain.（即使氣象預報說可能會下雨，他還是決定要出門。）根據題意，前方提及比賽將會持續，為假定情況，因此選(B)。

35 (A)。政府提供划算的低利率貸款給符合資格、想要創業的年輕人。
(A)interest(n.)利息
(B)financial (a.)金融的
(C)funds(n.)資金
(D)money(n.)金錢
解 此題考的是一固定用法，interest rate為「利率」之意，根據後方提及的loan（貸款），應填入(A)interest（利息）。

36 (A)。珍有極糟的方向感，她常常迷路。

(A)sense of direction 方向感

(B)feeling of map 地圖的感覺

(C)old vehicle 老舊的汽車

(D)distance perception 距離感知

解 後面的句子解釋了空格處之意，提及她常常會迷路，因此應填入(A)sense of direction（方向感）。sense of direction為固定用法，建議背起此慣用詞。

37 (A)。 使用信用卡線上購物很方便，但會有個人資料遭竊的風險。

(A)risk(n.)風險

(B)perhaps (ad.)或許；可能

(C)good chance 很棒的機會

(D)unlucky (a.)不幸的

解 依照句型，空格處應填入名詞。依據題意應選(A)risk（風險）。(B)(C)(D)皆不符合題意。

38 (D)。 賽門一直在受訓泳渡日月潭。他承認這很難。

(A)over 在……之上

(B)on 在……之上

(C)in 在……裡面

(D)across 橫越；穿過

解 此題考了四個介系詞，根據題意應選(D)across（橫越；穿過）。

39 (D)。 日本對台灣人來說是最受歡迎的旅遊勝地之一。

(A)nations 國家

(B)attractions 有吸引力的事物

(C)locations 位置

(D)destinations 目的地

解 此題考的是一固定用法，travel destination為「旅遊目的地；旅遊勝地」之意。

40 (B)。 由於北極的冰塊持續在融化，北極熊正在失去牠們的棲息地。「Habitat」代表了＿＿＿＿＿。

(A)everyday habits 每天的習慣

(B)place to live 居住的地方

(C)space polar bears are used to 北極熊習慣的空間

(D)houses 房屋

解 此題詢問habitat的意思為何，前方提及北極的冰持續在融化，因此北極熊正在失去的是他們居住的地方，habitat的意思為「棲息地」，因此選(B)。

109年 臺灣自來水新進職員（工）

一、字彙

( ) **1** A _____ operated robot was sent to a place where no human can safely reach in order to take those breath-taking pictures.
(A)stiffly
(B)remotely
(C)candidly
(D)tentatively

( ) **2** Inadequate or poor-quality sleep is a common cause of _____; people who do not sleep well usually feel tired.
(A)tremor
(B)verdict
(C)fatigue
(D)discharge

( ) **3** The two women in the picture _____ from their home with more than half a million dollars in jewelry. Now everyone is looking for them.
(A)vanished
(B)entrenched
(C)articulated
(D)dilated

( ) **4** The market has changed so much that company executives today are facing new challenges that their _____ have never known.
(A)referrals
(B)transmitters
(C)predecessors
(D)capturers

( ) **5** The _____ policy has sparked disagreements among various groups, and fierce debates about its effects followed.
(A)controversial
(B)gregarious
(C)affable
(D)submerged

二、文法測驗

(　　) **6** After hearing about his accident, I regret _____ those cruel words to him before he left.
(A)to say
(B)said
(C)having said
(D)have said

(　　) **7** The study analyzed six previous studies _____ nearly 30,000 people.
(A)that including
(B)which including
(C)to include
(D)that included

(　　) **8** You will not be able to see the result until four weeks later, but I think it will definitely _____.
(A)be worth the wait
(B)worth waiting
(C)be worthy to wait
(D)worthwhile your wait

(　　) **9** A: What can I get you for dinner?
B: _____ meat. I can't eat any more meat.
(A)Everything no
(B)Anything but
(C)All not
(D)Nothing but

(　　) **10** Sales statistics _____ by the company showed that the new product brought in a record $11.5 billion in the second quarter this year.
(A)were released recently
(B)releasing recently
(C)that recently released
(D)recently released

三、閱讀測驗

　　Do you play video games on the Internet in excess? Are you compulsively shopping online? Can't physically stop checking Facebook? Is your excessive computer use interfering with your daily life – relationships, work, school? If you answered yes to any of these questions, you may be suffering from Internet Addiction Disorder, also commonly referred to as Compulsive Internet Use (CIU), Problematic Internet Use (PIU), or iDisorder. Originally debated as a "real thing," it was satirically theorized as a disorder in 1995 by Dr. Ivan Goldberg, who compared its original model to pathological gambling. Since then, the disorder has rapidly gained ground and has been given serious attention from many researchers, mental health counselors, and doctors as a truly debilitating disorder.

Like most disorders, it's not likely to pinpoint an exact cause of Internet Addiction Disorder. This disorder is characteristic of having multiple contributing factors. Some evidence suggests that if you are suffering from Internet Addiction Disorder, your brain makeup is similar to those that suffer from a chemical dependency, such as drugs or alcohol. Interestingly, some studies link Internet Addiction Disorder to physically changing the brain structure—specifically affecting the amount of gray and white matter in regions of the prefrontal brain. This area of the brain is associated with remembering details, attention, planning, and prioritizing tasks.

Biological predispositions to Internet Addiction Disorder may also be a contributing factor to the disorder. If you suffer from this disorder, your levels of dopamine and serotonin may be deficient compared to the general population. This chemical deficiency may require you to engage in more behaviors to receive the same pleasurable response compared to individuals not suffering from addictive Internet behaviors.

Predispositions of Internet addiction are also related to anxiety and depression. Oftentimes, if you are already suffering from anxiety or depression, you may turn to the Internet to relieve your suffering from these conditions. Similarly, shy individuals and those with social awkwardness might also be at a higher risk of suffering from Internet addiction. If you suffer from anxiety and depression, you might turn to the Internet to fill a void. If you are shy or socially awkward, you may turn to the Internet because it does not require interpersonal interaction and it is emotionally rewarding.

(　　) **11** What is the passage mainly about?
(A)The true definition of Internet addiction.
(B)What causes Internet addiction.
(C)Whether or not Internet addiction is officially recognized as a disorder.
(D)Who are the most likely to cure Internet addiction.

(　　) **12** Which of the following is true about Internet addiction?
(A)Scientists have proven the relationship between Internet disorder and people's physical strength.
(B)Though hard to define, it is clearly caused by problems in genes.
(C)It has been receiving a lot of serious attention from medical professionals.
(D)So far researchers can only say that it is related to biological factors.

(　　) **13** According to the passage, which of the following might be related to Internet addiction?
(A)A person's emotional state.
(B)Which part of the world a person lives in.
(C)Whether a person has a gambling parent or not.
(D)A person's height and blood pressure.

(　　) **14** Which of the following questions can the passage answer?
(A)Is Dr. Ivan Goldberg the first one to treat Internet addiction?
(B)What medical procedures can cure Internet addiction?
(C)Is Internet addiction an urgent medical condition?
(D)What factors can lead to Internet addiction?

(　　) **15** According to the passage, what kind of people are most likely to suffer from Internet addiction?
(A)People with higher levels of dopamine.
(B)People who are shy and do not have many friends.
(C)People who are usually happy and satisfied with their lives.
(D)People whose family members have gambling problems.

解答與解析　答案標示為#者，表官方曾公告更正該題答案。

一、字彙

1 (B)。 遠端操作的機器人會被送往一個人類無法安全抵達的地方來拍這些令人讚嘆的照片。
(A)僵硬的　　　　(B)遙遠地
(C)率直地　　　　(D)暫時地
解 線索為人類無法安全到達的地方，因此可推論是遠端操作的機器人，此題選(B)。

2 (C)。 缺乏睡眠和低品質的睡眠是造成疲倦的常見因素，睡不好的人通常會覺得疲勞。
(A)（因興奮緊張）而顫抖
(B)裁決
(C)疲勞
(D)允許……離開
解 睡眠不足和低品質的睡眠兩者的共通點就是會覺得累，且後面也提到"people who do not sleep well usually feel tired"，可判斷空格也是和「疲累」相關的詞，答案選(C)。

3 (A)。 照片中的兩名女性帶著價值超過50萬元的珠寶從她們家消失得無影無蹤，現在大家都在找她們。
(A)消失
(B)使牢固
(C)清楚地表達
(D)（使身體的某部分）擴張
解 此題可從句義和介系詞判斷出答案，後面那句表示大家都在

找他們，因此可以確定他們一定是「消失」所以大家才會找他們，且從介系詞為to可以知道答案應為vanish，"vanish from somewhere"是vanish這個動詞最常見的用法，為「從某處消失」之意，此題選(A)。

4 (C)。 市場改變之大讓現今的公司主管面臨以往前輩所不知的新挑戰。
(A)提及　　　　(B)發射機
(C)前任　　　　(D)捕獲者
解 前面提到市場改變很大，且強調"today"和"new challenges"，都在表示現今和以往的對比，因此可判斷答案為predecessors，此題選(C)。

5 (A)。 廣受爭議的政策引起眾多族群的反對和隨之而來的激辯。
(A)爭議性的
(B)（人）愛交際的
(C)和藹可親的
(D)淹沒的
解 從"spark disagreement"和"fierce debates"可看出此政策引起很多不滿和反對聲浪，因此是具爭議性的政策，此題選(A)。

二、文法測驗

6 (C)。 聽到他發生的意外後，我後悔在他離世前曾對他說那些傷人的話。
(A)to say　　　　(B)said
(C)having said　　(D)have said

解 從句義可知道要表達對於生前說過的話感到後悔，"regret＋Ving"為「後悔前曾做過某事」，答案選(C)。

7 (D)。這份研究分析了以往六份包括將近30,000人的研究。
(A)that including
(B)which including
(C)to include
(D)that included

解 參與研究的人是「被」涵蓋在這六份研究裡，因此要用被動式，此題選(D)。

8 (A)。四個月後你才能看見成果，但我想絕對是值得等待的。
(A)be worth the wait
(B)worth waiting
(C)be worthy to wait
(D)worthwhile you wait

解 此題考的是容易混淆的相似用法，此題要先了解句義要表達的為值得花時間等待，「be worth＋名詞/代名詞」的用法指「值得花時間、金錢或精力等等」，worth的用法都有be動詞在前，因此(B)不正確，而(D)的worthwhile多用it當形式主語，沒有(D)的用法，通常用法為「something be worthwhile」或「something be worth one's while」，而(C)的worthy如果搭配to使用的句型為「something be worthy to be done」，因此(C)的時態錯誤，此題選(A)。

9 (B)。 A：晚餐我要幫你買什麼？
B：除了肉以外什麼都好，我吃不下更多的肉了。
(A)Everything no
(B)Anything but
(C)All not
(D)Nothing but

解 此題可從B的後面一句判斷答案，B表示他吃不下肉了，因此可以知道前面一句應為「除了」肉以外的食物，沒有(A)和(C)的用法因此可直接刪去，nothing but通常不會放在句首，且套用在此句意思會變成「除了肉以外的食物都不要」，與後面要表達的內容不符，此題選(B)。

10 (D)。近期公司發表的銷售統計數字顯示新產品在今年的第二季創下獲利115億的紀錄。
(A)were released recently
(B)releasing recently
(C)that recently released
(D)recently released

三、閱讀測驗

　　你是否過量地上網玩遊戲呢？是不是有網購強迫症？無法停止查看臉書？如果你對這幾個問題之一的答案為是的話，你可能得了嗜網症，也通稱為網路成癮症（CIU）、不當網路使用（PIU）或是網路症候群，原先因是否為「真實事物」而引起激辯，在1995年由Ivan Goldberg博士以理論諷刺性地將網路成癮解釋成一種疾病，他將網路成

癮與病態賭博相互比較，從那時起此疾病迅速地普及化且受到許多研究人員、心理咨詢師和醫生正視其為一項真的會使人衰弱的疾病。

此疾病的特徵為擁有多項的影響因素，有些證據指出如果患有網路成癮症，你的大腦結構會相似於那些依賴如毒品和酒精這類化學物品的人，有趣的是，有些研究顯示網路成癮與大腦構造的生理改變之間的關聯——尤其是對額葉區塊的皮質和髓質數量的影響，大腦的此區塊關係到細節記憶力、注意力、計算能力和工作次序。

生理因素也可能是網路成癮症的影響因素之一，如果你罹患此疾病的話，你的多巴胺和血清素的水平相較於一般人可能會較低，這種化學物質的不足會使你比起那些沒有罹患網路成癮症的人需要做更多才能得到相同的愉悅感。

網路成癮症也和焦慮及憂鬱傾向有所關聯，當你感到焦慮或抑鬱時經常會透過上網來緩解這些狀況，相似地，較內向的人和不善交際的人患有網路成癮症的風險也較高，如果你覺得很焦慮或憂鬱，你可能會轉而上網來填補空虛，如果你很害羞或不擅交際，你可能也會因為上網不需與人互動且在情感上得到慰藉而上網。

11 (B)。 此篇文章主旨為何？
(A)網路成癮症正確的解釋
(B)什麼會導致網路成癮
(C)不論如何，網路成癮已經被承認為一種疾病
(D)誰最可能治癒網路成癮

解 此篇文章主旨環繞在導致網路成癮的原因以及網路成癮會影響到什麼，此題選(B)。

12 (C)。 下列何者關於網路成癮的敘述為真？
(A)科學家已證明網路成癮和人們體力的關連
(B)雖然難以解釋，不過此疾病顯然是由基因問題所造成的
(C)這個疾病受到很多醫療專業人士的重視
(D)到目前為止，研究員只能説此疾病與生理因素相關

解 本文第一段後面有提到從Ivan Goldberg博士於1995年諷刺性地將網路成癮視為一項疾病後，網路成癮就受到許多研究員、心理咨詢師和醫生的重視，此題選(C)。

13 (A)。 根據本文，下列何者與網路成癮有關聯？
(A)人的情緒狀態
(B)人居住的區域
(C)是否有愛賭博的父母
(D)人的身高和血壓

解 此題最後一段有提到人感到焦慮或抑鬱時更傾向於尋求網路的慰藉，焦慮和憂鬱都屬情緒狀態，此題選(A)。

14 (D)。 下列哪個問題能在文章找到答案？
(A)Ivan Goldberg博士是第一位治療網路成癮的人嗎？
(B)透過哪種醫療程序能治癒網路成癮？

解答與解析

(C)網路成癮會危及到醫治狀況嗎？

(D)什麼因素會造成網路成癮？

解 本文主旨即為網路成癮的成因，此題選(D)。

15 (B)。 根據本文，哪種人最可能罹患網路成癮症？

(A)多巴胺水平高的人。

(B)害羞且朋友少的人。

(C)快樂且對生活感到滿意的人。

(D)家人有賭博問題的人。

解 本文最後一段有提到不擅交際且內向的人罹患風險較高，此題選(B)。

109年　桃園捷運新進人員

一、閱讀測驗

　　Do you want to bolster your chances of maintaining your New Year's resolution? Then consider heeding these tips from scholars at Stanford University: we should ingrain "tiny habits" for ourselves rather than try to rework our behaviors outright. Tiny goals like "flossing one tooth" may sound like ridiculously small achievements, but broad goals like "eating healthy" are more **elusive** because they're more abstractions than achievable feats. Instead, desired behaviors incorporated as day-to-day habits are much more effective since you'll carry them out without thinking about it.

　　Keeping a scorecard could also help you track your progress since this will keep you tuned in on your efforts. It'll also create a sense of satisfaction if you manage to keep your resolution. Besides, maintaining a sense of purpose in the face of temptation is key to achieving goals; practicing mindfulness through meditation might help promote self-regulation. Last, you should keep your resolution to yourself. Announcing your goal implies a sense of completion, meaning you're less likely to follow through. Lifehacker, however, counters this suggestion, advising that you tell friends or family members. Having social support helps people achieve difficult goals and holds them accountable for following through with their resolution.

(　) **1** What is the main purpose of the passage?
　　(A)To explain the difficulty of keeping New Year's resolution.
　　(B)To illustrate the benefits of making New Year's resolution.
　　(C)To provide advice on how to stick to New Year's resolution.
　　(D)To compare New Year's resolution to a daunting task.

(　) **2** What does the word "**elusive**" in the second paragraph most likely mean?
　　(A)feasible　　　　　　　　(B)vague
　　(C)crucial　　　　　　　　 (D)apparent

(   ) **3** According to the passage, which of the following tips may have pros and cons?
(A)announce your goals to friends
(B)keep a scorecard
(C)make modest change in habits
(D)do mindfulness practice

二、字彙

(   ) **4** If you are _____ to run errands for me, just tell me. I won't force you to do things you don't want to.
(A)indifferent   (B)reluctant
(C)sympathetic   (D)willing

(   ) **5** Jenny really _____ the prize because she has spent a great amount of time and effort doing research on the cure for the rare disease.
(A)inherits   (B)manipulates
(C)retains   (D)deserves

(   ) **6** For those who do not _____ the traffic regulation, they must pay a fine of NT$1,800.
(A)abide by   (B)call for
(C)bring in   (D)depend on

(   ) **7** The door of this convenience store slides open _____ when you push the button, so you don't have to open it yourself.
(A)intentionally   (B)originally
(C)automatically   (D)frequently

(   ) **8** On Christmas day, many people have fun in gift _____ activities. They feel excited when they receive the gifts they want.
(A)exchange   (B)wrapping
(C)recruitment   (D)refund

( ) **9** Housing prices in Taipei City have soared extremely in recent years, which _____ younger households from purchasing houses there.
(A)deters
(B)alerts
(C)encourages
(D)increases

( ) **10** They went to the same high school and college. Now they even work in the same company. What a _____!
(A)probability
(B)revolution
(C)farewell
(D)coincidence

( ) **11** The actress feels very delighted and _____ to be able to work with some of the most talented and world-renowned directors.
(A)impoverished
(B)depressed
(C)frustrated
(D)privileged

( ) **12** It's difficult for people to function well when they're sleep _____. They can't focus well if they don't have enough sleep.
(A)deprived
(B)occupied
(C)replaced
(D)starved

( ) **13** No one can say with _____ certainty that the world economy will undoubtedly turn better next year. The future is unpredictable.
(A)accurate
(B)absolute
(C)additional
(D)appropriate

( ) **14** To save time in a conference, please do not talk about things that are not _____ to the main topic.
(A)relevant
(B)sensible
(C)accurate
(D)condensed

( ) **15** Reading can broaden your _____. So, read as many different kinds of books as you can.
(A)atmospheres
(B)horizons
(C)surfaces
(D)mechanisms

( ) **16** Exercising for thirty minutes is one of Anita's daily _____. She does it every day and that's how she keeps fit.
(A)accessories (B)belongings
(C)routines (D)capacities

( ) **17** For information _____, users should change their passwords at least once every three months.
(A)leakage (B)security
(C)flow (D)processing

( ) **18** It was my teacher who _____ me to study abroad, and it turned out to be the best time in my life.
(A)dissuaded (B)rescued
(C)inspired (D)conveyed

( ) **19** The contract will not be legally binding until it has been _____ agreed to by both parties.
(A)evidently (B)nearly
(C)liberally (D)formally

( ) **20** You can add the fluid to the powder, or _____, you can add the powder to the fluid.
(A)conversely (B)namely
(C)generally (D)precisely

解答與解析 答案標示為# 者，表官方曾公告更正該題答案。

一、閱讀測驗

你想要提升維持新年願望的可能性嗎？那麼參考史丹福大學學者們的建議吧：我們應該為自己內化「小習慣」，而非將我們既有的行為砍掉重練。像「用牙線清理一顆牙齒」這樣的細微目標可能聽起來小到有點可笑，但是像「健康飲食」這樣的大目標又顯得過於籠統，因為這當中抽象的成份多於可行的成果。因此，將目標行為融入每天的習慣才是比較有效的方式，因為這些行為不用特別考慮，你自然就會去做了。

使用計分卡可幫助你追蹤自己的進步歷程，因為這方法會讓你留意自己的努力，而且當你努力達成願望時，它也提供了滿足感。此外，保持目的導向不

受當前誘惑也是達成目標的關鍵；透過打坐時靜觀冥想可能有助於自我調整。最後，建議將這些願望讓自己知道即可；公開自己的目標則暗示某種成就感，意味著自己不太可能想達成目標。不過，生活黑客反對這種說法，他們建議應該要將願望告知家人親友；他們相信社群支持可幫助人們達成困難的目標，並且以負責任的態度完成他們的願望。

1 (C)。本篇短文的主要目的為何？
(A)解釋維持新年願望的困難處。
(B)說明立下新年願望的好處。
(C)提供如何堅持新年願望的建議。
(D)將新年願望比喻為艱鉅的任務。
解 本題為主旨題。文章第一段中Then consider heeding these tips from scholars at Stanford University可知作者將提供一些專家學者的建議，故選(C)。

2 (B)。第二段中的"elusive"最有可能指何意？
(A)可行的 　　(B)模糊的
(C)關鍵的 　　(D)明顯的
解 本題為字義題。該字在第一段倒數第二句，句中出現關鍵字broad「廣泛的；籠統的」及more abstractions「更多抽象事物」，可推測較接近的選項為(B)vague。

3 (A)。根據本篇短文，下列哪種建議可能有正反兩面的看法？
(A)將你的目標宣布給朋友知道
(B)使用計分卡
(C)慢慢改變習慣
(D)進行靜觀冥想

解 本題為細節題。文章中第二段Announcing your goal implies a sense of completion, meaning you're less likely to follow through. Lifehacker, however, counters this suggestion, advising that you tell friends or family members. 上述兩句說明大家對「將個人願望公告周知」的看法不一，故選(A)。

二、字彙

4 (B)。如果你不願意幫我跑腿，跟我說沒關係。我不會勉強你做不想做的事。
(A)冷漠的 　　(B)不願意的
(C)同情的 　　(D)願意的
解 本題考字義。第二句提到you don't want to，暗示這是對方「不想」做的事情，故選(B)reluctant。

5 (D)。Jenny的確該得到這份獎勵，因為她花了很多心力在研究罕見疾病的治療上面。
(A)遺傳 　　(B)操縱
(C)保持 　　(D)該得到
解 本題考字義。由文意可知，由於Jenny的付出，推知這份獎勵「應當」讓她獲得，故選(D)deserves。

6 (A)。對於那些不遵守交通規則的人，他們必定會遭受一千八百元台幣之罰款。
(A)遵守 　　(B)呼籲
(C)產生 　　(D)依靠

解 本題考字義。句中提到會遭罰款，暗示這些人不「遵守」交通規則，故選(A)abide by。

7 (C)。 當你按下按鈕時，這家超商的門會自動開啟，因此不須要手動開門。

(A)故意地　　　(B)原本地

(C)自動地　　　(D)常常地

解 本題考字義。該句說明超商的門不用手動打開，意指它可以「自動」開關，故選(C)automatically。

8 (A)。 聖誕節當天，大家喜歡玩交換禮物的活動。當他們拿到自己想要的禮物時會非常開心。

(A)交換　　　　(B)包裝

(C)招募　　　　(D)退款

解 本題考字義。由第二句when they receive the gifts they want可知大家拿到的不是自己的禮物，暗示禮物透過「交換」的方式進行，故選(A)exchange。

9 (A)。 台北市房價這幾年漲得很離譜，這也阻止了年輕家庭在那裡買房子。

(A)阻止　　　　(B)警告

(C)鼓勵　　　　(D)增加

解 本題考字義。本句提到北市房價大漲，常理推論年輕家庭所得有限，可能對在那裡購屋產生「卻步」，故選(A)deters。

10 (D)。 他們上同一所高中及大學，甚至目前還在同一家公司上班。這真是巧合！

(A)可能性　　　(B)革命

(C)道別　　　　(D)巧合

解 本題考字義。文意描述兩人念書及工作機構皆相同，暗示這屬於「巧合」的情況，故選(D)coincidence。

11 (D)。 能跟一些有才華的國際知名導演合作，這位女演員感到十分開心及榮幸。

(A)貧困的　　　(B)沮喪的

(C)挫折的　　　(D)榮幸的

解 本題考字義。句中提到跟國際名導合作，推知以正面的詞彙描述女演員心情較合理，故選(D)privileged。

12 (A)。 當人們睡眠被剝奪時，就很難正常運作；他們如果睡眠不足，就無法集中專注力。

(A)剝奪　　　　(B)佔據

(C)取代　　　　(D)飢餓

解 本題考字義。第二句關鍵詞don't have enough sleep暗示睡眠品質被「剝奪」，故選(A)deprived。

13 (B)。 沒有人能絕對肯定明年全球經濟一定會好轉。

(A)正確的　　　(B)絕對的

(C)額外的　　　(D)適當的

解 本題考字義。句中say with certainty表示「肯定地說」，而absolute則適合用來修飾certainty的程度，故選(B)。

14 (A)。 為了把握研討會的時間，請勿討論跟主題不相關的事情。

(A)相關的　　　　　(B)明智的

(C)正確的　　　　　(D)濃縮的

解 本題考字義。該題前句提到研討會時間有限，引導出後句希望只針對「相關」議題討論，以免時間不夠用，故選(A)relevant。

15 **(B)**。閱讀可以開拓你的視野，因此盡可能地廣泛閱讀吧！

(A)氣氛　　　　　(B)視野

(C)表面　　　　　(D)機制

解 本題考字義。文意表示鼓勵大家多閱讀，推知閱讀可打開人的「視野」，故選(B)horizons。

16 **(C)**。Anita每天固定作息之一就是運動半小時；她靠天天運動保持身材。

(A)配件　　　　　(B)財物

(C)例行事務　　　(D)能力

解 本題考字義。由句中關鍵詞daily及every day可知運動是Anita「固定從事」的項目，故選(C)routines。

17 **(B)**。基於資訊安全考量，網路使用者應該至少每三個月更換一次密碼。

(A)洩漏　　　　　(B)安全

(C)流動　　　　　(D)處理

解 本題考字義。該句提到應定期更換密碼，表示這行為目的為保障資訊「安全」，故選(B)security。

18 **(C)**。鼓勵我出國念書的人是我的老師，結果這成為我人生最棒的時光。

(A)勸阻　　　　　(B)解救

(C)鼓勵　　　　　(D)傳達

解 本題考字義。從本句關鍵詞to study abroad及the best time in my life推知老師對作者採取較正向的行為，故選(C)inspired。

19 **(D)**。這份合約在未經雙方正式同意之前，都不具有合法的效力。

(A)明顯地　　　　(B)幾乎地

(C)自由地　　　　(D)正式地

解 本題考字義。該句說明合約只有在雙方都「正式」認可後才開始生效，故選(D)formally。

20 **(A)**。你可以將液體倒入粉末中；反之，你也可以將粉末倒入液體中。

(A)相反地　　　　(B)也就是

(C)一般地　　　　(D)精確地

解 本題考上下文。由題目的文意可知前後兩句呈現相對關係，操作順序正好相反，故選(A)conversely。

解答與解析

109年 桃園捷運新進人員（第二次）

一、字彙、文法

(　　) **1** That rich man is very _____. He never donates even a penny to those in need.
(A)stingy
(B)generous
(C)irritable
(D)humble

(　　) **2** These drills will _____ you with the skills needed in carrying out the task through repeated practice.
(A)alienate
(B)familiarize
(C)disconnect
(D)distinguish

(　　) **3** Before you sign a _____, read "terms of agreement" carefully to ensure that your rights are protected.
(A)contract
(B)resume
(C)reference
(D)petition

(　　) **4** The financial crisis we faced was difficult to deal with, but experienced managers _____ came up with a solution after a thorough discussion.
(A)currently
(B)eventually
(C)originally
(D)initially

(　　) **5** This is a secret between you and me. Please do not _____ it to other people.
(A)conceal
(B)instill
(C)guard
(D)reveal

(　　) **6** If the relation between the two countries keeps _____, they may sever all the diplomatic links.
(A)strengthening
(B)deteriorating
(C)restoring
(D)establishing

diving for food, so it's unlikely that an eel would jump into the nose of a seal. The other idea scientists were considering was vomiting, but again it's unlikely that an eel would have been pushed through the nasal cavity.

Littman has another idea. It seems that juvenile seals may not be all that different from human teenagers. It may be a "teenage trend"—one seal accidentally got an eel up its nose, and then others started copying it because they thought it was "cool." There's no evidence to truly back this up, but at this point, it's as good an idea as any.

(　　) **18** How many hypotheses are mentioned in this passage?
(A)one　　　　　　　　(B)two
(C)three　　　　　　　(D)four

(　　) **19** What does the word "malevolent" in the second paragraph most likely mean?
(A)considerate　　　　(B)diligent
(C)vicious　　　　　　(D)amiable

(　　) **20** What can be inferred from the passage?
(A)Juvenile monk seals may imitate others because they think it's fashionable.
(B)None of the monk seals who had eels stuck in their nostril survived
(C)Young monk seals cannot swim with their nostrils shut.
(D)No more monk seals will be found with an eel up their nose because it is dangerous.

解答與解析　答案標示為# 者，表官方曾公告更正該題答案。

一、字彙、文法

1 (A)。那個有錢人非常吝嗇，他對窮人幾乎是一毛不拔。
(A)吝嗇的　　　(B)大方的
(C)煩躁的　　　(D)謙虛的

解 本題考字義。其中第二句提到 He never donates...，表示其特質為小氣吝嗇，故選(A)stingy。

2 (B)。透過反覆練習，這些演練會讓你熟悉執行任務時所需的技能。

(A)疏遠　　　　　(B)使熟悉
(C)切斷　　　　　(D)分辨

解 本題考字義。由文中最後關鍵詞repeated practice推知本句強調熟能生巧的概念,故選(B)familiarize。

3 (A)。在你簽約之前,記得先仔細看過協議條款,以確保你的權益。
(A)合約　　　　　(B)履歷
(C)參考書目　　　(D)請願書

解 本題考字義。該句中出現terms of agreement推測應為契約相關文件,因此較接近的選項為(A)contract。

4 (B)。我們面臨到棘手的財務危機,但資深經理們最後在充分討論後想出了解決辦法。
(A)目前地　　　　(B)最後地
(C)原本地　　　　(D)開始地

解 本題考上下文。前一句提到difficult to deal with,後一句提到but... a solution,表示事件隨著時間推移有了轉變,故選(B)eventually。

5 (D)。這是我們之間的祕密,請別讓其他人知道。
(A)隱藏　　　　　(B)灌輸
(C)捍衛　　　　　(D)透露

解 本題考字義。其中第一句關鍵詞a secret between you and me暗示不能讓其他人知道,故正解為(D)reveal。

6 (B)。如果這兩國的關係持續惡化,他們可能會切斷所有的外交連結。
(A)強化　　　　　(B)惡化
(C)恢復　　　　　(D)建立

解 本題考字義。由後半句關鍵詞sever ... links推知雙方國家關係應該變差,故選(B)deteriorating。

7 (C)。早點睡吧,不然你隔天精神會變差。
(A)因此　　　　　(B)然而
(C)否則　　　　　(D)但是

解 本題考上下文。文中第一句提到早睡,第二句提到隔天沒精神,前後兩句呈對比關係,暗示如果不早睡會帶來的可能後果,故選(C)otherwise。

8 (A)。Emily的醫生建議她要多運動讓自己更健康。
(A)做(原形動詞)
(B)做(現在式第三人稱單數動詞)
(C)做(過去式動詞)
(D)做(過去分詞)

解 本題考suggest用法。表示建議或命令的動詞,如suggest、advise等,後面所接的that子句須搭配原形動詞,因該原形動詞前方省略了助動詞should。故由空格前方suggested that ...可知後面須接原形動詞(A)do。

9 (B)。由於一直被日曬又沒擦防曬乳,Regina被曬傷了。
(A)曝曬(原形動詞)
(B)曝曬(過去分詞)
(C)曝曬(現在分詞)
(D)曝曬(不定詞)

解 本題考分詞構句。由於expose的意思為「使曝曬」,主詞多半為太陽或光線;而該句以人做為主

詞表示被動，故應將動詞改為過去分詞，故選(B)Exposed。

10 (A)。有的研究顯示出有正面效果，然而其他的研究則無。
(A)然而　　　　(B)所以
(C)因為　　　　(D)也不
解 本題考上下文。由該題的前後兩句文意相反，推知兩者為對比關係，故較合適的選項為(A)while。

11 (D)。Steve很清楚表示他收集的公仔是非賣品，因為他非常珍惜。
(A)探索　　　　(B)操作
(C)組織　　　　(D)珍惜
解 本題考字義。從文中的關鍵詞not for sale表示Steve對公仔的態度是正向的，故選(D)treasured。

12 (B)。這名政治家要求這報社為不實的報導道歉，該報導影射他接受了富商的賄賂。
(A)適當的　　　(B)不正確的
(C)真正的　　　(D)誠懇的
解 本題考字義。該句出現apologize及後半段提到的負面報導，表示修飾該報導的形容詞為負面字義的可能性較高，故選(B)incorrect。

13 (C)。小孩的注意力很短；也就是說，他們無法專注在某件事物上太久。
(A)力氣　　　　(B)儲存
(C)時間長度　　(D)設定
解 本題考字義。其中後半句最後出現for a long time推知主題跟時間長度有關，故較合理的選項為(C)span。

14 (B)。Tiffany兩個月前升為秘書長；前一位秘書長則因政治醜聞而辭職。
(A)挖空的　　　(B)空缺的
(C)有彈性的　　(D)遙遠的
解 本題考字義。該題第一句提到promoted to...而第二句提到The former ... resigned ... ，暗示前一位辭職後的職缺由Tiffany接任，故選(B)vacant。

15 (A)。這病毒不會只出現在老年人身上，統計顯示老少人口病毒感染人數近期都達到高峰，主要在20至39歲年齡層之間。
(A)侷限　　　　(B)保證
(C)孤立　　　　(D)佔據
解 本題考字義。文中前半句雖提到the elderly，但後半句提到年輕及老年人患者數量都很多，暗示老年人非唯一的族群，故選(A)confined。

16 (C)。對於恐怖份子的攻擊，政府在機場及火車站採取更嚴謹的安檢措施。
(A)組成　　　　(B)離開
(C)檢查　　　　(D)執行
解 本題考字義。由前半句出現的關鍵字terrorist attacks推測政府將嚴加戒備此現象，故應會加強大眾運輸的安全及篩檢管制，因此選(C)screening為正解。

17 (C)。Josh的不安全感，可能來自童年目睹雙親不斷肢體衝突的悲慘經驗。
(A)履行　　　　(B)分離
(C)來自　　　　(D)阻止

解 本題考字義。該題空格前面提到 sense of insecurity，後面提到 tragic childhood experience，暗示前後兩者為因果關係，且後面的原因產生前面的結果，故選(C)spring。

二、閱讀測驗

　　幾年前，一位研究夏威夷僧海豹計畫的頂尖科學家查爾斯‧李南（Charles Littnan），收到一則不尋常的電子郵件，而標題只有簡短的三個字：鼻子裡的鰻魚。在幾次信件來回之後，李南了解有一隻鰻魚在海豹的鼻子裡。當研究者試著把鰻魚從海豹的鼻孔中移除，並將這件事視為一個罕見的意外；但這件事又連續發生了幾次，次數多到排除單一個案的可能。事實上，這件事直到最近才被報導，更令人不解的是，這只發生在未成年的海豹身上。

　　然而，有些關於這種奇怪行為的理論已經被排除了。這個島嶼相當偏遠，只有生物學家來過，不可能是人為的惡意造成；海豹的鼻孔在潛水覓食時是關閉的，因此鰻魚不太可能跳進海豹的鼻子裡；科學家想到的另一個可能性是嘔吐，但是同樣地，鰻魚不太可能被推進鼻腔中。

　　李南則有不同的想法。未成年的海豹或許和人類青少年階段相似，這或許是青少年的潮流－－一隻海豹不小心將一隻鰻魚困在鼻腔中，其它海豹因為覺得這很「酷」所以開始仿效。目前雖然尚未有證據可支持這說法，但就目前為止，它是最能夠解釋的理論。

18 (D)。 本篇短文提到幾項假設？
(A)一項　　　　　(B)兩項
(C)三項　　　　　(D)四項
解 本題為推論題。其中文章第一段提到一種假設，第二段則說明其他科學家所提的兩項理論，最後一段則為李南本人的另一個假設，因此本文共提到四項假設，故選(D)。

19 (C)。 第二段中的"malevolent"最有可能指何意？
(A)體貼的　　　　(B)勤勞的
(C)惡意的　　　　(D)親切的
解 本題為字義題。該字出現在第二段第二行... couldn't be the hand of a malevolent human中，否定句表示它們不可能落入人類手中，暗示malevolent最有可能為負面的語詞，故選(C)。

20 (A)。 本篇短文可推論哪項敘述？
(A)未成年僧海豹可能有模仿的習性，因為牠們覺得很酷。
(B)只要鼻孔有鰻魚卡住的僧海豹，最後都無法存活。
(C)年輕僧海豹游泳時無法關閉鼻孔。
(D)之後不會再發現有僧海豹的鼻孔有鰻魚卡住，因為這情況是危險的。
解 本題為推論題。從文章中第三段第二行...others started copying it because they thought it was "cool"推知未成年海豹可能也有類似人類模仿及認知的行為模式，而(B)(C)(D)選項的敘述在文章中並無提到，故選(A)。

109年 臺灣菸酒從業評價職位人員

一、字彙

( ) **1** In the movie, the _____ of all mankind, to live or to die, is counting on this superhero.
(A)fate　　　　　　　(B)scar
(C)pace　　　　　　　(D)muse

( ) **2** My niece screamed in _____ on seeing her birthday gift—AirPods she had dreamed of receiving.
(A)peace　　　　　　　(B)terror
(C)sorrow　　　　　　(D)delight

( ) **3** As the violent typhoon raged on, we were _____ in the house, unable to go anywhere.
(A)reserved　　　　　(B)confined
(C)absorbed　　　　　(D)inspected

( ) **4** As the head _____ of this award-winning restaurant, Archie is always creating new recipes.
(A)chef　　　　　　　(B)maid
(C)butler　　　　　　(D)customer

( ) **5** Before sharing news, search online for facts and _____ the information so that you won't become one who spreads misinformation.
(A)adore　　　　　　(B)verify
(C)expose　　　　　　(D)predict

( ) **6** Anna found it hard to adjust to the _____ climate when she moved to Thailand. The heat was too strong to bear.
(A)smooth　　　　　　(B)tropical
(C)pleasant　　　　　(D)changing

(   ) **7** Considering consumers' tighter budget, Apple is expected to release a more _____ model this spring.
(A)essential   (B)conscious
(C)affordable   (D)prosperous

(   ) **8** As the government is stepping up efforts to put the disease under control, the tourist industry is _____ resuming business.
(A)suddenly   (B)gradually
(C)randomly   (D)frequently

二、文法測驗

(   ) **9** The singer Elton John apologized to his fans after he lost his voice and _____ to cut a concert short.
(A)forced   (B)had forced
(C)was forced   (D)was forcing

(   ) **10** Allen looked upset when he gazed at the picture, _____? I wonder what he was thinking about then.
(A)did he   (B)was he
(C)didn't he   (D)wasn't he

(   ) **11** Your brother seems to have a crush on the girl _____ father owns the restaurant across the road.
(A)who   (B)whom
(C)which   (D)whose

(   ) **12** All you need to do when preparing for big exams _____ study hard and do enough practices.
(A)is   (B)to
(C)are   (D)will

(   ) **13** _____, the more mental workouts you get. That is, regular reading keeps your brain active.
(A)You often read more   (B)You read more often
(C)The more you often read   (D)The more often you read

( ) **14** _____ the spread of COVID-19, one must ensure that their hands are free from germs. Washing hands with soap and water is the most effective.

(A)Prevent (B)To prevent

(C)Preventing (D)By preventing

( ) **15** Willy is filled with regrets. If he _____ smoking years ago, he might not have lung cancer now.

(A)quit (B)had quit

(C)would quit (D)would have quit

三、克漏字測驗

Young smokers beware: On Monday, it became illegal in Iowa for anyone under 18 to smoke a cigarette. If ____16____ smoking, chewing or even possessing tobacco by the police, an under-aged offender could be ____17____ as much as $100, yanked off the street or out of the shopping mall and taken home in the backseat of a police car. The law is part of the state's campaign to ____18____ tobacco use greatly among all Iowans. The police are ordered to enforce the law, but some are skeptical. On their long list of priorities, this measure shares a spot with the neighbor's cat stuck in a tree. "We're ____19____ busy to enforce a law like that," said the Des Moines Police Department. Forty-four states have laws that ban selling cigarettes to minors or ____20____ minors from possessing tobacco, but these laws are rarely enforced.

( ) **16** (A)catch (B)caught (C)catching (D)to be caught

( ) **17** (A)given (B)rewarded (C)fined (D)frowned

( ) **18** (A)reduce (B)increase (C)allow (D)perform

( ) **19** (A)very (B)much (C)too (D)extremely

( ) **20** (A)encourage (B)prohibit (C)let (D)take

四、閱讀測驗

　　I am one of those people who spend much time in coffeehouses talking to and observing others. One time I met half a dozen gentlemen who were talking about the different kinds of people in Europe. One of these men stated that he had all of the wonderful qualities of the English in his person. He went on to say that the Dutch were all greedy and hungry for money. The French were not to be trusted. The Germans were a bunch of drunks. The Spanish were too proud. In bravery, kindness, generosity, and every other virtue the English were better than the rest of the world.

　　The rest of the company, all Englishmen, accepted his statements as truth. I sat there and said nothing, so a companion of mine asked me if what that man said was not true. I replied that I could not judge until I had spent some time in those countries. Perhaps I might find that the Dutch were thrifty and saved their money, that the French were very polite, that the Germans are hard-working, that the Spanish were very calm and quite, and even that the English, although brave and generous, might be too bold and free-swinging when things went well and too sad when they did not. Soon after I said this, I lost the goodwill of my companions, and they all left me alone.

　　I paid my bill and went home. There I began to think about the silliness of national prejudice. I thought of the ancient wise man, when asked the country of his citizenship, replied that he was a "citizen of the world." We have now become so English, French, Dutch, Spanish, or German that we are no longer citizens of the world. We are so much the citizens of one small society that we no longer think of ourselves as members of that grand society that includes all of humankind.

(　　) **21** Which of the following would be the most appropriate title for the passage?
　　(A)Coffee Shops in Europe　　(B)Story of an Ancient Wise Man
　　(C)Citizen of the World　　(D)Prejudice against Gentlemen

(　　) **22** Where did the author meet these English gentlemen?
　　(A)At a steak house.　　(B)At a barbershop.
　　(C)At a theater.　　(D)At a coffeehouse.

( ) **23** Of the following counties, which was **NOT** mentioned in the passage?

(A)France　　　　　(B)Denmark

(C)Germany　　　　(D)Spain

( ) **24** According to the passage, which of the following statements is true?

(A)The author did not talk to others in coffeehouses.

(B)The English gentlemen did not like what the author said and left.

(C)These gentlemen all agreed on the good qualities of other nations.

(D)The author went home without paying the coffeehouse.

( ) **25** Which of the following ideas is supported by the passage?

(A)National prejudice prevents us from being part of all humankind.

(B)The Englishmen are not citizens of the world.

(C)The Dutch do not get along with the French.

(D)The English are flawless and are far better than others.

解答與解析　答案標示為#者，表官方曾公告更正該題答案。

一、字彙

1 (A)。在這部電影中，人類生死存亡的命運都仰賴這位超級英雄。

(A)命運　　　　(B)瘡疤

(C)速度　　　　(D)靈感

解 本題考字義。從句中關鍵詞to live or to die及counting on this superhero表示只有該超級英雄能掌握全人類的「命運」，故選(A)fate。

2 (D)。我姪女看到生日禮物時開心地尖叫—她夢寐以求的藍芽無線耳機。

(A)和平　　　　(B)驚恐

(C)悲傷　　　　(D)開心

解 本題考字義。該句提到seeing her birthday gift及had dreamed of 推知姪女當下的心情應該非常「開心」，故選(D)delight。

3 (B)。當颱風正猛烈地肆虐時，我們被困在家中無法外出。

(A)保留　　　　(B)侷限

(C)吸收　　　　(D)檢查

解 本題考字義。本題後半句同位格 unable to go anywhere描述這些人應被「困」在某空間裡無法出門，故選(B)confined。

4 (A)。身為這家得獎餐廳的大廚，Archie總是發明新的食譜。

(A)廚師　　　　　(B)女僕
(C)管家　　　　　(D)顧客

解 本題考字義。由句中的關鍵詞 the head、restaurant及creating new recipes暗示Archie的身分應為「廚師」，故選(A)chef。

5 (B)。 在分享訊息之前，先上網搜尋真相並確認資訊，才不會變成散播假訊息的人。
(A)愛慕　　　　　(B)證實
(C)曝露　　　　　(D)預測

解 本題考字義。該句後半段提到you won't become one who spreads misinformation推測前半段說明我們該「確認」資訊的真實性，故選(B)verify。

6 (B)。 Anna移居泰國時，她發現很難適應熱帶氣候；那裡天氣熱到讓她受不了。
(A)平順的　　　　(B)熱帶的
(C)宜人的　　　　(D)改變的

解 本題考字義。由文中第二句The heat was too strong to bear. 可知該國應屬「熱帶型」氣候，故選(B)tropical。

7 (C)。 考量顧客的荷包縮水，蘋果公司可望在今年春季推出較平價的款式。
(A)基本的　　　　(B)有意識的
(C)買得起的　　　(D)繁榮的

解 本題考字義。句子前半段出現關鍵字consumers' tighter budget，推知後半段介紹的產品應會提

到有關價位的訊息，故選(C) affordable。

8 (B)。 當政府正努力控制疾病的同時，旅遊業也逐漸復甦中。
(A)突然地　　　　(B)漸漸地
(C)隨機地　　　　(D)常常地

解 本題考字義。該題說明隨著政府努力控制疾病，旅遊業景氣也「逐漸」回溫，因此較適合的選項為(B)gradually。

二、文法測驗

9 (C)。 歌手艾爾頓·強在演唱會上因失聲而被迫縮短表演時間後，他跟歌迷們道歉。
(A)強迫（過去式）
(B)已強迫（過去完成式）
(C)被強迫（過去式被動）
(D)正強迫（過去進行式）

解 本題考被動式。本句後半段提到歌手失聲的因素，因此表演時間縮短的決定是不得已的結果，故選(C)was forced。

10 (C)。 Allen在看這張照片時，看起來好像不快樂，不是嗎？我不知道他當時在想什麼。
(A)是嗎（過去式助動詞）
(B)是嗎（過去式be動詞）
(C)不是嗎（過去式助動詞）
(D)不是嗎（過去式be動詞）

解 本題考附加問句。逗點前方的主要子句Allen looked upset...為過去式一般動詞的肯定直述句，可

判斷附加問句須為時態一致的否定疑問句，故選(C)didn't he。

11 (D)。你哥似乎對這女孩有好感，而她爸爸在對街有一家餐廳。
(A)她（表示人的關代主格）
(B)她（表示人的關代受格）
(C)那個（表示物的關代主／受格）
(D)她的（表示人／物的關代所有格）

解 本題考關係代名詞。由該子句先行詞the girl及空格後father owns the restaurant可推知兩者屬於所有格關係，也就是the girl's father owns the restaurant，故選(D)whose。

12 (A)。當準備大考時，你需要做的就是努力唸書及充分練習。
(A)是（be動詞單數形）
(B)朝向；對著
(C)是（be動詞複數形）
(D)將會

解 本題考主要動詞之判斷。雖然空格後出現study hard and do enough practices兩件事，但依文意仍當作一個單位，意即將all視為everything，故選(A)is。

13 (D)。你越常閱讀，你就越能鍛鍊思考；也就是說，經常閱讀讓大腦保持靈活。
(A)你常多閱讀　　(B)你更常閱讀
(C)你越常多閱讀　(D)你越常閱讀

解 本題考形容詞雙重比較級。該句型的結構為「the形容詞/副詞比較 +（主詞+動詞）」，依照上述句型所述，較合語法的選項為(D)The more often you read。

14 (B)。為了預防新冠病毒擴散，每個人都要確保雙手沒有細菌；使用肥皂洗手是最有效的方式。
(A)預防（動詞原形）
(B)為了預防（不定詞）
(C)預防（現在分詞）
(D)藉由預防（介詞+現在分詞）

解 本題考不定詞。句中敘述保持雙手清潔之「目的」在於防止病毒擴散，因此前半句應以不定詞開頭表達目的，故選(B)To prevent。

15 (B)。Willy現在後悔萬分；他幾年前如果戒菸的話，現在可能就不會得肺癌了。
(A)戒掉　　　　　(B)之前已戒掉
(C)將會戒掉　　　(D)當時就會戒掉

解 本題考假設語法。文中第二句後半段提到he might not have lung cancer now，表示Willy之前已有抽菸的習慣，且已得肺炎，而該假設法類型為與過去事實相反，須以過去完成式had V-pp表達，故選(B)had quit。

三、克漏字測驗

年輕的吸菸族群請注意：從週一起，愛荷華州將未滿十八歲吸菸視為違法行為。如果未滿十八歲且被警方抓到抽菸、咀嚼或甚至持有香菸者，可能會被開罰美金一百元，並強行從街上或

購物中心坐警車回家，該州也已立法希望州民能大量減少香菸的使用。雖然警方被下令要確實執法，但一些警察仍持懷疑的態度；在警方的一長串執法待辦項目中，這部分就跟處理「鄰居的貓卡在樹上」一樣瑣碎。德梅因警局表示：「我們忙到沒辦法執行這樣的法律」。儘管全美有44州都明文規定禁止賣菸給未成年者及禁止他們持有香菸，但警察卻很少強制執行這些法令。

16 (B)。 (A)抓到（動詞原形）
(B)抓到（過去分詞）
(C)抓到（現在分詞）
(D)抓到（不定詞被動）
解 本題考分詞構句。原句可還原為
If she/he is caught smoking...，由
於前後句子主詞相同，故可將連
接詞if引導的該句主詞省略，並
依語態將動詞改為被動的V-pp形
式，因此選(B)。

17 (C)。 (A)被給予　(B)獲獎　(C)被
罰　(D)被看不慣
解 本題考字義。該句主詞為offender
「違法者」，後面又提到as much
as $100，可推知本題說明違法者
的處罰方式，故選(C)。

18 (A)。 (A)減少　(B)增加　(C)允許
(D)表現
解 本題考字義。本句敘述該州立
法的目的即在「減少」州民香
菸的使用量，依照句意可知答
案選(A)。

19 (C)。 (A)非常　(B)許多　(C)太
(D)極端地
解 本題考慣用語詞。too busy to
enforce...表示「忙到無法嚴格執
行……」之意，故選(C)，其餘
選項無相關搭配用法。

20 (B)。 (A)鼓勵　(B)禁止　(C)讓
(D)帶著
解 本題考字義。依據空格前的關
鍵字ban「禁止」及後面出現的
possessing tobacco「持有香菸」
可推測該句為描述有關香菸的禁
令，故選(B)。

四、閱讀測驗

　　我習慣花時間坐在咖啡廳跟人聊天及觀察人群。有一次我遇到六位男士聊到不同類型的歐洲人，其中一位提到英國人集所有優點於一身，他接著說荷蘭人貪心且愛錢、法國人不可靠、德國人一堆酒鬼、西班牙人太驕傲，而英國人在勇敢、仁慈、大方等美德上都優於其他國家。

　　其他五位英國男士聽了都表示有道理。我坐在那邊不發一語，因此其中一位同行友人便問我他說的哪部分並非如此；我回答無法判斷，除非我在那國家待一段時間。或許我可能認為荷蘭人很節省、法國人很有禮貌、德國人工作勤奮、西班牙人很淡定，而英國人雖然勇敢且大方，但太容易受到外界事物的變化而影響心情；我一說完後，同行友人們便悻悻然地離開咖啡廳，留我一人在那邊。

我結帳後就回家了，我開始想到國家偏見有多愚蠢；想起某位古代智者說過：假如有人問你是哪一國人，就回答「世界公民」。我們都太執著在英國人、法國人、荷蘭人、西班牙人或德國人的刻版印象，以至於讓自己不再是世界公民；我們都太把自己放在小團體中，而忘了我們都是這世界大家庭的一份子。

21 (C)。下列何者最適合作為本篇短文的標題？
(A)歐洲的咖啡店
(B)一位古代智者的故事
(C)世界公民
(D)對紳士的偏見
解 本題為主旨題。文章最後一段提到作者對那次經驗的反思，並兩次強調citizen of the world之重要性，因此較合適的答案為(C)。

22 (D)。作者在哪裡遇到這群英國男士？
(A)牛排館　　　(B)理髮店
(C)戲院　　　　(D)咖啡廳
解 本題為細節題。文章第一段提到I am one of those people who spend much time in coffeehouses... One time I met half a dozen gentlemen who were...可知作者當時在咖啡遇到這六位男士。

23 (B)。本篇短文沒有提到下列哪個國家？
(A)法國　　　　(B)丹麥
(C)德國　　　　(D)西班牙

解 本題為細節題。文章中每一段皆提到English、Dutch、French、German、Spanish，唯獨沒提到Denmark「丹麥」，故選(B)。

24 (B)。根據本篇短文，下列何者為真？
(A)作者在咖啡廳沒有跟其他人說話。
(B)這群英國男士不喜歡作者所說的，之後便離開了。
(C)這群男士都認同其他國家好的特質。
(D)作者沒付錢給咖啡廳就回家了。
解 本題為除外題。(A)由I am one of those people who spend much time in coffeehouses talking to and observing others. 可知作者會在咖啡廳跟人聊天；(C)由The rest of the company...accepted his statements as truth. 提到這群男士認同的是對其他國家的偏見；(D)由I paid my bill and went home. 可知作者在咖啡廳付了錢才回家；而文中第二段最後一句Soon after I said this, I lost the goodwill of my companions, and they all left me alone. 說明作者的言論讓同行的友人們聽了之後不歡而散，符合文章所敘述，故選(B)。

25 (A)。本篇短文支持下列哪項論點？
(A)對國家的偏見，讓我們無法成為全人類的一份子。
(B)英國人不是世界公民。
(C)荷蘭人跟法國人合不來。
(D)英國人毫無缺點，且遠遠優於其他國家人民。

解 本題為細節題。(B)並沒說明英國人非世界公民;(C)並未提到荷蘭人跟法國人的相處問題;(D)此敘述為其中一位英國男士的看法,不代表本篇文章的立場;而從文章第三段最後一句 We are so much the citizens of one small society that we no longer think of ourselves as members of that grand society that includes all of humankind. 可推知一般人對世界各國仍有狹隘的刻版印象,因此無法有國際觀的心胸,故選(A)。

109年 臺灣菸酒從業職員

一、字彙

( ) **1** Ever since she watched that horror movie, Irene has being suffering from _____.
(A)diseases   (B)thrills
(C)nightmares   (D)wounds

( ) **2** Many major news stations have been _____ the presidential debates live on the evening news.
(A)televising   (B)condensing
(C)commemorating   (D)persuading

( ) **3** _____ from working overtime for three days, Justin slept for almost twelve hours.
(A)Lingered   (B)Occupied
(C)Exhausted   (D)Troubled

( ) **4** Due to global warming, many natural disasters have become more _____ and have resulted in more damage and losses.
(A)drastic   (B)drowsy
(C)memorable   (D)ineffective

( ) **5** Forgetting to have his coat with him, the man _____ in the heavy snow while waiting for the bus.
(A)refused   (B)shivered
(C)behaved   (D)exploded

( ) **6** The parcel was mailed last Monday. It _____ arrived last week, but we haven't received it until now.
(A)inevitably   (B)eventually
(C)apparently   (D)supposedly

( ) **7** The airline tickets are non-exchangeable; they cannot be _____ for cash, but you may be able to apply its value toward a future flight.
(A)released (B)respected
(C)rehearsed (D)redeemed

( ) **8** Kevin had to work extra hours in order to pay the monthly _____ for his new car.
(A)belongings (B)installments
(C)perspectives (D)establishments

二、文法測驗

( ) **9** You _____ clean your teeth twice a day to avoid tooth cavity or other problems.
(A)rather (B)do
(C)had better (D)have better

( ) **10** The company says the package was mailed two weeks ago but it _____ hasn't arrived.
(A)yet (B)still
(C)already (D)only

( ) **11** My daughter loves curry as much as her father _____.
(A)is (B)will
(C)do (D)does

( ) **12** _____ the disease is highly contagious, the government has advised the public to take cautions to protect themselves.
(A)With (B)As
(C)Whereas (D)Due to

( ) **13** The principal _____ with Tim's parents for more than half an hour. Tim is now feeling very worried.
(A)talks (B)talked
(C)has talked (D)was talking

( ) **14** Before John left for Germany, he said he would stay in contact, but he _____ called _____ wrote.
(A)both; and (B)either; or
(C)neither; nor (D)not only; but

( ) **15** As iron sharpens iron, so one person sharpens _____. From the saying, we know friends should sharpen and improve each other.
(A)other (B)another
(C)the other (D)one another

三、克漏字測驗

The sun is a huge, fiery globe of gas. Every now and then, it sends out massive waves of charged particles that hit Earth ___16.___ speeds upwards of a million kilometers an hour. These charged particles interact with our magnetic northern and southern poles, ___17.___ a breathtaking light show that enthralls all its viewers.

These light shows are known as auroras. Since Earth's magnetic field is strongest at its poles, auroras appear most brightly near the North and South Pole. They are not ___18.___ because they occur at any time of the year. Auroras appear as slowly moving curtains, bands, spots of color, and a variety of other shapes that shift across the sky. They can also exhibit more than one color at a time. The colors, ranging from purple to green, ___19.___ on the altitude of oxygen and nitrogen penetrated by solar energy. The most common color on view is green because it is at lower altitudes and people can see green the easiest. Photographing the breathtaking auroras is not difficult, but photos don't do them ___20.___. Viewing auroras is something that needs to be experienced in person.

( ) **16** (A)at (B)by (C)in (D)from
( ) **17** (A)serving as (B)checking out (C)reporting to (D)resulting in
( ) **18** (A)regional (B)seasonal (C)universal (D)normal
( ) **19** (A)to depend (B)depend (C)depending (D)dependent
( ) **20** (A)harm (B)wonders (C)justice (D)favors

四、閱讀測驗

If you've ever tried famous Taiwanese dishes Gua bao（刈包）, aka the Taiwanese hamburger, and Oyster Vermicelli Noodles（蚵仔麵線）, or the dessert which can only be best translated as ice cream burritos（花生捲冰淇淋）, you've probably eaten cilantro. Not just in Taiwanese cuisines, this plant is actually used in cuisines around the globe, including South Asian, Middle Eastern, and Latin American. Its seeds, called coriander, are found in the plant's fruit and used as a spice, and its leaves are used as an herb. It gives a fresh, citrus-like taste to foods.

Although many people think cilantro is tasty, some people hate it so much that there's even a website called ihatecilantro.com. People who don't like cilantro usually compare its taste to soap or dirt. It is likely that this widespread disgust with the herb is related to genetics. A study by an American behavioral neuroscientist in the early 2000s found that 80% of pairs of identical twins shared a common like or dislike for the herb, while fraternal twins only agreed about half of the time. In 2012, the genetic testing firm 23andMe did a study on the subject and found that about 12-14% of participants with European ancestry reported that cilantro had a soapy taste, whereas only 4-8% of Latino, East Asian, and South Asian participants did. The people who hated cilantro shared a genetic variation that affects a receptor of the gene OR6A2, which detects the compounds in cilantro's characteristic flavor.

While some people hate cilantro, it does have health benefits. Coriander can help lower cholesterol levels. Moreover, cilantro contains a natural compound that helps fight off food poisoning caused by salmonella. Cilantro's essential oils also aid in digestion. Whether you find yourself loving or hating this fragrant ingredient, there's no denying that cilantro's distinct taste has made its mark on the world.

(　　) **21** What is the main idea of this passage?
      (A)Taiwanese cuisine has made its mark on the world.
      (B)There are cultural differences in the use of cilantro.
      (C)Genes may explain likes and dislikes of a certain herb.
      (D)Using herbs creates pleasant food tastes and improves health.

( ) **22** How does the writer support the argument in the second paragraph?
(A)By sharing personal experiences.
(B)By pointing out possible problems.
(C)By giving examples in different places.
(D)By citing results from scientific studies.

( ) **23** What is true about Gua bao, Oyster Vermicelli Noodles, and Taiwanese ice cream burritos?
(A)They have a shared ingredient.
(B)They are sold at fast-food restaurants.
(C)They are very popular around the globe.
(D)They are all eaten as a dessert in Taiwan.

( ) **24** Which of the following words is NOT used to describe the taste of cilantro?
(A)spicy
(B)soapy
(C)fragrant
(D)citrus-like

( ) **25** Which of the following is **NOT** mentioned as one of cilantro's health benefits?
(A)Aiding digestion.
(B)Boosting your bones.
(C)Relieving food poisoning.
(D)Reducing cholesterol levels.

解答與解析 答案標示為# 者,表官方曾公告更正該題答案。

一、字彙

1 (C)。自從看了那部恐怖片之後,Irene便一直做惡夢。
(A)疾病
(B)激動
(C)惡夢
(D)傷口
解 本題考字義。前半句出現watched that horror movie,而後半句提示 suffering from,推知該恐怖片可能造成當事者的心理陰影,故選(C)nightmares。

2 (A)。許多大的新聞台,這陣子都在晚間新聞時段實況轉播總統辯論會。
(A)電視轉播
(B)濃縮
(C)紀念
(D)說服

解 本題考字義。由該句中關鍵詞 news stations及live on the evening news推測情境應為電視台「播放」某節目，故選(A)televising。

3 (C)。在連續加班三天後，Justin累到睡了將近十二小時。
(A)逗留　　　(B)佔據
(C)疲憊　　　(D)困擾

解 本題考字義。後半句slept for almost twelve hours推知Justin當時的精神狀態應非常「疲倦」，故選(C)exhausted。

4 (A)。由於全球暖化現象，許多天災變得更劇烈且帶來更多傷亡。
(A)劇烈的　　　(B)想睡的
(C)難忘的　　　(D)無效的

解 本題考字義。由關鍵詞resulted in more damage and losses可知本句描述天災已到了「極端」氣候的程度，故選(A)drastic。

5 (B)。因為忘記帶大衣，這名男子在大雪中等公車時全身發抖。
(A)拒絕　　　(B)顫抖
(C)表現　　　(D)爆炸

解 本題考字義。由文中提到 forgetting to have his coat及in the heavy snow兩個詞組，該名男士當下應該會冷到「發抖」，故選(B)shivered。

6 (D)。包裹上週一寄出，照理說上週就已送達了，但我們現在才收到。
(A)難免地　　　(B)最後地
(C)顯然地　　　(D)據推測

解 本題考上下文關係。從第一句 was mailed last Monday至第二句前半arrived last week，推測前後兩句為承接關係，在理論上是合邏輯的，故選(D)supposedly。

7 (D)。航空公司的機票是無法轉移的，它們無法折現，但可以在之後搭機時使用。
(A)釋放　　　(B)尊敬
(C)排練　　　(D)兌換

解 本題考字義。該題主詞為the airline tickets，中間一句提到 cannot be ... for cash，暗示機票跟現金之間無法進行「移轉或兌換」，故選(D)redeemed。

8 (B)。為了要負擔買新車的每月分期費用，Kevin不得不加班。
(A)財物　　　(B)分期付款
(C)觀點　　　(D)機構

解 本題考字義。句中提及pay the monthly ... for his new car，表示Kevin買新車需要付每月的車貸，故選(B)installments。

二、文法測驗

9 (C)。你最好一天清理牙齒兩次，以避免蛀牙或其他問題。
(A)寧可　　(B)做
(C)最好　　(D)最好（無此用法）

解 本題考慣用語詞。文意中針對牙齒保健之方法提出建議，故較合適的選項為(C)had better；此為固定用法，且並無(D)have better這樣的句型。

10 (B)。 公司說包裹兩週前已寄出，但目前仍未送達。

(A)但是、尚未　　(B)仍然
(C)已經　　　　　(D)只有

解 本題考上下文關係。本文前句提到was mailed two weeks ago，後句則敘述but it...hasn't arrived，前後兩句為轉折關係，推知包裹應仍未送達，故選(B)still；而(A)yet雖然有「然而、尚未」之意，但在本句後半段應改為but yet it hasn't arrived或but it hasn't arrived yet較合語法。

11 (D)。 我女兒跟她爸爸一樣都愛咖哩。

(A)是（be動詞單數形）
(B)將會（未來式）
(C)是（助動詞複數形）
(D)是（助動詞單數形）

解 本題考動詞之判斷。本句前半段動詞loves為一般動詞之現在簡單式，而後半句主詞her father為第三人稱單數，故依照其時態及主詞屬性應選(D)does。

12 (B)。 因為這疾病傳染力很強，因此政府已呼籲大眾採取謹慎措施以自我保護。

(A)有了　　　　　(B)既然
(C)然而　　　　　(D)由於

解 本題考上下文關係。由前半句的疾病現況及後半句的政府對策，可知兩句屬於因果關係，故選(B)As；而(D)Due to後面應接名詞，而非完整句子。

13 (C)。 校長已經跟Tim的爸媽談了超過半小時，Tim目前感到非常擔心。

(A)談話（現在式）
(B)談話（過去式）
(C)已經談（現在完成式）
(D)正在談（過去進行式）

解 本題考動詞時態。由第一句時間副詞for more than half an hour可知該句時態應為完成式（had/has＋V-pp），因此合適的選項為(C)has talked。

14 (C)。 John去德國前，他說會保持聯絡；不過他後來沒回電也沒寫信。

(A)兩者都　　　　(B)兩者任一
(C)兩者皆無　　　(D)不但……而且

解 本題考上下文關係。前半句提到John出國前答應會保持聯繫，後半句出現連接詞but，表示答應的事情都沒做到；依題意判斷，合理的答案為(C)neither ... nor ...。

15 (B)。 鐵磨鐵更利，而一個人也可磨塑另一個人；此格言告訴我們，朋友間應該要互相磨練彼此成長。

(A)其他
(B)另一個（非限定）
(C)另一個（限定）
(D)互相

解 本題考不定代名詞。本句並無設定總共有幾人，屬非限定；而非限定中的分開描述時用one... another，故選(B)。至於(D)的句子表達須改為They sharpen one another.「他們之間互相磨練彼此」才合乎語法。

解答與解析

三、克漏字測驗

　　太陽是一顆巨大的、充滿氣體的火球。有時它會將強大的帶電粒子波，以百萬公里的時速撞擊地球。這些帶電粒子跟地球的南北極產生電磁作用後，就成為迷人的光芒秀了。

　　這些光芒秀就是我們熟知的極光。由於地球兩極的磁場最強，極光在靠近兩極時也最亮；極光的形成非季節性的，因為它們一年四季隨時都會出現。極光劃過天際時形狀不一，有的像緩慢飄動的幕簾，有的則像帶狀物或光點；它們一次可產生不只一種顏色，從紫色到綠色都有，就看氧和氮被太陽能穿透後所在的高度而定。極光最常見的顏色是綠色，因為它出現的高度最低，且一般人也比較容易看到綠色；雖然拍下令人驚豔的極光畫面並不難，但照片的呈現效果仍有落差，欣賞極光需要親自體驗會比較好。

16 (A)。(A)在……；以……
　　(B)藉由……
　　(C)在……裡面
　　(D)從……
　　解 本題考介詞。at speeds of ... 為慣用語，表示「以……的速度」之意，其餘選項無相關搭配用法，故選(A)。

17 (D)。(A)擔任　(B)看看　(C)報告
　　(D)導致
　　解 本題考字義。該句提到帶電粒子跟地球南北極產生作用，因此「導致」極光的產生，依照句意

可知空格應填入(D)resulting in「導致；造成」，合乎文意。

18 (B)。(A)區域的　(B)季節性的
　　(C)全球的　(D)正常的
　　解 本題考字義。空格後句提到 because they occur at any time of the year，表示極光不是週期性或固定時間才出現，故選(B) seasonal較接近文意。

19 (B)。(A)依賴（不定詞）
　　(B)依賴（動詞原形）
　　(C)依賴（現在分詞）
　　(D)依賴的
　　解 本題考主要動詞判斷。該句主詞為複數形the colors，表達既定的事實，時態用現在簡單式即可，故選(B)。

20 (C)。(A)傷害　(B)驚奇　(C)公平
　　(D)恩惠
　　解 本題考慣用語詞。本句說明透過照片看到極光，仍無法完全呈現極光壯觀的感覺，故選(C)do ... justice「公平處理；合理對待」。

四、閱讀測驗

　　如果你吃過台灣有名的美食如刈包（亦稱台式漢堡）、蚵仔麵線或花生捲冰淇淋的話，你可能就會吃到香菜；不只有台灣美食，香菜其實在世界各地佳餚都會用到，包括南亞、中東及拉丁美洲。它的種子稱作芫荽籽，存在於植物的果實中並作為香料，而它的葉子則當作藥草，它可讓食物聞起來有柑橘的香味。

　　雖然許多人覺得香菜很美味，但仍有一些人非常討厭香菜，甚至網路上還有「我討厭香菜」這樣的網站；不喜歡香菜的人通常會將它的味道比喻成肥皂或灰塵，這麼多人覺得香菜噁心的原因可能跟本身的基因有關。2000年初，美國有一位行為神經科學家做了研究，他發現有八成的同卵雙胞胎會對藥草的好惡一致，而只有四成的異卵雙胞胎有這現象；2012年，一家名叫「23andMe」的基因檢測公司研究發現，如果受試者的祖先來自歐洲，有12%到14%會認為香菜有肥皂的味道，但如果祖先來自拉丁美洲、東亞或南亞的，僅4%到8%的受試者有這樣的感受。討厭香菜的人有某種相同的基因變異，這會影響OR6A2基因的接收，而OR6A2就是負責檢測香菜味道中的合成物。

　　雖然有些人討厭香菜，不過它卻有益於身體健康。香菜的種子可幫助降低膽固醇濃度，此外，它本身含有一種天然成份，可去除由沙門氏菌引起的食物中毒，而它提煉出的精油也可幫助消化。不管你本身喜愛或討厭這種香味食材，我們得承認香菜獨特的味道已經讓全世界留下深刻的印象了。

21 (C)。　本篇短文的主旨為何？
(A)台灣菜已在全世界打出名號。
(B)香菜的使用會因文化而有差異。
(C)基因或許能解釋對藥草喜好差異的原因。
(D)使用藥草可製造食物香味且有益健康。

解 本題為主旨題。雖然本文提到世界各地對香菜的喜好程度不同，而第二段從這句It is likely that this widespread disgust with the herb is related to genetics. 便開始探討跟基因的關聯性，故選(C)。

22 (D)。作者如何在第二段支持自己的論點？
(A)藉由分享個人經驗。
(B)藉由點出可能的問題。
(C)藉由舉出各地的例子。
(D)藉由引用科學研究結果。

解 本題為細節題。第二段中分別出現a study by an American behavioral neuroscientist及the genetic testing firm 23andMe did a study，可知作者引用之前做過的研究提供佐證，故選(D)。

23 (A)。關於刈包、蚵仔麵線及台灣花生捲冰淇淋的敘述，下列何者為真？
(A)它們有共通的食材。
(B)它們可在速食店買到。
(C)它們在全世界大受歡迎。
(D)它們在台灣都被當成點心來吃。

解 本題為除外題。(B)文中並未提到速食店有賣這些食物；(C)文中只有提到famous Taiwanese dishes，並未提到世界知名；(D)由the dessert which can only be best translated as ice cream burritos 可知只有花生捲冰淇淋被當成點心吃；而從文章中第一段第一句If you've ever tried famous Taiwanese dishes Gua Bao...and Oyster Vermicelli Noodles or...as ice cream burritos, you've probably eaten cilantro. 提到這些美食都可以吃到香菜，故選(A)。

24 (A)。下列何者並無拿來描述香菜的味道？

(A)辛辣的　　　　(B)滑膩的

(C)香味的　　　　(D)像柑橘的

解 本題為細節題。文章第一段有提到citrus-like taste，第二段出現soapy taste，第三段則使用fragrant ingredient；雖然文中也提到spice「香料」，卻並無描述spicy「辛辣的」之意，故選(A)。

25 (B)。有關香菜的保健功能中，下列何者在本文中並無提到？

(A)幫助消化。

(B)強健骨骼。

(C)減緩食物中毒。

(D)減少膽固醇濃度。

解 本題為細節題。文章第三段分別提到help lower cholesterol levels、helps fight off food poisoning及aid in digestion，卻沒出現任何有關bones「骨頭」或skeleton「骨骼」等關鍵字，故選(B)。

109年 臺灣糖業新進工員

一、字彙

( ) **1** Handing in your report late is not _____. If you miss the deadline, you will fail this course.
(A)adequate
(B)acceptable
(C)patient
(D)imaginative

( ) **2** Alex was eager to buy a car at first, but he _____ canceled the plan because he couldn't afford one.
(A)originally
(B)frequently
(C)eventually
(D)similarly

( ) **3** My sister and I had a heated _____ last night. She still refused to talk to me this morning.
(A)argument
(B)movement
(C)environment
(D)discouragement

( ) **4** Japan failed to _____ the Olympic Games in Tokyo this year due to the covid-19 pandemic.
(A)recognize
(B)host
(C)judge
(D)design

( ) **5** The warm winter had a very _____ impact on the clothing industry. The sale of coats dropped over 30%.
(A)popular
(B)convenient
(C)classic
(D)negative

( ) **6** Success is not totally _____ by how hard we work. Luck sometimes plays a part.
(A)surveyed
(B)analyzed
(C)determined
(D)defeated

( ) **7** Albert proudly _____ his gold medal to his family. His parents took great pride in their son's achievement.
(A)displayed (B)volunteered
(C)attracted (D)divorced

二、文法測驗

( ) **8** When it comes to _____ a foreign language, constant practice is most important.
(A)learn (B)learned
(C)learning (D)be learning

( ) **9** The lost tourist stood on the corner, _____ which road to take.
(A)wondering (B)wondered
(C)he wondered (D)and wondering

( ) **10** This apartment is excellent for three reasons. One is its closeness to schools, _____ is its large space, and _____ is its affordable price.
(A)one, another (B)one, the other
(C)another, the other (D)another, other

( ) **11** I really don't know where Jessie is now. If I _____ her whereabouts, I would tell you at once.
(A)know (B)will know
(C)knew (D)had known

( ) **12** The online game is so popular that _____ of players will continue to grow.
(A)a number (B)the number
(C)an amount (D)the amount

( ) **13** The customer _____ at the corner kept complaining about the food.
(A)sat (B)sitting
(C)seating (D)who sitting

( ) **14** Lauren screamed loudly _____ she saw a cockroach on her shoes.
(A)though   (B)upon
(C)unless   (D)as soon as

( ) **15** The foreigner is having a hard time _____ the sign. Let's help him out.
(A)read   (B)to read
(C)reading   (D)on reading

三、克漏字測驗

Temple University's history began in 1884, when a young working man asked Russell Conwell if he could tutor him at night. A well-known Philadelphia minister, Conwell quickly said yes. It wasn't ____16.____ before he was teaching several dozen students—working people who could only attend class at night but had a strong desire to make something of themselves.

Conwell recruited volunteer faculty to ____17.____ in the burgeoning night school, and in 1888 he received a charter of incorporation for "The Temple College." His founding vision for the school was to provide superior educational opportunities for academically talented and highly motivated students, ____18.____ their backgrounds or means.

The fledgling college continued to grow, ____19.____ programs and students throughout the following decades. Today, Temple's more than 35,000 students continue to follow the university's official ____20.____ —Perseverantia Vincit, or "Perseverance Conquers"—with their supreme dedication to excellence in academics, research, athletics, the arts and more.

( ) **16** (A)fun   (B)true   (C)bad   (D)long

( ) **17** (A)participate   (B)anticipate   (C)affect   (D)intimidate

( ) **18** (A)accounting for   (B)regardless of   (C)related to   (D)based on

( ) **19** (A)seducing   (B)deducting   (C)adding   (D)manipulating

( ) **20** (A)guilty   (B)tattoo   (C)logo   (D)motto

四、閱讀測驗

Newspapers have traditionally been made from wood for many years. But what would happen if the process were reversed? Could wood be made from newspapers to complete the full cycle? A Dutch designer sought out the answer to this question.

Mieke Meijer was a student when she first began exploring a way to extend the life of newspapers and make something useful from waste. The result of her project was the creation of a new material called NewspaperWood, which reversed the traditional wood-to-paper process and results in a wood-like product from recycled newspapers. She later joined a design team that helped her simplify the process so that it was less time-consuming and less complicated.

The process of making NewspaperWood involves coating each sheet of newspaper with environmentally friendly glue and then rolling the sheets up together tightly to form logs. The logs are then milled into planks just like wood. The result is a product that can be sanded, nailed, cut, and treated just like any other wood product. It can be used to make many items but cannot be used for largescale construction. If you cut open a NewspaperWood log, you can see the layers of paper that look like the lines of grain in a piece of real wood.

NewspaperWood is not invented to be a replacement for wood. It aims at making use of the surplus of waste paper and creating something more valuable out of it. Meijer calls the process "upcycling." NewspaperWood is being used by several designers to create products ranging from small pieces of jewelry to larger pieces of furniture.

( ) **21** Which two of the following can explain the main idea of the passage? （本題為複選題）

(A)The future of the newspaper business.

(B)The process of making newspapers.

(C)Newspapers are more useful than you think.

(D)How to turn newspapers back to wood.

( ) **22** According to the passage, which two of the following are LESS likely to be made of NewspaperWood?（本題為複選題）
(A)A chair.　　　　　　　　(B)A bicycle.
(C)A bookshelf.　　　　　　(D)A church.

( ) **23** Which two of the following statements are True?（本題為複選題）
(A)Mieke Meijer worked alone to design products from NewspaperWood.
(B)NewspaperWood is not a suitable material for the construction of skyscrapers.
(C)NewspaperWood is now a useful material for a variety of products.
(D)The process of making NewspaperWood has always been the same.

( ) **24** Based on this passage, which two of the following are **NOT** the steps for making NewspaperWood?（本題為複選題）
(A)Mixing the mud with dried grass.
(B)Rolling the sheets up together tightly to form logs.
(C)Sanding the wood for making a desk.
(D)Milling the logs into planks just like normal wood.

( ) **25** According to the passage, why did Meijer invent Newspaper Wood?（本題為複選題）
(A)To replace wood.
(B)To make use of waste paper.
(C)To reduce the use of newspapers.
(D)To make something useful out of waste paper.

五、非選擇題

1. 中翻英

只要你不在意感到無聊或是在排隊的陌生人之間睡覺，代客排隊是一個完美的職業。

_____

_____

_____

_____

2. 英翻中

When the word "mother" comes to mind, we tend to refer to our own moms. Nevertheless, animals of all shapes and sizes have mothers, too. Not all mothers in the animal world take care of babies in the same way as we humans do. Each species has its own unique approach.

_____

_____

_____

_____

解答與解析 答案標示為# 者，表官方曾公告更正該題答案。

一、字彙

1 (B)。 遲交報告是無法接受的；如果你錯過繳交期限，這門課就會被當掉。
(A)足夠的　　(B)可接受的
(C)耐心的　　(D)想像的
解 本題考字義。第二句提到miss the deadline的後果是fail this course，可見遲交報告的行為是不「被接受的」，故選(B) acceptable。

2 (C)。 Alex原本超想買一台車，不過最後他因為買不起而取消這計畫。
(A)原本地　　(B)常常地
(C)最後地　　(D)相似地

解 本題考上下文關係。前一句的at first及後一句的but暗示了事件的轉折，故選(C)eventually。

3 (A)。 昨晚我跟我姊起了激烈的爭執，她今早仍不想跟我說話。
(A)爭執　　　　　(B)運動
(C)環境　　　　　(D)阻止
解 本題考字義。由第二句refused to talk to me推知兩人之前應該有不愉快的互動，故較接近的選項為(A)argument。

4 (B)。 日本由於今年新冠流感因素而無法主辦東京奧運。
(A)認可　　　　　(B)主辦
(C)判斷　　　　　(D)設計
解 本題考字義。由該句的關鍵字Japan及the Olympic Games推測本題在敘述有關日本「主辦」奧運的事件，故選(B)host。

5 (D)。 暖冬對服飾業帶來負面的影響，大衣的銷售量下滑超過三成。
(A)受歡迎的　　　(B)方便的
(C)經典的　　　　(D)負面的
解 本題考字義。由第二句the sale of...dropped over 30%推測第一句應該描述較「負面」的事件，故選(D)negative。

6 (C)。 成功不完全取決於我們的努力，有時候運氣也會有影響。
(A)調查　　　　　(B)分析
(C)決定　　　　　(D)打敗
解 本題考字義。該題第二句Luck sometimes plays a part. 可知「決

定」成功的因素不只有一個，故選(C)determined。

7 (A)。 Albert自豪地將金牌秀給家人看，他爸媽對兒子的成就感到驕傲。
(A)展示　　　　　(B)自願
(C)吸引　　　　　(D)離婚
解 本題考字義。從第二句爸媽的驕傲可推知他們應該有看到Albert的金牌，意即Albert已將獎牌「展示」給爸媽看，故選(A)displayed。

二、文法測驗

8 (C)。 當談到學習外語，不斷練習是最重要的。
(A)學習（動詞原形）
(B)學習（過去分詞）
(C)學習（現在分詞）
(D)學習（be+現在分詞）
解 本題考慣用片語。When it comes to後面須接「名詞」或「現在分詞」（V-ing），故選(C)learning。

9 (A)。 這位迷路的觀光客站在角落，不知道該走哪條路。
(A)想知道（現在分詞）
(B)想知道（過去分詞）
(C)他想知道
(D)並且想知道
解 本題考分詞構句。後一句可還原為... and he wondered which road to take. 由於前後句子主詞相同，故可將連接詞and引導的該句主詞省略，並依語態將動詞改為主動的V-ing形式，因此選(A)wondering。

10 (C)。這間公寓有三個很棒的優點：一個是離學區近，另一個是空間寬敞，最後另一個是價格親民。
(A)一個；另一個
(B)一個；另一個（限定）
(C)另一個；另一個（限定）
(D)另一個；另一個（非限定）
解 本題考不定代名詞。由於第一句有先限定three reasons，因此第二句分別描述時，先介紹的用one，中間的會用another，剩下的則用the other，故選(C)。

11 (C)。我真的不知道Jessie目前在哪裡；如果我知道她的下落，一定馬上告訴你。
(A)知道（動詞原形）
(B)知道（未來式）
(C)知道（過去式）
(D)知道（過去分詞）
解 本題考假設語法。由第一句I really don't know...可知事實以現在式呈現，則假設語法設定為與現在事實相反，用過去式表示，故選(C)knew。

12 (B)。這款線上遊戲太受歡迎，以致玩家人數將會持續增加。
(A)一些（可數名詞）
(B)數量（可數名詞）
(C)一些（不可數名詞）
(D)數量（不可數名詞）
解 本題考冠詞及名詞類型。其中關鍵詞players為可數名詞，另外continue to grow表示持續成長的是玩家的「數量」，故選(B)the number of。

13 (B)。坐在角落的這位顧客不斷地抱怨食物。
(A)坐（過去分詞）
(B)坐（現在分詞）
(C)使就坐（現在分詞）
(D)坐（關係代名詞）
解 本題考關係代名詞。本句可還原為The customer who sat...，其中who可省略，而後面sat則須依語態將動詞改為主動的V-ing形式，故選(B)sitting。

14 (D)。Lauren一見到她鞋子上面的蟑螂，馬上大聲尖叫。
(A)雖然　　　　(B)一旦
(C)除非　　　　(D)一……就……
解 本題考上下文關係。由本題空格前後關鍵詞screamed loudly及saw a cockroach可推知前後事件幾乎是同時發生，故選(D)as soon as；而(B)upon後面只能接名詞或V-ing，無法接完整句子。

15 (C)。這位外國人正吃力地看著牌子，咱們去幫他一下吧。
(A)閱讀（動詞原形）
(B)閱讀（不定詞）
(C)閱讀（現在分詞）
(D)閱讀（介詞+現在分詞）
解 本題考慣用字詞。句中片語have a good/hard time後面須接地方副詞（如at the party）或現在分詞（V-ing），故選(C)reading。

三、克漏字測驗

天普大學的歷史起源於1884年,剛開始有一位年輕上班族問羅素·康威爾是否願意晚上當他的家教老師;身為費城的長官,康威爾馬上答應了。不久他就教到好幾十位學生——他們白天工作,只能用晚上進修,但企圖心強烈。康威爾招募志工團隊加入當時很夯的夜校行列,後來在1888年政府核准成立了「天普學院」;他創校目的是為了提供優秀的教育機會給學術人才及學習動機強的學生,不管他們的背景或財力如何。

這所剛起步的學院後來持續成長,在之後的幾十年間增加了課程及招生人數。目前天普大學擁有超過三萬五千名學生,他們都遵循這所學府的校訓——有毅力才會成功,也就是「毅力能戰勝一切」,並將卓越的奉獻投入在學術、研究、體育、人文藝術等各方面。

16 (D)。 (A)好玩的 (B)真實的 (C)壞的 (D)久的
　解 本題考字義。本句描述康威爾老師從原本一位家教到數十位學生,這當中間隔的時間不長,因此用not long before...「不久」來表達,故選(D)。

17 (A)。 (A)參與 (B)預期 (C)影響 (D)威脅
　解 本題考字義。本句表達康威爾老師招募志工加入夜校團隊,比較接近的詞彙為participate in「參加」,故選(A)。

18 (B)。 (A)解釋 (B)無論 (C)有關 (D)基於
　解 本題考字義。本句敘述該學府不限師生的背景皆可加入,較適合的片語為regardless of「不管;無論」,故選(B)。

19 (C)。 (A)誘惑 (B)推斷 (C)增加 (D)操縱
　解 本題考字義。前一句提到The fledgling college continued to grow,推論可知本句表達課程及招生人數也隨之成長,故選(C)adding。

20 (D)。 (A)有罪的 (B)刺青 (C)標誌 (D)座右銘
　解 本題考字義。空格前出現continue to follow,而空格後出現Perseverantia Vincit, or "Perseverance Conquers",表示本句應為該校的重要格言,故選(D)motto。

四、閱讀測驗

傳統以來,報紙一直是由木材做的,但如果將這順序反轉會發生什麼事?木材是否也可由報紙做成,讓生態循環回到原點呢?有一位荷蘭設計師想找出答案。

當蜜克·梅潔還是學生的時候,她就開始嘗試透過廢紙再利用的方式延長報紙的壽命;她這想法結果創造出新的材料,稱作「報紙木材」,這種木材保留了傳統由木頭到紙張的過程,並且從回收的報紙做出類似木材的產品。她後

來加入了一個設計團隊，可協助將這流程簡化為省時且較單純的步驟。

　　關於製造報紙木材的步驟，首先先用環保膠水塗在每張報紙上，讓這些報紙緊密黏合並捲成原木，接著將原木削成一片片木板。最後的產品可供打磨、釘東西及切割，就跟其他木製品沒兩樣；它可以用來製造許多物品，但無法作為大型建築。如果你將報紙原木切開，你會看到裡面有一層層紙張，就像真的木材內部紋理一樣。

　　發明報紙木材並非要取代木頭，而是想再利用廢紙創造更有價值的物品。梅潔將這流程稱作「升級再造」。而目前，有一些設計師將報紙木材做成不同的產品，包括小件珠寶到大型家具都有。

21 (C)(D)。下列哪兩項可作為本篇短文的大意？
(A)報紙產業的未來。
(B)報紙的製作過程。
(C)報紙的用途比你知道的還更多。
(D)如何將報紙回復為木材。
解 本題為主旨題。關鍵句在本篇第一段Could wood be made from newspapers to complete the full cycle? 及第二段exploring a way to extend the life of newspapers and make something useful from waste. 表示報紙除了當廢紙外還有其他的功能，以及這位設計師如何將報紙轉變為再生木材的方法，故文章主旨應選(C)和(D)。

22 (B)(D)。根據本篇短文，下列哪兩項比較不可能由報紙木材做成？
(A)椅子。　　　(B)腳踏車。
(C)書架。　　　(D)教堂。
解 本題為除外題。從文章中第三段It can be used to make many items but cannot be used for largescale construction. 表示非木製品及大型建築不能用報紙木材當材料，故較適合的答案為(B)和(D)。

23 (B)(C)。下列哪兩項敘述是真的？
(A)Mieke Meijer獨自將報紙木材設計成產品。
(B)報紙木材不適合用來蓋摩天大樓。
(C)報紙木材目前可做成許多產品。
(D)報紙木材的製作過程始終如一。
解 本題為除外題。(A)由She later joined a design team...可知Meijer非獨自完成；(D)由simplify the process so that it was less time-consuming and less complicated可知製作過程有經過簡化；而從文章中第三段It can be used to make many items but cannot be used for largescale construction. 可知報紙木材用途廣泛但不適合大建築，符合文章之敘述，故選(B)和(C)。

24 (A)(C)。根據本篇短文，下列哪兩項不是製造報紙木材的步驟？
(A)將泥漿倒入乾草中攪拌。
(B)將紙張緊密捲起形成原木狀。
(C)將木材打磨做成書桌。
(D)將原木磨成一般木板。

解 本題為除外題。文章中並無出現 mud「泥漿」或pulp「紙漿」等相關字,也沒提到desk或table這類詞彙,故選(A)和(C)。

25 **(B)(D)**。 根據本篇短文,Meijer為何要發明報紙木材?

(A)為了取代木材。

(B)為了利用廢紙。

(C)為了減少報紙的使用量。

(D)為了將廢紙做成有用的物品。

解 本題為細節題。從文章中最後一段NewspaperWood is not invented to be a replacement for wood. It aims at making use of the surplus of waste paper and creating something more valuable out of it.可知這位設計師的本意是希望報紙能再利用,故較適合的選項為(B)和(D)。

五、非選擇題

1.中翻英

Being a hired queuer is an ideal job as long as you don't mind feeling bored or taking a nap among strangers in a line.

2.英翻中

當想到「母親」這個字時,我們多半會指自己的母親;不過,所有的動物也都有母親。在動物界中,不是所有的母親照顧寶寶的方式都像我們人類一樣;每種動物都有其獨特的做法。

解答與解析

109年 經濟部所屬事業機構新進職員

一、字彙

( ) **1** That van is the ideal vehicle for carpooling because it can _____ nine passengers and two pets.
(A)abstain
(B)enumerate
(C)commemorate
(D)accommodate

( ) **2** Fifty nations have banned the use of _____ punishment of children.
(A)admonition
(B)corporal
(C)divine
(D)secular

( ) **3** This study is the _____ of the whole research program.
(A)cornerstone
(B)corner
(C)hailstone
(D)cornerback

( ) **4** Old English is the direct _____ of English modern tongue.
(A)ancestor
(B)bachelor
(C)creation
(D)descendant

( ) **5** The nation's economy grew 3.55 percent in the first quarter, more than the 2.54 percent increase the government forecast in May, as local semiconductor firms stepped up investment to meet global _____ for AI chips, the Directorate-General of Budget, Accounting and Statistics (DGBAS) said yesterday.
(A)discharge
(B)demand
(C)desire
(D)index

( ) **6** Helping high school students _____ to college and university leads to higher enrollment.
(A)apply
(B)employ
(C)graduate
(D)imply

(　　)　**7** Justice must be ＿＿＿＿＿ with mercy.
(A)tampered　　　　　　　(B)timbered
(C)tempered　　　　　　　(D)tumbled

(　　)　**8** When the shocking news reached us, we were completely ＿＿＿＿.
(A)happy　　　　　　　　(B)bewildered
(C)unsurprised　　　　　　(D)tired

(　　)　**9** An ecosystem is a community of living ＿＿＿＿ in conjunction with the nonliving components of their environment, interacting as a system.
(A)companies　　　　　　(B)institutes
(C)mortalities　　　　　　(D)organisms

(　　)**10** The new design is a ＿＿＿＿ from the norm.
(A)similarity　　　　　　(B)separate
(C)distinction　　　　　　(D)departure

二、文法及慣用語

(　　)**11** Jasmine was originally from Mexico, ＿＿＿＿ is a Spanish-speaking country blended with various tribal languages.
(A)which　　　　　　　　(B)where
(C)that　　　　　　　　　(D)so much as

(　　)**12** Not until the early years of the 20th century ＿＿＿＿ what divorce means to them.
(A)did women realize　　　(B)people has known
(C)didn't men figure out　　(D)women did know

(　　)**13** David seems to like Esther, and ＿＿＿＿.
(A)does so Norvin　　　　(B)so does Norvin
(C)Norvin does so　　　　(D)Norvin so does

(　　)**14** Liam gave many books to his brother, while Chris gave ＿＿＿＿.
(A)some books to anyone　(B)any book to no one
(C)anyone no books　　　(D)no books to anyone

(　　) **15** Even if the book _____ available in English, nobody would read it.
(A)was　　　　　　　　　　(B)were
(C)will be　　　　　　　　(D)would be

(　　) **16** To attract _____ students from around the world, this university is planning to establish full scholarships for 25 international students annually.
(A)brightest　　　　　　　(B)the brightest
(C)the more bright　　　　(D)the most bright

(　　) **17** It is important for a university magazine to ask questions of research, _____ simply accepting the claims of researchers at face value.
(A)except for　　　　　　(B)in terms of
(C)rather than　　　　　　(D)to an extent

(　　) **18** Freedom of speech is a fundamental human right, enshrined _____ Article 19 of the Universal Declaration of Human Rights.
(A)with　　　　　　　　　(B)in
(C)to　　　　　　　　　　(D)at

(　　) **19** The boxer is notorious for the obnoxious taunts he uses to _____ his opponents.
(A)psych out　　　　　　　(B)cheer up
(C)encourage　　　　　　　(D)push-up

(　　) **20** The best way to deal with burns is to prevent them _____ in the first place.
(A)happen　　　　　　　　(B)happening
(C)from happening　　　　(D)to happen

(　　) **21** The old lady has been learning ballet for years _____ the fact that she had been suffering from arthritis for more than 30 years.
(A)so as to　　　　　　　　(B)with so much so
(C)in spite of　　　　　　　(D)as much as

(　) **22** There are _____ changes when the new system is introduced.
(A)bound together by　　　(B)bound to be
(C)bound up in　　　(D)bound up with

(　) **23** Searching for one man in this city is like looking for _____.
(A)a pain in the neck　　　(B)a balloon in the air
(C)pins and needles　　　(D)a needle in a haystack

(　) **24** The experimenter told the students that she _____ later to explain how each problem was solved.
(A)returns　　　(B)will return
(C)would return　　　(D)would have returned

(　) **25** Little is known about what truly matters in searching for information, _____ what strategies users exploit.
(A)also　　　(B)as
(C)but　　　(D)nor

三、克漏字

　　Accreditation does not guarantee that you will be satisfied with a particular college or degree program. ____26.____ , it does mean that an independent, trustworthy source has checked that standards are being met and that your graduation ____27.____ in greater esteem by future employers, higher education providers and industry peers. Accreditation is a tool usable for ____28.____ to make an accurate evaluation of their options. It also rewards and publicly acknowledges those institutions that ____29.____ a benchmark in their education provision. It rewards the institution and the communities ____30.____ they are based and retains a focus on achievement.

(　) **26** (A)However　　　(B)In addition
(C)Therefore　　　(D)Hence

(　) **27** (A)will hold　　　(B)will be held
(C)holds　　　(D)be held

(   ) **28** (A)future schools   (B)selective college
            (C)prospective teachers   (D)would-be students

(   ) **29** (A)are achieved   (B)achieved
            (C)have achieved   (D)have been achieved

(   ) **30** (A)where   (B)when
            (C)what   (D)how

Among all the sciences, psychology is perhaps the most ____31.____ to the general public, and the most ____32.____ to misconceptions. Even though its language and ideas have ____33.____ everyday culture, most people have only a hazy idea of what the subject is about, and what psychologists actually do. For some, psychology conjures up images of people in white coats, either staffing an institution for mental disorders or ____34.____ laboratory experiments on rats. Others may imagine a man with a middle-European accent psychoanalyzing a patient on a couch or, if film scripts are to be believed, plotting to exercise some form of ____35.____ control.

(   ) **31** (A)straightforward   (B)mysterious
            (C)lucid   (D)transparent

(   ) **32** (A)immune   (B)sensitive
            (C)prone   (D)similar

(   ) **33** (A)violated   (B)demanded
            (C)observed   (D)infiltrated

(   ) **34** (A)working   (B)conducting
            (C)mocking   (D)launching

(   ) **35** (A)mind   (B)body
            (C)motor   (D)classroom

四、閱讀測驗

There's a fun game I like to play in a group of trusted friends called "Controversial Opinion". The rules are simple: Don't talk about what was shared during Controversial Opinion afterward and you aren't allowed to "argue" — only to ask questions about why that person feels that way. Opinions can range from "I think James Bond movies are overrated" to "I think Donald Trump would make an excellent president". Usually, someone responds to an opinion with, "Oh my god! I had no idea you were one of those people!" Which is really another way of saying "I thought you were on my team!" In psychology, the idea that everyone is like us is called the "false-consensus bias". This bias often manifests itself when we see in politics or polls.

Online it means we can be blindsided by the opinions of our friends. Over time, this morphs into a subconscious belief that we and our friends are the sane ones and that there's a crazy "Other Side" that must be laughed at — an Other Side that just doesn't "get it", and is clearly not as intelligent as "us". But this holier-than-thou social media behavior is counterproductive, it's self-aggrandizement at the cost of actual nuanced discourse and if we want to consider online discourse productive, we need to move past this.

What is emerging is the worst kind of echo chamber, one where those inside are increasingly convinced that everyone shares their world view, that their ranks are growing when they aren't. It's like clockwork: an event happens and then your social media circle is shocked when a non-social media peer group public reacts to news in an unexpected way. They then mock the Other Side for being "out of touch" or "dumb".

( ) **36** What is the main idea of this article?
   (A)Playing Controversial Opinion with trusted friends is simple and fun.
   (B)To have a constructive discussion, we need to talk to "the other side".
   (C)Having "false-consensus bias" is common among friends.
   (D)We should defend ourselves when others disagree with us.

( ) **37** What can you do when playing Controversial Opinion?
(A)Defend your opinions.
(B)Judge your friends' opinions.
(C)Ask your friends why they feel the way they do.
(D)Defend your friends' opinions.

( ) **38** What does it mean to have a holier-than-thou social media behavior?
(A)Listen to others' opinions without being judgmental.
(B)Interact only with people in your social echo chamber.
(C)Being condescending when listening to others' opinions.
(D)Try to reach a common ground when debating with people online.

( ) **39** What is likely to happen in an echo chamber on social media?
(A)People would believe that they may be misguided by misinformation on social media.
(B)People believe that everyone shares a common view toward the world.
(C)People are ready to talk to others who hold a different view from their own.
(D)People remain skeptical about online information.

( ) **40** What does it mean to be blindsided by the opinions of our friends?
(A)Defending our friends' opinions forcefully.
(B)Not paying attention to our friends' opinions.
(C)Adopting our friends' opinions without independent and critical thinking.
(D)Trying to persuade our friends to adopt our opinions.

解答與解析 答案標示為#者，表官方曾公告更正該題答案。

一、字彙

1 (D)。那台貨車非常適合共乘，因為它可以容納九位乘客和兩隻寵物。
(A)放棄　　　(B)列舉
(C)紀念　　　(D)容納

解 本題考字義。由題目中關鍵字 carpooling「共乘」及passengers and pets「乘客和寵物」可以得知題目在敘述貨車的功能，故正確答案為(D)accommodate。

2 (B)。 五十個國家已禁止對孩童實施體罰。
(A)警告　　　　(B)身體的
(C)神聖的　　　(D)世俗的
解 本題考名詞搭配字。由空格後方的punishment可知前面須填入形容詞，選項中只有(B)corporal可搭配punishment表示「體罰」。其他選項無相關搭配用法。

3 (A)。 這項研究是這整個研究計畫的基礎。
(A)基礎　　　　(B)角落
(C)冰雹　　　　(D)（橄欖球）後衛
解 本題考字義。該句中的關鍵詞this study及the whole research program說明了兩者間的關係，故較合適的選項為(A)cornerstone。

4 (A)。 古英文是現代英語的直系始祖。
(A)祖先　　　　(B)單身漢
(C)創作　　　　(D)後代
解 本題考字義。文中提到old English和modern English tongue之間的關係，可知前者為後者的源頭，故較接近的答案為(A)ancestor。

5 (B)。 行政院主計處昨日表示，由於當地半導體公司加速投資以因應全球人工智慧晶片的需求，全國第一季經濟成長百分之3.55，高於政府五月預估的百分之2.54。
(A)釋放　　　　(B)需求
(C)慾望　　　　(D)指數
解 本題考字義。由關鍵詞stepped up investment及global...for AI chips，推知半導體公司投資海外市場的目的，應是由於全球都需要用到人工智慧晶片，故選(B)demand。

6 (A)。 幫助中學生申請大專院校就讀，會提高他們的註冊率。
(A)申請　　　　(B)僱用
(C)畢業　　　　(D)暗示
解 本題考字義。該題說明中學生進入大學的管道，故較適合的選項為(A)apply。

7 (C)。 正義跟寬容必須並行使用（恩威並濟）。
(A)損害　　　　(B)以木材支撐
(C)調和　　　　(D)倒塌
解 本題考字義。文中justice和mercy為互補的概念，表示兩者需要調和才可相輔相成，故選(C)tempered。

8 (B)。 當我們得知這令人震驚的消息時，我們感到非常困惑。
(A)快樂的　　　　(B)困惑的
(C)不訝異的　　　(D)疲倦的
解 本題考字義。本題前半句提到shocking news，可推知後半句主詞的反應可能為錯愕或覺得不解，依文意判斷選(B)bewildered較合適。

9 (D)。 生態系統是指生命有機體跟所在環境的非生命元素連結成的共同體，且在同一個系統中互動。
(A)公司　　　　(B)機構
(C)死亡率　　　(D)有機體

解答與解析

解 本題考字義。由空格前方出現的living可推測後面接的名詞字義應和生物有關，故選(D)organisms。

10 (D)。 這款新的設計已脫離傳統模式獨樹一格。

(A)相似　　　　(B)分開

(C)區別　　　　(D)脫離

解 本題考字義。由句中關鍵字new design及norm可知兩者為對比的概念，而空格後接from則暗示新設計已離開傳統的框架，故選(D)departure。

二、文法及慣用語

11 (A)。 Jasmine來自墨西哥，那是一個說西班牙文並參雜許多部落語言的國家。

(A)那個（物的關代主／受格）

(B)那裡（關係副詞）

(C)那個（人或物的關代主／受格）

(D)到這程度（常用否定）

解 本題考關係代名詞。前方空格為名詞（先行詞）Mexico，空格後方出現逗點及缺主詞的不完整子句，可判斷空格處應填入表物的關係代名詞which，引導形容詞子句修飾先行詞。

12 (A)。 直到二十世紀初，女人才了解離婚的意義為何。

(A)女人才了解　　(B)人們已知道

(C)男人無法理解　(D)女人真的知道

解 本題考倒裝句。本題倒裝句開頭為否定詞Not until，則後面的主

詞跟be動詞或助動詞的位置須互換，且不用否定表達，故較合適的選項為(A)did woman realize。

13 (B)。 David似乎喜歡Esther，Norvin也是。

(A)Norvin也是（無此用法）

(B)Norvin也是

(C)Norvin這麼做

(D)Norvin也是（無此用法）

解 本題考附和句。文中前半句為肯定語氣，則附和句開頭為So，主詞與be動詞或助動詞須倒裝，故選(B)so does Norvin。

14 (D)。 Liam給他弟弟許多書，而Chris一本都沒給。

(A)一些書給任何人

(B)任何書給沒人

(C)任何人沒有書

(D)沒有書給任何人

解 本題考不定代名詞。該題前半句為肯定句，推知while後面應接否定句，而該否定句並無出現not，則否定詞no須放在後面緊接的受詞上，故選(D)no books to anyone。

15 (B)。 就算這本書有英文版的，也沒人想看。

(A)是（過去式be動詞單數）

(B)是（過去式be動詞複數）

(C)將會（未來式）

(D)將會（過去式）

解 本題考假設法。If 條件句若表達與現在事實相反，則be動詞須用

過去式were，表示目前這本書並沒有英文版，故選(B)were。

16 (B)。為了吸引世界頂尖學生就讀，這所大學計畫每年提供全額獎學金給25位國際生。

(A)最聰明的

(B)最聰明的（含the）

(C)比較聰明的（無此用法）

(D)最聰明的（無此用法）

圖 本題考形容詞最高級。文中提到提供獎學金的目的為吸引世界最聰明的學生，形容詞最高級的用法為the＋most開頭或est結尾之形容詞，而bright為短音節單字，故選(B)the brightest。

17 (C)。對於大學雜誌來說，提出研究問題是很重要的，而非將研究者的看法照單全收。

(A)除了之外　　(B)根據

(C)而非　　(D)到某種程度

圖 本題考連接詞。該題空格前後ask questions及accepting the claims為相對的概念，推知空格應填入表示轉折或相對的語詞，故選(C)rather than。

18 (B)。言論自由是基本人權，且世界人權宣言的第十九條中有保障此權利。

(A)和……一起　(B)在……裡面

(C)對於……　　(D)在……範圍

圖 本題考動詞片語。enshrine有珍藏、銘記之意，後面須接介係詞in，故選(B)in。

19 (A)。這名拳擊手習慣用惹人厭的挑釁動作來嚇對手，因此惡名昭彰。

(A)嚇住　　(B)振作

(C)鼓勵　　(D)提高

圖 本題考慣用語。由文中關鍵字notorious、obnoxious及taunts可知對該拳擊手多為負面的評價，推知空格的動詞字義也較負面，故選(A)psych out。

20 (C)。處理燒燙傷最好的方法就是不要讓它發生。

(A)發生（動詞原形）

(B)發生（現在分詞）

(C)發生（介詞+現在分詞）

(D)發生（不定詞）

圖 本題考動詞片語。空格前出現動詞prevent，後面須接介係詞from，意思為「防止（某人或物）發生（某事）」，故選(C)from happening。

21 (C)。儘管這名老婦人患有關節炎已超過30年，她仍持續學芭蕾舞好幾年。

(A)為了　　(B)到……程度

(C)儘管　　(D)和……一樣多

圖 本題考連接詞。該題前半段提到老婦人持續練舞多年一事，後半段為名詞子句，說明她其實長期患有某疾病，暗示該疾病並無影響她練舞，故選(C)in spite of。

22 (B)。當引進新的系統時，必定會產生改變。

(A)因……而在一起

(B)必定

(C)投入於……

(D)與……有密切關聯

解 本題考形容詞片語。本句說明產生改變對於新系統的必然性，依題意較接近的選項為(B)bound to be。

23 (D)。 要在這城市找一個人，等於跟大海撈針一樣。

(A)眼中釘　　　(B)苦盡甘來

(C)如坐針氈　　(D)大海撈針

解 本題考慣用語。文中提到在大地區找某人，暗示事情難以達成，故選(D)a needle in a haystack。

24 (C)。 這名實驗者跟學生說，她待會將回來解釋怎麼解決每一個問題。

(A)回來（現在式）

(B)將回來（未來式）

(C)那時會回來（過去式）

(D)那時已回來（過去完成式）

解 本題考時態。該句主要動詞為過去式told，後面接的名詞子句時態須一致，故選(C)would return。

25 (D)。 目前關於搜尋資訊的重要性所知甚少，對於用戶的使用策略也知道的不多。

(A)也　　　　　(B)一樣

(C)但是　　　　(D)也不

解 本題考附和句。前半段開頭Little在語意上為否定句，暗示後半段的語詞亦表示否定，故選(D)nor。

三、克漏字

學校評鑑並不保證你會對某大學或學位感到滿意；然而，它的確意味著某獨立、可靠的資源已經確認符合那些評鑑標準，而且你畢業後更能得到未來雇主、研究所和企業界的器重。學校評鑑對於準入學生而言，是一項可用的工具，他們可對自己的選擇做出準確的評估；而這種評鑑制度也獎勵及肯定辦學績效卓越的教育機構，除了有獎勵作用外，也會聚焦在這些學校及其領域的成就。

26 (A)。 (A)然而　(B)此外　(C)因此　(D)所以

解 本題考上下文。由前後句子的關鍵詞does not guarantee及it does mean可知兩者為對比關係，須填入轉折詞作為連接，故選(A)However。

27 (B)。 (A)將持有　(B)將被持有　(C)持有　(D)被持有

解 本題考被動語態。空格後出現by future employers暗示該句應以被動式表示，故選(B)will be held。

28 (D)。 (A)未來的學校　(B)菁英大學　(C)準教師　(D)準入學生

解 本題考字義。該句表示學校評鑑可做為評估選項的工具，這裡的「他們」指涉對象為即將進入大學就讀的學生，故選(D)would-be students。

29 (C)。 (A)被達成　(B)達成　(C)已達成　(D)已被達成

解 本題考時態。本句意思為「那些機構已達成辦學績效」，屬於單純事實的陳述，以現在式或現在完成式表達即可，且該句並無被動式結構，故選(C)have achieved。

30 (A)。(A)哪裡　(B)哪時　(C)什麼　(D)如何

解 本題考關係代名詞。空格前出現communities，而後面出現完整子句they are based，推知該空格應填入表示地方的關係副詞，故選(A)where。

　　在所有科學中，心理學對大眾而言是最神秘也最容易被誤解的學科了。即使它的語言和觀念在日常生活與文化中無所不在，大部分的人對這學科的內涵及心理學家的工作並不十分清楚。對一些人而言，心理學令人聯想到一群穿白色大衣的人，不是在精神障礙機構工作，就是在實驗室裡拿老鼠當實驗品；有些人則可能想像一位有中歐口音的男子，將躺在沙發上的病患進行心理分析，要不然就是像電影所敘述的，暗中策劃對某人進行洗腦。

31 (B)。(A)直接的　(B)神秘的　(C)清楚的　(D)透明的

解 本題考字義。由該句關鍵詞misconceptions可推知一般人對心理學仍為會產生誤解，故選項中較接近的答案為(B)mysterious。

32 (C)。(A)免疫的　(B)敏感的　(C)易於……的　(D)相似的

解 本題考字義。文中所要表達的意思為「心理學容易引起大眾的錯誤認知」，故較合適的選項為(C)prone。

33 (D)。(A)違反　(B)要求　(C)觀察　(D)滲透

解 本題考字義。該題後半句說明人們對心理學仍有模糊的概念，而前半句出現Even though及everyday culture，推測其語言思想應與日常生活有某程度的影響，故選(D)infiltrated。

34 (B)。(A)工作　(B)執行　(C)嘲笑　(D)發起

解 本題考搭配字。空格後的受詞為experiments，常搭配的動詞有conduct、carry out或perform，故選(B)conducting。

35 (A)。(A)心智　(B)身體　(C)馬達　(D)教室

解 本題考字義。由空格前出現的相關字mental及psychoanalyzing暗示敘述的情境較有可能與心理或心智有關，故選(A)mind。

四、閱讀測驗

　　我喜歡跟一群可信任的朋友中玩「爭議意見」的遊戲。規則很簡單：在你被允許表達意見之前不能談論觀點，只能夠詢問對方為何有這樣的想法。這些意見可以從「我覺得007電影系列的評價

過高」到「我覺得川普將會是很棒的總統」。人們通常的回應是：「我的天啊！我不知道你跟那些人是一國的！」，其實它表示「我以為你是站在我這邊的！」在心理學上，這種覺得大家跟我意見類似的想法稱作「錯誤共識偏見」。這種偏見常表現在政治或民意調查中。

在網路上，這表示我們會被朋友的意見找出盲點而加以攻擊。久而久之，它便成為我們潛意識的信念：我跟我朋友都是正常的，而「另一方」是不正常的、可笑的──另一方「不瞭解」我們、不像我們那麼「聰明」。然而，這種自以為是的社交媒體行為往往是適得其反的；這種自我膨脹的想法會犧牲真實、細微的對話。如果我們想將網路論述視為有建設性的對話，我們得需要超越這個層次。

回音室（同溫層）是目前出現最糟的類型。在這裡，越來越多人相信每個人有同樣的看法，並且共鳴等級越來越高，但其實不然。這現象已成為常態：當某個事件讓你的社群感到傻眼，而不在你社群的人可能覺得沒什麼，則前者可能會嘲笑後者是「狀況外」或「愚蠢的」。

36 (B)。 本篇文章的主旨為何？
(A)跟信得過的朋友玩爭議意見遊戲，是簡單又好玩的。
(B)為了能讓討論有建設性，我們必須跟「另一方」談話。
(C)「錯誤共識偏見」在朋友之間是很常見的。

(D)當別人意見跟我們不同時，我們應該要捍衛自己的立場。

解 本題為主旨題。本文從一款遊戲中說明現代人對議題討論時該有的態度，文章中第二段後面提到…this holier-than-thou social media behavior is counterproductive, it's self-aggrandizement at the cost of actual nuanced discourse and if we want to consider online discourse productive, we need to move past this. 表示當討論事情時，必須摒除堅持己見的想法且跟不同意見者溝通，故選(B)。

37 (C)。 在進行爭議意見遊戲時，你可以做什麼事情？
(A)捍衛自己的意見。
(B)評斷你朋友的意見。
(C)詢問朋友為何會這樣想。
(D)捍衛朋友的意見。

解 本題為細節題。在第一段第3行…only to ask questions about why that person feels that way說明了該遊戲規則，故選(C)。

38 (C)。 表現出「自以為是」的社群媒體行為，指的是何意？
(A)傾聽別人的意見且不作判斷。
(B)只跟同溫層的人互動。
(C)當傾聽別人意見時，採居高臨下的姿態。
(D)當跟人在網路上辯論時，試著彼此達成共識。

解 本題為細節題。在第二段第3行...an Other Side that just doesn't "get it", and is clearly not as intelligent as "us". 中敘述了這種行為的特質，暗示我們帶著優越感的心態看待另一方，故選(C)。

39 (B)。 社交媒體中的同溫層有可能會發生何事？

(A)人們會相信，他們可能會被社交媒體的錯誤資訊所誤導。

(B)人們相信每個人對世界的看法是一致的。

(C)人們會願意跟不同看法的人交談。

(D)人們對於網路資訊仍持懷疑的態度。

解 本題為細節題。第三段第1、2行...one where those inside are increasingly convinced that everyone shares their world view. 描述了同溫層的人的行為表現，故選(B)。

40 (C)。 被朋友的意見所攻擊，指的是何意？

(A)強烈捍衛朋友的意見。

(B)並無專心聽朋友的意見。

(C)無獨立或批判性思考，全盤接受朋友的意見。

(D)試著說服朋友接受我們的意見。

解 本題為推論題。文中第二段第1-3行提到Over time, this morphs into a subconscious belief that we and our friends are the sane ones and that there's a crazy "Other Side" that must be laughed at...表示我們會不自覺地相信自己的想法才是合理的，而覺得對方的想法是可笑的，推測我們並無經過客觀思考判斷，故選(C)。

110年 台灣電力新進僱用人員

(　) **1** What's the best answer when someone says, "How are things?" to you?
(A)What things?　　　　　(B)Same as usual.
(C)I don't have a clue.　　(D)I like them.

(　) **2** Earthquakes are not predictable, but new detectors _____ you to have 10 extra seconds to respond.
(A)give　　　　　　(B)allow
(C)let　　　　　　(D)make

(　) **3** Due to its success in fighting the COVID-19 pandemic, Taiwan is now a _____ for other countries.
(A)learning subject　　(B)object to copy
(C)standard nation　　(D)role model

(　) **4** The company was founded four decades ago; in other words, it has been in operation for _____.
(A)40 years　　　　(B)40 months
(C)80 years　　　　(D)80 months

(　) **5** Taiwan _____ approximately 400 kilometers from north to south.
(A)measures　　　　(B)longs
(C)has　　　　　　(D)goes to

(　) **6** Which is the most appropriate response to "Why aren't you going to lunch with us?"?
(A)I'm not friends.　　(B)I had a late breakfast.
(C)Is it a question?　　(D)It's my problem.

(　) **7** Possessing a skill can be more _____ than having a pretty diploma sometimes.
(A)better　　　　　(B)valuable
(C)impressed　　　　(D)convenient

( ) **8** Cathy is extremely _____ because she has exercised regularly for years.
(A)fit
(B)satisfaction
(C)likable
(D)suitable

( ) **9** Junk food is unhealthy, but it is usually quite _____ ; that's why a lot of people like it.
(A)good taste
(B)smells wonderful
(C)flavorful
(D)attractive

( ) **10** Tom and Jerry are identical twins and it's hard to _____ between them.
(A)tell the difference
(B)separate
(C)know who
(D)confirm the identity

( ) **11** It's difficult to achieve the goal of same work same pay between men and women although _____ is a government policy.
(A)salary fairness
(B)equal wages
(C)gender equality
(D)equality for all

( ) **12** Talk to the _____ if you have any question about the amount of pay you received last week.
(A)chairperson
(B)chief secretary
(C)accounting office
(D)personal office

( ) **13** "Do you have minute? I need to _____ you."
(A)hear a story from
(B)tell a lie to
(C)have a chat with
(D)play some music with

( ) **14** You have to _____ if you want to play the game.
(A)enjoy the atmosphere
(B)follow the rules
(C)know the results
(D)take the money

( ) **15** "There is no need to _____ ; the movie already started half hour ago."
(A)arrive
(B)rush
(C)race
(D)choose

(　　) **16** Jack admitted that he should have listened to you. It means
　　　(A)He didn't hear you.　　　(B)You didn't speak.
　　　(C)He didn't listen to you.　　(D)You had told him.

(　　) **17** "We're celebrating Jimmy's birthday this Friday. He's _____ 26."
　　　(A)turning　　　　　　　　(B)been
　　　(C)gone to　　　　　　　　(D)arrived

(　　) **18** Mark is an interesting person and people like to be _____ him.
　　　(A)besides　　　　　　　　(B)as
　　　(C)around　　　　　　　　(D)for

(　　) **19** Jay has trouble managing his money and he always _____ at the end of the month.
　　　(A)runs out of money　　　(B)uses cash
　　　(C)in need of money　　　　(D)has to lend money

(　　) **20** Matthew and Tony are buddies. They have known each other _____ childhood.
　　　(A)from　　　　　　　　　(B)since
　　　(C)in　　　　　　　　　　(D)during

(　　) **21** Taiwan Power Company is a _____ company under the Ministry of Economic Affairs.
　　　(A)private　　　　　　　　(B)state-owned
　　　(C)electric　　　　　　　　(D)publicity

(　　) **22** Many sports events are held without _____ because of the pandemic.
　　　(A)guests　　　　　　　　　(B)tickets
　　　(C)spectators　　　　　　　(D)people

(　　) **23** Gary spends three hours _____ between home and work each day, but he doesn't mind.
　　　(A)riding　　　　　　　　　(B)coming
　　　(C)commuting　　　　　　　(D)transporting

(　　) **24** Ken is really a good _____ although he doesn't seem to have a
lot of muscles.
(A)athlete　　　　　　　　　(B)cook
(C)game player　　　　　　　(D)gulf player

(　　) **25** "You'd better hurry if you want to _____. It leaves in half hour."
(A)get the airplane　　　　　(B)meet the bus
(C)take the taxi　　　　　　(D)catch the train

(　　) **26** The weather has been _____. Sometimes the temperature
drops ten degrees in one day.
(A)inconvenient　　　　　　(B)unbalanced
(C)inconsistent　　　　　　(D)unstable

(　　) **27** Some people are addicted to _____ and they upload several
posts everyday.
(A)internet　　　　　　　　(B)social media
(C)intranet　　　　　　　　(D)blogs

(　　) **28** It's impossible to _____ fashion because new models come
out so quickly.
(A)keep up with　　　　　　(B)pay attention to
(C)focus on　　　　　　　　(D)hold on to

(　　) **29** Norma's eyes are all red and swollen; she _____ all night
because of not passing the test.
(A)has cried　　　　　　　　(B)must cry
(C)cries　　　　　　　　　　(D)must have cried

(　　) **30** "Look at all the dark clouds coming in. It _____ rain."
(A)will seem to　　　　　　(B)will like to
(C)must to　　　　　　　　(D)is about to

(　　) **31** Taipei 101 _____ the tallest building in the world, but it is still
an important landmark in the city.
(A)has been　　　　　　　　(B)used to be
(C)is　　　　　　　　　　　(D)is once

(   ) **32** "Jake didn't ____, so the teacher thought he was not interested in the class."
(A)sign up   (B)write down
(C)turn in   (D)call out

(   ) **33** No motor vehicles are allowed to enter the pedestrian zone. What is a pedestrian?
(A)a person   (B)a walker
(C)a passerby   (D)a bicycle rider

(   ) **34** Children learn to speak by _____ their older family members.
(A)learning   (B)studying
(C)imitating   (D)seeing

(   ) **35** Which one is the closest to "find out" in meaning?
(A)learn about   (B)identify
(C)look for   (D)uncover

(   ) **36** My best friend's father wanted to _____ me a job, but I said no to him.
(A)provide   (B)supply
(C)suggest   (D)offer

(   ) **37** The customer who made the complaint accepted my explanation without _____ questions.
(A)further   (B)answering
(C)worst   (D)little

(   ) **38** By _____ garbage, we can reduce the amount of garbage put into our environment.
(A)keeping   (B)giving away
(C)hiding   (D)sorting

( ) **39** The workers have been instructed to follow the SOP. "SOP" stands for
(A)simple operation process　(B)single operational plan
(C)standard operating procedure (D)singular operative progress

( ) **40** Heather is a _____ person. She doesn't talk much.
(A)talkative　　　　　　(B)mute
(C)speechless　　　　　　(D)quiet

解答與解析　答案標示為#者，表官方曾公告更正該題答案。

1 (B)。當有人跟你說「你好嗎？」時，最佳回答為何？
(A)什麼事　　　(B)老樣子
(C)我沒頭緒　　(D)我喜歡它們
解 How are things ?為How are things with you ?的縮寫句，意為「你最近如何?」，因此回答Same as usual.（老樣子。）最為合適。

2 (B)。地震是無法預測的，但最新的偵測器能讓你有10秒的反應時間。
(A)給　　　　　(B)允許
(C)讓　　　　　(D)使
解 空格後方接續受詞you以及不定詞to V，選項中僅有allow合乎文法，allow的用法為allow sb. to V。give的用法應改為give you 10 extra seconds to respond；let的用法應為let you have 10 extra seconds to respond；make的意思為「使某人做某事」，因此不適合放在此處。

3 (D)。由於在對抗新冠肺炎方面的成功，台灣現在成為其他國家的典範。
(A)學習對象（無此用法）
(B)複製的物件（無此用法）
(C)標準國家（無此用法）
(D)榜樣；模範
解 此題考的是固定用法role model，意為「榜樣；典範」，因此選(D)。

4 (A)。該公司於40年前成立；也就是說，它已經營運40年了。
(A)四十年　　　　(B)四十個月
(C)八十年　　　　(D)八十個月
解 本題考的是decade的詞意，decade意為「十年」，因此four decades就是40年，應選(A)。

5 (A)。台灣從北到南長約400公里。
(A)量；有……長　(B)渴望
(C)有　　　　　　(D)去
解 本題考「有……長度」的說法該怎麼說，應用measure一字，measure意為「測量；有……

長」，因此應選(A)。long作為形容詞為「長的」，但作為動詞為「渴望」之意，固定用法為long for sth.（渴望某事物）。has並不能直接用在「有……公里」的用法上，此為中文上的講法，但英文中無此用法。

6 (B)。 對於「你為何不跟我們去吃午餐呢？」的最佳回答為何？
(A)我不是朋友。
(B)我很晚才吃早餐。
(C)這是個問題嗎？
(D)這是我的問題。
解 此題詢問「你為何不跟我們去吃午餐呢?」詢問對方理由,(B)回答我很晚才吃早餐,進而推論回答我不餓才拒絕。此種題型需注意,第一眼可能無法看出回答,需仔細判斷因果細節才能作答。

7 (B)。 懷有一項技能，有時比擁有一個漂亮的學歷有價值。
(A)更好的　　　(B)有價值的
(C)感到印象深刻的　(D)方便的
解 依據題意，應填入(B)有價值的。(A)並不符合文法，better本身即是比較級，前面不能再放more；(C)impressed是用來形容人「感到印象深刻的」；(D)不符合題意。

8 (A)。 凱西非常健康、強健，因為她多年規律運動。
(A)健康的；強健的　(B)滿意；滿足
(C)可愛的　　　(D)合適的

解 依照句型，空格處應填入形容詞當主詞補語。fit為「健康的；強健的」之意，依據題意應填入(A)。(B)不符合文法；(C)(D)皆不符合題意。

9 (C)。 垃圾食物不健康，但通常都很好吃；這就是為什麼很多人喜歡垃圾食物。
(A)好的味道　　(B)聞起來很棒
(C)美味的　　　(D)吸引人的
解 依照句型，空格處應填入形容詞當主詞補語，前面說垃圾食物不健康，後方說很多人喜歡，應題意應填入flavorful（美味的）。(A)(B)不符合文法；(D)不符合題意。

10 (A)。 湯姆和傑瑞是雙胞胎，要辨認他們很困難。
(A)區別
(B)將……分開
(C)知道誰<無此用法>
(D)確認身份
解 tell the difference意為「區別、辨別（差別）」，因此因題意應填入(A)。(B)(D)不符合題意；並無(C)的用法。

11 (C)。 要落實男女間同工同酬的目標是很困難的，儘管性別平等是政府政策。
(A)薪水公平<無此用法>
(B)平等薪資
(C)性別平等
(D)人人平等

解 此題考的是固定用詞gender equality（性別平等），故選(C)。並無(A)的說法；(B)為複數，不符合文法；(D)不符合文意。

12 (C)。 對於你上禮拜收到的薪資若是有問題，請去詢問會計部門。
(A)議長；主席　　(B)首席秘書
(C)會計部門　　　(D)個人辦公室

解 依據題意，對於薪資若有問題，應去詢問(C)accounting office（會計部門）。(A)(B)(D)皆不符合題意。

13 (C)。 「你有時間嗎？我需要跟你聊一下。」
(A)聽故事　　　(B)說謊
(C)聊一下　　　(D)播音樂

解 依據題意，應填入(C)have a chat with（聊一下）。(A)(B)(D)皆不符合題意。

14 (B)。 如果你要玩這個遊戲，你就必須遵守規則。
(A)享受氣氛　　(B)遵守規則
(C)知道結果　　(D)拿錢

解 依據題意，應填入(B)follow the rules（遵守規則）。(A)(C)(D)皆不符合題意。

15 (B)。 「不用趕了；電影在半小時前就已經開始了。」
(A)抵達　　　　(B)趕緊；匆忙
(C)競賽　　　　(D)選擇

解 依據題意，應填入(B)rush（趕緊；匆忙）。(A)為不及物動詞，不符文法；(C)(D)皆不符合題意。

16 (C)。 傑克承認他當初應該聽你的。這表示
(A)他沒有聽到你說的。
(B)你沒有說話。
(C)他沒有聽你的。
(D)你已經告訴過他了。

解 此題詢問should have p.p.的語意為何，should have p.p.表示當時應該做什麼，但卻沒有這麼做的事情。he should have listened to you表示他當初應該要聽你的（實際上卻沒有），因此應選(C)。

17 (A)。 「我們這禮拜五要慶祝吉米的生日。他要滿26歲了。」
(A)轉變為；滿
(B)是（be動詞的過去分詞）
(C)去
(D)抵達

解 本題考「年齡滿……歲」的用法，英文的動詞會用「turn＋年齡」，因此應選(A)。

18 (C)。 馬克是一個很有趣的人，大家都喜歡在他身邊。
(A)除……外　　(B)作為；當作
(C)在……身邊　(D)為了……

解 此題考的是介系詞用法，表示「在……身邊；周圍」用around這個介系詞，因此選(C)。另一個易混淆用法是介系詞beside，意思同為「在……旁」，但通常是指物理上的在旁邊；而besides作為介系詞意為「除了……之外」，作為副詞則是「此外」之意。

解答與解析

19 (A)。傑在管理金錢方面很有困難，他總是在月底就把錢用完。

(A)用完錢 　　　(B)使用現金

(C)缺錢 　　　　(D)必須借出錢

解 本題根據題意，前面提及傑在管理金錢方面有困難，因此應填入(A)runs out of money，run out of 意為「將……用完；耗盡」。(B)不符合題意；in need of表示「需要、缺乏」，但(C)不符文法；lend意思為「借出……」，因此(D)不正確，若是誤會成「借錢」則可能誤選此選項，若是要表示「借錢」則應用borrow（借入）這個詞。

20 (B)。馬修和湯尼是好兄弟，他們從孩提時期就認識彼此了。

(A)從…… 　　　(B)自從……

(C)在…… 　　　(D)在……期間

解 本題考時間上的介系詞，前方說道他們是好兄弟，因此推斷是「自從」孩提時期便認識彼此，since通常會加過去時間點，表示「自從何時開始便……」，因此選(B)。

21 (B)。台灣電力公司是一間國有企業，隸屬於經濟部。

(A)私人的 　　　(B)國有的；國營的

(C)電力的 　　　(D)名聲；宣傳

解 空格後方提到，台灣電力公司隸屬於經濟部，因此可推論為「國有企業」，因此選(B)。

22 (C)。因為疫情的關係，很多運動賽事是以沒有現場觀眾的方式舉辦的。

(A)賓客 　　　　(B)票券

(C)觀眾 　　　　(D)人

解 本題敘述因為疫情的關係，可推論運動賽事是用沒有「現場觀眾」的方式舉行，spectator表示運動賽事、演講等的觀眾，因此選(C)。

23 (C)。蓋瑞每天花三小時在公司與家之間通勤，但他不在意。

(A)騎乘 　　　　(B)來

(C)通勤 　　　　(D)運送；運輸

解 本題考的是在公司與家之間「通勤」，commute即為「通勤」之意，應選(C)。(D)transport可能會讓人以為是「交通」的意思，但其實transport作為動詞是「運送；運輸」之意，而其名詞transportation才是「交通」之意。

24 (A)。肯真的是一位很棒的運動員，儘管他看起來沒有很多肌肉。

(A)運動員 　　　(B)廚師

(C)球員 　　　　(D)高爾夫球員

解 空格後方提及，雖然肯看起來沒有很多肌肉，可推斷他應是一位優秀的「運動員」，選(A)。

25 (D)。「如果你要趕上火車，你最好快一點。火車再半小時就要開了。」

(A)得到飛機 　　　(B)碰見公車

(C)搭計程車 　　　(D)趕上火車

解 此題考的是「趕上……交通工具」的用法，通常會用catch這個詞，如catch the train/airplane（趕搭火車／飛機），因此應選(D)。

26 (D)。天氣不太穩定。有時候一天內溫度就下降了十度。
(A)不方便的　　(B)不平衡的
(C)不一致的　　(D)不穩定的
解 空格後方提到有時溫度在一天內就掉了十度，因此可判定天氣「不太穩定」，因此選(D)。

27 (B)。有些人對社群媒體成癮，他們每天都會上傳一些貼文。
(A)網路　　　　(B)社群媒體
(C)內部網路　　(D)部落格
解 空格後方提到，他們每天都會上傳貼文，因此可判斷是使用「社群媒體」成癮，選(B)。

28 (A)。要跟上流行是不太可能的，因為新的款式總是出來得很快。
(A)跟上；不落後　(B)專注於
(C)聚焦在　　　　(D)堅持
解 空格後方提到，新的款式機型總是出來得很快，因此可判斷要「跟上」流行是不太可能的，keep up with意為「跟上；不落後」，選(A)。

29 (D)。諾瑪的眼睛又紅又腫；她一定因為沒通過考試哭了整晚。
(A)has cried　　(B)must cry
(C)cries　　　　(D)must have cried
解 本題考不同時態所代表的不同語境，must have p.p.表示推斷「過去一定是……」，空格前方提到諾瑪的眼睛又紅又腫，因此說話者根據此現象判斷她昨晚「一定是哭了整晚」，因此選(D)。

30 (D)。「看看那些靠近的烏雲，就要下雨了。」
(A)will seem to　(B)will like to
(C)must to　　　(D)is about to
解 be about to表示「即將要……」，本題空格前方提到有烏雲靠近，可判定就快要下雨了，因此選(D)。並無(A)(B)(C)的用法。

31 (B)。台北101曾是世界上最高的建築物，但現在仍是城市中很重要的一個地標。
(A)has been　　(B)used to be
(C)is　　　　　(D)is once
解 本題表示台北101「過去曾是」世界上最高的建築，used to be表示「過去曾經……」，因此選(B)。(A)has been表示「過去曾是而現在仍持續是」，因此(A)不正確；(C)表示「現在式」，現在式表示事實，因此也不正確；並無(D)的用法。

32 (A)。「傑克沒有報名，所以老師以為他對這堂課沒有興趣。」
(A)報名　　　　(B)寫下
(C)繳交　　　　(D)呼叫
解 空格後方提到老師以為他對這堂課沒興趣，所以可判定傑克應是沒有報名這堂課，sign up表示「註冊；報名」，因此選(A)。(B)(C)(D)不符合題意。

33 (B)。人行徒步區禁止機動車輛進入。pedestrian指的是什麼？
(A)人　　　(B)行走的人；步行者
(C)路人　　(D)騎腳踏車的人

解 本題考pedestrian的意思，pedestrian指的是「行人；步行者」，因此選(B)。

34 (C)。 孩童透過模仿家中較年長的成員來學習說話。

(A)學習　　　　　(B)研讀
(C)模仿　　　　　(D)看

解 本題依據題意，孩童透過_____家中較年長的成員來學習說話，因此應填入(C)imitating（模仿）。

35 (A)。 在意義上，下列何者最接近「find out」？

(A)打聽到；得悉　(B)辨識；識別
(C)尋找　　　　　(D)揭露

解 find out意思為「發現；找出；查明（真相等）」，因此(A)learn about（打聽到；得悉）在意義上最接近，選(A)。看到find，可能會有人會聯想到「尋找」而選(C)，但需注意find out此一片語為「發現」之意。

36 (D)。 我最好的朋友的爸爸想給我一份工作，但我拒絕了他。

(A)提供　　　　　(B)供給
(C)提議　　　　　(D)給予；提供

解 提供給某人工作，通常會使用offer sb. a job，因此選(D)。provide也是「提供」之意，但其用法為provide sb. with sth.。

37 (A)。 投訴的顧客接受了我的解釋，沒有進一步的疑問。

(A)進一步的　　　(B)回覆
(C)更糟的　　　　(D)很少的

解 根據題意，投訴的顧客接受了解釋，因此可判定沒有「進一步的」疑問，選(A)。

38 (D)。 透過垃圾分類，我們可以減少投入環境的垃圾量。

(A)保持　　　　　(B)分送
(C)隱藏　　　　　(D)分類

解 根據題意，能夠達到減少投入環境的垃圾量，可推測是透過「分類」垃圾，因此選(D)。

39 (C)。 工人被指導要遵守SOP。「SOP」代表

(A)simple operation process
(B)single operational plan
(C)standard operating procedure
(D)singular operative progress

解 SOP表示「標準作業程序」，也就是standard operating procedure，因此選(C)。

40 (D)。 海瑟是一個 _____ 的人，她不太多話。

(A)喜歡說話的
(B)靜音的
(C)一時說不出話的；不會說話的
(D)安靜的

解 空格後方說道海瑟不多話，因此可判定她是安靜的人，因此選(D)。

110年 台中捷運新進人員（運務類、維修類）

( ) **1** Tom: How is the graduation trip planning going?
Mary: We've had a few _____ , but it's going well.
Tom: I'm sure it'll be perfect. I am looking forward to it.
Mary: We are too. I can't believe that it's next week.
(A)drills (B)pillars
(C)hurdles (D)thrones

( ) **2** Drunk driving is strongly prohibited in Taiwan; those who are caught driving under the influence will be _____ punished.
(A)reluctantly (B)objectively
(C)severely (D)mildly

( ) **3** The famous café _____ a Christmas sales promotion, trying to attract more people to buy its drinks.
(A)launched (B)acquired
(C)translated (D)dismissed

( ) **4** To remember the soldiers who lost their lives in the war, the government decided to build a huge _____ on which their names were inscribed.
(A)reservoir (B)monument
(C)cradle (D)furniture

( ) **5** It's _____ that everyone should get adequate sleep and eat a balanced diet to stay healthy.
(A)disputable (B)considerable
(C)preventable (D)advisable

( ) **6** When Mark's wife accused him of cheating on her, he was _____ by her lack of trust in him.
(A)incensed (B)entranced
(C)manifested (D)assassinated

(　) **7** New laws have been enacted by the legislature to reduce carbon dioxide _____ from vehicles and factories.
(A)portraits　　　　　　　　(B)applications
(C)emissions　　　　　　　　(D)sensations

(　) **8** This liquid is very _____ , so it shouldn't be used near an open fire.
(A)exhaustive　　　　　　　(B)flammable
(C)complimentary　　　　　　(D)elastic

(　) **9** Anna was _____ from her job after she failed to deal with customer complaints and yelled at her client.
(A)assumed　　　　　　　　(B)registered
(C)dismissed　　　　　　　　(D)conveyed

(　) **10** Your report is impressive, and the ideas are _____ and clear. In brief, it leaves nothing to be desired.
(A)frequent　　　　　　　　(B)vague
(C)temporary　　　　　　　　(D)concrete

(　) **11** Mary decided to _____ her career when she determined to stay home and take care of her kids.
(A)sacrifice　　　　　　　　(B)advertise
(C)publicize　　　　　　　　(D)criticize

(　) **12** That politician is a _____ man. He successfully convinced the public to vote for him.
(A)persuasive　　　　　　　(B)current
(C)sensitive　　　　　　　　(D)democratic

(　) **13** Within 24 hours, the video went _____ on YouTube and Facebook, with hundreds of likes and thousands of views.
(A)viral　　　　　　　　　　(B)civil
(C)typical　　　　　　　　　(D)internal

(　) **14** Rita wears a device around her wrist to _____ her heart rate so that she can monitor her health conditions.
(A)track　　　　　　　　　　(B)spoil
(C)involve　　　　　　　　　(D)consume

( ) **15** Mr. Lin wanted you to call him back _____ . He seemed to be very worried.
(A)globally　　　　　(B)immediately
(C)regretfully　　　　(D)awkwardly

( ) **16** Global warming poses a _____ to the survival of many creatures.
(A)threat　　　　　(B)demand
(C)sense　　　　　(D)chat

( ) **17** The tourists got lost because they were not _____ with the streets in the city.
(A)tense　　　　　(B)determined
(C)innovative　　　　(D)familiar

( ) **18** It is against the _____ to use the printer in the office for personal affair.
(A)intelligence　　　(B)property
(C)regulation　　　　(D)sustainability

( ) **19** You can call the technicians if the machine _____ . They will come and fix it as soon as possible.
(A)passes away　　　(B)gives up
(C)takes off　　　　(D)breaks down

( ) **20** The train is _____ Taipei. If you are heading for Tainan, you should go to Platform 2.
(A)bound for　　　　(B)related to
(C)preparing for　　　(D)prone to

( ) **21** Chris: What do you usually do on weekends?
Grace: _____ I'm actually quite flexible.
Chris: I see. Are you interested in going hiking with me this Sunday? Grace: Sure. Where do you want to go?
(A)It matters a lot.　　(B)It's my pleasure.
(C)It depends.　　　　(D)It's interesting.

(　　) **22** Sharon: Do you know when the meeting will start?

Kevin: _____

Sharon: I asked when the meeting would begin.

Kevin: Oh, it'll start at three o'clock.

(A)I'm sorry. I didn't catch it.

(B)Excuse me. That was kind of rude.

(C)Thanks. It's really nice of you.

(D)Yes, it is a good timing.

閱讀測驗（第23～25題）

　　Cyber Monday, created in 2005, is the biggest online shopping day in the US. It is basically the online version of Black Friday, the Friday next to Thanksgiving. It is a time when businesses compete to sell their products with all sorts of deals. The offers can be so attractive that people just couldn't stop themselves from making a purchase.

　　Cyber Monday takes place on the Monday following Thanksgiving, mostly falling in November, but if Thanksgiving is on November 27 or 28, it may take place in December. In fact, online shopping sites sometimes extend Cyber Monday into "Cyber Week" in order that they can make more money.

Figure : Online Spending around Thanksgiving

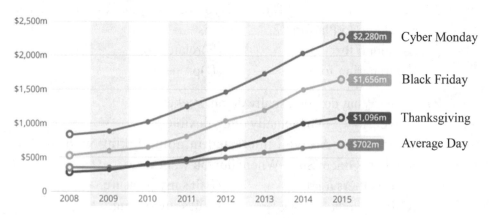

( ) **23** What does the word "deal" in the first paragraph most likely mean?
(A)Issue (B)Discount
(C)Exchange (D)Money

( ) **24** Which of the following is true about online spending around Thanksgiving from 2008 to 2015?
(A)People have spent more on Black Friday than on Cyber Monday over the years.
(B)People spent more on Thanksgiving than on average days before 2010.
(C)Online spending on Thanksgiving dropped over the years.
(D)Online spending has increased more on Cyber Monday than on Thanksgiving over the years.

( ) **25** According to the passage, why is Cyber Monday sometimes extended into "Cyber Week?"
(A)To increase sales (B)To save money
(C)To celebrate traditions (D)To correct mistakes

解答與解析 答案標示為# 者，表官方曾公告更正該題答案。

1 (C)。
湯姆：畢業旅行的規劃進行得如何了？
瑪麗：我們碰到一些阻礙，但進行得還不錯。
湯姆：我相信會很完美的，我非常期待。
瑪麗：我們也是，我不敢相信就是下禮拜了。
(A)訓練 (B)柱子
(C)困難；阻礙 (D)王座
解 本題空格位置a few之後，可判斷應填入名詞，hurdle原意為跨欄賽跑的「跳欄」，可引申為「障礙；阻礙」之意，選(C)。

2 (C)。酒駕在台灣是嚴格禁止的；被抓到酒後駕車的人將會被嚴厲地懲罰。
(A)不願地 (B)客觀地
(C)嚴厲地 (D)溫和地
解 本題空格前後架構完整，空格應填入一副詞來形容動詞punished，依題意應填入severely（嚴厲地），選(C)。

3 (A)。那個知名的咖啡館發起了一個聖誕節促銷活動，希望能吸引更多人來買他們的飲品。
(A)發行；發起 (B)獲得
(C)翻譯 (D)解散

262 Chapter 3 近年各類試題及解析

解 本題空格依結構應填入一動詞，
launch有「發起」活動之意，同
時也有「推出」新產品的意思，
選(A)。

4 (B)。 為了紀念那些在戰爭中失去生
命的軍人們，政府決定建造一個大型
紀念碑，並把他們的名字刻在上面。
(A)蓄水庫　　　　(B)紀念碑
(C)搖籃　　　　　(D)家具

解 本題空格依結構應填入一名詞，
由前方形容詞huge來修飾，依
題意應填入monument（紀念
碑），選(B)。

5 (D)。 建議每個人都要有足夠的睡
眠，並保有均衡的飲食才能維持健康。
(A)可質疑的　(B)值得考慮的
(C)可預防的　(D)可取的；明智的

解 本題空格應填入一形容詞，來形
容後方由that帶出的子句，依題
意應填入advisable（可取的；適
當的；明智的），選(D)。

6 (A)。 當馬克的老婆控訴他背叛她
時，他因她缺乏對他的信任而被激
怒了。
(A)激怒了的；憤怒的
(B)狂喜的；著迷的
(C)被表明的
(D)被暗殺的

解 本題空格應填入一形容詞接續
was，incense作為動詞有「激
怒」之意，incensed則為「被激
怒了的」之意，選(A)。

7 (C)。 立法機關頒布了新法條，要降
低汽車與工廠的二氧化碳排放量。
(A)肖像　　　　　(B)申請
(C)排放物　　　　(D)感覺

解 本題空格接續了carbon dioxide
（二氧化碳），依題意應放置
emission（排放物），選(C)。

8 (B)。 這個液體非常易燃，所以絕
對不可以放靠近明火。
(A)徹底的　　　　(B)易燃的
(C)贈送的　　　　(D)有彈性的

解 本題空格應放置一形容詞作為前
方liquid的補語，而後句說道不
可以放靠近明火，可判斷是非常
「易燃的」，選(B)。

9 (C)。 安娜在無法處理好客訴並對
客戶大吼之後被解僱了。
(A)假設　　　　　(B)登記
(C)解僱　　　　　(D)傳播

解 本題後句提到安娜無法處理客訴
並對客戶大吼，因此可判斷是被
解僱，dismiss有「解散；解僱」
之意，選(C)。

10 (D)。 你的報告讓人非常印象深
刻，而且想法很具體明確。簡短來
說，相當完美無缺。
(A)頻繁的　　　　(B)模糊的
(C)暫時的　　　　(D)具體的

解 本題空格應填入一形容詞且與
clear對等，前方說道很讓人印
象深刻，後方則提到it leaves
nothing to be desired（完美無
缺），可判斷是正向的形容詞，依
題意選(D)concrete（具體的）。

11 **(A)**。 當瑪麗決心要待在家裡照顧她的孩子時，她已決定要犧牲她的事業。
(A)犧牲　　　　　(B)廣告
(C)宣傳　　　　　(D)批判
解 本題應填入一動詞，後方接續受詞career（事業、生涯），後方提到瑪麗決定要待在家照顧小孩，可判斷是要「犧牲」事業，選(A)。

12 **(A)**。 那位政客是相當具有說服力的人。他成功說服大眾投票給他。
(A)具有說服力的　(B)目前的
(C)敏感的　　　　(D)民主的
解 本題空格應填入一形容詞形容後方的man，後句說道這位政客成功說服大眾投給他，可判斷他是「具有說服力的」人，選(A)。persuasive的動詞為persuade（說服）。

13 **(A)**。 在24小時之內，這個影片就在YouTube跟臉書上被瘋傳了，有著數百個讚數與數千的瀏覽數。
(A)病毒性的　　　(B)市民的
(C)典型的　　　　(D)內部的
解 本題考一固定用法，go viral意思是某事物像病毒一樣瘋傳，也就是在網路上瘋傳、爆紅之意，選(A)。

14 **(A)**。 瑞塔在手腕戴著一個裝置來追蹤她的心率，這樣她就可以監控她的健康狀況。
(A)追蹤　　　　　(B)寵溺
(C)牽涉　　　　　(D)消耗
解 本題空格應填入一動詞，後方接續受詞her heart rate，依題意應選track（追蹤），選(A)。

15 **(B)**。 林先生希望你立即回電給他，他看起來非常擔憂。
(A)全球地　　　　(B)立即地
(C)後悔地　　　　(D)尷尬地
解 本題空格前方結構完整，空格應填入一副詞形容動詞call，後方提到他看起來很擔心，因此應是要「立即」回電給他，選(B)。

16 **(A)**。 地球暖化對許多生物的生存都造成了威脅。
(A)威脅　　　　　(B)要求
(C)感官　　　　　(D)聊天
解 本題考一固定用法，pose a threat to意為「對……造成威脅」，選(A)。

17 **(D)**。 這群遊客迷路了，因為他們對這個城市的路不熟悉。
(A)繃緊的　　　　(B)決心的
(C)創新的　　　　(D)熟悉的
解 空格前提到遊客迷路，可判斷是對這城市的路不「熟悉」，be familiar with意為「對……熟悉」，選(D)。

18 **(C)**。 在辦公室使用印表機印私人文件是違反規定的。
(A)智慧　　　　　(B)財產
(C)規定　　　　　(D)永續
解 空格前方有介系詞against，有「違反;反對」之意，後方提到在辦公室用印表機印私人的東西，可判斷為違反「規定」，選(C)。

解答與解析

19 (D)。 如果機器故障的話,你可以叫
技師過來。他們會盡快過來修理。
(A)過世　　　　　(B)放棄
(C)起飛　　　　　(D)故障
解 本題考動詞片語,前方提到呼叫
技師,可判斷是若機器「故障」
的話,break down通常用來形容
機械故障,選(D)。

20 (A)。 這台火車開往台北。如果你
要前往台南,你應該去第二月台。
(A)前往　　　　　(B)與……有關
(C)為……準備　　(D)傾向於……
解 空格前方的主詞是the train,後
方是Taipei,可推知是「前往」
台北,be bound for有前往某地
之意,意同head for,選(A)。

21 (C)。
克里斯:妳週末通常都在幹嘛?
葛瑞絲:要看情況。我其實都很彈性。
克里斯:了解。那妳這星期日要跟
　　　　我一起去健行嗎?
葛瑞絲:好啊,你想要去哪裡?
(A)這相當重要。
(B)這是我的榮幸。
(C)要看情況而定。
(D)這真有趣。
解 本題考依據對話前後文填入適當
的語句,前方克里斯問道週末
通常都在幹嘛,葛瑞絲後面說
都很彈性,可判斷應是「要看狀
況」,It depends.意為「要視狀
況而定」,選(C)。

22 (A)。
雪倫:你知道會議幾點會開始嗎?
凱文:抱歉,我沒聽清楚。
雪倫:我問說會議幾點會開始。
凱文:喔,會於三點開始。
(A)抱歉,我沒聽清楚。
(B)不好意思,那有點沒禮貌。
(C)謝啦,妳人真好。
(D)是的,這是個好時機。
解 本題考依據對話前後文填入適當
的語句,前方雪倫問會議幾點
開始,後方又說了一次類似的
話,可見凱文請雪倫再說一次,
not catch something意指「沒有
聽清楚;沒有聽懂」,選(A)。

閱讀測驗(第23~25題)

　　網購星期一創建於2005年,是美國
最大的線上購物日。它基本上就是黑色
星期五的線上版本,黑色星期五在感恩
節的下個星期五。這是企業透過各種交
易競爭來銷售產品的時代。這些優惠都
非常有吸引力,以致於人們無法阻止自
己購買。

　　網購星期一在感恩節後的星期一
舉行,大部分時間在11月,但如果感恩
節在11月27日或28日,則可能在12月舉
行。事實上,線上購物網站有時會將網
購星期一延長為「網購週」,以賺取更
多收入。

圖片：感恩節前後的線上購物情況

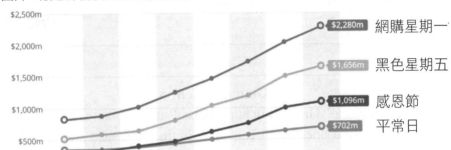

23 (B)。 第一段的「deal」最可能是什麼意思？
(A)議題　(B)折扣　(C)交換　(D)金錢

解 文章中提到business compete to sell their products with all sorts of deals，各家企業用各種「交易價格」來競爭販賣其商品，deal為「交易」之意，(B)discount（折扣）的意義最為接近。

24 (D)。 關於2008年至2015年感恩節前後的線上購物情形，下列何者為真？
(A)在這些年，人們在黑色星期五消費的金額比網購星期一還多。
(B)在2010年之前，人們在感恩節花費的金額比平常日還多。
(C)這些年來，在感恩節的線上購物逐年下降。
(D)這些年來，網購星期一的線上購物增加得比感恩節還要多。

解 由圖表可看出，網購星期一在這些年增加的幅度比感恩節還來得多，因此(D)正確。黑色星期五的額度沒有比網購星期一還多，因此(A)錯誤；在2010年以前，可以發現感恩節比平常日還要少，因此(B)不正確；這些年來，感恩節的金額持續在增加，因此(C)不正確。

25 (A)。 根據本文，為什麼網購星期一有時候會延展成「網購週」？
(A)為了增加銷售
(B)為了省錢
(C)為了慶祝傳統
(D)為了糾正錯誤

解 根據本文最後一段最後一行，文章提及網購星期一有時會延長成「網購週」的目的為：in order that they can make more money，這些網購商家為的是能賺更多的錢，因此選(A)。

解答與解析

110年 台中捷運新進人員（身障類、原住民類）

1~3為題組

Announcement A

Hello everyone! This is Taichung Mass Rapid Transit Green line service terminating at High Speed Rail Taichung Station. The next station is Daqing. Change here for Taiwan Railways services. Upon arrival, the front set of doors will not open. Customers in each carriage, please move towards the rear doors to exit. Mind the gap between the train and the platform.

(　　) **1** Which of the following statements based on Announcement A is False?
(A)High Speed Rail Taichung Station is the last stop.
(B)Mind the gap is a warning telling people to be cautious when stepping off the MRT.
(C)Those who need to change trains need to get off at Daqing station.
(D)The back doors won't open.

Announcement B

This is a platform announcement for passengers for the 0102 train to Taichung City Hall. This train is delayed by approximately 8 minutes.

Announcement C

The 0102 train will now depart from Platform 2. Passengers for the 0102 train to Taichung City Hall, please make your way to Platform 2. Currently the metro Green Line is partly closed between Yinghua Wunsin and Wenhua Senior High School due to the construction. Thank you.

(　　) **2** Based on the Announcement B and C, which of the following statements is True?
(A)The delay is less than eight minutes.
(B)The delay mainly results from the construction.
(C)Passengers cannot get off at Yinghua Wunsin station.
(D)The train for Taichung City Hall will leave at a quarter past twelve.

( ) **3** What is the purpose of the Announcement B and C?
   (A)To inform passengers of the delay and partial disclosure in some stops.
   (B)To cancel some of the trains leaving for Wenhua Senior High School.
   (C)To announce the duration of the construction.
   (D)To encourage the passengers to transfer to other lines.

( ) **4** Henry got up early this morning _____ he could take the first bus to school.
   (A)lest   (B)so that
   (C)as soon as   (D)despite the fact that

( ) **5** To remember the soldiers who lost their lives in the war, the government decided to build a huge _____ on which their names were inscribed.
   (A)reservoir   (B)monument
   (C)cradle   (D)furniture

( ) **6** New laws have been enacted by the legislature to reduce carbon dioxide _____ from vehicles and factories.
   (A)portraits   (B)applications
   (C)emissions   (D)sensations

( ) **7** Zak spent an hour looking for his electric car in the parking lot, _____ realize that he hadn't driven to work that morning.
   (A)with an eye to   (B)so as to
   (C)only to   (D)in addition to

( ) **8** This liquid is very _____ , so it shouldn't be used near an open fire.
   (A)exhaustive   (B)flammable
   (C)complimentary   (D)elastic

( ) **9** The infertile woman _____ wanted a child, so she adopted one from the nearby orphanage.
   (A)desperately   (B)technically
   (C)optionally   (D)thoroughly

(　　) **10** The movie star's rapid rise to _____ was triggered by an action film that sold very well.
(A)infancy (B)goodness
(C)explosion (D)fame

(　　) **11** Due to significant _____ in medical technology over the past few decades, people are able to survive diseases and injuries that would have caused death in the past.
(A)occasions (B)borders
(C)substances (D)advances

(　　) **12** Jessica came up with a _____ idea and successfully solved her client's problem.
(A)brilliant (B)regional
(C)crispy (D)sufficient

(　　) **13** The employee needs to make a few adjustments to the _____ before presenting it to the boss.
(A)disease (B)proposal
(C)avenue (D)channel

(　　) **14** The reason why Amy quit her job was that she couldn't tolerate her _____ boss.
(A)literary (B)demanding
(C)accessible (D)technical

(　　) **15** If you ever _____ things such as clothing online, you should be prepared for some disappointment since you do not always get what you think you ordered.
(A)recover (B)assist
(C)purchase (D)dodge

(　　) **16** Joanne will have her dog _____ in a pet beauty salon next week.
(A)cleaning (B)cleaned
(C)to clean (D)to be cleaned

(　) **17** Rita wears a device around her wrist to _____ her heart rate so that she can monitor her health conditions.
(A)track (B)spoil
(C)involve (D)consume

(　) **18** Before setting off, you should _____ the tourist information center for details about your trip.
(A)conclude (B)educate
(C)consult (D)respond

(　) **19** He spent almost an hour at the station _____ for the train.
(A)wait (B)waiting
(C)waited (D)to wait

(　) **20** If you need further _____, you can visit our Facebook page and learn more.
(A)information (B)expectation
(C)condition (D)situation

(　) **21** Mr. Lin wanted you to call him back _____. He seemed to be very worried.
(A)globally (B)immediately
(C)regretfully (D)awkwardly

(　) **22** The manager is _____ the new project. He is the one who makes the final decision.
(A)by means of (B)in honor of
(C)at the sight of (D)in charge of

(　) **23** You can call the technicians if the machine _____. They will come and fix it as soon as possible.
(A)passes away (B)gives up
(C)takes off (D)breaks down

( ) **24** Passengers are not allowed to open this window _____ there is an emergency.
(A)unless 　　　　　　　(B)so that
(C)whereas 　　　　　　(D)as if

( ) **25** The man was sitting on the chair _____ his eyes closed. He appeared to be exhausted.
(A)for 　　　　　　　　(B)by
(C)as 　　　　　　　　　(D)with

解答與解析　答案標示為# 者，表官方曾公告更正該題答案。

1~3為題組

廣播A

大家好！您正搭乘的是台中捷運的綠線，終點是高鐵台中站。下一站是大慶。如欲轉乘台鐵，請於本站換車。抵達後，前組的門不會開啟。每節車廂內的乘客，請往後門走至出口。請注意列車和站台之間的空隙。

1 (D)。根據廣播A，下列何者敘述不正確？
(A)高鐵台中站是最終站。
(B)「請注意空隙」是警告人們在跨出捷運時要小心。
(C)需要轉搭火車的旅客，須在大慶站下車。
(D)後門不會開啟。
解 本廣播倒數第二至三句説道，前組門不會開啟，乘客須由後門下車，因此(D)不正確。其餘敘述皆有於廣播中提到。

廣播B

這是給欲搭乘0102班次列車前往台中市政府之旅客的月台廣播。這班列車估計晚8分鐘。

廣播C

0102班次列車將從2號月台出發。欲搭乘0102班次列車前往台中市政府的乘客，請前往2號月台。目前捷運綠線的文心櫻花站與文華高中站之間因施工部分封閉。謝謝您。

2 (C)。根據廣播B和C，下列敘述何者正確？
(A)延誤時間小於8分鐘。
(B)延誤主要是由施工造成。
(C)乘客無法在文心櫻花站下車。
(D)前往台中市政府的列車將於12點15分出發。
解 廣播C的最後提到，文心櫻花站因施工封閉，因此乘客無法在此站下車，(C)正確。廣播B

提到列車估計晚8分鐘，因此(A)不正確；兩則廣播並沒有提到列車延誤是因為捷運施工造成，因此(B)不正確；兩則廣播並無提到列車於幾點出發，因此(D)不正確。

3 (A)。 廣播B和C的目的為何？
(A)要告知旅客延誤時間以及部分車站關閉。
(B)要取消部分前往文華高中站的列車。
(C)要公告施工的持續時間。
(D)要鼓勵乘客轉乘至其他線別。
解 廣播B主要在告知列車延誤時間，廣播C主要在告知列車發車時間，以及部分捷運車站因施工封閉，因此選(A)。

4 (B)。 亨利今天早上很早起床，這樣他才能搭第一班公車去學校。
(A)以免 (B)以便；為的是
(C)與……同時 (D)儘管……
解 本題空格應填入一連接詞來連接兩個句子，依語意應填入so that，意為「以便……」，選(B)。

5 (B)。 為了紀念那些在戰爭中失去生命的軍人們，政府決定建造一個大型紀念碑，並把他們的名字刻在上面。
(A)蓄水庫 (B)紀念碑
(C)搖籃 (D)家具
解 本題空格依結構應填入一名詞，由前方形容詞huge來修飾，依題意應填入monument（紀念碑），選(B)。

6 (C)。 立法機關頒布了新法條，要降低汽車與工廠的二氧化碳排放量。
(A)肖像 (B)申請
(C)排放物 (D)感覺
解 本題空格接續了carbon dioxide（二氧化碳），依題意應放置emission（排放物），選(C)。

7 (C)。 柴克花了一小時在停車場找他的電動車，結果卻發現他那天早上根本沒有開去上班。
(A)為了…… (B)為了……
(C)結果卻…… (D)除了……還有
解 本題空格前方說柴克在找電動車，後方說道他沒開去上班，only to通常用來接續表達意外或不幸的結果，因此選(C)。

8 (B)。 這個液體非常易燃，所以絕對不可以放靠近明火。
(A)徹底的 (B)易燃的
(C)贈送的 (D)有彈性的
解 本題空格應放置一形容詞作為前方liquid的補語，而後句說道不可以放靠近明火，可判斷是非常「易燃的」，選(B)。

9 (A)。 這位不孕的女士極度想要小孩，所以她在附近的孤兒院領養了一個孩子。
(A)極度地 (B)技術上
(C)可選擇地 (D)徹底地
解 本題空格前後結構完整，因此空格應填入一副詞形容後方的動詞wanted，根據語意應填入desperately（極度地），選(A)。

解答與解析

10 (D)。這位電影明星之所以會名氣快速上升，是因為一部動作片電影相當賣座。
(A)嬰兒期　　　　(B)良善
(C)爆炸　　　　　(D)名氣
解 本題空格應填入一名詞，接續前方的rapid rise to（……的急速上升），後方提到電影賣座，因此可判斷是「名氣」快速上升，選(D)。

11 (D)。由於過去幾十年醫療科技的重大進步，人們可以在過去會導致死亡或傷害中的疾病生存下來。
(A)場合　　　　　(B)邊界
(C)物質　　　　　(D)進步；發展
解 本題空格應填入一名詞，由前方形容詞significant形容，後方提到人們在過去會死亡、受傷的疾病中生存下來，可判斷醫療科技應是大幅「進步」所致，選(D)。

12 (A)。潔西卡想到了一個絕佳的點子，並成功地解決她客戶的問題。
(A)絕佳的　　　　(B)地區的
(C)脆的　　　　　(D)足夠的
解 本題空格應填入一形容詞來形容後方的idea，後方提到她成功解決客戶的問題，可判斷應是正向的形容詞，依題意應選brilliant（絕佳的），選(A)。

13 (B)。這名員工需要在呈交給老闆前，針對提案做一些修改。
(A)疾病　　　　　(B)提案
(C)巷　　　　　　(D)頻道
解 空格應填入一名詞，接續前方的adjustments to the...（……的修

改），題目提到員工和老闆，可判斷為要修改「提案」，選(B)。

14 (B)。艾美辭職的原因是因為她無法再忍受她那苛刻的老闆。
(A)文學的　　(B)苛刻的；高要求的
(C)可接近的　(D)技術的
解 本題空格應填入一形容詞，來形容後方的名詞boss，前方提到這是她辭職的原因，可判斷應是負面的形容詞，依題意應選(B)demanding（苛刻的）。

15 (C)。如果你曾在網路買過像是衣服的東西，你就應該準備可能會失望，因為你不一定總是會拿到你想像中的東西。
(A)恢復　　　　　(B)協助
(C)購買　　　　　(D)躲避
解 本題空格應填入一動詞，後方接續名詞things such as clothing，後方提到可能會因為拿到不是自己想像的東西而失望，可得知是在網路「購買」東西，選(C)。

16 (B)。喬安下週會把她的狗帶到寵物美容做清理。
(A)cleaning　　　(B)cleaned
(C)to clean　　　(D)to be cleaned
解 本題考使役動詞的被動用法，have為一使役動詞，意思為「把……、讓……做……」，後方的動作若是主動的動作則接原形動詞，而若是被動的動作則接過去分詞；本題是喬安讓她的狗去「被」清理，因此應用過去分詞cleaned，選(B)。

17 (A)。 瑞塔在手腕戴著一個裝置來追蹤她的心率，這樣她就可以監控她的健康狀況。

(A)追蹤　　　　　(B)寵溺

(C)牽涉　　　　　(D)消耗

解 本題空格應填入一動詞，後方接續受詞her heart rate，依題意應選track（追蹤），選(A)。

18 (C)。 在出發之前，你應該向旅客資訊中心諮詢一些旅程的細節。

(A)下結論　　　　(B)教育

(C)向……諮詢　　(D)回答

解 空格應填入一動詞，接在should之後，後方接續受詞the tourist information center，根據語意應填入consult（向……諮詢），本字通常會用於向專業人士（如律師、顧問）等諮詢時使用，選(C)。

19 (B)。 他花了近乎一小時在火車站等火車。

(A)wait　　　　　(B)waiting

(C)waited　　　　(D)to wait

解 本題考spend的用法，spend的用法為「人＋spend＋時間／金錢＋V-ing」或「人＋spend＋時間／金錢＋on名詞」；後方應使用現在分詞，因此選(B)。

20 (A)。 如果你需要更多資訊，可以上我們的臉書專頁得到更多。

(A)資訊　　　　　(B)期待

(C)狀況　　　　　(D)情況

解 空格應填入一名詞，由前方形容詞further（進一步的）接續，依題意應選information（資訊），選(A)。

21 (B)。 林先生希望你立即回電給他，他看起來非常擔憂。

(A)全球地　　　　(B)立即地

(C)後悔地　　　　(D)尷尬地

解 本題空格前方結構完整，空格應填入一副詞形容動詞call，後方提到他看起來很擔心，因此應是要「立即」回電給他，選(B)。

22 (D)。 主管負責新的專案，他是做最終決定的人。

(A)透過　　　　　(B)紀念

(C)一看見就……　(D)負責

解 本題考填入適當的片語，後方提到主管是做最終決定的人，可判斷他是「負責」這個最新的專案，選(D)。

23 (D)。 如果機器故障的話，你可以叫技師過來。他們會盡快過來修理。

(A)過世　　　　　(B)放棄

(C)起飛　　　　　(D)故障

解 本題考動詞片語，前方提到呼叫技師，可判斷是若機器「故障」的話，break down通常用來形容機械故障，選(D)。

24 (A)。 除非有緊急狀況，否則乘客不能打開這個窗戶。

(A)除非　　　　　(B)以便

(C)然而　　　　　(D)彷彿

解 空格應填入一連接詞接續兩個句子，前方說乘客不能打開窗戶，後方說有緊急狀況，可判斷是「除非」有緊急狀況，選(A)。

解答與解析

25 (D)。那名男子坐在椅子上、眼睛閉著，他看起來累壞了。

(A)for　　　　　(B)by

(C)as　　　　　(D)with

解 本題考with用來表示「有著……的狀態」的用法，句型為「with ＋受詞＋現在分詞／過去分詞」，若是受詞的動作為主動則用現在分詞，若受詞的動作是被動則用過去分詞，本題his eyes是「被」關上的，因此題目用過去分詞，故選(D)with。

110年 中華郵政職階人員（專業職(二)內勤）

一、字彙

( ) **1** It is everyone's _____ to save the earth's natural environment for future generations.
(A)responsibility (B)condition
(C)motivation (D)temperature

( ) **2** Wearing sunglasses on sunny days is important because if our eyes are _____ to too much sunlight, they could be hurt.
(A)connected (B)absorbed
(C)exposed (D)tightened

( ) **3** Water is _____ to life on Earth. All plants and animals must have water to survive.
(A)distinctive (B)transparent
(C)statistical (D)indispensable

( ) **4** Betty's kitchen is equipped with all the _____ she needs for cooking.
(A)nutrients (B)barriers
(C)appliances (D)vessels

( ) **5** Cell phones are _____ to some people because they can't do anything without one.
(A)essential (B)defensive
(C)noticeable (D)constructive

( ) **6** He knew she was holding back on her _____ to let out his love affairs in front of his wife.
(A)expression (B)manners
(C)status (D)urge

(　) **7** Tina walks ＿＿＿ for an hour every day in hope of losing some pounds in a few months.
(A)comparatively　　　　　(B)passively
(C)vigorously　　　　　　(D)absolutely

二、文法測驗

(　) **8** He sat still in front of the TV, ＿＿＿ by the news of the violent attack on the United States Capitol.
(A)shocked　　　　　　　(B)been shocked
(C)having shocked　　　　(D)to have been shocked

(　) **9** The designer dresses in this store are more affordable than ＿＿＿ in that store.
(A)ones　　　　　　　　(B)these
(C)those　　　　　　　　(D)which

(　) **10** The leftover is no longer edible for it ＿＿＿ on the table for hours.
(A)was left　　　　　　(B)is being left
(C)has been left　　　　(D)had been left

(　) **11** I suggest Jim ＿＿＿ the fastest route instead of the shortest one to his destination.
(A)take　　　　　　　　(B)takes
(C)be taking　　　　　　(D)taking

(　) **12** Most residents in this community are aged World War Two soldiers, ＿＿＿.
(A)many of them live alone
(B)many of them living alone
(C)and many of whom live alone
(D)and many of whom living alone

(   ) **13** It was not until I raised the alert to Debbie _____ to take action to deal with her mother's aging problems.
(A)who started   (B)did she start
(C)when she started   (D)that she started

(   ) **14** Dealing with so many customers at a time _____ not easy to me because their needs are quite different.
(A)being   (B)are
(C)is   (D)to be

(   ) **15** Jane is a shy girl. She has difficulty _____ to people in her workplace or neighborhood.
(A)talking   (B)talk
(C)to talk   (D)talks

三、克漏字測驗

    Fashion is the second most polluting industry on Earth. It is right behind oil. The pressure to reduce costs and _____16._____ production time means that the environment is sacrificed in the name of profit. Fast Fashion's bad impact includes the use of cheap, poisonous dyes. The fashion industry is the second largest polluter of clean water globally.

    The speed at which clothes are produced also means that more and more clothes are _____17._____ by consumers, creating a huge amount of waste. In Canada, the average person throws out 81 pounds of clothes annually, _____18._____ North Americans send 9.5 million tons of clothing to the landfill every year. Most of the clothes which are disposed of could be reused.

    There are about 40 million garment workers in the world today, many of _____19._____ do not have rights or protections. They are some of the lowest paid workers in the world and 85% of all garment workers are women.

Actually, it's possible to find stylish, affordable, and ethical clothing if you just know where to start. So, next time when you shop new clothes, be sure to buy from eco-fashion companies who are ____20.____ the production of clothing with more environmentally friendly methods. Also, make sure those companies provide fair working conditions and offer reasonable wages to the workers.

( ) **16** (A)slow down   (B)speed up
      (C)check out   (D)put away

( ) **17** (A)worn out   (B)thrown away
      (C)taken over   (D)passed down

( ) **18** (A)whether   (B)if
      (C)while   (D)since

( ) **19** (A)them   (B)that
      (C)who   (D)whom

( ) **20** (A)comparing   (B)pursuing
      (C)benefiting   (D)informing

四、閱讀測驗

The sandwich as we know it was popularized in England in 1762 by John Montagu, the 4th Earl of Sandwich. Legend has it, and most food historians agree, that Montagu had a gambling problem that led him to spend hours on end at the card table. During a particularly long binge, he asked the house cook to bring him something he could eat without getting up from his seat, and the sandwich was born. Montagu enjoyed his meat and bread so much that he ate it constantly, and as it grew popular in London society circles, it also took on the Earl's name.

Of course, John Montagu (or rather, his nameless cook) was hardly the first person to think of putting fillings between slices of bread. In fact, we know exactly where Montagu first got the idea for his creation. Montagu traveled abroad to the Mediterranean, where Turkish and Greek mezze platters were served. Dips, cheeses, and meats were all "sandwiched" between and on layers of bread. In all likelihood Montagu took inspiration from these when he sat at that card table.

Montagu's creation took off immediately. Just a few months later, a man named Edward Gibbon mentioned the sandwich by name in a diary entry, writing that he'd seen "twenty or thirty of the first men of the kingdom" in a restaurant eating them. By the Revolutionary War, the sandwich was well established in England. You would expect American colonists to have taken to the sandwich as well, but there's no early written record of them in the new country at all, and a sandwich recipe didn't appear in an American cookbook until 1815.

Why would this creation go **unsung** in the nation for so long? It seems early American cooks tended to avoid food trends from their former ruling state. And the name "sandwich" itself comes from the British upper class system, something that most Americans wanted to forget. Once memory faded and the sandwich appeared, the most popular version wasn't ham or turkey, but tongue!

Of course, most Americans today wouldn't dream of eating a tongue sandwich. But that's ok, since so many pretty excellent sandwich ideas have popped up since then.

( ) **21** What is the passage mainly about?
(A)The process of making the sandwich.
(B)The history of the sandwich
(C)The story of John Montagu.
(D)The ingredients of the sandwich

( ) **22** Where did John Montagu get the inspiration of making the sandwich?
(A)From Chinese dumplings.
(B)From American hamburgers.
(C)From Korean beef bulgogi.
(D)From Turkish and Greek mezze platters.

( ) **23** Which of the following statements about John Montagu is **NOT** true?

(A)He was the 4th Earl of Sandwich.

(B)He was said to have a gambling problem.

(C)He travelled abroad to the Mediterranean.

(D)Edward Gibbon was his cook.

( ) **24** Which of the following words is closest in meaning to the word **"unsung"** in Paragraph 4?

(A)overlooked   (B)established

(C)emphasized   (D)popularized.

( ) **25** Which of the following statements about the sandwich is true?

(A)It was not until 1815 that the sandwich became popular in England.

(B)John Montagu was the first person to put fillings between slices of bread.

(C)Early American cooks tended to avoid food trends from England.

(D)For Americans today, their favorite version of the sandwich is a tongue sandwich.

解答與解析　答案標示為# 者，表官方曾公告更正該題答案。

一、字彙

1 (A)。 為下個世代保存地球的自然環境，是每個人的責任。

(A)責任   (B)狀況

(C)動機   (D)溫度

解 本題考應填入哪個名詞，空格後方提到為下個世代保存自然環境，依題意應選(A)。

2 (C)。 在晴朗的天氣戴太陽眼鏡是很重要的，因為如果我們的眼睛曝曬於過量的陽光之下，可能會受傷。

(A)連接   (B)吸收

(C)曝曬   (D)使變緊

解 本題考一固定用法，be exposed to意為「曝曬於……之下」，應選(C)。

3 (D)。 水對於地球上的生物是不可或缺的。所有的動植物都必須要有水才能生存。

(A)有特色的   (B)透明的

(C)統計的   (D)必不可少的

解 本題後句說道所有動植物都需要有水，可判斷水對地球的生物是「必不可少的」，選(D)。

4 (C)。 貝蒂的廚房裝備有她烹飪所需的所有器具。
(A)營養　　　　　(B)障礙
(C)器具　　　　　(D)船隻
解 本題空格應填入一名詞，appliance意為「器具；裝備」，因此選(C)。

5 (A)。 手機對某些人來説是必要的，因為他們沒有手機的話就做不了任何事。
(A)必要的　　　　(B)防禦的
(C)顯著的　　　　(D)建設性的
解 本題空格應填入一形容詞補充説明cell phones，essential意為「必要的；必不可少的」，因此選(A)。

6 (D)。 他知道她在抑制自己不要讓他老婆知道他的婚外情。
(A)表達　　　　　(B)禮儀
(C)狀態　　　　　(D)衝動
解 本題空格應填入一名詞，hold back意為「退縮；壓制」之意，而後面的to let out...則是補充說明此空格之名詞，依題意應是「抑制衝動」，選(D)。

7 (C)。 提娜每天都很有活力地走路一個小時，以期能在幾個月內瘦個幾磅。
(A)比較地　　　　(B)被動地
(C)精力旺盛地　　(D)絕對地
解 本題空格應填入一副詞，來形容前面的動詞walks，依題意應填入vigorously（有活力地），選(C)。

二、文法測驗

8 (A)。 他靜坐在電視前，被美國國會大廈的恐怖攻擊新聞驚嚇到了。
(A)shocked
(B)been shocked
(C)having shocked
(D)to have been shocked
解 本題為分詞構句，動詞為shock（使驚嚇），因為he應是「被驚嚇」，因此應選p.p.的shocked，選(A)。

9 (C)。 這間店的設計師洋裝比那間店的還可負擔。
(A)ones　　　　　(B)these
(C)those　　　　 (D)which
解 本題考比較的句型，因比較的事物重複出現，後者可用that（單數）或those（複數）代替，dresses為複數，因此選(C)。

10 (C)。 這些廚餘已經不能吃了，因為已經放在桌上好幾個小時了。
(A)was left　　　 (B)is being left
(C)has been left　 (D)had been left
解 本題考文法時態，因為後方有持續性時間for hours（好幾小時），因此可判斷應用現在完成式has been left，選(C)。請注意，此句的for為連接詞，意為「因為」。

11 (A)。 我建議吉姆搭那條最快的路線到達目的地，而不是那條最短的。
(A)take　　　　　(B)takes
(C)be taking　　　(D)taking

解 本題考suggest的固定用法，建議某人的句型為「suggest(that)＋主詞＋(should)＋原形動詞」，因為此句型其實有一個隱藏的should，因此後方動詞應使用原形動詞，選(A)。

12 (B)。 這個社區大部分的居民都是上了年紀的二戰軍人，他們許多人都是獨居。

(A)many of them live alone

(B)many of them living alone

(C)and many of whom live alone

(D)and many of whom living alone

解 本題考句型結構，因為英文一個句子只能有一個動詞，若是要有兩個動詞則需要有連接詞。本句使用連接詞的原始句型應為：，and many of them live alone.，若是去掉連接詞and，則須將動詞改成現在分詞living，因此(B)正確。而若是要使用whom，whom有身兼關代與連接詞的功能，因此若有了whom則不再需要多接一個連接詞，因此若使用whom的句型應為：，many of whom live alone.。

13 (D)。 直到我向黛比提出警告，她才採取行動處理她母親的老化問題。

(A)who started　　(B)did she start

(C)when she started　(D)that she started

解 本題考not until的分裂句句型，句型為「It is＋not until...+that+S＋V」，因此正確為(D)。

14 (C)。 同時面對這麼多顧客對我來說並不容易，因為他們的需求不盡相同。

(A)being　　　(B)are

(C)is　　　　(D)to be

解 本題考句型結構，前面是一動詞現在分詞dealing作為主詞，因此本句尚缺一動詞，應填入單數be動詞is，選(C)。

15 (A)。 珍是一個害羞的女孩。她對於在工作場合或與鄰居交談感到有困難。

(A)talking　　　(B)talk

(C)to talk　　　(D)talks

解 本題考對於做某事有困難的句型，為「S+have difficulty+V-ing」，後面固定加現在分詞，因此選(A)。

三、克漏字測驗

　　時尚是地球上第二大污染的產業。其就緊跟在石油產業之後。降低成本和加快生產時間的壓力意味著為了利潤而犧牲環境。快時尚的不良影響包括使用廉價、有毒的染料。時裝業是全球第二大淨水污染者。

　　衣服生產的速度也意味著越來越多的衣服被消費者扔掉，造成了極大量的浪費。在加拿大，平均每人每年扔掉81磅的衣服，而北美人每年將950萬噸的衣物送到垃圾掩埋場。大部分被丟棄的衣服都可以重複再使用。

當今世界上約有4000萬名服裝工人，其中許多人沒有權利或被保護。他們是世界上收入最低的工人之一，85%的製衣工人是女性。

事實上，如果你知道如何開始，就有可能找到時尚、實惠且合乎道德的服裝。所以，下次買新衣服時，一定要從追求以更環保方式生產服裝的環保時尚公司購買。此外，確保這些公司提供公平的工作條件，並為工人提供合理的工資。

16 (B)。 (A)慢下來　(B)加快　(C)檢查　(D)收起來
解 本題考一動詞片語，後面接續受詞production time，依題意應是「加快」生產速度的壓力，選(B)。

17 (B)。 (A)損壞　(B)丟掉　(C)接管　(D)傳遞
解 本題考一動詞片語，接續在be動詞are之後，為被動語態，主詞為衣物，後面接續動作人by customers，可判斷衣服是被顧客「丟掉」，選(B)。

18 (C)。 (A)是否　(B)如果　(C)然而　(D)自從
解 本題考一連接詞，連接前後兩個句子，前句在談加拿大的丟棄衣物情況，後句則是在談北美的狀況，在做兩個國家的對比，由此可知應選(C)，while常被用來當作兩個比較句型的連接詞。

19 (D)。 (A)them　(B)that　(C)who　(D)whom

解 本題考文法，前方提到先行詞garment workers，進而接續本句，說他們很多都沒有權利或被保護，兩個句子間沒有連接詞，因此不可用(A)，應使用(D)的關係代名詞whom，whom同時兼有連接詞與關係代名詞的功用，指涉前方的garment workers，選(D)。

20 (B)。 (A)比較　(B)追求　(C)使受益　(D)通知
解 本題考動詞詞彙，前方的主詞為eco-fashion companies，後方受詞為the fair working conditions，可判斷環保時尚公司是「追求」公平的工作環境，選(B)。

四、閱讀測驗

我們所知道的三明治是於1762年，由第四代三明治伯爵約翰蒙塔古在英格蘭所推廣。傳說，大多數的食物歷史學家都同意，蒙塔古有賭博問題，導致他會在牌桌上花好幾個小時。在一段特別長的狂歡之中，他叫廚師給他端來一些他不用從座位上起身就能吃的東西，而三明治就這樣誕生了。蒙塔古非常喜歡他的肉和麵包，以致於他經常吃，隨著它在倫敦社會圈中的流行，它也冠上了伯爵的名字。

當然，約翰蒙塔古（或者更確切地說，他的無名廚師）並不是第一個想到在麵包片之間放入餡料的人。事實上，我們確切地知道蒙塔古最初是從哪裡獲得創作靈感的。蒙塔古曾前往地中

海，在那裡會供應土耳其和希臘的梅茲（mezze）拼盤。沾醬、奶酪和肉類都「夾在」麵包層之間和麵包層上。當蒙塔古坐在那張牌桌上時，他很可能是從這些之中獲得靈感。

蒙塔古的創作立刻就流傳開來。僅僅幾個月後，一個名叫愛德華吉本的人在日記中提到了這個三明治的名字，並寫道他在一家餐館看到「二十或三十個王國的第一批人」在吃它們。到革命戰爭時期，三明治在英國已經很盛行了。你會認為美國殖民者也會吃三明治，但在這個新國家根本沒有關於他們的早期書面紀錄，而且三明治食譜直到1815年才出現在美國的食譜中。

為什麼這個創作會默默無名在國內這麼久？似乎早期的美國廚師傾向於避免他們以前的統治國家的食物潮流。而「三明治」這個名字本身就來自英國的上流社會制度，這是大多數美國人想要忘記的。一旦記憶消失，三明治出現了，最受歡迎的版本不是火腿或火雞，而是舌頭！

當然，今天的大多數美國人都不會夢想吃舌頭三明治。但這沒關係，因為從那以後出現了很多非常優秀的三明治創意。

21 (B)。 本文主要與什麼有關？
(A)製作三明治的過程
(B)三明治的歷史
(C)約翰蒙塔古的故事
(D)三明治的成分
解 本文主要在講解三明治的歷史演變進程，因此選(B)。

22 (D)。 約翰蒙塔古是從哪裡獲得製作三明治的靈感？
(A)從中國的餃子
(B)從美國的漢堡
(C)從韓國的韓式烤牛肉
(D)從土耳其和希臘的梅茲（mezze）拼盤
解 本文第二段提到，約翰曾到過地中海，那裡會供應土耳其和希臘的梅茲（mezze）拼盤，因此選(D)。

23 (D)。 關於約翰蒙塔古的敘述，下列何者錯誤？
(A)他是第四代三明治伯爵。
(B)據稱他有賭博問題。
(C)他曾去過地中海。
(D)愛德華吉本是他的廚師。
解 本文第三段提到，愛德華吉本是記錄下三明治流傳開來的人，並非約翰的廚師，因此(D)不正確。其他選項皆有在文中提及。

24 (A)。 下列何者意義最接近於第四段的「unsung」？
(A)忽略　　　　(B)建立
(C)強調　　　　(D)流行
解 unsung本身為「未被讚頌的；被埋沒的」之意，因此overlooked（被忽略的）意義與之最接近，選(A)。

25 (C)。 下列關於三明治的敘述何者正確？
(A)直到1815年，三明治才在英格蘭盛行起來。
(B)約翰蒙塔古是第一個在麵包夾層中放入餡料的人。

(C)早期的美國廚師傾向於避免來自英格蘭的食物。

(D)對於今日的美國人來說，他們最喜歡的三明治版本是舌頭三明治。

解 本文倒數第二段提到，似乎早期的美國廚師傾向於避免他們以前的統治國家的食物潮流，而三明治便是英格蘭流傳過來的名字，因此(C)正確。

110年 經濟部所屬事業機構新進職員

一、字彙

( ) **1** In the literary history of the world, two of the greatest love stories have always been very popular and _____ - Shakespeare's Romeo and Juliet and the Chinese folk tale: The Cowherd and the Weaver Girl.
(A)intertwining　　　　(B)influential
(C)arguable　　　　(D)sensible

( ) **2** Some critics argue that if people rely on alternative medicine too much, they could delay getting treatment for potentially serious problems or possibly _____ illness.
(A)well-known　　　　(B)eye-catching
(C)life-threatening　　　　(D)long-lasting

( ) **3** Sarah _____ Marian's help. She is thankful for her assistance.
(A)obtains　　　　(B)endures
(C)motivates　　　　(D)appreciates

( ) **4** Police are still _____ how the accident happened. They try to find more clues.
(A)puzzling　　　　(B)investigating
(C)stalking　　　　(D)reinforcing

( ) **5** _____ food does not contain any meat or fish.
(A)Country　　　　(B)Processed
(C)Greasy　　　　(D)Vegetarian

( ) **6** Simon is _____. He is aggressive and prone to cause an argument.
(A)manipulative　　　　(B)confrontational
(C)unanimous　　　　(D)dubious

(　) **7** The United Nations Educational, Scientific and Cultural Organization is usually _____ to UNESCO.
(A)abbreviated　　　　　(B)associated
(C)abstracted　　　　　(D)affiliated

(　) **8** The extinction of bees would have _____ effects for all other living things on earth.
(A)hypocritical　　　　(B)extroverted
(C)vulnerable　　　　　(D)catastrophic

(　) **9** The delivery person was instructed to handle the _____ package with the utmost care.
(A)fragile　　　　　　(B)fertile
(C)famished　　　　　(D)fatigue

(　) **10** Everyone has been talking about the hyper-violent thriller that has become a massive _____ ever since it launched on Netflix two weeks ago.
(A)cast　　　　　　　(B)fling
(C)medium　　　　　(D)hit

二、文法及慣用語

(　) **11** The couples make vows and promises to _____ each other in sickness and in health, through good and bad times.
(A)embark on　　　　(B)result in
(C)care for　　　　　(D)come up with

(　) **12** Medicines should be _____ the reach of children.
(A)kept out of　　　　(B)kept in with
(C)cut off　　　　　　(D)caught out

(　) **13** Nowadays there are plenty of different methods teaching us how to live longer, from impossible diet plans to rigorous yoga routines, _____ suggest that you sleep before 10:00 p.m. and wake up at 4:00 a.m. to practice yoga daily.
(A)that　　　　　　(B)which
(C)what　　　　　　(D)whom

(　　) **14** You don't have to pay for your first drink; it's _____.
　　(A)on sale　　　　　　　　　(B)in season
　　(C)on the house　　　　　　　(D)on the go

(　　) **15** Stress relief is one of the most important factors for a longer life, and _____ suitable methods for releasing stress is important.
　　(A)have　　　　　　　　　　(B)having
　　(C)being having　　　　　　　(D)has

(　　) **16** Simon is working on three jobs while attending school. I hope he does not _____.
　　(A)bring the community to his knees
　　(B)go to the end of the earth
　　(C)make mountains out of molehills
　　(D)bite off more than he can chew

(　　) **17** With her loud voice and colorful outfit, Martha always _____. She gets all the attention.
　　(A)cuts it out　　　　　　　　(B)takes a hike
　　(C)takes center stage　　　　　(D)stays put

(　　) **18** The current white rhino population _____ at only 17,000 to 18,000.
　　(A)is estimated　　　　　　　(B)estimated
　　(C)is estimating　　　　　　　(D)estimates

(　　) **19** I would have bought a house last year if I _____ money then.
　　(A)have　　　　　　　　　　(B)had
　　(C)would have　　　　　　　　(D)had had

(　　) **20** Sally likes vegetable in general, and broccoli _____.
　　(A)in particular　　　　　　　(B)on the other hand
　　(C)in truth　　　　　　　　　(D)for example

(　) **21** _____ no denying that the quality of service is the main standard hotels are judged on.
(A)It is   (B)They are
(C)There has   (D)There is

(　) **22** The billionaire is happy to donate one million to the charity because it's just _____ for him.
(A)a drop in the bucket   (B)a pipe dream
(C)the lion's share   (D)a long shot

(　) **23** If we _____ our trip in advance, we would have booked the seats.
(A)should have planned   (B)had planned
(C)plan   (D)planned

(　) **24** It is essential _____ these instructions carefully to ensure his computer system has the technical capabilities he needs to fulfil the task.
(A)that he reads   (B)he reads
(C)that he read   (D)he must read

(　) **25** Please note that all applications must be received _____ Friday, December 10. Any late submission will not be accepted.
(A)no later than   (B)no less than
(C)no more than   (D)no sooner than

三、克漏字測驗

　　Numerous opportunities exist for people who want to travel abroad to experience a foreign culture. Homestays, study abroad programs, student exchanges, and international competitions all offer rich opportunities for cross-cultural ____26.____ . There are also government-run programs, such as the Peace Corps. ____27.____ US president John F. Kennedy in 1961, the organization has sent volunteers all over the globe to take part in community enriching programs.

Since its inception four decades ago, the Peace Corps has sent 200,000 Americans abroad. They've traveled to 139 countries, with the majority serving in Africa and Latin America. Volunteers ____28.____ 27 months of service, which includes pre-service training and time spent overseas. Their assignments may be in one of many fields, such as education, agriculture, health, business, and youth development. Since many of these fields require ____29.____ knowledge, 89% of volunteers hold university ____30.____ .

(　　) **26** (A)competition　　　　(B)interview
　　　　(C)interaction　　　　　(D)business

(　　) **27** (A)Established by　　　(B)Declared by
　　　　(C)Establishing　　　　(D)Announced

(　　) **28** (A)make up　　　　　(B)commit to
　　　　(C)consist of　　　　　(D)depend on

(　　) **29** (A)general　　　　　(B)personal
　　　　(C)political　　　　　(D)specialized

(　　) **30** (A)documents　　　　(B)degrees
　　　　(C)papers　　　　　　(D)proofs

The Stanford Marshmallow experiment is a psychological experiment to ____31.____ children's ability to control their impulses. The idea was to see ____32.____ the difference was between children who managed to control their impulses and those who could not. The results showed that those who succeeded in ____33.____ the immediate temptation to eat the marshmallow were able to perform better at exams and ____34.____ in other aspects of their lives than those who had grabbed the marshmallow directly. The researchers were also able to show that the impulsive group also seemed to suffer more ____35.____ stress and problems in relationship in later life.

(　　) **31** (A)look away　　　　(B)look after
　　　　(C)look into　　　　　(D)look for

(　　) **32** (A)what　　　(B)how　　　　(C)where　　　(D)in which

(　　) **33** (A)resisting　(B)accepting　(C)identifying　(D)insisting

(　　) **34** (A)being more stable　　　(B)be more stable
　　　　　 (C)was more stable　　　　(D)were more stable

(　　) **35** (A)of　　　　(B)with　　　　(C)from　　　　(D)in

四、閱讀測驗

Recent biological research indicates that there is a biochemical basis to love, which explains why people in love feel as if they were in a more beautiful world. Psychologists such as Dr. Elaine Hatfield, Robert Sternberg and Zick Rubin posit that love consists of three or more stages. The three main stages are lust, attraction, and **attachment**, while some of the other stages are intimacy, trust, and jealousy. Each stage is ruled or initiated by specific hormonal controllers. In their studies, every love passes through some of these stages and occurs due to the mediation of certain molecules in these specific chemical controllers.

Biological research has shown that the hormones dominant in the different phases include testosterone and estrogen (the sexual hormones); dopamine, norepinephrine and serotonin (these are the "pleasure chemicals" - the hormones invoking feelings of pleasure and excitement); and oxytocin (the "cuddle chemical" - the hormone producing feelings of **attachment** to another person). For example, in the second phase of attraction, when people have the feeling of being in love, the little molecule phenylethylamine (known as PEA), controlling the love chemicals dopamine and noreinephrine, can cause feelings of elation, exhilaration and euphoria. People feel excited and fulfilled.

Additionally, biological anthropologist Helen Fisher, an expert on romantic love, discusses what happens in the brain when people are in love and proposes that there is a dramatic increase in the amount of dopamine and norepinephrine present in the brain when one first becomes infatuated with another person.

(　) **36** What is the passage mainly about?
　　(A)Variations of love
　　(B)Love in different cultures
　　(C)Chemistry of love
　　(D)Psychological effects of love

(　) **37** According to the researchers, which of the following chemicals is
　　most closely related to the feeling of being in love?
　　(A)testosterone　　　　　　(B)oxytocin
　　(C)estrogen　　　　　　　 (D)dopamine

(　) **38** Which of the following is closest in meaning to the word
　　"attachment"?
　　(A)assistance　　　　　　　(B)concentration
　　(C)connection　　　　　　　(D)enclosure

(　) **39** According to the scientists, which of the following about how
　　love occurs is **NOT** true?
　　(A)Every love passes through three or more stages - lust, attraction,
　　　　attachment, etc.
　　(B)PEA is a hormone our bodies produce that promotes mutual
　　　　feelings of connection and bonding.
　　(C)There is an increase in the amount of dopamine present in the
　　　　brain when people are in love.
　　(D)People's brains are influenced by hormones and chemicals that
　　　　cause them to feel the way they feel.

(　) **40** What does the passage imply about love?
　　(A)Most people are not controlled by love.
　　(B)Science may help explain how love takes place.
　　(C)Love can be expressed precisely by words or actions.
　　(D)People can easily find the right person everywhere.

解答與解析　答案標示為# 者，表官方曾公告更正該題答案。

一、字彙

1 (B)。 在世界文學史上，兩個最偉大的愛情故事一直都很廣為人知且具有影響力——莎士比亞的「羅密歐與朱麗葉」和中國民間故事：「牛郎織女」。
(A)糾纏的　　　(B)有影響力的
(C)可辯論的　　(D)敏感的
解 本題空格依文法應填入與popular對應的形容詞，依題意應填入(B)。

2 (C)。 一些批評家認為，如果人們過度依賴替代醫學，他們可能會延遲對潛在嚴重問題或可能危及生命疾病的治療。
(A)知名的　　　(B)引人注目的
(C)危及生命的　(D)持續很久的
解 空格應填入一形容詞形容後方的illness，依題意應填入(C)。

3 (D)。 莎拉感激瑪麗安的幫忙。她很感謝她的協助。
(A)獲得　　　　(B)忍受
(C)激勵　　　　(D)感激
解 依照後句可判斷，本句空格是想考thankful的同義詞，應填入(D)appreciate（感激；感恩）。

4 (B)。 警方仍在調查意外是如何發生的，他們嘗試找到更多線索。
(A)使困惑　　　(B)調查
(C)跟蹤　　　　(D)加強
解 本題依據前後文可推知，警方應是「調查」意外如何發生，應選(B)。

5 (D)。 素食食物不含任何的肉或魚。
(A)鄉村　　　　(B)加工過的
(C)油膩的　　　(D)素食的
解 本題根據後方「不包含魚或肉」可推知，應是指「素食」食物，選(D)。

6 (B)。 賽門相當咄咄逼人，他攻擊性強且容易造成糾紛。
(A)操作的
(B)對抗的；咄咄逼人的
(C)一致同意的
(D)半信半疑的
解 根據後句陳述他攻擊性強且易引起糾紛，可判斷應選(B)。

7 (A)。 聯合國教育、科學及文化組織通常會縮寫為UNESCO。
(A)縮寫　　　　(B)有關的
(C)抽象化　　　(D)附屬的
解 依據空格前後方，可判斷後面的UNESCO為前面整串的縮寫，選(A)。

8 (D)。 蜜蜂的滅絕可能會對地球上其他生物帶來毀滅性的影響。
(A)偽善的　　　(B)外向的
(C)脆弱的　　　(D)毀滅性的
解 根據題意，蜜蜂絕種應是對其他生物帶來「毀滅性的」影響，選(D)。

9 (A)。 送貨的人被指示要很小心地處理易碎的貨物。
(A)脆弱的；易碎的　(B)多產的
(C)非常飢餓的　　　(D)疲累的

解 根據前後文，送貨的人應是被指示小心地處理「易碎的」包裹，因此選(A)。

10 (D)。 每個人都在討論那部變成大受歡迎的超暴力恐怖片，自從其兩週前在網飛上映後。

(A)卡司

(B)揮動

(C)媒體

(D)成功而風行一時的事物

解 根據前後題意，可判斷該部恐怖片變成大家都在討論的熱門片，massive hit意為大受歡迎的電影／影集等，選(D)。

二、文法及慣用語

11 (C)。 這對情侶許下誓言，承諾無論是生病或健康、光景是好是壞，都會照顧彼此。

(A)著手；開始　　(B)造成；引起

(C)照顧；照料　　(D)想出

解 根據題意，情侶應是承諾無論生病健康、狀況是好是壞，都會「照顧」彼此，選(C)。care for與take care of皆為「照顧；照料」之意。

12 (A)。 藥物應放置於孩童拿不到的地方。

(A)遠離　　　　　(B)與……友好相處

(C)去除；切除　(D)看出；看破

解 空格前方提到藥物，後方提到孩童，判斷應是要讓藥物「遠離」孩童，選(A)。

13 (B)。 現今有很多種不同的方法教導我們如何更長壽，從不可能達成的飲食計畫到嚴峻的瑜伽行程，也就是代表你每天要在晚上10點前入睡，並在清晨4點醒來練習瑜伽。

(A)that　　　　　(B)which

(C)what　　　　　(D)whom

解 空格後句結構不完整，因此空格處應選一關係代名詞，指涉前面的rigorous yoga routines，指涉事物的關係代名詞有which和that，但that不能放在逗點後方銜接，因此選(B)which。

14 (C)。 你不需要支付第一杯飲料的錢；這是免費的。

(A)特價中　　　　(B)當季的

(C)免費的　　　　(D)特別忙的

解 第一句說明你不需要付第一杯飲料的錢，代表這是「免費的」，on the house即為free（免費的）之意，選(C)。

15 (B)。 紓解壓力是長壽其中一個最重要的因素之一，而擁有紓解壓力的適當方法相當重要。

(A)have　　　　　(B)having

(C)being having　(D)has

解 本題考文法，根據句型結構，應填入動詞的現在分詞V-ing，才能銜接後方的is important，選(B)。

16 (D)。 賽門在學期間還同時兼三份工作，我希望他不會不自量力。

(A)搞垮社群　　　(B)<無此用法>

(C)<無此用法>　　(D)不自量力

解 本題在考固定用語，根據題意應填入(D)，bite off more than one can chew表示「承擔力所不及的事；不自量力」。(A)bring something to its knees表示「搞垮……」之意；(B)正確用法應為go to the ends of the earth，意為「去到天涯海角」；(C)正確用法應為make a mountain out of a molehill，意為「小題大作」。

17 (C)。 有著大嗓門與鮮豔服裝，瑪莎總是成為眾人的目光焦點，她得到所有人的關注。

(A)停止……　　(B)滾開
(C)成為眾人的焦點　(D)留在原地

解 本題考固定用法，take center stage原意為「站在舞台的中央位置」，也就是「成為眾人的焦點」之意，與get all the attention同義，選(C)。

18 (A)。 目前白犀的數量預估只有17,000至18,000隻。

(A)is estimated　　(B)estimated
(C)is estimating　　(D)estimates

解 本題考文法，主詞為the current white rhino population，數量應是「被估計」，應使用被動語態，選(A)。

19 (D)。 如果我去年有錢，我那時就會買一間房子了。

(A)have　　　　(B)had
(C)would have　　(D)had had

解 本題考文法時態，句型為與過去事實相反的假設語氣，

句型為「If主詞had+p.p.，主詞would/could/should/might+have p.p.」，因此空格處應填入had+p.p.，選(D)。

20 (A)。 莎利喜歡大部分的蔬菜，尤其是花椰菜。

(A)尤其是　　　(B)另一方面
(C)事實上　　　(D)舉例來說

解 本題固定用法，前面說道喜歡大部分的蔬菜，後面提到花椰菜，可判斷是「尤其是」花椰菜，選(A)。

21 (D)。 服務品質是飯店被評判的主要標準，這點是無庸置疑的。

(A)It is　　　　(B)They are
(C)There has　　(D)There is

解 本題考固定用法，「There is no denying（that）+完整子句」意為「某事物是不容置疑的；……是不可否認的」，選(D)。

22 (A)。 這名億萬富翁很樂意捐款一百萬做公益，因為這對他來說僅是很小的金額。

(A)很小或微不足道的量
(B)幻想；白日夢
(C)最大份額或最大的一份
(D)希望不大的嘗試

解 本題考固定用語，drop是「一滴；水滴」的意思，bucket是「水桶」的意思，a drop in the bucket意為「很小或微不足道的量」，因此選(A)。

23 (B)。 如果我們有事先規劃行程，我們就可以先訂位了。

解答與解析

(A)should have planned

(B)had planned

(C)plan

(D)planned

解 本題考與過去事實相反的假設語氣，句型為「If主詞had+p.p.,主詞would/could/should/might+have p.p.」，因此空格處應填入had+p.p.，選(B)。

24 (C)。 他必須仔細閱讀這些說明，以確保他的電腦系統具備完成任務所需的能力。

(A)that he reads　　(B)he reads

(C)that he read　　(D)he must read

解 本題考「某件事是重要／必要的」句型，句型為「It is+adj.+that+主詞+（should）+原形動詞」，這種句型其實中間隱藏了一個should被省略，因此後方的動詞應使用原形動詞，選(C)。

25 (A)。 請注意所有申請必須在12月10日星期五之前收到，任何遲交的申請將不被接受。

(A)不晚於　　　(B)不少於

(C)不多於　　　(D)<無此用法>

解 此題考文法語意，後句說到遲交的申請不會被接受，因此可判斷是要在12月10日以前繳交申請，也就是必須「不晚於」12月10日，選(A)。

三、克漏字測驗

對於想要出國旅行體驗外國文化的人來說，存在著許多機會。寄宿家庭、

留學計畫、交換學生和國際比賽都為跨文化交流提供了豐富的機會。還有政府營運的計畫，例如和平工作團。該組織由美國總統約翰·甘迺迪於1961年創立，已在全球範圍內派遣志工參與社區豐富計畫。

自40年前成立以來，和平工作團已將200,000名美國人派往海外。他們去過139個國家，其中大部分在非洲和拉丁美洲服務。志工們承諾服務27個月，其中包括服務前培訓和在海外度過的時間。他們的任務可能是許多領域的其一，例如教育、農業、健康、商業和青年發展。由於其中許多領域都需要專業知識，因此89%的志工都擁有大學學位。

26 (C)。 (A)競爭　(B)訪談　(C)互動　(D)商業

解 空格前方在談論出國體驗外國文化，因此可判斷是跨文化「交流」，選(C)。

27 (A)。 (A)由⋯⋯所創立　(B)由⋯⋯所宣告　(C)創立　(D)宣布

解 本句主詞為後方的the organization，組織應是「被創立」，因此選(A)。

28 (B)。 (A)化妝　(B)承諾　(C)包括　(D)依靠

解 本句主詞為Volunteers，空格後方為27 months of service，可推斷是「承諾」27個月的服務。

29 (D)。 (A)一般的　(B)個人的　(C)政治的　(D)專業的

解 空格前方談到了許多領域，因此可推斷是需要「專業」知識，specialized有「專業的；專門的」之意，選(D)。

30 (B)。 (A)文件 (B)學位 (C)論文 (D)證明

解 空格前方說道89%的人都擁有大學……，可推斷是擁有大學學歷，選(B)。學位、文憑的另一個用字還有diploma。

　　史丹佛的棉花糖實驗是一項研究兒童控制衝動能力的心理實驗。這個想法是想看看能控制衝動的孩子和不能控制衝動的孩子之間有什麼區別。結果表明，那些成功抵制了直接吃棉花糖誘惑的人，在考試中表現得更好，在生活的其他方面也比直接抓棉花糖的人更穩定。研究人員還能夠證明，衝動的群體似乎在以後的生活中也更容易受到壓力和人際關係問題的影響。

31 (C)。 (A)移開視線 (B)照顧 (C)調查 (D)尋找

解 空格前方提到實驗，可推斷是要「調查」孩童的能力，選(C)。

32 (A)。 (A)what (B)how (C)where (D)in which

解 本句主詞為the idea，動詞為was to see，後方又出現一結構完整的句子（有主詞difference、動詞was），可判斷應填入複合關係代名詞what作為受詞，選(A)。

33 (A)。 (A)抵抗 (B)接受 (C)辨明 (D)堅持

解 空格後方的受詞為the immediate temptation，可判斷是要「抵抗」誘惑，選(A)。

34 (B)。 (A)being more stable
(B)be more stable
(C)was more stable
(D)were more stable

解 本句主詞為the results，動詞為showed，後方接續that子句，子句主詞為those（後方who succeeded in resisting the immediate temptation to eat the marshmallow作為形容詞子句），子句動詞為were able to，後方接續了一個動詞perform，後方又出現一連接詞and，因此可判斷應與perform平行，也是原形動詞，選(B)。

35 (C)。 (A)of (B)with (C)from (D)in

解 空格前方為suffer more，後方為stress and problems，suffer的固定用法為suffer from...，意為「受……之苦」，選(C)。

四、閱讀測驗

　　近期的生物學研究表明，愛是有生理基礎的，這就解釋了為什麼戀愛中的人會覺得自己彷彿置身於一個更美麗的世界。Elaine Hatfield博士、Robert Sternberg和Zick Rubin等心理學家認為，愛情由三個或更多階段組成。三個

主要階段是慾望、吸引力和依戀，而其他一些階段是親密、信任和嫉妒。每個階段都由特定的荷爾蒙控制器管制或啟動。在他們的研究中，每一次愛情都會經歷其中一些階段，並且由於這些特定化學控制器中某些分子的調解而發生。

生物學研究表明，在不同階段占主導地位的激素包括睪酮和雌激素（性激素）；多巴胺、去甲腎上腺素和血清素（這些是「愉悅化學物質」——引起愉悅和興奮感的激素）；和催產素（「擁抱化學物質」——產生對另一個人的依戀感的激素）。例如，在吸引的第二階段，當人們有戀愛的感覺時，控制愛情化學物質多巴胺和去甲腎上腺素的小分子苯乙胺（稱為PEA）會引起興奮和愉快的感覺。人們會感到興奮和滿足。

此外，浪漫愛情專家、生物人類學家海倫‧費舍爾討論了人們戀愛時大腦中發生的情況，並提出當一個人第一次迷戀上另一個人時，大腦中的多巴胺和去甲腎上腺素的含量會急劇地增加。

36 (C)。 本文主要與什麼有關？
(A)愛的變化
(B)不同文化中的愛
(C)愛的化學作用
(D)愛的心理效應
解 本文主要在談論人們經歷愛情的生理變化情形，因此選(C)。

37 (D)。 根據研究人員的說法，下列哪個化學物質與戀愛的感覺最密切相關？
(A)睪酮　　　　(B)催產素
(C)雌激素　　　(D)多巴胺

解 最後一段提到，當迷戀上另個人時，大腦中的多巴胺和去甲腎上腺素的含量會急劇地增加，因此選(D)。

38 (C)。 下列何者與「attachment」意義最為接近？
(A)協助　　　　(B)專注
(C)連結　　　　(D)附件
解 attachment意為「依戀；依附」，因此與(C)connection意義最為接近。

39 (B)。 根據科學家的說法，下列關於愛是如何發生的敘述何者為非？
(A)每段愛情都經過三個或更多階段——慾望、吸引、依戀等。
(B)PEA是我們身體產生的一種激素，可以促進相互聯繫和結合的感覺。
(C)當人們戀愛時，大腦中多巴胺的含量會增加。
(D)人們的大腦受到荷爾蒙和化學物質的影響，這些荷爾蒙和化學物質使他們產生自己的感覺。
解 根據第二段結尾，PEA會引起興奮和愉快的感覺，因此(B)不正確。

40 (B)。 本文對於愛有何暗示？
(A)多數人不受愛的控制。
(B)科學可能可以幫助解釋愛是如何發生的。
(C)愛可以精確地透過語言或行動表達。
(D)人們可以輕易地在任何地方找到合適的人。
解 本文主要在解釋，透過生理學的角度來闡述愛的發生過程，因此可推斷為(B)。

111年 台北捷運新進人員（控制員(二)(運務類)）

一、選擇題

( ) **1** If we _____ earlier, we would have gotten better seats for the movie.
(A)have arrived   (B)have been arriving
(C)had arrived   (D)have been arriving

( ) **2** The doctor of the local clinic _____ his patient to a specialist in the teaching hospital.
(A)referred   (B)deferred
(C)inferred   (D)interfered

( ) **3** The defendant _____ that he was innocent, but all evidence pointed in the opposite direction.
(A)inserted   (B)deserted
(C)exerted   (D)asserted

( ) **4** More women are now being _____ to do jobs that were once male dominated.
(A)recruit   (B)to recruit
(C)recruited   (D)recruiting

( ) **5** Because local taxes were too high, many companies _____ much of the labor in countries overseas.
(A)resourced   (B)resold
(C)outsold   (D)outsourced

( ) **6** This monument was dedicated _____ all the brave men and women who lost their lives defending the country.
(A)in memory of   (B)in place of
(C)in charge of   (D)in terms of

(　　) **7** My boss was not _____ with my job performance and, therefore, gave a negative review.
(A)satisfy (B)satisfied
(C)satisfying (D)satisfactory

(　　) **8** Soon after the outbreak of the COVID-19 pandemic, infected patients were needed to be quarantined _____ they would not spread the virus which they carried.
(A)unless (B)in case
(C)so that (D)in order to

(　　) **9** The UK, EU and US have imposed _____ on Russia because of its military invasion of Ukraine.
(A)sanctions (B)transactions
(C)transitions (D)sensations

(　　) **10** The new supervisor is going to _____ all the staff to make sure everyone is doing a good job.
(A)evacuate (B)evaluate
(C)elevate (D)eliminate

(　　) **11** A number of scientists _____ questioned the research methods used in the report.
(A)has (B)have
(C)was (D)is

(　　) **12** Before you purchase the software, you should check its _____ with the operating system.
(A)sensibility (B)complexity
(C)identity (D)compatibility

(　　) **13** While microwaves heat up food more quickly, most food tastes better when it is cooked in a _____ oven.
(A)conventional (B)conversational
(C)conditional (D)commercial

( ) **14** With the new and talented team members, the coach _____ that the team would win the championship.
(A)predicting
(B)predicted
(C)predict
(D)will predict

( ) **15** What's the name of the man _____?
(A)whose car you borrowed
(B)which car you borrowed
(C)you borrowed his car
(D)his car you borrowed

( ) **16** Blue-collar workers are paid a _____ wage of NT$ 168 per hour in Taiwan.
(A)premium
(B)minimum
(C)maximum
(D)optimum

( ) **17** When there is a change in temperature, some people are _____ to sneezing and sniffing.
(A)convertible
(B)perceptible
(C)susceptible
(D)eligible

( ) **18** The company decided to _____ redundant employees whose jobs have been done by robots.
(A)lay off
(B)take off
(C)show off
(D)put off

( ) **19** When he returned home, he found his house _____ and all his valuables stolen.
(A)break into
(B)breaking into
(C)to break into
(D)broken into

( ) **20** Most physicians suggest _____ vitamins on a full stomach.
(A)taking
(B)to take
(C)taken
(D)take

( ) **21** The instructions on the ticket vending machine were confusing. They were not _____ at all.
(A)users-friendly
(B)user-friendly
(C)user-friends
(D)friendly-users

(　) **22** Every employee in our department ___ come up with solutions to lower the company's budget.
(A)is supposing to 　　　　　(B)supposed to
(C)is supposed to 　　　　　(D)supposing to

(　) **23** A growing number of international companies including McDonald's, Coca-Cola and Starbucks _____ trading in Russia because of its invasion of Ukraine.
(A)have extended 　　　　　(B)have suspended
(C)have intended 　　　　　(D)have defended

(　) **24** Where _____? Which hairdresser did you go to?
(A)did you cut your hair 　　(B)have you cut your hair
(C)did you have your hair cut (D)did you have cut your hair

(　) **25** The host showed great _____ toward his guests by preparing a terrific feast.
(A)credibility 　　　　　　(B)possibility
(C)hospitality 　　　　　　(D)ambiguity

(　) **26** The _____ for electric cars and clean energy storage are brightening.
(A)reductions 　　　　　　(B)respects
(C)prospects 　　　　　　(D)reflections

(　) **27** The two political parties could not reach a _____ on the best methods for reducing carbon emissions.
(A)consensus 　　　　　　(B)circus
(C)construction 　　　　　(D)containment

(　) **28** I _____ a walk because it is such a nice day.
(A)want taking 　　　　　　(B)feel like taking
(C)would like taking 　　　　(D)feel like to take

(　　) **29** After Carl pointed out the problem, he went on _____ some ways to solve it.
(A)to suggest　　　　　　(B)suggesting
(C)suggested　　　　　　(D)being suggested

(　　) **30** She _____ on many outfits before she realized she didn't have enough money.
(A)has been tried　　　　(B)has tried
(C)had tried　　　　　　(D)had been tried

(　　) **31** The young artist's work was considered _____ because it was hard to understand.
(A)contract　　　　　　(B)attract
(C)extract　　　　　　　(D)abstract

(　　) **32** Man:That'll be NT$ 5000. Would you like to have this printer delivered? It'll be free of charge because your purchase is more than NT$1000.
Woman:Wow, that's great. Could you deliver it by next Monday? I need to use it as soon as possible.
Man: No problem. Could you fill out this form, please?
What does the man offer the woman?
(A)A full refund　　　　(B)Free repair
(C)Free delivery　　　　(D)A special discount

(　　) **33** Man:Hi, I'd like to make an appointment for a dental exam. The last time I had a checkup was about half a year ago.
Woman:We're fully booked this week. How about next Friday afternoon?
Man:OK, Next Friday suits me fine. Can I have the appointment at 3 o'clock?
Woman: Sure, 3 o'clock is fine.
Where does the woman probably work?
(A)A bookstore　　　　　(B)A dental clinic
(C)A convenience store　　(D)A bank

( ) **34** Man: Sandy, did you find a new apartment?

Woman: Not yet, Ronald. I want to move into a place with good access to public transportation. The apartment I'm living in now is too far from the office.

What does the woman complain about?

(A)Her apartment is far from her office.

(B)Her room is too small.

(C)There is only one bus stop near her apartment.

(D)The street is too noisy.

( ) **35** Woman: Hi, welcome to Wendy's Kitchen. Is this your first time here?

Man: Yes, it is. Do you have a daily special here?

Woman: Of course, we do. Today's specials are pasta with mussels, a cream of mushroom soup, and a chicken warm salad. How does it sound?

Man: They all sound great. But first, could I have a soft drink first while I decide what to eat?

What does the man ask the woman about?

(A)A discounted item   (B)A special dish

(C)A cookbook   (D)A gift

( ) **36** Woman: I've been trying to look for Jason all morning. I know he's not in his office because he's not answering the phone, and he hasn't returned any of my e-mails either.

Man: He is in trouble with the manager because he's lost an important client's file. I think the manager is talking to him now.

According to the man, where is Jason now?

(A)In his office   (B)In the storage room

(C)In the restroom   (D)In the manager's office

( ) **37** Woman: Good afternoon, this is the front desk. How may I help you?

Man: Yes, this is Allen Lee in room 301. My shower's not working. I called this morning, but no one's been in to fix it.

Woman: Let me apologize, Mr. Lee. I'll call maintenance and check for you right away.

Why did the man contact the woman?
(A)To order a meal (B)To confirm an appointment
(C)To ask for a repair (D)To make a reservation

( ) **38** Woman: How would you like your hair done? Do you want to keep your style or go for a different look?

Man: I'd like to try a new look. I think I need a perm. Also, can you cut the sides short?

Woman: No problem.

Where does this conversation most likely take place?
(A)At a party (B)At a hair salon
(C)At a clinic (D)At a fashion show

( ) **39** Man: Do these shoes come in different sizes?

Woman: Let me see. We only have sizes 10 to 12 right now, but we'll have a full stock by Wednesday. What size are you looking for?

Man: I need a size 9, but I guess I could wear a 10 as well. Sometimes the sizes aren't exactly the same.

Woman: OK, let me get you a pair of size 10s and you can try them on to see if they fit.

What will the man do next?
(A)Try on the shoes (B)Wait until Wednesday
(C)Visit another store (D)Buy the shoes

( ) **40** Woman: Excuse me. Does a Sarah Wang work here? I have a couple of boxes for her.

Man: You just missed her. She's left to attend a meeting, and it'll take about one hour.

Woman: Would it be possible for you to sign for the delivery? If not, I could come back in two hours.

Man: I think I can sign for it.

Where is Ms. Wang?
(A)At lunch (B)At home
(C)At a bank (D)At a meeting

二、閱讀測驗

【第一篇】

March 11, 2020. That's a day for the history books. On that date, the World Health Organization (WHO) gave the spread of the coronavirus a new title — pandemic. So, we have now been living in a pandemic for two years.

A lot changed after March 11, 2020. People began wearing masks and went into lockdown. They went to work — and school — online. We all worked together (by staying apart) to stay safe. Now in its third year, the COVID-19 pandemic is still affecting millions of people. Yet life is slowly returning to normal.

By March 2022, about 500 million people have tested positive for COVID-19. More than 6 million people have died. Those include more than 1 million in Asia and more than 900,000 in the United States. Millions more got sick from the virus, many of whom are still dealing with the long-term effects of the illness.

The virus itself has changed over the past two years as well. It has mutated several times into different variants. Those include delta and omicron, both of which are very contagious. That caused new waves of COVID-19 — and resulted in the spread of the disease to more places. By now, it has reached nearly every corner of the globe. Even the isolated islands in Tonga, Vanuatu, and Micronesia have had some cases.

The COVID-19 vaccine helped to protect a lot of people. It kept patients from getting very sick (or dying). A 90-year-old woman in Britain got the first approved shot on December 8, 2020. By now, most Americans have gotten the vaccine. However, poorer areas of the world do not have as much access. More than 1 billion people in Africa (more than 90% of the population) still have not had any shots of the vaccine.

The numbers of COVID-19 cases have dropped in the United States. As a result, people do not have to wear masks anymore in most areas of the country. This month, thousands of schools removed their mask **mandate**. However, travelers on planes, trains, or public buses will still have to wear masks until at least April 18.

However, the pandemic is far from over. More than 1 million people worldwide are testing positive for COVID-19 each day. And some areas are seeing a record number of cases. Those include the city of Hong Kong, China, which is currently facing its worst outbreak ever. And, of course, we will feel the effects of the pandemic for many years. For example, recent studies show that closed schools caused millions of young students to fall behind in their reading skills.

What will the third year of the pandemic look like? No one can be sure. There will likely be new treatments for COVID-19 (including pills). Some experts believe that the pandemic will officially end in 2022. But that doesn't mean the virus will go away. Instead, it will likely become endemic in most areas. That means the disease will continue to spread at different times. And we will learn to live with this virus as part of our world.

( ) **41** According the article, why did the COVID-19 pandemic begin on March 11, 2020?
(A)That was when the pandemic first spread to other countries.
(B)That was when the WHO first called it a pandemic.
(C)That was when the first person got sick with COVID-19
(D)That was when the first person died from COVID-19.

( ) **42** About how long after the start of the pandemic did people begin getting approved vaccines for COVID-19?
(A)one year and three months　(B)2 years
(C)3 months　　　　　　　　　(D)9 months

( ) **43** What does it mean that the coronavirus mutated?
(A)It changed.　　　　　　　(B)I spread quickly.
(C)It became more dangerous.　(D)It caused many people to die.

( ) **44** What was mentioned in the passage about the impact of closed schools caused by the COVID-19 pandemic on the young students?
(A)Young students liked studying online.
(B)Young students didn't like studying at all.
(C)Young students fell behind in their reading skills.
(D)Young students preferred playing video games to studying.

(　　) **45** What does the word **"mandate"** mean?

(A)randomization (B)freedom

(C)resistance (D)rule

【第二篇】

Obesity is a medical condition in which excess body fat has accumulated to the extent that it may have an adverse effect on health, leading to reduced life expectancy and/or increased health problems. Body mass index (BMI), a measurement which compares weight and height, defines people as overweight (pre-obese) when their BMI is between 25 kg/m^2 and 30 kg/m^2, and obese when it is greater than 30 kg/m^2.

Obesity increases the likelihood of various diseases, particularly heart disease, type 2 diabetes, breathing difficulties during sleep, certain types of cancer, and osteoarthritis. Obesity is most commonly caused by a combination of excessive dietary calories, lack of physical activity, and genetic susceptibility, although a few cases are caused primarily by genes, blood disorders, medications or illness. Evidence to support the view that some obese people eat little yet gain weight due to a slow metabolism is limited; on average obese people have a greater energy expenditure than their thin counterparts due to the energy required to maintain an increased body mass.

The primary treatment for obesity is dieting and physical exercise. Sometimes, anti-obesity drugs may be taken to reduce appetite or inhibit fat absorption. In severe cases, surgery is performed or a balloon is placed to reduce the stomach size/or bowel length, leading to people eating less.

Obesity is a leading **preventable** cause of death worldwide, with increasing prevalence in adults and children, and authorities view it as one of the most serious public health problems of the 21st century. Obesity is hated in much of the modern world (particularly in the Western world), though it was widely perceived as a symbol of wealth and fertility at other times in history, and still is in some parts of the world.

( ) **46** The article implies that _____.
  (A)although obesity is prevalent, it is not considered as a serious illness
  (B)obesity is considered as a serious illness
  (C)obesity only affects men
  (D)obesity is only from genetics

( ) **47** Obese people _____.
  (A)may suffer from severe illnesses
  (B)may suffer from mild ailments
  (C)are all rich
  (D)only live in the West

( ) **48** Modern medicine _____.
  (A)is the best way to stop obesity
  (B)is the worst way to cure obesity
  (C)can sometimes cure obesity
  (D)cannot cure obesity at all

( ) **49** The first treatment for obesity is _____.
  (A)gene therapy   (B)medication
  (C)surgery   (D)related to individuals' lifestyle

( ) **50** The term **"preventable"** means _____.
  (A)unstoppable   (B)affordable
  (C)avoidable   (D)predictable

解答與解析　答案標示為#者，表官方曾公告更正該題答案。

一、選擇題

1 (C)。如果我們早點到達，我們就能坐到比較好的位子看電影。
  (A)have arrived(v.)到達（現在完成式）
  (B)have been arriving(v.)到達（現在完成進行式）

  (C)had arrived(v.)到達（過去完成式）
  (D)have been arriving(v.)到達（現在完成進行式）
  解 這題是考If假設語氣的句型，特別是「與過去事實相反的假設」語氣句型，常用在表達對過去未

達成的行為的後悔。句型是：If+主詞＋過去完成式（had+過去分詞），主詞+would/could/should/might＋現在完成式（have+過去分詞）。如何判斷這題是考「與過去事實相反的假設」句型，看此句的後半部：we（主詞）+would+have gotten（have+過去分詞），因此可知，講這句話的人，懊悔如果早點抵達，可以坐到更適合看電影的位子。但是已無法改變，在過去的某一段時間點，未達成的行為。故選(C)。

備註：除了本題考的「與過去事實相反的假設」語氣句型，If假設語氣的句型還包括了：(1)與現在事實相反的假設語氣，且未來不太可能會發生。句型是：If+主詞+過去簡單式，主詞+would/could/should+might+原形動詞。例句：If I had time, I would visit you（如果現在我有時間，我會去拜訪你），但事實上，我的行程很忙碌，講話的當下或是未來一段時間內，很難去拜訪你。(2)表達未來可能會發生的假設語氣。句型是：If+主詞+原形動詞，主詞+will+原形動詞。例句：If I have time this weekend, I will go to the library（如果這週末我有空，我會去圖書館）。語意

上可以解讀，這週末我或許有空，只要我有時間，我將去圖書館。(3)表達現在的事實、真理，或習慣。句型是：If+主詞+原形動詞，主詞+原形動詞。例句：If I have time, I often go to the library（如果我有空，我常去圖書館）。語意上解讀，這是一個習慣。

2 (A)。地方診所的醫生，已經把他的病患轉介到教學醫院裡的專門醫生了。
(A)refer(v.)使求助於
(B)defer(v.)推遲
(C)infer(v.)推斷
(D)interfere(v.)妨礙
解 地方上的診所的醫生，若求診的病人病況需要更近一步的診斷及醫療，會將病人轉介到教學醫院。這題是考「轉介」refer這個動詞，句型是：refer to，比如這句中的 "the doctor of the local clinic referred his patient to a specialist..."。故選(A)。
備註：specialist(n.)專門醫生
teaching hospital(n.)教學醫院

3 (D)。這位被告聲稱他是無罪的，但是所有的證據卻指向相反的方向。
(A)insert(v.)插入　(B)desert(v.)拋棄
(C)exert(v.)施加　(D)assert(v.)聲稱
解 這題是考「以強有力的態度來聲明某件事」的動詞，例如assert，雖然是強有力的態度，

但未必擁有強而有力的證據，尤其此句後半部指出，所有證據都不利於被告，故選(D)。

備註：defendant(n.)被告
innocent(adj.)無罪的
opposite(adj.)相反的

4 (C)。 現今有更多的女性被僱用而從事那些以往是由男性支配的工作。

(A)recruit(v.)僱用（原形動詞，現在式）

(B)僱用（to+recruit的原形動詞）

(C)僱用（動詞過去式，過去分詞）

(D)僱用（動詞的進行式）

解 這題是考「現在進行式的被動語態」，句型是：主詞+is/am/are being+過去分詞，被動語態用於強調受詞。這題句子要強調的是「女性」，換句話說，女性被雇主僱用而從事之前只會僱用男性的工作，力求達到在職業上，性別平等的精神。故選(C)。

備註：dominate(v.)支配，統治

5 (D)。 因為地方稅太重，許多公司外包給更多在海外的勞動力。

(A)resource(v.)為……提供資源

(B)resell(v.)轉售

(C)outsell(v.)賣得比……多

(D)outsource(v.)外購，將……外包

解 這題是考「將……外包」的動詞outsource，因為本地的稅太重，

為了節稅，故將某些工作外包給海外的勞力，故選(D)。

備註：overseas(adj.)國外的

6 (A)。 這座紀念碑是紀念那些為保衛國家而失去生命的勇敢的男性與女性。

(A)in memory of(phr.)紀念

(B)in place of(phr.)代替

(C)in charge of(phr.)負責

(D)in terms of(phr.)就……方面來說

解 紀念碑的建設是為了紀念那些為國捐軀的勇敢國民，故選(A)。

備註：monument(n.)紀念碑
dedicate(v.)以……奉獻
brave(adj.)勇敢的

7 (B)。 我的老闆不滿意我的工作表現，所以給了負面的評價。

(A)satisfy(v.)滿意（原形動詞）

(B)satisfied(v.)滿意（動詞過去式）

(C)satisfying(v.)滿意（動詞的進行式）

(D)satisfactory(adj.)令人滿意的

解 這題是考be satisfied with這一慣用法，意思是「對……感到滿意」。

備註：review(n.)評價

8 (C)。 在新型冠狀病毒肺炎大流行爆發後，被感染的病患必須被隔離，以至於他們不會到處散播病毒。

(A)unless(conj.)除非

(B)in case(phr.)假使

(C)so that(phr.)以至於

(D)in order to(phr.)為了

解 這題是考 "so that" 這個副詞連接詞的用法，後面接副詞子句。語意上，因為句子的前半部的原因，而導致句子的後半部的結果的發生。在此句中，因為新冠肺炎爆發期，確診者需要被隔離，以至於這些人不在社區內活動散播病毒。故選(C)。

(D)"為了in order to" 後面接原形動詞，故不能選。(B)"假使in case" 是連接詞片語，後面接子句，放在這題中，語意不通，故不能選。

備註：outbreak(v.)爆發
pandemic(n.)大流行
infect(v.)感染
quarantine(v.)隔離
spread(v.)擴散

9 (A)。 因為俄羅斯對烏克蘭的軍事侵略，英國、歐盟及美國對俄羅斯進行國際制裁。
(A)sanctions（n.複數）國際制裁
(B)transaction(n.)交易
(C)transiti on(n.)變遷
(D)sensation(n.)感覺

解 impose sanctions on是一慣用法，意思是「進行制裁」，請注意：sanction是制裁的意思，複數名詞sanctions是國際制裁的意思。

備註：impose(v.)將……強加於人
military(adj.)軍事的
invasion(n.)侵略

10 (B)。 新主管將對所有的職員進行評量，以確保每個人都做好工作。

(A)evacuate(v.)撤離
(B)evaluate(v.)評價，評量
(C)elevate(v.)舉起
(D)eliminate(v.)淘汰

解 這題是考「評量、評估」的動詞，故選(B)。

備註：supervisor(n.)主管

11 (B)。 一些科學家已經質疑這份報告中所使用的研究方法。
(A)has（助動詞、用於第三人稱單數）已經
(B)have（助動詞、用於第一人稱或第二人稱單複數）已經
(C)was（助動詞、過去式、用於第一人稱或第三人稱單數）是
(D)is（助動詞、現在式、用於第一人稱或第三人稱單數）是

解 這題是考「現在完成式」，句型是：主詞+has/have+過去分詞。題目中科學家scientists是名詞複數型，故選(B)。

備註：question(v.)對……表示疑問

12 (D)。 在你購買軟體之前，你應該確認作業系統的相容性。
(A)sensibility(n.)感覺
(B)complexity(n.)複雜性
(C)identity(n.)身分
(D)compatibility(n.)兼容性

解 在購買軟體前，應該確認此軟體與目前使用的作業系統是否相容，故選(D)。

備註：operating system(n.)作業系統

13 (A)。微波爐能更快速加熱食物，然而，大部分用一般烤箱料理的食物，嘗起來更美味。

(A)conventional(adj.)普通的

(B)conversational(adj.)會話的

(C)conditional(adj.)附有條件的

(D)commercial(adj.)商業的

解 conventional oven是一慣用法，意思是「一般烤箱」。

備註：while（連接詞）然而、和……同時

microwave(n.)微波爐

14 (B)。因為這些新加入且具有天分的成員們，教練預測隊伍會贏得冠軍。

(A)predicting（v.進行式）預測

(B)predicted（v.動詞過去式）預測

(C)predict（v.原形動詞）預測

(D)will predict將預測

解 這題選擇(B)predict這個動詞的過去式，是因為句子後半部的子句（the team would win the championship）裡用的是will這個助動詞的過去式would，語意上來說，代表教練「預測」的這個動作，已經發生在過去某一個時間點，故選(B)。

備註：with（介系詞）由於、因為

talented(adj.)有天才的

coach(n.)教練

15 (A)。你向他借車的那個男人叫什麼名字？

(A)那輛你向他借來的車

(B)哪輛是你借來的車

(C)你向他借來了車

(D)錯誤句子，因為沒有關係代名詞。應該是：his car that you borrowed（那輛你向他借來的車）

解 這題是考關係代名詞whose的用法。whose是關係代名詞who的所有格，後面接名詞，當名詞子句裡的主詞或受詞，比如題目中的：whose（關係代名詞）+car（名詞）。關係代名詞whose具有連接詞的功能，可以把兩個獨立但相關聯的句子合併成一個句子，比如題目中的句子可以拆成兩個單句：What's the name of the man?以及The man whom you borrowed the car from.（請注意：關係代名詞whom是關係代名詞who的受格）。這兩個單句中，重複的名詞子句是：the man，更仔細地説：The man who has the car（這個有車的男人）。要將兩個單句合併成一個句子，我們需要關係代名詞who的所有格whose來做連接詞，修飾這個名詞子句：the man，因此可以寫成以下這個句子：The man whose car you borrowed，然後 The name of the man whose car you borrowed，寫成問句：What is the name of the man whose car you borrowed? 故選(A)。

不能選(B)，因為關係代名詞who的所有格是whose。關係代名詞which代替的是「事物」，

而不是「人」（例如題目中的 the man）。

不能選(C)，因為沒有關係代名詞whom。

備註：whose（關係代名詞）那個人／那些人的，他/她的，他們／她們的

Which（關係代名詞）那一個、那些、這一個、這些

borrow(v.)向（某人）借入／借來……

16 (B)。 在台灣，藍領勞工的最低薪資是每小時新台幣168元。

(A)premium(adj.)優質的

(B)minimum(adj.)最低的

(C)maximum(adj.)最大的

(D)optimum(adj.)最理想的

解 minimum wage是一慣用語，意思是「最低薪資」。

備註：blue-collar(adj.)藍領階級的

17 (C)。 當氣溫有變動時，有些人容易打噴嚏及抽鼻涕。

(A)convertible(adj.)可轉換的

(B)perceptible(adj)可感知的

(C)susceptible(adj.)易受影響的

(D)eligible(adj.)有資格當選的

解 be susceptible to是「對……很敏感，易患……」的意思，故選(C)。

備註：sneeze(v.)打噴嚏
　　　sniff(v.)抽鼻涕

18 (A)。 公司決定裁減那些工作能以機器人完成的冗員。

(A)lay off(phr.)解僱

(B)take off(phr.)起飛

(C)show off(phr.)炫耀

(D)put off(phr.)延遲

解 員工的工作，若可以用機器人來完成，為節省人力成本，公司決定解僱這些人員，故選(A)解僱。

備註：redundant(adj.)多餘的

whose（關係代名詞who的所有格）他／她的，他們／她們的

robot(n.)機器人

19 (D)。 當他回到家時，發現他的房子被人闖入，且所有他的貴重物品都被偷了。

(A)break into(phr.)闖入

(B)breaking into(phr.)闖入

(C)to break into(phr.)闖入

(D)broken into(phr.)闖入

解 這題是考find（動詞）表示「發現」時的句型，其中一個句型是：found（find的過去式）+受詞+過去分詞，這裡的過去分詞用來形容前面的受詞。在這題的句子中，"his house"（他的房子）接在find（動詞）後面，是為受詞，而broken into（broken是break動詞的過去分詞）來補充說明他的房子被闖入了，故選(D)。

這題的句子可以這樣變化：He found that someone broke into his house → He found that his house was broken into by someone → He found his house broken into.

備註：valuable(n.)貴重物品

20 (A)。 大部分的內科醫生建議吃飽了再服用維他命。

(A)taking（v.現在式）服用

(B)to take(v.)服用

(C)taken（v.過去分詞）服用

(D)take（v.動詞原形）服用

解 suggest是及物動詞，若後面接動詞，動詞形式是動名詞（V-ing），不能接不定詞（to+V），故選(A)。

備註：physician(n.)內科醫師

on a full stomach(phr.)吃飽了，飽著肚子

21 (B)。 自動售票機的使用說明令人困惑。它們並不易於使用。

(A)users-friendly（錯誤，應該是user-friendly）

(B)user-friendly易於使用的

(C)user-friends（錯誤）

(D)friendly-users（錯誤）

解 這題是考複合形容詞的一種，句型是：名詞+形容詞，其中名詞常使用單數，例如：sugar-free（無糖的）。故選(B)。

備註：instruction(n.)使用說明

ticket vending machine(n.)自動售票機

22 (C)。 我們部門的每個雇員，應該想出對策以降低公司預算。

(A)is supposing to（錯誤，應該是is supposed to）

(B)supposed to（錯誤，少了be.動詞，應該是is supposed to）

(C)is supposed to應該，理應當

(D)supposing to（錯誤，應該是is supposed to）

解 這題是考動詞suppose（應該、理應當、期盼）的用法，句型是：be supposed to。

備註：employee(n.)雇員

come up with(phr.)想出

solution(n.)解決方法

23 (B)。 因為俄羅斯入侵烏克蘭，越來越多的跨國公司，包括麥當勞、可口可樂及星巴克，已經暫停在俄羅斯的貿易往來。

(A)have extended(v.)已經延長

(B)have suspended(v.)已經暫停

(C)have intended(v.)已經打算

(D)have defended(v.)已經防禦

解 因為俄羅斯對烏克蘭的侵略，不少國際公司已經暫停在俄羅斯境內的貿易往來，故選(B)。

另外，extended的原形動詞是extend，suspended的原形動詞是suspend，intended的原形動詞是intend，defended的原形動詞是defend。

備註：a growing number of（數目、數量）越來越多的、不斷成長的

trading(n.)貿易、交易

24 (C)。 你在哪裡剪頭髮的？你指定哪一位設計師？

(A)錯誤，應該是did you have your hair cut

(B)錯誤，應該是did you have your hair cut

(C)did you have your hair cut

(D)錯誤，應該是did you have your hair cut

解 have是使役動詞，頭髮是被剪的，故後面接過去分詞，句型是：have+受詞+過去分詞。故選(C)。

備註：cut(v.)修剪，剪斷

（動詞變化：動詞原型或現在式cut→過去式cut→過去分詞cut）

hairdresser(n.)美髮師

25 (C)。 這位主人備妥盛宴來熱烈款待他的客人。

(A)credibility(n.)可靠性

(B)possibility(n.)可能性

(C)hospitality(n.)款待、招待

(D)ambiguity(n.)模稜兩可

解 在英文中，款待或招待客人的動詞是hospitality，故選(C)。

備註：host(n.)主人

terrific(adj.)極度的

feast(n.)盛宴

26 (C)。 電動車及清淨能源儲存的前景是光明的。

(A)reduction(n.)減少

(B)respect(n.)尊敬

(C)prospect(n.)前景

(D)reflection(n.)反射

解 能源節約是目前看好的發展之一，故選(C)。

備註：electric car(n.)電動車

clean energy(n.)清潔能源

storage(n.)儲存

27 (A)。 這兩個政黨，在如何減少碳排放的最好處理方法上，未能達成共識。

(A)consensus(n.)共識，合意

(B)circus(n.)馬戲團

(C)construction(n.)建設

(D)containment(n.)遏制

解 依題意選(A)。

備註：reduce(v.)（數量上的）減少

carbon emission(s)(n.)碳排放

28 (B)。 我想來去散步，因為今天天氣多美好。

(A)want taking（錯誤，應該是want to take）

(B)feel like taking想要去做某件事

(C)would like taking（錯誤，應該是would like to take）

(D)feel like to take（錯誤，應該是feel like taking）

解 這題是考 "feel like想要（做某件事）、感覺好像……" 的用法，句型是：feel like+名詞/V-ing。feel是動詞，like在這裡當作介係詞，後接現在分詞（V-ing），故選(B)，不能選(D)。(A)應改成want to take。(C)，句型應該是would like to+原形動詞，意思

也是「想要做某事」，或句型為would like+sth.，意思是「想要某物」，故(C)應改成would like to take才對。

29 (A)。在卡爾點出問題後，他進一步建議了些解決方法。
(A)to suggest建議
(B)suggesting（v.進行式）建議
(C)suggested（v.過去式）建議
(D)being suggested(v.)被建議

解 這題是考 "go on繼續（剛剛從事的某件事）" 的用法，句型是：go on+V-ing，例如：He went on talking for 30 minutes.（他繼續講了30分鐘的話）。另一句型：go on+to+原形V.，意思是下一步將從事新的、不同的事情，例如：After cleaning the house, he went on to take a shower.（在打掃房子後，他接著去洗澡。）這題題目中提到，卡爾已經點出問題，他的下一步是建議一些解決方法，這前後兩個動作不一樣，所以用go on to+V的句型，故選(A)。
備註：point out指出，點出

30 (C)。在她了解她沒帶足夠的錢之前，她已經試穿了不少件套裝。
(A)has been tried（現在完成被動式）已被嘗試過（主詞通常是「事、物」）
(B)has tried（現在完成式）嘗試過了
(C)had tried（過去完成式）嘗試過了
(D)had been tried（過去完成被動式）已被嘗試過（主詞通常是「事、物」）

解 這題是考英文文法「完成式」的句型及意義。(C)是正確答案，是因為：題目後半段提到，她後來才瞭解到她沒帶足夠的金錢，這裡的動詞realize是用過去式realized，因此可得知，試穿這件事情是已經發生在過去某一時間點。所以選(C)，而不能選(B)。
(A)[現在完成被動式]及(C)[過去完成被動式]，主詞得是某件事情，或是沒有生命的物品。若主詞是「人」的話，意思則變成「某人已被受審」。
備註：try on試穿
outfit(n.)套裝、全套服裝
realize(v.)理解到、了解到

31 (D)。這位年輕藝術家的作品被認為太抽象，因為它太難懂了。
(A)contract(v.)訂契約
(B)attract(v.)吸引
(C)extract(v.)提煉
(D)abstract(adj.)抽象的

解 題目中提到這位年輕藝術家的作品太難懂了，可猜測其作品或許很抽象，故選(D)。
備註：consider(v.)考慮、認為

32 (C)。
男性：這總共新台幣5000元。請問要將這台影印機寄送到貴府嗎？因為你購買金額超過新台幣1000元，所以免運費。
女性：哇，太好了。影印機是否能在下個禮拜一之前寄到？我需要能盡快使用影印機。

男性：沒問題。可以請你填寫這張
　　　表格嗎？

這位男性提供什麼給這位女性？

(A) 全額退款　　　(B)免費修理

(C)免費寄送　　　(D)特別折扣

解 題目中提到因為這位女性此次購
　　物超過新台幣1000元，可獲得免
　　運費寄送影印機，故選(C)。

　　備註：printer(n.)印表機

as soon as possible盡快、越快
越好

deliver(v.)寄送

fill out填寫

repair(v.)修理、修復

33 (B)。

男性：嗨，我想要預約牙齒檢查。
　　　我上次檢查大約是半年前。

女性：這禮拜都被預約光了。下禮
　　　拜五的下午，可以嗎？

男性：可以，下禮拜五，我可以。
　　　我可以預約下午三點嗎？

女性：當然，下午三點，沒問題。

這位女性可能在哪裡工作？

(A)書店　　　　(B)牙科診所

(C)便利商店　　(D)銀行

解 題目中提到這位男性想預約一
　　次的牙齒檢查（dental exam），
　　可猜測這位女性是在牙醫診所
　　工作。

　　備註：dental exam(n.)牙齒檢查

book(v.)預約

suit me fine符合我的需求

34 (A)。

男性：珊蒂，你找到新公寓了嗎？

女性：還沒，羅納德。我想要搬
　　　到距離大眾運輸交通近的地
　　　點。我現在住的公寓離我的
　　　辦公室太遠了。

這位女性在抱怨什麼？

(A)她的公寓距離她的辦公室太遠。

(B)她的公寓房間太小。

(C)她公寓附近只有一個公車站。

(D) 街道太吵了。

解 題目中這位女性希望找到靠近大
　　眾運輸系統的公寓，因為她現在
　　住的公寓離她的辦公室太遠了，
　　故選(A)。

　　備註：public transportation(n.)
公共交通運輸、大眾交通運輸

35 (B)。

女性：你好，歡迎光臨溫蒂廚房。
　　　這是你第一次來嗎？

男人：是，是第一次。你們這裡有
　　　每日特餐嗎？

女人：當然，我們有。今天的特餐
　　　是貽貝義大利麵，奶油蘑菇
　　　湯，以及雞肉溫沙拉。這聽
　　　起來如何？

男人：聽起來很棒。但首先，當我
　　　決定點什麼時，可以來杯汽
　　　水嗎？

這位男性詢問女性什麼資訊？

(A)打折項目　　　(B)一份特餐

(C)一本食譜　　　(D)一個禮物

解 這位男性第一次到溫蒂廚房用餐，詢問有沒有今日特餐，這位女性回答有，是貽貝義大利麵，奶油蘑菇湯，及雞肉溫沙拉，故選(B)。

備註：daily special(n.)今日特餐

pasta(n.)義大利麵

mussel(n.)貽貝

mushroom(n.)蘑菇

warm salad(n.)溫沙拉

soft drink汽水

36 (D)。

女性：我整個早上都試著聯絡傑森。我知道他不在他的辦公室裡，因為他沒有回電話，他也還沒有回我的電子郵件。

男性：他被經理盯上了，因為他弄丟了一位重要客戶的檔案。我想，經理現在正責備他。

根據這位男性的回答，現在傑森在哪裡？

(A)在他的辦公室　(B)在儲藏室

(C)在廁所　　　　(D)在經理辦公室

解 這男性說傑森因為弄丟了一位重要客戶的檔案，經理正在責備他，可猜測傑森在經理的辦公室裡，故選(D)。

備註：人be. in trouble 某人犯錯，導致他／她的頂頭上司生氣，而被責備

talk to人責備某人

37 (C)。

女性：午安，這是服務台。請問有什麼我能幫忙的？

男性：是的，我是301室的李艾倫。我的淋浴器壞了。今天早上我已經聯絡你們了，但還沒人來修理。

女性：請容我向您道歉，李先生。我會馬上連絡維修部，請他們立即為您檢查。

這位男性為什麼要聯絡這位女性？

(A)為了訂餐點

(B)為了確認一個約會

(C)為了修理東西

(D)為了預約

解 題目中提到這位男性已經聯絡櫃檯說他的房間淋浴器壞了，但還沒有人來修理，所以這位男性是再次聯絡櫃檯，請求幫忙，故選(C)。

備註：front desk(n.)服務台

shower(n.)淋浴器

maintenance(n.)維修

38 (B)。

女性：您希望做什麼髮型？您想要保持原來的髮型，還是換個不一樣髮型？

男性：我想嘗試新髮型。我想我需要燙髮。還有，你可以把兩側頭髮修短一點嗎？

女性：沒問題。

這個對話最可能發生在什麼地方？

(A)在派對　　　　(B)在髮廊

(C)在診所　　　　(D)在時尚秀

解 女人問男人想要什麼髮型，男人想嘗試新髮型，想要燙髮，可見對話發生在髮廊，故選(B)。

備註：perm(n.)燙髮

39 (A)。

男性：這雙鞋有進不一樣的尺寸嗎？

女性：我來看看。我們現在只有10到12號，但在禮拜三之前，我們會有完整的尺寸存貨。您想找什麼尺寸？

男性：我想要9號，但我猜我也可以穿10號。有時候尺寸不見得都一樣大小。

女性：好，讓我拿10號給您試穿，您可以試試看合不合腳。

這位男性下一步會做什麼事？

(A)試穿鞋子　　　(B)等到星期三
(C)去另一家店看看　(D)買鞋子

解 題目中提到這位男性詢問有沒有其他尺寸，這位女性回答目前只有10到12號，要到星期三才會有齊全的尺寸，這位男性平常都穿9號，也可穿10號，但是因為尺寸會有誤差，所以這位女性拿10號鞋給這位男性試穿，故選(A)。

備註：stock(n.)存貨

40 (D)。

女性：不好意思。請問王莎菈在這裡工作嗎？我有些箱子要給她。

男性：你正好錯過她了。她剛離開去參加一個會議，而這會議會持續大約一個鐘頭。

女性：是否能請你為這次的快遞遞送簽名嗎？若沒辦法，我將在兩個小時內回來這裡。

男性：我可以為這次的快遞遞送簽名。

王小姐在哪裡？

(A)在吃午餐　　　(B)在家裡
(C)在銀行　　　　(D)在開會

解 題目中提到王莎菈剛離開去參加一個會議，且會議將持續大約一個鐘頭，所以王莎菈在開會，故選(D)。

備註：sign(v.)簽名
delivery(n.)快遞

二、閱讀測驗

【第一篇】

　　2020年3月11號，這是史書上的一天。那一天，世界衛生組織將冠狀病毒的擴散定義了新的名詞－－傳染疫情（流行疫情）。從那天起，人類世界已經在這個傳染疫情中生活兩年了。

　　在2020年3月11號後，很多都改變了。人們開始戴口罩，且進入封城狀態。他們如常工作－－及上課－－在網路上。我們都一起工作（在不同的地方），為了保持安全。如今，在疫情傳染的第三年中，新型冠狀病毒肺炎的流行仍持續影響數百萬人的生活。即使，生活慢慢地回復正常。

　　在2022年3月底前，大約有5億人確診新型冠狀病毒肺炎，超過600萬人過世。這包括了，在亞洲超過1百萬人，在美國超過90萬人。數以百萬計的人們被病毒侵襲而生病，當中很多人仍在與癒後的長期後遺症奮鬥。

　　過去2年，病毒本身也變種過。它已突變了數次，產生不同的變異株。這些變異株包括delta及omicron－－這兩種變異株都有極強的傳染力。已造成了新型冠狀病毒肺炎的幾波新高峰－－且疾病擴散到更多地區。目前，新型冠狀病毒幾乎已到達地球的每個角落。甚至是如東加、萬那杜及密克羅尼西亞這些獨立的島嶼國家，也傳出確診案例。

　　新型冠狀病毒肺炎疫苗可以保護許多人。疫苗可以使感染的人避免轉為重症患者（或死亡）。在2020年12月8號，一位90歲的英國女士，接種了第一支通過許可的疫苗。現今，大部份美國人已完成疫苗接種。然而，世界上的貧窮地區，沒辦法提供足夠的疫苗給人民接種。在非洲，超過10億人（超過非洲人口的90%），仍沒有接種過任何疫苗。

　　在美國，新型冠狀病毒肺炎的確診數字已經下降了。因此，美國許多地方的人們不再戴口罩。這個月，數千所學校已解除口罩命令。然而，直到4月18號，搭乘飛機、火車及公共巴士的旅客，還是需要戴口罩。

　　然而，疫情離結束之日還很遠。每一天，世界各地有超過1百萬人確診新冠肺炎。某些地方面臨創紀錄的確診數字。這些地區包括香港，及近來遭遇最嚴重疫情爆發的中國。當然，往後幾年，我們仍會感受到疫情的副作用。例如，近期的幾項研究顯示了，學校關閉已造成數百萬名年輕學子的閱讀能力落後。

　　疫情大流行的第三年會是如何？沒有人知道。或許會有治療新型冠狀病毒肺炎的新療法（包括藥丸）。一些專家相信疫情大流行會正式地在2022年結束。但這不代表病毒將會消失。反而，新冠肺炎極可能在大部分的地區，轉變成地方型流感。這表示，新冠肺炎將在不同的時間點，繼續擴散。而我們將學習與病毒共存，成為生活一部分。

　　備註：pandemic(n.)流行病，傳染中的疫情
lockdown(n.)（尤指監獄暴動時的）嚴防禁閉，封城
affect(v.)影響
positive(adj.)（醫學測驗的）陽性反應的
virus(n.)病毒
deal with處理
long-term長期的
effect(n.)結果，後果，影響
mutate(v.)產生改變，變化
variant(n.)變形，轉化
contagious(adj.)接觸傳染性的，（可能）帶接觸傳染原的
remove(v.)脫掉（remove from）
mandate(n.)命令，指令
worldwide(adj.)遍及全球的
outbreak(n.)爆發（outbreak of）
endemic(n.)地方流行疾病

41 (B)。根據此篇文章，為什麼新型冠狀病毒肺炎大流行在2020年3月11號開始？

(A)這是疫情大流行第一次擴散到其他國家的時間。

(B)這是世界衛生組織第一次稱它為流行疫情的時間。

(C)這是第一個人得到新型冠狀病毒肺炎的時間。

(D)這是第一個人死於新型冠狀病毒肺炎的時間。

解 根據第一段，世界衛生組織在2020年3月11號定義了冠狀病毒的擴散，故選(B)。

42 (D)。 疫情大流行後大約多少時間，人們開始接種通過許可的新型冠狀病毒肺炎疫苗？

(A)1年又3個月　　(B)2年

(C)3個月　　　　(D)9個月

解 根據第五段，英國一名90歲的女人在2020年12月8號接種第一支通過許可的疫苗，所以在2020年3月11號之後約九個月，人們開始接種疫苗，故選(D)。

43 (A)。 冠狀病毒突變是什麼意思？

(A)它改變了。

(B)它擴散地很快。

(C)它變得更危險。

(D)它造成很多人死亡。

解 mutate(v.)是突變的意思，故選(A)。

44 (C)。 文章中提到，因新型冠狀病毒肺炎大流行，學校關閉對年輕學生的影響是什麼？

(A)年輕學生喜歡線上閱讀。

(B)年輕學生一點都不喜歡閱讀。

(C)年輕學生的閱讀能力落後。

(D)比起閱讀，年輕學生更喜歡電動遊戲。

解 根據第七段，近期研究顯示關閉學校造成數百萬名年輕學生閱讀能力落後，故選(C)。

45 (D)。「命令」一詞是什麼意思？

(A)隨機化　　　　(B)自由

(C)反抗　　　　　(D)規定

解 mandate(n.)意思是「命令，指令」，選項中只有rule（規定，規則）最接近mandate的意思。

【第二篇】

肥胖是過多的體脂肪累積到極大值、對健康造成損害、導致預期壽命減短及／或增加健康問題的醫療狀況。身體質量指數（BMI），一種由體重及身高衡量的數值，定義了身體質量指數數值介於15公斤/身高的平方及30公斤／身高的平方之間是超重（肥胖前期），而超過30公斤/身高的平方是過胖。

肥胖會增加不同疾病發生的可能性，特別是心臟疾病、第2型糖尿病、睡眠呼吸困難、某些癌症及骨關節炎。肥胖通常是因攝取過量的卡路里、缺少體能運動、遺傳易感性這些綜合因素造成的，即使一些案例主要是由基因、血液不正常病癥、藥物治療，或疾病所造成。有論點以為一些過胖人士，因為新陳代謝慢，即使吃不多，體重卻仍增加，支持這項論點的證據有限；平均來說，對應纖瘦者，過胖者消耗更多的能量，因為需要這麼多的能量來維持增加的體重。

治療肥胖最有效的方法是節食及體能運動。有時候，服用減肥藥物來減少

食慾或抑制脂肪吸收。嚴重的案例則會執行手術，或放入一顆氣球到胃中以減少胃的大小／或腸子的長度，可讓人們吃少一點。

　　由於肥胖現象普遍存在於成人及孩童之中，肥胖是世界上最能被預防的致死因素，且政府相關權力機構視肥胖為21世紀最嚴肅的公共衛生問題。在現代社會中（尤其是西方社會），肥胖是被仇視的，即使在過往歷史中，肥胖被廣泛地認為是財富及生育力的表徵，而這樣的想法，依然存在世界某些地區。

　　備註：obesity(n.)肥胖，過胖
medical(adj.)醫學的，醫療的
excess(adj.)過量的
accumulate(v.)累積
adverse(adj.)有害的，相反的
reduce(v.)減少，減輕體重
expectancy(n.)期望，預期
measurement(n.)測量
compare(v.)比較，對照（compare with/to）
obese(adj.)過胖的
increase(v.)增加，增強
diabetes(n.)糖尿病
osteoarthritis(n.)骨關節炎
susceptibility(n.)敏感性，易受影響的氣質
disorder(n.)混亂，無秩序
medication(n.)藥物，藥物治療
metabolism(n.)新陳代謝
expenditure(n.)消費，支出額
inhibit(v.)抑制，妨礙
absorption(n.)吸收，吸收過程

preventable(adj.)可阻止的，可預防的
prevalence(n.)（疾病等的）流行程度

46 (B)。 這篇文章意指＿＿＿＿。
(A)雖然肥胖很普遍，但它不被認為是嚴重的疾病
(B)肥胖被視為一嚴重的疾病
(C)肥胖只影響男人
(D)肥胖只來自遺傳
解 第二段提到肥胖會增加不同疾病發生的可能性，特別是心臟疾病、第2型糖尿病、睡眠呼吸困難、某些癌症及骨關節炎。另外，第四段提到肥胖現象普遍存在於成人及孩童之中，且政府相關權力機構視肥胖為21世紀最嚴肅的公共衛生問題，故選(B)。
不能選(D)是因為：第二段中提到肥胖是因為攝取過多的卡路里，缺乏體能運動，遺傳易感性等眾多原因造成的，另外少部分是因為基因，血液病癥或疾病造成，所以肥胖是許多因素造成。

47 (A)。 肥胖者＿＿＿＿。
(A)會受苦於嚴重的疾病
(B)會受苦於輕微的疾病
(C)都很有錢
(D)只存在在西方社會
解 第二段中提到肥胖會增加不同疾病發生的可能性，特別是心臟疾病、第2型糖尿病、睡眠呼吸困

難、某些癌症及骨關節炎，這些疾病是需要積極治療、得嚴肅面對的疾病，故選(A)。

備註：ailment(n.)（輕微的）疾病、病痛

48 (C)。現代醫學＿＿＿＿＿。
(A)是停止肥胖的最好方式
(B)是治療肥胖的最糟方式
(C)或能治療肥胖
(D)完全沒辦法治療肥胖

解 第三段提到治療肥胖最有效的方法是節食及體能運動。服用減肥藥物也可以減少食慾或抑制脂肪吸收。某些嚴重案例則會執行手術，或放入一顆氣球到胃中以減少胃的大小／或腸子的長度，可讓人們吃少一點，故選(C)。

49 (D)。首要治療肥胖的方式是＿＿＿＿＿。
(A)基因治療
(B)藥物治療
(C)手術
(D)跟個人生活型態有關

解 第三段提到主要治療肥胖的方法為節食及運動，故選(D)。

50 (C)。這個字 "preventable" 是什麼意思？
(A)無法阻擋的　　(B)負擔得起的
(C)能避免的　　　(D)可預料的

解 preventable(adj.)意思是「可預防的，可阻止的」，而選項中(C) avoidable（能避免的）意思與之最接近。

111年　台灣電力新進僱用人員

(　)　**1** Many people are environmentally _____ and they choose to use YouBike to travel around the city.
(A)kind
(B)friendly
(C)considerable
(D)thinking

(　)　**2** Take an umbrella because _____ , according to the weather forecast.
(A)it rains
(B)it has been raining
(C)it was raining
(D)it is going to rain

(　)　**3** Jay does the cooking and his wife _____ the dishes.
(A)has
(B)prepares
(C)is in charge of
(D)finishes

(　)　**4** The Harry Potter movies are among the most _____ movies in history.
(A)profitable
(B)money
(C)paying
(D)liking

(　)　**5** You should register your bike _____ stolen.
(A)in case it will be
(B)in case it is
(C)if it will be
(D)if it is

(　)　**6** Nina is a _____ , so she doesn't eat meat or fish.
(A)artist
(B)Buddhist
(C)dentist
(D)socialist

(　)　**7** Sometimes less is more, so _____ is not always the most important.
(A)volume
(B)quality
(C)number
(D)shape

(　　) **8** Jean is bad at _____ her money; she runs out of money at the end of each month.
(A)spending　　　　　　　　(B)keeping
(C)calculating　　　　　　　(D)handling

(　　) **9** Ken's car is still running _____ although it is already 23 years old.
(A)wisely　　　　　　　　(B)speedily
(C)smoothly　　　　　　　(D)verily

(　) **10** Mary loves _____ and wants to become a vet.
(A)animals　　　　　　　(B)plants
(C)food　　　　　　　　(D)nature

(　) **11** Ken's father _____ at a chicken farm for a long time when he decided to start his own fifteen years ago.
(A)worked　　　　　　　(B)has stay
(C)had helped　　　　　　(D)employed

(　) **12** Many people in Taipei choose to ride motorcycles because _____ is easier.
(A)transportation　　　　　(B)stopping
(C)trafficking　　　　　　(D)parking

(　) **13** Sally _____ to university, but instead she chose to work to help her parents financially.
(A)went　　　　　　　　(B)had gone
(C)could have gone　　　　(D)didn't go

(　) **14** Many young people choose to _____ nowadays because they realize having a good skill can be better than having a diploma.
(A)take vocational training　(B)go to college
(C)receive foreign education　(D)study science

(　) **15** More and more countries have requested _____ and magazines to hire very thin models because of the bad influence on young girls.
(A)newspapers　　　　　　(B)artists
(C)performers　　　　　　(D)designers

( ) **16** People today like to use electronic _____ and reading is becoming a dying habit.
(A)writing   (B)devices
(C)items   (D)pieces

( ) **17** Jimmy _____ to pass the exam after all the time and energy he has spent preparing for it.
(A)hopes   (B)wishes
(C)likes   (D)looks forward

( ) **18** The food looked so _____ that I felt hungry right away.
(A)well   (B)wonderfully
(C)inviting   (D)shining

( ) **19** To _____ such data, you need special approval from the manager.
(A)enjoy   (B)accept
(C)understand   (D)access

( ) **20** I missed the bus this morning and _____ take a taxi to go to work.
(A)must to   (B)need to
(C)had to   (D)wanted to

( ) **21** Don't forget to turn off all electrical _____ before you leave home.
(A)wires   (B)users
(C)appliances   (D)properties

( ) **22** As a result of aging population, more and more countries plan to _____ the retirement age to sixty-eight or even seventy.
(A)regulate   (B)extend
(C)maintain   (D)remove

( ) **23** Willy wastes a lot of time playing online games because he is _____ them.
(A)addicted to   (B)improved with
(C)entertained in   (D)enjoyed by

(　　) **24** It took Judy a year to _____ the Civil Service Examination and she passed it.
(A)ready for　　　　　　　　(B)get over
(C)prepare　　　　　　　　　(D)prepare for

(　　) **25** All workers applying for technical positions _____ to complete related training in three months.
(A)are advised　　　　　　　(B)has got
(C)should　　　　　　　　　(D)have need

(　　) **26** After _____ the matter for two days, we were still unable to reach any conclusion.
(A)discussed　　　　　　　　(B)having been discussed
(C)discussing　　　　　　　　(D)being discussed

(　　) **27** Because of _____ oil prices and the COVID-19 pandemic, things that people need in everyday life are becoming more and more expensive.
(A)raising　　　　　　　　　(B)rising
(C)difficult　　　　　　　　　(D)extending

(　　) **28** It is very unusual that the Japanese ramen shop _____ since last week.
(A)is close　　　　　　　　　(B)does not open
(C)has been closed　　　　　　(D)will not be open

(　　) **29** Frank is taking a one-year _____ to go to study in Australia next year.
(A)holiday　　　　　　　　　(B)leave of absence without pay
(C)paid vacation　　　　　　　(D)trip

(　　) **30** Live streaming is very popular and has made many Internet _____ become rich.
(A)reds　　　　　　　　　　(B)stars
(C)famous　　　　　　　　　(D)celebrities

(　) **31** You should hurry if you want to apply for a scholarship because the _____ is this Friday.
(A)end (B)finish time
(C)deadline (D)time table

(　) **32** There's no need to rush; we're already late _____ the movie.
(A)to (B)for
(C)at (D)from

(　) **33** Don't prepare _____ for dinner because Jack is a big meat eater.
(A)too many vegetables (B)so much beef
(C)too many fruit (D)so many seafoods

(　) **34** Being parents for the first time, Tim and Diana do not know how to stop _____ .
(A)the baby to cry (B)the baby cries
(C)the baby from crying (D)the baby cry

(　) **35** Our department encourages all workers to get professional licenses and _____ to improve their knowledge and skills.
(A)documents (B)instructions
(C)requirements (D)certificates

(　) **36** Studies show females usually surf the Internet for _____ reasons and males just do it for fun.
(A)practical (B)unthinkable
(C)questionable (D)valuable

(　) **37** It took Brian more than six months to bicycle _____ the USA all by himself.
(A)cross (B)in
(C)on (D)across

(　) **38** The mayor said last week he would increase the pay for every city government employee _____ 3% next year.
(A)by (B)to
(C)out of (D)in

( ) **39** Mom doesn't feel like cooking tonight, so we'll have some spaghetti _____ .
(A)bought (B)delivered
(C)to deliver (D)to buy

( ) **40** There's a bottle of dish soap _____ if you need more.
(A)in the bathroom (B)under the kitchen sink
(C)in the living room (D)in the refrigerator

解答與解析　　答案標示為# 者，表官方曾公告更正該題答案。

1 (B)。 許多人是環境友好的，他們選擇騎YouBike探訪這座城市。
(A)kind(adj.)親切的
(B)friendly(adj.)友好的
(C)considerable(adj.)相當的
(D)thinking(adj.)理性的
解 environmentally friendly是一慣用法，意思是「保護生態環境的，對生態環境無害的」。

2 (D)。 根據氣象預報，快要下雨了，帶把雨傘吧。
(A)下雨（現在式）
(B)已經下雨了（現在完成進行式）
(C)下雨（過去進行式）
(D)快要下雨（未來進行式）
解 這題選(D)因為：題目中提到氣象預報（weather forecast），說話的當下，天氣將會有變化（下雨）。另外，it在英文中，可當作天氣的代名詞。
(A)不能選，因為現在式（或現在簡單式）表達現在時間的動作、狀態或是短時間內不會變化的事實。

(B)不能選，因為題目中建議攜帶雨傘，可推測，講話當下並沒有下雨。
(C)不能選，因為這表示這場雨已經下了，在過去某段時間。
備註：weather forecast(n.)天氣預報

3 (C)。 傑負責煮飯，而他的太太負責洗碗。
(A)has(v.)有
(B)prepare(v.)準備
(C)is in charge of(phr.)負責
(D)finish(v.)結束
解 do the dishes有「洗碗」的意思，故選(C)。

4 (A)。 電影「哈利波特」是歷史上票房最賣座的電影。
(A)profitable(adj.)有利潤的
(B)money(n.)錢
(C)paying(adj.)有利的
(D)liking(n.)喜歡
解 電影哈利波特的票房很好，故選(A)。

5 (B)。 你應該登記你的腳踏車，以防萬一它被偷。
(A)（錯誤，應該是in case it is）
(B)以防萬一它被
(C)（錯誤，應該是in case it is）
(D)（錯誤，應該是in case it is）
解 這題是考 "in case"（連接詞片語）的用法。in case表示「要做好準備，以防萬一發生什麼事」，後面接子句，而子句的動詞時態是簡單現在式，句型為：in case+子句，例如：Order some food, in case he is hungry after taking the exam.（點些食物，以防萬一他考完試後會肚子餓。）in case of是介系詞片語，有「若發生事情，我們該做什麼」的意思，後面接名詞，句型為：in case of+名詞，例如：In case of the emergency, press the red button.（萬一發生意外，按下紅色按鈕。）
備註：register(v.)登記，註冊

6 (B)。 妮娜是佛教徒，所以她不吃肉跟魚。
(A)artist(n.)藝術家
(B)Buddhist(n.)佛教徒
(C)dentist(n.)牙醫
(D)socialist(n.)社會主義者
解 佛教徒不吃肉跟魚，所以選(B)。

7 (A)。 有時候少即是多，所以數量絕對不是最重要的事。
(A)volume(n.)量
(B)quality(n.)品質

(C)number(n.)數字
(D)shape(n.)形狀
解 less is more有「少即是多」，少及多是指數量的多寡，故選(A)。

8 (D)。 珍不擅長管理她的錢，她每個月底都會把錢花光。
(A)spend(v.)花錢
(B)keep(v.)持有
(C)calculate(v.)計算
(D)handle(v.)處理
解 珍是個月光族，可猜測她不擅長管理她的金錢，故選(D)。
備註：be bad at不擅長……
run out of用完，耗盡

9 (C)。 雖然肯的車子已經開了23年了，它依然跑得很流暢。
(A)wisely(adv.)聰明地
(B)speedily(adv.)迅速地
(C)smoothly(adv.)流暢地，順利地
(D)verily(adv.)真實地
解 這題是考 "although（連接詞）雖然、儘管、然而" 的用法，although連接的前後子句，語意應該相反。因此，雖然是高齡車，但開起來依然順手，故選(C)。

10 (A)。 瑪莉熱愛動物，她想成為一名獸醫。
(A)animal(n.)動物
(B)plant(n.)植物
(C)food(n.)食物
(D)nature(n.)自然
解 瑪莉想成為獸醫，可見她喜歡動物，故選(A)。
備註：vet(n.)獸醫

11 (C)。十五年前當肯的爸爸決定開始自己的事業時，他已經在一座雞場工作很長一段時間了。
(A)work(v.)工作
(B)（錯誤，應該是has stayed已經停留了）
(C)had helped已經幫忙了
(D)employ(v.)僱用

解 這題是考過去完成式的用法。過去完成式表達某一動作或經驗已經在過去某段時間完成了。句型是：had+過去分詞。過去完成式的句子通常描述過去發生的兩件事情，先發生的事情用「過去完成式」，而後發生的事情則用「過去簡單式」來表達。比如：在這考題，兩件事情都發生在過去，但是這子句 "when he decided to start his own" 裡用的動詞decided，其時態是「過去簡單式」，可知肯的爸爸的決定是後來發生的事情，因此在雞場工作的事情是先前發生的事情，故選(C)過去完成式。

12 (D)。在台北許多人選擇騎摩托車，因為停車比較容易。
(A)transportation(n.)運輸
(B)stopping(n.)停止
(C)trafficking(n.)非法交易
(D)parking(n.)停車

解 騎摩托車比較容易停車，故選(D)。

13 (C)。莎莉原本可以進大學讀書，但她卻選擇工作，以在財務上幫忙她的父母。

(A)went（v.過去式）前往
(B)had gone（v.過去完成式）已經前往
(C)could have gone(v.)可前往
(D)didn' t go(v.)沒去

解 這題是考「could have+過去分詞」的意思及用法。 "could have+過去分詞" 表示「過去可以做到，卻沒有去做」，例如：I could have got up earlier this morning, but I decided to lie in till noon.（我今天可以早點起床，但我決定賴床到中午。）莎莉本來可以進大學，但沒有進去而是去工作，所以用此句型。

14 (A)。現在許多年輕人選擇參加職業訓練，因為他們了解到擁有好的技能比擁有畢業文憑還重要。
(A)參加職業訓練 (B)進入大學
(C)接受外國教育 (D)研讀科學

解 題目提到擁有好的技能比擁有畢業文憑重要，故選(A)參加職業訓練以培養好的技能。
備註：diploma(n.)畢業文憑
vocational training(n.)職業訓練

15 (#)。越來越多的國家要求設計師及雜誌不要僱用過瘦的模特兒，因為這對年輕女性有不好的影響。
(A)newspaper(n.)報紙
(B)artist(n.)藝術家
(C)performer(n.)演出者
(D)designer(n.)設計師

解 這題因考題有瑕疵，故官方公佈無正確答案。題目的瑕疵之

處在於：... have requested _____ "and" magazines to hire... 中的連接詞and，應該改成 介系詞 of，而成為 designers of magazines（雜誌的設計師），因為動詞request（要求、請求）後面通常接「人」，請求某人做某事（politely ask someone to do something.）。

備註：request(v.)要求

16 (B)。 今日人們喜歡電子設備，閱讀成為消失的習慣。
(A)writing(n.)寫作
(B)device(n.)設備
(C)item(n.)項目
(D)piece(n.)一片
解 electronic devices是「電子設備」的意思，現今人們習慣用手機、電腦等電子設備閱讀資訊，書本閱讀恐成為一消失的習慣，故選(B)。

17 (A)。 在花了所有的時間及精力準備考試後，吉米希望能通過考試。
(A)hope(v.)希望
(B)wish(v.)希望
(C)like(v.)喜歡
(D)look forward(phr.)期待
解 hope意思是希望，表示未來很可能發生，例如：I hope our team will win.（我希望我們的隊伍可以贏。）而wish，意思也是希望，但希望的事情發生可能性很低，或與事實相反，例如：I wish I were here last night（我

希望昨天晚上我在這裡。[但事實上我昨天晚上不在這裡]）。look forward to，表示期待，這裡的to是介係詞，後面要接動名詞（V-ing），例如：look forward to passing the exam。

18 (C)。 這食物看起來如此吸引人，讓我當下覺得肚子餓。
(A)well(adj.)好的
(B)wonderfully(adv.)極好地
(C)inviting(adj.)吸引人的
(D)shining(adj.)光亮的
解 這題是考「連綴動詞」的意思及用法，比如這題中的look（看起來）。連綴動詞後面接的補語必須是形容詞，句型為：主詞+look/sound/smell/taste/feel+主詞補語（形容詞），例如：It smells inviting.（這聞起來很吸引人）。
(A)well當形容詞時，常指身體狀況良好，例如：She is not well.（她身體不舒服。）故不選(A)。
備註：so... that... 如此……以至於……

19 (D)。 你需要經理的特別同意，才能讀取這些資料。
(A)enjoy(v.)享受
(B)accept(v.)接受
(C)understand(v.)理解
(D)access(v.)接近，存取

解 access有「讀取，存取」的意思，故選(D)。

備註：approval(n.)同意，批准

20 (C)。我今天早上錯過巴士了，得搭計程車去工作。

(A)must to必須

(B)need to需要

(C)had to必須

(D)wanted to想要

解 這題是考must to、have to、need to三者的差別及用法。這三者的意思都可以是「必須」，但是must to表示（義務、必要性的）必須，比較主觀，例如：I must to leave for work early.（我得早點去工作。）have to也表示（義務、必要性的）的需要，但比較客觀，例如：I have to fasten the belt.（我得繫好安全帶。）但must沒有時態問題，若要表示過去某段時間所應盡的義務，要用had to，故選(C)。而need to表示為了達到目的，某事必須要做，但不一定得優先做，例如：I need to clean my dirty shirt.（我需要洗我的髒襯衫。）

21 (C)。在出門之前，別忘了關掉所有電子設備。

(A)wire(n.)金屬線

(B)user(n.)使用者

(C)appliance(n.)設備

(D)property(n.)財產

解 electronic appliance是「電子設備」的意思。

備註：turn off關掉

22 (B)。人口老化的因素，越來越多國家計畫延長退休年齡至68或70歲。

(A)regulate(v.)控制，管理

(B)extend(v.)延長

(C)maintain(v.)維持

(D)remove(v.)移動

解 現今許多國家，面對人口老化的問題，考慮提升高齡者工作參與的可能性，故選(B)。

23 (A)。因為沉迷於線上遊戲，威力花費很多的時間打線上遊戲。

(A)addicted to沉迷於……

(B)improved with改進……

(C)entertained in使……快樂

(D)enjoyed by享受……

解 be addicted to意思是「沉迷，沉溺」，故選(A)。

備註：waste(v.)浪費，花費

24 (D)。茱蒂花了一年的時間來準備公務員考試，而她通過了考試。

(A)ready for預備……

(B)get over克服……

(C)prepare(v.)準備

(D)prepare for（為什麼事情作）準備

解 prepare當及物動詞，是要提供這樣東西，可以有「籌備、製作」的意思，例如：I am preparing the quiz.（我正在出這份測驗的考題。）。而prepare for有「為了某事準備」的意思，例如I am prepare for the quiz.（我正在為測驗作準備。）故選(D)。

25 (A)。所有申請科技職位的員工被建議在三個月內完成相關訓練。
(A)are advised(v.)建議
(B)has got(v.)必須
(C)should(aux.)應該
(D)（錯誤，應該是have to）
解 advise+人+to+原形動詞，意思是「建議某人去做……」，故選(A)。不能選(B)是因為：所有的員工（all workers）是複數，而(B)has的主詞得是單數。不能選(C)是因為：助動詞should後面直接加動詞，不需要介系詞to。
備註：apply for申請
position(n.)職位
complete(v.)完成

26 (C)。在討論這項議題兩天後，我們仍然沒有達成任何結論。
(A)discussed（v.過去式）討論
(B)（錯誤）
(C)discussing（v.動名詞）討論
(D)being discussed(v.)被討論
解 這題是考「分詞構句」的概念。分詞構句指的是：主要子句與從屬子句的主詞是一樣的，若把從屬子句的主詞及連接詞省略，而假使從屬子句的語態是主動的，可把動詞改成現在分詞V-ing；若從屬子句的語態是被動的，可把動詞改成過去分詞Vp.p.。例如此題目的原始句子是：After we discussed the matter for two days, we were still unable to reach any conclusion. 可改成

After discussing the matter for two days, we were still unable to reach any conclusion.

27 (B)。因為油價上升及新型冠狀病毒肺炎大流行，人們每天生活需要的物資越來越貴。
(A)raise(v.)提高，舉起
(B)rising(adj.)上升的
(C)difficult(adj.)困難的
(D)extending（v.動名詞）延長的
解 rise是不及物動詞，指某件東西自己上升，例如太陽上升、價格上漲、數量增加、站起來、起床，都可以用rise，故選(B)。而raise是及物動詞，後面接受詞，舉起東西、提高稅金／標準、引起疑惑／問題，都可以用raise。
備註：pandemic(n.)疾病大流行

28 (C)。這家日本拉麵店從上禮拜就關閉了，這很不尋常。
(A)is close(adj.)接近的
(B)does not open(v.)沒有開
(C)has been closed（v.現在完成式）關閉
(D)will not be open(v.)將不會開
解 這題是考開門營業（be. open）或關門休息（be. closed）的觀念。題目中已經提到，這家店從上個禮拜（since last week），就關門沒營業，是不尋常的事，故選(C)has been closed，因為關門沒營業這件事已經在上禮拜就發生了，直到說這句話的當下。

不能選(D)是因為，題目中提到關門沒營業是從上禮拜就開始了。

備註：ramen(n.)拉麵

29 (B)。 法蘭克即將留職停薪一年，明年前往澳洲讀書。

(A)holiday(n.)假期

(B)leave of absence without pay(n.)留職停薪

(C)paid vacation(n.)帶薪假日

(D)trip(n.)旅行

解 前往異國進修，可能需要較長的時間，而(A)(C)(D)較適合短期旅遊或短期計畫，故選(B)。

30 (D)。 網路直播十分流行，且讓不少網路名人成為有錢人。

(A)red(n.)紅色

(B)star(n.)明星

(C)famous(adj.)著名的

(D)celebrity(n.)名人

解 celebrity常指的是社交圈有名的人，或是因自有媒體網路（如YouTube）而出名的素人（如網紅）。而star常指的是有名，成功，重要的人，特別是藝術方面的表演者，例如：歌星、影視明星、運動明星等。故選(D)。

備註：live streaming(n.)網路直播

31 (C)。 如果你想申請獎學金，你得加快速度，因為禮拜五就是截止日了。

(A)end(n.)結束

(B)finish time(n.)完成時間

(C)deadline(n.)截止日期

(D)time table(n.)時刻表

解 在英文，截止日期的說法是deadline或是due date，故選(C)。而(B)finish time，是指某件事情完成的時間。

備註：scholarship(n.)獎學金

32 (B)。 不用急；我們已經趕不上電影了。

(A)to(prep.)向

(B)for(prep.)為了

(C)at(prep.)在……地點

(D)from(prep.)從……起

解 late for(phr.)意思是「趕不上，遲到」，因為已經趕不及電影，所以不用急。

33 (A)。 晚餐不用準備太多蔬菜，因為傑克是個無肉不歡的人。

(A)太多蔬菜

(B)如此多的牛肉

(C)太多水果

(D)如此多的海鮮

解 題目中提到傑克是喜歡吃肉的人，所以不用準備太多蔬菜，故選(A)。這題也是考形容詞many、much的差別，many及much都是「很多的、許多的」意思，但是many用來形容可數名詞，例如vegetables、beefs，而much則用來形容不可數名詞，例如fruit、seafood。

34 (C)。 第一次當父母，提姆跟黛安娜不知道如何使寶寶停止哭泣。

(A)錯誤，應該是the baby from crying

(B)錯誤，應該是the baby from crying

(C)寶寶停止哭泣

(D)錯誤，應該是the baby from crying

解 這題是考stop+受詞+from+V-ing，意思是「阻止……做某事」，故選(C)。

35 (D)。 我們的部門鼓勵所有員工取得專業證照及執照，以提升他們的知識及技能。

(A)document(n.)文件

(B)instruction(n.)教導

(C)requirement(n.)必要條件

(D)certificate(n.)執照

解 依題意選(D)。License（證照）是指通過政府等主管機關的考試後，讓你可以去從事某（專業）工作，沒有license就無法從事那件工作，例如：driving license（駕駛執照）、medical license（醫師執照）、教師執照（teaching license）。Certificate（執照）則是指通過某項技能訓練後或通過某項技能考試後，證明你有從事某項工作的能力。certificate也可以證明一些事實的存在，例如：graduate certificate（畢業證書）、birth certificate（出生證明）。

備註：license(n.)執照

36 (A)。 研究顯示女性常為了現實需要而上網瀏覽，男性上網只為了打發時間。

(A)practical(adj.)實際的

(B)unthinkable(adj.)難以想像的

(C)questionable(adj.)可疑的

(D)valuable(adj.)有用的

解 題目中講述男性多半只（just）為了打發時間而上網，從副詞just中可推測女性或許有不一樣的原因上網，故選(A)。

備註：surf(v.)上網瀏覽

37 (D)。 布萊恩花了超過六個月的時間，自己騎腳踏車橫越美國。

(A)cross(v.)橫穿

(B)in(prep.)在……裡

(C)on(prep.)在……之上

(D)across(prep.)橫越，穿過

解 這題中的bicycle是不及物動詞，意思是騎腳踏車，後面應該選介系詞，故選(D)。

38 (A)。 上星期，市長說了每個市府雇員明年的薪水增加3%。

(A)by(prep.)按

(B)to(prep.)向

(C)out of(phr.)在……範圍外

(D)in(prep.)在……裡

解 表示幅度，可以用by，例如：The unemployment rate has decreased by 1%.（失業率已經下降1%。）故選(A)。

39 (B)。 媽媽今天晚上不想煮飯，所以我們將點義大利麵外送。

(A)buy(v.)買

(B)delivered（v.過去分詞）送到

(C)to deliver(v.)送貨

(D)to buy(v.)買

解 這題是考未來完成式的觀念。句型是：will+have+動詞的過去分詞（v. pp），意思是：在未來某個時間點，某件事將會完成。題目中提到，因為媽媽不想準備晚餐，今晚將點外送，講話的當下，外送這件事情還未完成，但將在今天晚上某個時間點完成，故選(B)。

備註：spaghetti(n.)義大利麵條

40 (B)。 如果你需要更多的洗碗精，在水槽下有一瓶洗碗精。

(A)在浴室 　　　(B)在水槽下

(C)在客廳 　　　(D)在冰箱

解 洗碗精通常放在靠近洗碗的地方，像是廚房的洗碗水槽下。

備註：dish soap(n.)洗碗精

sink(n.)水槽

refrigerator(n.)冰箱

111年 臺灣菸酒從業評價職位人員

一、字彙

( ) **1** This store does not have _____ hours. It opens when the owner feels like it.
(A)eager　(B)capable　(C)similar　(D)regular

( ) **2** The local people are trying to raise _____ to improve the park and make it a better and safer place for children.
(A)funds　(B)tourists　(C)products　(D)purchases

( ) **3** We decided to take more days off and _____ our vacation.
(A)exaggerate　(B)exclude　(C)explain　(D)extend

( ) **4** The president felt confident before the _____ , but finally she only won by a few votes.
(A)security　(B)community　(C)election　(D)generation

( ) **5** In the meeting before the travel, the tour guide _____ a map, a cap, and a travel bag for each guest.
(A)provided　(B)featured　(C)repaired　(D)considered

( ) **6** Jacob was _____ to his friends for helping him when he was out of work.
(A)grateful　(B)dependent　(C)practical　(D)significant

( ) **7** Some experts believe that colors have a(n) _____ on our feelings. For example, blue makes us calm and helps us relax.
(A)faith　(B)impact　(C)exhibition　(D)indication

( ) **8** The severe water _____ last summer taught the people a lesson about water conservation.
(A)shortage　(B)evidence　(C)participation　(D)depression

二、文法測驗

(   ) **9** _____ hard the work is, you need to have enough patience to finish it.
(A)Whatever   (B)Whenever   (C)Wherever   (D)However

(   ) **10** Sometimes good chances are worth _____ .
(A)to wait   (B)to be waited   (C)waiting   (D)of waiting

(   ) **11** Study hard, _____ you will fail the exam.
(A)and   (B)or   (C)but   (D)so

(   ) **12** Your room is such a mess _____ someone had just dropped a bomb inside.
(A)as if   (B)even though   (C)even if   (D)as long as

(   ) **13** Judy misses her life in Paris, a beautiful city _____ she studied French literature and met her husband.
(A)that   (B)which   (C)where   (D)when

(   ) **14** _____ carefully in advance, the activity should be very successful.
(A)Planning   (B)If planned   (C)To plan   (D)When planning

(   ) **15** He wrote many poems, most of _____ were about nature.
(A)them   (B)those   (C)that   (D)which

三、克漏字測驗

Valentine's Day is a well-known holiday in many countries. In Japan, it's celebrated a little _____16._____ from elsewhere, though. It's not a day when men buy their loved ones chocolate and flowers and take them out to dinner._____17._____ , it's a day when women are expected to buy chocolate for their male colleagues as well as their boyfriends or husbands. Chocolate for male workers, called giri choco, or "obligation chocolate," is not a practice _____18._____ every Japanese woman is fond, however. Many think it's unfair and expensive. The practice started in 1958, created by a company trying to sell more of their sweets and chocolate. The company was very successful in this marketing scheme. Today, 25% of all the chocolate sold in Japan is purchased around Valentine's Day. In 2019, though, many Japanese women said they'd _____19._____ giri choco. A majority of Japanese women said that they _____20._____ purchase the sweet stuff for themselves on Valentine's Day.

( ) **16** (A)casually　(B)similarly　(C)seriously　(D)differently

( ) **17** (A)Besides　(B)Instead　(C)Therefore　(D)Otherwise

( ) **18** (A)in that　(B)that　(C)of which　(D)which

( ) **19** (A)scan　(B)skim　(C)skip　(D)spot

( ) **20** (A)would like　(B)rather than　(C)prefer　(D)would rather

四、閱讀測驗

There have been a lot of silly lawsuits in the past, but Anton Purisima's definitely takes the cake. After he was bitten by a dog on a bus and had his photo taken without permission during treatment for that bite, Anton, 62, decided to sue New York City for two undecillion dollars. Written out, it looks like this: US$2,000,000,000,000,000,000,000,000,000,000,000,000. That's more money than that held by every person and nation on the planet combined. Anton wrote the 22-page lawsuit out by hand and said that no amount of money could meet his listed demands and settle his grievances. Well, apparantly two undecillion dollars is a good enough start.

Anton has jumped right to the top of the ridiculous lawsuit rankings with his legal action. The one that started it all was Stella Liebeck's lawsuit against McDonald's. She accidentally spilled a cup of coffee in her lap, and suffered third-degree burns. She ended up being awarded around US$500,000. Another amusing lawsuit is the case brought against the Warner Bros.studio by the mayor of a Turkish city called Batman. The mayor said there is only one Batman in the world, and it's his city. Warner

Bros., of course, owns the rights to the popular Batman movies that star Christian Bale. There is one more to marvel at. In 2004, a woman decided to sue a shopping center because she was attacked by a squirrel in the parking lot outside. According to the woman, the shopping center encouraged the squirrel and didn't warn customers properly that "squirrels live outside sometimes."

Crazy lawsuits such as these are both funny and sad. As for Anton Purisima's case, even if he wins, all one can say is good luck for collecting.

(   ) **21** What is the best title for the passage?
(A)A Lucky Man Who Won Two Undecillion Dollars
(B)Some of the World's Craziest Lawsuits
(C)Ridiculous Lawsuits Against Famous People
(D)The Most Expensive Lawsuits in History

(   ) **22** What is so unusual about Anton Purisima's court case?
(A)He filed a lawsuit against all the nations on the planet.
(B)He demanded an impossible amount of money for what had happened to him.
(C)His lawsuit against New York City cost him two undecillion dollars.
(D)He represented himself in his lawsuit against a dog on the street.

(   ) **23** What is said about Stella Liebeck?
(A)She was a former employee of McDonald's.
(B)She sued a shopping center for being attacked by a squirrel.
(C)She took legal action agaist a fast food chain and won.
(D)She was burned in a fire that occurred at a coffee shop.

(   ) **24** What did a Turkish mayor accuse the Warner Bros. studio of doing?
(A)Modeling the character Batman on him.
(B)Letting Christian Bale play the role of Batman.
(C)Producing Batman movies without giving him credit.
(D)Using his city's name without permission.

( ) **25** According to the passage, which of the following statements is true?

(A)The author gives three examples of ridiculous lawsuits.

(B)None of the people mentioned in the passage won their lawsuit.

(C)All of the lawsuits involve animals.

(D)Stella Liebeck was the first one to start a ridiculous lawsuit.

解答與解析　答案標示為# 者，表官方曾公告更正該題答案。

一、字彙

1 (D)。這家商店沒有固定營業時間。它會在主人想開的時候開門。

(A)渴望的　　　(B)有能力的

(C)相像的　　　(D)固定的

解 eager(adj.)熱心的；熱切的；渴望的；急切的

capable(adj.)有能力的；有……的能力；能幹的；有才華的

similar(adj.)相像的；相仿的；類似的

regular(adj.)固定的；規則的；有規律的；正常的；定期的；定時的

2 (A)。當地人正在努力籌集資金來改善公園，使其成為對兒童更好、更安全的地方。

(A)資金　　　(B)旅遊者

(C)產品　　　(D)購買

解 tourist(n.)旅遊者；觀光者；（飛機、輪船等的）旅遊艙

product(n.)產品；產物；產量；出產；結果

purchase(n.)購買；所購之物

fund(n.)資金；基金；專款

3 (D)。我們決定多休幾天假，延長假期。

(A)誇大

(B)把……排除在外

(C)解釋

(D)延長

解 exaggerate(v.)誇張；誇大；對……言過其實；使增大；使擴大

exclude(v.)把……排除在外；拒絕接納；不包括；排斥；逐出

explain(v.)解釋；說明；闡明；為……辯解

extend(v.)延長；延伸；擴大；擴展；伸出

4 (C)。總統在選舉前信心滿滿，但最終她僅贏了少許的票。

(A)安全　　　(B)社區

(C)選舉　　　(D)生成

解 security(n.)安全；防備；保安；防護

解答與解析

community(n.)社區；共同社會；共同體；（一般）社會
generation(n.)世代；一代；同時代的人；一代人
election(n.)選舉；當選

5 (A)。 旅行前的見面會上，導遊提供地圖、帽子、旅行包給每位客人。

(A)提供　　　　　(B)特色
(C)修復　　　　　(D)考慮

解 feature(v.)以……為特色；是……的特色；（電影）由……主演
repair(v.)修理；修補；補救；糾正
consider(v.)考慮；細想；考慮到；認為
provide(v.)提供；裝備；供給

6 (A)。 雅各很感激他的朋友們在他失業時幫助他。

(A)感激的　　　　(B)依賴的
(C)實用的　　　　(D)有意義的

解 dependent(adj.)依賴的；依靠的；取決於……的
practical(adj.)實用的；實踐的；實際的；有實用價值的
significant(adj.)有意義的；意義（或意味）深長的
grateful(adj.)感激的；感謝的；令人愉快的

7 (B)。 一些專家認為顏色對我們的感覺有影響。例如，藍色讓我們平靜，幫助我們放鬆。

(A)信仰　　　　　(B)影響
(C)展覽　　　　　(D)指示

解 faith(n.)信念；信任；完全信賴；保證；諾言；信仰
exhibition(n.)展覽；展覽會；展示會；展覽品
indication(n.)指示；指點；表示；徵兆；跡象；暗示
impact(n.)影響；衝擊；撞擊；碰撞

8 (A)。 去年夏天的嚴重缺水給人民上了一堂水資源保護的課。

(A)缺少　　　　　(B)證據
(C)參與　　　　　(D)沮喪

解 evidence(n.)證據；證詞；證人；物證
participation(n.)參加；參與；分享
depression(n.)沮喪；意氣消沉；不景氣；蕭條
shortage(n.)缺少；不足；匱乏；不足額

二、文法測驗

9 (D)。 無論工作如何艱鉅，你需要有足夠的耐心去完成。

(A)無論怎麼的
(B)無論何時
(C)無論何地
(D)無論如何

解 whatever(adj.)無論怎麼的；任何……的；凡是……的；不管什麼樣的
whenever(adv.)無論什麼時候
wherever(adv.)無論什麼地方；去任何地方

however(adv.)無論如何；不管怎樣；不管用什麼方法

形容詞whatever之後要接名詞，但空格之後是形容詞hard（困難的），所以選項(A)為非。

選項(B)是表時間的副詞，選項(C)是表地方的副詞，都不能用來修飾空格後的形容詞hard，故均為非。

副詞however可以用來修飾形容詞，例如：However hot it is, she will not take off her coat. 天氣無論多熱，她不會脫下她的外套。故選項(D)為正確答案。

10 **(C)**。 有時候好機會值得等待。
(A)等待（不定詞）
(B)被等待（不定詞被動語態）
(C)等待（動名詞）
(D)等待（介系詞＋動名詞）
解 worth 當形容詞時，意指「值得（做……）；有……的價值」，其後必須接動名詞，例如：The book is worth reading. 這本書值得一讀。故選項(C)為正確答案。

11 **(B)**。 努力學習，否則你會考試不及格。
(A)和　(B)否則　(C)但　(D)所以
解 連接詞or可以用來警告或建議某人不好的事情可能會發生，例如：Hurry up, or you will not catch the bus. （快點，否則你會趕不上公車。）故選項(B)為正確答案。

12 **(A)**。 你的房間一團糟，好像有人剛剛在裡面扔了一顆炸彈。
(A)好像　　　　　(B)雖然
(C)即使　　　　　(D)只要
解 even though 雖然；即使
even if 即使；儘管；縱然
as long as 只要；既然；由於
as if 好像；似乎；彷彿

13 **(C)**。 朱蒂懷念她在巴黎的生活，她在那座美麗的城市裡，學習法國文學並遇到了她的丈夫。
(A)那　　　　　　(B)哪一個
(C)在那裡　　　　(D)當……時
解 空格前的先行詞是city（城市），所以空格內應該填入關係副詞where，來引導關係子句，故選項(C)為正確答案。

14 **(B)**。 如果事先精心策劃，這活動應該會非常成功。
(A)計劃（現在分詞）
(B)如果計劃
(C)計劃（不定詞）
(D)當計劃時
解 空格後的子句主詞是活動，活動是被計劃的，不會做計劃這個動作，而選項(A)(C)和(D)都是主動的動詞，故均為非。
If planned carefully in advance, the activity should be very successful. =
If the activity is planned carefully in advance , the activity should be very successful.

解答與解析

15 (D)。他寫了許多詩，其中大部分的詩是關於自然的。
(A)他們 　　　　(B)那些的
(C)那 　　　　　(D)那一個

解 空格前的先行詞是poem，因此空格內應該填入關係代名詞which，來引導形容詞子句修飾先行詞，故選項(D)為正確答案。

三、克漏字測驗

情人節在許多國家都是眾所周知的節日。不過，在日本，它的慶祝方式與其他地方略有不同。這不是男人給他們所愛的人買巧克力和鮮花，並帶他們出去吃飯的日子。反而，這一天女性應該為她們的男同事以及她們的男朋友或丈夫購買巧克力。然而，給男性員工的巧克力被稱為 giri choco 或「義理巧克」，這並不是每個日本女性都喜歡的習慣。許多人認為這是不公平而且又昂貴的。這種習慣始於 1958 年，由一家試圖銷售更多糖果和巧克力的公司創立。該公司在這個營銷計畫中非常成功。如今，在日本銷售的所有巧克力中有 25% 是在情人節前後被購買的。然而，在 2019 年，許多日本女性表示她們會略過 giri choco。大多數日本女性表示，她們更願意在情人節為自己購買甜食。

16 (D)。(A)隨意地　(B)同樣地　(C)認真地　(D)不同地

解 casually(adv.)隨意地；偶然地；無意地；若無其事地

similarly(adv.)同樣地；相仿地
seriously(adv.)認真地；嚴肅地；當真地
differently(adv.)不同地；相異地

17 (B)。(A)除了　(B)反而　(C)因此　(D)否則

解 besides(adv.)此外；而且；加之
therefore(adv.)因此；因而；所以
otherwise(adv.)用別的方法；不同樣地；在其他方面；除此以外
instead(adv.)反而；作為替代；卻

18 (C)。(A)因為　(B)那　(C)of＋哪個　(D)哪個

解 空格前的先行詞是practice，所以關係代名詞用which或that都可，但是空格後的動詞片語是is fond of（喜歡），其中的of被移到關係代名詞的前面，此時that就不能當關係代名詞，故選項(C)為正確答案。

19 (C)。(A)掃描　(B)略讀　(C)略過　(D)弄髒

解 scan(v.)掃描；細看；審視
skim(v.)瀏覽；略讀；撇去；去除；提取
spot(v.)弄髒；使沾上汙點；用聚光燈照
skip(v.)略過；漏掉；換來換去；跳躍；快速處理

20 (D)。(A)想要　(B)而不是　(C)更喜歡　(D)寧願

解 would like 想要
rather than 而不是

prefer(v.)更喜歡；寧可；寧願
would rather寧願、較喜歡
空格後已經有動詞purchase（購買），所以空格內不能再填入動詞，故選項(A)和(C)均為非。

四、閱讀測驗

過去曾發生過很多愚蠢的訴訟，但安東‧普利斯瑪（Anton Purisima）的訴訟無人能及。62歲的安東在公共汽車上被狗咬傷，並且在治療期間未經允許被拍攝了照片後，他決定起訴紐約市，要求賠償「2萬億億億億」美元。寫出來，它看起來像這樣：2,000,000,000,000,000,000,000,000,000,000,000,000美元。那是比地球上每個人和國家所擁有的錢加起來還要多。安東手寫了長達22頁的訴訟書，並表示再多的錢也無法滿足他的訴求，解決他的冤屈。好吧，顯然2後面加上36個0的美元是一個足夠好的開始。

安東憑藉他的法律行動躍居荒謬訴訟排行榜的首位。這一切的始作俑者是史黛拉‧里貝克（Stella Liebeck）對麥當勞的訴訟。她不小心將一杯咖啡灑在膝上，結果造成三度燒傷。她最終被判獲得大約50萬美元的賠償金。另一個有趣的訴訟是土耳其城市蝙蝠俠的市長，對華納兄弟工作室提起的訴訟。市長說世界上只有一個蝙蝠俠，而那就是他的城市。當然，華納兄弟擁有由克里斯汀‧貝爾主演的熱門蝙蝠俠電影的版權。還有一個值得驚嘆的案例。2004年，

一名婦女決定起訴一家購物中心，因為她在外面的停車場被一隻松鼠襲擊了。根據女人所言，購物中心鼓勵松鼠，沒有適當地警告顧客「松鼠有時住在外面。」

諸如此類的瘋狂訴訟，讓人覺得既有趣又可悲。至於安東‧普利斯瑪的案子，即使他贏了，我們能說的也只有祝催款好運。

21 (B)。 本文最佳的標題是什麼？
(A)一個幸運的人贏得了2後面加上36個0的美元
(B)一些世界上最瘋狂的訴訟
(C)一些針對名人的荒謬訴訟
(D)史上最昂貴的訴訟
解 本文談到的不只一個荒謬訴訟，故選項(A)和(D)均為非。
本文談到的不是針對名人的訴訟，故選項(C)為非。

22 (B)。 安東‧普利斯瑪的法庭案件有何不同尋常之處？
(A)他對地球上的所有國家提起訴訟。
(B)對於發生在自己身上的事情，他索求多到不可能的賠償金。
(C)他對紐約市的訴訟使他損失了2後面加上36個0的美元。
(D)他代表自己對街上的一隻狗提起訴訟。
解 從第一段第四句："That's more money than that held by every person and nation on the planet combined."可知，選項(B)為正確答案。

23 (C)。 關於史黛拉‧里貝克人們說些什麼？
(A)她是麥當勞的前僱員。
(B)她因被松鼠襲擊起訴一家購物中心。
(C)她對一家快餐連鎖店提起法律訴訟並獲勝。
(D)她在一家咖啡店發生的火災中被燒傷。
解 從第二段第二到第四句："The one that started it all was Stella Liebeck's lawsuit against McDonald's. She accidentally spilled a cup of coffee in her lap, and suffered third-degree burns. She ended up being awarded around US\$500,000 "可知，選項(C)為正確答案。

24 (D)。 一位土耳其市長指責華納兄弟工作室做了什麼？
(A)以他為模型塑造蝙蝠俠這個角色。
(B)讓克里斯汀‧貝爾扮演蝙蝠俠的角色。
(C)在沒有稱讚他的情況下製作蝙蝠俠電影。
(D)未經允許使用他的城市名稱。
解 從第二段第六句："The mayor said there is only one Batman in the world, and it's his city."可知，選項(D)為正確答案。

25 (D)。 根據本文，下列哪一項敘述是正確的？
(A)作者舉出三個荒謬的訴訟例子。
(B)文中提到的人都沒有打贏官司。
(C)所有訴訟都涉及動物。
(D)史黛拉‧里貝克是第一個發起荒謬訴訟的人。
解 從第二段第二句："The one that started it all was Stella Liebeck's lawsuit against McDonald's."可知，選項(D)為正確答案。

111年 臺灣菸酒從業職員

一、字彙

( ) **1** We'll find out what happens to the leading character in the next _____ of the TV show.
(A)episode　(B)finalist　(C)commercial　(D)interface

( ) **2** He's definitely not a man of _____. He's always talking about his achievements and never misses a chance to show off.　(A) destiny　(B)penalty　(C)bravery　(D)humility

( ) **3** The young actress _____ for a role in the new movie, hoping she would be able to appear on the big screen.　(A)excused　(B) formatted　(C)auditioned　(D)instilled

( ) **4** The number of people affected is _____ to reach 4,000 in the next 5 months if nothing is done soon.　(A)winced　(B)loaned (C)projected　(D)collided

( ) **5** You'd better go to a doctor immediately if you're showing _____ of lung diseases.　(A)diameters　(B)motivations　(C)symptoms　(D) advertisements

( ) **6** You can find the latest numbers on line as they are _____ every ten minutes.　(A)subsisted　(B)updated　(C)restrained (D)hissed

( ) **7** The special device can _____ huge amounts of data from one place to another 500 miles away in just a few seconds.　(A) transmit　(B)bend　(C)invert　(D)linger

( ) **8** The man could only take the seat next to the bathroom because all the others were not _____.　(A)dimmable　(B)available (C)huggable　(D)readable

二、文法測驗

(　) **9** _____ is made from environmental friendly materials. 　(A) Nearly all of what you see here 　(B)Near all of you see here 　(C) Nearly here of you see 　(D)All can you see nearly

(　) **10** Taking trips abroad was _____ a luxury that only wealthy families could enjoy. 　(A)thought once was 　(B)once to think as 　(C)thought once be as 　(D)once thought to be

(　) **11** While some of the rich kids drove to school every day, _____ could only walk or take the school bus. 　(A)the rest of us 　(B) rest of we all 　(C)we all the rest 　(D)rest of the us

(　) **12** Protesters argued that the contractors tasked with caring for children weren't qualified for the job, and _____ they shouldn't be allowed to continue their practice. 　(A)which 　(B)it 　(C)that (D)for

(　) **13** The plane, _____ Tokyo 16 hours ago, will arrive in New York soon. 　(A)departed from 　(B)which departing to 　(C)that was departed to 　(D)departing from

(　) **14** Considering the possible danger involved, _____ .
(A)the less you know the better
(B)you know less better than
(C)better you know less than
(D)less than you know the better

(　) **15** If the police had not arrived in time, the poor man _____ .
(A)would dead 　　　　　　(B)have been died
(C)would have been dead 　(D)had died

三、克漏字測驗

Parents, educators, and the community have a responsibility to support all children as they reach for their personal best. It is essential to support the growth and development of gifted children, ____16____ their intellectual, social, emotional, and physical domains. That support ____17____ at home. Parents and caregivers are usually the first to ____18____ a child's extraordinary gifts and talents. Parents recognize above norm abilities, interests, and passions that are different in other children they see. Being gifted often comes with ____19____ like asynchronous development or social and emotional problems. Parents can engage with their children to provide rich stimulation and learning experiences and discover ways to __ ____20____ schools and resources in the broader community to nurture their child's specialized learning needs.

(   ) **16** (A)dependent   (B)except   (C)including   (D)above

(   ) **17** (A)begins   (B)sinks   (C)pays   (D)halts

(   ) **18** (A)identify   (B)exclude   (C)broil   (D)mix

(   ) **19** (A)benefits   (B)challenges   (C)decorations   (D)teams

(   ) **20** (A)send to   (B)look after   (C)take on   (D)partner with

四、閱讀測驗

Space X—the American technology company—launched 60 satellites into space in January 2020. Space X plans to create a network of 12,000 satellites. The company says that the network, known as Starlink, will help provide better Internet service to remote parts of the world. But astronomers say the growing number of satellites orbiting the Earth is making it harder for them to observe and learn from the universe.

Satellites are made of metal that reflects sunlight. This makes them show up in the night sky as bright, slow-moving dots. After the launch, the Starlink satellites appeared in images taken by telescopes and deep-space cameras as a line of bright lights flying across the sky. Astronomers learn about space by using large telescopes and special cameras to observe light coming from very far away. The information they collect can help them understand things like how galaxies are formed or which planets might be able to support life.

Some astronomers also use radio telescopes, which record radio waves coming from space. This makes it possible to study things that give off low energy and would not show up as light—like dust and gases. In April 2019, astronomers used information collected by several radio telescopes to produce the first image of a black hole. Large groups of satellites—known as "satellite constellations" —give off radio signals of their own and reflect radio waves coming from Earth. These extra signals interfere with radio waves coming from further away in the galaxy. While it might be possible to build satellites with surfaces that don't reflect light, it will be very difficult to make satellites that don't interfere with radio waves.

(   ) **21** What is the passage mainly about?   (A)Space X the technology company   (B)Satellites and their contribution to communication (C)The problems with too many satellites in space   (D)What satellite constellations really are

(   ) **22** What's the intended benefit of the Starlink project?   (A)Better internet connection in far-off places   (B)More income for major companies providing internet service   (C)Easier ways to collect information for astronomers   (D)Cheaper ways to keep off sunlight and radiation

(   ) **23** Which of the following is true?   (A)Space X has successfully made satellites that do not reflect sunlight.   (B)The first image of a galaxy was made with the help of Space X.   (C)Satellite constellations can help astronomers solve the problem of reflected sunlight interfering with their studies.   (D)The Starlink satellites could be seen in images taken by telescopes and deep-space cameras.

(　) **24** How are the second and third paragraphs related to the first paragraph?　(A)They give examples of the benefit described in the first paragraph.　(B)They provide details on an issue mentioned at the end of the first paragraph.　(C)They each describe a solution to the problem mentioned at the end of the first paragraph.　(D)They explain a term that appears in the first paragraph.

(　) **25** What can be inferred from the passage?　(A)Space X will probably stop its Starlink project in the near future.　(B)The light reflected from the satellites will interfere with internet connection on earth.　(C)Satellite constellations give off radio signals that will hurt people in remote places.　(D)There is currently no easy way to completely prevent the satellites from interfering with astronomical studies.

解答與解析　答案標示為#者，表官方曾公告更正該題答案。

一、字彙

1 (A)。 我們將會在電視連續劇的下一集中看出主角發生了什麼事情。
(A)（連續劇的）一集
(B)參加決賽的人
(C)商業廣告
(D)界面
解 finalist(n.)參加決賽的人；決賽選手
commercial(n.)商業廣告
interface(n.)界面；分界面；接合部；介面；接口；連繫裝置
episode(n.)（連續劇的）一集；插曲；片段；一節；一個事件

2 (D)。 他絕對不是一個謙虛的人。他總是談論他的成就，而且從不錯過任何炫耀的機會。
(A)命運　(B)處罰　(C)勇敢　(D)謙虛
解 destiny(n.)命運；天數；天命；神意
penalty(n.)處罰；刑罰；罰款
bravery(n.)勇敢；勇氣；華麗；華麗的衣服；壯觀
humility(n.)謙虛；謙卑；謙遜

3 (C)。 這位年輕的女演員試鏡了新電影中的一個角色，希望她能出現在大銀幕上。
(A)原諒　　　(B)格式化
(C)試鏡　　　(D)逐漸灌輸

解 excuse(v.)原諒；辯解；成為……的理由

format(v.)格式化；為……編排格式

instill(v.)逐漸灌輸；徐徐地教導；徐徐滴入

audition（演員、樂手、舞蹈演員等的）試鏡；試奏；試唱；試演；聽力；聽覺；試聽

4 (C)。 如果不盡快採取措施，受影響的人數將在未來5個月內預計達到4,000人。

(A)畏縮　　　　　(B)借出
(C)預計　　　　　(D)相撞

解 wince(v.)畏縮；退避

loan(v.)借出；貸與

collide(v.)碰撞；相撞；衝突；抵觸

project(v.)預計；推斷；計畫；企劃；投擲；發射；噴射

5 (C)。 如果出現肺部疾病的症狀，你最好立即就醫。

(A)直徑　　　　　(B)動機
(C)症狀　　　　　(D)廣告

解 diameter(n.)直徑；倍

motivation(n.)動機；刺激；推動；積極性；幹勁

advertisement(n.)廣告；宣傳；公告；啟事

symptom(n.)症狀；徵候；徵兆；表徵

6 (B)。 你可以在網上找到最新的數字，因為它們每十分鐘更新一次。

(A)維持生計　　　(B)更新
(C)抑制　　　　　(D)發出嘶嘶聲

解 subsist(v.)維持生活；活下去；存在；繼續存在

restrain(v.)抑制；遏制；控制；限制；約束；阻止

hiss(v.)發出嘶嘶聲；發出噓聲

update(v.)更新；使現代化；使……合乎時代

7 (A)。 特殊設備可以在幾秒鐘內將大量數據從一個地方傳送到500英里以外的另一個地方。

(A)傳送　　　　　(B)彎曲
(C)使倒轉　　　　(D)徘迴

解 bend(v.)彎曲；轉彎；折彎；使低垂

invert(v.)使倒轉；使上下顛倒；使前後倒置；使反向

linger(v.)徘徊；繼續逗留；持續；緩慢消失

transmit(v.)傳送；傳達；傳（光、熱、聲等）；傳動

8 (B)。 那個男人只能坐到洗手間旁邊的座位，因為其他座位都是不可用的。

(A)陰暗的　　　　(B)可用的
(C)逗人喜愛的　　(D)可讀的

解 dimmable(adj.)陰暗的；昏暗的；不明亮的；可調光的

huggable(adj.)逗人喜愛的

readable(adj.)可讀的；（讀起來）有趣味的；（字跡）清晰的；易辨認的

available(adj.)可用的；在手邊的；可利用的；可得到的；可買到的；有空的

二、文法測驗

9 (A)。 幾乎你在這裡看到的所有東西都是由環保材料製成的。

(A)Nearly all of what you see here

(B)Near all of you see here

(C)Nearly here of you see

(D)All can you see nearly

解 選項(A)是一個當主詞的名詞片語，其中名詞子句"what you see here"是介系詞of的受詞，of＋what子句是用來形容代名詞all。空格後已經有被動語態的動詞片語，所以空格內只要填入主詞即可，故選項(A)為正確答案。

選項(B)和(C)的錯誤在於介系詞of之後的名詞子句不完整，因為動詞see之後沒有受詞，造成語意不清，故均為非。

選項(D)的錯誤在於助動詞can不應該放在you的前面，因為本句不是倒裝句，也不是問句。

10 (D)。 出國旅行曾經被認為是只有富裕家庭才能享受的一種奢華。

(A)thought once was

(B)once to think as

(C)thought once be as

(D)once thought to be

解 選項(A)中有兩個動詞（thought和was）同時存在，沒有連接詞連接，故為非。

選項(C)中有兩個動詞（thought和be）同時存在，沒有連接詞連接，故為非。

選項(B)中的不定詞to think是主動語態，但本句主詞不是人，所以不能做to think這個動作，故為非。

was once thought意指「以前曾被認為」，主詞是出國旅遊這件事情，故選項(D)的寫法是正確的。

11 (A)。 當有些富家子弟每天開車上學，我們其餘的人只能走路或坐校車。

(A)the rest of us

(B)rest of we all

(C)we all the rest

(D)rest of the us

解 名詞rest當「其餘部分或其餘的人」解釋時，要寫成：the rest of＋名詞，故選項(B)(C)和(D)的寫法都錯了。

12 (C)。 抗議者爭辯説，負責照顧兒童的承包商不具備這份工作的資格，而且不應該讓他們繼續從事他們的工作。

(A)which　(B)it　(C)that　(D)for

解答與解析

解 空格前有that子句和對等連接詞and，所以空格內也應該要填入that才對，故選項(C)為正確答案。

空格前沒有先行詞，所以空格內不能填入關係代名詞which，故選項(A)為非。

空格後已經有主詞they，所以空格內不能再填入代名詞it，故選項(C)為非。

空格前已經有對等連接詞and，所以空格內不能再填入對等連接詞for，故選項(D)為非。

13 (D)。 16小時前從東京離開的飛機，很快即將抵達紐約。

(A)departed from

(B)which departing to

(C)that was departed to

(D)departing from

解 depart（離開；出發）在此是不及物動詞，沒有被動語態，故選項(C)為非。

過去分詞departed表示被動語態，故選項(A)為非。

選項(B)which departing to之中沒有主動詞，故為非。

14 (A)。 考慮到可能涉及的危險，你知道得越少越好。

(A)the less you know the better

(B)you know less better than

(C)better you know less than

(D)less than you know the better

解 the＋比較級……，the＋比較……（越……，越……）

選項(B)中less better是錯誤的寫法，兩個比較級不能寫在一起。

選項(C)和(D)都多了連接詞than，故均為非。

15 (C)。 如果警察沒有及時趕到，這個可憐的人早就死了。

(A)would dead

(B)have been died

(C)would have been dead

(D)had died

解 if子句中的動詞片語是過去完成式had not arrived，所以主要子句的動詞片語要用would＋have＋p.p.，故選項(C)would have been dead為正確答案。

這是跟過去事實相反的假設語句，事實上當時警察及時趕到，而那人當時沒有死。

三、克漏字測驗

父母、教育工作者和社區有責任當所有孩子達到個人最佳狀態時，支持他們。支持天才兒童的成長和發展至關重要，包括他們的智力、社交、情感和身體的領域。這種支持始於家中。父母和照顧者通常是第一個確認孩子的非凡天賦和才能的人。父母認識到超越一般的能力、興趣和熱情，這跟他們在其他孩子身上看到的不同。有天賦往往會伴隨而來的是發展不同步或社交和情感問題的挑戰。家長可以跟孩子一起，提供豐

富的刺激和學習體驗，並找到與學校和更廣泛社區的資源合作的方式，以培養孩子的專業學習需求。

16 (C)。(A)依靠的　(B)除了……之外　(C)包括　(D)在……上面
解 dependent(adj.)依靠的；依賴的；取決於……的
except (prep.) 除……之外
above (prep.) 在……上面；在……之上；超過
including (prep.) 包括；包含

17 (A)。(A)開始　(B)下降　(C)支付　(D)停止
解 sink(v.)下沉；（日、月）落；沒；（面頰等）下陷
pay(v.)支付；付款給；償還；補償
halt(v.)停止；停止行進；終止
begin(v.)開始；開始進行；始於；源於

18 (A)。(A)確認　(B)把……排除在外　(C)烤　(D)使混合
解 exclude(v.)把……排除在外；拒絕接納；不包括；逐出
broil(v.)烤；炙；使受到灼熱；曝曬
mix(v.)使混和；攪和；使結合；使結交
identify(v.)確認；識別；鑑定；驗明

19 (B)。(A)好處　(B)挑戰　(C)裝飾　(D)隊
解 benefit(n.)好處；利益；優勢；津貼；救濟金
decoration(n.)裝飾；裝潢；裝飾物
team(n.)隊；組；班
challenge(n.)挑戰；邀請比賽；質疑；指責

20 (D)。(A)發送給　(B)照顧　(C)承擔　(D)合夥
解 send to 傳送給；寄給
look after 照顧；照看；看管
take on 承擔；取得；接受
partner with 合夥；合股；成為搭檔

四、閱讀測驗

美國科技公司Space X於2020年1月向太空發射了60顆衛星。Space X計劃創建一個由12,000顆衛星組成的網絡。該公司表示，這個名為Starlink（星鏈）的網絡將有助於為世界偏遠地區提供更好的聯路服務。但天文學家表示，越來越多繞地球運行的衛星使他們更難觀察和了解宇宙。

衛星由反射陽光的金屬製成。這使得它們在夜空中以緩慢移動的明亮點形式出現。發射後，星鏈衛星在望遠鏡和深空相機拍攝的圖像中，呈現出一排亮光劃過天空。天文學家透過使用大型望遠鏡和特殊照相機，觀察來自遠方的光以便了解太空。他們收集的信息可以幫助他們了解銀河是如何形成的，或者哪些行星能夠維持生命。

解答與解析

某些天文學家也使用電波望遠鏡記錄來自太空的無線電波。這使得研究那些發出低能量且不會以光出現的事物成為可能，例如灰塵和氣體。2019年4月，天文學家利用多台電波望遠鏡收集的信息，製作了第一張黑洞圖像。被稱為「衛星星座」的大群衛星會發出自己的無線電信號，並反射來自地球的無線電波。這些額外的信號會干擾來自銀河更遠地方的無線電波。雖然製造表面不反射光的衛星是可能的，但製造不會干擾無線電波的衛星將是非常困難的。

21 (C)。本文主要講的是什麼？
(A)Space X科技公司
(B)衛星及其對通信的貢獻
(C)太空中衛星太多的問題
(D)真正的衛星星座是什麼
解 從第一段最後一句：''But astronomers say the growing number of satellites orbiting the Earth is making it harder for them to observe and learn from the universe.''可知，衛星太多會使得天文學家們更難觀察和了解宇宙，故選項(C)為正確答案。

22 (A)。Starlink項目的預期好處是什麼？
(A)在遙遠的地方有更好的聯路連接
(B)為提供互聯網服務的主要公司帶來更多收入
(C)為天文學家收集信息的更簡單方法
(D)避免陽光和輻射的更便宜的方法

解 從第一段第二句：''The company says that the network, known as Starlink, will help provide better Internet service to remote parts of the world.''可知，選項(A)為正確。

23 (D)。下列敘述何者為真？
(A)Space X已成功製造出不反射陽光的衛星。
(B)在Space X的幫助下拍攝了第一張銀河圖像。
(C)衛星星座可以幫助天文學家解決反射太陽光干擾其研究的問題。
(D)在望遠鏡和深空照相機拍攝的圖像中可以看到星鏈衛星。
解 從第二段第三句：''After the launch, the Starlink satellites appeared in images taken by telescopes and deep-space cameras as a line of bright lights flying across the sky.''可知，選項(D)為正確答案。

24 (B)。第二段和第三段與第一段有什麼關係？
(A)他們舉例說明了第一段中描述的好處。
(B)他們提供了關於第一段最後提到的問題之詳細信息。
(C)他們各自描述了第一段最後提到的問題之解決方案。
(D)他們解釋了第一段中出現的術語。
解 從第三段最後一句：''While it might be possible to build satellites with surfaces that

don't reflect light, it will be very difficult to make satellites that don't interfere with radio waves." 可知，問題並沒有解決，故選項(B)為正確答案。

25 (D)。從本文可以推斷出什麼？
(A)Space X 可能會在不久的將來停止其星鏈項目。
(B)衛星反射的光會干擾地球上的互聯網連接。
(C)衛星星座發出的無線電信號會傷害偏遠地區的人們。
(D)目前沒有簡單的方法可以完全防止衛星干擾天文研究。

解 從本文最後一句可知，製造不會干擾無線電波的衛星是非常困難的，故選項(D)為正確答案。

解答與解析

111年 台中捷運新進人員

( ) **1** In total, there are about 1000 people _____ this year's singing contest. (A)attending to (B)participating in (C)making up (D)abiding by

( ) **2** _____ I have known the ending of the story, I am still touched by it. (A)Even though (B)If (C)Unless (D)As long as

( ) **3** The young teacher is an _____ person; he has made up his mind to establish his own school before 30. (A)odd (B)intense (C)extensive (D)ambitious

( ) **4** After spending the whole afternoon cleaning up his house, Mark thought he _____ a good rest and a hearty meal. (A)preserved (B)reserved (C)conserved (D)deserved

( ) **5** Frank didn't know the answer to the _____ math question, so he turned to the smartest student in his class for help. (A)dynamic (B)complicated (C)residential (D)optimistic

( ) **6** If I _____ you, I would not accept Tom's proposal. (A)am (B)were (C)to be (D)can be

( ) **7** Due to the COVID-19 pandemic, whether the book fair will be held as scheduled _____ still under discussion. (A)is (B)are (C)has (D)have

( ) **8** Scientists have successfully developed a _____ for the infectious disease, so few children are suffering from it now. (A)vaccine (B)portfolio (C)cushion (D)momentum

( ) **9** The _____ of the two small companies will create the world's largest computer manufacturers. (A)texture (B)merger (C)orientation (D)cradle

( ) **10** The TMRT corporation requires that every passenger _____ by the safety regulations. (A)abides (B)abide (C)to abide (D)will abide

( ) **11** Passengers are prohibited from carrying dangerous items, such as _____ , firearms, and knives.
(A)highlighters (B)popsicles (C)explosives (D)bulletins

( ) **12** _____ an emergency, use the intercom in the car immediately, and some crew member will come to the assistance.
(A)In case of (B)Thanks to (C)At risk of (D)Except for

( ) **13** The seats in the MRT car are _____ for the disabled, the elderly, and pregnant women.
(A)reserved (B)confined (C)exhibited (D)prevented

( ) **14** The _____ you have to pay from Wenhua Senior High School to Wenxin Yinghua is NT$20 dollars.
(A)fabric (B)feat (C)fare (D)ferry

( ) **15** When the train is about to pull in, the signals on the platform will _____ . (A)flare (B)flash (C)fling (D)flush

( ) **16** If you are confused about the route map, you can _____ help from the information center.
(A)seek (B)look (C)make (D)keep

( ) **17** The escalator is not _____ properly, so you had better take the stairs.
(A)uplifting (B)progressing (C)cooperating (D)functioning

( ) **18** In order not to be caught in a traffic jam, Steve chose to take the MRT _____ driving his car. (A)owing to (B)aside from (C)compared with (D)instead of

( ) **19** When the Taichung Mass Rail Transit (Taichung MRT) opens, people can _____ travel around the city. They can also easily go to the Taiwan High Speed Rail Station in Taichung to journey to the northern and southern parts of Taiwan.　(A)traditionally (B)conveniently　(C)similarly　(D)desperately

(　　) **20** Ben liked the TV show very much because he felt he could ___ _____ with the characters,some of whom were going through the same experiences as he was.　(A)murmur　(B)launch　(C) identify　(D)blend

(　　) **21** To bridge the gap between the two different political parties, the young politician proposed a new law that would require both sides' _____ .　(A)cooperation　(B)circulation　(C) calculation　(D)congestion

(　　) **22** The company _____ all its older automobiles with electric vehicles as part of its efforts to go green.　(A)absorbed　(B) substituted　(C)trembled　(D)pronounced

(　　) **23** Some people _____ with the virus look and feel healthy, but still can pass the virus to others.　(A)who infected　(B)infecting (C)infected　(D)are infected

(　　) **24** A person with a computer addiction thinks his "Cyber friends" are important, so he spends _____ time with his family and friends.　(A)more　(B)less　(C)much　(D)fewer

(　　) **25** Alice: I need to do some shopping. Is there any supermarket in the community?

Terry: Yes. There is one opposite the elementary school.

Alice: _____

Terry: About ten minutes on foot. Maybe you'd better go there by car.

(A)How long have you been there?

(B)How far is the supermarket from here?

(C)How do you do?

(D)How can I apply for the job?

解答與解析　答案標示為# 者，表官方曾公告更正該題答案。

1 (B)。 總共有大約1,000人參加今年的歌唱比賽。
(A)注意　　　　(B)參加
(C)組成　　　　(D)遵守
解 attend to 注意；致力於；關心；照料；護理
make up 組成；補足；編造
abide by 遵守；遵從；承擔……的後果；承受
participate in 參加

2 (A)。 雖然我已經知道了故事的結局，但我仍然為之感動。
(A)雖然　　　　(B)如果
(C)除非　　　　(D)只要
解 if(conj.)如果；要是
unless(conj.)除非；如果不
as long as 只要……；既然；由於；在……期間
even though 雖然；即使；縱然；儘管

3 (D)。 這位年輕的老師是一個有雄心的人；他已經下定決心，要在30歲之前創辦自己的學校。
(A)奇特的　　　(B)強烈的
(C)廣泛的　　　(D)有雄心的
解 odd(adj.)奇特的；古怪的；單隻的；不成對的；零散的
intense(adj.)強烈的；劇烈的；極度的；熱情的；熱切的
extensive(adj.)廣泛的；廣大的；廣闊的；大規模的；大量的

ambitious(adj.)有雄心的；野心勃勃的

4 (D)。 在花了整個下午清掃他的房子後，馬克認為他應該好好休息和享用豐盛的一餐。
(A)保存　　　　(B)預約
(C)用糖保存　　(D)應得
解 preserve(v.)保存；保藏；防腐；保護；維護
reserve(v.)預約；儲備；保存；保留；預訂
conserve(v.)用糖保存；保存；保護；節省；將……做成蜜餞
deserve(v.)應受；該得

5 (B)。 法蘭克不知道這道難懂的數學題的答案，所以他向班上最聰明的學生求助。
(A)動態的　　　(B)難懂的
(C)住宅的　　　(D)樂觀的
解 dynamic(adj.)動態的；強有力的；有活力的；有生氣的；動力的；力學的
residential(adj.)住宅的；居住的；作住所用的；適合於居住的
optimistic(adj.)樂觀的；樂觀主義的；樂天的
complicated(adj.)複雜的；難懂的；結構複雜的

6 (B)。 如果我是你，我不會接受湯姆的求婚。

(A)am　　　　　(B)were
(C)to be　　　　(D)can be
解 從主要子句的動詞片語would＋
V和前面的if子句可知，本句是
與現在事實相反的假設語句，所
以選項(B)為正確答案。

7 (A)。由於COVID-19疫情，書展
是否如期舉行仍在討論中。
(A)is　(B)are　(C)has　(D)have
解 whether名詞子句當主詞時，其
後的動詞必須用is，故選項(A)
為正確答案。
例：Whether the news is true
or not is our main concern.（消
息是否屬實是我們的主要關注
點。）

8 (A)。科學家們已經成功研製出一
種針對這種傳染病的疫苗，因此現
在很少有兒童患上這種疾病。
(A)疫苗　(B)文件夾　(C)墊子
(D)氣勢
解 portfolio(n.)文件夾；卷宗夾；公
事包；代表作選輯；投資組合
cushion(n.)墊子；坐墊；靠墊；
墊狀物；緩衝器
momentum(n.)氣勢；衝力；動
力；推動力
vaccine(n.)疫苗；牛痘苗

9 (B)。這兩家小公司的合併將創建
世界上最大的電腦製造商。
(A)質地　　　　(B)合併
(C)方向　　　　(D)發源地

解 texture(n.)質地；組織；結構；
（材料等的）構造
orientation(n.)方向；定位；適
應；熟悉；（對新生的）情況
介紹
cradle(n.)發源地；搖籃；策源地
merger(n.)合併

10 (B)。MRT公司要求每位乘客遵守
安全規定。
(A)遵守（現在式單數）
(B)遵守（動詞原形）
(C)遵守（不定詞）
(D)將遵守（未來式）
解 動詞require（要求）之後可以
接that子句當受詞，但這子句中
的動詞要用原形動詞，因為省
略了should，故選項(B)為正確
答案。
其他類似的動詞有：request,
demand, ask

11 (C)。旅客被禁止攜帶危險品，如
炸藥、槍支、刀具等。
(A)螢光筆　　　(B)冰棒
(C)炸藥　　　　(D)公報
解 highlighter(n.)螢光筆；輪廓色
popsicle(n.)冰棒
bulletin(n.)公報；公告；會報；
學報；期刊；新聞快報
explosive(n.)炸藥；爆炸物

12 (A)。萬一有緊急情況，可立即使
用車內對講機，會有乘務員前來
協助。

(A)萬一

(B)感謝

(C)冒……險

(D)除了……以外

解 thanks to 幸虧；多虧；由於；託……福

at risk of 冒……險

except for 除了……以外；要不是由於

in case of 萬一；假使；如果發生

13 (A)。 這些捷運車廂內的座位是保留給殘疾人士、老人和孕婦的。

(A)保留　　　　(B)限制

(C)展示　　　　(D)阻止

解 confine(v.)限制；使局限；禁閉；幽禁

exhibit(v.)展示；陳列；表示；顯出

prevent(v.)阻止；防止；預防；制止；妨礙

reserve(v.)保留；預約；儲備；保存；預訂

14 (C)。 從文華高中到文心櫻花的票價是新台幣20元。

(A)織物　　　　(B)功績

(C)票價　　　　(D)渡輪

解 fabric(n.)織物；織品；布料；構造

feat(n.)功績；業績；英勇事跡；武藝；技藝

ferry(n.)渡輪；聯運船；擺渡船；擺渡

fare(n.)票價；車（船）費

15 (B)。 當列車即將進站時，站台上的信號燈會閃爍。

(A)（火焰）閃耀　(B)閃爍

(C)擲　　　　　(D)沖洗

解 flare(v.)（火焰）閃耀；燃燒；閃亮

fling(v.)擲；扔；拋；丟；猛衝；直奔；急行

flush(v.)用水沖洗；使注滿；湧；湧流；（臉）發紅

flash(v.)閃爍；閃光；（想法等）掠過；閃現

16 (A)。 如果你對路線圖有疑惑，可以從服務台尋求幫助。

(A)尋求　　　　(B)看

(C)製造　　　　(D)保有

解 look(v.)看；注意；留神

make(v.)製造；做；建造

keep(v.)保有；持有；擁有；保管

seek(v.)尋求；探索；追求

17 (D)。 自動扶梯運作不正常，所以你最好走樓梯。

(A)振奮　　　　(B)進步

(C)合作　　　　(D)運作

解 uplift(v.)振奮；舉起；抬起；使上升；使隆起

progress(v.)進步；前進；進行；上進；提高

cooperate(v.)合作；協作；配合

function(v.)運作；工作；起作用

18 (D)。為了不被堵車，史蒂夫選擇乘坐捷運，而不是開車。
(A)由於
(B)除此之外
(C)與……比較
(D)而不是

解 owing to 由於；因為
aside from 除此之外
compared with 與……比較
instead of 而不是；代替

19 (B)。台中捷運（Taichung MRT）通車後，市民可以方便地周遊全市。也可輕鬆前往台中的台灣高鐵站，暢遊南北兩地。
(A)傳統上　　　(B)方便地
(C)同樣地　　　(D)絕望地

解 traditionally(adv.)傳統上；傳說上；習慣上
similarly(adv.)同樣地；相仿地
desperately(adv.)絕望地；不顧一切地；拼命地
conveniently(adv.)方便地；便利地；合宜地

20 (C)。班非常喜歡這部電視劇，因為他覺得自己與其中的角色感同身受，其中一些人和他有著相同的經歷。
(A)發出輕柔持續的聲音
(B)開始
(C)識別
(D)混合

解 murmur(v.)發出輕柔持續的聲音；私語，小聲說話

launch(v.)開始；積極投入；猛力展開；（船）下水；出海
blend(v.)混和；混雜；交融；協調
identify(v.)感同身受；（與……）認同；一致

21 (A)。為了縮短兩個不同政黨之間的分歧，這位年輕的政治家提出了一項需要雙方合作的新法律。
(A)合作
(B)（貨幣、消息等）流通
(C)計算
(D)擁塞

解 circulation(n.)（貨幣、消息等）流通；循環；環流；運行；發行量
calculation(n.)計算；計算結果
congestion(n.)擁塞；擠滿；充血
cooperation(n.)合作；協力；合作社

22 (B)。該公司用電動汽車代替其所有舊汽車，以當作綠色環保努力的一部分。
(A)吸收　　　(B)代替
(C)發抖　　　(D)宣稱

解 absorb(v.)吸收；汲取；理解
tremble(v.)發抖；震顫；焦慮；擔憂
pronounce(v.)宣稱；斷言；表示；發……的音
substitute(v.)用……代替；代替

23 (C)。某些被感染病毒的人看起來和感覺都很健康，但仍然可以將病毒傳染給其他人。
(A)誰感染了
(B)感染（現在分詞）
(C)感染（過去分詞）
(D)被感染（現在式被動語態）
解 選項(A)who infected是錯誤寫法，因為infected是形容詞，句中少了動詞，故為非。
選項(B)infecting是現在分詞，表示主動，但人是被感染的，應該用過去分詞，故亦為非。
選項(D)are infected雖然被動語態正確，但因為空格後已經有動詞look和feel，所以空格內不能再填入動詞are，故為非。
Some people infected with virus look and feel healthy, ... = Some people who are infected with virus look and feel healthy, ...

24 (B)。一個有電腦成癮的人認為他的「網絡朋友」很重要，所以他花在家人和朋友身上的時間較少。
(A)較多
(B)較少（接不可數名詞）

(C)很多
(D)較少（接可數名詞）
解 選項(A)和(C)的語意跟原句不符，故均為非。
選項(D)fewer（較少）之後應該接可數名詞，但time是不可數名詞，應該用less修飾之，故為非。

25 (B)。
愛麗絲：我需要去買點東西。這社區裡有超市嗎？
特里：是的。小學對面就有一家。
愛麗絲：_____
特里：步行大約十分鐘。也許你最好開車去那裡。
(A)你在那裡多久了？
(B)超市離這兒有多遠？
(C)你好嗎？
(D)我怎樣才能申請這份工作？
解 空格後的回答說走路大約十分鐘，所以選項(B)的問題是正確答案。
opposite(prep.)在……對面
　　　　(adj.)相反的；對立的；對面的；相對的
　　　　(adv.)在對面
　　　　(n.) 對立面；對立物

解答與解析

111年　中華郵政職階人員（專業職(二)內勤）

一、字彙測驗

(　) **1** Judy is one of my most valued friends; our friendship has _____ over thirty years.
(A)spared　(B)spread　(C)scattered　(D)spanned

(　) **2** The geopolitical situation demands a reduction in tension in the _____relationship between the two countries.
(A)responsive　(B)friendly　(C)frosty　(D)dazzling

(　) **3** Although air travel has resumed in many parts of the world, airline _____ shortages continue to create flight cancellation and airport chaos.
(A)staffing　(B)polluting　(C)promoting　(D)tracking

(　) **4** No one takes him at his word because he is a _____ individual.
(A)courageous　(B)critical　(C)bold　(D)noncredible

(　) **5** Migrants who have fled instability and uncertainty in their home countries have arrived at the border in _____.
(A)crowds (B)motion　(C)hills　(D)humidity

(　) **6** The unprecedented heatwaves in different parts of the world represent a _____ of climate change.
(A)cheap　(B)passion　(C)fingerprint　(D)revision

(　) **7** _____ unpopular, the scandal-ridden politician was hardly able to finish his speech in the booing of the audience.
(A)Cautiously　(B)Shapely　(C)Massively　(D)Technically

(　) **8** The school administration has promised to strengthen security to _____ the concerns of parents.
(A)double　(B)relieve　(C)shoulder　(D)knee

二、文法測驗

(　　) **9** As back-to-school season begins, the national teacher shortage crisis in the US emerges, and it _____ that it's only going to get worse.
(A)seemed　(B)seems　(C)is to seem　(D)had seemed

(　　) **10** The man _____ by the big India laurel tree is the person your sister talked about.
(A)standing　(B)stands　(C)stood　(D)who stand

(　　) **11** We find _____ really hard to believe that Mr. White is the man pickpocketing tourists at the museum.
(A)that　(B)it　(C)him　(D)the thing

(　　) **12** Too much time with digital devices (such as computers, tablets, and cellphones) has been linked to a lot of problems, _____ sleep disorders, low self-confidence, and poorer academic performance.
(A)includes　(B)included　(C)including　(D)to include

(　　) **13** According to the research reports, the loss of mass from Antarctica's ice shelves has been twice as _____ as previously estimated.
(A)extensive　　　　　　　(B)extensively
(C)being extensive　　　　(D)being extensively

(　　) **14** Not only _____ the American student speak Chinese well, but she also understands Taiwanese.
(A)do　(B)will　(C)did　(D)does

(　　) **15** To build a new building, we need materials like steel and concrete, the production of _____ takes out big amounts of carbon dioxide.
(A)what　(B)which　(C)that　(D)where

三、克漏字測驗

There is much we can learn from dogs. In childhood, they are our best companions, ___16___ to understand our every emotion.

Capitan was a beloved German shepherd with a glossy, dark coat and kind, knowing eyes. He was always ___17___ Miguel's side, the two of them inseparable as Miguel pushed into his later years.

When Miguel passed away, Capitan disappeared — only to turn up later at the cemetery, lying on Miguel's grave. He grieved the separation ___18___ death brought. Despite many attempts ___19___ him home, Capitan always ran away, back to the cemetery 15 blocks from the house.

After 12 years at Miguel's gravesite, Capitan also passed away. He was mourned as a community member, ___20___ to many in the town and an example of the love that connects all living things.

(　) **16** (A)seem　(B)seeming　(C)seemed　(D)to seem

(　) **17** (A)for　(B)in　(C)with　(D)at

(　) **18** (A)that　(B)when　(C)of　(D)if

(　) **19** (A)bring　(B)to bring　(C)bringing　(D)brought

(　) **20** (A)belove　(B)to belove　(C)beloved　(D)beloving

四、閱讀測驗

Early in 2021, a little-known app called Clubhouse exploded in popularity. The app had been around since the previous summer, but was only being used by a small handful of wealthy employees at American technology companies. Today, it has millions of users around the world.

Clubhouse is unlike any other app on the market. It allows users to create a room where they can invite others to participate in discussions. The chats are not done through text, but through audio. This way, everyone in the room can literally have a voice and participate in conversations with strangers. Clubhouse differs from other platforms in that the chat rooms are created with certain topics. These can range from the stock market to cooking to politics to...well, there is no limit. One difference, and major benefit, of Clubhouse is that the audio isn't saved after it's heard. People can chat without much fear of their opinions being recorded, shared, and saved on the Internet.

People in China and Taiwan took advantage of that feature early in the app's emerging popularity. It provided an opportunity for people in both countries to talk honestly and peacefully with each other. Some Chinese citizens seemed to express support for Taiwan, mentioning that their schools had forced them to learn only the Chinese side of Taiwan's history. Many users wanted to know more about Taiwan, and people on both sides had a civil dialogue about their cultures and governments. The heartwarming chats ended soon after, though, when the Chinese authorities blocked the app. Elsewhere, politicians, such as South Korea's prime minister, are beginning to use Clubhouse, believing it might one day become essential for keeping in touch with voters. If you're interested in joining, be aware that you must be invited into the service by an existing user. The same was true for Facebook in its early days, so there is a chance that the invitationonly feature could be dropped in the future.

(　　) **21** What is the main idea of the article?
　　(A)A new Chinese social media app has created problems in South Korea and Taiwan.
　　(B)People in China and Taiwan have found a new way to discuss their problems.
　　(C)The government of China has banned the use of a popular new app.
　　(D)A new social media app has become popular because of how it works.

(　　) **22** According to the article, how is Clubhouse different from other apps?
　　(A)You can discuss in groups.
　　(B)You can communicate either by sending messages or talking to others.
　　(C)Everyone can use it for free.
　　(D)It provides topics for each chat room to talk about.

（　）**23** What did Clubhouse do for people in Taiwan and China?
(A)It helped them talk openly online.
(B)It helped them search for information.
(C)It taught them more about their own countries.
(D)It helped them understand their governments.

（　）**24** Why does the author mention Facebook in the article?
(A)To explain where Clubhouse came from.
(B)To describe how important Clubhouse is getting.
(C)To suggest that Clubhouse might change later on.
(D)To warn that Clubhouse has a lot of competition.

（　）**25** Which statement about Clubhouse is NOT true?
(A)It was created in 2020.
(B)It has chat rooms for a wide variety of topics.
(C)It is a very useful tool for a meeting because it helps save people's opinions.
(D)You cannot enjoy its service unless you are invited by a Clubhouse user.

解答與解析　　答案標示為# 者，表官方曾公告更正該題答案。

一、字彙測驗

1 (D)。 朱蒂是我最重要的朋友之一；我們的友誼已經持續了三十年。
(A)赦免　　　　　(B)使伸展
(C)使分散　　　　(D)持續
解 spare(v.)赦免；饒恕；不傷害；分出；剩下
spread(v.)使伸展；使延伸；張開；展開；攤開；塗；敷；分布
scatter(v.)使分散；使消散；使潰散；撒
span(v.)持續；延伸到；橫跨；跨越；在……架橋；用手環繞

2 (C)。 地緣政治形勢需要緩和兩國之間關係冷若冰霜的緊張狀態。
(A)反應的　　　　(B)友好的
(C)冷若冰霜的　　(D)耀眼的
解 responsive(adj.)反應的；回答的；應答的；響應的；敏感的
friendly(adj.)友好的；親切的；支持的；贊成的
dazzling(adj.)耀眼的；眼花繚亂的
frosty(adj.)冷若冰霜的；霜凍的；結霜的；嚴寒的；灰白的

3 (A)。儘管世界許多地方的航空旅行已經恢復，但航空公司人員編制短缺持續造成航班取消和機場混亂。
(A)人員編制　　(B)污染
(C)促進　　　　(D)跟蹤
解 polluting 汙染；玷汙；敗壞
promoting 促進；鼓勵；促銷；推銷
tracking 跟蹤；追蹤；（學生依能力編排的）組；班
staffing 人員編制；配備人員

4 (D)。沒有人相信他的話，因為他是一個不可信的人。
(A)勇敢的　　(B)批判的
(C)大膽的　　(D)不可信的
解 courageous(adj.)勇敢的；英勇的
critical(adj.)批判的；緊要的；關鍵性的；危急的；批評的
bold(adj.)大膽的；英勇的；無畏的；放肆的
noncredible(adj.)不可信的；不可靠的
take somebody at one's word 相信某人的話；照某人的話去做

5 (A)。移民們逃離他們自己動盪和變化多端的國家，成群結隊地抵達邊境。
(A)人群　　(B)運動
(C)丘陵　　(D)濕度
解 motion(n.)運動；移動；（天體的）運行；動作；姿態
hill(n.)丘陵；小山；（道路等的）斜坡
humidity(n.)濕氣；濕度

crowd(n.)人群；一伙；一幫
in crowds 成群地；大群地

6 (C)。世界不同地區前所未有的熱浪代表氣候變化的一個特色。
(A)便宜的　　(B)熱情
(C)特色　　　(D)修訂
解 cheap(adj.)便宜的；價廉的；劣質的；廉價品的
passion(n.)熱情；激情；戀情
revision(n.)修訂；校訂；修正；修訂本；訂正版
fingerprint(n.)特色；特徵；特點；指紋；指印

7 (C)。這位醜聞纏身的政治家極度不受歡迎，在觀眾的噓聲中幾乎無法完成他的演講。
(A)謹慎的　　(B)豐滿勻稱的
(C)極度地　　(D)技術上
解 cautiously(adv.)謹慎地；小心地
shapely(adv.)豐滿勻稱的；樣子好看的；形狀美觀的
technically(adv.)技術上；工藝上；技巧上；嚴密地來說
massively(adv.)極度地；大規模地；沉重地；大大地；大量地
ridden(adj.)充滿……的

8 (B)。校方已承諾加強安保，以解除家長的顧慮。
(A)變成兩倍　　(B)解除
(C)肩起　　　　(D)膝蓋
解 double(v.)變成兩倍；增加一倍
shoulder(v.)肩起；挑起；擔負；承擔

knee(n.)膝蓋；膝；膝部
relieve(v.)解除；緩和；減輕；
換⋯⋯的班；接替

二、文法測驗

9 (B)。 隨著開學季的開始，美國出現了全國教師短缺危機，而且這似乎只會變得更糟。
(A)似乎（過去式）
(B)似乎（現在簡單式單數）
(C)將似乎
(D)似乎（過去完成式）
解 因空格前的動詞時態都是簡單現在式單數，故選項(A)和(D)均為非。
be to＋V.表示計畫或安排，有未來的含意，故選項(C)為非。

10 (A)。 站在那棵大的印度月桂樹旁的那個人就是你姐姐說的那個人。
(A)站著（現在分詞）
(B)站著（現在簡單式單數）
(C)站著（過去式）
(D)站著的那個人
解 空格後的動詞時態是現在式，所以選項(C)為非。
空格後已經有動詞is，又沒有對等連接詞，所以空格內不能再填入另一個動詞，故選項(B)為非。
空格前的主詞是單數第三人稱的the man，所選項(D)的動詞stand應該在字尾加上s才對。
The man who stands by the big India laurel tree is the person your sister talked about.

= The man standing by the big India laurel tree is the person (whom) your sister talked about.

11 (B)。 我們很難相信懷特先生就是在博物館扒竊遊客的人。
(A)那 (B)它
(C)他 (D)那件事
解 find it hard to believe that+子句（發現很難相信⋯⋯）
本句中的it是虛受詞，真正的受詞是不定詞（to+V.+that子句），因為真正的受詞太長，所以用it代替。

12 (C)。 過長時間使用數位設備（如電腦、平板電腦和手機）與許多問題有關，包括睡眠障礙、自信心不足和學習成績較差。
(A)包括（現在式單數）
(B)包括（過去分詞）
(C)包括（現在分詞）
(D)為了包括（不定詞）
解 空格前是逗點，而且前面已有動詞，因此不能再填入另一個動詞，故選項(A)為非。
選項(B)的過去分詞表示被動語態，與空格後的幾個受詞不相容，故為非。
選項(D)的不定詞通常表示目的，與原句語意不符，故為非。

13 (A)。 根據研究報告，南極洲冰棚大量消失是先前估計的兩倍大。
(A)廣大的 (B)廣大地
(C)是廣大的 (D)是廣大地

解 空格前的動詞是been，所以空格內應該填入形容詞，
故選項(A)為正確答案。
twice(adv.)兩倍；兩次；兩回
extensive(adj.)廣大的；廣闊的；廣泛的；大規模的；大量的；龐大的

14 (D)。 這位美國學生不僅中文說得很好，而且她也聽得懂台灣話。
(A)do　　　　　(B)將
(C)did　　　　　(D)does
解 do在此處當助動詞，以構成倒裝句，其本身沒有任何意義。
not only放在句首時，表示加強語氣，其後的主詞和動詞要交換位置成倒裝句，若動詞是一般動詞，則需要在主詞前面加上助動詞，而助動詞的時態必須跟一般動詞的時態一致。本句空格後的動詞是speak和understands，所以空格內必須填入助動詞does，故選項(D)為正確答案。

15 (B)。 要建造一座新建築，我們需要鋼鐵和混凝土等材料，那些原料的生產會釋放大量二氧化碳。
(A)什麼　　　　(B)那一些
(C)那個　　　　(D)在哪裡
解 空格前的先行詞是steel和concrete，所以選項(A)和(D)為非。
因空格前有逗點，是非限定用法，所以關係代名詞不能用that，故選項(C)為非。

三、克漏字測驗

　　從狗身上我們可以學到很多東西。小時候，他們是我們最好的伙伴，似乎能理解我們的每一種情緒。

　　蓋普丹是一隻深受喜愛的德國牧羊犬，擁有光滑的深色皮毛以及親切聰明的眼睛。他一直在米格爾身邊，隨著米格爾步入晚年，他們倆形影不離。

　　當米格爾去世時，蓋普丹消失了——沒想到後來卻出現在墓地，躺在米格爾的墳墓上。他為死亡帶來的分離而悲傷。儘管多次嘗試把他帶回家，蓋普丹總是逃跑，回到離房子15個街區遠的墓地上。

　　在米格爾墓地待了12年之後，蓋普丹也去世了。他像一位社區成員一樣被哀悼，鎮上許多人喜愛他，他也是一個用愛聯繫所有生物的榜樣。

16 (B)。 (A)似乎（動詞原形）
(B)似乎（現在分詞）
(C)似乎（過去式）
(D)似乎（不定詞）
解 空格前有逗點，而且也有動詞，所以空格內不能再填入動詞，故選項(A)和(C)為非。
選項(D)的不定詞通常表示目的，與原句語意不符，故為非。

17 (D)。 (A)對於
(B)在……裡
(C)和……
(D)在……地點
解 at one's side = standing beside someone 在某人的旁邊

解答與解析

18 (A)。 (A)那
　(B)當……時
　(C)……的
　(D)如果
　解 空格前的先行詞是separation
　（分離），所以選項(A)that為正
　確答案。

19 (B)。 (A)帶來（動詞原形）
　(B)帶來（不定詞）
　(C)帶來（現在分詞）
　(D)帶來（過去分詞）
　解 attempt (n.)+to+V意指「做某事的
　企圖」，故選項(B)為正確答案。

20 (C)。 (A)愛（動詞原形）
　(B)愛（不定詞）
　(C)心愛（過去分詞）
　(D)愛（現在分詞）
　解 beloved (adj.)被喜愛的；心愛
　的；親愛的；受鍾愛的狗是被愛
　的，所以選項(C)為正確答案。

四、閱讀測驗

　2021年初，一款鮮為人知，名為
Clubhouse的應用程式大受歡迎。該應
用程式自去年夏天就已出現，但僅被美
國科技公司的少數富有員工使用。如今
它在全球擁有數百萬用戶。

　Clubhouse不同於市場上的任何其
他應用程式。它允許用戶創建一個房
間，他們可以在那個房間裡邀請其他人
參與討論。聊天不是透過簡訊進行的，
而是透過聲音。這樣，房間裡的每個人
都可以真實地發表意見並與陌生人對
話。Clubhouse與其他平台的不同之處

在於，聊天室是以特定主題創建的。這
些主題範圍可以從股市到烹飪到政治到
……好吧，這裡沒有限制。Clubhouse
的一個不同之處以及主要好處是語音在
聽到後不會被保存下來。人們可以聊天
而不用擔心他們的意見被記錄、分享和
保存在互聯網上。

　中國大陸和台灣的人們在該應用程
式開始流行的早期，就利用了該功能。
它為兩國人民提供了彼此坦誠相待、和
平對話的機會。一些中國公民似乎表達
了對台灣的支持，提到他們的學校強迫
他們只學習關於台灣歷史的中國方面說
法。許多用戶想更了解台灣，兩岸的人
對於他們的文化和政府方面進行了民間
對話。然而，當中國官方封鎖了這個應
用程式時，溫暖的談話很快就結束了。

　在其他地方，像韓國總理等這樣
的政客開始使用Clubhouse，他們相信
有一天它可能成為與選民保持聯繫的必
要條件。如果你有興趣加入，請注意你
必須受到現有用戶的邀請才能加入該服
務。早期的Facebook也是如此，因此未
來有可能取消僅限邀請的功能。

21 (D)。 本文的主要思想是什麼？
　(A)一款新的中國社交媒體應用程式
　　在韓國和台灣產生了問題。
　(B)在中國大陸和台灣的人們已經找
　　到了一種新的方式來討論他們的
　　問題。
　(C)中國政府已禁止使用一款新流行
　　的應用程式。
　(D)一種新的社交媒體應用程式因其
　　如何運作的方式而變得流行。

解 選項(A)的論點並未出現在文章中，故為非。

選項(B)的論點不是事實，故為非。

選項(C)的論點只在文章的第三段提到，這並不是全文的重點，故為非。

本文每一段都在談如何使用這種新的應用程式，故選項(D)為正確答案。

22 (D)。根據這篇文章，Clubhouse與其他應用程序有何不同？

(A)你可以分組討論。

(B)你可以透過發送消息或與他人交談來進行交流。

(C)每個人都可以免費使用。

(D)它提供了每個聊天室可以談論的話題。

解 從第二段第五句："Clubhouse differs from other platforms in that the chat rooms are created with certain topics."可知，選項(D)為正確答案。

23 (A)。Clubhouse為台灣和中國大陸的人們做了什麼？

(A)它幫助他們在網上公開交談。

(B)它幫助他們搜尋信息。

(C)它教了他們更多關於自己國家的知識。

(D)它幫助他們瞭解他們的政府。

解 從第三段第二句："It provided an opportunity for people in both countries to talk honestly and peacefully with each other."可知，選項(A)為正確答案。

24 (C)。為什麼作者會在文章中提到Facebook？

(A)解釋Clubhouse的由來。

(B)描述Clubhouse會變得多重要。

(C)建議Clubhouse以後可能會改變。

(D)警告Clubhouse有很多競爭者。

解 從第四段的最後一句話："The same was true for Facebook in its early days, so there is a chance that the invitation-only feature 從第二段倒數第二句："One difference, and major benefit, of Clubhouse is that the audio isn't saved after it's heard."可知，Clubhouse不會儲存說過的話，故選項(C)的說法是錯誤的。

25 (C)。下列關於Clubhouse的說法何者不正確？

(A)它創建於2020年。

(B)它有各種主題的聊天室。

(C)這是一個非常有用的會議工具，因為它有助於保存人們的意見。

(D)除非你被Clubhouse用戶邀請，否則你不能享受它的服務。

解 從第二段倒數第二句："One difference, and major benefit, of Clubhouse is that the audio isn't saved after it's heard."可知，Clubhouse不會儲存說過的話，故選項(C)的說法是錯誤的。

111年 中華郵政職階人員（專業職(二)外勤）

一、字彙測驗

( ) **1** The doctor _____ that I exercise at least three times a week in order to stay healthy.
(A)avoided (B)obeyed (C)recommended (D)depended

( ) **2** Eating moon cakes during the Mid-Autumn Festival is an old _____.
(A)tradition (B)spirit (C)rumor (D)generation

( ) **3** Employees in this company are allowed to wear _____ clothes to work such as T-shirts and jeans.
(A)casual (B)emotional (C)automatic (D)imaginary

( ) **4** Bill has changed so much these years that I could hardly _____ him yesterday.
(A)represent (B)recognize (C)determine (D)perform

( ) **5** The city has one of the world's largest subway systems.The subway system is so _____ that many first-time travelers get lost in it.
(A)appropriate (B)complicated (C)essential (D)enthusiastic

( ) **6** As a(n) _____ of getting into a big argument with his boss, Alex was fired and had to look for a new job.
(A)consequence (B)interruption
(C)contact (D)entertainment

( ) **7** It's important to have enough money to live on, but money alone doesn't _____ that you will have a happy life forever.
(A)compare (B)guarantee (C)replace (D)issue

( ) **8** After you read my composition, please give me some _____ so that I can improve it.
(A)charity　(B)delight　(C)feedback　(D)crisis

二、文法測驗

( ) **9** He was heard _____ a love song to his girlfriend.
(A)sing　(B)sang　(C)singing　(D)to singing

( ) **10** This is the school from _____ I graduated.
(A)that　(B)what　(C)which　(D)where

( ) **11** Jack's dog ran out of his house, _____ by another dog.
(A)was chased　(B)chasing　(C)to be chased　(D)chased

( ) **12** He has many pen pals.One is from America, another is from Canada, and _____ is from England.
(A)other　(B)the other　(C)others　(D)still another

( ) **13** The Internet _____ for us to communicate with people all over the world.
(A)makes it possible　　(B)makes it possibly
(C)makes that possible　(D)makes that possibly

( ) **14** At least 33 coastal cities are sinking by over one centimeter per year.That's _____ the rate of current sea level rise.
(A)fifth time　　(B)five times
(C)five times than　(D)five times as much

( ) **15** Sam prefers spending time outside _____ video games inside all day long.
(A)to play　(B)than playing　(C)than play　(D)to playing

三、克漏字測驗

Many people have the experience of feeling sleepy on rainy days. Simply watching the rain fall on the window makes them lazy and sleepy. There may be two reasons that ___16___ such a sleepy feeling. First, people have a habit of going to sleep when it is dark and quiet. On rainy days, the clouds make the sky darker and ___17___ our brain, so we think nighttime is coming. Second, because the sound of rain drops is static, it makes people feel quiet. To understand this, we have to know more about our hearing. Our ears can hear many different sounds at the same time, but our brain chooses only ___18___ . Think of a classroom. There may be the sounds of a clock , a computer, and fans, but you may only notice the teacher's voice. When there is static noise, or white noise, you will stop ___19___ distracting noises because it works as a magic screen, which ___20___ distracting noises and makes you feel quiet.

(　) **16** (A)result from　　　　(B)step on
　　　　　(C)lead to　　　　　　(D)run into

(　) **17** (A)play a trick on　　　(B)do harm to
　　　　　(C)make fun of　　　　(D)take part in

(　) **18** (A)a little to listen　　　(B)a little to listen to
　　　　　(C)a few to listen　　　(D)a few to listen to

(　) **19** (A)to hearing from　　　(B)hearing
　　　　　(C)to hear from　　　　(D)from hearing

(　) **20** (A)comes up with　　　(B)puts up with
　　　　　(C)blocks out　　　　　(D)depends on

四、閱讀測驗

I grew up on a farm in Colombia, a poor country in South America. The lack of rain has been killing many of the people who live around here. My friends and I have been helping them survive, but we're not superheroes. We are just beans, little beans that grow in the dirt. Yet it's our ability to grow in the dirt that makes us so special.

We're called guajiro beans, and we don't need much water. In fact, sometimes we can sprout from dry land.There are lots of nutrients in the soil that we can take in and grow from.When we're fully developed in our pods, we contain vitamins, minerals, and proteins.

That is why we have been able to help so many people. As you know, Earth's climate is changing. Here in Colombia, we're feeling the effects. About ten years ago, the rain stopped coming. Our rivers have dried up, our forests have burned down, and our farms can't grow many types of food. So, for many people here, we guajiro beans are giving them some of the nutrients they need. In addition to that, we're also giving farmers a product to sell.

We're especially important to the Wayuu people, a local tribe. The Wayuu have been farming the land here for centuries. However, they can't grow and raise animals like they used to. But beans like my friends and me are keeping the tribe and its culture alive. In fact, we even help people grow other foods, too. We add nitrogen to the soil, which helps foods like pumpkins and corn grow. We can't do all this by ourselves, though. We sometimes need a bit of water, and the farmers here have found ways to get small amounts out of wells, clean it, and spread it on our land.

I'm proud to be a guajiro bean. I'm strong, healthy, and easy to get along with. I'm so happy that I can help my Wayuu friends survive.

(　　) **21** Who is the author?
　　(A)A talking plant.
　　(B)A Wayuu tribesperson.
　　(C)A Colombian farmer.
　　(D)A guajiro bean seller.

(　　) **22** According to the article, why are guajiro beans special?
　　(A)They only grow in Colombia.
　　(B)They grow faster than other plants.
　　(C)They do not need much water to grow.
　　(D)They supply nitrogen as nutrition for people.

( ) **23** What does the author imply about the Wayuu people?
(A)They also grow pumpkins and corn.
(B)They came to Colombia ten years ago.
(C)They have trouble digging wells to find water.
(D)They bought the guajiro beans from somewhere else.

( ) **24** Which statement about the guajiro beans is true?
(A)A single bean contains all the nutrients a person needs.
(B)They are starting to be considered a "superhero."
(C)People can feed them to farm animals.
(D)They can be sold as a farm product.

( ) **25** Which statement about life in Colombia is **NOT** true?
(A)Climate change has a serious impact on farming.
(B)Many people have died because there has been little rain these years.
(C)The Wayuu have been living only on guajiro beans for centuries.
(D)Guajiro beans are important crops there because they are nutritious and help people grow other plants.

解答與解析　答案標示為# 者，表官方曾公告更正該題答案。

一、字彙測驗

1 (C)。醫生建議我每週至少運動3次以保持健康。
(A)避免　　　　(B)服從
(C)建議　　　　(D)依靠
解 avoid(v.)避開；躲開；避免
obey(v.)服從；聽從；執行；遵守；按照……行動
depend(v.)依靠；相信；信賴；依賴；依……而定；取決於

recommend(v.)建議；推薦；介紹；勸告
動詞recommend之後若接子句當受詞，此子句中的動詞要用原形，因為動詞前面的助動詞should被省略了。

2 (A)。中秋節吃月餅是一個古老的傳統。
(A)傳統　　　　(B)精神
(C)謠言　　　　(D)一代

解 spirit(n.)精神；心靈；靈魂；精
靈；幽靈
rumor(n.)謠言；謠傳；傳聞；
傳說
generation(n.)一代；世代；同
時代的人；一代人；一代事物
tradition(n.)傳統；傳統思想；
慣例；常規

3 (A)。該公司允許員工穿著休閒服
上班，例如T恤和牛仔褲。
(A)休閒的
(B)感情（上）的
(C)促進
(D)想像中的
解 emotional(adj.)感情（上）的；
易動情的；感情脆弱的
automatic(adj.)自動的；自動裝
置的；習慣性的；無意識的
imaginary(adj.)想像中的；虛構
的；幻想的
casual(adj.)休閒的；非正式
的；偶然的；碰巧的；隨便
的；漫不經心的；臨時的

4 (B)。比爾這些年變化太大了，昨
天我都快認不出他了。
(A)表示
(B)認識
(C)決定
(D)執行
解 represent(v.)表示；表現；象
徵；描繪；作為……的代表
determine(v.)決定；使下決心；
確定；判決
perform(v.)執行；履行；完成；
做；演出；表演；演奏

recognize(v.)認出；識別；認
識；正式承認；認可

5 (B)。這座城市擁有世界上最大的
地鐵系統之一。地鐵系統如此複
雜，以至於很多初次旅遊的人都迷
路了。
(A)適當的
(B)複雜的
(C)必須的
(D)熱情的
解 appropriate(adj.)適當的；恰當
的；相稱的
essential(adj.)必要的；不可缺
的；本質的；實質的；基本的
enthusiastic(adj.)熱情的；熱烈
的；熱心的
complicated(adj.)複雜的；難懂
的；結構複雜的

6 (A)。由於跟老闆大吵一架，亞歷克
斯被解僱了，然後不得不另謀高就。
(A)結果
(B)中斷
(C)接觸
(D)娛樂
解 interruption(n.)中止；阻礙；障
礙物；打擾；干擾
contact(n.)接觸；觸碰；交往；
聯繫；聯絡
entertainment(n.)娛樂；消遣；招
待；款待；遊藝；演藝；餘興
consequence(n.)結果；後果；重
大；重要

7 (B)。有足夠的錢過日子很重要，
但只有錢並不能保證你會永遠有幸
福的生活。

解答與解析

(A)比較　　　　　(B)保證
(C)取代　　　　　(D)發行

解 compare(v.)比較；對照；比喻為；比作

replace(v.)取代；把……放回；以……代替

issue(v.)發行；發布；發給；配給；核發

guarantee(v.)保證；擔保；保障

8 (C)。 看完我的作文後，請給我一些反饋，以便我能改進它。
(A)慈善　　　　　(B)欣喜
(C)反饋　　　　　(D)危機

解 charity(n.)慈善；慈悲；仁愛；博愛；施捨；善舉

delight(n.)欣喜；愉快；樂事；樂趣

crisis(n.)危機；緊急關頭；轉折點；病情危險期

feedback(n.)反饋；回饋；返回；反饋的信息

二、文法測驗

9 (C)。 有人聽到他正在對著他的女朋友唱情歌。
(A)唱（動詞原形）
(B)唱（過去式）
(C)唱（現在分詞）
(D)唱（錯誤寫法）

解 感官動詞hear之後可以接原形動詞或現在分詞，如果表示正在進行的動作，則要用Ving，故選項(C)為正確答案。

10 (C)。 這就是我畢業的學校。
(A)那　　　　　(B)什麼
(C)那一個　　　(D)哪裡

解 空格前是介系詞from，而介系詞前面是先行詞school，所以關係代名詞要用which，故選項(C)為正確答案。

This is the school from which I graduated.＝This is the school where I graduated.

雖然關係代名詞that和which有時可以互換，但介系詞之後不可用關係代名詞that。

11 (D)。 傑克的狗跑出屋外，然後被另一隻狗追逐。
(A)被追逐
(B)追逐（現在分詞）
(C)追逐（不定詞被動）
(D)追逐（過去分詞）

解 從空格後的by可知，這隻狗是被追逐的，故選項(B)=的現在分詞為非。

選項(A)是動詞片語，但空格前已經有動詞，卻沒有對等連接詞，所以不能再填入另一個動詞，故為非。

不定詞片語通常表示目的，此與原句語意不符，故選項(C)亦為非。

12 (D)。 他有許多筆友。一位來自美國，另一位來自加拿大，還有另一位來自英國。

(A)兩者中另一個人（物）

(B)另一方

(C)其餘的人（物）

(D)還有另一個

解 other (pron.) 兩個中的另一個人（物）；另一方

others (pron.) 其餘的人（或物）

another (pron.) 另一個；又一個；再一個

本句指出他的筆友很多，而other當代名詞時，通常指兩個中的另一個人（物）或另一方，故選項(A)和(B)為非。

代名詞others是複數名詞，而空格後的動詞是is，故選項(C)為非。

13 (A)。 網際網路使我們能跟全世界的人們交流。

(A)使之成為可能

(B)使它也許

(C)使那個成為可能

(D)使那個也許

解 make it possible 使之成為可能；使它變成可能

此處的it是虛受詞，而possible是形容詞，用來當修飾受詞的補語，選項(B)和(D)的possibly是副詞，不能用來修飾名詞，故均為非。

that不能用來當替代不定詞片語的虛受詞，故選項(C)為非。

14 (B)。 每年至少有33個沿海城市下沉超過1厘米。這是目前海平面上升速度的五倍。

(A)第五次 　　(B)五倍

(C)五倍比 　　(D)五倍多

解 time當「倍」解釋時，其用法如下：

(1)She earned three times as much as I did last year.（去年她賺的錢是我的三倍。）

=She earned three times more than I did last year.

(2)The earth is 49 times the size of the moon.（地球是月球的49倍大。）

選項(A)fifth time中的time意思是「次」，故為非。

因空格後是名詞the rate of，此與上面的(2)例句類似，故選項(B)為正確答案。

選項（C）和（D）的寫法都不完整，也與原句句型不符，故均為非。

15 (D)。 比起整天在裡面玩電動遊戲，山姆更喜歡在外面消耗時間。

(A)玩（不定詞）

(B)寧願玩（不定詞）

(C)寧願玩（動詞原形）

(D)玩

解 prefer...to...更喜歡；寧可；寧願，其用法如下：

(1)John prefers red wine to white. 比起白葡萄酒，約翰更喜歡紅葡萄酒。

(2)He prefers watching tennis to playing it. 比起打網球，他更喜歡看網球比賽。

空格前是spending time，所以空格內不能填入原形動詞，故選項(A)和(C)均為非。

prefer與to連用，而不是than，故選項(B)為非。

三、克漏字測驗

很多人都有下雨天想睡覺的經歷。光是看著落在窗戶上的雨滴，就使得他們懶散和想睡。造成這種睏倦感的原因可能有兩個。

首先，人們有在天黑且安靜時就入睡的習慣。下雨天，烏雲使天空變暗，然後欺騙了我們的大腦，所以我們認為夜晚來臨了。第二，因為雨滴的聲音是靜態的，使人覺得安靜。要了解這一點，我們必須更深入地了解我們的聽力。我們的耳朵可以同時聽到許多不同的聲音，但我們的大腦只會選擇少數幾個來聽。想想一間教室。可能有時鐘、電腦和風扇的聲音，但你可能只會注意到老師的聲音。當有靜態噪音或白噪音時，你將不再聽到令人分心的噪音，因為它就像一個神奇的屏幕，可以阻擋分心的噪音並讓你感到安靜。

16 (C)。(A)起因於　(B)踩　(C)導致　(D)偶然碰到

解 result from 起因於

step on 踩；踩在

run into 偶然碰到；陷入；達到；合計；撞上；跑進

lead to 導致；引起；通向某目的地；帶到某處

17 (A)。(A)欺騙　(B)傷害　(C)嘲笑　(D)參加

解 do harm to 傷害；損害

make fun of 嘲弄；嘲笑

take part in 參加；出席

play a trick on 欺騙；迷惑；捉弄；開……的玩笑

18 (D)。(A)聽一點（不可數）

(B)去聽一點（不可數）

(C)聽一點（可數）

(D)去聽一點（可數）

解 動詞listen（聽）必須與to連用，例：My mother liked to listen to the radio. 我母親喜歡聽收音機廣播。

選項(A)和(C)都沒有to，故均為非。

空格前的名詞是複數的，而a little（少量；些許）其後必須接不可數名詞，故選項(B)為非。

19 (B)。(A)得到……的消息（現在分詞）　(B)聽　(C)得到……的消息（動詞原形）　(D)從聽

解 動詞片語hear from的意思是「得到……的消息；接到……的電話」，與空格後的受詞不相關，故選項(A)和(C)均為非。

動詞stop的用法：

(1)stop＋Ving表示「不再做某事；停止正在做的事情」

(2)stop＋to do something 表示「停下正在做的然後去做另外一件事情」

(3)stop somebody (from) doing something 表示「阻止某人做某事」

根據上述(3)的用法，選項(D)的from之前應該要有某人，但空格之前是動詞stop，並沒有人，故選項(D)為非。

20 (C)。(A)想出　(B)容忍　(C)阻擋　(D)依賴

解 come up with 想出；提供；趕上

put up with 容忍；忍受

depend on 依賴；確信；堅信；信賴；視某事物而定；取決於某事物

block out 阻擋；擋住；抑制；屏蔽；忘掉；抹去

四、閱讀測驗

我在哥倫比亞的一個農場長大，那是一個南美洲的貧窮國家。

雨水稀少已經讓許多住在附近的人喪生。我和我的朋友們一直在幫助他們生存下來，但我們不是超級英雄。我們只是豆子，長在泥土裡的小豆子。然而，就是我們在泥土中成長的能力使我們如此特別。

我們被稱為瓜吉羅豆（guajiro beans），我們不需要太多的水。

事實上，有時我們可以從乾燥的土地中發芽。土壤中有很多我們可以從中吸收和生長的養分。當我們在豆莢中完全成熟時，我們含有維生素、礦物質和蛋白質。

這就是為什麼我們能夠幫助這麼多人。如你所知，地球的氣候正在發生變化。在哥倫比亞，我們感受到了影響。大約十年前，雨停止了。我們的河流已經乾涸，我們的森林被燒毀，我們的農場無法種植許多食物。因此，對於這裡的許多人來說，我們瓜吉羅豆為他們提供了一些他們需要的營養。除此之外，我們還為農民提供了一種產品來銷售。

我們對當地部落瓦尤人特別重要。幾個世紀以來，瓦尤人一直在這裡耕種土地。然而，他們現在不能像以前那樣種植和飼養動物。但是像我和我的朋友們這樣的豆子正在使這個部落和它的文化存活下去。事實上，我們甚至還幫助人們種植其他食物。我們在土壤中添加氮，這有助於像南瓜和玉米這樣的食物生長。可是，我們不能自己完成所有這些事情。有時我們需要一點水，這裡的農民已經想找到方法從井裡取出少量水，弄乾淨之後，把它灑在我們的土地上。

我很驕傲能成為瓜吉羅豆。我強壯、健康，而且容易相處。我很高興能幫助我的瓦尤朋友們活下來。

解答與解析

21 (A)。作者是誰？
(A)一種會說話的植物。
(B)一位瓦尤族的人。
(C)一位哥倫比亞的農夫。
(D)一位瓜吉羅豆的銷售者。

解 從最後一段第一句："I'm proud to be a guajiro bean."可知，選項(A)為正確答案。
這是擬人化的寫作手法，作者把自己當成這種豆類植物，來敘述自己的生長環境、特性和優點。

22 (C)。根據這篇文章，瓜吉羅豆為何特殊？
(A)它們只在哥倫比亞生長。
(B)它們比別種植物生長得更快。
(C)它們生長不需要太多的水。
(D)它們為人們提供氮當作營養素。

解 從第二段第一句："We're called guajiro beans, and we don't need much water."可知，選項(C)為正確答案。

23 (A)。關於瓦尤人，作者暗示什麼？
(A)他們也種植南瓜和玉米。
(B)他們十年前來到哥倫比亞。
(C)他們在挖井找水時遇到困難。
(D)他們從其他地方購買瓜吉羅豆。

解 從第四段第四句："But beans like my friends and me are keeping the tribe and its culture alive."可知，選項(A)為正確答案。

24 (D)。關於瓜吉羅豆，下列何者為真？
(A)一顆豆子含有人體所需的全部營養。
(B)他們開始被視為「超級英雄」。
(C)人們可以把它們餵給農場動物。
(D)它們可以當做農產品出售。

解 從第三段的最後一句話："In addition to that, we're also giving farmers a product to sell."可知，選項(D)為正確答案。

25 (C)。關於在哥倫比亞的生活，下列說法何者不正確？
(A)氣候變化對農業產生嚴重影響。
(B)因為這些年雨很少，所以許多人已經死了。
(C)幾個世紀以來，瓦尤人一直只靠瓜吉羅豆為生。
(D)瓜吉羅豆是那裡的重要農作物，因為它們有營養，而且還可以幫助人們種植其他植物。

解 從第四段第五和第六句："In fact, we even help people grow other foods, too. We add nitrogen to the soil, which helps foods like pumpkins and corn grow."可知，瓦尤人還有種植南瓜和玉米，並不是只靠瓜吉羅豆為生，選項(C)的說法是錯誤的。

111年 經濟部所屬事業機構新進職員

一、字彙

(　) **1** Different scientists, analyzing the same data, may arrive at wholly different and sometimes＿＿＿＿interpretations.　(A)unsuitable (B)unintelligible　(C)conflicting　(D)invalid

(　) **2** In some developing countries, the sales of imported brands are severely affected by the widespread availability of cheaper＿＿＿＿goods that look almost exactly the same. (A)counterfeit　(B)smuggled　(C)circulated　(D)predominated

(　) **3** The French philosopher Jean-Paul Sartre's＿＿＿＿writing theme was that man is alone in the world and has to shape his own life. (A)phenomenal　(B)observant　(C)superficial　(D)dominant

(　) **4** Some safe＿＿＿＿methods are recommended by doctors to get fertility control.
(A)counteractive　　　　　　(B)contradictory
(C)contrastive　　　　　　　(D)contraceptive

(　) **5** The prices of goods are soaring, and the government is trying very hard to fight the＿＿＿＿.
(A)inflation　(B)deflation　(C)reflation　(D)conflation

(　) **6** His interpersonal relationship does not take place in physical reality. Most of his friends are＿＿＿＿.
(A)fantastic　(B)realistic　(C)imaginary　(D)imaginative

(　) **7** John lost his life in a＿＿＿＿effort to save the child from drowning.
(A)consequential　　　　　　(B)conscientious
(C)contemporary　　　　　　(D)contemptuous

(　) **8** How did a man of so little personal_____get to be prime minister?　(A)aversion　(B)affection　(C)charisma　(D) affliction

(　) **9** She's been in the_____recently, following her heated debate on some political issues.　(A)limelight　(B)daylight　(C)fanlight (D)apple light

(　) **10** I didn't_____my high school classmate until she introduced herself to me at the conference.　(A)recognize　(B)forget　(C) overlook　(D)neglect

二、文法及慣用語

(　) **11** The suspect denies_____into the house, but there is quite enough convincing evidence_____him guilty.
(A)to break, proving 　　　　(B)break, proven
(C)broken, having proven 　　(D)breaking, to prove

(　) **12** Each of them_____to bring_____own book to the next class.
(A)are, his　(B)is, their　(C)is, his　(D)are, them

(　) **13** I'm not surprised that they are good students. They do nothing but _____.　(A)study　(B)studied　(C)studying　(D)to study

(　) **14** _____, inform their parents.　(A)The children misbehave (B)Would the children misbehave　(C)Were the children to misbehave　(D)Should the children misbehave

(　) **15** Supposing no one _____, what would you do with all the food you have prepared?
(A)comes　(B)came　(C)had come　(D)would come

(　) **16** Adam has a lot of experience_____teaching young children; moreover, he has considerable patience_____them.
(A)at, from　(B)for, for　(C)with, towards　(D)in, with

( ) **17** If Kim thinks that I'm going to let her copy my math homework, she's _____. (A)beating around the bush (B)getting stuck between a rock and a hard place (C)barking up at the wrong tree (D)standing up for herself

( ) **18** I cannot_____my new boss. He is too demanding. (A)get up (B)get over (C)get on with (D)get out

( ) **19** As a customer service representative, he has to deal with complaints from clients,_____are hard to please. (A)many of who (B)many of which (C)many of them (D)of whom many

( ) **20** We feel very sorry to cancel the appointment_____, and we will do everything within our power to make up for it. (A)at your earliest convenience (B)at your own risk (C)for your own trouble (D)on such short notice

( ) **21** The monthly rent is the same_____how many occupants there are. (A)irrespective of (B)despite of (C)according to (D)in proportion as

( ) **22** Animal rights groups are opposed_____health and beauty products on animals. (A)to test (B)testing (C)tests of (D)to testing

( ) **23** A number of automobile_____agencies are located on the lower level of the airport. (A)renting (B)rents (C)rental (D) rented

( ) **24** Some construction firms look for ways to_____in order to earn a greater profit. (A)cut short (B)cut corners (C)cut off (D) cut down

( ) **25** You should have avoided_____her divorce. (A)to talk about (B)mentioning (C)to mention (D)being mentioned

三、克漏字

The antismoking lobby succeeded __26__ people knew without being told that cigarettes were killing their friends and families. They demanded hard data about the risks of breathing in secondhand smoke.

They disbelieved glib assurances that cigarettes were __27__ and that the right to smoke __28__ the right to breathe clean air. More important, antismoking activists changed our idea of what smoking is all about.

They uncooled the cigarette companies and their brands, forever __29__ smoking and death in all of our minds. It was, perhaps, the first victory in the fight for our mental environment—an ecology as rife with __30__ as any befouled river or cloud of smog. We long ago learned to watch what we dump into nature or absorb into our bodies; now we need to be equally careful about what we take into our minds.

(　　) **26** (A)that　(B)because　(C)although　(D)if

(　　) **27** (A)safe　(B)dangerous　(C)difficult　(D)commercial

(　　) **28** (A)superseded　　　　(B)superimposed
　　　　　(C)substituted　　　　(D)outnumbered

(　　) **29** (A)connect　(B)connected　(C)connecting　(D)connective

(　　) **30** (A)creatures　(B)illnesses　(C)myths　(D)pollutants

Insomnia, also known as sleeplessness, is a __31__ disorder in which people have trouble sleeping.

They may have difficulty falling asleep, or staying asleep __32__ desired. Insomnia is typically followed by daytime sleepiness, low energy, __33__ , and a depressed mood. It may result in an increased risk of motor vehicle collisions, as well as problems __34__ . Insomnia can be short term, lasting for days or weeks, or long term, lasting more than a month. The concept of the word insomnia has two possibilities : insomnia disorder and insomnia symptoms, and many __35__ of randomized controlled trials and systematic reviews often underreport on which of these two possibilities the word insomnia refers to.

(　　) **31** (A)sleeping　(B)sleepy　(C)sleep　(D)asleep

(　　) **32** (A)as long as　　　(B)as soon as
　　　　　(C)as more as　　　(D)no sooner than

(　　) **33** (A)irritating　(B)irritable　(C)irritability　(D)irritative

(　　) **34** (A)study and to work　　　(B)studying for work
　　　　　(C)focusing and learning　　(D)focus and learn

(　　) **35** (A)abstracts　(B)subtracts　(C)distracts　(D)attracts

四、閱讀測驗

　　For a long time, many psychologists embraced a victim narrative about trauma, believing that severe stress causes long-lasting and perhaps irreparable damage to one's psyche and health. In 1980, post-traumatic stress disorder (PTSD) was added to the list of mental disorders and has since received a lot of attention in the media and among ordinary individuals trying to understand what happens to people **in the wake** of tragic life events. Yet psychologists now know that only a small percentage of people develop the full-blown disorder while, on average, anywhere from one half to two-thirds of trauma survivors exhibit what's known as post-traumatic growth. After a crisis, most people acquire a newfound sense of purpose, develop deeper relationships, have a greater appreciation of life, and report other benefits.

　　In American culture, when people are feeling depressed or anxious, they are often advised to do what makes them happy; they are encouraged to distract themselves from bad news and difficult feelings, to limit their time on social media and to exercise. However, the happy feelings one gets by doing pleasant things fade fast, and soon the sad mood takes over, plunging one into a deeper abyss of melancholy. A better strategy to cope with trauma has to do with meaning-seeking. When people search for meaning, they often do not feel happy, because the things that make our lives meaningful, like volunteering or working, are stressful and require effort. But months later, the meaning seekers not only reported fewer negative moods but also felt more enriched, inspired and part of something greater than themselves. Therefore, although none of us can avoid suffering, we can still learn to suffer well.

(　　) **36** What is this passage mainly about?　(A)PTSD as a widespread mental disorder.　(B)A good way to deal with trauma.　(C)How to find happiness in life.　(D)Suffering as a meaning of life.

(　　) **37** Which of the following statements is true about the first paragraph?　(A)Stress inevitably causes permanent damage to one's mind and body.　(B)PTSD should have been listed earlier as one of the mental disorders.　(C)Most people are able to survive and grow from a traumatic experience.　(D)The more serious one's crisis is, the more growth one can exhibit.

(　　) **38** According to the second paragraph, which of the following options can best help one to recover from a traumatic experience?　(A)To do something cheerful as distraction.　(B)To find meaning in the unhappy experience.　(C)To seek help from a professional psychologist.　(D)To eat well, exercise well, and sleep well.

(　　) **39** Which of the following is closest in meaning to the phrase in the wake of in the first paragraph?　(A)before　(B)after　(C)conscious of　(D)suffering from

(　　) **40** Which of the following has the least to do with post-traumatic growth?　(A)To awaken to the futility of all struggles.　(B)To discover new sense of purpose in life.　(C)To appreciate the meaning of life better.　(D)To develop a closer bond with loved ones.

解答與解析　答案標示為# 者，表官方曾公告更正該題答案。

1 (C)。不同的科學家分析相同的數據，可能會得到完全不同的而且互相矛盾的解釋。
(A)不合適的　(B)難理解的　(C)互相矛盾的　(D)無效的
解 unsuitable(adj.)不合適的；不適宜的；不相稱的
unintelligible(adj.)難理解的；晦澀難懂的；不可理解的
invalid(adj.)無效的；作廢的；殘廢的；有病的
conflicting(adj.)互相矛盾的；衝突的

2 (A)。在某些發展中國家，進口品牌之銷售嚴重地受到廣泛分布的便宜仿冒品影響，那些仿冒品看起來幾乎完全一樣。
(A)仿冒的　　(B)走私的
(C)流通的　　(D)佔優勢的
解 smuggled（smuggle的動詞過去分詞）走私的
circulated（circulate的動詞過去分詞）流通的
predominated（predominate的動詞過去分詞）佔主導地位的
counterfeit(adj.)仿冒的；偽造的；假冒的；假裝的；虛偽的

3 (D)。法國哲學家尚－保羅‧沙特（Jean-Paul Sartre）的主要寫作主題是，人在世界上是孤獨的，而且必須計劃自己的生活。

(A)現象的
(B)（觀察）仔細的
(C)表面的
(D)主要的
解 phenomenal(adj.)現象的；非凡的；傑出的；驚人的
observant(adj.)（觀察）仔細的；細心的；嚴格遵守……的；觀察力敏銳的
superficial(adj.)表面的；外表的；面積的；粗略的；膚淺的
dominant(adj.)主要的；主導的；佔優勢的

4 (D)。醫生推薦一些安全的避孕方法來控制生育。
(A)中和性的　　(B)矛盾的
(C)對比的　　(D)避孕的
解 counteractive(adj.)中和性的；反對的
contradictory(adj.)矛盾的；對立的
contrastive(adj.)對比的
contraceptive(adj.)避孕的

5 (A)。商品價格飛漲，政府正在努力抗擊通貨膨脹。
(A)通貨膨脹　　(B)通貨緊縮
(C)通貨再膨脹　(D)合併
解 deflation(n.)通貨緊縮；抽出空氣
reflation(n.)通貨再膨脹
conflation(n.)合併；合成
inflation(n.)通貨膨脹；充氣；膨脹

6 (C)。 他的人際關係並不發生在自然現實中。他的大多數朋友都是想像中的。
(A)（口語）極好的　(B)現實的
(C)想像中的　　　(D)有想像力的
解 fantastic(adj.)（口語）極好的；難以置信的；驚人的；奇異的
realistic(adj.)現實的；注重實際的；實際可行的；逼真的
imaginative(adj.)有想像力的；富於想像的；幻想的；有創造力的
imaginary(adj.)想像中的；虛構的；幻想的

7 (B)。 約翰為了盡心盡責的救孩子免於溺水而失去了生命。
(A)隨之發生的
(B)盡心盡責的
(C)當代的
(D)表示輕蔑的
解 consequential(adj.)隨之發生的；必然的；間接的
contemporary(adj.)當代的；同時代的；同年齡的
contemptuous(adj.)表示輕蔑的；瞧不起的；藐視的
conscientious(adj.)盡心盡責的；認真的；勤勤懇懇的；謹慎的

8 (C)。 一個如此缺乏個人魅力的人是如何成為首相的？
(A)厭惡　　　(B)喜愛
(C)魅力　　　(D)苦惱
解 aversion(n.)厭惡；反感；討厭的人
affection(n.)喜愛；愛；情愛；鍾愛
affliction(n.)苦惱；折磨；苦事
charisma(n.)魅力；非凡的領導力；神授的能力

9 (A)。 在對一些政治問題激烈辯論之後，她最近成為眾目矚目的焦點。
(A)焦點　　　(B)日光
(C)風扇燈　　(D)蘋果燈
解 daylight(n.) 日光；白晝[U]；黎明
fanlight(n.) 扇形窗；天窗；扇形氣窗
apple light 蘋果燈
limelight(n.) 眾人矚目的中心；石灰光；石灰光燈

10 (A)。 直到我的高中同學在會議上向我介紹她自己，我才認出她。
(A)認出　　　(B)忘記
(C)眺望　　　(D)忽視
解 forget(v.)忘記；忘記帶；忽略
overlook(v.)眺望；俯瞰；看漏；忽略
neglect(v.)忽視；忽略；疏忽；玩忽
recognize(v.)認出；識別；認識；正式承認；認可

二、文法及慣用語

11 (D)。 嫌疑人否認闖入屋內，但有足夠令人信服的證據證明他有罪。

(A)to break, proving

(B)break, proven

(C)broken, having proven

(D)breaking, to prove

解 及物動詞deny（否認）之後須接名詞或動名詞當受詞，故選項(A)(B)(C)均為非。

不定詞片語to prove（證明）用來修飾前面的名詞evidence（證據）。

12 (#)。 他們每個人都將自己的書帶到下一堂課。

(A)are, his　　　　(B)is, their

(C)is, his　　　　(D)are, them

解 each＋of之後接複數名詞，但是複數名詞之後的動詞必須用單數語態，故選項(A)和(D)均為非。

官方原公告選項(C)為解答，但his（他的）指男性，但是本句中的them也有可能包含女性，所以his不是最好的用字，故為非。

從以下兩個例句可知，選項(B)為正確答案：

例：Everyone chooses what they want to have for dessert.

（每個人都選擇他們想要的甜點。）

Everybody puts their own dishes in the dishwasher.

（每個人都將他們自己的盤子放入洗碗機。）

後官方釋疑選(B)或(C)均給分。

13 (A)。 他們是好學生，我並不感到驚訝。他們除了學習以外，什麼都不做。

(A)學習（動詞原形）

(B)學習（過去分詞）

(C)學習（現在分詞）

(D)學習（不定詞）

解 do nothing but＋V. 意指「除了……以外，什麼都不做」，其中的V.是原形動詞，故選項(A)為正確答案。

14 (D)。 如果孩子行為不端，請通知他們的父母。

(A)The children misbehave

(B)Would the children misbehave

(C)Were the children to misbehave

(D)Should the children misbehave

解 選項(A)(B)和(C)的子句之後，沒有連接詞，無法連接兩個子句，故均為非。

把should放在句首，用來代替if連接詞，變成倒裝句，強調不確定的語氣，例：Should you have any questions, ... = If you have any questions, ...Should the children misbehave, ... = If the children should misbehave, ...故選項(D)為正確答案。

15 (B)。 假若沒有人來，你會用你準備的所有食物做什麼？

(A)來（現在式單數）

(B)來（過去式）

(C)已經來了（過去完成式）

(D)會來（過去式未來）

解 當我們不太確定時，我們使用 suppose、supposing和what if＋過去式來表示未來的可能性，例如：Supposing someone else wrote the essay. How would we know?（假若其他的人寫了這篇論文。我們怎麼會知道？）故選項(B)為正確答案。

16 (D)。亞當在教幼兒方面有豐富的經驗；而且，他對他們相當有耐心。
(A)at, from
(B)for, for
(C)with, towards
(D)in, with

解 experience in（有經驗；有……的經驗）其後接名詞或者動名詞，表示在某方面有經驗或經歷，故選項(D)為正確答案。
have patience with 對……有耐心

17 (C)。如果金認為我會讓她抄我的數學作業，那她就是找錯了人。
(A)拐彎抹角
(B)進退兩難
(C)找錯了原因
(D)捍衛她自己

解 beating around the bush（説話）轉彎抹角；兜圈子；旁敲側擊
getting stuck between a rock and a hard place 進退兩難；左右為難
standing up for oneself 捍衛自己；維護自己；為自己挺身而出
barking up at the wrong tree 找錯了原因；用錯了方法；罵錯人

18 (C)。我無法與我的新老闆和睦相處。他太苛刻了。
(A)起床
(B)克服
(C)與某人和睦相處
(D)出去

解 get up 起床；變得猛烈；籌備；打扮
get over 克服；恢復常態
get out 出去；離開；滾開；出版；漏出；解答出
get on with 與某人和睦相處；與某人關係良好；繼續做某事

19 (D)。作為客戶服務代表，他要處理客戶的投訴，這些投訴中有很多是難以取悅的。
(A)many of who
(B)many of which
(C)many of them
(D)of whom many

解 因空格前的先行詞是複數可數名詞complaints（投訴；抱怨），不是人，故選項(A)的who和(D)的whom均為非。
空格前後都是子句，而選項(C)沒有連接詞，無法連接兩個子句，故為非。
which是關係代名詞，代替前面的先行詞complaints，並引導形容詞子句，來修飾所替代的先行詞，官方公告解答為(D)，但筆者認為選項(B)為正確答案。

20 (D)。我們感到非常抱歉，在這麼短的時間內通知你取消預約，因此我們將盡我們的全力來彌補。

(A)在你方便的時候盡早

(B)自擔風險

(C)為了你自己的麻煩

(D)在這麼短的時間內通知

解 at your earliest convenience 得便請盡快；盡早

at your own risk 自擔風險；風險自負

for your own trouble 為了你自己的麻煩

on such short notice 在這麼短時間內的通知；這麼急的通知；臨時通知

21 (A)。不管有多少居住者，每月的租金都是一樣的。

(A)不管　　　　(B)儘管

(C)根據　　　　(D)按比例

解 despite of 儘管；雖然

according to 根據；按照；取決於

in proportion as 按……的比例；依……程度而變

irrespective of 不管；不考慮；不論

22 (D)。保護動物權利組織反對在動物身上測試健康和美容產品。

(A)測試（不定詞）

(B)測試（現在分詞）

(C)……的測試（名詞）

(D)測試

解 object to（反對；對……反感），這個to是介系詞，所以後面要接名詞或動名詞當受詞，例如：They object to dumping substandard machines on the market.（他們反對把次級品機器傾銷到市場上。）故選項(D)為正確答案。

23 (C)。許多出租汽車經銷處位於機場的下層。

(A)出租（現在分詞）

(B)出租（現在式單數）

(C)出租的

(D)出租（過去式）

解 空格後已經有動詞，所以空格內不能再填入動詞，故選項(B)和(D)均為非。

汽車出租公司的英文是a car rental company 或 a rental car company，不是a car renting company，故選項(C)為正確答案。

24 (B)。一些建築公司想方設法偷工減料以賺取更大的利潤。

(A)打斷……的話

(B)偷工減料

(C)切除

(D)縮減

解 cut short 打斷……的話；縮短

cut off 切除；切斷；中斷；停止

cut down 縮減；削減；砍倒

cut corners 偷工減料；走捷徑；圖省事；貪便宜

25 (B)。 你應該避免提及她的離婚。
(A)談論（不定詞）
(B)提及（動名詞）
(C)提及（不定詞）
(D)被提及

解 及物動詞avoid（避免）之後要接名詞或動名詞當受詞，例如：The taxi driver swerved to avoid hitting the bus.（計程車司機急轉彎以免撞上公共汽車。）故選項(B)為正確答案。

三、克漏字

禁煙遊說團取得了成功，因為人們在沒有被告知的情況下就知道香煙正在殺死他們的朋友和家人。他們要求提供有關吸入二手煙風險的明確數據。他們不相信那些油嘴滑舌的保證，即保證香煙是安全的，還有吸煙的權利取代呼吸清潔空氣的權利。更重要的是，反吸煙活動家改變了我們對抽煙是什麼的想法。他們使得香煙公司及其品牌變得不受歡迎，並且讓我們所有人的腦海中將吸煙與死亡永遠聯繫在一起。這也許是我們為精神環境而戰的第一個勝利——一個充滿污染物的生態，像任何被污染的河流或雲霧一樣。我們很久以前就學會注意我們向自然傾倒了什麼東西，或我們吸收入身體的是什麼東西；現在，我們需要同樣小心注意，我們記在腦海裡的是什麼東西。

26 (B)。 (A)那　(B)因為　(C)雖然
(D)如果

解 空格前後都是子句，所以空格中必須填入連接詞，故選項(A)為非。
選項(C)和(D)的從屬連接詞語意跟原句不符，故為非。

27 (A)。 (A)安全的　(B)危險的　(C)困難的　(D)商業的

解 dangerous(adj.)危險的；不安全的；招致危險的
difficult(adj.)困難的；難相處的；不隨和的
commercial(adj.)商業的；商務的；營利本位的；商業性的
safe(adj.)安全的；無危險的；保險的；無害的；不能為害的

28 (A)。 (A)取代　(B)加上去　(C)用……代替　(D)數目超過

解 superimpose(v.)加上去；使疊映；把……套錄在某物上
substitute(v.)用……代替；代替
outnumber(v.)數目超過；比……多
supersede(v.)取代；代替；接替

29 (C)。 (A)連接（動詞原形）　(B)連接（過去式）　(C)連接（現在分詞）　(D)連接的

解 空格前已經有動詞，所以空格內不能再填入動詞，故選項(A)和(B)均為非。
形容詞connective是用來修飾名詞的，但空格後沒有名詞，故選項(D)為非。

30 (D)。 (A)生物　(B)疾病　(C)神話
(D)污染物

解 creature(n.)生物；動物；家畜
illness(n.)疾病；患病；身體不適
myth(n.)神話；虛構的人（或事
物）
pollutant(n.)汙染物；汙染源

失眠，又稱缺乏睡眠，是一種睡眠
障礙，在這障礙中人們難以入睡。他們
可能入睡困難，或很難想睡多久就能睡
多久。失眠之後通常會出現白天嗜睡、
精力不足、易怒和情緒低落。 這可能
會導致車禍增加的風險，以及注意力和
學習的問題。失眠可能是短期的，持續
數天或數週，也可能是長期的，持續一
個多月。失眠這個詞的概念有兩種可能
性：失眠障礙和失眠症狀，許多隨機對
照試驗和系統化文獻回顧的摘要，往往
漏報了失眠這個詞所提及的是這兩種可
能性的哪一種。

31 (C)。（A）睡覺（現在分詞）
(B)睏了　(C)睡眠（名詞）　(D)
睡著的

解 睡眠障礙的英文是 s l e e p
disorder，故選項(C)為正確答案。

32 (A)。(A)只要　(B)一經……　(C)多
達　(D)剛……就……

解 as soon as 一經……；立即
……；一……就……
as more as 多達
no sooner than 剛……就……；
一……就……

as long as 只要……；既然；由於
（註）根據Wikipedia原文，
as long as desired之前有
for。

33 (C)。 (A)令人惱怒的　(B)易怒的
(C)易怒　(D)刺激性的

解 空格前後都是名詞，所以選項
(C)的名詞為正確答案。

34 (C)。 (A)學習和工作　(B)為工作
學習　(C)專注和學習（動名詞）
(D)專注和學習（動詞原形）

解 動詞片語have problems (in)
doing something（做某事有困
難）其中的介系詞in被省略，所
以problems後面直接接動名詞，
故選項(C)為正確答案。

35 (A)。 (A)摘要　(B)減　(C)分散
(D)吸引

解 subtract(v.)減；減去；去掉
distract(v.)分散；轉移；岔開；
使分心；使轉向
attract(v.)吸引；引起注意
abstract(n.)摘要；抽象概念；抽
象派藝術作品

很長一段時間以來，許多心理學家
都接受了關於創傷的受害者敘述，認為
嚴重的壓力會對一個人的心理和健康造
成長期而且可能無法彌補的損害。1980
年，創傷後壓力症候群（PTSD）被加
入到精神障礙的列表中，此後受到媒體
和普通人的許多關注，試圖了解繼悲慘

解答與解析

生活事件之後人們會發生什麼事情。然而，心理學家現在知道，只有一小部分人會發展成全面失調，而平均而言，有一半到三分之二的創傷倖存者表現出所謂的創傷後成長。危機過後，大多數人獲得了新找到的使命感，發展了更深層的關係，有了更好的人生體會，以及報告其他的好處。

在美國文化中，當人們正感到沮喪或焦慮時，通常會建議他們做讓他們開心的事情；鼓勵他們從壞消息和困難情緒中分心出來，限制他們在社交媒體上的時間，然後去鍛鍊身體。然而，做愉快的事情所帶來的快樂感覺很快就消失了，而且很快地悲傷的情緒就佔據了心頭，使人陷入更深的憂鬱深淵。應對創傷的更好策略與尋求意義有關。當人們尋找意義時，他們往往不會感到快樂，因為讓我們的生活變得有意義的事情，比如志工服務或工作，都是有壓力的，並且需要努力。但幾個月後，尋求意義的人不僅報告了更少的消極情緒，而且感到更加充實、受到啟發，並且成為比自己更偉大的事物的一部分。因此，雖然我們誰都無法避免受苦，但我們仍然可以學會忍辱負重。

36 (B)。 本文主要談的是什麼？
(A)PTSD 作為一種普遍的精神障礙。
(B)處理創傷的好方法。
(C)如何找到生活中的快樂。
(D)受苦作為生命的意義。

解 從第二段第三句：''A better strategy to cope with trauma has

to do with meaning-seeking."可知，選項(B)為正確答案。

37 (C)。 關於第一段，下列哪一項敘述是正確的？
(A)壓力不可避免地會對人的身心造成永久性傷害。
(B)PTSD應該更早地被列為精神障礙之一。
(C)大多數人都能從創傷經歷中生存和成長。
(D)一個人的危機越嚴重，他就越能表現出成長。

解 從第一段最後一句：''After a crisis, most people acquire a newfound sense of purpose, develop deeper relationships, have a greater appreciation of life, and report other benefits."可知，選項(C)為正確答案。

38 (B)。 根據第二段，以下哪一個選項最能幫助一個人從創傷經歷中恢復過來？
(A)做一些快樂的事情來分散注意力。
(B)在不愉快的經驗中尋找意義。
(C)尋求專業心理學家的幫助。
(D)吃得好，運動得好，以及睡得好。

解 從第二段第四句：''When people search for meaning, they often do not feel happy, because the things that make our lives meaningful, like volunteering or working, are stressful and require effort.

39 (B)。 以下哪一項與第一段中的片語"in the wake of"的含義最接近？
(A)之前　　　　　(B)之後
(C)意識到　　　　(D)受……之苦
解 in the wake of = happening after or as result of event 繼……之後，故選項(B)為正確答案。

40 (A)。 以下哪一項跟創傷後成長無關係？
(A)認識到所有奮鬥的徒勞。
(B)發現新的人生使命感。
(C)更好地體會生命的意義。
(D)與親人發展更緊密的聯繫。
解 從第一段最後一句："After a crisis, most people acquire a newfound sense of purpose, develop deeper relationships, have a greater appreciation of life, and report other benefits."可知，選項(A)不在本句中，故為正確答案。

解答與解析

112年 台灣電力新進僱用人員

(   ) **1** It's not a surprising fact that education levels are_____related to income. (A)deeply (B)heavily (C)largely (D)strongly

(   ) **2** The deadline was announced. The manager made us_____our project proposal by next Monday. (A)submit (B)to submit (C)submitting (D)to be submitted

(   ) **3** Today's news included the results of a study by Veterans General Hospital on the rise in alcoholism_____the country. (A)over (B)cover (C)across (D)cross

(   ) **4** Many smartphone manufacturers are developing user-friendly mobile devices with many features for a different_____of the local market. (A)sector (B)section (C)segment (D) intersection

(   ) **5** As the meeting is going to end in 15 minutes, the chairperson suggests we_____the details and get to the last item on the agenda.
(A)go over (B)skip over (C)hop over (D)move over

(   ) **6** The HR manager_____back from his business trip when we have our meeting next Monday.
(A)is coming   (B)is going to come
(C)will have come   (D)has come

(   ) **7** You should_____me to change lanes so that I could turn left at the intersection.
(A)allow (B)let (C)have allowed (D)have let

(   ) **8** The representatives of two labor unions haven't reached a consensus and_____a solution after months of negotiation.
(A)come by   (B)come up with
(C)come forth   (D)come down with

( ) **9** _____other forms of energy, the cost of producing solar energy is relatively economical. (A)Unlike (B)Dislike (C)Alike (D)Not like

( ) **10** "What do you do for a living?"Choose the best response.
(A)I live just a few blocks from here.
(B)I enjoy living here.
(C)I used to work for an international trading company.
(D)I'm a computer programmer in an IT company.

( ) **11** Some people think that using English is a way of_____ communication, so that people don't have to negotiate which language they are going to use. (A)changing (B)discussing (C)neutralizing (D)understanding

( ) **12** A lot of research shows that health problems_____poor diet and a relative lack of exercise. (A)are linked to (B)link with (C)are linked with (D)link to

( ) **13** Too much sun damages the skin,_____many people still do not use sunscreen. (A)since (B)and (C)or (D)yet

( ) **14** All new employees enroll in an intensive English program designed to_____the amount of time they are exposed to spoken English.
(A)change (B)broaden (C)maximize (D)reduce

( ) **15** The team_____all the best players you can find in this country.
(A)is made of (B)is composed of
(C)is consisted of (D)composes of

( ) **16** Dian is so pleased to be informed of an opening in Taipei's branch since she has been thinking of_____for a while. (A)to transfer (B)to be transferred (C)transferring (D)being transferred

(   ) **17** "Susan is all dressed up. I'd say she's fishing for compliments."What does the speaker think about Susan?
(A)Fishing is her favorite activity.
(B)She looks pretty.
(C)She deserves compliments.
(D)She wants to be praised.

(   ) **18** "Everyone, we're just pulling in to our stop at Austin. We'll be here for ten minutes to take on some more passengers."Where is the speaker?   (A)At a store.   (B)On a bus.   (C)On a boat.   (D)On a plane.

(   ) **19** Since the files are regarded as strictly_____, you should save them with a password.   (A)confide   (B)confident   (C)confidential   (D)confidence

(   ) **20** Interestingly, the painting on the wall is_____upside down in that restaurant.   (A)hung   (B)hanged   (C)hang   (D)to hang

(   ) **21** Any attempt to influence the referees during the game will be regarded as a(n)_____of the rules.   (A)fraction   (B)infraction   (C)intrusion   (D)malfunction

(   ) **22** The newly-appointed CEO is known not only for her integrity _____for her decisiveness.
(A)or   (B)but also   (C)nor   (D)and

(   ) **23** Don't be troubled by Kate's frequent angry remarks. It's just _____of her illness.
(A)a clarification   (B)a consistency
(C)an enforcement   (D)a manifestation

(   ) **24** Everyone can be creative. Creativity is a tool we can all equip ourselves with and_____.
(A)futile   (B)utilize   (C)possession   (D)take advantage

( ) **25** "Believe it or not, Fred's new novel has been selling like hot cakes."Choose the best explanation for the sentence.
(A)Fred likes to bake cakes.
(B)Fred's novel is about baking cakes.
(C)Fred has been selling cakes.
(D)Fred's new novel sells well.

( ) **26** Marc Chagall's masterpieces are currently_____at the national museum. (A)on screen (B)in display (C)on exhibit (D)in exhibition

( ) **27** The best way to protect the skin_____is to avoid the sun when it is at its hottest or wear sunscreen.
(A)to injure   (B)to be injured
(C)from injuring   (D)from being injured

( ) **28** Being a good listener involves more than just the ability to speak. Your body language also_____. (A)counts (B)accounts (C)calculates (D)depends

( ) **29** General Motors announced yesterday that sales of its vehicles have increased_____five percent over the last two years.
(A)for (B)to (C)with (D)by

( ) **30** The success of our ad campaign for the new products_____our expectation.
(A)accumulated (B)exceeded (C)overwhelmed (D)procured

( ) **31** According to a recent survey, the amount of time_____to leisure is dropping.
(A)devoted (B)sacrificed (C)taken (D)spent

( ) **32** Audrey Hepburn will always be the favorite film actress of all time and a(n)_____to style, elegance,and humanitarianism.
(A)idol (B)icon (C)figure (D)signal

(　) **33** Pop art,＿＿＿developed in the late 1950's, is the 20th century art movement.　(A)it　(B)that　(C)X　(D)which

(　) **34** Only after I had arrived at the office＿＿＿that I had forgotten to take the office keys with me.
(A)did I realize　　　　　　(B)I realized
(C)have I realized　　　　　(D)I had realized

(　) **35** ＿＿＿, I think the conference has been a great success.
(A)One for all　(B)One in all　(C)All for all　(D)All in all

(　) **36** Long exposure to second-hand smoke can be＿＿＿to anyone, particularly those who have never smoked before.
(A)detrimental　　　　　　(B)meticulous
(C)incremental　　　　　　(D)sentimental

(　) **37** The company has＿＿＿telemarketing as an effective means of seeking potential customers for years.
(A)found　(B)adopted　(C)hired　(D)understood

(　) **38** The government has decided to＿＿＿the ban on the import of US beef until the end of next year.
(A)extend　(B)expand　(C)launch　(D)release

(　) **39** All staff are required to＿＿＿these new safety regulations.
(A)comply with　　　　　　(B)abide with
(C)conform with　　　　　　(D)obey with

(　) **40** "Who's going to fill the position of Mike Andrews?"Choose the best response.
(A)He should fill out the form first.
(B)He wants a higher position.
(C)They're considering an intern from the Marketing Department.
(D)He went to the Accounting Department.

解答與解析　答案標示為# 者，表官方曾公告更正該題答案。

1 (D)。教育水準與收入非常相關這一事實不足為奇。
(A)深刻地　　　(B)沉重地
(C)大部分　　　(D)非常
解 deeply(adv.)深刻地；在深處；到深處；強烈地
heavily(adv.)沉重地；沉悶地；鬱悶地；厲害地；濃密地
largely(adv.)大部分；主要地；大量地；廣泛地
strongly(adv.)(= very much) 非常；堅固地；結實地；強烈地；激烈地

2 (A)。截止日期已經宣布。經理讓我們在下週一之前提交項目提案。
(A)提交（原形動詞）
(B)提交（不定詞）
(C)提交（現在分詞）
(D)提交（不定詞被動與態）
解 動詞make（讓；使）當使役動詞時，其句型結構為：S.＋make＋O.＋V.，故選項(A)為正確答案。

3 (C)。今天的新聞包括榮民總醫院對全國酗酒增加的研究結果。
(A)在……之上
(B)遮蓋
(C)遍及……各處
(D)越過
解 over(prep.)在……之上；越過
cover(v.)遮蓋；覆蓋
cross(v.)越過；渡過

across(prep.)遍及……各處；橫越；穿過；在……那邊
across the country 在全國各地

4 (C)。許多智能手機製造商正在為本地市場的某個不同部分，開發具有多功能且容易使用的行動裝置。
(A)扇形　　　　(B)地區
(C)部分　　　　(D)十字路口
解 sector(n.)扇形；部門；部分；行業
section(n.)地區；地段；部門；處；科；股；（事物的）部分；階層；（文章等的）節
intersection(n.)十字路口；橫斷；交叉；交叉點；道路交叉口
segment(n.)部分；部門；切片；斷片

5 (B)。由於會議將在15分鐘後結束，主席建議我們跳過細節，並直接進入議程的最後一項。
(A)審查　　　　(B)省略
(C)跳過　　　　(D)挪開
解 go over審查；仔細檢查；溫習
hop over跳過
move over挪開；讓位；挪動
skip over省略；略過；遺漏；作短期旅行

6 (C)。下週一我們開會時，人力資源經理將已經出差回來了。
(A)將回來（現在進行式）
(B)將回來（未來式）

(C)將已經回來了（未來完成進行式）

(D)已經回來（現在完成式）

解 本句的時間是下週一，因此應該用未來式，故選項(D)的現在完成式為非。

be＋Ving現在進行式和be going to都可用來表達未來式，但在本句中若用未來式，意指「人力資源經理將回來」，這跟前面的時間副詞子句不相配，因未來式常搭配的時間副詞是tomorrow, next Monday, tonight, soon, later, someday等等，故選項(A)和(B)均為非。

未來完成式表示在未來某個時間點之前，將會已經完成的動作，本句有表示未來某個時間點的when時間副詞子句，因此選項(C)will have come為正確答案。

7 (C)。你當時應該讓我變換車道，這樣我就可以在十字路口左轉。

(A)允許（動詞原形）

(B)讓

(C)允許（完成式）

(D)讓（完成式）

解 動詞let（讓）之後，要用原形動詞，但本題空格後是不定詞 to change，故選項(B)和(D)均為非。

空格後的動詞片語could turn表示與現在事實相反的假設，現在的事實是「不能左轉」，因為當時沒有換車道，所以空格內要填入跟過去事實相反的假

設語氣動詞片語: should have＋p.p.，故選項(C)為正確答案。

8 (B)。經過數月的談判，兩個工會的代表們仍未達成共識以及提出解決方案。

(A)順道拜訪　　　(B)提出

(C)出現　　　　　(D)降落

解 come by順道拜訪；得到；獲得；接近

come forth出現；公布

come down降落，倒下；落下；降落；平靜下來

come up with提出；想出；趕上

9 (A)。和其他形式的能源不同，太陽能生產成本相對地節省。

(A)和……不同

(B)厭惡

(C)一樣地

(D)不喜歡

解 dislike(v.)厭惡；不喜愛

alike(adv.)一樣地；相似地

not like(v.)不喜歡

unlike(prep.)和……不同；不像；與……相反

介系詞unlike必須跟同質性的東西作類比，例：Unlike my brother, I cannot dance.（不像我兄弟，我不會跳舞。）unlike之後的brother和I都是人，可以作類比。

但本考題句unlike之後是other forms of energy（其他形式的能源），而主詞是the cost of producing solar energy（生產太陽能的成本），能源和成本不是同質性的東西，不能作類比，所以本考題句是錯誤的句子，本題應該沒有正確答案。本考題句應該改為：Unlike other forms of energy, solar energy is relatively inexpensive to produce.

10 (D)。「你做什麼工作？」選擇最佳回覆。

(A)我住在離這裡只有幾個街區的地方。

(B)我喜歡住在這裡。

(C)我曾經在一家國際貿易公司工作。

(D)我在一家資訊科技公司當電腦程式設計師。

解 選項(A)(B)和(C)的回覆與原問句無關，故均為非。

11 (C)。有些人認為使用英語是一種使溝通中立的方式，這樣人們就不必協商他們要使用哪種語言。

(A)改變　　　(B)討論

(C)使中立　　(D)理解

解 change(v.)改變；更改；交換；互換

discuss(v.)討論；商談；論述；詳述

understand(v.)理解；懂；熟諳；認識到

neutralize(v.)使中立；使無效；抵銷

12 (A)。許多研究表明，健康問題與不良飲食和相對地缺乏運動有關。

(A)與……有關

(B)與……聯合

(C)與……有關

(D)把……與……連在一起

解 動詞片語link with和link to的含意相同，意指「與……聯合；把……與……連在一起」，其用法是：to link A with B = to link A with B = to link A and B

本句主詞是健康問題，不是人，無法做link這個動作，因此要用被動語態，故選項(B)和(D)的主動用法均為非。

根據Longman Dictionary: be linked to/with something 與某物有關；與某物連繫在一起，故選項(A)和(C)應均為正確答案。

13 (D)。太多的陽光照射會傷害皮膚，可是許多人仍然不使用防曬霜。

(A)既然　　　(B)和

(C)或者　　　(D)可是

解 since(conj.)既然；因為；由於；自……以來

and(conj.)和；及；與；同；又

or(conj.)或者；還是；否則；要不然

yet(conj.)可是；然而；卻（表達轉折的語氣，其含意跟but接近）

空格前是肯定句，而空格後卻是否定句，因此要用表達轉折

語氣的yet來連接兩個子句，故
選項(D)為正確答案。

14 (C)。所有新員工都參加了密集英
語課程，該課程的目的是最大限度
地增加他們接觸口語英語的時間。
(A)改變
(B)使擴大
(C)使增加至最大限度
(D)減少
解 change(v.)改變；更改；交換；
互換
broaden(v.)使擴大；使寬；使
闊；
reduce(v.)減少；縮小；降低
maximize(v.)使增加至最大限
度；對……極為重視
（本句time之後是一個完整的
子句，而且time之後並沒有關
係代名詞，因此這個子句不是
形容詞子句；同時又沒有關
係副詞，因此也不能當副詞子
句，所以這個子句是錯誤的。
另外enroll in（參加）沒有必
需的含意，可以自由選擇參加
或不參加，這似乎不符合公司
的政策，因此建議改寫為：All
new employees are required to
complete an intensive English
program that exposes them to
spoken English for a maximum
amount of time.）

15 (B)。這個球隊由這個國家中所有
可以找到的最佳球員組成。
(A)由……材料做的
(B)由……組成
(C)（錯誤寫法）
(D)（錯誤寫法）
解 is made of 由……材料做的
consist of（由……組成）不能
使用被動語態，故選項(C)is
consisted of 為非。
動詞compose（組成）是及物動
詞，若是主動用法，其後要接
受詞，而不是接介系詞，故選
項(D)composes of為非。
is composed of由…組成

16 (#)。黛安很高興被告知台北分公
司有一個職位空缺，因為她已經考
慮調動有一段時間了。
(A)調動（不定詞）
(B)被調動（不定詞被動語態）
(C)調動（動名詞）
(D)被調動（現在分詞）
解 空格前的動詞片語think of之後
應該接名詞或動名詞，故選項
(A)和(B)均為非。
本題官方公告選(C)或(D)，均
給分。

17 (D)。「蘇珊盛裝打扮。我覺得她
是在尋求讚美。」説話者如何看待
蘇珊？
(A)釣魚是她最喜歡的活動。
(B)她看起來很漂亮。

(C)她值得讚美。

(D)她想要被稱讚。

解 I'll say 意指「我也這麼覺得；我也這麼想；我同意你說的」

fishing for compliments 意指「用一種巧妙的方法來讓別人恭維你、讚揚你」，故選項(D)為正確答案。

18 (B)。「各位，我們正要到達奧斯丁站。我們將在這裡停留十分鐘，以搭載更多乘客。」說話者在哪裡？

(A)在一家商店裡。

(B)在公共汽車上。

(C)在船上。

(D)在飛機上。

解 pull in 到達；到站；賺到；獲得；吸引

從「停留十分鐘來搭載更多乘客」可知，選項(B)為正確答案。

19 (C)。 由於這些文件被視為絕對機密的，因此你應該使用密碼保存它們。

(A)透露 (B)確信的

(C)機密的 (D)自信

解 confide(v.)透露；吐露；將……委託；將……託付

confident(adj.)確信的；有信心的，自信的

confidence(n.)自信；信心；把握

confidential(adj.)機密的；祕密的；表示信任的

20 (A)。 有趣的是，那家餐廳牆上的畫是倒掛著的。

(A)掛起（過去分詞）

(B)絞死（過去分詞）

(C)把……掛起（動詞原形）

(D)把……掛起（不定詞）

解 畫是被掛的，因此要用被動語態，故選項(C)和(D)的主動動詞均為非。

hanged的意思是「被絞死；被吊死」，與原句語意不符，故選項(B)為非。

21 (B)。 任何試圖在比賽中影響裁判的行為都將被視為違反規則。

(A)小部分 (B)違反

(C)侵入 (D)故障

解 fraction(n.)小部分；片段；碎片；些微；分數

intrusion(n.)侵入；闖入；打擾

malfunction(n.)故障；機能不全；疾病

infraction(n.)違反；侵害；違背；違法

22 (B)。 大家都知道這位新任命的首席執行官不僅正直而且果斷。

(A)或 (B)而且 (C)也不 (D)和

解 not only...but also（不僅……而且）是對等連接詞，可以用來連接兩個詞性相等的單字、片語或子句，本題空格前已經出現 not only，因此空格內要填入but also，故選項(B)為正確答案。

23 (D)。 不要被凱特頻繁的憤怒言論所困擾。那只是她生病的一種表現。
(A)澄清　　　　　(B)一致
(C)執行　　　　　(D)表現
解 clarification(n.)澄清；淨化；說明
consistency(n.)一致；一貫；符合；協調
enforcement(n.)實施；執行；強制；強迫
manifestation(n.)表現；顯示；表明；證實；表現形式

24 (B)。 每個人都可以有創造力。創造力是一種工具，我們都可以用它來裝備自己並加以利用。
(A)徒勞　　　　　(B)利用
(C)擁有　　　　　(D)利用
解 futile(adj.)無益的；無效的；無用的；無希望的
possession(n.)擁有；佔有；所有物；財產；領地
take advantage（of）利用；善用；佔便宜
utilize(v.)利用
選項(D)take advantage是錯誤的，應該改為take advantage of。

25 (D)。 「信不信由你，弗雷德的新小說已經非常暢銷。」選出此句子的最佳解釋。
(A)弗雷德喜歡烤蛋糕。
(B)弗雷德的小說是關於烤蛋糕的。
(C)弗雷德一直在賣蛋糕。
(D)弗雷德的新小說賣得很好。

解 sell like hot cakes = be sold quickly and in large quantities 非常暢銷；非常熱賣
這句話的含意與蛋糕無關，故選項(A)(B)和(C)均為非。

26 (C)。 馬克夏加爾的傑出作品目前正在國家博物館展出。
(A)在屏幕上
(B)（錯誤寫法）
(C)在展出
(D)在展覽會裡
解 on screen在屏幕上；屏幕上；銀幕上
put something on display 把某物陳列出來，故選項(B)in display是錯誤的。
in exhibition在展覽會裡
on exhibit展出；當期展覽

27 (D)。 保護皮膚免受傷害的最好方法是避免在最熱的時候曬太陽，或者塗防曬霜。
(A)受傷（不定詞）
(B)被傷害（不定詞被動）
(C)免於傷害（動名詞）
(D)免於被傷害（被動語態）
解 動詞injure（傷害；損害；毀壞）是及物動詞，其動名詞表示傷害這個動作，但本句空格前的名詞是皮膚，不是人，不會做傷害這個動作，而皮膚是被傷害的，選項(A)to injure和(C)from injuring都含有主動意味，故均

為非。protect...from...意指「保護……免受……」，故選項(D)為正確答案。

28 (A)。成為一個好的傾聽者需要的不只是說話的能力。你的肢體語言也很重要。

(A)重要　　　　(B)報帳
(C)計算　　　　(D)取決於

解 account(v.)報帳；解釋；說明；導致；產生
calculate(v.)計算；估計；預測；推測；計畫；打算；使適合
depend(v.)取決於；依靠；依賴；相信；依……而定
count(v.)重要；有價值

29 (D)。通用汽車昨天宣布其汽車銷量在過去兩年中增長了5%。

(A)為了　　　　(B)到
(C)與……一起　(D)by

解 for(prep.)為了；代替；代表；對於
to(prep.)到；向；往
with(prep.)與……一起；偕同；和……
by(prep.)相差；被，由；靠、用，透過介系詞"by＋百分比"表示上升或下降多少，故選項(D)為正確答案。（此片語中的by本身沒有適當的中文翻譯）

30 (B)。我們新產品廣告活動的成功超出了我們的預期。

(A)累積　　　　(B)超出
(C)戰勝　　　　(D)獲得

解 accumulate(v.)累積；積聚；積攢
overwhelm(v.)戰勝；征服；壓倒；覆蓋；淹沒
procure(v.)獲得；取得；採辦；引起；導致；實現；達成
exceed(v.)超出；超過；勝過

31 (A)。根據最近的一項調查，用於休閒的時間正在減少。

(A)用於　　　　(B)犧牲
(C)採取　　　　(D)採取

解 sacrifice(v.)犧牲；獻出
take(v.)採取；花費；佔用（be taken to＋V. 應採取）
spend(v.)花（時間，精力）（＋on）
devote(v.)將……奉獻給；把……專用於（be devoted to 將……用於；貢獻給；致力於）
因空格後有介系詞和受詞to leisure，只有選項(A)devoted最適合填入空格中，形成一個分詞片語devoted to leisure，用來修飾前面的主詞，這個分詞片語是由一個形容詞子句簡化而來：the amount of time which is devoted to leisure，故為正確答案。
其他三個選項的過去分詞都不能與空格後的to leisure連用，故均為非。

32 (B)。奧黛麗・赫本（Audrey Hepburn）將永遠是有史以來最受歡迎的電影女演員，也是時尚、優雅和人道主義的偶像。

(A)受喜愛的偶像
(B)受尊崇的偶像
(C)人物
(D)信號

解 figure(n.)人物；名人；外形；體形；數量；金額
signal(n.)信號；暗號
根據Oxford Dictionary：icon = a famous person or thing that people admire and see as a symbol of a particular idea, way of life, etc.（人們欽佩的名人或事物，並將其視為特定思想、生活方式等的象徵）idol = a person or thing that is loved and admired very much（人們非常喜愛和欽佩的人或事物）。雖然icon和idol都可以翻譯成受人崇拜的偶像，但是前者更有模範性和標誌性，而後者只是一般性，故選項(B)為正確答案。（icon和idol之後接介系詞of，例：a better icon of democracy（一個更好的民主象徵）、icons of fashion（時尚偶像）、the idol of young girls（年輕女孩們崇拜的偶像），因此本考題句空格後的to應該改為of才對。）

33 (D)。波普藝術始於 20 世紀 50 年代後期，是 20 世紀的藝術運動。
(A)它　(B)那　(C)X　(D)那一個

解 空格後有動詞developed（形成；發生；出現），前有先行詞Pop art，因此空格內應該填入關係代名詞which，以形成一個形容詞子句，來修飾Pop art，故選項(D)為正確答案。
雖然that也可當作關係代名詞，來取代who、whom和which，但是因為空格前有逗點，這是非限定的形容詞子句，所以不能用that當關係代名詞，故選項(B)為非。
develop在本句中是不及物動詞，developed不是被動語態，而是過去式動詞，因此前面不能沒有主詞，故選項(C)為非。
空格內若填入it，則造成兩個子句，沒有連接詞的錯誤寫法，故選項(A)為非。

34 (A)。到達辦公室後，我才意識到我忘記帶辦公室的鑰匙了。
(A)我意識到（倒裝句）
(B)我意識到（過去式）
(C)我已經意識到（現在完成倒裝句）
(D)我當時已經意識到（過去完成式）

解 從句首的副詞片語only after I had arrived at the office可知，本句是一個表示強調的倒裝句，其後的主詞和動詞必須要互換，採用疑問句的倒裝寫法，例：Only in this way can you save some money.（只有用這種方法，你才能存些錢。）

選項(B)和(D)都不是倒裝句，故均為非。

選項(C)是現在完成式，不能和空格前的過去完成式同時存在，故為非。

空格前是過去完成式，表示過去以前已經完成的事情，因此空格內必須填入過去式動詞，故選項(A)為正確答案。

35 (D)。總而言之，我認為這次會議獲得了巨大的成功。

(A)人人為我　(B)一共　(C)人人互助　(D)總而言之

解 one for all人人為我

one in all一共

all for all人人互助

all in all總而言之；總之；頭等重要的東西；一切

36 (A)。長期接觸二手煙對任何人都是有害的，尤其是那些以前從未吸煙的人。

(A)有害的　　　(B)過分精細的

(C)增加的　　　(D)多情的

解 meticulous(adj.)過分精細的；小心翼翼的；嚴密的；一絲不苟的

incremental(adj.)增加的；增值的

sentimental(adj.)多情的；情深的；感情用事的；多愁善感的

detrimental(adj.)有害的；不利的

37 (B)。多年來，公司一直採用電話營銷作為尋找潛在客戶的有效手段。

(A)發現　　　　(B)採納

(C)僱用　　　　(D)理解

解 find(v.)發現；找到；尋得

hire(v.)僱用；僱；租；租借

understand(v.)理解；懂；熟諳

adopt(v.)採用；採取；採納；吸收；過繼；收養

38 (A)。政府已決定將進口美國牛肉的禁令延長至明年年底。

(A)延長　　　　(B)展開

(C)使升空　　　(D)發布

解 expand(v.)展開；張開（帆，翅等）；使膨脹；使擴張

launch(v.)使升空；使（船）下水；發射；投擲

release(v.)釋放；解放；放鬆；鬆開；發射；投擲

extend(v.)延長；延伸；擴展；伸出

39 (A)。所有員工都必須遵守這些新的安全規定。

(A)遵守

(B)（錯誤寫法）

(C)（錯誤寫法）

(D)（錯誤寫法）

解 動詞abide當「遵守」解釋時，是不及物動詞，與介系詞by連用，故選項(B)abide with為非。

動詞conform當「遵守」解釋

時，是不及物動詞，與介系詞 to 連用，故選項(C)conform with 為非。

動詞 o b e y（遵守；服從；聽從）是及物動詞，其後直接接受詞，不需要介系詞，故選項(D)obey with為非。

解 comply with遵守；服從；依從

40 (C)。「誰來接任麥克·安德魯斯的職位？」選擇最佳的回覆。

(A)他應該先填寫表格。

(B)他想要更高的職位。

(C)他們正在考慮市場部的實習生。

(D)他去了會計部。

解 選項(A)(B)和(D)中所說的"he"不知是誰，不能解答考題句的疑問，故均為非。

112年 台中捷運新進人員

( ) **1** With the COVID-19 pandemic deteriorating, all public places like stores, restaurants, and MRT stations demanded that everyone _____surgical masks.
(A)wears (B)wore (C)wear (D)wearing

( ) **2** With the computer software, making complex calculations will not be time-_____ anymore.
(A)commuting   (B)consuming
(C)committing   (D)convincing

( ) **3** It took her a long time and a lot of hard work, but she finally achieved her _____of running a marathon.
(A)rank (B)crew (C)goal (D)jail

( ) **4** The _____music at the restaurant was too loud, making it difficult to hear each other.
(A)kingdom   (B)territory
(C)audience   (D)background

( ) **5** Drunk driving is a serious problem that can cause accidents and even_____death.
(A)figure out   (B)dress up
(C)result in   (D)look forward to

( ) **6** After a year of social distancing, it feels strange to return to _____social interactions.
(A)suspicious   (B)normal
(C)anxious   (D)potential

(　　) **7** The concept of love is _____and extends across all cultural boundaries.
(A)universal　　　　　　　(B)terrifying
(C)inferior　　　　　　　(D)doubtful

(　　) **8** There is no doubt that Taichung is a great city._____, you can enjoy the old buildings as well as the delicious food at the same time if you visit it.
(A)Besides　　　　　　　(B)However
(C)For instance　　　　　(D)In the end

(　　) **9** Person A: "I've completed the form. Here it is."
Person B: "Let me check it over. Oh, you forgot to sign it. Could you please sign your name here?"
Person A: "Oh, I'm sorry about that. Let me do that now."
Person B: "_____"
(A)No problem, take your time.
(B)That's very kind of you to say so.
(C)That's just a piece of cake.
(D)That means nothing to me.

(　　) **10** Located at Fukuoka's center is Maizuru Park, which is worth _____.
(A)of visiting　　　　　　(B)to be visited
(C)a visit　　　　　　　(D)being visited

(　　) **11** There are a wide variety of foods served on the table, three of _____are Korean dishes.
(A)what　(B)them　(C)which　(D)that

(　　) **12** Only the staff members of the company have access _____the data on the website.
(A)to　(B)for　(C)with　(D)of

(　　) **13** No one can deny _____.
(A)how important is it to go green

(B)how important it is to go green
(C)how it is important to go green
(D)how importantlyit is to go green

(　) **14** The monk sat under the tree, meditating with his eyes_____.
(A)closed　(B)closing　(C)close　(D)closely

(　) **15** Mushrooms and truffles are both classified as the fungus. The former are inexpensive, while the _____are invaluable.
(A)latter　(B)either　(C)later　(D)other

(　) **16** _____ an emergency, call 911 without delay.
(A)If it were not for
(B)Had it not been for
(C)When it comes to
(D)Should there be

(　) **17** _____ the bad news _____she burst into tears.
(A)Hardly she heard／before
(B)Hardly had she heard／when
(C)No sooner had she heard／before
(D)No sooner has she heard／than

(　) **18** _____ my grandfather couldn't speak English, he traveled around North America on his own.
(A)Because　　　　　　　(B)If
(C)Although　　　　　　　(D)As soon as

19~20為題組

Bowerbirds occur in many parts of New Guinea and Australia. Males weave intricate display areas (called bowers) out of twigs, decorating their bowers with saliva, charcoal, and colorful objects. A bower is an attractive "avenue" that male bowerbirds use to entice a female. Adult male and female satin bowerbirds share the same bright lilac-blue eyes but no other similarities in color, the male being black with a sheen of glossy purple-blue, and the female olive-green above, with off-white and dark scalloping on her lower parts, withbrown wings and tail. Juvenile males and females look similar to each other, known as "green" birds.

Satin bowerbirds inhabit most of the east and south-east coast of Australia, living in humid woodlands and forests and their edges. They can be found in nearby open regions as well. During winter, flocks occur in open habitats such as gardens, parks, and orchards. Bower sites are usually located in suitable rainforests and woodlands.

This bird species is diurnal. Adult males are mostly solitary; however, the "green" birds often are seen in groups or fairly large flocks. In winter, these birds move to more countryside that is more open and occasionally go into orchards, at which time mature males may enter the "green" bird flocks. They forage at all levels of trees, fruits often being taken from the canopy, about 18-20 meters above the ground. They catch insects by gleaning and sallying. These birds can make an amazing range of sounds, including buzzing, whistling, and hissing. Outside of the breeding season,flocks can be vocally noisy.

This species is polygynous. Males may mate with a number of females during one season. At the start of the mating season, a male builds and decorates a bower to attract female birds. It is an avenue built from sticks and twigs and sticks, woven into walls that run north to south. Platforms at each end are decorated with mostly blue objects, such as flowers, berries, and feathers. When a female arrives, the male begins a ritualized display, prancing and strutting around his bower. He will offer the female objects from his collection while making hissing, chattering, and scolding sounds. If impressed, the female enters the bower to mate and then goes off to perform nesting duties by herself.

(   ) **19** Which of the following statements is CORRECT according to the passage?

(A)Male satin bowerbirds look similar to female ones because of their colors.

(B)Male satin bowerbirds tend to live in dry woodlands.

(C)Male satin bowerbirds may mate with more than one female

(D)Male satin bowerbirds are often seen in groups.

( ) **20** Where is the satin bowerbird LEAST likely to be found?

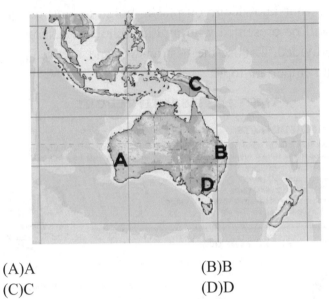

(A)A   (B)B
(C)C   (D)D

( ) **21** What chart can best organize the last paragraph?

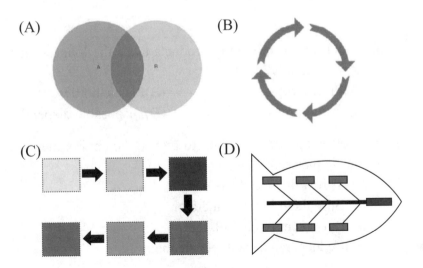

22~25為題組

Welcome to the TMRT Love Earth News Report. In this part, we will be testing your knowledge on plastic pollution and its environmental impact. You will be presented with multiple-choice questions based on the information provided. Choose the best answer and let's see how much you know about this important topic.

TMRT LOVE EARTH REPORT

SHOCKING PLASTIC FACTS:

Did you know that it takes hundreds of years for plastics to break down naturally? Here are some examples of the time it takes for commonly used plastic products to break down:

- Fishing lines: up to 600 years
- Plastic cups: up to 50 years
- Plastic bottles: up to 450 years
- Plastic bags: anywhere from 200 to 1000 years
- Disposable diapers: up to 550 years

WHAT CAN BE DONE?

- Reduce, reuse, and recycle plastic materials to minimize their environmental impact.
- Place more garbage and recycling containers in cities and along coastlines to encourage proper waste disposal.
- Redesign products to be more eco-friendly and consider their environmental impact before using them.

(　) **22** Which of the following products takes the longest time to break down naturally?
(A)Plastic cups
(B)Plastic bottles
(C)fishing lines
(D)Disposable diapers

(　) **23** What is the ideal solution to reduce the environmental impact of plastic materials?
(A)Throw them in the ocean
(B)Burn them in an incinerator
(C)Bury them in landfills
(D)Reduce, reuse, and recycle them

( ) **24** How can proper waste handling be encouraged in cities and along coastlines?

(A)By increasing the number of garbage and recycling containers

(B)By not providing any garbage and recycling containers

(C)By reducing the number of garbage and recycling containers

(D)By encouraging people to litter in cities and along coastlines

( ) **25** How can we reduce the environmental impact of products?

(A)Use products without considering their environmental impact.

(B)Design sustainable products before using them.

(C)Use products without any care for the environment.

(D)Encourage the use of single-use plastic products.

解答與解析　答案標示為# 者，表官方曾公告更正該題答案。

1 (C)。隨著COVID-19大流行的惡化，所有公共場所，像商店、餐館和地鐵站要求每個人都要戴醫用口罩。

(A)戴著（現在式單數）

(B)戴著（過去式）

(C)戴著（動詞原形）

(D)戴著（現在分詞）

解 及物動詞demand（要求）之後，動詞要用原形，例：Mary demanded that John (should) return the books he borrowed from her.（瑪莉要求約翰歸還那些他向她借的書。）故選項(C)為正確答案。

2 (B)。有了計算機軟體，做複雜的計算將不再費時。

(A)通勤　　　(B)消耗的

(C)承諾　　　(D)令人信服的

解 commuting（動名詞）通勤

committing（動名詞）承諾

convincing(adj.)令人信服的；有說服力的

consuming(adj.)消耗的；消費的

3 (C)。她花了很長時間，付出了很多努力，但她終於實現了跑馬拉松的目標。

(A)等級　　　(B)全體船員

(C)目標　　　(D)監獄

解 rank(n.)等級；地位；身分；社會階層；軍階

crew(n.)全體船員；（飛機或太空船的）全體機員；空勤人員；一組工作人員

jail(n.)監獄；拘留所；監禁

goal(n.)目標；目的；目的地

4 (D)。 餐廳的背景音樂太大聲，使得他們很難聽到彼此的聲音。

(A)王國　　　　　(B)領土
(C)觀眾　　　　　(D)背景

解 kingdom(n.)王國；君主身分；王權
territory(n.)領土；版圖；領地；地區
audience(n.)聽眾；觀眾；讀者群
background(n.)背景；遠因

5 (C)。 酒後駕駛是一個嚴重的問題，它可能導致意外事故甚至死亡。

(A)弄明白　　　　(B)打扮
(C)導致　　　　　(D)期盼

解 figure out 弄明白；理解；想出
dress up 盛裝；穿正裝；裝扮
look forward to 期盼；盼望；期望
result in 導致；結果造成

6 (B)。 經過一年的保持社交距離，回到正常的社交互動讓人感覺很奇怪。

(A)可疑的　　　　(B)正常的
(C)焦慮的　　　　(D)潛在的

解 suspicious(adj.)可疑的；引起懷疑的；懷疑的
anxious(adj.)焦慮的；掛念的；令人焦慮的
potential(adj.)潛在的；可能的
normal(adj.)正常的；正規的；標準的；精神正常的；身心健全的

7 (A)。 愛的概念是全世界的，跨越所有文化界限。

(A)全世界的　　　(B)可怕的
(C)低等的　　　　(D)懷疑的

解 terrifying(adj.)可怕的；駭人的
inferior(adj.)低等的；下級的；低於……的；次的；較差的
doubtful(adj.)懷疑的；有疑慮的；不能確定的；不大可能的
universal(adj.)全世界的；宇宙的；普遍的；一般的；整個的

8 (C)。 毫無疑問，台中是一個美好的城市。例如，如果你來這裡旅遊，你可以同時欣賞古老的建築以及品嘗美味的食物。

(A)此外　　　　　(B)然而
(C)例如　　　　　(D)最後

解 besides(adv.)此外；而且；加之；在其他方面
however(conj.)然而；可是；不過
in the end 最後；最終
for instance 例如；舉例來說

9 (A)。
A：「我已經填好了表格。在這兒，給你。」
B：「我檢查一下。哦，你忘記簽名了，可以在這裡簽個名嗎？」
A：「哦，我很抱歉。我現在簽。」
B：「沒問題，慢慢來。」
(A)沒問題，慢慢來。
(B)謝謝你的誇獎。
(C)這事情很簡單。
(D)這對我來說毫無意義。

解 選項(B)、(C)和(D)的回答跟空格前的句子無關，故均為非。
a piece of cake 一件容易的事；小事一樁……

10 (C)。位於福岡市中心的舞鶴公園
非常值得一遊。
(A)旅遊（動名詞）
(B)旅遊（不定詞被動）
(C)旅遊（名詞）
(D)被參觀（被動式）
解 形容詞worth（值得做……；有
……的價值）之後要接名詞或
動名詞，例：This book is worth
our attention.（這本書值得我們
的注意。）
名詞worth（價值）之後可接of
＋名詞，例：The worth of this
diamond is $80,000.（這顆鑽石
的價值是八萬元。）
形容詞worthy（有價值的；
值得的）之後可接不定詞或of
＋名詞，例：This business is
worthy of investment.（這生意
值得投資。）
故選項(C)(worth) a visit是正確
答案。

11 (C)。餐桌上的食物種類繁多，其
中三道是韓國菜。
(A)什麼　　　(B)他們
(C)那些　　　(D)那
解 空格前的先行詞是foods，因
此空格內應該填入關係代名詞
which，雖然that也可以當關係代
名詞，但是因為空格前有介系詞
of，所以空格內不能填入that，
故選項(C)為正確答案。
另外，限定性的關係子句可以

用that來當關係代名詞，取代
who或which，但是在非限定的
關係子句中，卻不能用that取代
who或which。

12 (A)。只有公司員工才能使用網站
上的數據。
(A)至　　　　　(B)為了
(C)與　　　　　(D)……的
解 have access to 可以使用；可以到
達；有接觸……的機會或權力

13 (B)。沒有人可以否認環保有多
重要。
(A)（錯誤寫法）
(B)環保有多重要
(C)（錯誤寫法）
(D)（錯誤寫法）
解 本句不是疑問句，因此選項(A)
how important is it to go green的
倒裝寫法是錯誤的。
how是副詞，用來修飾形容
詞important，因此應該放在
important的前面，不能分開，
故選項(C)how it is important to
go green是錯誤的。
形容詞important是用來修飾代
名詞it，而副詞importantly不能
用來修飾名詞，故選項(D)how
importantly it is to go green是錯
誤的。

14 (A)。那個和尚坐在樹下，閉目
打坐。
(A)閉著的（過去分詞）
(B)關閉（現在分詞）

(C)關閉（動詞原形）

(D)接近地

解 空格前有介系詞with，因此空格內不能填入動詞，故選項(C)close為非。

選項(D)closely是副詞，不能用來修飾名詞eyes，故為非。

選項(B)closing有主動的含意，不能用來修飾eyes，因為眼睛是被閉起來的，故為非。

15 (A)。蘑菇和松露都被歸類為真菌。前者價格低廉，後者則是非常貴重。

(A)後者的

(B)（兩者之中）任一的

(C)較晚的

(D)（兩者之中）另一個的

解 either(adj.)（兩者之中）任一的；每一方的

later(adj.)較晚的；以後的；更晚的 (adv.)後來；較晚地；以後

other(adj.)另一個的；其餘的；別的

latter(adj.)（兩者中）後者的；後面的；後半的；近來的

the former（前者）常與the latter（後者）連用，表示兩項事物的第一項和第二項，或者指兩個人的第一個人和第二個人。

16 (D)。如果有緊急情況，請立即撥打911。

(A)要不是有（與現在事實相反）

(B)要不是有（與過去事實相反）

(C)一說到

(D)如果有

解 If it were not for意思是「要不是有……，現在就會……」，其後的主要子句句型是：S.＋would/could/might＋V.，這是與現在事實相反的假設語法，本句空格後的主要子句並不是這種句型，故選項(A)為非。

If it had not been for意思是「要不是有……，過去就會……」，其後的主要子句句型是：S.＋would/could/might＋have p.p.，這是與過去事實相反的假設語法，本句空格後的主要子句並不是這種句型，故選項(B)為非。

when it comes to意思是「一說到；提及；當談到……時」，其後要接名詞或動名詞，此含意跟原句語意不相關，故選項(C)為非。

should there be = if there were to be意思是「如果有；萬一」，此句型用來強調此條件子句所敘述的情況極不可能或完全不可能發生，此含意跟原句語意相符，故為正確答案。

17 (B)。她剛聽到這個壞消息，就淚流滿面。

(A)（錯誤寫法）

(B)她一聽見／就

(C)（錯誤寫法）

(D)（錯誤寫法）

解 hardly...when (before) = no sooner...than意思是「一……就……」，表示兩個動作幾乎同時發生，但是先發生的事情要用過去完成式，後發生的事情要用過去式，若hardly或no sooner放在句首時，其後的主詞和動詞要倒裝，故選項(A)hardly she heard是錯誤的。

no sooner不能與before連用，故選項(C)是錯誤的。

選項(D)No sooner has she heard是現在完成式，不符合文法規定，故為非。

18 (C)。 雖然我的祖父不會說英語，但他獨自環遊了北美。

(A)因為　　　　(B)如果

(C)雖然　　　　(D)只要

解 because(conj.)因為

if(conj.)如果；假如；要是

as soon as 一……就……；不遲於

although(conj.)雖然；儘管；然而

19~20為題組

園丁鳥出現在新幾內亞和澳大利亞的許多地區。雄性鳥用樹枝編織複雜的展示區域（稱為涼亭），用唾液、木炭和彩色物品來裝飾它們的涼亭。涼亭是雄性園丁鳥用來引誘雌性鳥的一個有吸引力的「林蔭大道」。成年雄性和雌性緞紋園丁鳥有著相同的明亮的紫丁香藍色眼睛，但它們在顏色上沒有其他相似之處，雄性鳥是黑色，帶有發亮的紫藍色光澤，雌性鳥上半身是橄欖綠色，下半身有灰白色和深色扇形裝飾，並且有棕色的翅膀和尾巴。幼年的雄性和雌性鳥外觀相似，被稱為「綠色」鳥類。

緞紋園丁鳥棲息在澳大利亞東部和東南海岸的大部分地區，生活在潮濕的林地和森林及其邊緣。牠們也可以在附近的空曠地區找到。冬季裡，成群的動物出現在花園、公園和果園等開放棲息地。涼亭地點通常位於合適的雨林和林地中。

這種鳥是晝行性的。成年雄性鳥大多獨居；然而，「綠色」鳥類經常成群或以相當大的鳥群出現。在冬天，這些鳥會遷徙到更開闊的鄉村，偶爾進入果園，此時成熟的雄性可能會進入「綠色」鳥群。牠們在各種高度的樹木上覓食，通常從距地面約18-20米高的樹冠層上採摘果實。它們以撿拾和突圍的方式來捕捉昆蟲。這些鳥會發出各種令人驚嘆的聲音，包括嗡嗡聲、口哨聲和嘶嘶聲。除了繁殖季節之外，鳥群可能會製造很多噪音。

這物種是一夫多妻制。在一個季節裡，雄性鳥可能會與多隻雌性鳥交配。在交配季節開始時，雄鳥會建造並裝飾一個涼亭以吸引雌鳥。它是一個用一些枝條和細枝築成的林蔭大道，這些條枝被編織成從北到南的牆壁。兩端的平台大多裝飾著藍色的物體，如鮮花、漿果和羽毛。當雌性鳥到達時，雄性鳥開始進行儀式化的展示，在它的涼亭周圍昂首闊步炫耀。它會一邊發出嘶嘶聲、喋

喋不休的聲音和責罵的聲音，一邊奉上它收藏的女性物品。如果被感動了，雌性鳥就會進入涼亭交配，然後獨自去執行築巢任務。

19 (C)。根據本文，以下哪一項敘述是正確的？
(A)雄性緞紋園丁鳥的顏色與雌性相似。
(B)雄性緞紋園丁鳥往往生活在乾燥的林地中。
(C)雄性緞園丁鳥可以與不止一隻雌性交配。
(D)雄性緞紋園丁鳥經常成群出現。
解 從第四段第二句："Males may mate with a number of females during one season."可知，選項(C)為正確答案。

20 (A)。緞紋園丁鳥最不可能在哪裡被發現？
(A)A　(B)B　(C)C　(D)D
解 從第一段第一句："Bowerbirds occur in many parts of New Guinea and Australia."和第二段第一句："Satin bowerbirds inhabit most of the east and south-east coast of Australia, ..."可知，在選項(A)的地區最不可能發現緞紋園丁鳥。

21 (C)。下列哪一張圖表可以最好地組織最後一段？
解 筆者認為四個選項只有圖形，沒有文字説明，所以是沒有意義的，看不出有任何一個選項

的圖形跟本文的最後一段有任何關係，故本題無解。

22~25為題組

歡迎收看臺中捷運公司（TMRT）愛地球新聞報導。在這一部分中，我們將測試你對塑料污染及其對環境影響的了解。你將看到根據所提供的信息所做出的選擇題。請找出最佳答案，讓我們看看你對這個重要主題了解多少。

臺中捷運公司（TMRT）愛地球新聞報導令人震驚的塑料事實：

你知道塑料製品需要數百年才能自然分解嗎？以下是常用塑料製品分解所需時間的一些例子：

釣魚線：長達600年
塑料杯：長達60年
塑料瓶：長達450年
塑料袋：從200到1000年不等
一次性尿布：長達550年
可以做什麼？

減少、再利用和回收塑料材料，以盡量減少其對環境的影響。

在城市和海岸線放置更多垃圾和回收容器，以鼓勵適當的廢物處置。

重新設計產品，使其更加環保，並在使用前考慮其對環境的影響。

22 (C)。以下哪一種產品自然分解所需的時間最長？
(A)塑料杯　　　　(B)塑料瓶
(C)釣魚線　　　　(D)一次性尿布
解 釣魚線要花600年，是時間最長的，故選項(C)為正確答案。

23 **(D)**。 減少塑料材料對環境影響的理想解決方法是什麼？
(A)把它們扔進海裡
(B)將它們放入焚化爐中焚燒
(C)將它們掩埋在垃圾填埋場
(D)減少、再利用和回收它們
解 選項(A)(B)和(C)在原文中並未提到，故均為非。

24 **(A)**。 如何鼓勵城市和沿海地區進行適當的廢物處理？
(A)增加垃圾和回收容器的數量
(B)不提供任何垃圾和回收容器
(C)透過減少垃圾和回收容器的數量
(D)鼓勵人們在城市和沿海地區亂扔垃圾。
解 選項(B)(C)和(D)在原文中並未提到，故均為非。

25 **(B)**。 我們怎樣才能減少產品對環境的影響？
(A)使用產品時不考慮其對環境的影響。
(B)先設計可持續產品，然後再使用它們。
(C)使用產品時不在乎環境。
(D)鼓勵使用一次性塑料製品。
解 選項(A)(C)和(D)都跟原文論點不一致，故均為非。

解答與解析

112年　中鋼公司新進人員（員級）

(　) **1** The machine is designed to <u>collect</u> data.
(A)process　(B)plan　(C)gather　(D)share

(　) **2** If you'd like to join the club, please <u>fill out</u> the form first.
(A)mail　(B)complete　(C)send　(D)ask for

(　) **3** My neighbour always <u>takes care of</u> my dog when I am away.
(A)looks after　(B)takes after　(C)confirms　(D)sends

(　) **4** I am so thirsty. I need to drink <u>some</u> water.
(A)a few　(B)a little　(C)many　(D)few

(　) **5** Could you please <u>inform</u> me what to do next?
(A)tell　(B)ask　(C)obey　(D)follow

(　) **6** After you book a room in our hotel, you will receive an email to <u>confirm</u>.
(A)disapprove　(B)order　(C)make sure　(D)send

(　) **7** The modern term "robot" was first <u>introduced</u> by a Czech writer in his play in 1920.
(A)made　(B)addressed　(C)confirmed　(D)sent

(　) **8** If you buy more stock, I can offer you a bigger <u>discount</u>.
(A)price reduction　(B)number　(C)district　(D)economics

(　) **9** JFE Steel Corporation <u>provides</u> steel sheets, electrical sheets, shapes, pipes and tubes, stainless products, steel bars and wire rods etc.
(A)supplies　(B)sends　(C)prefers　(D)pulls

(　) **10** They <u>escaped</u> the cycle of poverty through education.
(A)admired　(B)acted　(C)avoided　(D)apologizes

( ) **11** Choose the correct meaning for the following signs.

> High speed trains pass platform without stopping. Please stand behindthe yellow line.

 The notice tells passengers....
(A)where to catch the fast train.
(B)to stay away from fast trains.
(C)about a change to the train service.
(D)not to stand at the platform.

12~15為題組

There is good news for people who hate passwords. Google has added a different way to log in to its services. This new feature __12.__ employs the use of "passkeys." Passkeys represent a safer __13.__ alternative to passwords and texted confirmation codes. All a person has to do is __14.__ confirm their identity on the device. This confirmation, also known as verification, can take several forms, including a PIN unlock code, a fingerprint or face __15.__ scan, or a physical security dongle on different devices like iPhones, Mac and Windows computers or Android phones.

( ) **12** (A)works   (B)lays   (C)uses   (D)pauses

( ) **13** (A)opinion   (B)option   (C) occupation   (D)parcel

( ) **14** (A)miss   (B)make sure   (C)minimize   (D)lose

( ) **15** (A)examination   (B)keyboard   (C) lecture   (D)operator

---

解答與解析　答案標示為#者，表官方曾公告更正該題答案。

1 (C)。這機器旨在收集數據。
(A)處理   (B)計畫
(C)收集   (D)均分
解 process(v.)處理；辦理；加工；消化；沖洗加工

plan(v.)計畫；打算；設計
gather(v.)收集；召集；使聚集；積聚
share(v.)均分；分攤；分配；分享；分擔；共有

collect(v.)收集，採集；使集合；領取；接走

2 (B)。如果你想加入俱樂部，請先填寫表格。
(A)郵寄　　　　(B)填寫
(C)發送　　　　(D)要求
解 mail(v.)郵寄
complete(v.)填寫；使齊全；使完整；完成；結束
send(v.)發送；寄；派遣；打發
ask for 要求；索取；請求
fill out 填寫；發福；長胖

3 (A)。當我不在的時候，我的鄰居總是照顧我的狗。
(A)照顧　　　　(B)與……相像
(C)確定　　　　(D)發送
解 look after 照顧；照看；看管
take after 與……相像
confirm(v.)確定；證實；堅定；加強
send(v.)發送；寄；派遣；打發
take care of 照顧；負責；處理

4 (B)。我好渴。我需要喝點水
(A)一些　　　　(B)一點
(C)許多　　　　(D)很少
解 a few 一些；幾個（用來修飾可數名詞）
a little 一點（用來修飾不可數名詞）
many 許多（用來修飾可數名詞）
few 很少；不多；幾個（用來修飾可數名詞）

some 一些；若干（用來修飾可數名詞或不可數名詞）
water是不可數名詞，故選項(B) a little為正確答案。

5 (A)。能不能請你告訴我下一步該怎麼做？
(A)告訴　　　　(B)問
(C)服從　　　　(D)跟隨
解 tell(v.)告訴；講述，説
ask(v.)問；詢問；請求准許；要求
obey(v.)服從；聽從；執行；遵守
follow(v.)跟隨；接在……之後；追趕
inform(v.)告知；通知；報告
could you please是禮貌的請求，也可以用would you please來表達。

6 (C)。在你預訂我們飯店的房間後，你將收到一封確認的電子郵件。
(A)　　　　　　不贊成
(B)命令　　　　(C)確定
(D)發送
解 disapprove(v.)不贊成；不同意
order(v.)命令；指揮；定購；叫（菜或飲料）
make sure 確定；查明；設法確保
send(v.)發送；寄；派遣；打發
confirm(v.)確定；證實；堅定；加強

7 (B)。現代術語「機器人」是由一位捷克作家在1920年他的戲劇中首次提出的。

(A)被做　　　　(B)被提出

(C)被證實　　　(D)被寄

解 made 被做；被製造

addressed 被提出；被寫

confirmed 被證實；被確定

sent被寄；被發送

introduced 被提出；被製定；被推行

以上五個單字可表示動詞的過去式或過去分詞，如何分辨其真實詞性，就看其前面是否有be動詞，若有be動詞，該字則為過去分詞，若沒有，它基本上就是過去式。因本句的introduced之前有be動詞was，所以這五個單字都是表被動語態的過去分詞。

8 (A)。如果你買更多的存貨，我可以給你更大的折扣。

(A)降價　　　　(B)數

(C)轄區　　　　(D)經濟學

解 price reduction 降價

number(n.)數；數字；號碼

district(n.)轄區；行政區；地區；區域

economics(n.)經濟學；（國民的）經濟情況

discount(n.)折扣；打折扣；貼現；貼現率

stock(n.)存貨；供應物；儲備物；股份；股票；庫存

9 (A)。JFE鋼鐵公司提供鋼板、電工板、型材、管道和管材、不鏽鋼製品、金屬棒、和線材等。

(A)供給　　　　(B)發送

(C)寧可　　　　(D)拉

解 supply(v.)供給；供應；提供；補充

send(v.)發送；寄；派遣；打發

prefer(v.)寧可；寧願；更喜歡

pull(v.)拉；拖；牽；拽；搬走；拔

provide(v.)提供；裝備；供給；規定

10 (C)。他們透過教育擺脫了貧窮的循環。

(A)欽佩　　　　(B)扮演

(C)避開　　　　(D)道歉

解 admired (動詞過去式) 欽佩；欣賞；稱讚；誇獎

acted (動詞過去式) 扮演；裝出；舉動像

avoided (動詞過去式) 避開；躲開；避免

apologize(v.)道歉；認錯；賠不是；辯解

escaped (動詞過去式) 擺脫；避免；逃避；逃脫

11 (B)。選出下列標誌的正確意義。

> 高速列車過站不停。請勿超越黃線。

該通知告訴乘客……

(A)搭乘快速列車的地方。

(B)別靠近快速列車。

(C)關於列車班次的變更

(D)不要站在月台上。

解 stand behind the yellow line 勿超越黃線；站在黃線後面
stay away 別靠近；離開；遠離；別碰
選項(A)、(C)和(D)的含意都跟標誌的意思無關，故均為非。

12~15為題組

對於討厭密碼的人來說有個好消息。谷歌增加了一種不同的方式來登入其服務。這個新功能使用了「通行金鑰」。通行金鑰（數位認證憑證）是密碼和簡訊確認碼的一種更安全的選擇。一個人要做的就是在設備上確認自己的身分。這種確認（也稱為驗證）可以採取多種形式，包括一個PIN（personal identification number 個人身分確認碼）解鎖碼、一個指紋或臉部掃描，或一個安裝在iPhone、Mac和Windows電腦或Android手機等不同裝置上的實體安全適配器。

12 (C)。(A)工作　(B)放　(C)使用　(D)中斷
解 work(v.)工作；勞動；幹活；（機器等）運轉
lay(v.)放；擱；鋪設；砌磚；塗
use(v.)使用；發揮；行使
pause(v.)中斷；暫停；停頓；猶豫；考慮
employ(v.)使用；僱用；利用

13 (B)。(A)意見　(B)選擇　(C)工作　(D)包裹

解 opinion(n.)意見；見解；主張；評價
option(n.)選擇；選擇權；選擇自由；可選擇的東西
occupation(n.)工作；職業；消遣；日常事務
parcel(n.)包裹；（土地的）一塊；一片
alternative(n.)選擇；二擇一

14 (B)。(A)未擊中　(B)確定　(C)使減到最少　(D)使失去
解 miss(v.)未擊中；未得到；未履行；未出席；未趕上；錯過
make sure確定；查明；設法確保
minimize(v.)使減到最少；使縮到最小；低估；小看；極度輕視
lose(v.)使失去；失；丟失；喪失
confirm(v.)確定；證實；堅定；加強

15 (A)。(A)審查　(B)鍵盤　(C)授課　(D)操作者
解 examination(n.)審查；檢查；調查；考試
keyboard(n.)鍵盤；鍵盤樂器；鑰匙板
lecture(n.)授課；演講；冗長的訓話；告誡；責備
operator(n.)操作者；作業員；技工；司機；接線生
scan(n.)掃描；審視；細看；粗略一看；瀏覽

112年　中鋼公司新進人員（師級）

( )　**1** Endurance workouts—generally defined as two hours or more of <u>vigorous</u> activity—can be tough on the body, draining it of electrolytes, stored carbs, and protein.
(A)intense　(B)lengthy　(C)groundbreaking　(D)difficult

( )　**2** With the massive national and international audiences that some sports are able to <u>achieve</u>, media companies are eager to sign up the rights to show the events.
(A)persuade　(B)reach　(C)please　(D)applaud

( )　**3** The technological tools that enabled people around to <u>function</u> during the pandemic have contributed to a growing sense of isolation.
(A)operate　(B)undergo　(C)undertake　(D)understand

( )　**4** Western Canada is bracing for a "heat dome" weather system that will push temperatures to new records over the weekend, and is likely to worsen wildfires that have already <u>displaced</u> tens of thousands of residents.
(A)emigrated　(B)compelled　(C)relocated　(D)replaced

( )　**5** The deaths of dozens of civilians in fighting in the far south of Sudan and an outbreak of communal violence in the restive Darfur region have <u>fuelled</u> fears that communities across the frontier regions of
Africa's third biggest country are being drawn into the bloody contest between two rival generals.
(A)burned　(B)kindled　(C)extinguished　(D)eliminated

( )　**6** Body positivity was originally based on the work of fat-acceptance activists from the 1960s. The movement was focused entirely on fighting for the equality of opportunities, treatment, representation, safety, and dignity of all people living in marginalized bodies.

(A)extraordinary　(B)diagnosed　(C)insignificant　(D) peripheral

(　)　**7** When Microsoft incorporated ChatGPT into its Bing search engine, the large number of factual errors triggered a tsunami of criticism.

(A)confronted　(B)generated　(C)endured　(D)solved

(　)　**8** Exchange programs are intended to _____ employees to offshore knowledge and practices.

(A)create　(B)compromise　(C)expose　(D)examine

(　)　**9** It can be frustrating to hear that learning a complex skill takes a long time, but try not to _____ to impatience.

(A)make　(B)compare　(C)defeat　(D)succumb

(　)　**10** Some people lie to increase their sense of importance, to _____ punishment, or to gain an end that would otherwise be unattainable.

(A)escape　(B)capture　(C)liberate　(D)elaborate

(　)　**11** In law, homicide is the _____ term for any act of killing.

(A)general　(B)middle　(C)moderate　(D)maleficent

(　)　**12** Educational research has shown that your I.Q. is _____ related to your cultural knowledge.

(A)intimately　(B)quickly　(C)democratically　(D)reluctantly

13～15為題組

A holiday can be a break from normality, a chance to be away from the familiar and to experience new places and meet new people. Free from responsibilities and routine, we can connect with the more playful parts of ourselves. The time-limited and transient nature of a holiday means our usual **social norms** and inhibitions are cast aside. The desire to share and connect can be intense and effortless. And in the strangeness of a new country, there is the unexpected and the unpredictable, and with this comes the opportunity for **spontaneity**, adventure, and risk – and the chance to dip our toes into a different version of ourselves.

(　　) **13** According to the passage, what is a holiday?
(A)A festival　　　　(B)A tradition
(C)An honor　　　　(D)An opportunity

(　　) **14** According to the passage, what does the author NOT believe about social norms?
(A)Social norms are restrictive
(B)Social norms are part of everyday life
(C)Social norms are familiar
(D)Social norms are transient

(　　) **15** Which word is the closest in meaning to **spontaneity**?
(A)impulse　　　　(B)transience
(C)application　　　(D)familiarity

解答與解析　答案標示為# 者，表官方曾公告更正該題答案。

1 (A)。耐力訓練－－通常定義為兩個小時或更長時間的劇烈活動－－對身體來說可能很艱難，它會耗盡身體裡的電解質、儲存的碳水化合物和蛋白質。
(A)劇烈的　　(B)長的
(C)開創性的　(D)困難的
解 intense(adj.)劇烈的；強烈的；極度的；熱情的；熱切的
lengthy(adj.)長的；冗長的；囉唆的

groundbreaking(adj.)開創性的
difficult(adj.)困難的；難相處的；不隨和的
vigorous(adj.)劇烈的；有力的；壯健的；強有力的

2 (B)。由於某些運動能夠接觸到大量的國內和國際觀眾，媒體公司渴望簽下該賽事的轉播權。
(A)說服　　(B)接觸
(C)使高興　(D)向……鼓掌
解 persuade(v.)說服；勸服；使某人相信

reach(v.)接觸；達到；延伸；與
……取得聯繫

please(v.)使高興；使喜歡；使
滿意

applaud(v.)向……鼓掌；稱讚；
贊成

achieve(v.)達到；獲得；取得

3 (A)。在疫情期間，使人們能夠正
常工作的科技方法加劇了孤立感。

(A)工作　　　　　(B)經歷

(C)試圖　　　　　(D)理解

解 operate(v.)工作；運作；運轉；
營業；營運

undergo(v.)經歷；經受；忍
受；接受

undertake(v.)試圖；著手做；進
行；從事；承擔；接受

understand(v.)理解；懂；熟
諳；認識到；了解

function(v.)工作；運行；起作用

4 (C)。加拿大西部正在準備迎接
「熱蓋現象」天氣系統，該系統將
在週末將氣溫推至新紀錄，並且可
能會加劇野火，這些野火已經導致
好幾萬名居民流離失所。

(A)移居國外　　　(B)強迫

(C)遷移　　　　　(D)替換

解 emigrate(v.)移居國外

compel(v.)強迫；使不得不；強求

relocate(v.)遷移；搬遷；調動；
重新安置

replace(v.)替換；代替；接替；
更新；放回原處

displace(v.)迫使……離開常居
地；轉移；替換

5 (B)。在蘇丹最南端的戰鬥和在躁
動不安的達爾富爾地區爆發的社區
暴力，造成許多平民死亡，激起了
人們的擔憂；在非洲第三大國家的
邊境各處社區，正捲入於兩軍之間
的血腥較量。

(A)燒毀　　　　　(B)激起

(C)熄滅　　　　　(D)排除

解 burn(v.)燒毀；燒傷；燒壞；燒
焦；燙傷

kindle(v.)激起；點燃；燃起；
煽動

extinguish(v.)熄滅；使破滅；使
消失

eliminate(v.)排除；消除；消
滅；淘汰；不加考慮

fuel(v.)激起；刺激；給……加
油；對……供給燃料

6 (D)。身體自愛最初是起源於1960
年代的肥胖接受運動者的運作。這
項運動完全專注於為所有社會邊緣
化的群體爭取機會、待遇、代表
權、安全和尊嚴的平等。

(B)　　　　　　　非凡的

(B)被診斷的　　　(C)不重要的

(D)邊緣的

解 extraordinary(adj.)非凡的；特別
的；意想不到的；令人驚奇的

diagnosed(adj.)被診斷的

insignificant(adj.)不重要的；無
足輕重的；瑣碎的；無意義的

peripheral(adj.)邊緣的；周邊的；次要的；附帶的

marginalized(adj.)被邊緣化的

7 (B)。當微軟將ChatGPT納入其Bing搜尋引擎時，大量事實錯誤引起了海嘯般的批評。

(A)面臨　　　　(B)引起

(C)忍耐　　　　(D)解決

解 confront(v.)面臨；遭遇；勇敢地面對；正視；對抗

generate(v.)引起；造成；產生；發生

endure(v.)忍耐；忍受

solve(v.)解決；解釋；闡明；解答

trigger(v.)引起；觸發；發射；扣板機開槍

8 (C)。交流計畫旨在讓員工接觸到國外的知識與工作。

(A)創造　　　　(B)妥協

(C)使接觸到　　(D)檢查

解 create(v.)創造；創作；設計；創建；創設

compromise(v.)妥協；讓步

expose(v.)使接觸到；使暴露於；揭露；揭發

examine(v.)檢查；細查；診察；審問

9 (D)。聽到學習一項複雜的技能需要很長的時間，這可能會令人沮喪，但盡量不要屈服於沒耐心。

(A)做　　　　　(B)比較

(C)戰勝　　　　(D)屈服

解 make(v.)做；製造；建造；做出

compare(v.)比較；對照；比喻為；比作

defeat(v.)戰勝；擊敗；使失敗；挫敗

succumb(v.)屈服；委棄；聽任；被壓垮；死

10 (A)。有些人說謊是為了增加自己的重要性、逃避懲罰或得到原本無法實現的目的。

(A)逃避　　　　(B)捕獲

(C)解放　　　　(D)精心製作

解 escape(v.)逃避；逃脫；避免

capture(v.)捕獲；俘虜；佔領；奪得；獲得

liberate(v.)解放；使獲自由；釋放

elaborate(v.)精心製作；詳盡闡述；發揮

11 (A)。在法律上，殺人是任何殺戮行為的總稱。

(A)總的　　　　(B)中間的

(C)適度的　　　(D)作惡的

解 general(adj.)總的；首席的；一般的；全體的；大體的

middle(adj.)中間的；中等的；中級的

moderate(adj.)適度的；有節制的；不過分的；普通的

maleficent(adj.)作惡的；犯罪的；有害的；惡毒的

12 (A)。教育研究顯示你的智商跟你的文化知識有密切關係。

解答與解析

(A)密切地　　　(B)迅速地

(C)民主地　　　(D)不情願地

解 intimately (adv.) 密切地；熟悉地；私下地；祕密地；詳盡地

quickly (adv.) 迅速地；快；立即；馬上

democratically (adv.) 民主地

reluctantly (adv.) 不情願地；勉強地

13～15為題組

假期可以是一種正常狀態的暫停，也就是一個遠離熟悉的地方、體驗新環境、和認識新朋友的機會。沒有責任和例行公事，我們可以跟我們自己更有趣的部分連接起來。假期的有限時間和短暫性意味著我們把一般的社會規範和禁忌拋到一邊。分享和聯繫的願望可能是強烈且毫不費力的。在一個陌生的國家裡，有意想不到的事情和不可預測的事情，隨之而來的是自然發生、冒險和風險的機會－－以及那個讓我們探索不同版本的自己的機會。

13 (D)。根據本文，假期是什麼?

(A)節日　　　(B)傳統

(C)榮譽　　　(D)機會

解 festival(n.)節日；喜慶日；（定期舉行的）音樂節

tradition(n.)傳統；傳統思想；慣例

honor(n.)榮譽；名譽；面子；信譽

opportunity(n.)機會；良機

從第一句："A holiday can be a break from normality, a chance to be away from the familiar and to experience new places and meet new people."可知，選項(D)為正確答案。

14 (D)。根據本文，關於社會規範作者不相信什麼？

(A)社會規範具有限制性。

(B)社會規範是日常生活的一部分。

(C)社會規範是常見的。

(D)社會規範是短暫的。

解 從第三句："The time-limited and transient nature of a holiday means our usual social norms and inhibitions are cast aside."可知，假期才是短暫的，故選項(D)為正確答案。

15 (A)。下列哪一個字的含意最接近"spontaneity"？

(A)衝動　　　(B)頃刻

(C)應用　　　(D)熟悉

解 impulse(n.)一時的念頭；衝動；推動力

transience(n.)頃刻；無常；短暫；稍縱即逝

application(n.)應用；適用；運用；申請

familiarity(n.)熟悉；通曉；親近；親暱

spontaneity(n.)自然發生；自發性

"Oxford Dictionary describes spontaneous behavior as: performed or occurring as a result of a sudden inner impulse or inclination and without premeditation or external stimulus."由此可知，impulse跟 spontaneity的含意最接近。

重要單字片語

a. normality(n.)正常狀態；常態

b. transient(adj.)短暫的；一時的；瞬間的

c. social norm 社會規範

d. inhibition(n.)禁止；抑制

e. cast aside 拋棄；消除；唾棄

f. intense(adj.)強烈的；劇烈的；極度的；熱情的；熱切的

g. effortless(adj.)不費力的；容易的

h. dip our toes into 探索；小心嘗試；摸索

112年　經濟部所屬事業機構新進職員

一、字彙

(　) **1** The famous scientist lost all _____ once his fabricated data came to light.
(A)credibility
(B)credence
(C)credulity
(D)credo

(　) **2** Nicole's _____ that she had stolen the money had shocked everyone.
(A)adjustment
(B)admission
(C)admittance
(D)adoption

(　) **3** Public _____ to the problem of litter has left the city's park in a total mess.
(A)disbelief
(B)dispute
(C)fastidiousness
(D)indifference

(　) **4** The cars are _____ in price, but far apart in terms of performance.
(A)communicative
(B)compact
(C)comparable
(D)compassionate

(　) **5** No new business can succeed without hard-working and ___ employees.
(A)compatible
(B)competent
(C)complacent
(D)complimentary

(　) **6** In a laboratory, it is important to be _____ when measuring substances.
(A)potential
(B)peculiar
(C)precise
(D)primary

(　　) **7** The _____ for setting the drinking age at 18 is that self-control and good judgement are still being developed before that age.
(A)rationale (B)recession
(C)retort (D)revulsion

(　　) **8** A microscope can _____ a cell and make it large for our eyes to see.
(A)modify (B)maintain
(C)mislead (D)magnify

(　　) **9** The _____ child was found safe after a week-long search, but the criminal demanded $1 million in exchange for the child.
(A)invested (B)defeated
(C)performed (D)kidnapped

(　　) **10** This country's military _____ near the border have raised concerns about a possible invasion, despite the claim to test their readiness of the armed forces.
(A)outskirts (B)wardrobes
(C)maneuvers (D)parameters

二、文法及慣用語

(　　) **11** The doctor _____ the patient's cancer for several months now, and the patient is responding well to the treatment.
(A)has been treating (B)has been treated
(C)is treating (D)treats

(　　) **12** This year, only two applicants joined the job interview, but _____ of the candidates was qualified for the job.
(A)both (B)either (C)neither (D)all

(　) **13** There are lots of cover-ups in the business world, _____ involve fraud and corruption.

(A)one of them   (B)some of them

(C)one of which   (D)some of which

(　) **14** Dell was struggling _____ the demands of his boss.

(A)to keep up   (B)to keep down

(C)to keep in   (D)to keep up with

(　) **15** The keys to happier marriage include not _____ change from your spouse.

(A)demand   (B)demanding

(C)to demand   (D)by demanding

(　) **16** It is intriguing to travel in foreign lands _____ cultures are different from our own.

(A)with   (B)which

(C)whose   (D)what

(　) **17** _____ you have any questions, please do not hesitate to contact us.

(A)Should   (B)Would

(C)Could   (D)Will

(　) **18** Zoey moved to New York on her own when she was 17, _____ her family in Louisiana.

(A)left aside   (B)leaving behind

(C)leaving aside   (D)to leave behind

(　) **19** If you have something to say about his notorious behavior, _____ . It is no use to complain to me.

(A)say nothing of it   (B)enjoy yourself

(C)like it or not   (D)say it to his face

(　) **20** _____ entering the concert hall, I noticed that refreshments were being served.

(A)On   (B)About   (C)To   (D)Of

(　　) **21** Only if the arrogant man sees the world through the eyes of a child ＿＿＿＿ truly appreciate natural beauty.
(A)he (B)that he
(C)he does (D)does he

(　　) **22** Though Abby may seem like a simple person when you first meet her, there's more to her ＿＿＿＿ .
(A)than meet the eyes (B)than meets the eye
(C)then meets the eye (D)yet meets the eye

(　　) **23** That restaurant managed to survive the pandemic ＿＿＿＿ .
(A)one way or another (B)by no means
(C)in no way (D)at all

(　　) **24** "My son doesn't mind fruit, but vegetables are a whole different story." That means ＿＿＿＿
(A)My son doesn't like fruit, but he likes vegetables.
(B)My son doesn't like either fruit or vegetables.
(C)My son eats fruit but not vegetables.
(D)My son doesn't eat fruit, but he eats vegetables.

(　　) **25** "Tyler is no less intelligent than his brother" means the same as "Tyler is ＿＿＿＿ his brother."
(A)more stupid than (B)as smart as
(C)sharper than (D)as stupid as

三、克漏字

　　Jane and Philip are in general a happily married couple; however, they do struggle over one point of ＿＿26.＿＿ .They disagree as to how their family should follow the traditions of seasonal holidays. In her opinions, the emphasis ＿＿27.＿＿ presents has made the season lucrative for all those mercenary retailers who overcharge at holiday time. In addition, people should be watching their expenses and avoid unnecessary ＿＿28.＿＿ in their budgets. Therefore, she aspires to keep her home free of all such customs and wants her children to ＿＿＿29.＿＿＿ from traditions such as gift-giving and dyeing Easter eggs. Although Philip understands her concerns, he prefers the conventional way of celebrating holidays. He believes that children enjoy the customary ＿＿＿30.＿＿＿ that are connected with the holidays.

(　) **26** (A)dissent　(B)relief　　(C)deficit　　(D)harmony

(　) **27** (A)at　　　(B)on　　　(C)by　　　(D)of

(　) **28** (A)wealth　(B)surplus　(C)shortfall　(D)adequacy

(　) **29** (A)desire　(B)affiliate　(C)prompt　　(D)abstain

(　) **30** (A)burdens (B)sections　(C)downers　(D)activities

　　Memorizing information is something we all need to do. There are ＿＿ 31.＿ ways to improve our memory, one of which is known as mind-mapping. A mind map is like a ＿＿32.＿ of thoughts, starting from a single idea, and spreading ＿＿33.＿ to new ideas, showing the connections between them. The theory behind it is that by drawing the map on paper, we are made to ＿＿34.＿ the information clearly. Later as we look at the mind map again and again, we ＿＿35.＿ our knowledge of the information and then memorize it.

(　) **31** (A)vulnerable　　(B)inevitable (C)various　　(D)identical

(　) **32** (A)drill　　　(B)diagram　(C)frontier　(D)machine

(　) **33** (A)inside　　(B)over　　　(C)outward　(D)downward

(　) **34** (A)minimize　　(B)isolate　(C)schedule　(D)visualize

(　) **35** (A)reinforce　　(B)reverse　(C)reward　　(D)terminate

四、閱讀測驗

　　Ocean waves represent our planet's last untapped large-scale renewable energy resource. Over 70 % of the earth's surface is covered with water. The energy contained within waves has the potential to produce up to 80,000 TWh (10^{12} watt-hours) of electricity per year—sufficient to meet our global energy demand five times over.

　　No wonder the idea of extracting energy from ocean waves and turning it into electricity is an alluring one. The first serious attempt to do so dates back to 1974, when Stephen Salter of Edinburgh University came up with the idea of "ducks": house-sized buoys tethered to the sea floor that would convert the swell into rotational motion to drive generators. It failed, as have many subsequent efforts to perform the trick. But the idea of wave power will not go away, and the latest attempt—the brainchild of researchers at Oscilla Power, a firm based in Seattle—is trying to address head-on the reason why previous efforts have foundered.

　　This reason, according to Rahul Shendure, the firm's boss, is that those efforts took technologies developed for landlubbers (often as components of wind turbines) and tried to modify them for marine use. The consequence was kit too complicated and sensitive for the rough-and-tumble of life on the ocean waves, and also too vulnerable to corrosion. Better, he reckons, to start from scratch.

　　Instead of generators with lots of moving parts, Oscilla is developing ones that barely move at all. These employ a little-explored phenomenon called magnetostriction, in which ferromagnetic materials (things like iron, which can be magnetized strongly) change their shape slightly in the presence of a magnetic field. Like many physical processes, this also works in reverse. Apply stresses or strains to such a material and its magnetic characteristics alter. Do this in the presence of permanent magnets and a coil of wire, such as are found in conventional generators, and it will generate electricity.

(　　) **36** What are NOT true about ocean waves?

(A)They can be turned into electricity.

(B)Stephen Salter successfully used "ducks" to convert them into electricity.

(C)There have been attempts to convert them into electricity.

(D)Oscilla Power is one of the firms to convert them into electricity.

(　　) **37** What is true about Oscilla Power?

(A)It is based in Seattle.

(B)Its boss is Stephen Salter.

(C)It adopts a similar approach to other previous efforts.

(D)It copies some of the previous designs.

(　　) **38** What are true about Oscilla's generators?

(A)They have many moving parts.

(B)They move along with the waves.

(C)They do not have coils of wire.

(D)The phenomenon magnetostriction is employed.

(　　) **39** What are the advantages of ocean wave energy?

(A)It's easily available.

(B)It's easily tapped.

(C)It's renewable.

(D)It can be recycled.

(　　) **40** Why had the previous ocean wave energy conversion efforts failed? (A)Because they all relied on buoys.

(B)Because they were vulnerable to corrosion.

(C)Because they were not modified for marine use.

(D)Because they were not tethered to the sea floor.

解答與解析　答案標示為# 者，表官方曾公告更正該題答案。

一、字彙

1 (A)。一旦他捏造的數據曝光，這位著名科學家就失去了所有的可信性。
(A)可信性　　　　(B)相信
(C)輕信　　　　　(D)信條
解 credibility(n.)可信性；確實性
credence(n.)相信；信用；祭器臺；供桌
credulity(n.)輕信；易受騙
credo(n.)信條；信條的伴奏曲

2 (B)。妮可承認自己偷了錢，這讓所有人都感到震驚。
(A)調節　　　　　(B)承認
(C)進入　　　　　(D)採納
解 adjustment(n.)調節；調整；校正；調節器
admission(n.)承認；坦白；（學校、會場等的）進入許可；入場券
admittance(n.)進入；入場許可
adoption(n.)採納；採用；正式通過；收養

3 (D)。公眾對垃圾問題的漠不關心導致該市的公園一團糟。
(A)不信　　　　　(B)爭論
(C)挑剔　　　　　(D)漠不關心
解 disbelief(n.)不信；懷疑
dispute(n.)爭論；爭執；爭端
fastidiousness(n.)挑剔；過分講究
indifference(n.)漠不關心；冷淡；不感興趣；不重要

4 (C)。這些車在價格上可比，但在性能上卻相差甚遠。
(A)愛說話的　　　(B)緊密的
(C)可比的　　　　(D)有同情心的
解 communicative(adj.)愛說話的；暢談的；愛社交的；愛交際的
compact(adj.)緊密的；結實的；緊湊的；小巧的
comparable(adj.)可比的；比得上的；相當的；差不多的
compassionate(adj.)有同情心的；憐憫的；慈悲的

5 (B)。沒有辛勤工作和有能力的員工，任何新企業都無法成功。
(A)相容的　　　　(B)有能力的
(C)滿足的　　　　(D)讚賞的
解 compatible(adj.)相容的；可並立的；適合的；兼用式的
competent(adj.)有能力的；能幹的；能勝任的；稱職的
complacent(adj.)滿足的；自滿的
complimentary(adj.)讚賞的；恭維的；表示敬意的；問候的；贈送的

6 (C)。在實驗室中，測量物質時保持精確非常重要。
(A)潛在的　　　　(B)奇怪的
(C)精確的　　　　(D)首要的
解 potential(adj.)潛在的；可能的
peculiar(adj.)奇怪的；罕見的；特有的；獨特的
precise(adj.)精確的；準確的；確切的；明確的；清晰的

primary(adj.)首要的；主要的；初級的；初等的；基層的

7 (A)。 將飲酒年齡定為18歲的基本理由是，在該年齡之前，自我控制力和良好的判斷力仍在發展中。
(A)基本理由　　　(B)後退
(C)反擊　　　　　(D)突變
解 rationale(n.)基本理由；原理的闡述；邏輯依據
recession(n.)後退；退回；凹處；衰退
retort(n.)反擊；回嘴；反駁
revulsion(n.)突變；劇變；嫌惡；強烈反感

8 (D)。 顯微鏡可以放大某個細胞，讓我們的眼睛可以看到它。
(A)更改　　　　　(B)維持
(C)把……帶錯方向　(D)放大
解 modify(v.)更改；修改；緩和；減輕
maintain(v.)維持；保持；使繼續；維修；保養
mislead(v.)把……帶錯方向；把……引入歧途；使產生錯誤想法；使迷離
magnify(v.)放大；擴大；誇張；誇大

9 (D)。 經過一週的搜尋，人們發現那個被綁架的孩子是安全的，但犯罪者要求100萬美元來交換那個孩子。
(A)投入的　　　　(B)擊敗的
(C)執行的　　　　(D)被綁架的

解 invested(adj.)投入的；投資的
defeated(adj.)擊敗的
performed(adj.)執行的
kidnapped(adj.)被綁架的

10 (C)。 該國在邊境附近的軍事演習引發了人們擔憂可能會入侵，儘管該國聲稱是為了測試其武裝部隊的準備狀態。
(A)市郊　　　　　(B)衣櫥
(C)軍事演習　　　(D)參數
解 outskirt(n.)市郊；郊區；邊界
wardrobe(n.)衣櫥；衣櫃；藏衣室；全部戲裝
maneuver(n.)軍事演習；機動演習；調動；策略
parameter(n.)參數；因素；特徵；界限

二、文法及慣用語

11 (A)。 醫生已經治療這位癌症患者幾個月了，患者對治療的反應良好。
(A)已經治療（現在完成進行式）
(B)已經被治療（現在完成式）
(C)正在治療（現在進行式）
(D)治療（現在式）
解 本句的主詞是醫生，不是被治療的病人，所以選項(B)的被動語態為非。
本句的時間副詞片語是for several months，因此動詞時態要用現在完成式，故選項(A)has been treating為正確答案。

動詞的現在完成進行式（have/has＋been＋Ving）意指一件事「從過去一直持續至今，目前仍在進行的動作，而且可能會持續下去」。

12 (C)。今年，只有兩名應徵者參加了面試，但兩位應試者都不符合該職位的條件。

(A)兩者（都）

(B)（兩者之中）任何一個

(C)（兩者之中）無一個

(D)全體

解 both(pron.)兩者（都）；兩個（都）；雙方（都）

either(pron.)（兩者之中）任何一個

neither(pron.)（兩者之中）無一個

all(pron.)全體；一切；全部

對等連接詞but意指「但是、相反、對比」，用來表達轉折或是相反的語氣，之後所連接的子句通常有否定詞，而這四個選項中，只有neither有否定含意，故選項(C)為正確答案。

13 (D)。商業世界中有很多掩蓋行為，其中一些涉及欺詐和腐敗。

(A)它們中的一個

(B)它們中的一些

(C)那些中的一個

(D)那些中的一些

解 空格後是動詞和受詞，空格前沒有連接詞和主詞，若填入選項(A)或(B)，則形成一個沒有連接詞的兩個子句，這是錯誤的寫法，故均為非。

空格後的動詞是複數的，故選項(D)some of which為正確答案。

空格前的先行詞是複數名詞cover-ups，因此關係代名詞要用which。

（去年第19題也考類似的問題）

14 (D)。戴爾當時正在努力跟上老闆的要求。

(A)保持　　　　(B)壓制

(C)隱藏　　　　(D)跟上

解 to keep up 保持；繼續；使人熬夜

to keep down 壓制；保持低調；躺低；臥下

to keep in 隱藏；抑制；隱瞞；不外出

to keep up with 跟上；不落後；保持聯繫；與……並駕齊驅

15 (B)。幸福婚姻的關鍵包括不要求配偶做出改變。

(A)要求（動詞原形）

(B)要求（動名詞）

(C)要求（不定詞）

(D)要求（介系詞＋動名詞）

解 動詞include（包括）之後要接動名詞Ving，故選項(B)為正確答案。

備註：考題句主詞"the keys to happier marriage"是錯誤寫法，應該改為"the keys to a happier marriage"才對。

16 (C)。 旅行在文化與我們不同的外國是很有趣的。
(A)和　　　　　(B)那一個
(C)它們的　　　(D)什麼
解 空格前的先行詞是foreign lands，空格後有名詞和動詞，所以空格內不能再填入關係代名詞which，而需填入所有格關係代名詞whose，故選項(C)為正確答案。

17 (A)。 如果你有任何疑問，請立即與我們聯繫。
(A)可能　　　　(B)將
(C)能　　　　　(D)將
解 Should you have any questions, …= If you should have any questions, ...
would, could, will這些助動詞放在句首時，都是疑問句，句尾應該要有問號，但本句句尾不是問號，故選項(B)、(C)和(D)均為非。

18 (B)。 佐伊17歲時，離開路易斯安那州的家人，獨自搬到了紐約。
(A)將……擱置（過去式）
(B)離開（現在分詞）
(C)將……擱置（現在分詞）
(D)離開（不定詞）
解 leave aside 將……擱置；將……放在一邊；不考慮
leave behind 離開；拋開；撇下；落下；留下
選項(A)和(C)的含意跟原句語義不符，故均為非。

本句中的"leaving behind ..."是一個分詞構句，由一個句子簡化而來：Zoey…was 17, leaving behind her family in Louisiana. = Zoey…was 17 and she left behind her family in Louisiana.當兩個子句的主詞相同時，可以將第二個子句簡化，省略連接詞和主詞，並且將動詞改為現在分詞，故選項(B)為正確答案。
不定詞片語"to leave behind..."放在本句句尾意指「為了離開」，用來說明move的目的，故選項(D)是正確答案。
本題官方解答為(B)，但筆者認為(B)(D)皆正確。

19 (D)。 如果你對他臭名昭著的行為有什麼話要說，請當著他的面說。向我抱怨是沒有用的。
(A)更不用說
(B)玩得開心
(C)不管你喜歡不喜歡
(D)當著他的面說
解 say nothing of it 更不用說；而且還；遑論
enjoy yourself 玩得開心
like it or not 不管你喜歡不喜歡
say it to his face 當著他的面說

20 (A)。 進入音樂廳的時候，我注意到正在提供茶點。
(A)在……的時候　(B)關於
(C)向　　　　　　(D)……的

解 on(prep.)在……的時候；在……
後立即
about(prep.)關於；對於
to(prep.)向；往；到
of(prep.)……的；屬於；用……
做成的
refreshment(n.)茶點；便餐；飲
料；恢復活力

21 (D)。 傲慢的人只有透過孩子的眼
睛看世界時，他才能真正欣賞自然
之美。
(A)他
(B)（連接詞）他
(C)他（助動詞）
(D)（助動詞）他
解 only if放在句首時，後面的主要
子句要變成倒裝句，助動詞要放
在主詞的前面，例: Only if you
study hard will you get good grades.
= Only when you study hard will
you get good grades. 你只有努力
讀書，才會得到好成績。
故選項(D)為正確答案。

22 (B)。 儘管當你第一次見到艾比
時，她可能看起來是一個簡單的
人，但她的內心遠比表面上看到的
要複雜。
(A)（錯誤寫法）
(B)比表面上看起來還要複雜
(C)（錯誤寫法）
(D)（錯誤寫法）
解 more than meets the eye 比表面
上看起來還要複雜

選項(A)的動詞meet沒有加s，
故為非。
選項(C)的then應該改為than才對。
選項(D)的yet應該改為than才對。

23 (A)。 那家餐廳想方設法在這場疫
情中存活下來。
(A)想方設法　　(B)一點也不
(C)決不　　　　(D)根本
解 one way or another 想方設法；用
某種方法；以某種方式；無論如何
by no means 一點也不；絕不；
絲毫不
in no way 決不
at all 根本；到底；完全

24 (C)。 「我兒子不介意水果，但蔬
菜就完全不同了。」這意思是我兒
子吃水果而不吃蔬菜。
(A)我兒子不喜歡水果，但他喜歡蔬
菜。
(B)我兒子不喜歡水果或蔬菜。
(C)我兒子吃水果但不吃蔬菜。
(D)我兒子不吃水果，但他吃蔬菜。
解 a whole different story 完全不
同；另一回事
doesn't mind fruit 不介意水果，
也就是吃水果的意思，故選項
(C)為正確答案。

25 (B)。 「泰勒並不亞於他的兄弟聰
明」與「泰勒和他的兄弟一樣聰
明」的意思相同。
(A)比……更笨
(B)與……一樣聰明

解答與解析

(C)比……更敏銳

(D)與……一樣笨

解 no less intelligent than 與……同樣聰明；聰明不亞於

as smart as 與……同樣聰明

三、克漏字

　　總的來說，簡和菲利普是一對幸福的夫妻。然而，他們確實為了一個不同的觀點而爭執。他們對於家人應該如何遵循季節性假期的傳統有不同意見。在她看來，對禮物的重視使得那些在假期期間過度收費且唯利是圖的零售商們賺很多錢。此外，人們應該留意自己的開支，並避免不必要的預算赤字。因此，她希望自己的家沒有這樣的習俗，並希望她的孩子們戒掉送禮和為復活節做彩色蛋等傳統。儘管菲利普理解她的擔憂，但他更喜歡傳統的慶祝節日的方式。他認為孩子們喜歡那些跟假期相關的習俗活動。

　　備註：本文第三句的in her opinions 是錯誤的寫法，應該改為in her opinion 才對。

26 (A)。(A)不同意　(B)緩和　(C)不足額　(D)和睦

解 dissent(n.)不同意；異議

relief(n.)緩和；減輕；解除；輕鬆；寬心

deficit(n.)不足額；赤字

harmony(n.)和睦；融洽；一致；和諧

27 (B)。(A)在……地點　(B)加之於　(C)被　(D)……的

解 at(prep.)在……地點；在……時刻

on(prep.)加之於；重疊於

by(prep.)被；由；靠；用

of(prep.)……的；屬於；用……做成的

名詞emphasis (強調)之後與介系詞on/upon連用，故選項(B)為正確答案。

28 (C)。(A)財富　(B)過剩　(C)赤字　(D)適當

解 wealth(n.)財富；財產；資源；富有；豐富；大量

surplus(n.)過剩；剩餘物；剩餘額；盈餘；公積金

shortfall(n.)赤字；不足額；差額

adequacy(n.)適當；恰當；足夠

29 (D)。(A)渴望　(B)使緊密聯繫　(C)促使　(D)戒掉

解 desire(v.)渴望；要求

affiliate(v.)使緊密聯繫；使隸屬於；接納……為成員

prompt(v.)促使；激勵；慫恿；引起；激起

abstain(v.)戒掉；避免；避開；棄權

30 (D)。(A)負擔　(B)部分　(C)鎮定劑　(D)活動

解 burden(n.)負擔；重負；重擔；沉重的責任

section(n.)部分；片；地區；
節；款；項
downer(n.)鎮定劑；掃興的人或事
activity(n.)活動；活躍；行動

　　記住訊息是我們所有人都需要做
的事情。提高記憶力的方法有很多種，
其中之一是心智圖。心智圖就像一張思
考圖，從一個單一的想法開始，然後向
外傳播新的想法，並顯示它們之間的連
結。其背後的理論是，透過在紙上繪製
地圖，我們可以清楚地把資訊視覺化。
以後，當我們一遍又一遍地查看心智圖
時，我們會強化對資訊的了解，於是就
記住它了。

31 (C)。(A)易受傷的　(B)不可避免
的　(C)許多的　(D)同一的
解 vulnerable(adj.)易受傷的；易受
責難的；有弱點的；難防守的；
脆弱的
inevitable(adj.)不可避免的；必
然的
various(adj.)許多的；不同的；各
種各樣的，形形色色的；好幾個的
identical(adj.)同一的；完全相
同的；完全相似的

32 (B)。(A)操練　(B)圖表　(C)國境
(D)機器
解 drill(n.)操練；訓練；鑽頭
diagram(n.)圖表；圖解；曲線圖
frontier(n.)國境；邊境；邊疆
新領域
machine(n.)機器；機械；計算機

33 (C)。(A)在裡面　(B)在上方　(C)
向外　(D)向下
解 inside (adv.) 在裡面；往裡面
over (adv.) 在上方；在上空；倒下
outward (adv.) 向外；出海；出港
downward (adv.) 向下；日趨沒
落地

34 (D)。(A)使減到最少　(B)使孤立
(C)將……列表　(D)使看得見
解 minimize(v.)使減到最少；使縮
到最小；低估；小看；極度輕視
isolate(v.)使孤立；使脫離
schedule(v.)將……列表；將
……列入計畫（或時間）表
visualize(v.)使看得見；使顯
現；使形象化；想像；設想

35 (A)。(A)加強　(B)顛倒　(C)報答
(D)使停止
解 reinforce(v.)加強；增援；增加；
補充
reverse(v.)顛倒；翻轉；使倒
退；使倒轉；使反向
reward(v.)報答；報償；酬謝；
獎勵
terminate(n.)使停止；使結束；
使終止；使結尾

四、閱讀測驗

　　海浪代表了地球上最後一個未開發
的大規模再生能源。地球表面70％以上
被水覆蓋。波浪中蘊含的能量每年有可
能產生高達80,000太瓦/時（10^{12}瓦時）

解答與解析

的電力，足以滿足全球能源需求的五倍以上。

難怪從海浪中提取能量並將其轉化為電能的想法是一個誘人的想法。第一次認真的嘗試可以追溯到1974年，當時愛丁堡大學的史蒂芬·索爾特（Stephen Salter）提出了「鴨子」的想法：將房屋大小的浮筒繫在海底，然後它們會將洶湧的浪濤轉化為旋轉的運動以驅動發電機。但它失敗了，隨後的許多嘗試也都失敗了。但波浪能的想法不會消失，最新的嘗試是總部位於西雅圖的Oscilla Power公司研究人員的創意，正試圖專門處理先前努力失敗的原因。

該公司老闆拉胡爾·謝杜爾（Rahul Shendure）表示，原因在於這些努力採用了不懂航海的人所開發的技術（通常作為風力渦輪機的組件），並試圖對其進行修改以用於海洋用途。結果是該套件對於海浪上坎坷的生活來說過於複雜和敏感，而且也太容易受到腐蝕。他認為最好從頭開始。

Oscilla正在開發幾乎不用移動的發電機，而不是有大量移動零件的發電機。它們採用了一種鮮為人知的現象，稱為磁致伸縮，意指鐵磁性材料（例如鐵，可以被強烈磁化）在磁場中會輕微改變其形狀。與許多物理過程一樣，這也是反向運作。對這種材料施加壓力或張力，其磁性特性就會改變。在永久磁鐵和線圈中如此做，例如在傳統發電機中發現的一樣，然後它將產生電力。

36 (B)。關於海浪的說法，下列何者是不正確的？

(A)它們可以被轉換為電能。

(B)史蒂芬·索爾特成功地利用「鴨子」將其轉化為電能。

(C)人們曾經嘗試將它們轉化為電能。

(D)Oscilla Power是將其轉化為電能的公司之一。

解 從第二段第三句："It failed, as have many subsequent efforts to perform the trick."可知，這個嘗試失敗了，故選項(B)的敘述不正確。

37 (A)。關於Oscilla Power公司，下列何者為真？

(A)總部位於西雅圖。

(B)它的老闆是史蒂芬·索爾特。

(C)它採用了與先前其他工作類似的方法。

(D)它複製了一些先前的設計。

解 從第二段最後一句："But the idea of wave power will not go away, and the latest attempt—the brainchild of researchers at Oscilla Power, a firm based in Seattle—is trying to address head-on the reason why previous efforts have foundered."可知，選項(A)的敘述是正確的。

Oscilla Power的老闆是Rahul Shendure，故選項(B)為非。

從第三段最後一句："Better, he reckons, to start from scratch."可知，這間公司要從頭開始，

並不會採用先前其他類似的方法，也不會複製先前的設計，故選項(C)和(D)的敘述均為非。

38 (D)。關於Oscilla發電機，下列何者為真？

(A)它們有許多移動的零件。

(B)它們隨著海浪移動。

(C)它們沒有電線圈。

(D)它們使用磁致伸縮現象。

解 從第四段第一句和第二句："Instead of generators with lots of moving parts, Oscilla is developing ones that barely move at all.These employ a little-explored phenomenon called magnetostriction, in which ferromagnetic materials (things like iron, which can be magnetized strongly) change their shape slightly in the presence of a magnetic field."可知，選項(A)、(B)和(C)的敘述均為非，只有選項(D)的敘述是正確的。

備註：

a.本題考題問句中的are是錯誤的，應該改為is才對。疑問詞what當主詞時，應該視為單數的名詞，例如第37題的考題句。

b.選項(D)phenomenon magnetostriction應該改為phenomenon of magnetostriction]

39 (C)。海洋波浪能源有哪些優點？

(A)它很容易取得。

(B)它很容易被開發。

(C)它是可再生的。

(D)它是可回收的。

解 從第一段第一句："Ocean waves represent our planet's last untapped large-scale renewable energy resource."可知，選項(C)為正確答案。

40 (B)。為什麼之前海浪能源轉換的努力都失敗了？

(A)因為他們都依賴浮筒。

(B)因為它們容易腐蝕。

(C)因為它們沒有改裝以供海洋使用。

(D)因為它們沒有被綁在海底。

解 從第三段第二句："The consequence was kit too complicated and sensitive for the rough-and-tumble of life on the ocean waves, and also too vulnerable to corrosion."可知，選項(B)為正確答案。

重要單字片語

a. untapped(adj.)未開發的；未利用的

b. TWH = Tera Watt Hour 太(拉)瓦時，1TWH = 10^{12}瓦時

c. sufficient(adj.)足夠的；充分的

d. extract(v.)取出；挑出；拔出

e. alluring(adj.)誘人的；迷人的；極吸引人的

f. buoy(n.)浮標；浮筒；救生圈；救生衣

g. tether(v.)(用繩、鏈等)拴

解答與解析

h. convert(v.)轉變；變換

i. swell(n.)(浪濤的)洶湧；(土地的)隆起鼓起；膨脹；腫脹；增大；壯大

j. rotational(adj.)旋轉的；輪流的；循環的；輪作的

k. motion(n.)運動；移動

l. generator(n.)發電機；產生器

m. subsequent(adj.)後來的；其後的；隨後的

n. brainchild(n.)創作；獨創的觀念

o. address(v.)處理；對付；向……致詞；稱呼；給……寫信

p. head-on (adv.) 正面針對地；迎頭；頭朝前地

q. founder(v.)失敗；垮掉；崩潰；(船)浸水而沉沒

r. landlubber(n.)不懂航海之人；新水手；不習慣航海的人

s. turbine(n.)渦輪機；葉輪機

t. marine(adj.)海的；海生的；海產的；船舶的，航海的；海運的；海事的

u. kit(n.)配套元件；成套工具；工具箱；服裝；用品

v. rough-and-tumble混戰；拼搶；爭奪；亂作一團

w. vulnerable(adj.)易受傷的；易受責難的；有弱點的；難防守的

x. corrosion(n.)腐蝕；侵入；漸失；衰敗

y. reckon(v.)認為；把……看作；覺得；猜想

z. start from scratch 從頭開始；從起跑線開始；從零開始

aa. magnetostriction(n.)磁致伸縮；磁性變化

bb. ferromagnetic(adj.)強磁性的

cc. reverse(n.)相反；背面；反面

dd. alter(v.)改變；修改

ee. coil(n.)線圈；繞組；一捲；一圈

112年　臺灣菸酒從業評價職位人員

一、字彙

( ) **1** Instead of _____ tasks, Paul prefers doing work that requires creativity.
(A)repetitive
(B)intelligent
(C)plastered
(D)momentary

( ) **2** Your annual subscription ends in two months. _____ your subscription now and get a 5% discount.
(A)Instill
(B)Renew
(C)Quarrel
(D)Vacate

( ) **3** The contract states that all _____ are required to pay the rent in full by the fifth day of each month.
(A)peddlers
(B)inspectors
(C)assistants
(D)tenants

( ) **4** People attribute his success to diligence and _____ . He always works hard and never gives up.
(A)variation
(B)deficiency
C)perseverance
(D)merriment

( ) **5** Not sure what her grandmother's diamond necklace was worth, Mary asked an expert to _____ it.
(A)appraise
(B)terminate
(C)remit
(D)indulge

( ) **6** As a football player, he has past his _____ and can no longer play as well as he used to.
(A)surface
(B)prime
(C)lineage
(D)clearance

( ) **7** It is _____ that all students take at least two years of Math before they graduate. Every student has to do that.
(A)mandatory   (B)extraneous
(C)figurative   (D)subsidized

( ) **8** The word may denote something too _____ to be understood by a middle school student.
(A)infiltrated   (B)rudimentary
(C)profound   (D)frugal

二、文法測驗

( ) **9** We have been committed to _____ the best service in town for the past 25 years.
(A)deliver   (B)being delivered
(C)be delivered   (D)delivering

( ) **10** Maybe we should just walk to the store. The bus is not coming___ , and the store is not that for away.
(A)sometimes near   (B)anytime soon
(C)sooner than sometime   (D)no time near

( ) **11** You _____ if you are going to be two hours late. The meeting will be over before you get there.
(A)might as well not go   (B)not go as well
(C)might not go to well   (D)as well as don't go

( ) **12** Mary said she wouldn't want to eat bamboo _____ a panda.
(A)even though she were   (B)even if she were
(C)even when she was   (D)even so being

( ) **13** _____ you waste, _____ you are going to reach your goal.
(A)More time...like less
(B)More than the time...less than likely
(C)The time more...like less than
(D)The more time... the less likely

(　) **14** Mrs. Wilma had her air conditioner _____ because it was starting to make loud noises again.

(A)checking　　　　　　　　(B)be checking

(C)been checking　　　　　　(D)checked

(　) **15** _____ he is taking art lessons says that he is serious about going to art school.

(A)That is　　　　　　　　(B)That is fact

(C)The fact that　　　　　　(D)The fact is

三、克漏字測驗

When the United States first fired a missile from an armed Predator drone in Afghanistan on November 14, 2001, it was clear that warfare had forever changed. During the two decades that followed, drones became the most iconic ____16.____ of the war on terror. Highly sophisticated, multimillion-dollar US drones were repeatedly used in targeted killing campaigns. But their use worldwide was __ ____17.____ powerful nations. Then, as the navigation systems and wireless technologies in hobbyist drones and consumer electronics ____18.____ , a second style of military drone appeared－not in Washington, but in Istanbul. And it caught the world's ____19.____ in Ukraine in 2022, when it proved itself capable of holding back one of the toughest militaries on the planet. The Bayraktar TB2 drone, a Turkish-made aircraft from the Baykar corporation, marks a new ____ 20.____ in the still-new era of drone warfare. Cheap, widely available drones have changed how smaller nations fight modern wars.

(　) **16** (A)gesture　　(B)instrument　　(C)partition　(D)misfortune

(　) **17** (A)limited to　(B)in contrast with (C)on top of　(D)separate from

(　) **18** (A)released　(B)invented　　(C)improved　(D)replaced

(　) **19** (A)emergence (B)criteria　　(C)trial　　　(D)attention

(　) **20** (A)dilution　(B)fence　　　(C)chapter　　(D)wafer

四、閱讀測驗

Is your glass half-empty or half-full? How you answer this age-old question about positive thinking may reflect your outlook on life, your attitude toward yourself, and whether you're optimistic or pessimistic, and it may even affect your health. Indeed, some studies show that personality traits such as optimism and pessimism can affect many areas of your health and well-being. The positive thinking that usually comes with optimism is a key part of effective stress management. And effective stress management is associated with many health benefits. If you tend to be pessimistic, don't despair. You can learn positive thinking skills.

Positive thinking doesn't mean that you ignore life's less pleasant situations. Positive thinking just means that you approach unpleasantness in a more positive and productive way. You can learn to turn negative thinking into positive thinking. The process is simple, but it does take time and practice. If you want to become more optimistic and engage in more positive thinking, first identify areas of your life that you usually think negatively about, whether it's work, your daily commute, life changes or a relationship. You can start small by focusing on one area to approach in a more positive way. Think of a positive thought to manage your stress instead of a negative one. Also, aim to exercise for about 30 minutes on most days of the week. Exercise can positively affect mood and reduce stress. Follow a healthy diet to fuel your mind and body. Get enough sleep. And learn techniques to manage stress. Next, surround yourself with positive people. Make sure those in your life are positive, supportive people you can depend on to give helpful advice and feedback. Negative people may increase your stress level and make you doubt your ability to manage stress in healthy ways. Finally, practice positive self- talk. Start by following one simple rule: Don't say anything to yourself that you wouldn't say to anyone else. Be gentle and encouraging with yourself. If a negative thought enters your mind, evaluate it rationally and respond with affirmations of what is good about you. Think about things you're thankful for in your life.

( ) **21** What is the best title for the passage?
(A)Age-old philosophical questions
(B)Ways to practice positive thinking
(C)The benefits of philosophical thinking
(D)Your sleep and stress management

( ) **22** Which of the following statements is **NOT** supported by the passage?
(A)People can learn to be positive thinkers.
(B)Your friends and family may influence your thinking.
(C)People are born to be optimistic or pessimistic.
(D)Your physical well-being is related to your thinking.

( ) **23** What can be inferred from the passage?
(A)People who think positively have encountered less difficulties in life.
(B)Your personality traits can be the result of your work and income.
(C)Physical exercise, food, and sleep may affect how people manage stress.
(D)Less healthy people often associate themselves with successful and supportive people.

( ) **24** Which of the following is mentioned as helpful to learning positive thinking?
(A)Practice yoga and meditate regularly.
(B)Eat fat-free food and get up early every day.
(C)Expect quick results when learning to think positively.
(D)Make friends with optimistic and supportive people.

( ) **25** Where is the passage most likely taken from?
(A)An article on how to manage stress and live a healthy life
(B)A paper about life philosophy and people's achievement
(C)A report of a comparison of healthy and unhealthy people
(D)An on-line advertisement for a fitness center

解答與解析　答案標示為# 者，表官方曾公告更正該題答案。

一、字彙

1 (A)。保羅更喜歡做需要創造力的工作，而不是重複性的作業。
(A)重覆的　　　　(B)聰明的
(C)爛醉的　　　　(D)短暫的
解 repetitive(adj.)重覆的；嘮叨的
intelligent(adj.)聰明的；有才智的；明智的；有理性的
plastered(adj.)爛醉的；抹過灰泥的
momentary(adj.)短暫的；瞬間的；隨時會發生的；時時刻刻的

2 (B)。你的年度訂閱將在兩個月後結束。立即續訂可獲得5%的折扣。
(A)逐漸灌輸　　　(B)續訂
(C)爭吵　　　　　(D)空出
解 instill(v.)逐漸灌輸；徐徐滴入；徐徐地教導
renew(v.)續訂；續借；重新開始；繼續；使更新；使復原；換新；重複
quarrel(v.)爭吵；不和；埋怨；責備；挑剔
vacate(v.)空出；搬出；使撤退

3 (D)。合約規定，所有房客必須在每月的第五天之前支付全額租金。
(A)小販　　　　　(B)檢查員
(C)助手　　　　　(D)房客
解 peddler(n.)小販；兜售者；傳播者
inspector(n.)檢查員；視察員；督察員；巡官

assistant(n.)助手；助理；助教；店員
tenant(n.)房客；佃戶；承租人；住戶；居住者

4 (C)。人們把他的成功歸功於勤奮和堅持不懈。他總是努力工作，從不放棄。
(A)變化　　　　　(B)不足
(C)堅持不懈　　　(D)歡樂
解 variation(n.)變化；變動；變化的程度；差別
deficiency(n.)不足；缺乏；不足的數額；缺點
perseverance(n.)堅持不懈；堅忍不拔
merriment(n.)歡樂；歡笑；歡鬧

5 (A)。瑪麗不確定祖母的鑽石項鍊值多少錢，於是請專家來估價。
(A)估價　　　　　(B)使停止
(C)寬恕　　　　　(D)沉迷於
解 appraise(v.)估價；估計；估量；評價
terminate(v.)使停止；使結束；使終止；使結尾；解僱
remit(v.)寬恕；赦免；豁免；免除
indulge(v.)沉迷於；滿足；使高興；縱容；遷就

6 (B)。作為一名足球員，他已經過了全盛時期，不能再像以前那樣踢球了。
(A)表面　　　　　(B)全盛時期
(C)家系　　　　　(D)清除

解 surface(n.)表面；水面；外觀；外表
prime(n.)全盛時期；最初；黎明；春天；青年；精華；最好的部分
lineage(n.)家系；後裔；世系
clearance(n.)清除；清掃；出空；空地；空隙；結關

7 (A)。所有學生在畢業前必須至少學習兩年的數學課程，這是強制性的。每個學生都必須這樣做。
(A)強制的　　(B)體外的
(C)比喻的　　(D)得到補貼的
解 mandatory(adj.)強制的；義務的；命令的；指令的
extraneous(adj.)體外的；外來的；無關的
figurative(adj.)比喻的；形容多的；修飾豐富的
subsidized(adj.)得到補貼的；有津貼的；受資助的

8 (C)。這個字可能表示一些太深奧的東西，以至於中學生無法理解。
(A)被滲透的　　(B)基本的
(C)深刻的　　(D)節約的
解 infiltrated(adj.)被滲透的
rudimentary(adj.)基本的；初步的；早期的；發展未完全的；退化的
profound(adj.)深奧的；深刻的；深切的；深度的；淵博的；造詣深的
frugal(adj.)節約的；儉樸的；花錢少的，廉價的

二、文法測驗

9 (D)。過去25年來，我們致力於提供城裡最好的服務。
(A)提供（動詞原形）
(B)提供（被動語態分詞）
(C)提供（被動語態動詞原形）
(D)提供（動名詞）
解 be committed to something致力於做某件事情，介系詞to之後要接名詞或動名詞Ving，故選項(D)為正確答案。

10 (B)。也許我們應該步行去商店。公共汽車不會很快來，而且商店也不遠。
(A)有時靠近
(B)很快
(C)比某個時候更快
(D)沒有時間靠近
解 sometimes near 有時靠近
anytime soon 很快；不久；立刻；即將；最近
sooner than sometime 比某個時候更快
no time near 沒有時間靠近

11 (A)。如果你要遲到兩個小時，你還不如不去。會議在你到達之前就結束了。
(A)還不如不去　　(B)也不去
(C)（錯誤寫法）　　(D)以及不去
解 might as well not go 還不如不去
not go as well 也不去
might not go to well 錯誤寫法，沒有意義。go to之後通常接名

詞，不會接副詞well。

as well as don't go 以及不去

12 (B)。瑪麗說，即使她是熊貓，她也不想吃竹子。

(A)（錯誤寫法）

(B)即使她是

(C)（錯誤寫法）

(D)（錯誤寫法）

解 even though she were錯誤寫法。

even though（雖然）其後所接的子句是事實，其含意是「雖然事實如此……」，但she were是假設語氣的句型，所以不能接在ever though之後。

even if she were 即使她是。

even if引導假設的事情，其所接的子句不是事實。

even when she were 錯誤寫法，even when不能引導假設語氣的句子。

even so being 錯誤寫法，even so（即使如此）通常放在句首，其後要接逗點，例：She had a fever yesterday. Even so, she went to work. 她昨天發燒。即使如此，她還是去上班。

13 (D)。你浪費的時間越多，你實現目標的可能性就越小。

(A)（錯誤寫法）

(B)（錯誤寫法）

(C)（錯誤寫法）

(D)更多時間…更少可能

解 the more...the more/less是一個特殊句型，表示「越……，越……」的意思。

選項(A)的錯誤有兩個，一是like應該改為likely，二是less應該放在likely的前面。

more than...less than的寫法是錯誤的，than是一個連接詞，其後要接子句，故選項(B)和(C)均為非。

14 (D)。威爾瑪夫人讓人檢查了她的空調，因為它又開始發出很大的噪音。

(A)檢查（現在分詞）

(B)檢查（現在進行式，be動詞原形）

(C)檢查（完成式現在分詞）

(D)檢查（過去分詞）

解 空格前的名詞是冷氣空調，它是被人檢查的，應該用過去分詞來修飾之，故選項(D)為正確答案。

15 (C)。他正在上藝術課這一事實表明他對於去讀藝術學校是認真的。

(A)那是　　　　(B)那是事實

(C)這……的事實　(D)這事實是

解 the fact that之後所接的子句就是前面的fact，文法中稱為同位語，可以當主詞或受詞，通常that不會省略。

空格後已經有主詞和動詞，因此空格內不能再填入動詞，故選項(A)、(B)和(D)的寫法都是錯誤的。

本句是由一個主要子句和兩的名詞子句組成的複雜句，説明如下：

主要子句的主詞	the fact that he is taking art lessons
主要子句的動詞	says（説明）
主要子句的受詞	that he is serious about going to art school
第一個名詞子句的主詞	he
第一個名詞子句的動詞	is taking
第一個名詞子句的受詞	art lessons
第二個名詞子句的主詞	he
第二個名詞子句的動詞	is
第二個名詞子句的主詞補語	serious

三、克漏字測驗

　　2001年11月14日，當美國首次在阿富汗用武裝「掠奪者」無人機發射飛彈時，戰爭顯然已經永遠改變了。在隨後的二十年裡，無人機成為反恐戰爭中最具代表性的工具。價值數百萬美元高度先進的美國無人機被多次用於定點清除行動。但它們在全球的使用僅限於強國。然後，隨著業餘無人機和消費性電子產品中導航系統和無線技術的改進，第二種軍用無人機出現了－－不是在華盛頓，而是在伊斯坦堡。2022年，它在烏克蘭引起了全世界的關注，證明了自己有能力阻止地球上最強大的軍隊之一。拜拉克塔爾TB2無人機是巴依卡爾（Baykar）公司在土耳其製造的飛機，它寫下無人機戰爭新時代的新篇章。廉價、廣泛使用的無人機改變了小國打現代戰爭的方式。

16 (B)。(A)姿勢　(B)工具　(C)分開　(D)不幸

解 gesture(n.)姿勢；手勢；姿態；表示
instrument(n.)工具；手段；儀器；器具；器械；樂器
partition(n.)分開；分割；劃分；部分；隔板；隔牆
misfortune(n.)不幸；惡運；不幸的事；災難

17 (A)。(A)限制在　(B)對照之下　(C)除……之外　(D)與……分離
解 limited to 限制在；受限於
in contrast with對照之下；與……成對比
on top of 除……之外
separate from 與……分離

18 (C)。(A)釋放　(B)發明　(C)改進　(D)把……放回
解 release(v.)釋放；解放；放鬆；鬆開；發射
invent(v.)發明；創造；捏造；虛構

improve(v.)改進；改善；增進
replace(v.)把…放回；取代；以……代替

19 (D)。(A)出現　(B)標準　(C)試
(D)注意
圝 emergence(n.)出現；浮現；露頭
criteria(n.)[criterion的複數] 標
準；準則；尺度
trial(n.)試；試用；試驗；考
驗；磨煉
attention(n.)注意；注意力；專
心；照料

20 (C)。(A)稀釋　(B)柵欄　(C)章
(D)晶圓
圝 dilution(n.)稀釋
fence(n.)柵欄；籬笆
chapter(n.)章；回；重要時期
wafer(n.)晶圓；薄片；圓片；
晶片；薄酥餅；威化餅；聖餅

四、閱讀測驗

你的杯子是半空的還是半滿的？
你如何回答這個關於積極思考的古老問
題，可能會反映你的人生觀、你對自己
的態度以及你是樂觀還是悲觀，甚至可
能影響你的健康。事實上，一些研究表
明，像樂觀和悲觀這些個性特徵會影響
你健康和福祉的許多方面。通常伴隨樂
觀而來的積極思考是有效壓力管理的關
鍵部分。有效的壓力管理與許多健康好
處有關。如果你傾向於悲觀，請不要絕
望。你可以學習積極思考的技能。

積極思考並不代表你忽略生活中
不太愉快的情況。積極思考只是意味著
你以更積極、更有成效的方式處理不愉
快的事情。你可以學習將消極思考轉變
為積極思考。這個過程很簡單，但確實
需要時間和練習。如果你想變得更加樂
觀並進行更積極的思考，首先要確定你
生活中經常產生消極想法的領域，無論
是工作、日常通勤、生活變化還是人際
關係上。你可以從小事做起，專注於一
個領域，以更積極的方式處理。想出一
個正面的想法來管理你的壓力，而不是
負面的想法。此外，以一週大約每天鍛
鍊30分鐘左右為目標。運動可以積極
影響情緒並減輕壓力。遵循健康的飲食
習慣，為你的身心提供能量。確保充足
的睡眠。並學習管理壓力的技巧。接下
來，跟積極的人相處。確定你生活中的
人都是積極的、給予你幫助的人，你可
以依靠他們提供你有用的建議和反饋。
消極的人可能會增加你的壓力水平，並
使你懷疑自己以健康方式管理壓力的能
力。最後，練習積極的自我對話。先從
遵循一個簡單規則開始：不要對自己說
任何你不會對別人說的話。溫柔地鼓勵
自己。如果你的腦海中出現了負面的想
法，請理性地評估它，並以肯定你的優
點來回應。想想生活中你所感激的事。

21 (B)。本文的最佳標題是什麼？
(A)古老的哲學問題
(B)學習積極思考的方法
(C)哲學思考的好處
(D)你的睡眠與壓力管理

解 本文第二段説明將消極思考轉變為積極思考的三個方法，故選項(B)為正確答案。

22 (C)。本文不支持下列哪一項敘述？
(A)人們可以學習成為正向的思考者。
(B)你的朋友和家人可能會影響你的想法。
(C)人生來就是樂觀的或悲觀的。
(D)你的身體健康與你的思考有關。

解 選項(A)、(B)和(D)的敘述在文章中都可以找到，只有選項(C)的敘述並非作者的觀點。

23 (C)。從本文可以推斷出什麼？
(A)積極思考的人在生活中遇到較少的困難。
(B)你的性格特徵可能是你的工作和收入的結果。
(C)體能活動、食物和睡眠可能會影響人們管理壓力的方式。
(D)比較不健康的人經常將自己與成功且支持他人的人聯繫在一起。

解 從第二段第9、10和11句話："Exercise can positively affect mood and reduce stress. Follow a healthy diet to fuel your mind and body. Get enough sleep."可知，選項(C)為正確答案。

24 (D)。下列哪一項被認為有助於學習積極思考？
(A)定期練習瑜珈和冥想。
(B)吃無脂肪食物並每天早起。
(C)學習正向思考時，希望能快速見效。
(D)跟樂觀和給予幫助的人交朋友。

解 從第二段第14句話："Make sure those in your life are positive, supportive people you can depend on to give helpful advice and feedback."可知，選項(D)為正確答案。

25 (A)。本文最有可能選自哪裡？
(A)一篇關於如何管理壓力與健康生活的文章
(B)一篇關於人生哲學和人們成就的論文。
(C)健康人和不健康人的比較報告。
(D)健身中心的線上廣告。

解 選項(B)、(C)和(D)的敘述和本文所談的內容沒有關係，故均為非。

解答與解析

112年 中華郵政職階人員（專業職（二）內勤）

一、字彙測驗

( ) **1** The latest _____ of this software is superior to all the previous ones.
(A)priority   (B)anniversary
(C)version   (D)fiction

( ) **2** To get hired in this _____ industry, you need to have some unique traits that make you stand out from your fellow candidates.
(A)obvious   (B)responsible
(C)imaginary   (D)competitive

( ) **3** An _____ to driving during rush hour is taking public transportation.
(A)achievement   (B)alternative
(C)objection   (D)inspiration

( ) **4** In the speech contest, Jane and Bill won first place and third place _____ .
(A)barely   (B)particularly
(C)gradually   (D)respectively

( ) **5** Walking in the city after the tragic event, you can see that many pedestrians were weighed down by a heavy sense of _____ .
(A)joy   (B)sorrow
(C)delight   (D)excitement

( ) **6** At the party, her delightful smile was so _____ that it influenced the mood of everyone present.
(A)dismal   (B)infectious
(C)unapproachable   (D)noncommunicable

( ) **7** In the company, he stood out as a _____ employee, consistently punctual and exceptionally responsible with tasks.
(A)tardy　　　　　　　　(B)lazy
(C)careless　　　　　　　(D)diligent

( ) **8** Regrettably, they decided to _____ the party due to unforeseen circumstances.
(A)cancel　　　　　　　(B)attend
(C)enhance　　　　　　 (D)decorate

二、文法測驗

( ) **9** _____ everybody's effort, the concert was a big success.
(A)In addition to　　　　(B)Because
(C)In spite of　　　　　 (D)Thanks to

( ) **10** It was an old friend _____ Tom came across in the park yesterday.
(A)which　　　　　　　(B)that
(C)what　　　　　　　 (D)where

( ) **11** She _____ all her homework assignments yet, has she?
(A)hadn't finished　　　 (B)hasn't finished
(C)don't finish　　　　　(D)didn't finish

( ) **12** Despite _____ incredibly tired, he continued working on the project.
(A)be　　　　　　　　(B)being
(C)been　　　　　　　 (D)to be

( ) **13** During the weekends, he likes hiking in the mountains, swimming in the local pool, and _____ in the park.
(A)to run　　　　　　　(B)run
(C)running　　　　　　 (D)ran

(　　) **14** I can't forget that memorable place _____ we shared our first conversation and laugh.
(A)where (B)which
(C)who (D)whose

(　　) **15** Not only did she sing a beautiful song, but she also _____ a graceful dance at the party.
(A)dance (B)dances
(C)danced (D)dancing

三、克漏字測驗

French fries are delicious. They are many people's favorite, because they are perfect comfort food. Sadly, there is a new study that ____16.____ fried foods are related to mental health.

The results of the study show that people who enjoy fried foods are more likely to experience negative emotions. ____17.____ with those who avoid fried snacks, they are more likely to have mental problems. They have a 12 percent higher chance of feeling ____18.____ and a 7 percent higher chance to feel depressed. The study was based on data ____19.____ over 11 years from the diets of more than 140,000 people. It reveals that those who ate more fried foods also ____20.____ depression more often. However, it's important to note that unhappy people may simply prefer eating fried snacks.

(　　) **16** (A)offers (B)delivers (C)rises (D)suggests

(　　) **17** (A)Comparing (B)Compared (C)To compare (D)Compare

(　　) **18** (A)anxious (B)luxurious (C)curious (D)various

(　　) **19** (A)collecting (B)collected (C)was collected (D)to collect

(　　) **20** (A)figured out (B)turned down (C)suffered from (D)relied on

四、閱讀測驗

There is an idea that's simple yet powerful. It's called The Fun Theory, and it states that things are better if they are more fun. Why? Because people are more willing to do the right thing if they can get some fun out of it.

Volkswagen announced The Fun Theory in 2009 and since then has organized contests for inventions that can prove The Fun Theory. One winner was the Speed Camera Lottery, designed to get people to obey the speed limit. It involves a camera that not only issues speeding tickets to cars that drive too fast, but also notices cars that come through at or under the speed limit. It then automatically issues a lottery ticket to those who obeyed the speed limit, giving them a chance to win some money. Best of all, the lottery is funded by money collected from speeding fines.

Another winner of The Fun Theory contest is The World's Deepest Trash Bin. It's a trash bin with a sound effect---when someone throws trash in, the bin makes the sound of a heavy object falling through the air and crashing to the ground.

The results of these inventions prove that The Fun Theory can indeed be used to change people's behavior. The Speed Camera Lottery led to a 22% **decrease** in people's average driving speed, and the World's Deepest Trash Bin collected more than seventy kilograms of garbage in one day. As The Fun Theory shows, things are better when they're more fun.

( ) **21** What is the purpose of this passage?
(A)To introduce an idea. (B)To compare two items.
(C)To solve a problem. (D)To tell a gruesome story.

( ) **22** According to the passage, which of the following statements about The Fun Theory is true?
(A)It was first proposed in the 19th century.
(B)It claims that people like to do interesting things.
(C)Volkswagen held contests to prove it was wrong.
(D)It is a powerful but complicated theory.

( ) **23** Which of the following is the benefit that the Speed Camera Lottery brought?

(A)There have been more and more car accidents.

(B)People were driving even faster than before.

(C)Fewer and fewer people got speeding tickets.

(D)Many people became millionaires.

( ) **24** Which of the following can best replace the word **"decrease"** in the last paragraph?

(A)Drop. (B)Improvement.

(C)Promotion. (D)Benefit.

( ) **25** Where does this passage most likely come from?

(A)A medical journal.

(B)A magazine named "Animal World."

(C)An ad about travel.

(D)A report on amazing inventions.

解答與解析　答案標示為#者，表官方曾公告更正該題答案。

一、字彙

1 (C)。軟體的最新版本優於所有先前的版本。

(A)優先權 (B)週年紀念

(C)版本 (D)小說

解 priority(n.)優先權；在先；居前；優先考慮的事

anniversary(n.)週年紀念；週年紀念日；結婚週年

version(n.)版本；說法；譯文；改寫本

fiction(n.)小說；虛構；捏造；想像

2 (D)。為了要在這個競爭激烈的行業中獲得聘用，你需要具備一些獨特的特質，使你能夠從其他候選人中脫穎而出。

(A)明顯的 (B)認真負責的

(C)想像中的 (D)競爭的

解 obvious(adj.)明顯的；顯著的；平淡無奇的

responsible(adj.) 認真負責的；可信賴的；需負責任的

imaginary(adj.)想像中的；虛構的；幻想的

competitive(adj.)競爭的；好競爭的

3 (B)。在尖峰時段替代開車的另一個選擇是搭乘大眾運輸工具。
(A)達成　　　　　(B)選擇
(C)反對　　　　　(D)靈感
解 achievement(n.)達成；完成；成就；成績
alternative(n.)選擇；二擇一；供選擇的東西
objection(n.)反對；異議；不喜歡；缺點
inspiration(n.)靈感；鼓舞人心的人或事物；吸氣

4 (D)。在演講比賽中，珍和比爾分別獲得第一名和第三名。
(A)僅僅　　　　　(B)特別
(C)逐步地　　　　(D)分別地
解 barely (adv.) 僅僅；勉強；幾乎沒有；貧乏地；公開地
particularly (adv.) 特別；尤其；詳細地；詳盡地；具體地
gradually (adv.) 逐步地；漸漸地
respectively (adv.) 分別地；各自地

5 (B)。悲劇發生後，走在城市裡，可以看到許多行人心中因為悲痛而感到頹喪。
(A)歡樂　　　　　(B)悲痛
(C)欣喜　　　　　(D)刺激
解 joy(n.)歡樂；高興；樂事；樂趣
sorrow(n.)悲痛；悲哀；悲傷；憂傷；傷心事；懊悔
delight(n.)欣喜；愉快；樂事

excitement(n.)刺激；興奮；激勵；令人興奮的事
weigh down 使頹喪；壓倒；沉重地壓在心頭

6 (B)。宴會中，她的笑容極具感染力，影響了在場所有人的心情。
(A)憂鬱的　　　　(B)有感染力的
(C)不易親近的　　(D)非傳染性的
解 dismal(adj.)憂鬱的；沉悶的；淒涼的；陰暗的
infectious(adj.)有感染力的；易傳播的；傳染的
unapproachable(adj.)不易親近的；孤高的；冷漠的；難接近的
noncommunicable(adj.)非傳染性的；無法在人與人之間傳播的

7 (D)。在公司裡，他是一名勤奮的員工，始終守時，並且對工作非常負責。
(A)遲到的　　　　(B)懶散的
(C)粗心的　　　　(D)勤奮的
解 tardy(adj.)遲到的；緩慢的；遲鈍的
lazy(adj.)懶散的；怠惰的；緩慢的；懶洋洋的
careless(adj.)粗心的；疏忽的；草率的；隨便的
diligent(adj.)勤奮的；勤勉的；用功的；費盡心血的

8 (A)。遺憾的是，由於不可預見的情況，他們決定取消宴會。
(A)取消　　　　　(B)出席
(C)提高　　　　　(D)裝飾

解答與解析

解 cancel(v.)取消；廢除；刪去；劃掉
attend(v.)出席；參加；前往；
照料；伴隨；陪同
enhance(v.)提高；增加；改善
decorate(v.)裝飾；粉刷；修飾

二、文法測驗

9 (D)。由於大家的努力，演唱會圓
滿成功。
(A)除了…之外　　(B)因為
(C)儘管　　　　　(D)由於

解 in addition to 除了……之外；還
有（其後必須接名詞或動名詞）
because (conj.) 因為（其後必須
接子句）
in spite to 儘管；不管（其後必
須接名詞或動名詞）
thanks to 由於；幸虧；託……福
（其後必須接名詞或動名詞）

10 (B)。湯姆昨天在公園裡遇到的是
一位老朋友。
(A)哪一個　　　　(B)那
(C)什麼　　　　　(D)哪裡

解 It is/was...that是分裂句，又稱強
調句，將要強調的部分放在be
動詞之後，例：It was Mary that
broke the window. 打破窗戶的就
是瑪莉。

11 (B)。她還沒有完成所有的家庭作
業，是嗎？
(A)還未完成（過去完成式）
(B)還未完成（現在完成式）

(C)未完成（現在式）
(D)未完成（過去式）

解 從附帶問句的has she可知，本句
的動詞時態是現在完成式，所以
選項(B)為正確答案。

12 (B)。儘管非常疲倦，他仍繼續研
究該項目。
(A)是（原形動詞）
(B)是（動名詞）
(C)是（過去分詞）
(D)是（不定詞）

解 despite當介系詞時，意指「儘
管；不管；任憑」，其後必須接
動名詞，例：She went to school
despite her illness. 儘管生病，她
還是去上學。

13 (C)。週末時,他喜歡去山上健行、
去當地的游泳池游泳、以及去公園
跑步。
(A)跑步（不定詞）
(B)跑步（原形動詞）
(C)跑步（動名詞）
(D)跑步（過去式）

解 對等連接詞and前面有hiking和
swimming，因此空格內也應該
填入動名詞，故選項(C)為正確
答案。

14 (A)。我無法忘記我們第一次歡聚
的那個令人難忘的地方。
(A)在那裡　　　　(B)哪一個
(C)誰　　　　　　(D)誰的

解 空格前的名詞是place，表示地
點，因此選項(A)where關係副詞
為正確答案。

15 (C)。她在晚會上不僅唱了一首優美的歌曲，還跳了一段優美的舞蹈。
(A)跳舞（動詞原形）
(B)跳舞（動詞原形單數）
(C)跳舞（過去式）
(D)跳舞（現在分詞）
解 not only...but also（不僅……而且）是對等連接詞片語，其所連接的動詞時態應該是相同的，本句not only之後是過去簡單式的did she sing，因此選項(C)danced為正確答案。
注意：not only之後的主詞和動詞要倒裝，如果動詞是一般動詞，則要在主詞之前加上與主動詞時態符合的助動詞。

三、克漏字測驗

炸薯條很好吃。它們是許多人的最愛，因為它們是完美的安慰食品。可悲的是，一項新研究顯示油炸食品與心理健康有關。

研究結果表明，喜歡油炸食品的人更容易產生負面情緒。與那些不吃油炸零食的人相比，他們更容易出現精神問題。他們感到焦慮的可能性高出12％，感到憂鬱的可能性高出7％。該研究是以收集了11年超過14萬人的飲食數據為基礎。研究表明，吃更多油炸食品的人也更容易罹患憂鬱症。然而，值得注意的是，不快樂的人可能只是更喜歡吃油炸零食。

16 (D)。(A)提供 (B)運送 (C)上升 (D)顯示
解 offer(v.)提供；給予；拿出；願意；出價；試圖
deliver(v.)運送；投遞；發表；履行
rise(v.)上升；升起；上漲；升高；增加
suggest(v.)顯示；表明；建議；提及；暗示

17 (B)。(A)比較（現在分詞） (B)被比較（過去分詞） (C)比較（不定詞） (D)比較（原形動詞）
解 動詞compare（比較）之後應該要有受詞，例：That seems expensive. Have you compared prices in other shops?那個好像很貴。你有沒有去其他商店裡比較價格呢？
因空格後沒有受詞，所以選項(A)(C)(D)的主動用法均為非。
過去分詞compared意指「被比較」，其後不需要受詞，故選項(B)為正確答案。

18 (A)。(A)焦慮的 (B)奢侈的 (C)好奇的 (D)不同的
解 anxious(adj.)焦慮的；掛念的；渴望的
luxurious(adj.)奢侈的；豪華的；非常舒適的
curious(adj.)好奇的；渴望知道的；奇怪的；難以理解的

解答與解析

various(adj.)不同的；各式各樣的；好幾個的；許多的

19 (B)。(A)收集（現在分詞）

(B)被收集（過去分詞）

(C)被收集（過去簡單式被動語態）

(D) 收集（不定詞）

解 空格前已經有動詞片語was based，卻沒有連接兩個子句的連接詞，所以空格內不能填入動詞片語was collected，故選項(C)為非。空格前的名詞是data（資料），資料是被收集的，故選項(B)為正確答案。

20 (C)。(A)想出　(B)拒絕　(C)患有 (D)依靠

解 figure out 想出；理解；明白；演算出；計算出

turn down 拒絕；關小；調低；向下折轉；使顛倒

suffer from 患有；受……之苦；受……困擾；因（疾病）而痛或不舒服

rely on 依靠；信賴

四、閱讀測驗

這有一個簡單而有效的想法。它就是所謂的「樂趣理論」，它說明，如果事情更有趣，那就更會變得更好了。為什麼呢？因為如果人們能從中獲得樂趣，他們就更願意去做正確的事情。

福斯汽車於 2009 年宣布了「樂趣理論」，然後從那時開始籌畫一些能夠證明「樂趣理論」的發明競賽。其中一

個獲勝者是超速相機彩券，這競賽是讓人們遵守車速限制。 它包含一個攝像機，不僅可以對行駛速度過快的車輛開出超速罰單，還可以注意到那些剛好達到或低於速限的車輛。然後，它會自動給那些遵守速限的人發出一張彩券，讓他們有機會贏得一些錢。最重要的是，彩票的資金來自超速罰款。

另一個趣味理論競賽的獲勝者是世界上最深的垃圾桶。這是一個帶有音效的垃圾桶--當有人往裡面扔垃圾時，垃圾桶就會發出某個重物從空中墜落到地面的聲音。

這些發明的結果證明，樂趣理論確實可以用來改變人們的行為。超速攝影機彩券導致人們的平均駕駛速度降低了22%，而且世界最深垃圾桶一天內收集了70多公斤的垃圾。 正如有趣理論所表明的，當事情變得更有趣時，事情就會變得更好。

21 (A)。本文的目的為何？

(A)介紹一個想法。

(B)比較兩個項目。

(C)解決一個問題。

(D)講述一個可怕的故事。

解 從第一段第一句："There is an idea that's simple yet powerful." 可知，選項(A)為正確答案。

22 (B)。根據本文，以下關於樂趣理論的敘述何者為真？

(A)它最先於19世紀被提出。

(B)它聲明人們喜歡做有趣的事。

(C)福斯汽車舉辦競賽證明其錯誤。

(D)這是一個強大但複雜的理論。

解 從第一段最後一句：："Because people are more willing to do the right thing if they can get some fun out of it."可知，選項(B)為正確答案。

23 (C)。下列哪一項是超速相機彩券帶來的好處？
(A)車禍越來越多。
(B)人們的駕駛速度比以前更快。
(C)收到超速罰單的人越來越少。
(D)許多人成為百萬富翁。
解 從第四段第二句：："The Speed Camera Lottery led to a 22% decrease in people's average driving speed,..."可知，選項(C)為正確答案。

24 (A)。下列哪一項最能取代最後一段的"decrease"一詞？
(A)降低　　　　(B)改進
(C)提升　　　　(D)好處

解 drop(n.)降低；下降；差距；摔落
improvement(n.)改進；改善；增進
promotion(n.)提升；晉級；提倡；促銷；發揚
benefit(n.)好處；利益；優勢；津貼；救濟金
decrease(n.)減少；減小

25 (D)。本文最有可能來自哪裡？
(A)一本醫學雜誌。
(B)一本名為《動物世界》的雜誌。
(C)關於旅行的廣告。
(D)關於驚人發明的報告。
解 本文提到了兩個發明競賽，故選項(D)為正確答案。

解答與解析

112年　中華郵政職階人員（專業職（二）外勤）

一、字彙測驗

(　) **1** It will take lots of work to _____ such a big event, so we need more people to help.
(A)organize　　　　　　(B)occur
(C)beat　　　　　　　　(D)warn

(　) **2** Everybody in the _____ clapped when the singer finished singing her song.
(A)adventure　　　　　(B)audience
(C)custom　　　　　　　(D)mystery

(　) **3** Peter has a very busy _____ today. He has to attend several meetings and hardly has time for lunch.
(A)option　　　　　　　(B)approach
(C)schedule　　　　　　(D)recipe

(　) **4** With house prices rising so high, most young people cannot _____ to buy an apartment in Taipei.
(A)divide　　　　　　　(B)afford
(C)recognize　　　　　　(D)connect

(　) **5** The hotel is so popular that it doesn't have any room _____ this weekend.
(A)original　　　　　　(B)familiar
(C)available　　　　　　(D)similar

(　) **6** There is a high _____ of accidents driving in the storm.
(A)risk　　　　　　　　(B)selection
(C)material　　　　　　(D)award

(　) **7** This machine doesn't _____ well. It needs repairing.
(A)function　　　　　　(B)limit
(C)mention　　　　　　(D)explore

( ) **8** The value of a diamond _____ on its qualities. Each factor can greatly affect the price.

(A)describes   (B)introduces

(C)displays   (D)depends

二、文法測驗

( ) **9** I have many foreign friends. Some are from Japan and _____ are all from South Korea.

(A)another   (B)other

(C)others   (D)the others

( ) **10** Jack taught his students _____ effective ways to improve their English.

(A)a little   (B)a great deal of

(C)a few   (D)an amount of

( ) **11** The workers were not _____ the result of the meeting.

(A)satisfying to   (B)satisfying with

(C)satisfied to   (D)satisfied with

( ) **12** My decayed tooth is killing me. I cannot wait to have it _____ out.

(A)to pull   (B)to be pulled

(C)pulling   (D)pulled

( ) **13** _____ the bad weather, the rescue team continued to search day and night for any survivor of the earthquake.

(A)Despite   (B)Though

(C)As soon as   (D)As long as

( ) **14** The harder you work, _____ to succeed.

(A)you are more likely   (B)you are more possible

(C)the more likely you are   (D)the more possible you are

( ) **15** Do you know the girl _____ at you?

(A) smiled   (B)smiles

(C)smiling   (D)who smiling

三、克漏字測驗

　　When you feel lonely and sad, you might need a nice, warm hug to cheer you up. But ____16.____ there is no one around to hug you? This is not a problem if you have a "hugging chair." This type of chair is a rocking chair that has a large doll ____17.____ into it. The doll resembles a woman in a funny hat, and it has extra-long arms that can wrap the person who is sitting in the chair. Although the chair can ____18.____ comfort for anyone, the Japanese company that designed it said it was meant ____19.__ older people. About 25 percent of all Japanese people are over the age of 65. This number is likely to rise, and many older people ____20.____ living alone. The hugging chair can help such people feel less lonely by hugging them and playing familiar music, which can be comforting for older people.

(　　) **16** (A) when (B)if (C)how about (D)what if

(　　) **17** (A) build (B)building (C)built (D)to build

(　　) **18** (A) prevent (B)provide (C)protect (D)pretend

(　　) **19** (A) for (B)to (C)on (D)of

(　　) **20** (A) put up (B)take up (C)end up (D)pick up

四、閱讀測驗

　　Nola Ochs was born in Kansas in 1911. Her life was not extraordinary by most measures. She grew and married, had children and grandchildren, taught in rural schools, and lived the quiet Midwest life. But she was different in one notable way: After her husband died in 1972, Nola began taking classes and eventually earned her associate degree at age 77.

　　"I still wanted to go to school. It was fun to go to classes. And if I had an assignment to do in the evening, that occupied my time in a pleasant way," she recalled. After some years went by, Nola again got the bug to learn.

Learning takes time, and moving through courses must be done on your own time, at your own pace. When Nola had 30 hours of school left to complete, she moved 100 miles away from her farm, got an apartment and attended classes in person. She graduated with her granddaughter in 2007.

Nola could have been finished then with her long life of learning. She was, after all, 95 years young. Nola decided to keep going. She lived in the student dorms and got her master's degree in liberal studies with an emphasis on history three years later, at age 98.

A hundred years yields a lot of wisdom. But it's the process that can teach us all. Learn everything you can. Share your crops with the neighbors. And never, never give up on yourself. At 105, Nola finished her memoir.

( ) **21** What did Nola do after her husband's death in 1972?
(A)She wrote a book.
(B)She started a business.
(C)She moved to a different country.
(D)She began taking classes and earned an associate degree.

( ) **22** Why did Nola enjoy attending classes?
(A)She wanted to make new friends.
(B)She wanted to become a teacher.
(C)She was forced to attend by her family.
(D)She found it to be a pleasant way to spend her time.

( ) **23** What did Nola do when she had 30 hours of school left?
(A)She took a break from studying.
(B)She moved 100 miles away and attended classes in person.
(C)She decided to study online.
(D)She dropped out of school.

( ) **24** When did Nola finish her memoir?
(A)At age 90   (B)At age 95
(C)At age 100   (D)At age 105

(　) **25** What is the main idea of the story about Nola Ochs?
　　(A)The challenges of moving to a new place.
　　(B)The importance of family ties and relationships.
　　(C)The lifelong pursuit of learning and never giving up.
　　(D)The process of writing a memoir.

解答與解析　　答案標示為#者，表官方曾公告更正該題答案。

一、字彙

1 (A)。籌辦這麼大的活動需要做很多工作，所以我們需要更多的人來幫忙。
(A)籌辦　　　　(B)發生
(C)打擊　　　　(D)警告
解 organize(v.)籌辦；組織；安排；使有條理
occur(v.)發生；出現；存在；浮現
beat(v.)打擊；敲；衝擊；拍打
warn(v.)警告；告誡；提醒

2 (B)。當歌手唱完她的歌曲時，觀眾中的每個人都鼓掌。
(A)冒險　　　　(B)觀眾
(C)習俗　　　　(D)神祕
解 adventure(n.)冒險；冒險精神；冒險活動
audience(n.)觀眾；聽眾；讀者群；愛好者
custom(n.)習俗；慣例；習慣；顧客；關稅；（大寫）海關
mystery(n.)神祕；謎；神祕的事物；推理小說

3 (C)。彼得今天的行程滿檔。他要參加好幾次會議，幾乎沒有時間吃午餐。
(A)選擇　　　　(B)接近
(C)日程安排表　(D)食譜
解 option(n.)選擇；可選擇的東西；選擇權
approach(n.)接近；靠近；即將達到；著手處理；開始對付
schedule(n.)日程安排表；時間表；清單；目錄；課程表
recipe(n.)食譜；處方；烹飪法；訣竅；方法

4 (B)。由於房價上漲如此之高，大多數年輕人買不起台北的公寓。
(A)劃分　　　　(B)買得起
(C)認出　　　　(D)連接
解 divide(v.)劃分；分發；分享；使對立；使分開
afford(v.)買得起；有足夠的……（去做……）；支付得起
recognize(v.)認出；識別；認定；正式承認；賞識；理睬
connect(v.)連接；聯想；聯繫；使有關聯

5 (C)。這家旅館太受歡迎了，以至於這個週末都沒有空房了。
(A)最初的　　　　(B)熟悉的
(C)可用的　　　　(D)相像的
解 original(adj.)最初的；本來的；原始的；原本的
familiar(adj.)熟悉的；常見的；親近的；世所周知的
available(adj.)可用的；在手邊的；可利用的；可得到的；有空的；有效的
similar(adj.)相像的；類似的

6 (A)。在暴風雨中駕駛發生事故的風險很高。
(A)風險　　　　(B)挑選
(C)材料　　　　(D)獎
解 risk(n.)風險；危險；危險率
selection(n.)挑選；選擇；選拔；選集；選手
material(n.)材料；原料；織物；料子；工具
award(n.)獎；獎品；獎狀；獎學金

7 (A)。這台機器無法運轉。它需要修理。
(A)運轉　　　　(B)限制
(C)提到　　　　(D)探測
解 function(v.)運轉；運作；工作
limit(v.)限制；限定
mention(v.)提到；說起
explore(v.)探測；探勘；探究；探索；探險

8 (D)。鑽石的價值取決於其品質。每個因素對其價格都有很大的影響。
(A)描寫　　　　(B)介紹
(C)陳列　　　　(D)取決於某事物
解 describe(v.)描寫；描繪；敘述；形容
introduce(v.)介紹；引見；傳入；採用；引出
display(v.)陳列；展出；顯示；表現
depend on 取決於某事物；視某事物而定；確信；依靠；信賴

二、文法測驗

9 (D)。我有很多外國朋友。有些來自日本，其他則全部來自韓國。
(A)又一（單數名詞）
(B)另一個人/物（單數名詞）
(C)其餘（複數名詞－－不限定範圍）
(D)其餘（複數名詞－－限定範圍）
解 another(pron.)又一個；再一個；另一個
other(pron.)（兩個中的）另一個人/物
others(pron.)其餘的人/物
the others 其餘的人/物
空格後的動詞是are，因此空格內不能填入單數名詞，故選項(A)和(B)為非。
從空格後的all（完全地）可以看出本句中所提到的外國朋友是限定在來自日本和韓國，而

不是其他任何一個國家，故選項(D)的限定用法為正確答案。

10 (C)。傑克教他學生幾個提高英語的有效方法。
(A)一點　　　　(B)大量
(C)幾個　　　　(D)一些
解 a little 一點；一些（只能接不可數名詞）
a great deal of 大量；很多（只能接不可數名詞）
a few 幾個；一些（只能接可數複數名詞）
an amount of 一些（只能接不可數名詞）
空格後的名詞是複數的可數名詞ways，故選項(C)為正確答案。

11 (D)。工人們對於會議的結果不滿意。
(A)令人滿意的（現在分詞＋to）
(B)令人高興的（現在分詞＋with）
(C)感到滿足的（過去分詞＋to）
(D)感到滿意的（過去分詞＋with）
解 現在分詞satisfying通常用來修飾其後的事物，例：a satisfying meal 令人滿意的一餐。本句的主詞是人，因此選項(A)和(B)均為非。
過去分詞satisfied例：He was not satisfied with his position in the company. 他對於他在公司的職位感到不滿意。

12 (D)。我的蛀牙讓我快痛死了。我迫不及待地想把它拔出來。

(A)拔（不定詞）
(B)被拔（不定詞被動語態）
(C)拔（現在分詞）
(D)被拔（過去分詞）
解 空格前的名詞是it（代名詞代替前面的decayed tooth），蛀牙是被拔的，所以選項(A)和(C)的主動動詞均為非。
使役動詞have的用法：
a.have someone do something 讓某人去做某事
He had the mechanic look at his brake. 他讓那位技師檢查他的煞車。
b.have something done 讓某事被完成（通常是指讓別人去做）
Mary had her hair cut yesterday. 瑪莉昨天剪了頭髮。
因此選項(B)的不定詞用法為非。

13 (A)。儘管天氣惡劣，救援隊仍日夜不停地搜尋地震倖存者。
(A)儘管　　　　(B)雖然
(C)一……就……　(D)只要
解 despite(prep.)儘管；不管；任憑；雖然
though (conj.) 雖然；儘管
as soon as 一……就……；不遲於；一經……
as long as 只要；在……期間；既然；由於
despite和though都有「儘管；雖然」的含意，但是它們的詞性不同，用法也不同，前者是

介系詞，只能跟名詞連用，例：I still enjoyed the day despite the weather. 儘管天氣不好，這一天我還是過得很愉快。而後者是連接詞，其後必須接子句，例：Though it was raining, she still went jogging yesterday. 雖然昨天下雨，她還是去跑步了。因此，選項(A)為正確答案。

14 (C)。你越努力，你就越有可能成功。
(A)（錯誤寫法）
(B)（錯誤寫法）
(C)你就越有可能
(D)（錯誤寫法）

解 形容詞possible和likely都有「可能的」含意，但是它們的用法不同，例：a.It is likely/possible that you will fail. 你可能會失敗。b.It is possible for you to fail. 你可能會失敗。c.You are likely to fail. 你可能會失敗。由此可知，possible與虛主詞it連用，故選項(D)為非，而選項(C)為正確答案。
句型"The more…, the more…"表示「越……，就越……」的含意，選項(A)和(B)都少寫了第二個the more，故均為非。

15 (C)。你認識那個對你微笑的女孩嗎？
(A) 微笑（過去分詞）
(B)微笑（動詞原形單數）
(C) 微笑（現在分詞）
(D)誰在微笑（主詞＋現在分詞）

解 空格前有先行詞the girl，這女孩會做smile (微笑)這個動作，所以空格內應該填入現在分詞smiling來修飾前面的名詞，不能用過去分詞，故選項(C)為正確答案。
空格前的名詞the girl是動詞know的受詞，不是句子的主詞，所以空格內不能填入動詞，故選項(B)為非。
選項(D)的who是關係代名詞，其後應該接動詞，不是現在分詞。

三、克漏字測驗

當你感到孤獨和悲傷時，你可能需要一個溫暖的擁抱來讓你振作起來。但如果周圍沒有人擁抱你，那該怎麼辦？如果你有一把「擁抱椅」，這就不是問題了。這種椅子是一張搖椅，它內建了一個大玩偶。這個玩偶就像一個戴著滑稽帽子的女人，有超長的手臂，可以環抱坐在椅子上的人。儘管這款椅子可以為任何人提供舒適感，但設計它的日本公司表示，它是為老年人設計的。約25%的日本人年齡超過65歲。這個數字可能還會上升，而且許多老年人會獨居終老。擁抱椅可以透過擁抱這些人，並播放熟悉的音樂來幫助這些人來減輕孤獨感，這可以讓老年人感到安慰。

16 (D)。(A)何時 (B)如果 (C)……怎麼樣 (D)如果…會如何

解答與解析

解 本句最後是問號，而選項(B)if不是疑問詞，故為非。

when若放在句首，而句尾是問號，則該句的主詞和動詞應該是倒裝的，但本句的主詞和動詞並未倒裝，因此選項(A)為非。

how about（……怎麼樣）此片語用來提出建議，其後接名詞（動名詞），例：How about going to the cinema?去看電影怎麼樣？本題空格後是一個句子，不是名詞，故選項(C)為非。

what if 如果…會如何；要是…怎麼辦

17 (C)。(A)建造（動詞原形）　(B)建造（現在分詞）　(C)建造（過去分詞）　(D)建造（不定詞）

解 空格前的名詞是a large doll，它是被建造的，不會做build這個動作，故選項(C)built為正確答案。

18 (B)。(A)防止　(B)提供　(C)保護　(D)假裝

解 prevent(v.)防止；預防；阻止；制止；妨礙

provide(v.)提供；裝備；供給

protect(v.)保護；防護

pretend(v.)假裝；自稱；假扮

19 (A)。(A)為　(B)到　(C)在……上　(D)……的

解 be meant for 是為了；注定給；意味著；用於；適合；是給

20 (C)。(A)建造　(B)開始學　(C)最終成為　(D)用汽車接某人

解 put up 建造；供給……住宿

take up 開始學；接受；佔（地方）；費（時間）

end up 最終成為；結果成為；以……終結；結束

pick up 用汽車接某人；責備某人；偶然結識某人

四、閱讀測驗

諾拉・奧克斯1911年出生於堪薩斯州。從大多數的標準來看，她的生活並不非凡。她長大成人，結婚生子，在鄉村學校教書，過著平靜的中西部生活。但她在某一方面有所不同：1972年她丈夫去世後，諾拉開始上課，並終於在77歲時獲得了副學士學位。

「我還是想去上學。上課很有趣。如果我晚上有功課要做，我的時間就過得非常愉快，」她回憶道。幾年過去了，諾拉再次著迷於學習。

學習需要時間，並且必須按照自己的時間和步調完成課程。當諾拉還剩30個小時的學校課程要完成時，她搬到了距離她的農場100英里遠的地方、租了一套公寓、然後親自上課。2007年，她和孫女一起畢業。

諾拉的漫長學習生涯在那時就應該已經結束。畢竟她已經95歲了。諾拉決定繼續前進。她住在學生宿舍，三年後，在98歲時，獲得了文科碩士學位，主修歷史。

一百年的歲月，孕育出許多智慧。但這個過程可以教導我們所有人。學習一切你所能學到的。與鄰居分享你的農作物收成。永遠、永遠不要放棄自己。105歲時，諾拉完成了她的回憶錄。

21 (D)。諾拉在1972 年丈夫過世後，做了什麼?
(A)她寫了一本書。
(B)她開始做生意。
(C)她搬到了另一個國家。
(D)她開始上課並獲得了副學士學位。
解 從第一段最後一句："After her husband died in 1972, Nola began taking classes and eventually earned her associate degree at age 77."可知，選項(D)為正確答案。

22 (D)。為什麼諾拉喜歡上課?
(A)她想結交新朋友。
(B)她想成為老師。
(C)家人強迫她參加。
(D)她發現這是一種愉快的消磨時間的方式。
解 從第二段第二和第三句諾拉所説的話："It was fun to go to classes. And if I had an assignment to do in the evening, that occupied my time in a pleasant way,"可知，選項(D)為正確答案。

23 (B)。諾拉在剩下30小時學校課程時做了什麼？
(A)她暫時停止了學習。

(B)她搬到了100英里外並親自上課。
(C)她決定在線學習。
(D)她輟學了。
解 從第三段第二句："When Nola had 30 hours of school left to complete, she moved 100 miles away from her farm, got an apartment and attended classes in person."可知，選項(B)為正確答案。

24 (D)。諾拉什麼時候完成她的回憶錄?
(A)90歲時　　　(B)95歲時
(C)100歲時　　　(D)105歲時
解 從本文最後一句："At 105, Nola finished her memoir."可知，選項(D)為正確答案。

25 (C)。關於諾拉‧奧克斯的故事，其主旨為和?
(A)搬到新地方的挑戰。
(B)家庭連結和人際關係的重要性。
(C)終身追求學習，永不放棄。
(D)寫回憶錄的過程。
解 從最後一段的第二、三和四句："1. Learn everything you can. Share your crops with the neighbors. And never, never give up on yourself."可知，選項(C)為正確答案。

解答與解析

113年　台灣電力新進僱用人員

(　) **1** After heavy rains, there is always a high _____ mudslides in this area.
(A)possibility with 　　　(B)risk of
(C)danger for 　　　(D)chance from

(　) **2** The landlord told us that the rent had to be paid at the _____ of each month.
(A)final 　　　(B)middle
(C)tenth 　　　(D)beginning

(　) **3** This model of car _____ three different colors: silver, red, and dark blue.
(A)comes with 　　　(B)comes in
(C)goes with 　　　(D)goes in

(　) **4** The crew must take a rest because they _____ from a long trip.
(A)have just been returning 　　　(B)have just been returned
(C) just return 　　　(D)have just returned

(　) **5** Ellie has a wide _____ of hobbies, including painting, hiking, and surfing.
(A)range 　　　(B)rank
(C)scope 　　　(D)extension

(　) **6** Would you rather _____ a promotion or a new job?
(A)get 　　　(B)to get
(C)getting 　　　(D)be gotten

(　) **7** Jake was told not to _____ the boat until the negotiations were finished.
(A)rattle 　　　(B)shake
(C)disturb 　　　(D)rock

( ) **8** Physical therapists use their professional knowledge to assist you _____ supportive devices like a crutch or cane.
(A)and use
(B)to use
(C)use
(D)in using

( ) **9** It's better to get a rental car for the trip because the two cities are more than 20 km _____ .
(A)apart
(B)afar
(C)apart from
(D)afar from

( ) **10** Figures _____ last year show that the number of online retailers has increased by 15.4% during the post-pandemic period.
(A)were published
(B)that published
(C)published
(D)publishing

( ) **11** If you would like to get a refund for a _____ product, you have to bring in the product and its receipt.
(A)affected
(B)fault
(C) defected
(D)flawed

( ) **12** The conclusion she made was _____ relevant to the discussion.
(A)highly
(B)closely
(C)deeply
(D)largely

( ) **13** Bonus payments based on productivity act as a(n) _____ for employees to work harder.
(A)stimulus
(B)incentive
(C)perk
(D)commitment

( ) **14** If you _____ on fat and sugar in your diet, you'll feel a lot healthier.
(A)cut back
(B)cut off
(C)cut out
(D)cut short

(　　) **15** I can't remember her name, but it'll _____ me in a minute.
(A)come in (B)come to
(C)come upon (D)come after

(　　) **16** I haven't the slightest idea _____ the moment I arrived this afternoon.
(A)what have they discussed (B)what were they discussing
(C)what they have discussed (D)what they were discussing

(　　) **17** Heavy fines have recently been _____ minor driving offences.
(A)exposed to (B)deposed from
(C)imposed on (D)composed for

(　　) **18** _____ increasing education about skin cancer, suntanned skin is no longer a desirable look in Western cultures.
(A)Despite (B)Except for
(C)In that (D)Due to

(　　) **19** Own-label products now _____ more than 20% of sales in some European supermarkets.
(A)account for (B)account as
(C)count in (D)count for

(　　) **20** "Have you ever been to the Grand Canyon?" Choose the best response.
(A)I have. Never I had seen such a wonder.
(B)I have. Never had I seen such a wonder.
(C)I have. I haven't ever seen such a wonder.
(D)I have. Ever have I seen such a wonder.

(　　) **21** The babies of lions and bears are called cubs, but a person or a monkey _____ has just been born is called a baby.
(A)that (B)who
(C)which (D)either

( ) **22** The proposal for lifting the trade restrictions set off a(n)_____ over the issue. Until now, no conclusion has been reached.
(A)debate (B)alarm
(C)riot (D)panic

( ) **23** I've been feeling a little _____ this week. I'm afraid I must go to see a doctor.
(A)out of my element (B) at a loss
(C)under the weather (D) behind the times

( ) **24** You should get to the sales early to avoid missing out_____ all the best bargains.
(A)in (B)from
(C)for (D)on

( ) **25** A series of experiments to test the new drug _____ carried out, but so far it still can't prove to be an effective drug.
(A)was (B)were
(C)has been (D)have been

( ) **26** The candidate insisted on finishing his speech even though there was hardly _____ left in the room.
(A)one (B)no one
(C)anyone (D)someone

( ) **27** A competitive market helps to _____ efficiency.
(A)adopt (B)develop
(C)generate (D)promote

( ) **28** My office is only a five-minute walk from the MRT station, so it's_____ taking a taxi.
(A)not worth (B)no sense in
(C)no point in (D)no reason to

( ) **29** The car industry's annual production _____ between 5.2 million and 8.5 million vehicles.
(A)adjusts (B)fluctuates
(C)expends (D)influences

( ) **30** A lot of manufacturing companies are trying to _____ by cutting the budget for equipment renewals.
(A)balance (B)economize
(C)limit (D)reduce

( ) **31** Because there wasn't sufficient time, data precision and accuracy were barely _____ and reported in carbon monitoring.
(A)acquired (B)accessed
(C)assessed (D)assumed

( ) **32** Chiufen is an old gold-mining town that _____ economically when the gold ran out in the middle of the last century.
(A)dropped (B)declined
(C)fell (D)disappeared

( ) **33** An example of a generation gap is when the old have a value judgement that _____ that of the young.
(A)compares to (B)changes to
(C)differs from (D)reverses into

( ) **34** When you have trouble sleeping, a cup of warm milk can do the _____ .
(A)tip (B)trick
(C)effect (D)act

( ) **35** The new lecture hall has a seating _____ of over 200.
(A)amount (B)capability
(C)capacity D)number

(　) **36** "Susan hasn't told you about her resignation, has she?" Choose the best response.
(A)Yes, she did. 　　　　(B)Yes, she hasn't.
(C)No, she has. 　　　　(D)No, she hasn't.

(　) **37** "Mr. Smith has worked here for a long time, hasn't he?" Choose the best response.
(A)Yes, at five o'clock. 　(B)No, he's working overtime.
(C) Yes, more than thirty years. (D)No. I don't have a watch.

(　) **38** It rained heavily this morning, but they finally _____ to the airport.
(A)left it 　　　　　(B)made it
(C)got it 　　　　　(D)reached it

(　) **39** It was when they started working together that they found they just weren't _____ .
(A)compatible 　　　(B)doable
(C)possible 　　　　(D)workable

(　) **40** The departure dates listed in this brochure for the summer tours _____ change.
(A)look up to 　　　(B)look forward to
(C)are subject to 　　(D)are based on

解答與解析　　答案標示為# 者，表官方曾公告更正該題答案。

1 (B)。大雨過後，該地區發生山崩的風險一直很高。
(A)可能性　　(B)風險
(C)危險　　　(D)運氣
解 possibility(n.)可能性；可能的事（常與介系詞of連用）
risk(n.)風險；危險（常與介系詞of連用）

danger(n.)危險；威脅；危險物（常與介系詞of/to連用）
chance(n.)運氣；僥倖；可能性；希望（常與介系詞of連用）

2 (D)。房東告訴我們，房租必須在每個月初支付。
(A)決賽　　　(B)中間
(C)月的第十日　(D)開始

解 final(n.)決賽；期末考；末版
middle(n.)中間；平分；分擔（in
the middle of 在……的中間）
tenth(n.)月的第十日；第十（on
the tenth of each month 每個月
的第10日）
beginning(n.)開始；起始；起
點；開端
at the end of each month = on
the last day of each month 每月
的最後一天

3 (B)。該車型有三種不同的顏色：
銀色、紅色和深藍色。
(A)附帶　　　　(B)有
(C)相配　　　　(D)進入
解 come with 附帶；配有；陪；跟著
come in 有（主要用於說明商品
以某種型態出現於市場）；進入；
流行
go with (something) 相配；與
……協調；同意；接受
go in 進入；進去；遮住

4 (D)。船員們因為剛從長途旅行回
來，所以必須休息
(A)（錯誤寫法）　(B)（錯誤寫法）
(C)（錯誤寫法）　(D)剛回來
解 現在完成進行式強調一個動作從
過去一直持續到現在，而且目
前仍然在進行，但本句的動詞
"return"（返回）不可能一直持
續，因此選項(A)have just been
returning是錯誤的寫法。
本句主詞是人，因此不是被返

回的，故選項(B)have just been
returned是錯誤的寫法。簡單現
在式不能表達一個剛完成的動
作，故選項(C)just return是錯誤
的寫法。

5 (A)。艾莉有廣泛的嗜好，包括繪
畫、健行和衝浪。
(A)範圍　　　　(B)等級
(C)領域　　　　(D)伸展
解 range(n.)範圍；幅度；一系列；
山脈；生長區
rank(n.)等級；地位；身分；社
會階層；軍階
scope(n.)領域；範圍；眼界；
觀察儀器
extension(n.)伸展；延長；延期
range 表示數量或種類的幅度，
例：age range（年齡層）,price
range（價格範圍）
scope 表示某事物所涉及的領
域，例：beyond the scope of
this dictionary（不在這本字典
的範圍內）

6 (A)。你寧願升職還是得到一個新
工作？
(A)得到（動詞原形）
(B)得到（不定詞）
(C)得到（現在分詞）
(D)被得到
解 空格之前有助動詞would，因此
空格內只能填入動詞原形，故選
項(B)to get和(C)getting均為非。
本句主詞是人，因此是得到某物，

不是被得到，故選項(D)be gotten
為非。

7 (D)。傑克被告知在談判完成前不
要惹麻煩。
(A)使惱火　　　　(B)搖動
(C)妨礙　　　　　(D)搖晃
解 rattle(v.)使惱火；使驚慌失措；
使覺醒；使發出咯咯聲
shake(v.)搖動；震動；抖動；握手
disturb(v.)妨礙；打擾；擾亂；
搞亂
rock(v.)搖晃；搖動；輕輕搖晃
rock the boat 惹麻煩；惹事；搞
亂；破壞現狀；無事生非

8 (D)。物理治療師利用他們的專業
知識來幫助你使用拐杖或手杖等輔
助裝置。
(A)和使用
(B)使用（不定詞）
(C)使用（動詞原形）
(D)在使用
解 動詞assist (幫助)的用法：
a. assist someone with something
例：Mary assisted her younger
brother with the heavy bag. 瑪莉
幫助她的小弟拿很重的袋子。
b. assist someone in + Ving
例：Can you assist me in moving
the refrigerator? 你能幫我移動
這個冰箱嗎？
故選項(D)為正確答案。

9 (A)。這兩個城市相距20多公里，
這趟旅（我們）最好租一輛車。

(A)相間隔地　　(B)在遠處
(C)除了　　　　(D)（錯誤寫法）
解 apart (adv.) 相間隔地；分開地；
有距離地
afar (adv.) 在遠處；遙遠地；從
遠方
apart from 除了
介系詞from通常放在副詞afar之
前，例: People came from afar
to see the show. 人們從遠方來
看這個表演。因此選項(D)afar
from是錯誤的寫法。

10 (C)。去年公佈的數據顯示，疫情
後網路零售商數量增加了15.4%。
(A)被公布
(B)那公布
(C)公布（過去分詞）
(D)公布（現在分詞）
解 因空格後已經有動詞show（顯
示），所以空格內不能再填入動
詞，故選項(A)were published為非。
本句的主詞是數據，不是人，
而數據是被公布的，所以選項
(B)that published和(D)publishing
的主動寫法都是錯誤的。

11 (D)。如果你想獲得瑕疵品的退
款，你必須攜帶該產品和收據。
(A)假裝的　　　　(B)缺點
(C)脫離的　　　　(D)有瑕疵的
解 affected(adj.)假裝的；嬌柔做作
的；不自然的；裝模作樣的；受
影響的
fault(n.)缺點；過錯；故障；缺陷

解答與解析

defected(adj.)脫離的；叛逃的
flawed(adj.)有瑕疵的；有錯誤的；有缺點的

12 (#)。她得出的結論與討論高度相關。
(A)高度地　　(B)密切地
(C)深刻地　　(D)大部分
解 highly (adv.) 高度地；非常；很；高額地
closely (adv.) 密切地；緊緊地；仔細地；祕密地；接近地
deeply (adv.) 深刻地；非常；極其；強烈地；至深地（去年第16題考過）
largely(adv.)大部分；主要地；大量地；廣泛地（去年第16題考過）
以上四個副詞若分別放在空格中都是一個語意完整的句子，只是第四個句子的語意跟前三句有些不同。本題官方公告選(A)或(C)均給分但因為考題句沒有前後句，所以筆者認為四個選項都是正確答案。

13 (B)。以生產力為基礎的紅利制度有鼓勵員工更努力工作的效果。
(A)刺激　　(B)鼓勵
(C)補貼　　(D)託付
解 stimulus(n.)刺激；刺激品；興奮劑
incentive(n.)鼓勵；動機；刺激
perk(n.)補貼；津貼
commitment(n.)託付；交託；委任；下獄；信奉；支持

名詞incentive的含意是「讓員工積極工作的鼓勵措施」，而名詞stimulus的含意是「讓感官做出反應的任何事物」，這兩個字的中文翻譯雖然類似，但是兩字的含意並不相同。

14 (A)。如果你減少飲食中的脂肪和糖，你會感覺更健康。
(A)減少　　(B)切除
(C)剪下　　(D)打斷……的話
解 cut back 減少；降低
cut off 切除；中斷；切斷
cut out 剪下；剪出；裁剪出
cut short 打斷……的話；提早結束；縮短

15 (B)。我不記得她的名字了，但過一會兒我就會想起來。
(A)有　　(B)想起
(C)偶然發現　　(D)追趕
解 come in 有（主要用於說明商品以某種型態出現於市場）；進入；流行
come to 想起；甦醒；恢復知覺；共計
come upon 偶然發現；碰上；邂逅
come after 追趕；位於……之後；跟隨；追蹤；尋找

16 (D)。今天下午我才到的時候，我完全不知道他們當時正在討論什麼。
(A)他們在討論什麼（現在完成式－倒裝）
(B)他們當時正在討論什麼（過去進行式－倒裝）

(C)他們在討論什麼（現在完成式）

(D)他們在討論什麼（過去進行式）

解 what疑問子句不是真正的疑問句，不需要將助動詞放在主詞前面，故選項(A)和(B)為非。

the moment (that) = when（當），其用法："The moment (that)＋S.＋V.,S.＋V."，但要注意的是，這兩個子句的動詞時態要相同，例：The moment she opened the window, she smelled something burning. 她一打開窗戶，就聞到東西燒焦的味道。

因為考題句the moment之後的動詞時態是過去式，因此選項(C)的現在完成式為非。

17 (C)。最近輕微的駕駛違規行為都被強制處以重罰。

(A)暴露在　　　　(B)被廢黜

(C)被強制執行　　(D)由……組成

解 be exposed to 暴露在；接觸

be deposed from 被廢黜；被罷免

be imposed on 被強制執行；被強加

be composed of 由……組成

18 (D)。由於皮膚癌教育的不斷增加，曬成古銅色的皮膚在西方文化中不再是一種理想的外觀。

(A)儘管　　　　(B)除了……以外

(C)因為　　　　(D)由於

解 despite(prep.)儘管；不管；任憑

except for 除了……以外；要不是由於

in that 因為；基於……的理由（其後接子句）

due to 由於；因為

19 (A)。目前自有品牌的產品在某些歐洲超市銷售額中佔20%以上。

(A)佔　　　　　(B)帳戶為

(C)把……算在內　(D)有重要意義

解 account for 佔；解釋；說明；對……負責

account as 帳戶為（非動詞片語）

count in 把……算在內；包括

count for 有重要意義；有價值

20 (B)。「你去過大峽谷嗎？」選擇最佳回應。

(A)我去過。我以前從來沒有見過這樣的奇觀。（過去完成式）

(B)我去過。我以前從來沒有見過這樣的奇觀。（過去完成式－倒裝）

(C)我去過。我從來沒有見過這樣的奇觀。（現在完成式）

(D)我去過。我從來沒有見過這樣的奇觀。（現在完成式－倒裝）

解 副詞never放在句首時，主詞和助動詞要倒裝，因此選項(A)和(C)為非。

本句問的是過去的經驗，因此選項(B)的過去完成式為正確答案。

21 (A)。獅子和熊的幼崽被稱為幼獸，但剛出生的人或猴子被稱為嬰兒。

(A)那　　　　　(B)誰

(C)哪個　　　　(D)任何一個

解 先行詞為「人+物」時，關係代名詞要用that，本句空格前的先

行詞是a person 和a monkey，故
選項(A)為正確答案。

22 (A)。取消貿易限制的提議引發了對
該問題的辯論。到目前為止，還沒有
結論。
(A)辯論　　　　(B)警報
(C)暴亂　　　　(D)恐慌
解 debate(n.)辯論；討論；爭論
（其後接介系詞on）
alarm(n.)警報；警報器；鬧
鐘；驚慌
riot(n.)暴亂；騷亂；大混亂；
喧鬧；狂歡
panic(n.)恐慌；驚慌；經濟大恐慌

23 (C)。這週我覺得身體不舒服。恐
怕我必須去看醫生。
(A)不習慣　　　(B)茫然
(C)身體不舒服　(D)過時
解 out of my element 不習慣；不適
應；不得其所
at a loss 茫然；困惑；不知如何
是好；虧本的
under the weather 身體不舒服；
生病
behind the times 過時；落後於
時代

24 (D)。你應該儘早去參加促銷活
動，以免錯過所有最便宜的商品。
(A)在……裡　　(B)從……起
(C)為　　　　　(D)在……上
解 miss out on (something)錯過；錯失

25 (C)。新藥已經進行了一系列的測
試實驗，但迄今為止仍無法證明它
是一種有效的藥物。
(A)was（過去式－單數）
(B)were（過去式－複數）
(C)has been（現在完成式－單數）
(D)have been（現在完成式－複數）
解 集合名詞"series"單複數同形。
當它具有「一組；一系列」的單
數含義時，即使後面跟著 of 和
複數名詞，其後的動詞也要用單
數，故選項(B)和(D)的複數動詞
均為非。
從本句的語意可知這一系列的
實驗從過去做到現在，故選項
(C)的現在完成式為正確答案。
如果用選項(B)were，則表示這
一系列的實驗只在過去某個時
間點做過，這樣第二個子句就
不合邏輯了。

26 (C)。儘管房間裡幾乎沒有人了，
這位候選人仍堅持完成他的演講。
(A)一個人　　　(B)沒有人
(C)任何人　　　(D)某一人
解 hardly anyone = almost no-one 幾
乎沒有任何人
hardly ever = almost never 幾乎
從不
hardly any = almost none 幾乎
沒有

27 (D)。一個有競爭性的市場有助於
提升效率。
(A)採取　　　　(B)發展
(C)產生　　　　(D)提升

解 adopt(v.)採取；採納；吸收；收養（去年52題考過此單字）

develop(v.)發展；展開；使成長；使發達

generate(v.)產生；發生；造成；引起

promote(v.)提升；晉升；促進；促銷；鼓勵；推廣

28 (A)。我的辦公室距離捷運站只有五分鐘步行路程，所以不值得搭乘計程車。

(A)不值得 (B)不必

(C)沒有意義 (D)沒有理由

解 not worth + Ving 不值得

no sense in 不必；無意義

no point in 沒有意義

no reason to 沒有理由

形容詞worth（值得的）後面通常接名詞或動名詞，例：It is always worth fighting for your freedom and independence. 為你的自由和獨立奮鬥總是值得的。

29 (B)。汽車工業的年產量在520萬輛至850萬輛之間波動

(A)調節 (B)波動

(C)花費 (D)影響

解 adjust(v.)調節；改變……以適應；校正；調停

fluctuate(v.)波動；變動；動搖

expend(v.)花費；消費；用光；耗盡

influence(v.)影響；感化；左右

30 (B)。許多製造公司正試圖以削減更新設備的預算來省錢。

(A)平衡 (B)節省

(C)限制 (D)減少

解 balance(v.)平衡；權衡；比較

economize(v.)節省；節約（常與介系詞by或on連用）

limit(v.)限制；限定

reduce(v.)減少；縮小；降低；迫使

31 (C)。由於沒有足夠的時間，碳監測中的數據精度和準確性幾乎沒有評估和報告。

(A)取得 (B)使用

(C)評估 (D)以為

解 acquire(v.)取得；獲得；學到；養成

access(v.)使用；接近；存取資料

assess(v.)評估；考核；估量；評定

assume(v.)以為；認為；假定為

32 (B)。九份是一個古老的金礦小鎮，它在上世紀中黃金被耗盡後，經濟開始衰退。

(A)滴下 (B)衰退

(C)落下 (D)消失

解 drop(v.)滴下；落下；下降；變弱

decline(v.)衰退；衰落；下降；減少；下跌

fall(v.)落下；降落；跌落；跌倒

disappear(v.)消失；不見；突然離開；滅絕

解答與解析

33 (C)。一個代溝的例子是老年人有的價值判斷與年輕人的不同。

(A)將…比作　　(B)變成

(C)與…不同　　(D)倒車到

解 compare to 將……比作

change to 變成；把……更改為

differ from 與……不同；與……意見不同

reverse into 倒車到……

He reversed into a lamppost and damaged the back of the car.

他倒車時撞到了路燈柱，把車尾撞壞了。

34 (B)。當你難以入睡時，一杯溫牛奶可以奏效。

(A)小費　　　(B)妙計

(C)效果　　　(D)行為

解 tip(n.)小費；告誡；提示

trick(n.)妙計；戲法；手法；竅門；詭計；騙局；花招

effect(n.)效果；效力；作用；結果；影響

act(n.)行為；行動

do the trick 奏效；起作用 達到目的

35 (C)。新的演講廳可容納200多個座位。

(A)總數　　　(B)性能

(C)容量　　　(D)數字

解 amount(n.)總數；數量

capability(n.)性能；功能；耐受力；才能；潛力

capacity(n.)容量；能力；才能；能量；資格；地位

number(n.)數字；號碼；數量

36 (D)。「蘇珊沒有告訴你她辭職的事，是嗎？」選擇最佳回應。

(A)是的，她有。（過去式）

(B)是的，她沒有。（現在完成式）

(C)不，她有。（現在完成式）

(D)不，她沒有。（現在完成式）

解 本題考附帶問句的回答，主要子句的助動詞是has，因此選項(A)的did是錯誤的回答。回答Yes時，後面要接肯定的句子，回答No時，後面要接否定的句子，因此選項(B)和(C)都是錯誤的回答。

37 (C)。「史密斯先生在這裡工作了很長一段時間，不是嗎?」選擇最佳回應。

(A)是的，在五點鐘。

(B)不，他正在加班。

(C)是的，三十多年了。

(D)不，我沒有手錶。

解 選項(A)、(B)和(D)的回答都跟考題句無關，故均為非。

38 (B)。今天早上下著大雨，但他們終於到達了機場。

(A)別管它　　(B)到達

(C)知道　　　(D)搆到它

解 leave it 別管它；放下

make it 到達；成功；趕上；及時趕到

get it 知道；理解；收到；得到

reach it 搆到它

39 (A)。當他們開始一起工作時,他們發現彼此不相容。

(A)相容的　　　(B)可行的

(C)可能的　　　(D)可使用的

解 compatible(adj.)相容的;能共處的;可並立的;兼用式的

doable(adj.)可行的;可做的

possible(adj.)可能的;有可能的;合理的;合適的

workable(adj.)可使用的;可運轉的;可經營的

40 (C)。本手冊中所列出的夏季旅遊出發日期可能會有所變動。

(A)敬仰

(B)期待

(C)易受……的

(D)以……為基礎

解 look up to 敬仰;尊重

look forward to 期待;盼望

are subject to 易受……的;可以……的;受支配;以……為條件的

are based on 以……為基礎;以……為根據

一試就中，升任各大
國民營企業機構
高分必備，推薦用書

題庫系列

編號	書名	作者	定價
2B021111	論文高分題庫	高朋 尚榜	360元
2B061131	機械力學(含應用力學及材料力學)重點統整＋高分題庫	林柏超	430元
2B091111	台電新進雇員綜合行政類超強5合1題庫	千華 名師群	650元
2B171121	主題式電工原理精選題庫	陸冠奇	530元
2B261121	國文高分題庫	千華	530元
2B271141	英文高分題庫　👑榮登金石堂暢銷榜	德芬	630元
2B281091	機械設計焦點速成＋高分題庫	司馬易	360元
2B291131	物理高分題庫	千華	590元
2B301141	計算機概論高分題庫　👑榮登金石堂暢銷榜	千華	550元
2B341091	電工機械(電機機械)歷年試題解析	李俊毅	450元
2B361061	經濟學高分題庫	王志成	350元
2B371101	會計學高分題庫	歐欣亞	390元
2B391131	主題式基本電學高分題庫	陸冠奇	600元
2B511131	主題式電子學(含概要)高分題庫	甄家灝	500元
2B521131	主題式機械製造(含識圖)高分題庫　👑榮登金石堂暢銷榜	何曜辰	近期出版

2B541131	主題式土木施工學概要高分題庫　👑榮登金石堂暢銷榜	林志憲	630元
2B551081	主題式結構學(含概要)高分題庫	劉非凡	360元
2B591121	主題式機械原理(含概論、常識)高分題庫 👑榮登金石堂暢銷榜	何曜辰	590元
2B611131	主題式測量學(含概要)高分題庫　👑榮登金石堂暢銷榜	林志憲	450元
2B681131	主題式電路學高分題庫	甄家灝	550元
2B731101	工程力學焦點速成＋高分題庫　👑榮登金石堂暢銷榜	良運	560元
2B791121	主題式電工機械(電機機械)高分題庫	鄭祥瑞	560元
2B801081	主題式行銷學(含行銷管理學)高分題庫	張恆	450元
2B891131	法學緒論(法律常識)高分題庫	羅格思 章庠	570元
2B901131	企業管理頂尖高分題庫(適用管理學、管理概論)	陳金城	410元
2B941131	熱力學重點統整＋高分題庫　👑榮登金石堂暢銷榜	林柏超	470元
2B951131	企業管理(適用管理概論)滿分必殺絕技	楊均	630元
2B961121	流體力學與流體機械重點統整＋高分題庫	林柏超	470元
2B971141	自動控制重點統整＋高分題庫	翔霖	560元
2B991141	電力系統重點統整＋高分題庫	廖翔霖	650元

以上定價，以正式出版書籍封底之標價為準

歡迎至千華網路書店選購
服務電話 (02)2228-9070

千華網路書店

更多網路書店及實體書店

博客來網路書店　PChome 24hr書店　三民網路書店
MOMO 購物網　金石堂網路書店　誠品網路書店

查詢實體書店

國家圖書館出版品預行編目(CIP)資料

國民營英文高分題庫/德芬編著. -- 第十七版. -- 新北
市：千華數位文化股份有限公司, 2024.12

面；　公分

國民營事業

ISBN 978-626-380-800-3 (平裝)

1.CST: 英文　2.CST: 讀本

805.18　　　　　　　　　　113017045

[國民營事業] 國民營英文高分題庫

編 著 者：德 芬

發 行 人：廖 雪 鳳
登 記 證：行政院新聞局局版台業字第 3388 號
出 版 者：千華數位文化股份有限公司
地址：新北市中和區中山路三段 136 巷 10 弄 17 號
電話：(02)2228-9070　　傳真：(02)2228-9076
客服信箱：chienhua@chienhua.com.tw

法律顧問：永然聯合法律事務所
編輯經理：甯開遠
主　　編：甯開遠
執行編輯：尤家瑋
校　　對：千華資深編輯群
設計主任：陳春花
編排設計：邱君儀

千華官網
／購書

千華蝦皮

出版日期：2024 年 12 月 20 日　　第十七版／第一刷

本書如有勘誤或其他補充資料，
將刊於千華官網，歡迎前往下載。